THE VALENBLADE

A Novel

Mark Ivan Cole

Cover designed by Mark Ivan Cole

This book is a work of fiction. Names, characters, places, and incidents either are products of the author's imagination or are used fictitiously. Any resemblance to actual persons, living or dead, events, or locales is entirely coincidental.

Mark Ivan Cole
Visit my website at www.thevalenblade.wordpress.com

Printed in the United States of America

First Printing: Aug 2017
Name of Company

ISBN- 9781973222330

To the many people who have encouraged me to make this book a reality. Thanks for your relentless support, faith and insistence. It's finally here, folks.

PROLOGUE

It was a cold day in December. It was always a cold day in December, or so it seemed to Brian P. Gruffenson. Every December was like this—frost or snow, ice or sleet, high clouds or fog. In any case, the gruffen was not happy. But then again, gruffens rarely are.

He tugged at the matted, brown fur on his hands and arms. Fur was supposed to keep him warm. It never seemed to be enough for the coldest days. He took a look at his dwindling wood pile and decided not to throw any more fuel on the glowing coals. The pile wouldn't last the winter.

Brian P. Gruffenson rubbed his knobby nose with a leathery fist and grunted. His empty stomach growled back. He'd have to go hunting again, too. Brian had ventured much further looking for game, and he was finding more goblin tracks and fewer animal tracks these days. At his height and weight, not even the bears would challenge him. That put him at the top of the food chain, but none of that mattered when food was scarce. With another grunt, he eased his massive frame up off of the old log he used as a seat and stood to his feet. Grumpily, he spread the remaining coals and headed out into the snow.

Ranging through the foggy woods on four-toed feet, the gruffen picked up bits and pieces of wood. It took him a long time to gather enough wood to make a full load. Halfway home, he saw the rabbit: a big white rabbit! He hadn't seen one for days. This one was upwind where it couldn't smell the heavy scent of gruffen, and it was downhill, right below the little cliff where he stood.

Brian stood stock still. The rabbit did not move. Maybe he could just jump on it, but he would have to hang onto the armload of wood, or the rabbit would hear him. He crouched at the edge of the drop, and then leapt off. The rabbit sprang nimbly out of the way as Brian P. Gruffenson landed hard. His load of wood flew everywhere. Howling with frustration, he grabbed the nearest tree branch and yanked on it, showering himself and his lost wood with thick snow. This, of course, made him even more angry.

By the time Brian got back to his cave, he was tired, cross, hungry, and cold. He'd lost almost half the wood he'd gathered. He'd missed the rabbit, too, and was in no mood for visitors. But that's what he found when he came home.

Something smelled funny as he approached the cave. Something animal-ish but sweet. Something that might be tasty but could be very dangerous. Something oddly familiar and unfamiliar all at once. The fire was nearly out but he knew it should have long since died. Someone had been feeding it his wood—as if he had enough to last! He growled deep in his furry chest. Gruffens used fire—gruffens, goblins and HUMANS! The smell was too sweet for either goblins or gruffens.

That must be what I'm smelling, he thought. Brian P. Gruffenson vaguely remembered humans. Nasty creatures. He stayed as far away from them as possible. In fact, he could no longer remember the last contact he had with a human. Whenever he thought of them, something in his stomach turned sour.

Gruffens can be very quiet when it suits them. Brian entered the cave without a sound. Peering to the darkness, he could make out the form of a little human lying asleep next to the burning embers. Just a little one; that was reassuring. Although even the biggest were no match for a gruffen, they were usually more clever and wary than the young. This one was hardly big enough to worry about at all, but it was also bigger than the rabbit and a whole lot easier to catch, thought Brian. Plus, he basically had this one trapped. As hungry as he was, he wondered if this one might just be the meal he really needed.

Brian crouched down over the small figure and looked it over. It was pretty skinny, really; not much meat, but it was better than nothing. It had no fur on its spindly arms and legs but it also had quite a long mane. Over most of its body was another loose covering of the sort humans seemed to favor. The word "clothes" came to mind.

"Wouldn't eat that," mumbled the gruffen, half under its breath.

"Is it time to eat?" asked the little thing as it rolled over sleepily. Brian P. Gruffenson was leaning over so close that the movement startled him. He lurched backward, slamming into the cave wall and reeling drunkenly into the pile of wood.

The little person sat up very quickly, now wide awake. "Who's there? Are you all right?"

"I'm here! I'm NOT all right!" roared Brian P. Gruffenson, shaking the cobwebs and dust from his hair. "And it IS time to eat!"

"I don't see any food. How can we eat with no food?" asked the child.

"What do you think YOU are?" growled the hungry gruffen.

"I'm a girl. My name is Annie. Who are you?" asked the girl.

"Brian P. Gruffenson," answered Brian, wrinkling his forehead a little at hearing his own name out loud. It hurt to wrinkle his forehead.

"Nice to meet you, Mr. Gruffenson," replied Annie. She looked at his hulking, furry frame with wide eyes. "What ARE you?" she asked.

"Gruffen! Hungry! Go roast yourself." The gruffen was in no mood for formalities. Then again, gruffens are never in the mood for formalities.

* * *

Gruffen, roughen, toughen, muffin, stuffing...

It was a little rhyming game Annie sometimes played when trying to solve a problem. Quickly, she shook it out of her head. She had to think fast.

"Mr. Gruffenson," she said, "if you don't mind my saying, it's not fair that you should have supper and that I should go hungry. It doesn't seem right."

Small as she was, Annie was used to danger. She had been lost in these woods for a long time and had learned to keep her wits about her.

Gruffens, on the other hand, spend little time thinking about "fairness." In fact, they spend little time thinking at all, but Brian understood the concept somehow. Regardless, he was still hungry.

"If I eat you, you won't be hungry. Me neither," he said.

"That's true," said Annie, "but if you eat me, I'll be all gone and then you'll have to hunt again and neither of us will have anything to eat. You see, I would be only one small meal for you, but you would be several meals for me!"

Brian P. Gruffenson looked at her closely. "You can't eat me," he said. "No big teeth. And I taste bad."

"How do you know you taste bad?" asked Annie showing him her teeth, hoping he could see them in the dim light.

"Don't know. Always thought gruffens taste bad. Never seen anybody eat one," replied Brian, taken aback.

"Well, it doesn't seem fair that I should eat you anyway," said Annie. "Why should I be fat and lazy for days because of all the meals I ate from you, when if you ate me you'd have to go hunting tomorrow? I don't think I shall eat you, Brian P. Gruffenson."

They sat for a little while without saying anything. Brian's stomach growled indignantly, but the little person looked less and less like a meal.

"So what can we eat?" he asked. "You're so smart, what can we eat?"

Annie reached into her pocket and pulled out some nuts. "Here, I've had as many as I can eat."

Brian took the nuts. They were so small, they almost slipped between his big, wrinkled fingers.

"Squirrel food!" he retorted. "I eat the squirrels that eat these and they're not enough for my belly."

"Could a meal as big as me fill your belly?" asked Annie quickly. She didn't want him to get too angry.

"Maybe," replied the gruffen.

"The nuts are enough for me, and I'm enough for you, so enough nuts should be enough for you," she said.

"Enough, enough!" yelled Brian. "Don't see enough nuts to fill my belly. I'm hungry!"

Annie reached into her pocket and pulled out more nuts. "This makes twice as many nuts as I ate," she said. "If this is more than I can eat, and I'm as much as you can eat, then this should be twice as much. Eat your food!"

They looked pretty small, but Brian ate every one. He ate the shells, too, but Annie didn't correct him anymore.

"Are you full?" she asked when he was done.

"Don't think so," said the gruffen. "Never eaten tree parts before." He didn't say so, but he wondered if he might grow a tree inside his stomach. Then he remembered that squirrels ate these all the time, and they never grew trees. That made him feel a little better.

All this thinking had made him very tired and, hungry or not, he was soon fast asleep, snoring noisily.

Annie stayed awake for some time. She'd have to come up with something for breakfast tomorrow or they might go through this whole ordeal again. She thought for quite a while before she, too, finally went to sleep. Even if he's a gruffen, she thought as she drifted off to the sounds of Brian's heavy breathing, it was nice not to be alone anymore.

* * *

When Brian P. Gruffenson woke up early the next morning, he expected another cold December day but he was quite warm. The fire crackled away beside him and he almost felt good enough to go back to sleep, but then he jumped up in a rage.

"Who burns wood?" he howled. "Not enough wood for winter!"

Somewhere toward the mouth of the cave he heard a giggle. Then he remembered the little person from the night before.

"You burning my wood?" he growled fiercely.

"No," she answered. "I'm burning *my* wood, but you may as well be warm too."

"You got wood?" asked the gruffen, genuinely interested.

"I've been out already this morning and I got wood and food for myself. What are you going to do?"

"You got food?" asked Brian

"Fish," said Annie, holding up a bright, silvery one.

"Bear food!" complained the gruffen.

"Not when I'm eating it," returned the little girl. "And it would be gruffen food if you ate it. Want some?"

Brian P. Gruffenson scrutinized the fish and cocked a suspicious eye at Annie. "Not enough for both of us," he said flatly.

"Well, you try some of mine and if you like it, I'll show you where you can get more."

The fish, roasting over the fire, smelled pretty good once Brian got used to it.

"Burning too much wood," he said, but Annie reminded him that it was her wood.

When the fish was done, Annie ate some and gave some to the gruffen. Brian looked at it for awhile, decided he was too hungry to pass it up and gulped it down, bones and all. It wasn't nearly enough to satisfy his appetite.

Annie took him out to the river and tried to show him how to fish with a spear she had made from a thin branch. He had no luck at all with it, but he proved very adept at fishing bear-style, scooping the scaly things out of the water with one hand. Too hungry to roast them, he ate them right there.

"Now I'm full," he said, as satisfied as any gruffen ever was.

Things would have probably been just fine if they had gone on like this forever.

* * *

"Gruffen," said the first goblin, sniffing the air.

"Ugh," said the second one. "Hate those things."

"What do *you* know about gruffens?" asked the first.

The second one pointed at the four scars that ran across his face from his cheek to his lower lip.

"Sure," said the first goblin. "How'd you get away?"

"Let him have the fox," said the other. "He was hungry."

"Coward," spat the first, slashing him across the face with a clawed hand. "There. Four more to match," he said.

The second one sneered back, ignoring the wetness dripping down his jaw. "You're so brave, you go find this one and bring him to the King."

"Not that stupid," said the first goblin, adjusting the load on his back. The terrified deer he carried could not break its tight bonds. "Pick up the pace, idiot!"

The second one slung a squirming sack over his shoulder and followed, wiping his bloody face on his sleeve.

* * *

Sitting on the dark throne, he rolled the glossy marble of utter blackness between his fingers. Today, it seemed to long for its missing counterpart more than ever.

Patience, he reminded himself. Time will bring it to me. They will reunite in my hands.

The wound in the back of his neck seeped a little. It was only a scratch, the nick of a knife, but in all these years, it had never healed. Not even the Stone could remove this one reminder of his vulnerability.

No matter. There was still time.

CHAPTER 1

Intruders

One day, several weeks after Annie and Brian P. Gruffenson first met in the cave, they came home to find their firewood gone and the store of nuts empty.

"You hid the wood!" howled the gruffen. "People are all the same! You take everything! I bet you scared away the rabbits and deer so we have to eat squirrel food!" He picked up a rock from the floor and hurled it at the empty storage area.

Annie was frightened. She didn't know where the wood and food had gone either.

"Wait, Brian!" she yelled over the clamor. "We were both outside, gathering wood. You could see me the whole time. How could I do this? I was with you!"

Brian bounced another big rock off the cave wall and sat down hard. "Then who stole it?" he growled.

"I don't know," said Annie quietly, looking around. "Brian, look! Goblin tracks!"

"There's goblin tracks everywhere, stupid." grumbled Brian.

"I know," retorted Annie wrinkling her eyebrows and pursing her lips. "But these tracks are bigger."

The gruffen came over, sniffing intently. "I just smell fish," he spat. "No, wait. You're right. Goblin tracks—and not small, not normal. Fresh. Why didn't I smell them?"

"You had the fish, remember?" offered the girl.

"Fish!" said the gruffen. "Working all day, carrying bear food, squirrel food, wood! No good! All because of you! No more! You're trouble. Goblins saw your tracks and smelled you and stole stuff because they thought this was YOUR cave! It's MY cave!" he roared. "Go find your own home, human! Leave me alone!"

Annie was hurt. Maybe Brian had thought to eat her when he first saw her, and, yes, he was grumpy much of the time, but he really wasn't a bad fellow. Besides, she had enjoyed having a friend to talk to after so much time alone, and he let her sleep near his warm body at night. Now he was sending her away. She'd have to make her own shelter, catch fish and carry wood all by herself again. She had done it before, but it was much better with someone else. For the first time in a long, long time, she thought she might cry.

Brian P. Gruffenson wasn't paying attention. "Need wood! When I come back, no more you! No more fish! Go away!"

He stormed off noisily into the woods, growling at every snow-covered bush. He was so angry that he kept forgetting he was supposed to be gathering wood and just kept forging forward. For several hours, he crashed through the underbrush, not caring where he went. When he finally looked around, he was far from home. Grumpily, he sat down right where he was and put his head in his hands.

His hands still smelled like fish, so he rubbed them in snow. It didn't help, so he rubbed them with pine needles. Then they smelled like fishy pine so he went to rinse them in the creek and there he remembered fish which reminded him of his empty stomach.

Brian P. Gruffenson was hungry again but he couldn't see any fish and he didn't want to scrounge for more nuts in the snow. Then he remembered Annie. He wouldn't eat her, of course, but maybe she could be made to do all the work! She could do the fishing and wood-gathering, and he could just eat and be warm! At the moment, this sounded like a good idea. He decided to go back to the cave and see if she was still there.

He dropped to all fours and ran swiftly and silently in a long, loping gait like some massive wolverine. Gruffens can cover great distances in rough terrain, even faster than a bear or mountain lion. Brian kept an eye out for anything that moved. A few fat little birds flitted among the brush, but he knew he couldn't catch those. He wondered again why there were no other animals. Usually, when he ran this quietly, he would surprise a deer or spook a rabbit, but the whole forest was hushed.

As he came over a low rise, the wind shifted slightly and he suddenly stopped dead still, sniffing the air with his great nose. Goblin! The scent was very strong here. He listened hard, but the only noise was the wind in the trees. Moving forward slowly, he peered around a thick bush. Goblin tracks! Lots of them! They were all moving together in the same direction, side by side, not helter-skelter with the largest in front.

Brian froze where he was, confused. This was odd behavior for goblins. Worse yet, they were well within his home range.

A cold chill made him forget his hunger. He dropped down to all fours again and continued homeward at even greater speed. The intruders had to be stopped. As he approached his shelter, he saw more and more goblin tracks. The acrid smell filled the air. He slowed to a creep. Goblin tracks led everywhere, mostly in pairs side by side.

Several paths converged and headed straight for his cave. These were only a couple of hours old. They must have come just after he left Annie at the entrance. Annie!

He wondered if she had been seen. A peculiarly un-gruffen-like thought occurred to him, and it made his stomach feel bad. What might they do to her?

Something threatened Annie! His thick eyebrows came down low on his forehead and his nostrils flared. The fur on his back bristled like a porcupine and his big hands clenched into fists like heavy stones. Without a sound, he worked his way around the hill and approached his cave from above and behind. The goblin smell almost made him sneeze. He stifled it and listened. Two gritty voices were talking.

"Looks like a good cave to me."

"Maybe the King will want to use it."

"Why?"

"Just look, stone brains! It's almost at the top of the hill, not far from the river, defensible from three sides—an excellent position!"

"You have the guts to walk up to the King and tell him? You with the big ideas?"

"More guts than you, you little rabbit. You didn't want to come out here when you heard there was a human. You were scared of a little girl!"

The conversation degenerated into howls, bites, squeals, scratches and grunts. Brian stole a look over the edge. They were too busy fighting to notice him. Annie's tracks were mostly covered, but he could see where they went. She had apparently begun to walk away but had gone only few paces when she abruptly changed direction and ran pell-mell. Her tracks stopped abruptly at the intersection where two paths of goblin tracks converged. There was evidence of a scuffle. The trampled snow was still white. No blood. The goblin tracks headed off, a bit deeper, as if they carried extra weight. So the goblins had her!

Brian eased his way out of earshot of the two fighting goblins and set off through the woods, keeping low, moving in the same direction as the goblin tracks. Soon, the tracks he was following joined those of a much larger company. The goblins were moving very fast, kicking up a lot of snow as they ran. Mixed in with the nasty goblin smell was the scent of other animals, but Brian could see no deer tracks, wolf tracks or badger tracks to go with those scents. Once or twice, he also picked up Annie's scent, but it was very faint.

He followed the trail along the mountainside, his sharp eyes searching the trampled snow for any sign of the little girl. There was nothing. Maybe she was slung on their backs. Maybe he was wrong and she wasn't with them at all. He was about to turn back and check when he saw a brown hair, too long for a scruffy goblin. He picked it up, rubbed it between his fingers and sniffed. Annie's, for sure! He followed the trail for some time without ever hearing the goblins. They must be traveling very fast, he thought. The trail was getting fresher, though.

The tracks turned abruptly uphill and then the trail got lost on the wind-scoured rocks that marked the crest of a cliff. Brian found a footstep here and there in the remnants of snow that lay in little drifts or cracks here and there, so he knew which direction the goblins were headed. Some distance up the ridge, he came to a vertical rift in the cliffs. He had to get all the way to the edge of it before he could see down into it. Some tough bits of hair and a little blood indicated that the goblins had climbed down the crevice, and at least one had lost some skin on the way in. The deep crack split the cold rock face as far as Brian could see before it became hidden by its own shadow.

From this vantage point, Brian couldn't see the valley floor, so he crept over to the very edge of the cliff and looked over. A band of goblins was heading away from him, out of the woods below the cliff, marching across a snowy meadow. They seemed to be carrying various animals on their shoulders, under their arms or suspended between them. The animals appeared to be dazed, but not dead. It was hard to tell from this distance. Four goblins carried a squirming bundle which Brian thought could be Annie wrapped up in something dark. In the middle of the meadow, the snow had somehow disappeared, leaving an almost perfect circle of matted grass with a strange pattern burned into it. A thin wisp of bluish smoke rose from the center of the pattern.

A terrible dread came over the gruffen. So many strange things at once: no animals, goblins traveling together in order, strange patterns in exposed grass in the middle of winter!

Raspy voices rose behind him. He raced along the rocky edge of the cliff until he found another crack in which to hide. As soon as he was wedged inside, he realized he had nowhere else to go. There was nothing to do now but wait it out. This group of goblins was a noisy lot, but suddenly, they all got quiet and stopped. The gruffen could hear them sniffing the air. He clung to the rock and tried not to breathe.

"Of course you smell gruffen, you lout!" yelled someone from the back. "Who knows what else they hauled out here?"

Shouts and catcalls followed as discipline broke down for a moment.

"Shut up, maggots! Get back in line!" barked the leader. "Down to camp!"

Still bickering, they followed the crevice down to the "camp." Brian stayed where he was until they were well away. At the base of the cliff, the goblins wound their way down a well-beaten path threading between snowy boulders as it continued down into the valley. By then, it was getting dark.

Brian climbed out of his hiding place, sneaked over to the crevice and began an icy descent. An ominous red glow from the clearing lit the fog that had rolled into the valley below. Brian could feel the wind picking up. It blew his fur about and made listening difficult.

At the bottom of the cliff, Brian carefully followed the goblins' beaten path, his heavy tread occasionally punching through a crust of snow that could hold their weight but not his. Time after time, he waited, holding his breath until he was certain no one had heard him. Then he worked himself out of the hole and quietly moved on.

The red glow in the valley had turned to purple, then blue. Now it was green. As the gruffen made his way down the talus slope, the colors in the clearing began to change more rapidly with no particular pattern. Brian moved quietly through the fog on all fours, a dark shadow against the steep, snowy slope. His eyes stared, his ears strained and his nose searched the air for enemies nearby. He was close enough to hear a few things—mostly goblin voices and muffled animal sounds. Brian pulled himself up the back of a large boulder near the bottom of the slope to get a better look before venturing into the woods. As he peered over the edge, the light in the valley went out completely.

Many voices squealed and howled at once. Brian's fur stood out all over. A low rumble shook the rock beneath him, rattling his very bones. The rumble grew into a loud roar and then became a voice, a rising shriek of horrific pleasure that drowned out all other sounds, echoing off the stone walls until it finally reverberated into terrible laughter. Despite the cold, sweat poured into Brian's fur. It seemed to him that the laughter had eyes that could see him as it ricocheted off the rocks around him. A powerful wave of heat surged through the forest. Brian could hear trees dumping snow. The heat wave rolled up the talus slope and over Brian. The boulder trembled under his chest. Then, once again, all was still and the air glowed red in the clearing. Summoning his courage, the gruffen dropped down from the boulder, hurried across the open snow and slipped into the shadowy woods.

He followed the goblin path through the trees toward the meadow. It was faster than plowing a new track through the snow, if a bit more dangerous. The whole area seemed charged with some kind of power that ebbed and flowed with the flickering, ever changing colors. The thick, sharp smell of goblin grew stronger the closer he got to the clearing. Another smell, more acrid and unfamiliar, assaulted his nose. Somewhere over there, he could also smell rabbit, badger, deer, coyote. His sensitive nose picked up very little blood, so he knew they were not being slaughtered. Why had they been brought here alive?

Hiding behind the thick trunk of an ancient fir, he stared into the clearing. The fog was so thick that, for a moment, he couldn't be sure of what he saw. A huge, squat object sat in the middle of the clearing where the smoke had been rising earlier in the day. The object looked almost like a steep hill, half as tall as the old fir trees, and it had apparently grown there since nightfall. The light source was on the far side of it, casting the object's great shadow past the hidden gruffen. Beyond the hulking object, just in front of the far woods, hundreds of shining goblin eyes stared back at the bright light. So many! They stood in straight, orderly rows.

The light changed colors. A couple of goblins brought out something all wrapped up and laid it in front of the huge object. Brian's heart raced until he realized it was too small to be Annie and he could hear a badger weakly trying to fight its way out. The goblins turned and ran back to the ranks.

Then the huge object moved, and Brian could make out monstrous shoulders and arms. The thing seemed to have no legs, as if it grew directly out of the ground. It reached toward the struggling badger with a sharp-nailed hand that was easily as big as Brian himself! Brian couldn't see what it was doing. The monster's head reeled back and the light began to change color faster and more frantically. Then, suddenly, the light went out altogether.

Once again, Brian heard the howling and screeching, the massive roar and the rising shriek. Once again, his fur stood on end. When the red light came back on, the monster's head was slowly leaning forward as the shriek wandered off among the peaks and turned into cackling laughter.

Brian P. Gruffenson stared, petrified. The badger was gone. In its place stood a large goblin, much larger than the two that had brought the badger. It quickly joined the crowded ranks on the edge of the clearing. When it turned around, its eyes were on the same level as many of the others. There were dozens of goblins that size! This explained the over-large footprints in the snow.

Another animal was brought out to the beast in the clearing, and Brian then realized why there were so many goblins and no animals. The thing with its back to him was making goblins from the other forest creatures by some frightful magic. He had to find Annie! Staying within the woods, he skirted the clearing, hoping to find where they held the future victims.

He got a better look at the thing in the clearing as he came alongside it. The colored light that floated in front of it had no clear point of origin, as if the air itself glowed of its own accord. The monster had no hair, and its hide or skin was somehow simultaneously dark and brilliant, cold and burning hot. It had powerful shoulders and arms. Its head sat directly on its shoulders with no neck to speak of. Its flaming eyes were narrow slits set wide apart, and its mouth either disappeared altogether or split the whole face with a searing grin. Its deadly teeth seemed to drip from above and splash up from below. Brian could see now that, indeed, it had no legs or feet. It sat upon squat haunches as it toyed with its victim.

Brian tried not to watch as it proceeded in its ugly business. He froze in his tracks again as the light extinguished and the roar shook the mountains once more. By now, he had come around behind the ranks of goblins and could see many animals bound to the trees. His nose picked up the scent of human just before the wind shifted and took it away from him. He had to come in closer. There were all sorts of animals there, many of which were mortal enemies but unable either to flee or pursue each other, all somehow dazed and unresponsive even to Brian's presence.

Finally, the gruffen could see Annie, standing upright, tied to a tree and staring at the ground. She had been crying and her cheeks were dirty. Whether she shivered more from fright or cold, he couldn't tell, but he could smell her sweat. Seeing her like this made his chest hurt and his throat tight.

Brian circled around from behind and reached the tree where Annie was bound with tough fibers.

"I knew you'd find me, Brian!" she whispered. "I knew you'd come! There's a village, they said. We have to warn them!"

The word "village" made the gruffen's already bristling fur stand up like spikes, but he ripped at her bonds with his tough nails until he got her loose. Just then, the light went out again and they were plunged into total darkness. Annie clung to the fur on the gruffen's thick forearm, pulling him on. Somehow they stumbled blindly forward until the light resumed. The shrieking laughter chased them deeper into the woods away from the clearing.

Annie was trying to run through the foggy woods, but her short legs couldn't carry her very fast in the snow. Brian grabbed her by the waist and slung her over his shoulder.

"Over the ridge!" hissed Annie. "That's where they said the village was! We have to warn them!"

Brian didn't care where they went, as long as it was far away from the monster behind them. They started uphill, heading for the top of the ridge across the valley from the cliff Brian had descended. It was hard going in the snow, but the gruffen kept on. They heard several goblin creations in the process. Despite himself, Brian always stopped and cringed as the laughter rattled through the hills.

Laboriously, he climbed above the tree line and out of the fog. The moon and stars were completely obscured by clouds, but in the eerie glow of the valley, Brian could make out a line of stony outcrops at the top of the ridge in front of him. Only vaguely could he remember being on the other side of this ridge, many, many years ago. Something in distant memory told him he didn't want to go back there. Suddenly, a great commotion started in the valley below. Apparently, he didn't have a choice.

Brian dropped to his knees in the snow. "Get on my back," he said. "Can't carry you anymore."

Annie scrambled up onto his broad back, wrapped her arms around his neck and held on with her legs as best she could.

"No neck!" croaked Brian. "Grab the fur!"

Annie quickly grabbed onto the fur on his shoulders as he pressed forward, groping his way up the steep, icy incline. Annie looked back and stifled a cry. Down in the fog, several dozen lights were spreading out and heading up all sides of the valley.

"They're searching for us," she hissed.

"Make a goblin out of you," wheezed Brian. "What is it?"

"The huge monster is really a man," she said. "He makes goblins out of animals, but I don't think he was going to make one out of me. When he saw me, he said something about a surprise. He's only the monster when he's in that circle, but he's ugly even when he's just a man. They were talking about a village. I think they're going there next. We have to go there, Brian. We have to warn them!"

Brian just grunted.

"It has to be *this* direction. I heard them talking about it. It can't be the other way; I came from there," said Annie.

Harsh voices called across the valley. There was much excitement down below. Some of the lights on the far cliffs retreated back down the hill, but the lights nearer to Brian and Annie continued to follow them.

Annie reported this to Brian. "Do you think they've spotted us?"

"Found tracks or got our scent," said Brian. "Can't see in the fog."

Even so, the pursuers were gaining all the time. How could they be so fast? Maybe they were already up on this ridge. It didn't matter. A couple of lights were getting close. Brian was upwind from them so he knew they could smell him.

Thick clouds scraped the tops of the peaks dropped a few flakes of cold, wet snow on Annie's hair and Brian's fur. A shout rose up as four goblins with torches burst through the trees below and saw the escapees. Brian slipped a bit and had to climb up again. To make matters worse, he was breaking trail for their pursuers. A thrown bit of a broken tree branch hit him on the backside. Annie ducked and buried her head in the back of Brian's neck. The gruffen kept going, not daring to turn around. In the goblins' torchlight, he could just see a narrow saddle between two crags on the top of the ridge. It wasn't far. He headed for it, scraping his way upward through heavy snow.

The flakes were really beginning to come down and the wind was picking up but Brian felt only the sense of urgency and the fire in his arms and legs. Growling with every breath, he dragged himself and his young friend upward. He could hear the goblins right behind him.

The wind blew fiercely at the top, right in their faces. It nearly blasted Brian and Annie back into the arms of their hunters. The gruffen crouched against the rocky outcrop next to the saddle, just out of the wind. An icy cornice had built up on this side. He kicked at it hard. A chunk of it slid down the hill, breaking loose a small avalanche that swept one or two of their pursuers into the woods below.

Brian was pretty sure the far side was a steep slope. With any luck, the snow should be deep enough, even with the wind. The torches that remained behind them were closing in quickly. He had little time to think.

"Get down!" he shouted over the wind.

"What?" shouted Annie, clinging to his back.

"Get off!" shouted Brian.

He helped her down and pulled her in front of him.

"Hang on!" he yelled. Annie hugged him tightly and hung on.

Clenching his arms around the little human, Brian struggled against the wind into the saddle. Turning to face their pursuers, he planted his feet, crouched down low and then simply launched himself backward over the crest of the mountain.

Down they fell, through the air and onto the blanket of snow. Brian landed on his back and almost had the wind knocked out of him, but somehow he kept hold of Annie. He rolled over several times and then realized that the snow was moving with him. Hugging the little girl to his chest, he kicked desperately to stay on top of the avalanche washing them down the slope. Trees and branches smacked against him as he flew over and past them. Finally, they slid to a stop. Brian was half buried but only partially embedded. He shifted back and forth to work himself and his precious cargo loose.

"You all right?" he asked.

The little girl did not answer. With a free hand, he dug the rest of her out of the snow and held her face close to his cheek. He could feel her breath, but she was not responding. Laying her aside, he continued to work himself out of the frozen trap. Snow was falling thick and fast by the time he got free. He dusted it off of Annie, picked her up and waded through the deep whiteness until he came found the upended root system of a fallen cedar. He crawled inside the natural hollow and wedged himself into a dry corner. Covering Annie as best he could, he finally succumbed to exhaustion.

* * *

When Brian woke up again, it was still snowing. He knew the sun was high already. It hurt to open his eyes. Actually, it hurt to move. His body ached from the long slide.

Slowly, it came back to him. A village. They were going to a village.

Men!

The old fear intruded into his consciousness. He sat up in the snow and sniffed the air. Nothing strange there. That was a relief.

Annie! Where was Annie? He could smell her, but where was she? He stood up and looked around, shielding his eyes from the brightness.

"Are you going to eat today or aren't you hungry?" asked Annie, blue with cold, but smiling and holding out a fistful of nuts. "I found a squirrel store."

Brian P. Gruffenson scowled and was going to grunt something, but taking a deep breath hurt his battered rib cage. He just held out his hand. Annie laughed and gave him the nuts which he crunched quietly for a little while.

"You're all banged up, Mr. Gruffenson," Annie said.

"You're blue," he replied.

"I've seen the village," said Annie, changing the subject. "It's down that way. We must get you fixed up and tell them about the Thing and his goblin army. Can you walk? Let's go!"

"Not going," he said.

"Why not?"

Brian made a face. "No village. Bad people," he growled. "You do it. No more humans for me."

Annie stood quietly for a little while and neither of them said anything. Then she ran to him and buried herself in his chest.

"I'm scared, too, Brian," she cried. "I don't know anybody, and I haven't seen any people for so long, and I don't know what will happen, even if we tell them. But we have to warn them. We have to!" She held onto his leathery, furry neck and sobbed without making a sound.

Brian P. Gruffenson was confused. Something in his mind told him that humans were horrible, vicious creatures. But Annie was human, and she had always treated him well. If not for her, he wouldn't have a friend in the world. On the other side of the mountain there were only goblins...and that Thing. What did he have to lose? He could always run away if things went badly. Maybe not all humans were bad. Maybe there were more like Annie.

"Okay," he said. "Let's go."

With considerable difficulty, he hefted Annie onto his shoulders and worked his way slowly but steadily through the snow, down the mountainside toward the village. As they descended, they crossed one set of boot tracks, then another. There were no goblin tracks on this side.

Suddenly, into their path sprang four men with heavy staves.

"Hey, you! Let the girl go!" snarled the largest one, brandishing his staff.

The fur on Brian's back stood up and his scalp prickled. He was already too battered for a good fight. Besides, weren't these the people they were going to warn of the danger at their doorstep? Brian took a breath.

"It's coming," he growled. "A monster, and goblins, coming to get you." He knew that hadn't come out right. Annie tried to say something but Brian kept her head buried in his chest.

"By the gods! It talks!" a second man stammered. "Drop her and get away! Back where you came from!"

"What 'monster?'" asked the first man. "Did this monster send you? Tell me, or you'll pay!" Swiftly, he shot out his staff and struck Brian on the shoulder.

"Ow! No! I'm Brian P. Gruffenson—!" he began.

"I don't care who you are," said the third man. "Put down the girl!"

"Annie's my friend. We're warning you! Seen rabbit or fox, deer or badger? No, you're hungry, too." He was talking as fast as he could think, hoping he could say something right. "Seen tracks? Goblin tracks. Big goblin tracks. Lots of them, and—"

Thud! The blow came from behind. Brian took a drunken swing at nothing as Annie flew from his arms. Another blow and all went black as he heard Annie crying, "No! No, don't!"

CHAPTER 2

Alliances

He was somewhere warm and quiet. Strange smells wafted in from everywhere, but there seemed to be no breeze. Brian P. Gruffenson moved tentatively. He ached all over. The ground was so soft and the blanketing snow seemed so cozy. Cozy? How odd! He wondered if he was still dreaming. His dreams had been very troubled.

He sat up quickly, too quickly, lost his vision for a second and collapsed back into the softness of his resting place. When he had a chance to collect his scattered consciousness again, he tried to piece together recent events. He remembered the flight from the magic circle in the fog, surviving the avalanche, and then heading for the village. Men. That's right. They met those men. Then what?

Humans! All these smells must be human, he thought. Maybe he was in a...what was the word? A dungeon, he thought. That was the word. Somehow he knew it.

But he seemed to remember that dungeons were cold and damp. This was warm and soft. Why did it seem familiar? He lay there in the dark, still wondering.

His thoughts were interrupted by a noise. Someone was being quietly greeted by someone else upon entering the dwelling. Both of them were human. Brian could tell from the sound that he, himself, was up on a higher level than the entryway. His nose told him he was surrounded by cut wood. How strange! Several people were talking in whispers below. He could make out at least five, all humans: two large, two middle size, and one small. Their scents wafted up to him.

The small one was Annie! He could smell her. She seemed all right. Brian wanted to call out to her, but he kept silent, motionless. A light flickered off to his right. Forgetting his aches, he sat up slowly and crouched, facing the hole up through which the light came. The wood beneath him creaked slightly. He froze.

There was more whispering below and then a little voice said: "Brian, I'm coming up."

Brian did not answer. He stared fixedly at the flickering light. Then he heard the soft padding of small, bare feet on wood, and saw Annie's little head poking up from the stairwell.

"Brian P. Gruffenson, are you still in bed? You've been asleep since yesterday morning!" She tried to look cross, but her face broke into a big grin. "Are you feeling okay?" she asked.

"Who's out there? What they do to you?" growled the gruffen quietly.

"Oh, I'm fine. The men who hit you don't know you're here," she said quickly. "These people like gruffens and they have been taking care of me. I've had so much to eat! So many different foods! I've had bread and cheese and...oh, but you're hungry, too, aren't you?"

"I'm hungry. How do I get food?" asked the gruffen, settling back slowly. The floor creaked beneath him again.

"You shouldn't be out now anyway," Annie said. "You're hurt. Mari and Lia have food if you want it, though. Shall I bring it up?"

"They safe?" he queried.

"The people? Of course, they're safe!" blurted Annie. "You have been asleep in their house for almost two days!"

"What if they're just waiting to...eat..." he stopped.

Annie wagged her head, "No one eats gruffens, Brian. I hear they taste bad. I'll get you some food." She went down below.

Soon she was back with a plate of food in one hand. In the other hand, she held the handle of a box with a little fire inside it. "It's a lamp!" she said. "So much easier than lighting a stick!" She set the food down on the floor and Brian gobbled it hungrily. "I'll go get more," she said, taking the empty plate back down the stairs. She made several trips before Brian declared he was full. The food was strange, but he liked it.

"Everyone else wants to meet you, but they don't want you to be scared," said Annie. "Can they come up?"

"All right," said Brian. He felt better now that his belly was full of warm food. He stood facing the stairwell while Annie called to the people downstairs.

"I'll go up first," said a man. Brian stiffened and waited as the heavy footsteps came up from below.

"Brian, this is Aaron," said Annie, taking the man's hand.

"Hello," said the man, nodding.

Aaron was a strong, burly man in his middle years. His forehead was balding, but the hair that remained was long and thick, tied behind him like a horse's tail. His thick beard nearly touched his collar bone. One look at his powerful hands and muscular arms told Brian that this man could be dangerous if he chose to be. In fact, if Annie were not so obviously comfortable with the man, Brian would have been afraid of him. He was glad to see that Aaron carried no weapon.

A lighter tread came up the stairs.

"Brian, this is Lia," said Annie. "She and Aaron are married and she's Mari's younger sister."

"What's...?" asked Brian. He was going to ask "what's 'married'" but he couldn't remember the word.

"Hello, Brian," said Lia with a nod and a smile.

She was tall and lean, and her measured movements reminded Brian of a strong buck: relaxed but aware, and able to leap into action at a moment's notice. Long, wavy hair the color of dark, rich honey flowed down her back, halfway to her waist. Had she been in the sunlight, Brian would have seen that her eyes were a bright blue rimmed with dark gray. She stood almost as tall as her husband. Brian figured she could also be dangerous in a fight, but, like a deer, her eyes were gentle, and she seemed genuine. The gruffen sensed the wariness that both she and her husband were feeling, but the scent of it was not strong, and neither of them moved aggressively.

"Mari, come up!" called Annie. More footsteps sounded on the stairs. "Brian, this is Mari," said Annie. "She's Lia's sister, and she's married to Holren."

"What?" asked Brian as another woman entered the room. 'What's 'married?'"

Mari, the older sister, was shorter than Lia, and shapelier, almost voluptuous. Her thick, black hair tumbled down her shoulders in a mass of loose curls. Her deep green eyes sparkled with intensity. She was earthy, with an air of wildness that showed in her face and her movements. Whether it was her demeanor or her scent, Brian found her the most intimidating of the three adults, but since Annie was unafraid, he figured Mari must be safe. The little girl stood with her arm around Mari's waist. Mari hugged her and nodded to Brian.

Someone else was coming up the stairs. Annie introduced him as: "Holren, Mari's husband. He's a wizard."

Brian didn't bother to ask what a "husband" was, much less a "wizard."

The old man was taller than most. Even with a slight stoop, he stood a full head above everyone else in the room save Brian. Holren was not a thick man but his frame belied considerable strength. His head was completely bald on top, but from the back and sides plenty of white hair flowed down, mingling with his beard in front and falling between his shoulder blades in back. He frowned slightly, apparently a habitual expression, his thick, white eyebrows dipping to the bridge of his long nose. His mouth was completely concealed behind a great mustache. He was robed in black, or at least it looked like black.

Holren's long fingers held a huge, bound book. Deep in his memory, Brian knew he had seen such a thing before, but I couldn't remember what it was.

"Annie tells us you are called Brian P. Gruffenson," said the wizard. He looked hard at Brian. "Is that your name?"

Stiffly, the gruffen rose to his full height. "Yes!" he said, a bit louder than he intended. Nearly everyone took a tiny step backward, including himself.

"Do you know who you are, Mr. Gruffenson?" asked Holren.

"Brian P. Gruffenson," answered Brian. "That's all."

The wizard smiled and shook his head. "That is hardly all, dear fellow," he said kindly as he set down the great book. "Let me tell you a story."

He took a deep breath and began. "Annie tells us you have seen a monster. You have seen the changing lights and heard the screaming laughter. You saw his horrid magic create goblin bodies with goblin minds from the flesh and blood of the forest animals. But the goblins he makes are no ordinary rabble. They walk in regimented troops. They obey. They are swift and sure. And they will be deadly.

"I know this monster. Though he now calls himself 'the King,' he was my apprentice, years ago, a young fellow named Taron Kaiss. His spells were powerful and his wits were keen, but he began to study the Dark Magic, despite my prohibitions, and I sent him away.

"Soon after I had banished him, there was a great fire which destroyed half the village and much of the surrounding forests. I was putting out flames when I saw my apprentice carrying a boy. Where this child came from, I did not know. He was not one of the local urchins. Suddenly, I felt the Dark Magic very strongly. All went black and I heard a scream, a roar of satisfaction, and then cackling laughter.

"Standing over the village was a dark shape with a visage I am loathe to recall. I knew it was Taron. Something writhed in his hands. He turned to look at me amidst the burning houses. Then he howled with glee and disappeared in a wind of cold and heat.

"There at my feet lay what appeared to be a bundle of fur not much bigger than a child. Turning it over, I was surprised to see it was a gruffen. I knew immediately what had happened and set about protecting the creature with spells of my own. It awoke in fear and ran away, but I caught it with one last spell before it escaped. I named it Brian P. Gruffenson and bade it remember that name. There isn't another gruffen within hundreds of miles of here, and I assure you no other gruffen has a name like yours."

Holren fixed his gaze on Brian. "You, sir," he said slowly; "are Brian P. Gruffenson. You were once a human boy. Your parents died when the jail burned down. Twenty years have passed since then, but I think the human remains strong in you, Brian P. Gruffenson. Yet you are gruffen. Look inside yourself. Do you understand?"

If Brian had been confused before, he was completely bewildered now, but strange things had been going on inside of him as this story was told. It was like dreaming in the daytime. He could see two beings in his heart, facing each other as if to fight. Several half-hearted blows landed on either side but neither seemed willing to harm the other. Gradually the two beings became more distinct. One was a man, the other a gruffen. The gruffen had the advantage of size and reach, but the man was cleverly feinting and ducking out of the way.

Then, between them, two eyes appeared, wide apart, like burning slits in the darkness. A great mouth below the eyes opened into a horrible grin. The gruffen and the man stopped and stared. Ominously, a mammoth hand reached out. It caught the man but the gruffen leapt in as well and became trapped in the same grip. Pressed tightly together, the two began to merge, and as they became one, the grip that held them weakened. The new creature they became had the body of a gruffen, but surely it was no gruffen. It began to grow until the hand could no longer hold it. The grip was released and the monster faded away.

"I say, Brian, do you understand?" asked Holren again.

"I don't know," said Brian. "I was human?"

Holren reached into a pocket somewhere in the folds of his robe and brought out something that looked like a bright pink rock about the size of a robin's egg. "Do you remember this?" asked the wizard.

Brian shook his head, but it did seem familiar. Now he knew what that other sweet smell was!

"Let me hand it to you and see if you don't remember," said Holren, holding it out at arm's length.

The gruffen approached hesitantly, and then snatched the thing from the wizard's hand and popped it in his mouth without thinking. His eyes grew wide. The thing made his mouth feel cold and the taste was wonderful! He couldn't think of the name for it.

"Pep!" he said. "Pep?"

"Peppermint," said Holren.

"Pep'mint!" said Brian. "MMmm!!" He rolled the hard candy around with his tongue. He felt like he was waking up. "I take these!" he said. "Pep'mint!"

"Indeed," said Holren. "I queried everyone I could find who might have known you when you were a boy. Only the shopkeeper remembered you because you had stolen peppermints from the jar on his counter."

The peppermint was soon gone. Brian looked at Holren, hoping for another. There was none forthcoming.

Holren picked up the large book again and opened it to a page somewhere in the middle. "This book writes itself," he said. "It speaks of things yet to come." Steadying the great volume with both hands, he began to read.

And when the Terror takes the land, the Changed One will bring her home. Against this Mountain rest your bones...

Holren stopped reading and looked up. "The book is empty after this, Brian P. Gruffenson," he said. "It says no more."

"So?" grunted Brian.

"Mr. Gruffenson," said Holren, taking up the book again. "You are 'the Changed One' the book mentions here. Though the book has stopped writing itself, there is apparently something very important for you to do."

Brian's forehead bunched up in confusion. "Do what?" he said. "I don't know anything."

"I do not know either, Brian," said Holren; "so I suggest we see what we can find out."

"What's that mean?" asked Brian.

Holren smiled a bit wearily. "Good question. I'm not sure of the answer myself. But if you'll come with me down below, maybe we'll all learn."

They all went down the stairs. Brian went last with Annie holding his hand. He was glad she was there. His fur bristled a little, but he reminded himself that she was not afraid.

Down below the house was a large underground laboratory with walls of earth. The ceiling was high enough for Brian to stand erect without bumping his head on the great beams of sweet smelling wood that supported it. Each beam was carved with strange scenes and symbols. A fireplace in the far wall gave light and heat, but no smoke. There was no chimney.

"No smoke," said Brian. "Why?"

The wizard chuckled. "A sorcerer makes smoke enough without a fire, and easily makes a fire without smoke. It keeps this place a secret."

"Good. No eye stings," said the gruffen. He wondered what a "sorcerer" was. Maybe it was a kind of "husband."

* * *

For several hours, Holren and the others carefully guided Brian through what it was like to be human. As they talked, Brian became more and more curious. He asked simple questions, some of which set the adults to arguing over the answers. The arguments usually ended with Holren declaring the last word, or when the five hundred pound gruffen grumpily said that was enough and changed the subject. For Brian, it was a long and tiring day, but he remembered many words he had forgotten, heard sounds he had not heard in many years, and tasted things he had once very much enjoyed eating.

That night, Brian had strange dreams, violent, fiery visions of a conflict with some evil foe, and a struggle with himself as well. At one point, he saw an image of a small boy crying all alone, but the scene changed in an instant of pain and terror. Then trees flew by as he raced through the woods.

He woke up and lay there stiffly, not wanting to move. It took him several minutes to get his bearings again. He was in a house. Annie was sleeping beside him. He could see lamplight flickering below the stairwell. Now he remembered. Everything was all right.

He rested again, glad for the warmth, vaguely listening to the conversation of the adults below.

"His thought process seems to be improving quickly," said Mari.

"I agree," said Holren. "I did not expect him to be willing to tax himself mentally as much as he has. He asks very good questions and he usually persists until he gets an answer."

"Yes," Mari said. "While his speech is primitive, he seems to grasp relatively complex ideas."

"Impressive," said Holren.

"But even more impressive is the little girl," said Mari. "Clearly, she is not a normal child."

"How old did she say she was?"

"She said she counted twelve winters," said Mari. "But then she said something like that was only since she had started counting. Annie is so alert, so fully aware of everything, I can't imagine she loses count easily. Either she's making up a fanciful tale, or there is something extraordinary about her."

"She can't be more than six or seven, from the looks of her," mused Holren. "But she acts like she has a great deal more experience. Even if she is as old as twelve or thirteen, she's been plucky and resourceful enough to survive in the woods and befriend a gruffen—no small feat. Imagine the courage it took to even approach a creature who could crush her in an instant!"

"Theirs is a unique friendship," said Mari. "Childlike, but surprisingly strong."

Brian drifted off to sleep again, listening to Annie's soft breathing beside him. He was happy she was there.

* * *

The following day, everyone focused on the apparent return of Holren's former apprentice. Brian and Annie learned that Holren had made several long journeys over the mountains in search of Taron Kaiss over the last two decades. The wizard did not recall exactly when he first found out the man had taken the title of "King." From time to time he found evidence of the King's passing—the remains of a sacrifice, or a symbol burnt into the ground—but he could never catch up with him. On one of his early searches, Holren had discovered a small clearing where the Dark Magic still hung heavily in the air, but he still had no success tracking down his former apprentice. Then, for a long time, there was no trace. Believing Taron to have moved eastward, the sorcerer eventually stopped looking for him.

"What is the Dark Magic?" asked Brian.

Holren frowned at him from under his great eyebrows and did not immediately reply. "It is the power of death, the strength of evil," he said, finally. "It is the enemy of the White Magic. Those who wield it become as evil as the power they wield and cannot escape."

Brian wasn't sure what he saw, but it seemed that everyone else in the room was very uncomfortable and he could smell a distinct change in everyone's scent. Mari stared into the fire, her face tight and her hands held very still. Lia and Aaron glanced at her quickly and said nothing.

Puzzled by Mari's demeanor, Annie leaned against her and whispered into her ear. Mari turned from the fire and smiled sadly at her, shaking her head.

Holren cleared his throat and continued. "I regret having abandoned the search for Taron. I should have been more watchful. Now I know he has returned, stronger than ever, and he is only over the ridge. With his arrival, the animals have disappeared. We see strange lights over the mountains. Some have heard howling laughter in the hills. The whole town is afraid. Why has he come back, we wonder. What is his aim? We must determine what he is about."

"He's making goblins out of the animals, like I told you!" blurted Annie. "Big, dangerous ones!"

"Yes," said Brian. "Nasty. And smart. They move together."

He explained the scene in the clearing.

"This confirms my fears," said Holren, gravely. "He makes goblins from badgers and deer. This is new: a higher form from a lower form. What could he do with man? That would truly be a fearsome monster, a dangerous servant indeed."

The wizard looked at the gruffen. "One factor he has not counted on. Perhaps because of my own spells, or by some stroke of fate, Brian, your human soul remains alive. Though it may have slept until now, I believe it is awakening. You are clearly more than what he intended to create. How much more, I do not know. Perhaps he himself began the process that will destroy him. If I read the Book correctly, you, yourself, may be part of his undoing." He indicated the large volume he had read from the day before.

"What's that mean?" asked Brian.

"You may be the one who stops the King," said Aaron.

"How? I can't fight him," said Brian.

"I do not know," said Holren. "The Book has been silent since it wrote last, some days ago; I do not know why or how. When it was entrusted to me by my teacher, he warned me that it was a thing outside of our control. Now that it has ceased to write itself, I cannot make it begin again. Since it also coincides with the King's reappearance, I fear Taron has learned its secret and shut its mouth." Holren's face grew hard and he said nothing more.

Aaron got up and leaned over the map on the table. "He is acting out in the open now, but that doesn't help much," he said. "We can't take the battle to the enemy until we know the enemy better. Who do we know who has been out there recently?"

"Me!" said Annie. Everyone stopped and then laughed at the tousled head peering up over the edge of the oaken table. Annie brushed her hair from her eyes and stood up. Then she started talking excitedly.

"If the monster can make goblins out of foxes and gruffens out of people, couldn't someone make a goblin out of me and then they wouldn't know it was me and I could go in and find out what he's doing and—?"

"No, child!" said Holren, vehemently. Everyone froze. He collected himself and continued more gently. "I would not wish to have to rescue you again. Brian succeeded once, but what if he was captured this time? Besides," he said, addressing the others; "what do we gain if Taron's actions are already easily followed?"

"The idea has merit," said Aaron. "It's a great disguise, though she's not the right one to be the spy."

Holren glared at him. "You know it should not be done."

Aaron let him glare a moment before he shrugged and let the matter drop.

Annie sat glumly in Mari's lap. Mari had not said anything this whole time, but now she bent down and whispered in the little girl's ear. The two smiled and Annie appeared to calm down. Brian noticed this exchange and wondered what it was about.

Aaron let out a deep breath. "One way or the other, we can't just sit around. We need information. No point in speculating. Once we know his strength and capabilities, we can make plans. Until then, it's all talk."

They decided to set out the next night at dusk. Aaron, Lia, Holren and Brian would go back to the clearing. Mari agreed to stay at the house with Annie and prepare in case the battle came closer to home. Annie seemed content to remain behind.

* * *

"I'm glad Annie didn't insist on going with us," said Lia later as she and Aaron prepared their gear. "I half expected her to. I would not want to take a child into this mess, even one as precocious as Annie."

"True, but it was good to have that much pluck in the room," said Aaron. "I agree, though: wouldn't want to have to keep an eye on her out there. Tangling with goblins is trouble enough." He took his baldric down from a peg on the wall and slipped a scabbard onto it. "I am curious to see how differently the new beasts fight."

Lia picked up a dagger and weighed it in her left hand. "One hopes they cut as easily."

"With any luck, we won't have to find out too soon," said Aaron, selecting a hand-and-a-half sword and checking its blade. It gleamed, spangling the wall with reflected candlelight. As with all his weapons, this one was clean, properly oiled, and wickedly sharp.

* * *

The next day, Annie and the gruffen stayed behind out of sight while the humans went into town. Aaron wanted provisions and they all wished to see how the village was responding to the increasingly strange goings on behind the mountains. They asked few questions, preferring to listen carefully to the chatter in the market.

"Strange lightning, I say," said a vegetable seller nearby.

"Lightnin' be blowed, it's the mountain itself goin' off," argued a customer. "Whole mountain goes up in flames and melts, that's what it be!"

"Have you seen the price of fish?" asked a great bulldog of a woman. "Any game you can find is too expensive to eat! Slaughter a cow or a pig and you make a fortune! Where's all the venison we get this time of year? And rabbit! I ain't seen rabbit in months! I think the hunters are spooked by there bein' so many goblins about. Ain't no goblins frightening me!"

"Oh, hold your tongue!" someone barked. Everyone turned toward the speaker, a homely man with a long face dominated by a drooping nose and wide mouth. His eyes were deeply set under his protruding brow, and despite his dark expression, his wrinkles suggested that he preferred to smile. He would have been considerably taller if he did not stoop so. The clothes on his back showed signs of a hard life out in the wild.

He stepped forward so he didn't have to shout. Aaron took one look at his lean muscles and guessed the man had often tested the limits of his endurance. Apparently, this complainer had brought him to the edge of it.

"I've not seen hide nor hair of big game since November," said the bent fellow. "And the goblins are no shoddy lot. I've fought goblins before, but these! These are dangerous. They have their wits about them. You'd swear one of them thought he was a fox, the way he stalked me. And they work together. No goblins I've ever seen had that kind of discipline."

"That's what I call a sorry tale to excuse your failure as a huntsman, Fortman Eldrich," said the bulldog lady. "Bring me back a goblin and we'll see if he's got wits enough to out-fox me! And if he does, I'll meekly serve you some of that beef none of us can afford!" She whipped her shawl around her shoulders and stormed off.

The crowd laughed but the huntsman simply shook his head and walked away. Aaron and Lia followed just behind him.

"Sir, what were the goblins doing when you found them?" asked Holren when he and Mari caught up with them.

The huntsman looked at each of them for a moment. Then he nodded. "That's the strangeness of it—they appeared to be hunting me. I know goblins; some are pretty crafty. But never have I seen any with such patience. These were hunters for sure."

"Where did you come across them?" Lia asked.

"Beyond the Pass of Bincharn," said the huntsman. "It was on the other side of the valley, near a cave where once I saw a gruffen. I rarely hunt there, but I've taken to ranging farther out. Why do you ask?"

Before they could respond, a passerby broke in. "Gruffen, eh? I hear tell Tom came upon a gruffen just outside the village. It had one of our little ones with it. Bet those nasty beasts are coming here looking for food! Better watch your step, Eldrich. There's more than goblins to worry about. Soon every cat, dog, and mouse is going to look at us with hunger! Ha! Almost better to eat the cat than have it turn on you, eh?"

Someone else yelled, "Ho! Did Eldrich say he caught a gruffen?"

"No, 'twas Tom!" cut in the interrupter. "Sold it for a fine fee, too, I hear. Tom's been eating beef for supper, I 'spect!"

Aaron motioned to the huntsman to follow them. They entered a small alley, well away from the market.

Holren lowered his hood. "Did you see anyone else in the wood?" he asked.

The disfigured man looked intently from one face to the next. "You ask very pointed questions," he said. "What are you looking for?"

"A greater enemy," answered Aaron. "There is something much more dangerous than goblins out there."

The huntsman grinned at this blunt statement.

"There was a man near the gruffen cave," he replied; " a small, thin fellow. Other than that, I couldn't describe him for you. He was busy talking to goblins so he didn't see me. They listened to him intently. They seemed surprisingly afraid of him."

"Did you catch what he said?" asked Lia.

"No, madam, I was in a hurry to get away. Soon afterward, I was set upon and barely escaped alive," the huntsman said.

"How long ago was this?" asked Mari.

"Only yesterday morning, madam. I may not have been so harsh with the lady back there had the memory not been so fresh." He glanced at them all again and then turned to Holren. "Friends, if you plan to investigate, I offer my services as a woodsman. I, too, am interested in what goes on back there. Besides, there is strength in numbers, and numbers we will need against these goblins."

Holren fixed him with the hard stare of a judge, but Mari simply gave the huntsman her hand.

"Aye, sir, your offer is welcome," she said. "But you should know this company is not complete as you see it. There is another member who hides for the sake of his skin. Would you join a company that includes a gruffen?"

The huntsman raised an eyebrow. "Does this gruffen have a name?"

"He has a name, surely. Haven't they all?" sputtered Holren, rising to his full height and stepping back into the center of the conversation.

Fortman Eldrich nodded. "Of course, but this particular name is—" He stopped as something moving in the alleyway caught his eye.

"Go!" said Holren, suddenly. "Each to his own direction! Mr. Eldrich, we will meet you at the river crossing tonight at dusk. He's here! Go!"

The warning rang true in everyone's ears and they scattered quickly back into the crowded streets.

CHAPTER 3

Forays

While the others were gone, Brian and Annie stayed down in the laboratory. They did not venture upstairs.

"Who knows what sort of spies Taron may have?" Holren had said. "As long as we're gone, you had best not be visible."

There wasn't much to do. After they'd sat around for as long as they could stand it, Annie got up and started leafing through the Great Book, looking at the pages.

Brian saw her lips moving silently. "Do you understand it?" he asked.

"Some of it," she said. "If I move my eyes along the page, it's like I can tell what it's saying, the way Holren does. I seem to be able to tell what the shapes mean."

Brian came over and stared at it with her, but no amount of straining lent the shapes any more meaning. Finally he gave up and sat against the wall, content to listening to Annie's uneven reading. The stories were kind of interesting. There were long sections of dull descriptions of battles and people being born and dying. The names were especially hard. Pretty soon, though, they got to certain places where Annie recognized the names Holren and Mari, Aaron and Lia.

"So this is about them, too," said Brian.

"It seems so," said Annie. "Look, here's the place where it talks about the 'son of thieves' and—Oh!" All at once she stopped short. She stared at the pages with wide eyes, both hands held out in front of her. She wasn't breathing. She just stood there frozen, as if trying to stop something from coming out of the pages.

The gruffen stood up quickly and growled, the fur on his shoulders and neck bristling. Thin wisps of smoke rose from the open Book like vapor from a hot spring. It smelled acrid. Brian was afraid to look at the Book, but he was more concerned about Annie who was beginning to shake soundlessly, still staring. Slowly, he approached the table beside the trembling girl and looked at the open pages.

The image of two burning slits, like two bright eyes, was searing itself into the paper, as if something inside the Book was trying to burn its way out by glaring through the pages. Below the eyes, a mouth suddenly split open, a sharp-toothed entrance to a vast abyss that opened up deep beneath the floor itself. Brian felt Annie bump against his arm. She was edging closer to the open mouth.

Now the whole table was mouth and eyes! It grew larger and larger until it almost filled the room! Several voices cried from within the apparition: a whining, wheedling voice—almost pitiful—mixed with a high pitched rising squeal and a low moan wafting up from the throat of the beast. The stench was awful.

Annie was getting pulled in by some invisible tug. Brian tried to push her away, but found himself fighting the inexorable pull. He howled with anger and beat on what was obviously no longer a table, feeling a strange kind of skin beneath his fists. The moaning turned to laughter as Annie was slowly dragged over the row of immense teeth. A liquid crimson tongue raced up the floor of the mouth to envelope her. Brian couldn't keep Annie from being gradually pulled inside the mouth. He jumped up onto the chin of the huge face. Then, with all the strength he could muster, Brian lunged over the gaping mouth and drove his arm deeply into one of the burning eye slits.

The laughter turned into a howl of pain. The blast of stale air venting from the mouth ejected Annie and threw her across the room. She landed in a crumpled heap in the corner. Brian wrenched his arm out of the eye and rolled off onto the floor. The laboratory shook with the sound of the monster's roar as the huge face began to shrink back into the table. Brian got to his feet and staggered back, his whole body trembling with pain, his arm hanging useless by his side. The monster was still shrinking away, trying desperately to turn and see who had wounded it. Soon it would see him. Brian reached down by the hearth and picked up the poker with his good hand. He threw the iron bar with all his might, burying it deeply in the other eye.

"Aaaauuuww! Whoo are yooouuu?!" cried the face, "Whoooo? Whooo are YOUUUUU?!!"

The words bounced around the room faster and faster until, with a flash of fire, the face disappeared into the Book. The voices stopped. All was quiet except for the gruffen's heavy breathing. The fire had gone out, but the ghost image of the King glowed on the Book's open pages. The monster's face was burnt over the writing. Both eyes soon turned black, and in place of the grinning mouth was singed an angry scowl with bared teeth. Beneath that, still smoking slightly, was a new inscription. The runes were different from those in the rest of the book.

Holding his arm, the gruffen hurried to the crumpled little figure in the corner.

"Annie," he called, "Annie, are you all right?"

The little girl did not respond. Brian picked her up gently with his uninjured arm and took her to the fireplace. Sitting down, he set the child in his lap and fed the red embers with a couple of fresh logs. A few long blasts from his powerful lungs set the timber burning. How odd, he thought, still no smoke. The heat seemed to soothe the pain in his injured arm. Slowly, however, it went numb until he could no longer feel it. When he touched it with his other hand, it felt frozen. He was still shaking.

The bundle in his lap lay motionless and cold. He bent down to the girl's face, listening carefully for the sound of her breath. He couldn't hear anything. Perhaps the crackling fire was too loud. Or maybe it was the ringing in his ears. He gently felt her tiny neck with his tough hand. He could just make out a pulse, slow and faint, but definitely a pulse. She was so cold. Brian cuddled her close to his chest next to the fire, rocking worriedly back and forth, one arm holding her tightly, and the other dangling awkwardly to the floor.

Great tears rolled down Brian's rutted checks and dampened his thick beard. The tightness and heaviness in his chest deepened as he looked at Annie lying unconscious in his lap. He hoped she was just sleeping. Brian let out a strangled whimper as one of his tears splashed on the girl's cheek. Closing his eyes, Brian P. Gruffenson began to rock back and forth, humming quietly but urgently in a low tone somewhere between a purr and song with no particular melody. The pain in his arm was getting worse again. He tried to ignore it. At some point, he lost consciousness.

* * *

The next thing he was aware of was Lia's soothing voice asking him if he could move his arm now. Brian opened his eyes to see her rubbing some sort of ointment on his furry forearm.

"Where's Annie? How's Annie?" he asked quickly.

Lia smiled. "She's asleep. She refused to leave the room until we promised you would be well cared for."

Holren was standing nearby. "Obviously the two of you had some sort of encounter. She could not tell us. What happened, Brian?"

Fumbling for words to describe everything, Brian told the whole tale.

Holren's eyebrows arched. "So that explains the solid black in the eyes and, perhaps, the reason for our escape," said the wizard.

Brian turned sharply. "Escape? From who?"

"From Taron Kaiss, I believe," said the sorcerer. He recounted their meeting with the huntsman. "After we were interrupted in the alley, I went no more than twenty paces when I was intercepted by a small man as thin as a young boy but with a very old face. I could sense Dark Magic about him. He stepped along beside me as if going my direction. Once he looked up into my face with flashing eyes and smiled at me as if I were an old friend. I went back to the market to lose him in the crowd, but he remained with me. No matter where I went, he was there. I could feel the Dark Magic building and I feared he might use it in the market, but just as I was about to confront him, I felt his magic crack, and he quickly disappeared. I waited for quite some time before I thought it safe to come here and join the rest of you."

"What does the Book say, under the face?" asked the gruffen.

"It is an ancient language. I don't think he meant to leave it. Perhaps the Book itself was released for a moment and left a message. I do not know what it means. It says:

> Eyes of ice
> Blinded twice
> Watch the watch
> And miss the mice.

"and then:"

> Goblins in
> Goblins out
> Goblins in the waterspout.

"I can't guess what it means, but I won't forget it," said Lia, with a wry smile.

"I'm not looking forward to 'Goblins in the waterspout,' though," said Aaron.

"I fear I have no choice but to silence the Book myself," said Holren, bringing down a smaller book from the far corner of the shelves. He thumbed through the worn pages, scanning them quickly until he found what he was looking for. Taking the book over to the table, he placed his index finger on the point on the Great Book where the last sentence ended. His lips moved soundlessly for a moment. Then he spoke several sentences in a strange tongue, each sentence more hushed than the last until the final words were barely whispered.

The wizard put down his book and tried to turn the pages of the Great Book. He could still view the previous leaves but he could not turn the next pages.

"It is done," said Holren; "and it shall not be undone unless I command it." Sadly, he replaced his small book on the shelf. "At least that is my hope."

In a few hours, Brian felt fit to travel. Lia's ointments had brought much of the warmth back into his hand. After a bite to eat, they all went above to prepare for the excursion into the mountains.

There was no pack large enough for the gruffen but he didn't need much, only food. Aaron figured out a way to sling a sack over Brian's shoulder in such a way that the gruffen's hands were left free. Aaron adjusted it as well as he could; no point starting a fight over a strap cinched too tightly. Finally, saying goodbye to Annie and Mari, they stepped out into the late afternoon sun.

It was good to be outside again, smelling the cold air and feeling the snow crunching underfoot. Brian was anxious to move and found it hard to go slowly enough for the humans. They took a wide path around the village and reached the river crossing by sunset. Only a red glow remained in the western horizon. The pale blue half moon overhead cast a hazy twilight on the river. Beneath the stone and beam bridge, the gravelly banks lay in shadow.

They waited in the cover of some thick evergreens until they saw a stone tossed into the river from the other side. Lia and Aaron crossed the bridge first and entered the woods on the far side. A moment later, Aaron came out into the open and beckoned to Holren and Brian.

Once they were all together, the hunter introduced himself more formally as Fortman Eldrich. To his credit, he treated Brian the same as the others. Brian asked about the cave. From Fortman's description, Brian knew the goblins had taken over his home; the huntsman had seen it.

They traveled as quickly as they could, following the huntsman's path. Some hours later, they had not yet reached the Pass of Bincharn, but the moon had set and they were very much in the dark.

To avoid lighting a torch, they each tied into a long rope with Brian in the lead, his night eyes and sensitive nose serving as they always did to help him find his way. How odd that he was now leading humans to his own cave where, some weeks ago, he had actually entertained the notion of eating one! The thought repulsed him now. He was surprised at his speedy recovery from the rough escape a few days ago and the encounter with the monster in the Book just that afternoon. Apparently, Lia was a skilled healer.

Suddenly, he stopped. The others bumped to a stop as well.

"Goblins," hissed the gruffen. "I can smell them."

Aaron reached down and felt in the snow. There were no tracks nearby.

"Get off the rope," he said, quietly. "Quickly."

Then all hell broke loose. The forest erupted with goblins.

Casting the rope aside, the company gathered into a circle, back to back, to stand and fight. Holren sent sparks and flames flying, torching several of the first wave of goblins, but they just kept coming. Aaron and Lia flanked Holren, keeping the rabble away from the sorcerer. Fortman Eldrich swung his hunting axe in a wide arc, cutting anything that came within reach. Brian's gruffen instincts took over and he just waded into the enemy, cracking skull against skull and swinging his fists like heavy hammers. His clawed feet stomped on any who fell, staining the snow with black blood. Howls, growls, shouts and squeals ricocheted off the cliffs.

Brian crushed one goblin only to face two more. Fortman leveled those two with a stroke of the axe and brought the butt crashing down on a third. Aaron took the shoulder off of one fiend and caught another in the throat with the back swing. Waving his long arms, Holren cast spells of fire, instantly reducing many to smoking ashes. Lia fended off all who approached, building a grizzly pile at her feet. The humans' weapons were superior, but there seemed to be no end of goblins.

Then, with a great hissing and rustling of branches, the enemy turned and disappeared into the woods leaving the dead and wounded bleeding on the ground. The five companions remained alone, breathing heavily and sweating in the cold and dark. The wind began to stir, blowing the stench of dead goblin up in their faces. Growling, Brian picked up some snow to clean his hands. All was quiet again except for their own sounds and the slight breeze. Amidst all the pungent odors, Brian picked up one he particularly did not like.

He turned to run, but was stopped in his tracks by a small, lonely figure.

"We meet again, Brian P. Gruffenson," said the small man. He sneered. "Well, what have we here? Judging from the stench, we are in the company of fighters. And is that smoke left behind by the average wizard defending himself? Ah, yes, I do sense some minor form of sorcery. Could it be the same worn out old man I met earlier in the day, perhaps?"

Holren came forward and peered into the darkness where the man stood. "Show yourself," he said.

"Why should I show myself to you when you cannot show yourselves to me?" came the sarcastic reply.

"The goblins had no trouble seeing us," said Aaron.

"Ah, but they have something I now lack," retorted the man. "These eyes see nothing. Keep a respectful silence, fool, as befits vassals before a King."

"What king?" asked Fortman Eldrich. "A blind man? Wandering in the woods?"

"No! No! NOOOO!" cried the small man, each syllable becoming louder, deeper and more piercing. The trees shook around him and everyone was knocked backward as the air split with a roar that exploded in a blinding light.

Then Brian saw again the monster that had sent such shivers down his back some nights ago. The huge haunches were only a few feet away. The flaming bright teeth burned in the open mouth, but this time there were no searing eyes.

"Blind! Yes, blind!" shouted the monster in a terrible voice. "But wandering I am not! I know where I go, and I will arrive even sooner now that I have you here." He swept a great hand over their heads and nearly knocked them all down.

"I cannot see you, but I know where you are. The four of you will come with me and we shall see what may become of you. Ah, my old master, Holren, you shall learn much in a short time. I fear your limited sight will not avail you of the true beauty of the Dark Magic. Now come, all of you, and see that you hand over your weapons carefully. I will brook no more bloodshed."

At this point, the monster disappeared and a fresh battalion of goblins sprang up around them. Fortman went for his axe again, but Aaron restrained him.

"Not this time," whispered the warrior.

Reluctantly, they all gave up their weapons. Several goblins appeared and bound the humans' hands behind their backs but no one could get close enough to Brian. They surrounded him with spear tips but they could not bind him.

"One bad move, gruffen, and we skewer you through!" yelled the goblin leader. "I'll make the last thrust myself! Now get in line. We're moving!"

Then they fell in behind the head goblin...

...all, that is, except Lia. Brian wondered when she had slipped away.

CHAPTER 4

"Eyes of Ice..."

I t began to snow. Out by the cliffs, great flakes were drifting down. After the moon had finally set, the wind picked up and clouds covered the sky, dropping a thick, wet blanket of snow. The lack of moon or starlight made traveling difficult. The goblin leader, a surly character named Snarg, was leading them well in spite of this. Moving swiftly, even for a goblin, he headed directly up the ravine despite the steepness of the ascent.

"Former wolf, perhaps," said Holren under his breath.

"Shut it!" ordered Snarg. "Nobody talks unless it's me giving orders!"

"I should think you have little choice if you intend to bring us in alive," said Holren, just behind him.

"Watch your tongue or I'll cut it out," spat the goblin, wheeling around mid-stride and grabbing the long white beard. He yanked the sorceror's face close to his own and opened his mouth to speak, but no sound came out. His eyes met the sorcerer's gaze in the dark and he froze.

Brian stood just behind the wizard. He could feel the vibration he had come to recognize as White Magic. The sensation was mingled the prickliness that he felt around the Dark Magic. He stepped back into the pointed tips of goblin spears. He stifled the instinct to strike back.

Holren was saying something to the goblin in low tones using a strange language. The creature answered him trance-like in the same language. Suddenly, the goblin leader let the wizard go.

"What are we standing around for?" he snapped. "Move it! We have a league to go!"

Brian dared not say anything the rest of the way to his old cave but his mind was racing as never before. His fur bristled and his glands were wide open, despite the cold. If he could, he would make a run for it when they got to the top. The spear tip in his backside made such a chance unlikely.

Snow fell thickly in the silent woods as they came out of the ravine. Brian kept wiping it off of his nose. Every tree they brushed past dropped even more. Still they kept on at a brisk pace.

Near dawn, they reached Brian's old familiar hillside, passing hundreds of goblins in camps of twenty to fifty each. Each of these had a sentry. The parade of prisoners stopped at each sentry point for a short exchange between Snarg and the guard on duty. Finally, they came to the mouth of the cave. Two goblins stood watch on either side. Snarg announced himself and was allowed admittance. A moment later, he returned and led them around to the back side of the hill where a clump of snowy evergreens and thick undergrowth surrounded by armed goblins made a temporary prison for the quartet.

The gruffen was wracking his brain for an escape route. Every safe path was covered by goblin troops.

"The King will see you one by one," said Snarg. "I'll escort you myself. Cooperate, if you know what's good for you. Oh, and thanks for the weapons and food," he sneered. He looked from one to the other before his eyes settled on Aaron. "You!" he growled. "Come with me!"

Aaron got to his feet and marched off downhill toward the cave.

Fortman was about to say something but Holren shushed him. "Listen," he hissed.

They heard nothing. Several minutes passed, and still there was no sound but their own breathing.

"When Snarg returns, follow him," said Holren, quietly. "No tricks."

"Why?" asked Fortman.

"Trust me," whispered the sorcerer.

"Shut up in there!" croaked a sentry on the other side of the thicket.

Another goblin shot back: "You shut up, loudmouth!"

"Keep talking and I'll shut your yacking hole myself!" rasped the first sentry.

"Keep talking and I'll shut ALL your holes!" spat Snarg. The others fell silent.

He poked his head into the little prison and thumped the huntsman with the butt of his spear. "Your turn," he grunted. "On your feet."

As soon as the huntsman was gone, the sorcerer came quickly over to Brian and whispered softly. "Listen, and say nothing. Snarg is under a spell which cannot last much longer. I ordered him to take us somewhere safe. I do not know where that is, and neither will he, once the spell wears off. When you reach the others, wait for me. I'll be along shortly."

"Silence!" Snarg was already back. "Wizard! You're next."

"I am weary," said Holren. "Take the gruffen next."

"Get up! Move!" snapped the goblin.

"Let me rest a little," said the wizard.

"I said MOVE!" growled Snarg. He prodded Holren with the sharp end of the staff.

The wizard got to his feet and followed. He was making some strange movements with his hands and Brian could feel that odd vibration again.

Brian P. Gruffenson sat by himself in the thicket. If he was going to make a run for it, he would have to go soon. Then he realized he had nowhere to go. Annie was a long way away in the village. He would have to take his chances out here with the others.

Snarg was back. "Up, gruffen!" he snarled. "We're going, and I'm taking no chances with you." He yelled to the sentries. "Everybody! Fall in!"

No one responded.

"Move it, you maggots! Fall in!"

Still no response.

"Not worth their own vomit," said Snarg. "Come on, gruffen. I'm not afraid of you."

Brian simply followed. When he looked back, he could see no goblins guarding the thicket.

Snarg led the gruffen down the hill, away from the cave entrance. Brian noticed that the goblin's breathing was uneven and strained. Snarg seemed to be having difficulty walking straight. He was going more and more slowly. Finally, he came to a complete stop. He was shaking violently.

Brian felt his own fir bristling. He could actually see light glowing around the goblin. Snarg lost his balance and pitched violently backwards at Brian's feet, foaming at the mouth and convulsing. His eyes were wide and his lips worked noiselessly as he thrashed in the snow. Just as suddenly, the fit stopped, and the goblin's body stiffened, every muscle frozen.

Snarg lay on his back, completely still, his head tilted backward toward the gruffen. The light around his body went out, but it still glowed in his wide open eyes which seemed to be the only part of him that was still alive. Each eye worked independently, roving about, searching for something. Brian knew one would soon find him. Quickly, he reached down, grabbed the goblin's head in both hands and whipped it hard to one side. The neck snapped, but one eye was now staring straight at Brian. He twisted the head the rest of the way and slammed it into the ground. He could feel the skull crack as it hit a rock, and he quickly let go.

Then he ran, following Holren's scent. He caught up with the others quickly.

"Follow me," he said, pushing past them. The smell of goblin was fainter here and there was no noise behind them yet, but they would be easily followed. Brian could think of only one place where they might be safe. He pressed on ahead, leaving the others behind. They couldn't get lost; all they had to do was follow his obvious trail through the snow. The white stuff was coming down more thickly than ever, but it would not hide their tracks.

He could smell his destination. As long as he didn't fall in first, they would be all right. He slowed to a walk as he came upon a thick stand of alder, half buried in the snow. He was in luck: he'd come upon the best possible entrance.

"Through there," he hissed when the others caught up. "Stop on the other side. Very steep!"

Fortman climbed through the thicket. Aaron looked back, scanned the area, and then followed the huntsman in. Holren seemed preoccupied.

"Hurry!" said Brian.

Holren paid him no mind.

Brian could feel the White Magic. What was he doing?

Finally, the wizard turned and climbed through the alder thicket. Brian looked back. Even with his keen night vision, he could see no trace of their passage. Their tracks had disappeared Amazing. With a shiver, he turned and went in. The others waited in a little clump. There was barely enough room for the four of them, surrounded as they were by huge boulders and thick brush.

The gruffen worked his way to the front of the group and led them a little further to a narrow, hidden ravine. Even with his superior eyesight, Brian had to feel his way down in the dark. The others followed slowly.

When they reached the sandy bottom, they were some fifty feet below the surface. Only a tiny bit of snow found its way down there. Even in the daylight, one would have looked straight up to see the undersides of bushes, so at night it was almost pitch black.

"Well, I hope Lia did not follow us," said Holren.

Brian felt his stomach tighten. He'd forgotten about Lia!

"She'll have me to deal with if she did," said Aaron. "But she knows better."

"She must be very clever to get away like that," said Fortman.

Brian sniffed the air and remembered why he never came down here. There was something musty and wet, not fish and not snake.

"No goblins down here," said Brian; "but there's something else."

"What?" asked Aaron.

"Don't know. Never saw it," said Brian. "There's water. A tunnel first, then a river."

"If so, this cut should lead to the Falls of Gashelt, the headwaters of the Matheron," said Fortman.

"I never went to the end," said the gruffen. "Very dark."

"If we can find the exit, we will completely bypass the goblin camps and be able to return to the village," said Fortman.

"Then I suggest we follow the river out of the mountain," said Holren. "We cannot go back. Just a moment, though. This should help."

Much to Brian's astonishment, the walls were lit softly with an iridescent green as Holren produced a sorcerer's torch on the tip of a fallen stick.

"More magic," Brian muttered to himself. "Don't worry about it." He still found it uncomfortable.

They could now see the steep, icicle laden walls on either side. Behind them was the jumble of boulders they had just descended. Before them, a sandy path wound around to the right. Centuries of erosion had worn this cut in the rock wide enough for two to pass abreast. Cautiously, the company started off around the bend, Holren in the lead with his torch, Brian right behind him. Fortman and Aaron picked up rocks, crude weapons but better than nothing.

Brian strained his senses for changes of sounds or scents in the air. The pale green torch light revealed nothing amiss but the musty scent was strong. They were coming to a much larger chamber when his sharp ears found what they had been hunting for: a faint shuffling of cold sand farther off in the cave. Brian tapped Holren on the shoulder and held up his hand. Everyone stopped.

There was that noise again, a heavy lateral movement, too heavy to be a lizard or a snake, neither of which would be active in this cold.

"Sssssstop where you are," said a hollow, hissing, raspy voice from somewhere in the chamber beyond. It was a huge sound that made Brian think it probably came from a very, very large throat. "There isssss a wizzzzard among you. I do not wisssssshhh to tangle with wizzzzzardsssss."

"There is, indeed," replied Holren, holding the torch high with one hand and working a strange pattern in the air with the other. "Come into the light. I warn you that I have a powerful spell ready, should you do any mischief."

"I cannot fffffffit in that sssssssmall sssssssspace," hissed the voice. "But I will sssshhhhhow my faccccccce. I mean you no hhhhhhhhhhhhhharm."

A lizard like snout appeared, followed by part of a long head and then a bright, golden eye.

"A dragon!" exclaimed Fortman Eldrich.

"Yesssss," said the creature. "I am Gassssssssssssslic. I mean you no hhhhharmmm. Have pity on me, if nothing elssssse.

"Pity? Why?" asked Aaron.

"Thissssss dragon sssshape wasssss not alwaysssss mine," the creature explained. "I wasssss once a trapper in thessssse hillssssss. About twenty yearsssssss ago, I came upon a poor ssssssssssoul wandering in the woodsssssssssssss during a terrible ssssstorm. I took him in, and I have regretted that kindnessssssss ever ssssssssince! Do you know the name Taron Kaissssssssss?" The worm hissed.

Holren nodded slowly. "Pity any who meet my former apprentice. He now calls himself 'the King.'"

"A missssssssnomer to be ssssssssssure," spat Gasslic. "When I met him, he wasssss near deathhhhhhh, in ssssssuch a ffffffever. He raved and mumbled nonsensssssse all night. If ever he wasss ssssssssane, it wassss during that ffffever. Many timesssssss he called out the names 'Holren' and 'Mari', and begged for protection."

"Protection?" Holren's eyebrows shot up. "I would not expect that. I am Holren, and Mari is my wife...but I interrupt you."

Gasslic regarded him for a moment and then went on. "He ssssssseemed plagued by sssssssome powerful forcccccce. When he came out of hissss ffffffever, I quesssssstioned him about the namessss and he fffflew into a rage! I thhhhhhought he would kill me. For yearssssss henccccccce I wisssssshed he had. 'Transssssmutation!' he sssssshouted over and over. He ssssssswore it would be the deathhhhhhh of the Whhhhhite Magic."

The dragon's great golden eye burned almost red-orange. "He began to gargle in ssssssome ssssssstrange language that hhhhhurt my earsssssssssss. Thhhhen he changed from a weak wayfarer to ssssssome hhhhhhorrid beasssssst with flaming eyessssss and an evil mouthhhhh. Hhhhhhe fffffffilled the cabin."

The worm turned its head away from the group and shot a hot flame into the chamber. "I fffffelt hisss cold fingersssss piercccccing thhhhhhrough me. Then there wasssss a blinding flasssssh that turned to hhhhhhhowling laughter." Wisps of black smoke issued from the dragon's mouth as he spoke.

"Hhhhhe made me into thisssss: a dragonnnnn. Then he cursssssssed me and bade me sssssssearch for Holrennnnn and tell himmmm thisssssss:

'The King livesss and breathesssss and ssssendsss thisssss warning: Interfere and die. Ssssssssssurrender and ssssssurvive.'

"Sssssso now I hhhave told you. It'ssssss donnnnnne. I did not sssssssearch asssss he bade me. He hassssssssn't the power over me that hhhhhhe wieldsssss over hissss goblinsssss. But a great weight isssssss lifffffted from me now that I have fffffound you and told you."

Aaron shook his head. "Another victim."

Brian approached the dragon but Gasslic pulled his head out of reach.

"Won't hurt you," said the gruffen.

The dragon's eyes grew wide. "Unexxxxpected ssssentimentssss fffrom a ssssstrange creature!" exclaimed Gasslic. "Who are you? And what are you, may I asssssssssk?"

"Brian P. Gruffenson," said Brian. "A gruffen."

"He was not always a gruffen," said Holren. "Brian was only a child when Taron Kaiss used his accursed magic on him."

The dragon's chest rumbled and he sent another tongue of flames licking at the chamber air. "Hassssssss he no sssssshhhhhammmmmme!" he hissed.

"It seems the King's magic works against him," said Holren, thoughtfully. "In your current forms, you are both powerful. Your bodies have strengths your human form did not. Somehow both of you have retained your human core."

"Hhhhhholren," said the dragon. "Issssss it possssssible, that you, the masssssster, could change me back to my former ssssself?"

Holren shook his head. "I do not deal in Dark Magic. But even if I did, I could not change you back. Only the one who transmutated you can return you to your former shape. I wonder, though, if you might survive the restoration after so many years in this shape."

The dragon nodded slowly, sadly. "Well, then...iffffff there isssssssss no returning to my former shhhhhhhape, I may yet prove ussssssseful. This dragon body hasssssssss lived far longer than I believe I would have. I wasssssss quite old when I wasssssss transsssssssmutated. Sssssssomehow, I have sssssssurvived. I may be weak from lack of fffffffood, but I am more crafffffffty than I ever wasssssss." The lizard grinned, a frightening sight that bared the sharp teeth in his glowing mouth.

"Gasslic, can you fly?" asked Fortman.

"Perhapssssssss. It hasssss been a long time sssssssincccccce I lasssst flew. I have not ventured from thisssssssss hole in yearssssssss. Even when I lived out in the open, I did not fly muchhhhhh. I fffffeared being ssssseen." The dragon shook his head sadly. "People do not take kindly to dragonsssss. But iffff you need to know a ssssssaffffffe exxxxxit from thissssssss placccccce, I can ssssssshow you to the ffffffallsssssss," continued the dragon.

"We will follow you, then," said Holren.

The dragon backed away and allowed them to come into the larger chamber. In Holren's torchlight, they could see the dragon in totality. Gasslic was easily forty five feet long from nose to tail. His scaly hide was stretched taut over a bony ribcage. Apparently, he had not eaten well for a long time. The sinews of its arms and legs were gnarled and lean, and his wings were wrinkled from lack of use, but the scales were magnificent! Even in the green light of the wizard's torch, they shone brightly. Blue and purple covered the dragon's back, from a deep indigo to a pale violet. The underside plates were yellow gold with streaks of white and other colors in thin shards throughout.

They followed the dragon to the water's edge and entered the underground passage. Brian learned that he had not gone even a quarter of the way into the tunnel on previous explorations. These were indeed the headwaters of the river Matheron. The aquifer was large enough to allow the dragon to pass easily. In some places, the water had carved out huge chambers where the sorcerer's torch lit only a small circle of the gently flowing river. At such times, one could not see the far wall of the cave.

It was cold and damp here but not as cold as outside in the wind and snow. Water dripped constantly but there was plenty of relatively dry space on which to walk.

"How much farther to the Falls of Gashelt?" asked Fortman.

"At this pacccccccce?" said the dragon. "Perhapssssssss another hour."

"So much faster underground!" said the huntsman.

They were in the largest area of the cavern yet. The green light of the torch could not reach the far wall. Up above and toward the closer wall was a gaping blackness where a great chunk of the ceiling had long ago fallen down, resulting in a high dome.

"The river curvessssss away to the right and then proceedesssss to the falls," said Gasslic.

"No other way out?" asked the gruffen.

"Perhapsssss," said Gasslic. "I have not bothered to look for another exxxxxxit. I usually ssssssswim thissssss channel where it'sssssss deeper. It's eassssssier than crawling."

"A dragon swimming?" said the huntsman. "I never expected to meet a dragon, much less one that swims!"

"I am not a normal dragon." drawled the worm.

"Stop!" ordered Brian, suddenly bringing everyone to a halt. His eyes peered upward and his nostrils flared. The air was different here, a bit colder. A small waterfall bubbled down the wall.

Holding the torch high over his head, the gruffen scanned the ceiling. He handed the torch back to the wizard and began scaling the slippery wall. He had heard something up there, a high, squealing noise that sounded like speech. A pebble came loose from above and bounced past him, narrowly missing his cheek.

The gruffen froze, sprawled out on a steep incline, listening intently. The squealing stopped for a moment and then returned with renewed vigor. Suddenly, with lightning quickness, Brian's long, furry arm reached out and grabbed something.

CHAPTER 5

Owls and Mice

Annie said goodbye to Brian and the others as they left for the bridge to meet the huntsman. Then she went with Mari through the trapdoor and down the steps to the laboratory. For several hours Mari taught the little girl some of the spells from the great leather and wood bound books: how to make fire burn blue or purple or red, or how to make heavy things light, or how to see with one's eyes shut.

Annie was exceptionally good at these things. Most children would not have been able to understand the subtleties of the White Magic. For Mari, it had taken hard work and concentration, and she was a quick learner. For Annie, the task seemed effortless.

"Mari?" called the child, bringing the woman's thoughts back to the room. "Will he come out of that book again?"

The Great Book in the middle of the table still lay open where the two eyes had burned into the pages. The woman stroked Annie's hair gently.

"No, dear, this book will do him no good: Holren has silenced it."

The little girl leaned against Mari. "If he catches Brian again, what will he do?" Annie asked.

"I don't know," answered Mari. "He knows how to change things into something they're not, but I don't know if he learned how to fix it, and only the one who cast the spell can reverse it. If there was a power great enough to change Brian back, he might die. I don't know if after so many years the spell could be reversed precisely. Not even magic can accurately predict the aging that would have occurred by now."

Annie looked at her quizzically. "How do you know all that?" she asked.

"I have studied a great deal," replied Mari. "Perhaps more than was wise." Her mind retraced the painfully familiar steps to a time many years ago.

* * *

Before Mari and Holren were married, he had spent many hours teaching her the ways of the White Magic. Almost immediately after they wed, everything changed. He took on an apprentice and she found herself alone much of the time.

To keep herself busy, she delved into the books of lore, devouring all she found with a voracious appetite. In several months, she had taught herself many things her husband had not shown her. When he did have time to spend with her, he was impressed with her progress, but he counseled her sharply against learning too much. She passed it off as his usual benign pomposity and continued to learn whatever she read.

Taron Kaiss, the apprentice, was first infatuated with her, then obsessed. Usually, he was kept far too busy to cause trouble. When he had the opportunity, though, he always found a way to be near Mari. He had a tongue that dripped with honey, and he spread it liberally whenever she was around. Mari paid his flattery little mind, but she found his attentions amusing, despite herself.

Years passed, and Holren's health began to suffer. Still, after long hours with the apprentice, he locked himself in the library where he would study long into the night. He began to take trips out into the woods, first for a day, then for a few days, ostensibly to rest, but when he returned, he was more exhausted than when he left. The trips became more and more frequent, though they never seemed to help.

Mari let him be. All her pleas had gone unanswered.

Taron Kaiss made the most of his master's absences. With the utmost sincerity, he convinced Mari that Holren wanted her to continue his apprentice's education while he was gone. Since she did not know what her husband had taught the young man, she did her best to teach him what she knew, but he was already very advanced. Taron begged her to show him something different. She knew there was only one book that he was forbidden to read, though she, herself, had studied it without her husband's knowledge or permission. Taron wheedled this information out of her and then begged her relentlessly, assuring her that this was precisely the kind of training she was to give him. Despite her misgivings, she found herself teaching him transmutation. He learned quickly.

From then on, his attitude toward her changed. No longer did he just fawn and flatter. "You are a great sorceress," he said. "You should be partnered with a master who is not weak or afraid. Come with me! We will grow even greater together."

Mari refused him. When he persisted, she began to weave spells to protect herself. Taron Kaiss was livid, yet he backed away. Within a few days, he was nowhere to be found.

After he was gone, Mari was could not imagine how the apprentice had convinced her to teach him but it was too late. When her husband returned a few days later, she went to him and told him everything.

Taron Kaiss struck out on his own, shortly after Holren returned. Before he left, he set the village on fire.

Mari knew that Holren had not forgiven her. Worse yet, he had been proven right: she had opened the world of Dark Magic to his apprentice and it had turned Taron Kaiss into a monster.

* * *

Though there were no windows, Annie felt a cold breeze go through the room. For awhile she dared not move. She looked up at Mari who was staring blankly at the wall. Something seemed dreadfully wrong. She could see flickering shapes within the room, but she couldn't make out what was going on. It looked like some sort of battle but she couldn't be sure if it was actually in the room or if she was seeing something from somewhere else.

She wished it would stop. Finally, Mari looked up again and the cold feeling left the room.

"What was that?" asked Annie.

"A fight," said Mari. "They're in trouble. I must go. You stay here!" She headed up the stairs.

"What's happened?" shouted Annie, hot on her heels.

"They've been captured," said Mari over her shoulder as she climbed up through the trapdoor.

"We have to help!" said Annie.

"No," said Mari. "You stay here. Go back downstairs and I will close the trapdoor behind you."

"I'm going with you!" Annie insisted.

The light from the laboratory below barely lit the upstairs room, but Annie could see Mari doing something with her hands. She felt tingly and a little sleepy, but she grit her teeth.

"NO!" she shouted. "You can't make me stay! I'm going with you!"

Mari continued her motions.

Annie balled her fists. "Stop!" she said. "Stop it! I'm not staying here, no matter what you do!"

"Annie, it's too dangerous!" said Mari.

"I don't care!" yelled Annie. "I'm going!"

"I'm sorry, dear," said Mari. "You really can't go." With that, she made a strange motion with one wrist and instantly disappeared.

Annie's quick eyes caught sight of a roach scuttling toward the door. She ran to the door and lay down in front of it. "You can't go past me!" she said to the cockroach which stopped just out of her reach.

"Annie, I have to go help!" squeaked the roach.

"Then take me with you!" said Annie. The roach ran this way and that, but Annie did not budge.

Suddenly, the roach disappeared and Mari stood there, looking down at the little girl barring the door. "All right then," she said. "You're coming with me, but we're going to have to fly as owls. Are you willing to be turned into an owl?"

"Yes!" said Annie, getting up. "Let's go!"

The sorceress waved the trapdoor shut and the light downstairs went out at the same time. Then she lifted the heavy latch on the door. Wind and snow blew in as Mari and Annie pushed their way outside into the storm. Mari locked the door behind them with another spell. Then she made another strange motion with her wrist.

To Annie's astonishment, the world grew suddenly big. She could see and hear everything much more clearly. She was surprisingly warm, despite the snow.

Another owl, much bigger than she, stood nearby. "Come, Annie," called the owl with a voice similar to Mari's. "This will be a tricky bit of flying." She took off ahead into the snow.

Without thinking, Annie found herself beating snowy white wings. She had been turned into an owl! She still felt like herself, though. Much to her surprise, she flew as if she had always known how.

"Stay just a bit behind me," said Mari's voice. "That way the wind won't be so hard in your face."

Annie wondered how Mari would find the others. They could be anywhere out there. Regardless, she worked hard to keep up as Mari dipped and swooped over the snowy countryside. Once they got to the base of the mountain and began to fly upward, they could feel the wind at their backs and underneath them. Annie was glad it wasn't so hard in their faces anymore.

As they came to the top of the ridge they flew low, almost touching the snow. Just on the other side, however, the wind shifted, driving them sharply downward. Annie struggled to recover, tumbling into the snowy woods below. Down she fell, falling from branch to snow-covered branch. Somehow, she made it all the way to the ground and landed in a heap, only to be buried by the snow sloughed off of the branches above. Her shoulder hurt and she couldn't breathe.

The sound of scratching paws broke through the blanket of snow and she found herself staring up at a fox! Instinctively, she let out a cry but the fox disappeared and Mari now knelt in its place.

The woman worked quickly to dig her the rest of the way out of the snow. Annie lay quietly and tried not to cry.

"Oh, if Lia were here, we could have you all fixed. I'm afraid if I change you back into a little girl, you'll freeze out here," Mari fretted. She thought for a moment. "Annie, I'm going to make a snow shelter to keep you out of the wind. I must find Lia. I think she escaped." She piled snow around and over the little owl, gave Annie a kiss, and then took off again flying on snowy owl's wings.

The wounded little owl lay there in the shelter. If she twisted her head around she could see out but there was nothing to see but falling snow. Her shoulder hurt badly and, even under the warm feathers, she was getting a bit cold. She thought about Brian and the others. What could she do now? She stared blindly out at the puffy, white flakes.

She didn't see the two hunched figures that came out of the cloud of swirling snow, heading straight for her little shelter.

* * *

She awoke in the dark to find herself lying on a pile of pine needles. The blankets covering her were rough and prickly, but at least she was warm. The place smelled strange, yet there was something familiar about it. Rolling over sleepily, she realized that the pain in her shoulder was gone. So were the feathers. She was a little girl again. There were voices talking around the corner. One of them was Mari's.

"Not to be rude," Mari was saying; "how would you know if I am as beautiful now as you remember me""

"If I had my eyes, my dear, I am certain they would prove me right," said a man. He had the most soothing voice Annie had ever heard. The soothing man's voice continued. "The hair I hold in my hand and the nose and cheeks I touch are smooth and lovely. Your neck is long and fair. Your chin, so fine, your ears: all these things I can explore and know without my eyes, and I say you are altogether desirable."

"I'm just an old woman," said Mari, bemused. "And a married old woman at that! No more touching."

In the other room, Annie frowned in the other room. Mari was not being terribly kind to this very nice man. It was almost hurt the ears to hear her chide him so.

"Ah, but you are so much closer to me than to him," said the nice man. "In age, there is less difference. Your spirit, I know, is closer to mine than to his. He is far too cautious. The flame of adventure burns hot inside you, I know. Was it not this very flame that opened you to the Dark Magic? He spurned us for our need to discover. But you taught it to me. Ah, the gift you gave me! We were partners then, weren't we, Mari?"

The nice man's voice continued: "Since then, I have learned much and built on the seed you planted in me. Should I not have done so? You also have become skilled in your Magic. Come now, Mari, we should have escaped together long ago, but I offer you my hand now. All you desire is yours, for such is the power of the King. You shall see wonders you never dreamed, feel power you always knew was there but were never allowed to touch. Give me your hand now as you should have done then, and all will be forgiven. What is your answer? Your hands tremble in mine, do they not?"

There was a dreadful silence. Annie was confused. The man seemed so wise and gentle but Mari said nothing.

"Well, think on it, my dear, if you must. We shall talk of it again. Give me your answer when I return," the man said. "Let me go to the little one you insisted that I bring here."

Annie could hear him shuffling along the wall. She could see nothing in the total darkness. She opened her eyes as wide as possible. He was in the room with her now. She wanted to burrow down into the covers, but found herself unable to move.

"Hello, Annie. Oh poor thing, you're shivering," he said. A deep warmth flowed over her, filling her with a sleepy happiness. "Do you have enough blankets?"

She nodded.

"You'll have to tell me, precious. I can't see with these eyes anymore," he murmured gently.

"Well, it's dark in here and I can't see, either," said Annie. He did sound so nice.

The man chuckled in the dark, the kind of laugh that made you feel silly for whatever you had done that caused it. "That's only fair now isn't it? If I am blind and it's too dark to see, we are on even terms. If you can see and I cannot, that puts us out of balance, does it not?"

Annie said yes, it seemed so.

"Now I understand you have learned quite a bit of Magic recently, is that true?"

"Yes sir, I have," said Annie, not wanting to seem foolish again.

"For a little girl, that's quite an accomplishment," he praised. "Did you find it fun?"

"Oh yes! It was such fun; we made glasses float and turned fire different colors and I even learned to see with my eyes shut!" blurted Annie, excitedly.

"Enough!" barked the man. "It is unfair that you can see and I can't! You said so, yourself!"

"Yes, sir, I'm so sorry!" said Annie, leaning forward earnestly.

She sat back immediately. Horrible faces with bulging, fiery eyes and jagged teeth began to spin around her, gaping at her hungrily. She tried to shut her eyes but she could still see them, spinning and spinning, constantly changing shape, one face melting into the next.

"Do you want to see anymore?" demanded the man.

"No! No! Make them go away! Make them stop!" cried the terrified little girl, squeezing her eyes shut and covering them with her hands.

Suddenly, all was black again. She opened her eyes again but could see only darkness.

"Isn't this much better here in the dark with me?" asked the man, his warm breath on her face.

"Yes sir, I like this much better," she answered, relaxing. Her eyelids drooped slightly. She felt very sleepy.

"It could always be dark," he said, soothingly. "You would always be safe from those awful things." He reached out and touched her cheek, stroking it softly again and again. She couldn't decide if she was hot and his hand felt cool or if he was warm and she was cold, but it felt wonderful on her face and she leaned into his hand.

"There now; it's all going to be all right. Wouldn't it be better if you gave me your eyes so I could keep them for you? Then you would never have to see those awful things again. Would you like that?" His hand continued to stroke her cheek. Stroke, stroke, stroke. She closed her eyes.

"Shall I keep your eyes for you, dear?" asked the nice man. "Wouldn't that be nice?"

It sounded like the loveliest offer in the whole world. Her body felt heavier and heavier. All she wanted to do was to sink into his arms and lie there forever and ever, not thinking about anything or anyone. Then everything would be fine.

"Yes," she said wanly; "that would be very nice."

"Ah, that's a good girl." It was the sweetest voice, wafting through the air like a soft song, driving all thoughts from her mind. "Now open your eyes for me and I will make sure you never see again."

"But I'm so sleepy," she said with a yawn.

"Open them now, my dear, or the monsters will come back." The tone was firmer and it brought her back to her senses a little. She could feel his fingers on her eyelids, gently prying them open. She was about to yield and open her eyes to him when the raspy voice of a goblin captain hollered from somewhere around the corner.

"Sir! The prisoners have escaped!" Footsteps thudded toward them.

"What?" yelled the King. The icy edge in his voice was like a sharp slap in Annie's face. What was she doing? She shut her eyes hard and shrank away. Something was wrong here.

"Watchman," rasped the King; "I'll eat your hide if they're gone!"

Annie felt a strangeness in her body. Somehow she could see better in the darkened room now. How had it become so huge?

"Quick! Run!" said a squeaky voice she somehow recognized as Mari's. A great nose and whiskers wriggled close to her cheek and two black eyes peered at her startled face. "Run! Run!" said the mouse.

"Let's go!" said another mouse nearby.

Then they were all scurrying over rocks and boulders. Their path was blocked by several goblins entering the room so the three mice turned tail and scampered along the base of the wall, out of sight.

"Negligent, fools!" the King raged. "Come here, sentry. You will not fail me again!"

A terrible caterwauling rose behind them, punctuated by tearing and cracking noises. The mice fled to the furthest corner of the cave. Just ahead, they found a split in the rocks barely wide enough for a mouse. They quickly squeezed through.

"They can't reach us here," said a mouse with a voice like Lia's, only squeakier.

"Keep going! Keep going!" cried Annie, plunging on ahead, petrified of the noises behind her.

"Annie! Annie, come back!" called Lia.

Annie continued her headlong rush down the cracks in the rocks. She could hear water running somewhere nearby. Without warning, she lost her footing and, with a cry, tumbled into a rushing stream.

Paddling hard, Annie struggled to keep her head above the freezing torrent. She could see nothing in the pitch blackness, but she could hear the relentless splashing of water on rocks. Finally, she was swept into an eddy and came to a dizzy stop at the hard edge of a pool. Coughing and gasping for breath, she dragged herself out of the water and lay shivering on the stone shelf. Only then did she realize her tail ached.

Two other mice, nearly drowned rats, climbed up out of the pool and flopped down beside her.

"Oh, I thought it would never end," groaned Lia.

Mari put a clawed hand on Annie's shoulder. "I'm sorry if your tail hurts," she said. "I was afraid I'd lose you in the water."

Annie was still catching her breath.

"Heaven knows where we are now," said Lia. "I feel a draft; do you?"

Mari sniffed around. "Yes!" she exclaimed, crawling quickly to the edge of the stream. "Smell that? White Magic! There is a sorcerer's torch nearby! There's the light now!"

"Yes, but is that good news or bad?" whispered Lia.

"Good news, I think," said Mari.

"I smell Brian for sure," said Annie, sniffing the air. Oh, her tail ached!

Lia sniffed, too. "No goblins," she said; "but I do smell gruffen...and Aaron. What is that other scent?"

"I don't know," said Mari.

"I'll go see," said Lia. "One mouse won't be noticed." She crawled around the corner and squeezed through another crack. A moment later, she was back.

"They're all there!" she hissed. "They're coming this way. No goblins, but there's a dragon with them! No one seems to be afraid of it. Brian's in front with the torch." She kicked hard to get out of the crack and dislodged a small rock that bounced down the wall. "Shall we join them? We can climb down easily enough."

"Yes!" cried Annie. She squeezed past Lia without waiting for a reply.

CHAPTER 6

The Falls of Gashelt

"**B**rian P. Gruffenson, set me down!" said whatever it was in his fist. Startled by the voice, the gruffen quickly obeyed. Two other voices down by his feet erupted in hysterical laughter.

"Eyes of ice
Blinded twice
Watch the watch
And miss the mice!"

Brian stood amazed as Annie, Mari and Lia materialized out of nowhere. Gasslic reared up on his hind legs and tail, towering over them like a cornered lion, claws bared and jaws wide.

"Gasslic! These are friends!" shouted Aaron. "Don't be afraid!"

Slowly, Gasslic relaxed.

Annie stared at the dragon in amazement. The scales and armor plates on his back and neck almost glowed with an insistent blue, and the marbled gold in his chest and underbelly was dazzling.

"I am Gassssssslic," hissed the dragon, lowering his wings and folding them neatly on his back.

"A recent ally," added Aaron.

"We are Annie, Lia and Mari," said the sorceress.

Holren stood off to one side, arms crossed, his face solemn.

Mari turned to him and nodded her head. "It was necessary," she said, quietly.

Holren bristled. "I thought we were done with all that," he said.

Something in the wizard's tone of voice made Brian's neck fur stand on end.

"We had an understanding," Holren continued. "This devilry is forbidden and you know full well why."

Mari did not flinch. "Transmutation is not devilry. We three escaped from the enemy because of it. We came from the village as owls, were captured and taken to the King's lair in human form, and we escaped as mice."

Holren shook his head. "Had you not come as owls, you would never have had to escape as mice," he said.

"But this is precisely as the Book foretold," said Mari.

"Nonetheless," said her husband, his eyes glittering darkly under his brow.

Mari took a deep breath. "Listen to me," she said. "The White Magic is weaker on its own. You know this. To use the two magics in tandem makes them both stronger. We need all the strength we can muster. One does not refuse a sword because it has been used for evil." She held out her hand. "My husband, do not fear the use of such power by one whose heart is pure."

Holren took two steps and came face to face with her but did not take her hand. "Tell me no lie," he whispered. "Do you serve the Dark Magic?"

"The Dark Magic serves me," said Mari, unshaken.

He beheld her for a moment. "For now. For now, at least," he muttered, and turned away. "Enough!" he said out loud. "We have no more time for this. Now onward, Gasslic, to the Falls, and let us construct a plan by which we may counter the enemy!"

Brian picked up Annie and held her in one arm as he lifted the sorcerer's torch with the other. He, the dragon and the wizard led the way along the bend as Aaron and Lia followed. Mari and Fortman Eldrich silently brought up the rear.

Just before the Falls of Gashelt, they came to another spacious cavern rimmed by a wide, level shelf of rock a few feet above the current water level. Here the river was calm and deep, collecting in a broad pool before it flowed out of the mountain. Near the mouth of the spring there were openings large enough to allow even Brian to get out without having to swim over the fall.

The plan was for Aaron and Fortman Eldrich to go to the village at dawn and return with weapons and provisions. That decided, they all found somewhere relatively comfortable to sleep. Brian held Annie close to his chest where she would be warmest. Holren sat against the wall with his head bowed. He did not look up when Mari lay by his feet. Gasslic slipped into the water and slowly patrolled it up and down.

Brian was awake for some time, listening to Annie's even breathing by his side and watching the dull glow of the dragon's eyes gliding across the water. When Annie was deep in slumber, the gruffen lifted her gently and placed her next to Mari. The older woman looked up and smiled as she covered the little girl with her skirt and settled back to rest.

The gruffen came and sat down by the water's edge. The glowing dragon eyes approached, reflecting off the cold lake surface.

"What keepssssss you awake?" whispered the dragon. "The watch hassssss hardly begun."

"I want to know," said Brian. "You're not dragon, not human. Me either. Didn't know this my whole life. Just little ideas about being human." He nodded to the dragon. "But you knew. What good is it?"

"Ah, you asssssk the very quesssssssssstion I asssssssked mysssssssself time and again," whispered Gasslic. "For me, it wasssss like a deathhhhhhhhhh. Only when I put the wayssssss of my fffformer ssssself to ressssst did I gain any peacccccce. I ssssssssspent daysssssss in dessssssspair, roving acrossssssss the hillssssside assssss a dragon, sssstill trying to tend to my trapsssss. Then I realizzzzed that I wanted the animalsss for their mussssscle and blood, not for their peltsssss. I fought it, but I had to eat ssssssssometime, and thesssssse are for flessssshhh," he said, baring the sharp teeth that lined his jaws.

"I grew weak from lack of food. I wassssss ssssssstill consciousssssss of the world and who I wasssssss. Sssssso I deccccccided to make a life asssss besssssssst I could, assssss what I wasssss: half-dragon, half-human. About that time, I came upon two huntersssssss, former acquaintancessss. This tongue had not learned sssssspeechhhhhh, and my attempt only frightened them. Their arrowsssss did me no harm, but I sssssssaw then that I wassssss truly a dragon, and I resssssssigned my old form to the deathhhhhh that issssss memory."

Brian was squatting next to the serpent, tracing a crack in the stone floor with his fingernail. "I got no memories like that," he murmured. "But something's still in there. What if I was a boy again?"

The dragon swung its jeweled head around toward Holren seated in the dark. "Would the sssssssorcerer allow it?" he asked. "I thhhhhhhink not."

They lapsed into silence. For several hours they said nothing as thoughts flitted about in Brian's head. He knew nothing about what it was to be a Man. He had survived all his life as a gruffen, but obviously he was not just a beast. He wondered how different things might have been.

Something disturbing brought his attention back to the dark cave. The gruffen's eyes searched the pitch blackness and his nose opened wide. There was no scent and he could see nothing. Turning to whisper to the dragon, he saw the tip of its tail slip noiselessly into the river. Seconds later, there was a small splash in the water and then Gasslic broke the surface.

The dragon lifted itself out of the water and laid a limp body on the stone shelf. In the light of the dragon's burning breath, Brian could make out the shape.

"Goblin!" he said in a hoarse whisper.

"A sssssssscout mosssssssst likely," said Gasslic.

"I doubt they would send one out alone," said Holren close by. "There may be another." He held his hand out over the water for a moment. "There!" With a flick of his gnarled wrist, he pointed. A ball of glowing green bubbles rose to the surface, carrying with it a stiff black body which began to drift downstream.

Brian's eyes grew large. He had felt a shiver when the sorcerer pointed. Even the White Magic was something to be feared.

"Catch him, Gasslic! He must not be washed over the Falls," said Holren. The dragon slipped in and caught the dead goblin before it had gone far. Bringing it back to the rocks, Gasslic laid it beside its companion.

Holren shook his white head. "This does not bode well. When these two do not return, the King will send more to look for them. If two can find their way down here, the rest will discover us sooner or later. The White Magic will be strong about this place for several days."

"I will bury them," said Gasslic. "Sssssssssunk deep into the channel and weighted down, they won't be found for a long time."

Gasslic dragged the bodies to the bottom of the deepest lake and buried them under heavy rocks. Then he and the gruffen traced the path of the goblins all the way to the rift where the goblins had entered. Faint sunlight drifted down between the walls of rock and icicle. Brian wanted to erase any evidence of the goblin intrusion. As he crawled up to take a look around, his nose warned him to be cautious. The scent that confronted him froze him more than the cold dawn. He clambered quickly down the wall.

"What isssss it?" hissed the dragon.

"Him," the gruffen answered, his fur bristling all over. "Goblins with him. Don't know where he's going."

"I'd rather not wonder," Gasslic whispered. "We shhhhhould report thissssss."

They headed back quickly. Neither spoke again until they were back to the others. They found Holren sitting off by himself. Mari, Lia and Anni sat in a little group a bit further on. Aaron and Fortman were nowhere to be seen.

"What's this?" grunted the gruffen.

Holren replied, stiffly: "She insists the Dark Magic must be used. I say no."

Mari shook her head. "Your intransigence may weaken our efforts to the point where we cannot overcome the true adversary. White Magic and Dark Magic are equals. Together, they are much stronger than either of them alone. The King himself wields both, but he serves the Dark Magic, so his White Magic is weaker. A White Magician with strength such as yours can bend the Dark Magic to increase his power."

"Permit me to underssssssstand," said Gasslic, twitching his tail like a great, scaled cat. "Ssssupposse two magicianssss wield bothhhhhh White Magic and Dark Magic. The White Magician, working for good, will not likely be overcome by the Dark Magic. But the Dark Magician, working for evil, might be overcome by White Magic. Isssssss thissssss asssss you ssssay?"

"Precisely," Mari acknowledged.

"What proof is there?" said Holren. "You are the least objective of all! I alone am untainted by the Dark Magic."

"Then you cannot provvvvve your claimsssssss either," interrupted the dragon. "I think it issss a quesssssssssstion of whether or not you choosssse to work with ussssss or without ussssss. If the ressssst do not hold to your point of view, you musssst decccccccide whether or not to ssssssssssssstay. Our goalssss are the sssssame: we would ssssstop the King. Can you ssssssucccccceed alone? Could we? It would sssssseem wisesssst for you to remain with ussssss and keep a shhhhharp eye on the usssssse of Dark Magic.

"Chooosssse then, Holren," continued Gasslic. "Remain with usssss, and recognizzzzze our mutual need; or be offffff, and sssssee ifffff either of ussss faresssss well on our own. We shhhhhall continue regardlessssssssss."

"It is not that clearly defined," countered Mari, sternly.

"No. It is quite clear," objected Holren. "The dragon speaks the truth. If I remain, I have little choice but to endure this accursed dabbling in Darkness, but if I leave, there is great danger that you will be swallowed up in that which you do not understand."

"I think the matter of underssssstanding is ssssstill open to quesssstion," said Gasslic dryly. "We have yet to ssssee whether or not the Dark Magic issss fully underssssssstood by anyone here."

"Stop!" barked Brian. "Where are the other two?"

"Off to the village for supplies," said the wizard; "but this is not the issue."

"Dead or caught, maybe," growled Brian. "When did they leave?"

"When you went to bury the goblins," said Lia.

"The King is moving," said Brian. "I'll go look for them."

"Give them time to sort this out," said Lia. "Aaron said they'd be back by nightfall. If they're not back, then we move."

"I agree," said Holren. He settled back down and leaned against the wall.

Brian sat down next to Annie and grunted. No one said anything for a long, long time.

* * *

It was not yet dark when Aaron and Fortman returned. Brian met them as they clambered through the crack by the waterfall. They were both breathing hard.

Lia saw the look at her husband's face and asked: "Can we help?"

"No." He shook his head. "Town's on fire," he said between breaths. "Goblins everywhere. Another battalion on the way. We came straight back."

Holren's eyes flashed. "Once again he takes out his anger on the village," he muttered. In a louder voice he asked: "What of our house?"

"Untouched," said Aaron; "for all we can see, anyway."

The sorcerer strode to the opening to the cavern. "I must save what I can from the laboratory, but I need great speed. Sir Gasslic, can you fly?"

"My wingsssss lack ussssssse," he replied; "but I shhhhhhhould like to try."

"I shall be light as a feather upon your back," assured the wizard.

"Let me firsssssst ssssssssee if I can sssssssupport my own ffffframe," suggested the dragon. He turned toward the lip of the falls and submerged into the water. The others quickly gathered at the entrance of the cave and watched for his head to appear from the thundering wall of falling water. The sky was a clear blue and the bright, white snow dazzled their eyes.

The dragon's head and neck emerged from the top of the falls and, with a great spray of water, Gasslic spread his leathery wings even as his shoulders emerged. The wings, seen completely open now for the first time, were much larger than anyone had suspected. The wet, sunlit scales took their breath away: deep indigo, brilliant blue and purple with subtle variances refracted the blinding light. The winter sun exploded off of every diamond drop of water that showered from the outstretched wings.

The flight itself was not so glorious. With great awkwardness and much struggle, the dragon strained his weakened sinews, but his violent thrashing barely slowed his descent. When he attempted to turn about, he stalled, slid sideways, and crashed in an ungainly heap on the ice covered rocks by the river. He did not rise.

Lia sprang from the cave and fairly tumbled down the steep, icy cliffs by the falls. When she got to the bottom, she raced along the ice to the dragon.

Gasslic was breathing hard and trembling. His left wing lay crumpled beneath him and Lea was urging him to roll over to free it. In obvious agony, Gasslic twisted himself so Lia could reach his wounded wing.

From their high vantage point, the rest of the company gasped as the full extent of the damaged was revealed. The upper joint of the wing had driven into the rocks and the main bone had split lengthwise as the socket separated. The tendons were torn and the cartilage was severely damaged. Splinters of skeleton had ripped through his tough hide, and blood—darker and redder than seemed possible—oozed steaming onto the white snow. Lia's experienced hands worked quickly, stretching the skin and muscle over the open blood vessels to stop the bleeding. The dragon's hot breath melted the ice by his head, sending clouds of mist drifting into the air.

Suddenly, Annie spoke up: "If I were a horse, I could carry Holren to the laboratory."

"You'll not be a horse nor any other such thing, young lady!" snapped the sorcerer, furiously.

"But the child has a point," said Mari. "If I could fly, I could carry you as easily as the dragon would have."

"I go alone and on foot," insisted the magician.

"A waste of time!" said Mari, firmly. "You shall ride on eagle's wings!" Without another word, she stepped out into the open and immediately became a huge eagle. To everyone's shock and surprise, she was now much taller than her husband, an imposing bird with dark brown plumage stark against the whiteness of the landscape.

"Amazing!" whispered Fortman, to no one in particular. "She can even choose the size of the creature she becomes."

Holren shot him a withering look and turned away.

"I will see what is the matter with our friend the dragon," said Mari and unfurled her wings, not waiting for an answer.

Brian clambered out and descended the icy cliff.

"This will take much more work," Lia was saying when he arrived few minutes later. "We must get him to shelter."

"I'll carry him," offered Brian. He bent over Gasslic's head. "Melt steps for me," he said.

"A sssssssmall fee for sssssssuch a ssssserviccccce," hissed the dragon between breaths. "Sssssspare me no pain, Brian. It issssss dreadfully cold."

"You will need a hand," said the eagle. Mari immediately transformed herself into another gruffen.

Brian looked at her with wonder. He had not seen another gruffen, except in his own reflection. Suddenly here was one right before his face. Her protruding jaw was bearded as his own and her fat nose hung down almost to her lower lip. How ugly, he thought.

Mari ignored his gaze. "One more thing," she said, and waved her hand at Gasslic. Then she stopped. "That's odd," she said. "Nothing happens." She tried again. Still nothing. She turned toward the cave and waved at her husband who did not respond. "One moment," she said.

Suddenly, she turned into an owl again and flew up to the cave mouth where she had a short conference with her husband and then returned to the river bank. Gasslic was shaking in pain. "I'm sorry," said Mari, when she was a gruffen again. "I cannot cast these two spells at once, but you shall be lighter on our backs in a moment, my dear, thanks to the wizard," she said to the dragon.

Indeed, Brian was surprised at how light Gasslic was on his shoulders. The dragon made no complaints but methodically burned steps deep into the ice so the gruffens could scale the steep slope by the falls. With great care and no little pain, they carried the dragon over the boulders at the entrance and laid him out on the stone floor.

"My friend, I did not intend this," said Holren to the dragon.

"Your intentionsssssss were not the causssssse." Gasslic's voice was a hoarse whisper. "I have been sssssssswimming too long."

Holren looked at the ragged end of the broken wing and gritted his teeth. "I have caused you great and unnecessary harm, and I know not how to repay you."

Gasslic turned his great, horned head and looked the sorcerer straight in the face. His burning breath hissed. "Then I charge you thisssssss: chide not your wife, for my sssssssake ifffff not your own. Go, and let her carry you in my ssssssssstead."

The sorcerer nodded silently and gave something to Lia who was already tending to the dislocated shoulder. Then he nodded to Mari and they left quickly. The thunder of eagle wings told everyone they had gone.

Lia opened a brown bottle Holren had just given her and poured a bit of powder onto the stones by Gasslic's mouth. "Lick up as much of this as you can," she said, and stood back while the dragon searched for it with his hot, forked tongue.

"Better," said Gasslic. His breathing slowed and became more even. "The pain isssss lesssssss," he said.

Brian brought water from the river in his cupped hands and helped Lia rinse the wounds. Aaron worked right beside her, holding the heavy wing for her and asking a whispered question every so often. Lia focused on the splintered, protruding wing bone. Her hands worked swiftly and carefully, tying off a broken blood vessel, pulling torn skin back around the joint. From a small pouch she always carried with her, she produced tiny bottles of various ointments and potions. She took out a bag of gray green herbs and poured some into her hand. As she spread it on the wounded muscle, the dragon winced. Lia did not wait for him to recover, rubbing it into the painful tissue; there was no time for comfort. Then she pulled out a stout needle and thread. With Aaron's help, she pushed the needle through the tough dragon hide and was able to sew some of the larger flaps of skin back into place.

Meanwhile, Brian squatted by the dragon's head and just stayed there with him, saying nothing. Annie stroked the scales of Gasslic's long neck and Fortman carried on a quiet, pleasant monologue, telling stories from earlier hunting days.

Hours later, as Aaron paced slowly from the curve in the tunnel to the fall's opening, Brian finally drifted off to sleep. Annie was lying close to his chest, buried in his fur and breathing quietly. Fortman Eldrich was to stand the next watch, so he had fallen asleep some time ago. Lia, exhausted, lay next to Gasslic whose shining eyes were tiny slits with pupils shifting slowly from one side to the other. He was as asleep as any dragon could be under such conditions.

* * *

A loud thumping outside the cave startled Brian. Fortman Eldrich was at the entrance dragging something inside. The whoosh of wings outside indicated that Mari was still an eagle. The sunrise in the east cast a finger of light through the cracks in the rocks and lit the falls from below. The others were still asleep. Even the dragon did not stir as Brian got up and helped the huntsman bring in a wooden chest.

"Where's Holren?" asked the gruffen quietly.

"The lady Mari will bring him with the rest of what they salvaged from the laboratory," said Fortman.

"What's this?" Brian asked as they set the chest on the floor.

"Heaven knows," said Fortman, shrugging; "probably a sorcerer's toolbox."

Neither of them dared risk a look inside, so they paced up and down to keep warm until the eagle returned. This time the wizard was with her. The two seemed to be on much better terms.

"How is the dragon?" Holren wanted to know.

"Better," hissed Gasslic from across the darkness. "My earsssss at leasssssst remain shhhhharp."

The others were awake now, and they all gathered together as Mari, back in human form, came in from outside. Lia showed the them all how the dragon's bone had repaired and the hide had begun to cover it again. The shoulder had been repositioned and the cartilage was returning. Still, the dragon was unable to move the wing and it could not be folded completely.

"How is it that wounds heal so quickly?" asked Fortman, astounded. "This is a great magic that you do, m'lady!"

The news from the village was less encouraging. The fires raged on but not a living soul was to be found. The spells surrounding the laboratory had spared it from fire but the chest in the watery cavern was all that the wizard dared to take with him. He destroyed the laboratory himself, leaving nothing behind to be plundered.

Mari had disguised herself as a goblin and searched the charred streets for survivors. She found only corpses. Most had died of a wound directly to the heart. All but a few were burned beyond recognition.

"The bodies that were only partially burned were the most grotesque," said Mari. "They were not wounded like the others, but they were terribly deformed. I fear the King attempted a few experiments as he passed through."

"If he makes goblins out of rabbits, what might he make of humans?" said Aaron.

"A new order with such power as none of us can guess," Holren said solemnly.

Aaron grunted. "We haven't the numbers to fight the goblins he has already, much less take on some new demon."

Fortman Eldrich crossed his arms. "That sounds hopeless. Is it true? Are we the last survivors? What recourse do we have?"

The sorcerer answered slowly. "Long ago, my teacher used to say there was one place to go when all else failed: the Mount of Taharah. I am told the Book is written from there and that the White Magic lives within it. I have brought maps and we gathered a few provisions. The journey is long, if we can find the mountain at all. Whatever hope we have will be there."

"We're hardly prepared for a long trek," Lia observed. "Snow travel is slow and we can't carry much, especially Gasslic and Annie."

"Those who can walk will carry those who cannot," said the wizard, stoutly. "We have little choice. Taron Kaiss and his goblins move swiftly; so must we. Aaron, take Brian and the huntsman with you and cut wood for a litter. We shall carry Sir Gasslic on our shoulders."

"Sensssselesssssss," said the dragon quietly, and then he rolled over the edge of the shelf and fell into the water.

"Gasslic!" cried Lia, but the dragon had already disappeared beneath the surface. They waited, holding their breath, but no one heard him come back up.

"I'll go find him," said Brian. Without waiting for an answer, he took off into the dark passageway, headed upstream.

By now the gruffen was so confused, he wanted only to do something active. Running down the dark tunnel was at least active. All this waiting and deliberating seemed so slow. His tough, four toed feet thumped on the cold stone. There was no other sound. Even his keen eyes could find no other movement in the tunnel. Up around the bend, however, he heard a rippling in the water and smelled the hot scent he had come to recognize as dragon's breath. Rounding a sharp corner, he saw the glowing slits of Gasslic's eyes. The two dark pupils slid around and found him. Gasslic was lying in the water with only his head resting on the sandy shore.

"I've lived here for yearssssss. I can live here sssssseveral more," wheezed the dragon.

"You'll die here," Brian countered. "Goblins will come. How many can you kill?"

"Who knowsssss," said the dragon letting out a meager flame. "Your chancesssssss of sssssurvival out there are lesssssss than mine here. Carrying me isss nonesenssse. Go. Tell them nothing, or tell them my mind isss made up. You need ssssspeed, sssstealth. Go! Talk wasstessss time."

Hesitating only a moment, Brian turned and loped down the tunnel. When he reached the others, everyone stopped and looked at him.

"He said 'go,'" Brian reported.

"I should stay and tend to him," said Lia.

Brian shook his head. "He said 'go,'" he repeated.

"No one wants to leave him behind, but Gasslic is right," said Aaron, flatly. "We should go."

In the end, it only made sense.

CHAPTER 7

Departure

Everyone agreed that the maps were vague. Most of the charts were based on hearsay. No one in generations had actually been to the Mount of Taharah. A note on one of the maps even questioned its existence. Still, what choice did they have?

Aaron and Fortman fashioned a harness so Annie could ride on Brian's back when she tired of walking. Holren had brought a couple of packs along with the wooden chest.

A great argument broke out when Mari suggested that they should go as birds, horses or deer which were better suited for such a journey. Aaron agreed that horses would allow them to make good distance and carry some provisions. Once again, Holren vehemently opposed this idea.

Brian was tired of all the arguing. Grabbing the old man by the shoulder with a strong clawed hand, he grunted: "Horses are better. Forget it."

The sorcerer turned slowly, still in the gruffen's grip. "Are you giving me choices now, Mr. Gruffenson?" he asked, bristling.

Brian just looked at him, not batting an eyelash. "Horses."

"Have you any idea what I am capable of doing to you for such an affront?" growled the sorcerer.

"No," Brian growled back. "Let's go." Then he took his hand off Holren's shoulder and walked away.

The sorcerer had heard enough. "I will not tolerate such insubordination and the use of forbidden magic! I will not set out with a company fashioned by such diabolical means. Gruffen, you are out of place! Follow the lead of men older and wiser than you."

"Like what?" said Brian over his shoulder. "Let's go."

"We can undertake the same task, but I'll not ride," came Holren's answer after a short silence.

Brian turned back around and looked him in the eyes. "Too slow. Ride, or don't come."

"You would exclude me?"

"You want out, stay out," said Brian. "No more fuss."

Holren looked from one face to the next.

"We need you," said Brian. "You need us." He shrugged. "Let's go."

"Onward then," replied Holren, gathering up the maps and carrying them toward the cave entrance. Everyone picked up what was within reach and went out through the opening. Mari turned herself into an eagle and carried everyone down, one by one.

When they were all on level ground below the falls, Mari returned to human form and once again began the magic. Holren would not watch. Lia became a lovely chestnut mare and Annie became a small hawk, but when Mari tried to turn Fortman into an eagle, she found she could not.

"What's wrong?" asked Aaron.

"I can't do it," she stammered. "I have no power now."

"Quickly! Turn her back!" shouted Aaron.

Mari did so, returning both Lia and Annie back to their human selves. They both felt fine. All was as it should be. After a moment, Mari turned Fortman into a horse. Nothing went awry. Lia became a horse also. Then Mari tried to make herself into a horse and it worked without a hitch. After that, though, she could not turn Annie into anything.

"I seem to have run out," said the sorceress. "Apparently, I cannot do more than this."

Holren turned around. "Indeed," he said. "Too many complex spells cannot be perpetuated simultaneously. Perhaps transmutation into a bird is too difficult once there are horses. I say enough is enough."

He was not particularly angry now and his advice was practical. They decided to leave well enough alone.

Brian climbed back up to the cave for one last look around as the horses were being loaded up. He was about to leave when a hiss in the blackness stopped him.

"Well done," said the dragon's voice. "Lead on, Brian P. Gruffenson."

"You good?" asked Brian.

"Perhapsssss, perhapssssss not. I do not give up easssssily. Now go. Trusssssst your inssssstinctssssss. They guide you well."

The gruffen nodded. The sound of water slipping past dragon scales told him Gasslic was leaving. Brian left the other way, out into the winter sun.

Down below, the horses were telling the men how best to shift the burdens so that they would be most comfortable. Fortman was too loaded down with gear to take a rider and Brian said he would be fast enough on his own, so Aaron mounted up on Lia. Despite everything, Holren mounted up without complaint. Annie sat in front of him and he seemed glad for her company. They headed north up the corridor of the mountain range, away from the village.

The first several miles were a mixture of nervous haste and frequent stops to adjust the loads on the horses. Then, having not seen more than an occasional goblin path, they slowed to a more even, sustainable gait.

The sun was setting to their left when they began to look for a place to spend the night. They had traversed the long ridge about midway up to avoid being seen from the valley. The sun had gone behind the western peaks awhile ago and the valley was now getting dark. The horses were tired, and so was Brian. He spotted an overhang some way ahead and set off to see if it might make a good shelter. The others continued on slowly as he plowed through hip deep snow.

When he reached the overhanging rock, he took a quick look around and sat down solidly on a snow covered log. Finally alone, he remembered his old, solitary gruffen existence. His stomach growled and he wondered if the horses could turn into deer and be roasted. A fat deer would taste so good! Then he remembered who they were and the thought of eating them repulsed him again. How frustrating to be hungry and have no appetite at the same time!

The weary gruffen inspected the area more carefully. A good bit of snow was piled above the overhang, but it seemed stable enough. Drifts surrounded an almost bare floor on both sides of the solid rock wall that propped up the overhang. It was tight but they would be out of the wind.

Brian trudged back to the others and brought them all to the natural bivouac. The horses were unloaded and returned to human form. Fortman asked for the first watch. This proposal was gratefully accepted. Not long after that, without much of a supper, they burrowed into the pine needles as best they could. Brian wrapped Annie in a blanket and held her next to him. She was asleep almost before he had a chance to get situated.

* * *

The sun was shining on the western peaks when Brian P. Gruffenson opened his eyes. Everyone else was still asleep. The huntsman, Eldrich, was still sitting at his watch post. His head was slumped over his chest and his shoulders lifted and drooped evenly. He was sound asleep also.

A smell in the crisp morning air brought Brian's senses ringing into focus. Rabbit! There were several rabbits just behind a small clump of brush. Leaving Annie wrapped in her blanket, the gruffen made his way silently past his sleeping comrades. If he could get one, they would eat meat for breakfast. His stomach reminded him how good breakfast could be.

The rabbits seemed unaware. With typical gruffen impatience, Brian lunged at the bush and thrust both hands through the prickly branches. He got a face full of snowy thorns and a handful of rabbit ear, but the prize he caught wasn't very big. He dragged the wriggling rabbit out of the brambles and gave its neck a quick snap. Then as cheers erupted behind him, he began to pluck the thorns from his cheeks and forehead. Annie came bounding through the snow behind him and nearly fell on him in her excitement.

"Look, Brian," she squealed, "Mari got one too!"

He extracted a particularly nasty thorn from his brow, and then turned to see an eagle with a large male rabbit firmly grasped in its talons. Looking at his own little catch, Brian shook his head and tossed it up the hill toward the bivouac.

"You hunt, then," he grumbled.

He received a lot of sympathy for his scratched face and hands. Eating the rabbits helped a bit, but he was still hungry.

Mari returned Lia, Aaron and herself to horse form and they all set off again.

They continued on this way for several days. If not for the cold, wet snow, the ride would have made a lovely holiday. The mountains on either side of the valley shone brightly in the open sunshine. They were heading steadily downhill as they came to the edge of the mountains. The further north they traveled, the warmer the air became. Spring was not expected in the upper altitudes for several months, but soon their heavy garments were too warm. Each time the humans became horses, their coats were a little bit sleeker and less woolly.

Periodically, they would consult the maps but it was hard to draw conclusions from the often indecipherable inscriptions. Everyone had an opinion as to what they meant. These discussions usually ended with Brian grunting and plunging on ahead.

Since the valley had guided them directly north, this had not been a problem. They were pretty sure that the Mount of Taharah was well north of them and quite some distance away, so it seemed expedient to continue on as they had. This plan came under reconsideration when the chain of mountains began to veer west. A great peak stood on their right. Brian made a steep climb part way up its rocky face and verified that the chain continued to curve until it led due west.

After a short discussion, they decided that Mari should become an eagle and go up for a look at the landscape. Once the load was removed from her back, the sorceress changed into bird form and soared up into the clear blue sky.

"Interesting," she called down as she rode the thermals higher up the slope; "I can make two horses and one bird, but not two birds and one horse!" A moment later, she disappeared over the peaks.

Back on the ground, everyone else huddled around the maps again to discuss whether this squiggle was that mountain, or if there might have been a river here years ago. An argument ensued over a certain smudge that several thought indicated a lake until Fortman Eldrich put his horse nose to it and informed them that it was not ink, but spilled tea. This discovery sent everyone into fits of laughter, including the horses, which made Aaron and Annie laugh all the harder. For the first time since they had set out, the mood was light.

If it could have remained so, with the sun shining, the snow melting and all engaged in merriment, everything would have been fine, but after half an hour passed and Mari had still not returned, the mood became somber. Strangely, so did the weather.

The afternoon wore on, and still there was no sign of the eagle. The sky became darker and darker as clouds began to move up from the south. Lit by the western sun, the towering thunderheads were beautiful, but below them one could see only black and gray as peak after peak slipped behind a veil of snow or rain. The storm would be upon them by nightfall.

Holren fretted about Mari's absence while Brian and Aaron scouted around for a suitable shelter. The huntsman was frustrated at having remained as a horse, but Lia reminded him that they were better prepared to handle the weather.

Annie had fallen asleep. She awakened to find everyone scurrying about, preparing for the oncoming storm.

"Look!" she called, pointing at the sky. It was dark with clouds by now. The setting sun glinted off the wings of a huge eagle that came soaring high over the peaks.

"Mari! Finally!" shouted Holren.

Even as they watched, the eagle wheeled about and dove straight for them.

"Not her!" shouted Brian, quickly scrambling down from the hillside, racing toward Annie.

This eagle was massive! With terrifying swiftness, it seized one of the horses. Fortman gave a terrified whinny as he was picked up and hauled over the ridge like a common rabbit. The contents of his pack trailed out behind him in an awkward stream.

"What was that?" exclaimed Aaron, still the woods.

"A huge eagle just took Fortman!" hollered Lia, rearing up on her hind legs and looking in all directions. "Is he alive? I couldn't see."

"Look out!" cried Brian as another bird of prey dropped out of the heavens.

Everyone scattered but the eagle fixed Lia in its grip, thundered back into the sky and sailed over the ridge with her.

Aaron bellowed in frustration, finally making it out of the woods. Brian scooped Annie into his furry arms and ran for the nearest tree. Holren followed, waving his arms and muttering some strange incantation. Aaron was retrieving his weapons that were still tied to Mari's saddle.

Just as suddenly as the first two, another eagle dove down out of nowhere. Aaron flung an axe at the diving bird, but with a slight shift, the eagle avoided it and it sailed off into the woods. Before he could draw a sword, the eagle pounced and smashed him into the ground. Then it grabbed him and lifted off with pounding wings.

The sorcerer finally finished his incantation, but the shock wave he sent out was too late. It merely ruffled the feathers of the fleeing predator.

Annie clung to Brian's fur.

"Stay where you are!" hollered Holren. "They may come back."

Sure enough, one of the eagles sailed over the ridge and dove toward the clearing. Surprised to find it empty, the predator lifted back into the air. Another eagle sailed over the ridge, then another. Soon there were five massive birds circling the stormy sky above the travelers, watching for anything that moved on the ground below.

One of them dropped deep into the valley and caught a deer. After what seemed like hours, the three huddled by the tree watched them leave. By now, night was nearly upon them and the storm was closing in. When no more eagles returned, Brian pointed to the ridge top. "I'll go up and see," he said.

Holren and Annie remained hidden under the tree and watched as the gruffen quickly scaled the slope. Once on the windy crest, Brian could make out the distinct shape of a large butte, several miles east. If any eagles lived nearby, that would be the best spot for an aerie, he thought. The storm was beginning to whip the trees by the time Brian got back to the two in the woods.

"Let's go," he suggested. "Other side will be drier, out of the wind."

They struggled up the steep hill as stinging drops of rain beat down. Brian held Annie and Holren clutched the remaining maps. The light was failing fast. Holren could not negotiate the same route Brian had taken to the ridge, so they had to traverse quite a distance before they could continue upward. By the time they reached the crest it was completely dark, the wind was so strong they kept one hand down to avoid being blown over the cliff. Good footing was hard to find. The other side was terribly steep at this point. They would have to backtrack along the ridge to find an easier way down.

"We have to get out of the wind!" shouted Holren.

They found a rocky place where it seemed like they might be able to get down. Brian went first, still holding Annie. He had to feel around for every foothold.

"I can't make it from here!" hollered the wizard. "I'll come around another way."

Brian finally found a solid ledge that sloped downward. He crept down it until it came to an end but it seemed to go nowhere so he turned back.

"Holren!" he hollered. The magician did not respond.

Brian called again but the wind blew away the sound before it went very far. Still hanging on to Annie, he searched the cliff face blindly until he was completely disoriented. Too exhausted to try anymore, he found a crevice deep enough to squeeze into and fell asleep with Annie tucked deep in beside him.

* * *

Morning arrived without the sun. The thick clouds from the night before remained, drifting like ghosts along the stones of the cliff, leaving a steady drizzle in their wake. The rocks, the sky, everything was cold, wet and gray. Brian extricated himself from the crack in the mountain and stretched. Annie! Where was Annie?

"Mr. Gruffenson, are you finally up?" said the little girl from around the corner. "If you don't come and get some of these berries now, there might not be any left for you. I've nearly eaten half the bush as it is."

"Berries," growled the gruffen, quite hungry, now that she brought it up. "Where did you find berries?"

"Come and see; and watch your step, your big feet might not fit as well as my small ones."

Gingerly working his way around the ledge, Brian wondered how he had gotten this far in the pitch blackness last night. Where was the wizard? He tried not to think of Holren lying broken and battered at the bottom of the foggy mountain.

Annie was several yards away, stretched out against the rock. One hand reached up to a tiny, spiny bush from which she picked small red berries. Her mouth was stained from the juice but she was grinning all the same.

"Are you going to come and get some or do I have to do everything for you?" she teased.

"Can't get there from here," said Brian. "Maybe Holren found a good way down." Or maybe not, he thought.

Annie stuffed another handful of berries into her mouth and filled her pockets. Then, easy as you please, she scrambled across to where Brian kept a tenuous perch on the ledge. He ate the berries gratefully enough but they were hardly more than a mouthful. There were no other bushes in sight. Perhaps they could find food of some sort in the valley.

"We better go" said the gruffen.

"Go where?" asked Annie. She wiped her mouth on her sleeve, staining her sleeve more than she cleaned her face. "We don't have the foggiest idea where anyone is."

"Maybe," grunted Brian. "Still better to get down."

They hollered Holren's name but got no answer. There was no point to looking for the wizard on the cliffs in the fog. Brian and Annie agreed that even if the sorcerer had spent the night up there, he would eventually climb down. Brian groped his way along the rocks with Annie behind him. Several times, they had to diverge and regroup because Annie couldn't reach a handhold or Brian couldn't use such a small foothold.

Hours later, much to their relief, the incline became less steep and they could walk upright without handholds. Annie said she was not feeling well, and she was beginning to lag behind so Brian carried her on his shoulders.

The slope gradually leveled out. They were glad to be off the mountain. Scraggly scrub oak trees dotted the hillside. Boulders of all sizes were randomly strewn about as if some massive giant had flung them. There was no snow at all on this side of the mountain; the air was considerably warmer.

Despite the bleak weather and the lack of food, Brian was in high spirits. In fact, he felt happy, giddy even. He wandered merrily along, swinging his arms and laughing, oblivious to the fact that the woods were getting thicker and the branches began to intertwine overhead. Carelessly forging through the ever more tangled brush, he didn't notice the gathering darkness.

Soon he was deep within the woods, hardly able to see in front of him, but singing at the top of his lungs. He talked to the trees, to himself, to the dirt. Splashing like a child through a creek, he slipped on the bank and fell face first into the mud. Howling with glee, he flopped back into the water and rinsed off only to turn and fall again.

He crawled out of the creek and was stumbling through thick brush when he slammed his forehead against a tree branch and sat down with a jolt. Dizzy and sick, Brian tried to sit up. It seemed unusually dark. He turned his head to look around and everything spun as if he had set the whole world in motion. Brian groaned and lay still.

* * *

He awoke to damp darkness. Brian listened hard but could hear only the ringing in his ears and the quiet burbling of a stream somewhere nearby. In this darkness, even his sensitive eyes could glean almost no light. Judging from the moisture, everything was enveloped in cool, dense fog. His nose told him he was deep in the woods, but even his sense of smell seemed dull and confused. His head hurt and his stomach was empty.

"Berries," said Brian, guessing the source of his headache. His muddled brain remembered having had trouble with berries once before. They had made him sick and forgetful then, also. How long had he been in this forest? Where was he?

And, most importantly, where was Annie?

"Annie?" Brian called into the fog. It muffled his voice. He didn't like this place; something about it felt like Dark Magic.

"ANNIE!" This time he bellowed it. The stream continued, heedlessly tumbling along.

Holding his aching head, Brian tried to piece together the events. They had come down from the mountain onto a slope with gnarled oaks. Eventually they had entered the wood. The rest was a blur. He remembered hitting his head, but he did not remember losing Annie. All he knew was that she had been riding on his shoulders before they got into the woods.

He did remember crossing a creek, so he decided to try to follow his own trail back to the mountains. Because of the berries, he couldn't easily sniff out his own footprints in the damp, pungent rot on the forest floor. After some scouting along the water's edge, he picked up his trail and fought his way through the brush trying to follow it.

A few paces later, he lost the trail again. It seemed to meander this way and that through the underbrush with no particular objective. After awhile, it became apparent that he was not likely to find the little girl by this method. If she had fallen off his shoulders in those woods, he might pass within two feet of her and never know she was there. The brush was too thick and the night too dark. Losing his trail for the last time, he decided to force his way out of the forest to see if he had lost her somewhere near the scrub oaks.

Try as he might, he could not escape the entanglements of the woods. He thrashed around in the dark, calling out for his friend. No one answered. No sound ever seemed to reach beyond the nearest tree trunk. He fought on, brambles and burrs embedding themselves in his fur. Spiny branches tore at his tough skin, and he wondered how large the forest really was.

How long he struggled in the woods he could never tell. The effort began to clear his head a bit. By now, he knew he had lost all sense of direction. He was about to stop and rest when he came to a talus slope that marked the edge of the forest. It also marked the edge of the fog. Moonlight filtered down onto the ferns and mosses. Although an uneasy sense of magic still hung in the air, Brian was relieved to be out of the woods.

Rising before him, wet and solid, was a stone cliff. In the moonlight, it appeared too smooth and steep to climb.

It took a moment for him to realize where he was. He had gone the wrong way to find Annie. This was the butte he had seen from the mountain.

Sinking to his knees, he let out a cry of anger and disappointment. For once, it felt like the sound penetrated the thick stillness. Finding some comfort in this, he filled his lungs and let loose another howl.

Above him on the cliffs, he heard a shrill scream, a rasping, brittle shriek: the cry of an eagle. Apparently, he had guessed the site of their nest correctly and had somehow found his way to it. Perhaps Lia, Mari, Aaron and the huntsman were trapped just above him at the top of the cliff. Maybe somehow Annie was up there, too. Maybe they were already long dead.

Hanging onto hope, he scrambled up the talus and felt along the wall for anything resembling a handhold or foothold. The wall yielded nothing for many yards, no cracks, no bumps, no indentations. The other eagles were crying overhead, circling in the moonlit sky, looking for the source of the howl. Brian found a clump of bushes at the base of the wall. Tucking himself away, he slumped down and succumbed to exhaustion.

* * *

Annie awoke to the smell of something awful. It tasted awful, too.

"Drink it all," said the hand holding the hollowed out branch. "It will feel better than it tastes, I hope."

Annie had already swallowed much of the foul liquid. It was gritty and full of pieces of crushed leaves and powders but she felt her stomach relax and the burning in her head began to cool. She opened her eyes a little. In the dim light she could see a great white beard and eyebrows.

"Now lie there quietly. It will be awhile before you get better," said the beard.

The little girl dropped off to sleep again, but her breathing was less labored and her heartbeat was smoother.

* * *

"I hope I got that right," Holren mumbled to himself. He had used whatever he could find on hand. It was hard to be sure what to she needed. Judging from the stains on her face and clothing, she had eaten some of the mountain berries. He was surprised she was recovering so well. The wizard laid his cloak on the girl and began to scavenge drier wood for a fire. Like it or not, they both had to stay warm.

He wondered how she had made it down from the cliffs. He, himself, had nearly fallen trying to descend in the fog. When the skies cleared later in the day, he had gone quickly from oak to oak, keeping out of sight as much as possible. The eagles had been circling most of the day. He discovered Annie lying in a heap beneath one of the trees, and he was glad to have found her so soon. Any later, she might have been much worse off. He had carried her a short distance into the woods. Though he found a few four toed tracks near Annie, they led nowhere, and he had seen neither hide nor hair of the gruffen.

Holren lit a small fire and cast the simple spell to eliminate the smoke. The sun was setting on the second day since his wife had gone up to survey the landscape. He had no idea if she had been attacked by the eagles or if she was still alive in some other form somewhere in the woods. Either way, finding her would be difficult. Finding *any* of the others would be difficult.

It was getting dark when he heard an unmistakable "whoosh." A huge eagle landed not more than fifty feet away in the clearing. It cocked its head and looked around. Holren held perfectly still, but the fire still burned. The eagle looked straight at him. Holren moved not a muscle. Raising its wings high over its head, the eagle thundered away toward the cliffs.

The wizard was sure he had been seen. The only escape was deeper into the woods. He was gathering Annie into his arms when he again heard the sound of feathers.

"Holren!" called a woman's voice. "I'm here!"

He turned quickly. There at the edge of the woods stood the most beautiful woman he had ever seen. She looked for all the world like a queen, so stately was her demeanor and so royal her apparel. In the waning daylight, the golden brocade on her purple cloak glittered with a light of its own. Her white dress was embroidered richly in purple and gold. The magician gasped.

"Mari?"

It *was* Mari. She walked into the grove and took Annie from her husband's arms.

"Are you safe? Where have you been?" Holren asked.

"In the citadel, up in the cliffs," she answered. "The eagles have not harmed me; in fact, they brought me here. I'm fine, as you can see. This bird will fly you to the citadel. I'll take the little one with me."

She had been leading him out to the clearing where the eagle waited patiently. Holren was too exhausted and relieved to question her. It was like a troubled dream in which, perhaps, things finally begin to go right.

Mari helped him onto the eagle's great back. Then the eagle took off.

The ride was marvelous, but Holren just hung on wearily. They circled about, rising into the sky until they could glide across the valley to the aerie.

The butte rose straight up from the surrounding woods to a nearly flat top like the stump of a tree. On one side, was a wooded rise, like a ramp leading to the top. A third of the way down the face there was a huge opening to a cave which had a paved ledge large enough for the five eagles guarding it to move about freely.

The two birds landed on the low wall bordering the ledge. Mari laid Annie gently on the stone floor and turned herself back into human form. In the dim light, Holren could see Aaron and Lia threading a path between the eagles. The birds allowed them to pass unhindered. Holren slid off the back of his mount as Lia whisked Annie away into the cave.

"Welcome to the citadel," said Aaron. "You'll find this place very comfortable."

Holren was led through the cavernous opening into the mountain. In the waning light, he could see the vaulted ceiling adorned with carvings, the marble floor inlaid with exotic stones. The entrance itself was a broad, low arch opening freely to the outside.

The eagles remained out on the ledge as Holren followed his wife and Aaron to a room off the main entrance through an ornate doorway.

"The huntsman is recovering nicely," said Mari.

"From what?" Holren asked, vaguely.

"He's fine," said Mari, dismissing any concerns with a wave of her bejeweled hand. "Everything is fine here."

"What is this place?" asked Holren. "How did you find it?"

Mari smiled. "I spied this place in the cliffs when I was up there circling around to get my bearings. The eagles confronted me when I landed on the stone porch, but when I returned to human form they let me come and go as I pleased. I was so happy to find beds and food!

"I finally got them to understand that there were more of us out in the valley. They set off immediately and brought the huntsman. I changed him back into his own body and they brought Lia. Aaron was the only one they brought back after that."

"I'm fine now," interjected Aaron. "It's actually too bad the rest of you were hiding."

"The eagles went out again and again to look for you, but you eluded them until I found you," continued Mari. "Well, take a look around. There is no one else here and the eagles treat us like we own the place. I think you will find it most satisfactory. Are you hungry?"

Holren was too tired for food.

They entered an adjoining room where the huntsman was seated on a bed of furs. "A little scouting was rewarded with this!" he beamed, raising a silver goblet and a highly decorated bottle. "This must be truly vintage."

Lia had laid Annie on another bed nearby. The little girl was resting on silken pillows. Holren noticed the color was back in her face but she appeared uneasy. Maybe that was an improvement; she was so still when he first found her.

He didn't have much chance to think about it. Aaron brought him into the next room where yet another bed was laid out. The sorcerer fell into it gratefully.

"Get some rest," said Aaron. "You'll feel better later."

Holren sank into the pillows and fell instantly asleep.

* * *

Annie awoke with a fright. A horrible howl had startled her out of a troubled sleep. It was followed by a cacophony of squalling and screeching that made her sit bolt upright in the soft bed. She was confused and disoriented. All she knew for sure was that it was pitch dark, and somewhere nearby were several monsters who sounded very upset about something.

"It's all right, Annie," said Mari's voice beside her. "The eagles are our friends. They will not harm you."

Mari picked her up and carried her out onto the landing where all the commotion was going on. As they came out into the night, Annie could see the silhouettes of six huge eagles up on the wall. Mari walked up to the largest one and touched its leg. The eagle moved aside to allow her to see over the edge. Just then, there was another howl from below.

"Brian!" crowed Annie, sliding out of Mari's arms. "That's Brian!"

"We should get him up here with us," said Mari.

She touched the wing of one of the eagles and it watched as she turned herself into a gruffen. Then Mari changed back into herself and pointed over the wall. Several eagles flew off to search for Brian. Mari took Annie back to the room and told her to lie down and try to go back to sleep.

Annie was still very weak so, she lay down. Try as she might, she couldn't keep her eyes open. She should really stay awake. There was something she had to tell Brian. Something not right. Something wrong. Something... Before she could figure it out, she fell fast asleep.

CHAPTER 8

Deeper In

"Brian P. Gruffenson, wake up."

The voice was right next to his ear.

"Brian P. Gruffenson, I refuse to wait for breakfast. If you want some, you'd better come and get it!."

He smelled food. Deer! How long had it been since he had tasted deer? How long had it been since he was this comfortable?

"I'm going without you, so don't be surprised if it's all gone when you get there!"

He couldn't decide whether to get up and eat the venison that smelled so good or stay there and enjoy the comfort. Rolling part way over, he saw Annie's hair bounce around the corner. This place smelled of something else besides good food, something odd. It smelled like earth, but a lot of other odors mingled strangely with it. Some smells he did not recognize at all.

He did smell bird, though. Eagles! He leapt out of bed and nearly fell in his rush to the door. Turning the corner, he entered a long hallway with a high ceiling. At the end of the hallway was a flat area of stone surrounded by a low wall on which sat five or six gigantic eagles. Annie was running straight for them.

"Annie, stop!" yelled Brian. All eagle eyes turned to see him and the little girl. Annie turned around and stood with her hands on her hips.

"I thought you'd come if I threatened to eat it all," she said with a laugh. She seemed totally unaware of the danger. Brian was about to scoop her up and run for it when he saw Holren come through a doorway next to Annie and snatch her out of his way. The gruffen came to a skidding halt and crawled in hastily on hands and knees.

Laughter greeted him. Four people in very fancy clothes sat at a sumptuous table set with objects made of bright metal and wood. Brian was dazzled. For a second, the fur on his neck remained standing straight out. Then he let the smell of food fill his nose.

"Join us," invited a tall women.

Brian hesitated. Maybe the berries hadn't quite worn off. The people looked familiar. Yes, this was Mari, Lia, Aaron and the huntsman.

"Come and eat!" said Aaron.

"The eagles—!" blurted Brian.

Everyone laughed again.

"Harmless," said Aaron. "See for yourself."

Brian went to the door and peeked out at the eagles on the stone porch. The great creatures ignored him.

"Sit down!" shouted the huntsman. "You need a good meal."

That was true. The gruffen was famished.

The fare was tremendous. Wine flowed freely and the table conversation was light and jovial, full of laughter. The meal went on and on until, finally, they all retired to their respective chambers for an early nap. The halls were silent except for the contented snoring.

But only the humans were content.

Brian was restless. The food had filled his empty belly but the atmosphere here made him uneasy. He stood up silently. He could hear the eagles shuffling around at the opening of the corridor. If the eagles lived here, why was everything arranged for humans? Who made all this food? Who left all these clothes? Why was no one here but themselves? Who lived here, and what if they came back?

He had asked some of these questions at the dinner but everyone just laughed. No one seemed curious enough to find out. Nor would they tell him anything they had learned about this place. Surely someone knew *something*. They all seemed so comfortable here. He went out to the hallway, determined to press them for answers. There had to be some explanation.

Much to his alarm, an eagle stood at each human's chamber door, yet his own door was unguarded. Bravely, he approached Holren's room. The eagle at the entrance remained motionless. Though it ignored him, it completely blocked his path.

"Holren!" called Brian, not too loudly. He didn't want to upset the eagle. Holren continued snoring.

"Holren!" Brian called, a bit louder. The eagle remained motionless and Holren remained asleep. Brian tried waking the others with no success. Finally, he decided to see what he could see from the mouth of the cavern. He stepped out into the open.

Directly overhead, the sky was still clear but great, flat-topped clouds towered in the south as another storm brewed. Lightning flashed. Peals of thunder rippled and crackled across the distant hills. On the one hand, Brian would be glad to be out of the rain when the storm arrived. On the other hand, this shelter felt strange, bad somehow. The fresh air cleared his head a little. Turning back to the cavernous citadel, the gruffen made up his mind to find out what was so wrong with this place.

The eagles made no move to stop him. His presence didn't seem to elicit any response from them at all. The humans slept quietly as Brian walked past their doors, his heavy, leathery feet making no sound on the smooth marble floor. No echo ricocheted off the arched ceiling of the vast hall.

He continued onward between tall columns with strange carvings. The likenesses of mighty men shouldered the buttresses that held up the high ceiling. This hall was joined by smaller ones at regular intervals. Fluted columns marked the corners of each intersection.

Further down, the main hall was lined on both sides with statues of what must have been former kings and queens. Between each human figure stood the statue of an eagle. The kings and queens were all different. Facing each one from across the hall stood a corresponding eagle which seemed to reflect the attitude and bearing of the human figure across from it. A strong king faced an equally powerful eagle. A beautiful and delicate queen stood across from a graceful and exquisite bird.

The hallway went deeper and deeper into the mountain, yet it never got darker. An eerie twilight came from nowhere—or everywhere—and left almost no shadows.

A flicker of fear stirred in Brian's chest. His breathing seemed to be swallowed up by the silence. It was almost as if he had gradually gone deaf just by walking down the hall. He stuck his finger into his ear to scratch.

There was no fooling his nose. Something smelled burnt—flesh, but not the usual burnt flesh smell. Very little of it lingered in the still air, but he could still catch a whiff of it. It grew slightly stronger as he continued on more quickly past row after row of kings and queens, one magnificent hall after another.

How long had he been walking? How many statues of eagles and humans had he passed? He felt like he'd been walking all day yet he was not really tired, so maybe he hadn't gone all that far. Looking back, he realized he could no longer see the opening of the cavern. He stopped and peered ahead into the semi-darkness but he couldn't see the end of the hall. There was no telling how much longer he would have to walk before he reached it.

He was about to head back when his nose picked up a subtle change in the atmosphere. It was not exactly a breath of fresh air. Actually, it was stale and dry, but somewhat cooler.

Wood. Dirt.

Brian looked around for the source. He had been walking down the very center of the hall, unconsciously wary of straying too close to either wall of statues, but now he carefully approached the figure of a queen where the scent was stronger.

She was smaller and more delicate than the other queens. Her face, though plain, was by far the most pleasant. Her skin seemed warmer than that of the others even though it was quite pale. Fine, thin hair flowed down past her slight shoulders nearly to her waist. Unlike the other statues which held weapons or strange implements in each hand, this queen held one empty hand facing forward, palm open. The other hand grasped a bristle branch which appeared to have pricked her skin. A drop of blood had left a dark stain on her white robe.

Brian looked around for the source of the woody dirt smell. It seemed to come from behind the statue, but he could see no holes or gaps.

At the base of the statue was a dusty inscription. Curious, Brian rubbed some dust away with his thumb, and then jumped back in alarm as a voice shouted out in an unknown language! He whipped around, fur bristling.

Nothing moved.

His eyes immediately fell on the eagle directly opposite him. It was leaning forward, glaring angrily. Brian dropped down and snarled before he realized it was still just a statue.

This one did not look like the delicate queen at all. One talon was placed slightly ahead of the other on its carved perch. The other talon crushed a simple daisy. One wing was depicted as having been broken. The other was partially unfurled as if about to unleash the fury that seemed to burn in the smoldering eyes. The other eagle statues were about the same size as their royal counterparts, but this raptor was much larger than the pale queen across from it. Its menacing attitude was all its own.

Brian scanned the walls, the floor, the ceiling. Nothing broke the ominous silence. When his fur finally settled back down again, he turned back to face the statue of the woman. Nothing had changed. The placard remained inscrutable. He gently brushed off the remaining dust with the back of his little finger.

"... the choice is yours," said a quiet voice. It was in his head!

Brian wheeled around again, just to be sure. Nothing moved. Nothing had changed. The crippled eagle across the hall still glowered silently.

Gingerly, he touched the inscription again. Nothing. Pulling his hand away he heard a quiet murmur, but no words. Then he dragged a finger slowly across the letters. As he did so, he could hear the quiet voice saying something in a foreign language with strange inflections. He did it again even more slowly, this time pressing a little harder, all the while watching the lady's face. Her expression did not change. The sound of the voice was louder and more firm, but it was still garbled and impossible to decipher. By now, he was sure he was hearing it in his head and not in the room.

Brian rubbed the placard in the other direction. This time it rang out clearly:

A wounded touch will spring the door.
Stay or go: the choice is yours.

The gruffen glanced about again and saw no one else. What was the voice talking about?

A new sound grabbed his attention. In the silence, it hissed like a snake. Standing back up to his full height, he listened carefully. There it was again—very quiet, but it was definitely a draft. The woody dirt smell was stronger, too.

Looking behind the statue of the queen again, he saw a fine, jagged crack in one of the elaborately carved and painted scenes covering the wall. The crack ran from floor to ceiling, dividing two armies about to meet in pitched battle. The draft was coming from a tiny hole where a spear that crossed the boundary had broken off. Looking around again to make sure no one was there, Brian ventured behind the queen and poked at the hole with his fingernail. His nose told him there was empty, earthy space behind the carved wall. As he looked more closely, he could tell that at one point, someone had entirely removed one horse from the scene, hastily painting over it with a grassy knoll and a bit of a bush. Brian could still make out the vague outline of a rearing horse, its rider pointing to a spot where some of the paint was smudged. An indentation had been worn into the wall at this point. Something had stained it dark. To Brian, it looked like dried blood.

Another new sound made his fur stand up again: feathers on a marble floor. For a moment, he thought he was being fooled again, but in the foggy half light, he thought he saw movement far down the hallway, coming from the same direction he had come. He crouched. For a short time, he could hide behind the line of statues, but not for long. Peering around the queen's statue, he could make out the silhouettes of several massive eagles approaching slowly. In front of them, a cart wheeled itself silently along. Brian's hide began to crawl as the now-familiar sensation of Dark Magic grew stronger. The burnt smell grew with it.

On the cart lay a crumpled body that looked more like a mass of clothing with an arm dangling askew. The sleeve was blue. Brian's fur bristled. The huntsman had been wearing something blue! As they approached, apparently either unaware of or ignoring the gruffen, Brian could make out the body more clearly. The fur on the right side of the cart was not a cap; it was human hair. The angle was unnatural. The huntsman's neck was broken.

As the procession drew closer, Brian looked for a better hiding place. There was nowhere to go. The bitter eagle across the hall glowered at him as if it would reveal him simply by staring. Brian reached back and inadvertently caught his finger on one of the bristles of the branch in the lady's hand. A drop of gruffen blood spilled on her dress.

"A wounded touch will spring the door," he seemed to hear again. "To stay or go, the choice is yours." What doors, he wondered.

The swishing of eagle feathers was growing louder.

Turning back to the carved wall, he searched for any sign of an opening. "A wounded touch?" He looked at the stained worn spot indicated by the pointing cavalryman. Maybe the dark smudge *was* blood.

He pressed his pricked finger into the indentation and was instantly sucked into blackness. The wall simply opened up and swallowed him.

He landed on all fours. Quickly, he looked in all directions, but all he could see was a faint, jagged line of light where the crack was behind him. He could hear the draft whistling softly through it.

The floor beneath him felt like dirty wooden boards. He was in a dark tunnel. From the sounds, it seemed to be about six feet high and three or four feet wide with one or more tributaries. Brian turned around quickly and peered through the tiny hole where the spear had broken off. He caught a glimpse of deep blue velvet, then nothing but feathers as the eagles paraded past. Finally, Brian could see over the shoulder of the frail queen to where the statue of the crippled eagle stared balefully back.

Brian had tried to count the eagles as they passed by. He wasn't entirely certain how many there were to begin with. Perhaps now the rest of his friends were not so well guarded. He had to get back. Silently, he felt around for some way to get back out. The rough wall yielded nothing.

"Brian!"

The gruffen whirled around in the darkness and stood up, slamming his head into the low rock ceiling. Despite the pain, he took a swipe with a clawed hand but struck nothing.

Just out of reach stood the ghostly figure of the queen whose statue stood on the other side of the wall. Brian dropped to all fours and growled deep in his chest.

"You can't go back, Brian," said the lady quietly. "You're not supposed to turn back."

"Who are you?" asked Brian, his head still smarting. "You know my name."

"My father knows many things and he sent me here to help you," said the pale figure. A soft light seemed to emanate from her. As Brian's eyes adjusted, he could see she was standing in one of several intersections to this tunnel.

"You wish to save your friends from the Citadel. That is good," she continued, not giving him any time to ask questions. "We also hope to save them. The huntsman's death could not be stopped and his loss will be doubly hard on you. We may yet save the others. Listen to me, Brian P. Gruffenson. What I will tell you is very important and you must do exactly as I say—"

The gruffen interrupted her.

"Wait," he said. "You know my name. You say you want to help. Why should I listen?"

The queen continued: "Brian, right now, you do not know where you are, what is happening, or what to do. I ask only that you listen first, then choose what you will do." She lifted the thorny branch she held in her hand. Breaking a thorn from it, she said: "You have already been pricked by this once. That was good. Keep this thorn with you. You will need it later." She held it out to him and he reached out hesitantly. Then suddenly, and without seeming to take a step, she came very close to him and placed the thorn in the thick mass of hair behind his left ear. He felt its sharp tip graze his temple, but it did not poke into him. Most of what he felt was her warm, soft hand by his face. She wasn't so mysterious up close. The statue of her in the great hallway did not do her justice. She was even kinder in person.

For a moment, Brian felt like he was dreaming. He saw two strange beings inside his body, both of them half man and half gruffen. Neither acknowledged the other.

Somehow in his heart, he could see the lady standing between them. She touched them both and, from opposite sides and brought their hands together. In that brief contact, one released a little of its humanity and the other relinquished some of the beast. As they each grew more distinct, a bond began to grow between them. The frail queen let go of their hands and allowed them to stand apart. Then she turned and gently kissed each on the cheek, first the man, then the beast.

Brian realized that he was actually still standing in the tunnel, staring into the eyes of the ghostlike figure of the lady.

"Anything else?" he mumbled.

"Yes," she replied smiling. "This tunnel has many channels. This one is the only path that will take you where you need to go. It will twist and turn, but never split. Do not take any tunnel to the left or right or you will be lost. There is only one place where you will be forced to decide which direction to take. By the time you reach it, it will be obvious to you what is right.

"Your friends are already moving deep within the mountain. Even now they are falling into an enchantment from which it will be difficult to save them. When you see them again, do not tell them you have met me. They will not understand. You must lead them out of the Citadel. Tell them that you know a better place to go; only then will they follow you. Such is the nature of the spell."

She paused for a moment. Then she said firmly: "When you strike, aim to kill. Now go. When you reach the end, you will find them. Remember: tell them you have a better place to go. Best of luck, Mr. Gruffenson."

With that, she vanished and Brian was left in total darkness. He did not hesitate. Groping along the walls, he came to the first intersecting tunnel and felt about the stone ceiling until he found where the passage continued and then kept on. Here the dirt and wood floor ended. The stone was cold to his hands and feet.

When he sensed a draft that announced the next adjoining corridor, he slowed again and carefully felt around to find the continuation. The tunnel began to curve gently to the right, then it took sharp turn to the left. Further on, it began to go uphill and down. Other tunnels now joined or intersected on different levels. Some had a damp smell to them. A trickle of water ran across his path, seeping from the wall. He continued on, as quickly as he could, wondering how long he had to go before he finally came out again. At times, the air grew sweeter, then more dank. In several sections, the tunnel had caved in and Brian had difficulty getting through the debris. More than once, he feared he might be too large to make it through a tight passage. Progress was painfully slow.

Crawling along the floor at one point, he could smell dry bones. The passage was so narrow that he could not avoid them. He found the tiny foot bones first, then the leg bones and the pelvis. Whoever had died there had been going the same direction he was but the flesh had long since turned to dust. He moved the skull aside and crawled past it.

Finally, the passage opened up again and he could stand. The air was much more fresh here and he breathed more easily. There seemed to be light ahead, a bright glow on the walls of stone. Brian loped forward, head down. He could hear water splashing.

The tunnel he had been following ended abruptly at a steeply sloping shaft about ten or twelve feet in diameter. Brian leaned out of the tunnel and peered upward to his right. Steps had been carved into the rocks, leading to the outside. Water poured down in a fine sheet from somewhere high above and struck the steps several yards up the shaft. Just now, the sun was shining directly down the hole through the thin waterfall, dancing on the roof and walls of the steep shaft. Never before had Brian been so relieved to see daylight.

Reluctantly, he looked to his left, down the shaft where the water tumbled continuously in the jagged channel it had cut into the stone steps. Brian took a deep breath of fresh air and let it out with a noisy rush. Then he stepped out onto the slippery steps and turned his back on daylight, casting his huge shadow before him.

Step, by step, he descended deeper into darkness, feeling around for purchase on the next slippery tread. It was tiring work. The further he went, the darker it got until, once again, he could see nothing in front of him.

After many, many steps, Brian could hear the water splashing into a deep pool in a large chamber below. Without warning, the staircase ended in thin air. There was nowhere else to go! Squatting on the last step, Brian searched the walls with his hands and feet, looking for a way down. He dared not simply drop into the water. A stronger vein of rock to his left provided a buttress which served as an awkward ladder. He climbed down until his foot found a boulder large enough to sit on. He rested a little bit and then gingerly worked his way down the boulder until his feet found flat, dry stone, polished smooth like the marble floors of the halls he had left hours before. Relieved, he stood upright and tried to get his bearings.

As he stared into the blackness, he thought he saw a fine slit of dim light. Was it a trick of the eyes? He moved toward it. For awhile, it seemed to recede, but then he realized that it was actually bigger than he had first thought, and much further away. As he drew closer, he could see that he was approaching a mammoth door that was slightly open. When he finally reached it, he opened it further. It swung silently on huge hinges. Before him lay another long hallway. The light was soft and thick as if the dust itself (of which there was a great deal) lit the walls and the air. This hallway also had high vaulted ceilings and ornately carved walls but there were no statues of kings, queens or eagles. As Brian stepped out into the hallway, the heavy layer of dust silently exploded with each footfall, leaving very clear gruffen tracks behind him.

Over his shoulder, he could barely make out the large room he had just left. The chamber was too dark and too vast for him to see the far wall or the trickling waterfall which echoed in the stillness. By chance, he had taken the most direct route to the door in which he now stood. He could see now that he had followed a straight path between long rows of empty banquet tables. Turning his back on the darkened chamber, he headed down the hallway, hoping to find his friends before they, too, suffered the fate of Fortman Eldrich.

At every corner, he checked for eagles or other predators but found no tracks. The heavy dust lay undisturbed. Brian kept walking, past hall after hall, until he came to an intersection where he had to turn one way or the other. In the center of the new hall, the dust on the floor was not as thick. Tail feathers had swept away all but the most obvious tracks, but Brian could see that both birds and humans had walked this hallway. Turning in the direction of the footsteps, he loped off after them.

CHAPTER 9

An Uncomfortable Party

With enough light to see by, the gruffen raced ahead. The eagle tracks turned off to one side and disappeared under a closed pair of massive doors but the human tracks continued on. Brian followed them to the end of the hall where they disappeared under another set of doors that was slightly ajar. He peeked inside. It took a few seconds for his eyes to adjust to the brightness of the room beyond.

It was a large, opulent banquet hall. Some revelry seemed to be going on inside. He could make out several figures that were splendidly dressed and dancing in swirling circles. There were no eagles in sight. Taking a quick look back over his shoulder, he opened the door and let himself in.

No one noticed him. They were too busy dancing on the polished marble floor which was cut throughout with designs in gold and inlaid with deep red and green gemstones. Gilded pillars studded with diamonds supported the frescoed ceiling, and bright crystalline lamps hung on long golden chains. Lush green plants grew from terraced, marble-edged gardens set in the corners of the room and in square, marble planters placed asymmetrically on the main floor. In the center of the wall farthest from the door was a raised area with three wide terraces leading up to it.

All along both sides of the way leading to the stairs were gilded tables draped with white silk and heavily laden with fine food and drink. The dancers wove in and out amongst the tables and each other, swirling around to music only they could hear. Every once in awhile, one would stop and eat a morsel. There must have been nearly a dozen merrymakers. Brian wondered who they all were, and whether his friends might be among them. He couldn't see anyone's face. Slowly, he drew closer.

As soon as he got within two or three paces of them, one of the women swirled away from her partner, grabbed Brian's big, hairy arm and spun him around to join the dance. At least that is what she meant to do. Spinning a gruffen is no easy task, and Brian was immovable. The woman jerked around and landed on the floor, laughing uproariously. Brian picked her up and set her back on her feet, which made her laugh all the more. Then he realized why he had not recognized her: her face was veiled and she avoided looking at him directly. In fact, everyone in the room was veiled.

"What's going on?" asked Brian.

The woman laughed merrily and waltzed away with another dancer. Someone else stopped to grab a bite from the table nearby and Brian watched him slip the food under his veil. A rough, dark beard barely showed; it looked like Aaron's. There were so many dancers, Brian had difficulty keeping track of them. Reaching out with a long arm, Brian grabbed the eater by the shoulder. The other tried to knock his hand off but Brian held him firmly and pulled him close.

"Aaron?" he asked.

"Ha! The joke's on you!" came the jolly reply. "Hey! Easy there!"

Brian was about to let go when he realized it was, indeed, Aaron's voice.

"Why the covered face?" Brian wanted to know.

"What? Don't be so serious! Here, have some wine!" Aaron grabbed a silver flagon and held it up, splashing some of it contents into Brian's face. The gruffen let go to wipe his stinging eyes as raucous laughter erupted from everyone else. Aaron drank the rest of the wine himself as he spun away and rejoined the dancing.

"There, there!," trilled one of the women. "Dry off and let's have no more of your antics!"

Brian took three steps to get into the middle of the group and bellowed, "Where's Annie?"

"Here I am!" piped another woman as they swirled around him.

"And here!" the rest chimed in.

"No, no, no!" boomed the gruffen. "A little girl! Annie! Where is she?"

"Oh, she's fine, wherever she is," crowed one of the men. "Probably dancing like the rest of us."

"Who are you?" growled Brian.

"Who cares?" they all said. "Such questions!"

Brian grabbed a male dancer and tore off his veil. It was Holren! The wizard was glassy-eyed and smiling vacantly. Bits of food dangled from his beard.

"Holren!" gasped the gruffen, letting go of him in alarm. "What—?"

The old man looked away and laughed. "What of it?" he whooped, dancing away into the crowd.

Brian began to chase the dancers around, pulling their veils off one by one until they were all exposed. The faces beneath were fixed in bizarre expressions of happiness. Holren, Aaron, Mari and Lea were there along with several others Brian did not recognize. The huntsman was not among them.

"What happened to Fortman Eldrich?" Brian shouted at them. No one responded as they whirled and danced away. All this time, they had been moving closer to the raised area at the far end of the banquet hall. When they reached the first terrace, one dancer after another began to dance on it.

"Annie," muttered Brian to himself. "Where's Annie?" He looked around for a little dancer but couldn't find one so he set off back toward the doors, checking both sides of the room. Finally, by one of the large stands of leafy, green plants, he spied a little body crumpled on the floor. He rolled the body over and quickly removed the veil. It was Annie! She was not smiling or dancing like the others. Her eyes were closed, her face was deathly pale, and her breathing was ragged. A little wine stained her beautiful dress.

"Annie!" said Brian, nudging her as gently as he could. "Annie! Wake up!"

Suddenly, there was a holler from the steps and a blinding flash lit the room. The gruffen turned to see an eagle on the top terrace, raising its wings high over its head. All the dancers applauded and shouted with glee as the eagle launched itself in Brian's direction.

The gruffen grabbed Annie and ducked behind a table. The eagle wheeled sideways and took a swipe at him, dashing several tables and their contents to the floor. Brian set Annie aside and leapt at the eagle. He caught the wingtip and they tumbled into the spilled food, claws and talons flying. Rolling away from the deadly beak, Brian bumped into one of the overturned tables. Grabbing the table by two legs, he smashed it against the raptor's skull. The eagle crumpled to the floor, shook and lay still.

Brian sat down hard on the cold stone, trembling. The blood of the dead eagle filled the air with a foul stench as it spilled onto the marble floor.

Brian looked up just in time to see a woman dance across the uppermost terrace. When she reached the center, there was another blinding flash. The dancer disappeared and another eagle stood in her place! Brian barely registered what had happened before the eagle bore down on him, just like the first one. He grabbed a broken table leg and threw it fiercely, burying it in the raptor's chest. The eagle crashed and slid across the floor, streaking blood until it stopped in a dead heap.

The gruffen had no time to appreciate his lucky throw. Another dancer was getting close to the uppermost terrace. Brian rushed across the hall, flew up the steps and tackled her. She lay there, stunned. Brian started to apologize but another bleary-eyed reveler was already dancing on the top terrace. He had yet to set foot on the curious design in the middle of the terrace. Brian leapt up and shoved the fellow back down the steps.

Now everyone was climbing the terraces at once! Every time Brian pushed one away, another came close to stepping into the design. He couldn't keep them all away. Angrily, he raised his hand against the woman closest to him. It was Lia, grinning at him with that maddening smile everyone wore. With a frustrated whimper, Brian firmly pulled her away from the magical center.

Then he saw Annie. Somehow, the little one had crawled all the way up the terraces. She was even more pale and her lips seemed unusually red. Despite the frozen smile on her face, she appeared to be in severe pain. Her little hand reached toward the design in the center of the floor.

All at once, Brian remembered the queen's advice.

"Wait!" he cried, scooping up the feverish little girl with one hand and grabbing Lia with the other. "Wait! I know someplace better!"

Everyone stared, their stupid grins tilted upward and their actions coming to a stilted halt.

"This stinks!" said Brian. "The food's no good!" He forced a smile and began to walk slowly away from the design on the top terrace. "There's better food! More drinks!" They all looked at him, hopefully. "Come! I'll show you!"

No one moved. All eyes were on him.

The gruffen laughed nervously and pulled Lia down the steps. "Come! It's better! Come!"

He looked over his shoulder, still smiling. He started skipping, big, clumsy dance steps, the best he could muster. Lia shrieked with laughter. So did the others. To his relief, they all fell in line behind him skipping and hopping with idiotic abandon. Soon they were skipping past the bloody carcasses of the eagles. As quickly as he could, Brian brought them out into the great dusty hallway and then raced back to shut the door behind them.

They were still skipping and hopping aimlessly in the middle of the hallway.

"Follow me! To the better place!" called Brian. He cradled Annie in his arms as he led the revelers back along their earlier tracks, past the door under which the eagle tracks disappeared. He knew he could not get them out the way he had come in. There was no way he could herd them all up the rock wall and up the shaft with its slippery stone steps.

Their pace seemed perilously slow. Brian danced about them, trying to keep everyone moving. He was beginning to tire. On and on they danced, ever in danger of being caught by the guardians of the palace. After awhile, most of them were shuffling along with considerably less exuberance and some of them looked ill. Brian kept Annie snug against his chest as he coaxed them along. Every now and then the little girl would mumble something unintelligible. The gruffen glanced over his shoulder down the hall. The eagles could be anywhere.

"I'm tired," said somebody.

Brian turned around. "We'll be there soon!" he said, trying to sound cheerful.

"But I don't feel like going," said a short, balding man Brian didn't recognize. "I'm going to bed." With that, he turned immediately to his right and pushed open one of the doors. There was a rushing sound as if some great beast had inhaled sharply, and then the man was gone. The door closed quickly and silently. The parade in the hallway ground to a halt.

"Too sleepy!" said Brian with a halfhearted laugh. There were nervous titters in reply. "Let's run!" he cheered. "Just for fun! Everyone grab hands!" Grabbing Aaron's hand, he set off down the hall. The group fell in behind him. When they were all in a chain, Brian picked up the pace. Looking at their faces, he could see that whatever had held them in its spell was losing its grip. Fear had crept in behind the gaiety. A few of them looked confused as if waking from deep sleep or stupor.

They ran in earnest now. The sweat on their skin and the blood pumping through their veins seemed to clear their heads. Finally, Aaron spoke.

"Where is the huntsman?" he asked.

"Don't know," huffed Brian, shaking his furry head. "Keep running. This looks familiar."

They had come to the hall of statues.

A terrified cry rose up behind him. Brian looked over his shoulder and came to a stuttering halt. People were dropping mid-stride, crumpling to the marble floor as they ran, their bodies suddenly wrinkled and aged beyond belief.

The only ones still standing were Lia, Aaron, Holren and Mari.

"They're dying!" Lia shouted, running back to help.

It was too late. Already, they had begun to decompose, filling the air with the stench of rotting flesh.

"Come on!" Brian hollered. "Let's get out of here!"

Lia wasn't listening. Kneeling beside one of the fallen bodies, she fumbled around for her medicine kit, not realizing she no longer carried it. She started to cry.

"Let's go!" shouted Brian.

Lia looked up at him and screamed.

Something slammed heavily into Brian's back, knocking Annie out of his arms. He hit the floor hard. He could feel the strength of the huge talons digging into his left shoulder, but he felt no pain. He twisted about and bit hard into the raptor's ankle. All hands and feet moved at once, scratching, tearing, looking for anything to grab. Somehow, he avoided the sharp beak. His right hand found the eagle's windpipe and ripped it out. Blood flew, some of it his, some of it the eagle's. The hold on his shoulder weakened. He kicked both feet over his head and caught the eagle in the cheek, snapping its head sideways and breaking its neck.

Brian pulled away from the dead raptor, suddenly aware of the searing pain in his arm and back.

Mari ran to Annie and picked her up. The little girl was barely breathing. Brian lay bleeding on the floor.

"Where are we?" asked Holren.

Brian's breath came in gasps but he rolled over and got to his knees. "Follow me," he said.

Forcing himself to his feet, he thumped down the hallway toward the opening, his left arm dangling limply beside him. The others followed.

Brian kept expecting to see day light. He knew there was an open ledge at the end of the hallway—at least he hoped that was where they were going. His memory of the place seemed like a dream now. Instead of getting lighter, it actually appeared to be getting darker, but the air was not as heavy and the dust was not as thick. Brian wondered if he was blacking out.

"Is it dark?" he asked breathlessly.

"Yes, quite," answered Holren; "but it is not magical; it's nighttime."

Even through the pain, Brian could smell fresh air. They must be close.

"Whoa! Stop!" hissed Aaron. They were on rougher stone now and it was suddenly breezy and damp. "We're here."

Night had fallen, indeed, and the fog was so thick Brian couldn't see much at all. Aaron's voice came from somewhere off to his right. The gruffen stopped and shut his eyes, consumed for the moment by the pain in his shoulder.

"Stroke of luck," said Aaron. "This is the stone wall at the cliff's edge. I say we go up and over the top. No sense climbing all the way down in this blackness."

Holren mumbled something repeatedly. Brian didn't understand it, but he thought he felt lighter on his feet.

"Good. That should help," said Aaron. "Follow me. There's a deep crack..."

From that point on, Brian remembered no more. All he knew was the cold hard stone, the throbbing in his left side, and the occasional sound of a rock dropping away into the darkness.

CHAPTER 10

Escape

Pain! Brian groaned.

"Don't move," said Lia's soothing voice. "You should rest until you get better."

"Where are we?" asked the gruffen. His shoulder was wrapped in some kind of cloth. He could smell his own blood, but it smelled old so he was pretty sure he wasn't bleeding anymore.

"We've found another cave. Holren and Aaron have gone to look for food."

"Where's Annie?"

"She's asleep on the other side of the fire," said Lia. "The spell was harder on her, perhaps because she is so young. We're keeping a close watch on her."

"What happened?" queried Brian.

"We're not sure," said Mari, coming from behind the cave wall with a bundle of sticks. Brian could smell her wet clothes. It was still raining outside. "We were hoping you could tell us."

Lia nodded. "We suspect we were bewitched by the food," she said. "I don't remember much after the meal you ate with us. In fact, none of us recalls anything after that. Next thing we knew, we were following you, running for our lives."

"The food didn't bother me," said Brian.

"Perhaps since your body is different, it did not respond to the magic," said Mari.

"Who were those people?" Brian asked.

"What people?" asked Mari.

"Other people with you," said Brian.

Mari and Lia looked at each other quizzically. They remembered no others.

Aaron and Holren came in from the rain with a batch of mud-covered roots.

"The best we could find," said Aaron; "At least it's real food."

"I see our friend the gruffen has risen from his long nap," said the wizard, squatting down to wash the roots in a puddle on the floor.

"When did I sleep?" asked Brian.

"You've been asleep since yesterday," replied Holren. "But I wonder what the rest of us missed before that. Are you strong enough to tell us what happened down there?"

Brian grimaced. Talking seemed to take his mind off the pain a little. With halting language, he told them about finding the tunnel and talking to the fragile queen. He skipped the whole ordeal in the tunnels and went straight to the part where he found them in the banquet hall. As best he could, he described the terraces and the appearance of the eagles. He finished simply by saying they had all left.

Lia vaguely remembered kneeling on the floor and looking up to see an eagle attacking Brian.

"When daylight returns, I will look for things that might help your shoulder," she said.

Brian forced himself to roll over. Cradling his left arm in his right, he sat up painfully. His wrinkled face twisted up whenever he moved but he didn't complain. He looked over at Mari who cradled Annie's tousled head in her lap. The woman's magnificent gown had was torn and dirty, but she looked all right otherwise. Annie's cheeks had more color in them and her lips were not quite so red, but she was very still.

"Well, I hope you get better," said Aaron to the gruffen. "I don't want to have to haul you the rest of the way, even with Holren's magical help. How's the wound?"

"Hurts," grunted Brian. "We should go."

"That's the dilemma," said Holren. "The storm continues in full force, so we're not likely to leave anytime soon, and the maps are gone, for better or worse, so we have no clearer destination than when we first became lost."

"But at least we all agree we're lost," quipped Aaron. "That's progress."

The others laughed. What a relief to hear genuine laughter again!

"We should go," Brian said again, but he couldn't get up without leaving his left arm unsupported.

"Here," said Aaron, stripping off his shirt. "You need a sling." He put on his ornate but soggy cloak. "Wish we had our own sensible clothes back."

He and Lia tied the shirt around Brian's neck and arm. The sleeves were barely long enough, but it was adequate support for the gruffen's heavy arm. Brian got to his feet and ambled stiffly to the other side of the fire to sit near Annie.

"She's looking better," he said to Mari.

Mari nodded. "Her breathing is deeper and she responds to touch, but I don't know how long she can go without water. I can't make her drink."

Brian reached out a large furry hand and stroked Annie's face. She twitched slightly, murmured something that sounded like what she had mumbled the other night, and then rolled over. Mari looked up at Brian.

"That's the most she has done all day!" she exclaimed, quietly.

The company spent the rest of the evening chewing on the fibrous roots and considering what to do next. In the end, they decided to continue northward and hope to meet someone who might know about the mountain where they might get help. All agreed that it was a poor plan, but it was better than returning south to face the King alone.

They would remain in the cave until the storm passed.

"Or until something more dangerous shows up," said Aaron.

The gruffen lay down next to Annie that night. At some point, he finally dozed off.

* * *

Brian awoke to thunder. Everyone else was asleep. Annie was breathing deeply and evenly. He could sense someone nearby. Staring hard, the gruffen could see a hunched figure standing in the rain just outside the cave, draped from head to foot in a heavy robe.

For no reason at all, Brian trusted this person. Maybe he was dreaming. The agony that seared through his whole body when he sat up suggested otherwise.

The figure remained motionless in the driving rain. Brian stood up painfully and walked to the mouth of the cave without disturbing his companions. Brian stood just inside and looked at the shadowy figure. The rain poured down in sheets and a curtain of water fell between him and the person outside. Lightning flashed, and Brian got a brief look at the old man's kindly face.

"Who are you?" the gruffen asked quietly.

The old man beckoned to him to come outside. Brian stepped out into the rain and was instantly drenched. He shuddered as the pelting raindrops bit into his torn flesh. The cold seeped into his fur. The old man reached up and touched Brian's chest. Brian could feel the warmth in that touch, even through his soaked fur. Taking Brian's right hand, the old man led the gruffen to a large boulder a few feet away. Then he climbed up on it so that he could look Brian in the eye. Saying nothing, the man deftly untied the makeshift sling and helped Brian lower his heavy arm until it hung there, limp. Another lightning flash lit up the old man's face. He was smiling sadly.

"This will hurt even worse," he said, in a thin voice that could somehow be heard over the storm. "Are you willing?"

Brian nodded.

Taking the gruffen's wounded arm in both hands, the old man raised it slowly over his head. Brian was nearly felled by the pain. Gently, but firmly, the old man stretched Brian's arm forward and back, in and out, up and down. With each motion, Brian experienced worse pain, but somehow his arm seemed to move more freely. When he thought he could stand it no more, the man placed his hand on Brian's forehead and the ache disappeared. To his astonishment, Brian could move his arm and hand at will. His back was neither stiff nor sore. He felt the fur. The hide was intact. It was as if he had never been wounded.

"Be well, Brian P. Gruffenson," said the man. "You met my daughter, Calicia, in the Citadel. You must trust me as you trusted her. I haven't time to explain. I give you these instructions: you must leave now. You are going to a place called Thihanan." He pointed to a faint trail in the darkness. "Follow this path down to the valley and turn west along the base of the hills. You will find a river flowing north. This will lead you to the Great Falls. Stay away from the still water. You must cross the Falls and the field beyond until you reach the forest on the western side. Look for a door in the brush and enter it immediately. Behind the door you will find help and more instructions. I will meet you in Thihanan."

He embraced Brian and the gruffen felt his strength return. "Do you remember what I said?" asked the man.

"Yes," said Brian. "Follow the path. Go west to the river. Stay away from still water. Cross the great falls and the field. Go to the west forest. Go in the door and get help. Meet you in—Thi—Thi—"

"Thihanan," said the man.

"Thihanan," repeated Brian.

"Good," the man replied. The lightning and thunder were growing even more intense. "One more thing: magic is NOT to be used, under any circumstances. It will draw your enemies to you faster than you can imagine. Only when you are behind the door in the woods will you be able to use it safely."

"No magic," said Brian. "What will happen to Annie?"

"She will recover," the man assured him. "Go quickly! The King is upon you and I cannot delay him. Beware of the still water! Beware of Wofrung. Now GO!"

With that he vanished.

"Brian! Get back inside!" shouted Aaron from inside the cave. Brian turned around and came in. The others were much alarmed.

"I'm fine!" said Brian, raising his arm over his head several times to prove it. "We have to go! Get Annie!"

No one could understand him until he took them all over to a quieter corner of the cave and explained what had happened.

"He fixed my arm," said Brian. "I trust him. He said to go. The King is here. We should go."

"What about Annie?" asked Mari.

"I'm here," said a little voice behind them.

"Oh, child!" cried Mari, reaching for her in the darkness. "You should not be up."

"We have to go," said Annie. "The old man said we have to go, so we should go."

"I would rather go out in the storm than be caught between the King and this place," said Aaron. "With Brian healed, we can at least make some distance."

"Fair enough," said Holren.

"I can carry Annie," said Brian. He brushed past the others in the dark and picked up the little girl. "Let's go."

"We should go as ferrets," said Mari.

"No!" said Brian, firmly. "The man said 'no magic.' We can't."

The water hit them like a wall as they came out into the open. The roiling sky shot thunderbolt after thunderbolt into the mountain. Feeling their way along, lit sporadically by lightning, they were barely able to follow the path leading over the ridge.

The slope on the northern side of the bluff was considerably less steep but the path followed a wash which was already half full with runoff. As they descended, the drainage deepened until the rock walls rose fifteen feet on either side. In several places, they had to hold hands and leap across water rushing in from adjoining cracks in the mountainside.

Drenched to the skin and shivering in the cold, they came upon a jumble of rocks at the bottom of the drainage. Brian found a route and led everyone across. Finally, they huddled to rest in the shelter of a huge boulder. The howling wind whipped the rain about and lashed at them mercilessly.

Suddenly the gruffen smelled something that made the fur stand up on his neck and shoulders. Somewhere on that whirling wind wafted the scent of goblin. Mixed with it was the smoky aroma he had grown to hate.

"Dark Magic!" shouted Holren, confirming it.

The howling rose to a shriek and rocks began to tumble down the slope. The earth around them shuddered, trembling like an erratic heartbeat. Brian set Annie down next to Mari and peered around the side of the boulder. Facing the stinging wind, he could just make out the shadows of falling stones. The crest above seemed to be breaking apart. A series of lightning flashes revealed the cause of the landslide: hundreds of goblins swarmed the bluff. They were rolling huge boulders off the edge and sending them tumbling down the drainage. The company had been discovered!

"West, the man said! West!" barked the gruffen.

He grabbed Annie and led them away from the drainage as an avalanche of rocks surged around the boulder that had given them shelter. He could feel Dark Magic all around him. He would have run in the dark, but the humans could not move so quickly so he led them forward as fast as they could manage.

Over the raging storm, there came a new howl, a howl of anger and desire, of vengeance and delight. More boulders came crashing down the slope behind them, but the howling voice seemed to follow them everywhere, around every tree, over every rock. No hiding place seemed safe. They kept moving.

Without warning, they came to the edge of a precipice. Far below, a rain-swollen torrent surged against the rocks as the river made a great bend northward, to the right. This river had scraped away at these mountains for millennia, leaving sheer cliffs on both sides.

Lightning revealed that the trail continued to their right along a narrow ledge until it disappeared around a knife-edged buttress. From there, they could not see if it continued. Brian set Annie down and loped sure-footedly along the ledge to see where it went. To his relief, it continued on, though it was just as narrow on the other side.

He was halfway back when Lia let out a cry: "Goblins!"

A sea of them swarmed around a bend a short distance behind them.

"You go first!" yelled Brian, picking up Annie and handing her to Aaron. Without hesitation, the warrior continued along the ledge, making slow, steady progress. Lia followed, then Mari, then Holren. Brian waited to be sure everyone made it. Then he raced along the ledge until he rounded the corner of the knife edge. On the other side, he turned and waited, just out of sight.

The first goblin reached the corner only to be pitched headlong into the foaming rapids. The next burst through only to go spinning into the same cauldron. The third stopped short, knocking two behind him off the ledge but a quick kick from Brian sent him over the edge. He fell with an ear-splitting shriek.

"Brian!" shouted Holren. "Stand back! Now!"

The gruffen shoved two more goblins off the cliff and leapt out of the way just as Holren threw a green fireball at the knife edge. The entire knife edge broke loose and thundered down into the river, taking several more goblins with it. Brian scrambled over to rejoin the others.

"No magic!" he said.

"We had little choice," said Holren. "Let's go."

There was only one direction to go now: forward.

They followed the narrow ledge first to the right and then back to the left along a horseshoe shaped cliff, following a tight bend in the river. Frequent flashes of lightning exposed the landscape in glaring light, and Brian could see that the company had not gone all that far in the dark. The entrance to the Citadel stared out at them like a shadowy eye.

They had just come off the ledge onto a steep, exposed ridge when a bloody howl from the high rocks above the Citadel made everyone turn to look. The electrical storm lit the shape of a strange figure that appeared to be twice Brian's height with the body of a man and the head of some carrion bird. A mass of goblins swarmed around it. As the lightning flashed again, the bird-man laughed and pointed his hand at them.

Holren pushed past everyone and stepped back onto the ledge, waving his arms in an intricate pattern and chanting in some unintelligible language at the top of his lungs.

"Get down!" cried Aaron. "It can see you!"

Holren ignored him, still chanting. Mari started after him despite Aaron's attempt to stop her.

The bird-man opened his palm and appeared to shove something toward them. A shock rippled through the air and hit everyone hard. Brian dropped to his knees and grabbed Annie. Aaron and Lia were already down low. Mari had just reached the ledge when it crumbled and gave way beneath her. She leapt back but could not keep her footing and started sliding down the steep side of the ridge.

Holren was standing on nothing but broken rock. It gave way completely. He was already falling into the abyss as he finished his spell. As he disappeared from sight, a green fireball shot from his arms, sizzled through the air and struck the bird-man full in the chest.

Rocks crashed into the river below as Brian and Aaron scrambled across the ridge, calling for Mari and Holren.

"Here!" Mari cried back. "Where's Holren? Can you see him?"

"No!" yelled Brian. "I'm coming to get you."

"Go on!" called Mari. "Run! Just run! Go!"

Brian ignored this and crossed the steep slope to where Mari was clinging to bits of brush and stone.

"My ankle," said Mari. "I think it's broken. Go, Brian!"

Before she could let go, Brian grabbed her around the waist and heaved her onto his shoulder.

"Follow me!" he bellowed at everyone else. "Run!"

They followed. The route down the ridge was treacherous in the rain. Aaron and Lia kept Annie between them. Brian carried Mari all the way down. Once they were down the ridge, they entered the forest. Thick underbrush kept them on the path. Wet and cold, they stumbled forward, one after the other, Brian in front with Mari on his back, Aaron bringing up the rear.

Eventually, the storm abated. For the rest of the night, there was no sight or sound of goblins or the bird-man. Finally, Aaron suggested that they stop to rest. Brian agreed. They found a rocky outcrop a short distance from the trail. Brian set Mari down and Lia did her best to make her comfortable. There wasn't much else she could do in the dark. Exhausted, Brian collapsed next to Annie, while Aaron kept watch.

CHAPTER 11

Owler

Brian awoke to the growling of his own stomach. He rolled over. A light drizzle was falling. Large drops collected on the branches and needles of the evergreens and dropped heavily on the ground. He was warm enough in his thick fur, but he wondered about the others.

Aaron, Lia and Annie still slept, drenched and muddied as they were from last night's flight. Mari was sitting against a tree, staring back at the empty trail. She must have taken the second watch. She smiled faintly as Brian made eye contact. He said nothing.

The others awakened soon and they set out again,eating whatever they could find along the way. The forest was rich with berries and greens. Even Brian could eat his fill, grazing as he went. Solemnly, they continued their northward march, the others taking turns helping Mari whose ankle was badly discolored and swollen. Most of the time, Brian carried her on his back. The slowly descending path led them closer and closer to the swollen river. Mari kept staring at the churning brown waters, as if she might see her husband somewhere along the banks.

"Put me down, Brian," she said quietly. "I'll turn myself into a swallow and look for him."

"No magic," said Brian, bluntly.

"If it draws the enemy to me, it may keep him from you," she said.

"No," said the gruffen.

For a moment, she was silent. Brian could feel her moving on his back, just a subtle shift.

"You're doing something!" he hissed. "Stop it!"

The movement stopped. A few paces later, he felt her shaking softly. She was crying.

"What?" he asked, as softly as he could.

"I can't," she said, choking back a sob.

"Can't what?" asked Brian.

"Magic," she said. "I can't do it."

"Why not?" asked Brian.

Mari took a deep breath and let it out. "I haven't the strength," she said. "Even if I wanted to, I don't have it in me."

Brian clumped onward as she buried her face in his furry back and fell silent. There was nothing more to say.

The day wore on, drizzling one hour and raining the next. They were discouraged, soaked through and weary, but all they could do was go on. When night fell, they slept further away from the river according to the old man's instructions.

Brian was on watch at dawn when he smelled something tantalizing. Slowly, he stood up. The rain had stopped. A little breeze stirred the morning mist. There was that smell again. Someone somewhere was cooking rabbit. The wind was so soft, it barely carried the scent, but Brian's nose could tease it out.

He woke Lia and said he was going to see if the cook was friendly. Without waiting for a reply, he set off quickly, following his nose. His heavy feet padded silently through the wet underbrush. His breath issued like steam from his nostrils. The scent was getting stronger. Mixed with it was the smell of human. Brian slowed as he saw a thin veil of smoke lingering high in the tree branches near a small clearing. Though he couldn't see the cooking fire, he was pretty sure somebody lived here.

The gruffen stopped and looked around, suddenly remembering what he looked like. His beard was matted down and dirty, and though the eagle blood had washed off in the rain, the rest of his fur was encrusted with mud and bits of brush. Maybe he should just look around and then go get one of the humans to make contact with the cook. He moved off to one side of the clearing and peered into the trees, looking for some sort of dwelling. He found none. Gently, he parted some of the underbrush. Nothing that looked like an entrance was to be found down there either.

Straightening up, he leaned back to ease his spine and felt the tip of a thin, sharp knife part the hair on the nape of his neck.

"Run, gruffen. Run fast, run far, and do not stop. Otherwise, I cut you deeply," said a steady voice behind him.

"Not just a gruffen," said Brian, as quietly as he possibly could. "Me and four humans. We're hungry. Been running since yesterday and need help. We mean no harm."

There was a pause.

"Step forward three paces and turn around slowly, please," came the reply.

Brian did so and saw very lean man, nearly seven feet tall, poised, but entirely at ease. He seemed quite old and quite young at the same time. His hair was short and light in color. He had no beard or mustache and did not look as if he ever needed to shave one. His clothes were green and brown like the surrounding woods. They seemed to shed water as easily as a leaf or goose feather.

"A gruffen with self control," said the man, studying Brian curiously. "Goblins have been causing trouble recently and gruffen sightings are unheard of here. I take no chances. You'll forgive the indignity." The man bowed slightly, but he kept his unusually long and intricately carved knife trained on the gruffen. "You flee the Citadel Guard, I presume," he continued, glancing skyward; "the eagles."

Brian growled. "If you are their friend, I will tear you apart."

"Were I their friend, I would deserve no less," answered the man, returning the stare and smiling grimly. "I can help you, but you may be as careful of me as you wish. I judge not the wary; I am myself a cautious man. You will do well to prove yourself trustworthy, however. Your life span could have been measured early only moments ago and is even now easily determined. But I will be a good friend if you are friendly. My name is Owler. Have you a name?"

"Brian P. Gruffenson," said the gruffen.

"Even more unusual," said Owler. "I would meet your friends, Mr. Gruffenson. Lead on." He sheathed his long knife.

"Fair enough," said Brian. "Your enemies are ours. Follow me."

They had not gone far when Owler stopped.

"My friends are over here..." Brian began, only to discover they were not.

Owler smiled. "You may come out now," he said aloud. No one appeared. "Very well then," Owler went on; "the man behind the fir tree, the woman in the bramble, and the other woman with the little girl in the small depression under the evergreen hedge may come out now."

Aaron appeared first, several yards away beside a large fir. He held a stout stick in his right hand and a rock in his left.

"Welcome," said Owler. "Weapons are unnecessary, unless you insist."

"You have yours; I have mine," Aaron returned.

Brian backed away.

"If this bothers you, I can put it someplace safer," Owler smiled. He unsheathed his knife, grasped the blade by the steel and flicked it into the trunk of the fir tree. It was deftly thrown, just out of Aaron's reach.

Aaron smiled, reached back and pulled it out without taking his eyes off Owler. He was impressed by how firmly the knife was embedded in the wood. "Then you are welcome to this," he said, flinging his short staff at Owler's feet. It buried itself into the soft ground just in front of the man's green boots.

Owler grinned. "A fine throw, but hardly a fair trade," he laughed. "If you are half as good with the rock as you are with the wood, I shall want my long knife back."

"You can have it," Aaron obliged. Casually, he lobbed it back. Owler whipped a hidden short dagger from his belt and sent it whistling into the same fir tree. Aaron ducked instinctively. Owler followed the arc of his long knife and caught it by the handle.

"If you are half as good with breakfast as you are with knives, we shall be well off indeed!" said Lia, coming out and pulling Owler's dagger from the tree. She handed it to him in person. Mari appeared behind the boulder with Annie.

"You're hurt," said Owler. "Foot or ankle?"

"Ankle," said Mari.

"You're in luck," said Owler. "I have some facility with the healing arts, especially broken limbs."

"Oh, good," said Lia. "We could use that just now. I've done what I can, but the healing is slow."

After short introductions, Owler led them just inside the forest near the clearing Brian had found. To everyone's amazement, he opened an ingeniously hidden door at the base of a nearby tree. A stone stairway led to a heavy wooden door braced with iron. It swung on silent hinges and opened up to a short entryway with heavily braced doors on either side. Owler opened the door on the right with a quick motion executed just out of sight. As the travelers entered the room, they were engulfed by warm, dry air and the smell of food freshly removed from a crackling fire.

"Where does the smoke go?" Brian wanted to know.

"It's routed through several trees," said their host. "That way no one traces it here."

Owler bade them sit down by the fire on wooden stools which he pulled out from under the pine bench against the far wall. Then he quickly set out dishes on the pine table that was draped with a simple, brown cloth.

"Rather oddly dressed for such a trek, aren't you?" he asked as he quickly tossed some clean vegetables into a larger stew pot full of water and hung it over the fire.

"Well, we wouldn't have chosen these clothes," replied Aaron. He told the story briefly and explained their purpose as Owler and Lia tended to Mari's injury.

They both agreed that the ankle wasn't broken, but it wouldn't be much use anytime soon. Lia was very happy that their host had several things handy that she knew how to use, and he was ingenious with his splinting. By the time the vegetables were cooked, Mari's ankle was encased in a light but stiff boot of cloth and wood. Aaron stacked some firewood near Mari's chair so she could rest her foot on it.

Brian observed their host carefully. Nothing about the tall, light-haired man seemed dishonest, but after the experience in the Citadel, Brian was paying closer attention. So far, so good.

Owler was an excellent and generous cook. They had not eaten so well in days.

Mari fell silent toward the end of the meal and sat staring into the fire. Owler noticed this and suddenly waved his hand.

"How rude of me!" he said. "You need baths and fresh clothing. Please allow me to lend you blankets until we can prepare something more fitting for you." He vanished into another room and returned with several quilts.

"We'll get them dirty," Lia protested.

"Nothing that can't be cleaned," said Owler. "Ladies, this place is blessed with a hot spring which I highly recommend. If you'll cross the entryway, you will find a door just inside and to the right which leads to a place where you and the little one may bathe in comfort. Leave your wet garments by the door; I'll use them for size." As the ladies crossed the entry to the other door he disappeared into another passageway and returned with fabric, scissors, needles and thread and all manner of buttons, clasps and belts.

"We can talk while I work, gentlemen. When the ladies are done with their bath, you may avail yourself of it also. Mr. Gruffen, the clean running water should do for your coat. For the rest, I can fashion serviceable clothing, but I have no skill that will suit you better."

By the time the women were done with their bath, Owler had already cut out and sewn a pair of breeches for Aaron and was halfway into a simple tunic. Aaron and Brian retired to the hot spring as the ladies came back wrapped in their blankets, cleaner and more relaxed.

Owler had built a stone pool which held enough water for both Aaron and Brian to sit comfortably. Fresh, hot water flowed in one side and out another, much of it splashing into a drainage ditch around the outside of the pool as Brian eased into the steaming bath.

Aaron groaned as he sank up to his neck in the hot water. "I'm as wary as you, Brian," he said; "especially after we were all fooled back there, but this Owler is solid."

Brian nodded. "He could have killed us by now."

"Yes," said Aaron; "but he hasn't. We have nothing to give him and he asks for nothing."

They didn't linger, soaking only long enough to get clean. Once they were done, Brian started to get out of the pool but then thought better of it.

"Go first," he said.

"Sure. Why?" asked Aaron.

"I have to shake," said Brian.

Aaron laughed. "Of course! Thanks for the warning!" He got out, wiped himself down, wrapped himself in a blanket and stepped out the door.

Brian hauled his big frame out of the pool, grinned and shook himself until his fur stuck out in all directions. He let out a long sigh and went back to join the others. Annie was asleep in front of the fireplace, and Aaron was trying on his new tunic when he got there.

Owler's hands continued to fly, fashioning very practical trousers, shirts and dresses right before their eyes. All the while, he fielded questions from his guests.

"I have watched the Citadel for many years," he said. "It was my father's task before me and my grandfather's before him. In the last century there has been little activity save for the regular departure of an eagle or two looking for food, but the palace was the epicenter of much more before ever I was born. You have made a remarkable escape. Let me tell you about the Citadel."

This was his tale.

CHAPTER 12

The Tale of the Citadel

At the end of the Rule of a Thousand Years the last Great King was dethroned and chaos ruled. No one stood for the people. No one trusted anyone. Justice and honor were spat upon in the streets. Death lay at every door, around every corner and on every dark road. Each day was one step deeper into despair.

Then, one day as the local townspeople were going about their dreary business, a massive eagle glided over the hillside. It cast such a shadow that everyone turned to see what it was. They barely caught a glimpse of it before it flew over the hill again and disappeared. The next day, it appeared again, briefly, but after a week, it was making daily, circling flights over the village.

There was much marketplace discussion over whether this omen was good or bad, whether the creature should be shot or tamed, and whether it was likely to have an appetite for human flesh. Someone said they had seen it eat an elk. Others claimed to have stalked it to its roost and never seen it actually eat anything. No one had proof.

One night, just after sundown, six friends were in the town square watching the eagle circling high overhead when it descended and landed on the ruins of the old fountain. The friends approached it carefully.

"Welcome," said one. The others nodded.

The eagle made a curious gesture with its left claw. Then it simply disappeared. The six friends glanced around in surprise. The eagle was nowhere to be seen. The only other occupant of the square was a small cat that quickly skittered up the steps to the abandoned town hall. The friends gathered into a little group and were mulling this over when the ancient bell in the town hall began to ring.

Villagers streamed out into the streets and converged on the square. The bell had not been rung since the end of the Thousand Years. Everyone gathered in front of the hall. They gasped and stepped back in alarm when suddenly lights appeared in all the windows and the front doors flew open. Standing in the entrance was the massive eagle.

"Be not afraid," it said with perfect enunciation. "I bring order and peace."

So saying, the bird made that peculiar gesture with its left claw and disappeared again. In its place stood a thin man in a dark, hooded robe that covered his head. The townspeople took a few more steps back.

He drew back his hood, exposing his gaunt, wrinkled face. Looking around, he pointed to each of the six young men who had first greeted him in the square

"Step forward," he said.

Trembling, but resolute, they all stepped forward.

"The rest of you, go home," said the thin man, waving his hand dismissively. The townspeople quickly dispersed.

The six stood bravely in the square. The thin man descended several steps toward them and then sat down and motioned for them to join him on the stairs. As they sat down, he introduced himself as "Nykos" and asked each of them their names. He seemed pleased that they would talk with him.

"Why are you here?" asked one of the six; "and why did you call us out to meet with you?"

"The world needs a new government," Nykos said simply. "I need you to go to each town and select six who will be wise leaders. Bring them to the cliffs at the edge of the valley. They will be trained in administration and defense."

"How will we know which will be wise leaders?" asked another one of the six.

"You will know from how they respond to you when you arrive," said Nykos.

"Why will they come with us? No one trusts anyone anymore," said another.

"Ah, they will come," said Nykos. "They will come because you will arrive as I did."

"How?" they asked.

"I will teach you the art of transmutation," replied the magician. "You will be as adept as I."

Despite their initial skepticism, they returned day after day for training. When they mastered the skill, they became instant heroes in the village.

From this stage onward, Nykos spent little time in public. Most of his orders were sent through his six governors. Soon they were sent out to recruit others from the surrounding towns. As stability and communication were restored, the sorcerer called for builders and artisans from all over. They were charged with carving out a citadel high in the bluff just outside the village

Soon, a great scaffolding was built on the cliff and hundreds of workers from all over labored at the site. Nykos would inspect the work every night, alone. It was rumored among the workers that he did some work himself at night, but no one was absolutely sure. There were stories of broken tools repaired overnight and damaged workmanship restored.

The sorcerer's plans for the Citadel were complex and detailed. Ornate fixtures were built to exact specifications. Doors were hewn from great planks of oak and cedar. Gold, sent from far and near was inlaid into the floors, the tables and the chairs. Fine gems and stones were gathered and set into silver utensils. Huge banquet halls were carved out of the rock of the mountain. It took three generations to complete the task. The work was handed down from father to son. The grandchildren were becoming parents when at last the Citadel of the Eagles was complete. Nykos was seen rarely, but he remained nearby throughout the construction.

By now, the governors were six hundred strong. Their authority extended far and wide. Nykos met with sixty of these every month in the Citadel. The other governors were welcome to come and go as they had requests or need of advice. Under Nykos, the land thrived, even through floods and a devastating pestilence. The governors ensured that justice was done, and the sick, the needy and the elderly were cared for properly. Communities came to each others' aid, and there was peace.

After a hundred and seventy years, Nykos appointed four young men to be his personal companions. For twenty more years, he trained them in all the ways of magic and leadership, then he presented them to the people.

"I have finished my work here," he declared to the crowd gathered below the Citadel. "Choose from these four whom you will have as king."

Three months later, the decision was made and Nykos disappeared northward, never to be seen again. The new ruler's first act as king was to appoint the other three candidates as supreme advisers. For three generations of kings, the land was ruled in peace from the Citadel.

The fourth king, Posaman, did not follow the same path. He dismissed the supreme advisers and installed officers from his army as governors throughout the land. Towns were ordered to pay tribute to the Citadel. Posaman's greed was matched by his paranoia, but he had reason to be afraid. The people were turning against him. Posaman isolated himself more and more. Leaving the affairs of state to his young son and his most trusted general, he would disappear for weeks on end. Some said he had gone northward to look for Nykos, the sorcerer. No one knew whether that was true, but each time Posaman returned, he seemed more haggard and afraid. In his absence, his son and the general tightened their grip on power. When Posaman returned, he summarily executed any officer or civilian they accused of disobedience. Sometimes Posaman, himself, would kill the accused without warning or preamble. It was said that the mere touch of his hand could kill.

When he returned from his last and longest expedition, he was no longer the same man who had assumed the throne after his father's death. He secluded himself in the Citadel, speaking to his son only through a locked door. Rumors circulated that he had gone mad.

The lower generals had begun to plot his overthrow when Posaman suddenly returned to the throne room accompanied by six massive eagles that would not leave his side. He called them the Guard and gave no further explanation. The lower generals were called into the throne room and were forced to watch as, one by one, each of them was eaten alive by the Guard. Any further thoughts of rebellion died with them.

Posaman lived for another year in rapidly failing health. Just before he died, he was taken to the room in which he had sequestered himself during his seclusion. The record states that after he had been placed in the room, he became an eagle, like one of the Guard, and lived on as an eagle for another twenty years. When his eagle form finally died, it was memorialized as a statue across from the statue of his human form in the great hall. His wife, his son, and all his children after him, were transformed in the same manner and lived on as members of the Guard for a time after their deaths.

The sons of Posaman were even more ruthless than their father. Dissent was brutally put down with the might of the army and the Citadel Guard. Over successive generations, they drove southward until the whole land was under the rule of the Citadel. Yet for reasons unexplained, they did not venture northward, nor would they allow any of their people to travel north.

Finally, factions in the army split the kingdom into three parts. The Guard remained with the Citadel but their king was weak and unable to maintain centralized power.

An uneasy truce followed. Then a king named Spakas rose up in the south and attacked the middle kingdom, destroying its capitol. Over the next few years, Spakas amassed a great army.

Gaff, the weak king of the Citadel, knew that he was next to fall. Just as his forefather, Posaman, had done, he began to make secret journeys. Unlike Posaman, however, Gaff had an eagle of the Citadel Guard to fly him northward so he was not away as long. Meanwhile, many of his people crossed the border to join Spakas. Those who did not, fled to the capitol and crowded into the city at the feet of the Citadel, clamoring for the protection of the Guard.

In the south, Spakas had built war engines designed to repel attacks from the air. His army was well-fed, well-equipped and well-trained. They marched across the border and entered town after town. The few straggling citizens they encountered offered no resistance. When the invaders finally gained the capital, they found the city entirely empty. Not a soul stirred. The markets, the squares, and even the thousands of temporary shelters built by refugees were all abandoned. The only residents were cats, dogs, rats and roaches. The great ramp that had been built to the Citadel had been blasted away by some incomprehensible force, obliterating the only route to or from the entrance high on the cliff.

The armies scoured the surrounding countryside but could find no trace of the people. Spakas concluded that all the inhabitants of the northern kingdom were sequestered in the Citadel. He set up his government in the city below, but he could not break into the fortress above. Soldiers who scaled the cliffs were repelled by the Guard as soon as they reached the opening to the Citadel. No one could get in. Once a month, the Guard would fly over the mountains to hunt for food but they ranged too far and were too clever to be captured or killed. Spakas kept the Citadel on constant watch, looking for a weakness. He found none.

Once, a watcher reported that a brilliant white dove had landed on the wall surrounding the stone terrace at the entrance to the Citadel. He said the Guard seemed afraid of it and let it enter the fortress unimpeded. No one else corroborated the story, but Spakas' extensive records included this report.

Determined to conquer the fortress, whether its inhabitants were living or dead, Spakas ordered a new earthen ramp to be built, not directly to the entrance but around the side. He intended to attack from above while the Guard was on its monthly hunt. The Citadel Guard could not stop the slow quarrying and transport of a mountain of rock and dirt, but the effort took decades.

Finally, as the Citadel Guard departed the fortress on its monthly hunt, the army surged up the ramp and dropped down into the Citadel by ropes. They entered the vast fortress unimpeded. It was deserted.

They wandered the great hallways searching for prisoners but found none to be taken. Everything appeared to have been abandoned. What looked like centuries worth of dust covered the floor, the fixtures and the furniture, but the place seemed to have been hurriedly abandoned. Tables were set for a banquet, beds were prepared, and fine clothing hung in wardrobes. Despite the thick layer of dust, everything was remarkably free of decay.

A flurry of wings on the terrace announced the return of the Citadel Guard. Spakas' soldiers attacked, but the monstrous eagles merely fended off the blows and did not fight back. In fact, the great birds laid down their kill and stepped back, as if to allow the intruders to examine their offerings.

Spakas ordered his soldiers to stand down. Boldly, he approached one of the great birds. It merely bobbed its head and let him examine the elk it had brought. Spakas inspected its kill and approached the second eagle. It bobbed its head and stepped back so he could examine its kill as well. With each of the Guard, the response was the same.

"Where are your masters?" he asked.

The eagles only nodded at him, picked up their kills and carried them into a side chamber. When Spakas entered behind them, he found a fresh banquet already set for many hundreds of people. The food was hot and steaming and the smell wafted out the door to where his army stood waiting. He called one of his men.

"Eat," he said. "Drink. If you survive, so will we all."

The soldier obeyed. After a few bites, he grabbed a chalice and touched his tongue to the wine. Then he grinned and drained the glass. Wiping his mouth on his sleeve, he said: "If I die, m'lord, I will die happy!"

He devoured his meal and sat back well satisfied.

"Are you ill?" asked Spakas.

"Only from my own excesses, m'lord!" said the soldier.

"Eat up!" cried Spakas. His army was all too happy to comply.

Spakas set up command in the Citadel and brought in reinforcements. Clearly, the victory was his, but possession of the Citadel did not unravel the mystery of the peoples' disappearance. He ordered every room searched. For six weeks, they hunted in the cavernous halls with no success. No one found a second entrance or exit, and while every room appeared to have been lived in, neither a survivor nor a corpse was ever found.

Deep in the Citadel, a vast library was discovered with copious written records. Spakas ordered that they also be searched.

"This makes no sense," said one of the researchers. "The records appear to show generation after generation of kings and queens, all descendants of Gaff, but by our calculations, he would be only seventy four years old today. Worse yet, the histories are nothing but gossip tales written by fools! They are full of doe-eyed romances and petty disagreements which are easily and quickly resolved. Every day appears to have been lived as if it were a holiday or festival. Nowhere is there mention of sickness, ill-will or mistrust. Death is but another excuse for a feast for the living. One cannot imagine why any writer would suffer the trouble of capturing such drivel—even if it is purely fiction—yet each tome is written by a separate hand, and there are hundreds of volumes, all of them essentially the same but for the details!"

This was puzzling, but Spakas was more interested in finding survivors, or at least in learning how they all escaped.

Then, one by one, day by day, the searchers themselves began to disappear. At first it was only a few, but every day there were more reports of others who had gone missing. After a few months, no one was willing to enter the Citadel. Spakas offered a reward to anyone who could bring back evidence of even one survivor. A few attempted it. None returned.

"I will search the palace myself!" he vowed. "The Guard attacks no one. There is nothing to fear. Anyone who will join me will be king when I die."

A wrinkled old man with a hunched spine and a withered hand stepped forward.

"Then let me be king when you die," he said.

Spakas laughed. "You are older than I, old man. If you are still alive when I die, you may be king. Who are you, and what is your name?"

"I am Korstad," said the old man. "I cast spells of itching and pustules on cats and small children. I drink the gall of dogs and leave them to die. For sport I turn husband against wife, father against son and brother against brother, even though they know it not. My favors come at a price, whatever my pleasure may be at the time."

"If you are half of what you claim, you are despicable," said Spakas.

"Yes," said Korstad; "but you have spoken. I will enter the Citadel with you, and I will be king when you die. That is my pleasure, and that is my price."

With this ill-willed companion, Spakas entered the Citadel. The kingdom awaited his return.

After ninety days, when neither Spakas nor Korstad had reappeared, the military appointed one of their officers as king. A great assembly was gathered in the main square at the foot of the Citadel. That night, as the scepter was being given to the newly-crowned king, a howl came from the Citadel. Terror struck all who heard it. Looking up, they saw a body falling from the entrance. The new king seized the scepter and ordered that the body be brought before him.

When they brought the body, everyone gasped. From the rings on his fingers and the clothes that he wore, everyone knew it was Spakas. Yet his face was almost unrecognizable. It was withered and ancient beyond belief. Even as they watched, the body decayed into dust at their feet.

All at once, the earth trembled beneath them and a huge explosion rocked the valley. The great ramp they had built to the Citadel began to crumble. The people panicked and ran from the square. Landslides roared into the city sweeping away trees and buildings. Many thousands were buried alive. Huge cracks in the earth opened up beneath those who could still run, swallowing them into untold depths. Fire broke out. The river suddenly changed course and surged into the city, washing people, animals, siege engines and structures into the great cracks, sweeping the rest away down the valley in a flood of turgid water. Those who were not drowned in the flood were burned in the fire or buried in the landslides. A few survived. By dawn's light the morning after, the entire countryside was burned to ash and buried under a thick layer of mud. The Citadel itself stood solid, isolated once again but for a steep ridge that was all that remained of Spakas' massive ramp.

A few months later, the Great Winter began, and it did not end until three hundred and thirty years later. When the ice finally melted, the remains of all three kingdoms had been scoured away. In time, the land became overgrown with dense forests.

Only a few know the stories of the survivors. I have inherited the responsibility of watching the Citadel. My father watched it for two hundred years and my grandfather for a hundred and fifty before him. The Guard remains, still waiting for something. Someday we shall know what it is.

* * *

"A strange tale indeed," said Lia. "I feel less foolish, knowing the strength of the magic in that place."

Owler listened with raised eyebrows as she and the others related their experience. "But the place held no sway over you, gruffen?" he asked.

"No," said Brian. "Just bothered me. I found all the kings and queens and eagles. One queen was different. Small, with a nice face. Her eagle was broken, ugly and dark. The eagles were coming, so I tried to hide. There's a tunnel behind the queen. She met me there and said how to find the others. Then she was gone."

Owler stopped what he was doing. "She was *inside* the Citadel?"

"And she knew where to go, where my friends were," Brian replied.

"Perplexing," said Owler, deftly tying a knot in the thread as he finished the third and smallest outfit, just suited for Annie. "My father saw three climbers scale the cliffs nearly a hundred and eighty years ago, but they were the last to enter and none ever returned, unless they found another exit. I have explored the forests around the bluffs, and several times narrowly escaped capture by the Guard, but I have found no such exit."

"There is one," Brian said. "I found it from inside. Don't know where it is outside. The sun came down a hole, so maybe it's on top. Water was coming in, like a waterfall."

"There is a pool on the surface, though I can never get a close look at it. The Guard is watchful and they quickly appear when there are intruders on the bluffs," said the tall man with the scissors as he cut out another pair of trouser legs. He chuckled. "Perhaps I will finally get a peek at the inside of the Citadel myself."

"I doubt that will happen anytime soon," said Aaron. "I expect it's overrun."

Owler frowned. "Goblins."

"And worse," Aaron continued. "They have a master who calls himself the King."

"Tell me more," said Owler.

"He's a wizard who turns animals into goblins," said Aaron. "Brian rescued Annie from him. Long story. We barely escaped from him ourselves on the way here."

"Maybe the bird-man and the King are one and the same," said Lia.

"That would ring true," said Mari. She stared into the fire. "It makes sense."

Owler stopped his stitching. "You have a personal reason for that belief," he observed.

"My husband defended us against this bird-man," she said. "I wondered why the creature stopped pursuing us after the magical blow he sent cast Holren into the river."

Owler nodded. "I wondered about your loss," he said.

Mari looked over at him. "How did you know?" she asked.

"A piece of you is elsewhere," said Owler. "That same piece is missing from the others as well, but yours is much greater. Silence says more than words in this case. Please accept my condolences, though I know they lessen the pain not at all."

Mari smiled briefly. "You are very kind," she said.

"Was that how you came to injure your ankle?" asked Owler.

"Right again," said Mari. "I was going to join him, but I was too late. The bird-man broke the ledge loose. I barely escaped."

Owler nodded. "But your husband did not," he said. "I'm sorry." He returned to his sewing. "I saw the bird-man down by the river yesterday afternoon. He seemed to be searching for something."

"I still hope to find my husband downstream," said Mari; "...before the King does."

"Or before he gets to the still water," said Aaron. "There's supposed to be something deadly in there. Owler, what is 'Wofrung?'"

"The monster who lives in the river," Owler replied. "He avoids the rapids, and nothing is safe on the banks of the still waters. He strikes like a snake, without warning and with great speed. Anything that dares to stop for a drink is at risk. In all the years I have lived here, I have seen the monster many times but I have never gotten a close look. It is too fast. A mother bear and her cubs can simply vanish from the shore, taken suddenly by a long, dark shape. How did you hear of him?"

"The old man who fixed my arm told me," said Brian.

Owler peppered Brian with questions about the small, old man.

"I don't know much," said Brian, but he told their host all he could.

"Fascinating," said Owler. "Over the years, I have often seen someone matching that description. He is very elusive. I have tracked him for days only to watch his trail suddenly end: a short trail of small footprints and no more. Clearly, he is a wizard of great power, but I have no clue what he does or where he goes." He tied off a seam, cut the thread and handed a pair of finished breeches to Lia. "Please try these on, m'lady, and let me know if they're suitable," he said. Then he got up and went to the kitchen.

When Lia came back wearing her new breeches and tunic, porridge was cooking in the big pot over the fire. Owler convinced them to stay until he could make outfits for both Annie and Mari. "It won't take long," he said. "I've got more practice now."

Aaron guffawed. "It didn't take long *without* the practice," he said.

They spent the afternoon learning about the surrounding landscape. Owler instructed them more precisely how to find the Great Falls and made sure they knew how far back to stay from the banks when the river was calm. Before he let them go, he also sewed simple packs and fitted them with tough leather straps so Lia and Aaron could carry some supplies.

"How can we thank you for all your help?" asked Mari.

"All I ask is that you never reveal the location of my dwelling," said Owler. "The last of the white water before the Great Falls is a day's journey away. After that, the river becomes smooth and deadly. Do not underestimate the monster. Now we must all be off. Many things have changed up on the hill and I need to know what they are."

"You should come with us," said Aaron as they stepped out into the clearing. "We could use your help, and I don't think you can get anywhere near the Citadel."

Owler smiled. "Yours is the first invitation I have actually fancied, my friend," he said; "but my work is here. I have many routes to the Citadel. If I cannot get close, I can still observe. The Guard has not caught me yet. I will ensure the goblins have no better luck."

With that, he bade them farewell and soundlessly slipped away, headed for the ridge. Almost immediately he vanished into the underbrush.

CHAPTER 13

Fire

They followed the high trail northward as it dropped lower and lower toward the watercourse. The forest canopy protected them from prying eyes above. Whenever there was an opening in the trees, everyone scanned the river banks below for any sign of Holren among the debris that lined the turbid, brown water. The river charged along, crashing into rocky outcrops that jutted their stone chins into the stream first on one side and then the other. The gray clouds had blown away and a warmer wind was whipping through the trees.

They spent the night in a thicket guarded by cottonwoods near a bubbling spring. Everyone was grateful for the clean, fresh water and the new clothes and food Owler had provided. After dark, Aaron kept watch while the others found soft, mossy places to sleep.

Aaron woke Brian sometime around midnight. "Do you smell something?" he whispered.

The gruffen sat up and shook off the sleep. "Smoke," he said. "Burning trees. Not close."

"I wasn't sure," said Aaron. "I'm going up the ridge to take a look."

Brian acknowledged and waited for Aaron to return. The others were sleeping relatively peacefully. The more rest they got now, the better. Brian wondered how the fire had started. There had been no lightning since the storm but the wind was getting stronger. The fire could have been touched off then and was only now catching up to them. Aaron came back.

"You were right," he said. "There's a long line of flames to the south of us. I can't tell how fast it's coming, but it is driven by this dry wind. I wonder if it was set to smoke us out."

"Maybe," said Brian. "Or maybe just lightning. Can we outrun it?"

"I don't think we need to run yet," said the other. "Besides, a few hours' sleep now may serve us better than trying to make slow progress in the dark. I say we wait."

The hours dragged by. Brian constantly sniffed the air but he could never decide if the scent was getting stronger or if he was merely more attuned to it. When the sun reached the top of the far ridge, he awakened the others. Aaron explained their predicament and they started out immediately, eating along the way. Brian hoisted Mari on his back and set a quick pace as they wound around the path which stayed well clear of the river. The water moved smoothly now, rippled only by the wind. The smoky haze cast a dark mood over the sky.

"I think we should go higher up the ridge," said Aaron. "We'll save all this sideways motion if we don't have to cross every drainage. Just this side of the top, we can maintain a fairly level path and straighten our route considerably."

Brian agreed. They left the path and began to climb gently upward, still heading north. By mid-afternoon, they had covered a substantial amount of territory, but they were all tiring. By evening, the smoke was burning their lungs. Ash soaked up the amber rays of sunset. About an hour later, the travelers stopped and settled in.

Brian climbed a high point on the ridge to see the fire's progress for himself.

Fire.

How long ago it seemed that he was living in his den, looking for firewood on the old old snow-laden hillside. How long ago it seemed that a little girl had appeared in his home and disrupted his life. That life seemed so far away. Yet even in his present predicament, he felt more alive than ever before.

He selected a sturdy tree on the hilltop and began to climb. Soon he could make out the red and gold glow of the fire line, snaking across the southern horizon. The long, hot tongue licked at the forest for several miles to the east and west. Trees exploded, sending sparks shooting up into the night sky. The river would probably bound the fire on the west, but Brian could not tell how far east the line extended. If it caught them, they would have nowhere to run but to the still water.

He climbed back down and joined the others where he took the first watch. Even after Lia relieved him for the second watch, he couldn't sleep. He kept smelling smoke. The wind was whipping up and the trees were blowing back and forth. In the smoke-tainted darkness, the snapping twigs sounded like fire. Annie slept uncomfortably by his side. Mari was awake most of the night, sitting with her back against a tree, staring down at the dull highway that was the river. Aaron, dozed nearby.

They were all up before it was light enough to see well and they set off immediately. They ate a little when they could see better, but no one wanted to stop for rest. The fire was gaining on them faster than they had thought possible.

Around noon, Brian climbed the ridge to scout the territory once again. His throat had been burning all day. The arid wind hurt his eyes and did little to keep him cool as he clambered up the hillside. Climbing a tree to get a better look, he saw the wall of smoke that had been showering them with ash for most of the day. Further back, behind the flames, lay a desolate landscape. Smoldering stumps and fallen tree trunks were strewn across the blackened hills. From where he was, Brian could see that the fire line did indeed stretch to the water's edge.

The gruffen was about to scramble down when he saw movement behind the wall of fire. Well back from the heat, but moving steadily northward was a large army raising another cloud of ash behind it. Goblins! They fanned out across the main breadth of the burned area searching the scorched remains of the forest. Brian thought of Owler and hoped the clever woodsman had somehow escaped.

Looking downstream, he could see that the river opened into a lagoon and, although it was hard to tell, he thought he could see mist rising in the distance. Perhaps he was seeing the Great Falls from behind but he could not be certain in the smoky daylight.

On the nearby banks, several deer fleeing the fire approached the water with their usual caution. Brian watched. The first deer took a quick drink and looked around. The next did the same. Brian felt thirsty just watching them. The other deer were equally skittish. Brian stared, uncertain as to whether he was actually seeing a shadow in the brown water. Then, with alarming speed, a huge, dark object shot from the water. The two closest deer were gone. Several more were knocked into the river and the rest scattered. Whatever it was had already slipped swiftly back under water but the swirling eddy it left behind sucked the struggling deer into the depths.

Wofrung!

Brian's heart raced as he began to register what he had seen. The ripples on the lagoon indicated a monstrous creature lay hidden below. The massive, dark shape he had seen must have been only the head and neck. Hastily, he returned to the others.

"Can't make it," said Brian. "We're a day away from the falls."

"You can see the falls from here?" asked Lia hopefully.

"I think so," he replied. "I saw Wofrung. Very big. It ate two deer and drowned some more."

"I think it's time we found a rock shelter or a deep ditch and let the fire blow over," said Aaron.

"Can't," said Brian.

"Why not?"

"Goblins," said the gruffen. "Right behind the fire. A whole army."

Aaron nodded grimly. "So we are being smoked out," he said. "On then."

They forged ahead. The smoke grew thicker by the hour. Everyone was coughing now, and Annie had to be carried. As the sun set, they scaled the ridge. They would spend the night at the highest vantage point so they could mark the progress of the fire. If it came too close, they might be able to wait it out. Plus, it was the most defensible position around, should the goblin army finally arrive.

Brian again took the first watch and climbed a tree. In the waning light, he could see where the lagoon simply stopped and a swirling mist began. That had to be the Great Falls. The ground rose steeply on either side of the lake. It would be a treacherous climb down to the falls. Worse yet, Brian could see no way to get across. The recent floods had swollen the lagoon. If there were rocks on the lip of the falls that one could traverse from one side to the other, they were buried underwater.

Brian looked at the dark, wind-raked lagoon and wondered if Wofrung swam somewhere down there.

All of this roiled around in Brian's head as he sat in the tree watching the flames marching toward him. He couldn't decide if they should struggle on in the darkness. Even if they reached the falls, they would have difficulty descending at night and they could not stay near the water. Around midnight, he climbed down and woke Aaron.

"Go look," he said. "I think we should move."

Aaron nodded and climbed the lookout tree. He came back quickly. "I agree," he said. "Let's put some distance between us and the flames. We'll need all the time we can get to figure out out how to cross the falls."

They went to the others. Lia had overheard the conversation and was already waking Mari. Annie was exhausted so Aaron lifted her onto his back. With the gruffen in the lead, they ventured again into the darkened forest.

Lia followed along just ahead of her husband. It crossed her mind how much she had always enjoyed walking through the woods with him. This was hardly such a walk, but in an odd way, she felt closer to him now than ever. He had told her some of his tales of battle and had taught her swordcraft, but she had always felt a little shut out of his world. When they had left the village to find the King, Lia was secretly thrilled at the chance to foray out with her husband.

Now, tired and hungry, with death hot on their heels, she was even more glad to be with him. He was in his element and she could tell. His movements were focused, both deliberate and quick. With Annie on his back and his pack in front, he marched steadily forward, never changing his gait even when the terrain was uneven. Dark though it was, he seemed to know where to place his feet.

She stumbled. Aaron's strong hand shot out and steadied her before she fell. Even with his concentration at its peak, he was mindful of her presence. They marched onward. Lia enfolded the memory deep in her heart.

The flames were closing in. They cast an eerie glow on the smoke above and behind them. Gingerly, the travelers picked their way along the now-jagged ridge. Great boulders jutted up out of the ground, blocking their way. The land dropped away sharply on either side but in the darkness no one could be sure which side was more dangerous. Finally, they made their way around to the west. Brian went first, without Mari, and then Aaron came over. When Aaron had a good solid footing, Brian continued until he found a secure stance further down. Aaron helped Mari through, and then Lia and Annie, handing them off to Brian who got them to more stable ground.

Progress was terribly slow. They had to stop often and rest. The advancing flames licked upward behind them and clouds of smoke billowing overhead. In the dim light of the red-orange glow, they inched forward. In time they heard the ominous rumble of the river thundering over the cliff edge. Behind them, the fire snapped and roared.

CHAPTER 14

The Race for the Door

A
s the blackened dawn broke, the party found themselves some five hundred paces from the edge of the Great Falls. Even from here they could see no way across to the other side. Lea cried out as she saw the river monster devour an elk that got too close to the water. Everyone watched in horror as the water grew still again.

After several hours of painful and dangerous climbing and descending, they could see the lip of the falls clearly. For the most part, they had continued to hold to the high ground. Now they had no choice but to descend toward the river. The sky was heavy with smoke and everything around them was gray with ash. By the time they worked their way to the cliffs above the falls, the fire had licked its way to the top of the ridge behind them. Beyond, the water plunged over the edge and thick spray boiled skyward.

They were trapped. The rocks on which they stood were undercut by years of erosion; there was no way down. Brian left Aaron with the others and went along the brink to try to find some other route. Peering over the edge into the mist, he fought back the anxiety that gnawed at him. The morning sky wallowed in a hazy twilight. On the hills, a mile back, the goblin army advanced over the burnt landscape. There had to be a way down to the falls. The man had told him to cross them.

The water was smooth right up to the edge of the cascade. Brian looked into its murky depths and saw the dark shadow of Wofrung patrolling quietly back and forth. The monster awaited them. Even if they were to reach the falls, they would be devoured. The gruffen shivered. We die quickly, he thought.

Winding around the cliff's edge, Brian found a place where he could look back at the face of the cascade from the north. The lip of the Great Falls was the edge of a massive, overhanging shelf of black rock. From there, the water plunged in a rippling, freefalling curtain for perhaps a hundred feet before it pounded heavily on a great pile of rocks that had been undercut from the shelf above. It thrashed about in a churning plunge pool before it overflowed once more and thundered down another three or four hundred feet where it disappeared into the mists.

From here, Brian could finally see how they might get across. A second shelf of rock lay underneath the first shelf, back just a bit from the curtain of water that launched off the lip. Between the two layers of rock was a deep and obvious gap. It appeared to be continuous, all the way to the far bank. If they could fit in the gap between these upper and lower shelves, they could cross behind the thundering falls, out of reach of the water and safe from the dark monster in the lagoon above.

First, he had to find a way down to the gap. Working a bit further forward, Brian found a small drainage that had cut a channel wide enough for them to climb down most of the way to the second shelf. It was risky, but it was all they had. Brian raced back to the others.

The lack of foliage on the ridge slowed the advancing fire. Mari hobbled along between Aaron and Lia without a word. Brian led them to the stream and they began their descent immediately. Once again, Brian went first and found somewhere safe to stand. Aaron lowered Annie to him and he set her aside. Then Lia helped Mari down to Aaron who sent her on to Brian at the bottom. On and on they continued like this, passing each other from one to the other, then scrambling down to do it again. Eventually they had to abandon the drainage and search along the sheer wall for another route downward. The thunder and hiss of the falls made it very hard to hear each other's shouted encouragement.

Brian brought them down to the gap between the first and second shelf and they all stopped to catch their breath. They were soaked through and nearly exhausted. It was difficult to see in the mist and gloom of spray and smoke. The Great Falls were a mere stone's throw away and the force of their pounding rumbled in everyone's chest. Brian was relieved to see that the gap was larger and deeper than he had first thought. They would almost be able to stand up in it.

"What about the far side?" shouted Lia. "I couldn't see a way down."

"Don't know!" bellowed the gruffen. "We have to try!"

Aaron climbed up into the gap between the rock shelves and motioned to Mari to follow. Lia helped her get up and the three of them started across the shelf behind the falls. They could just fit three abreast if they stooped. Annie insisted on climbing up by herself and Brian crawled in immediately behind her.

Once they were behind the waterfall, they were blinded and choked by the spray. The thundering water was now truly deafening. Aaron cracked his head against the rock ceiling and almost dropped to his knees, but he kept going. Mari stumbled blindly ahead between him and Lia. Brian had hold of Annie's hand as he half crawled through the gap.

He felt his head bump into Aaron from behind. The three ahead of him were stopped at a place where a rockfall blocked the way forward. No one could hear anyone else's shouts. Aaron explored both left and right, and finally tugged Mari and Lia toward the falling water on their right. One by one, they negotiated a tricky climb around the fallen boulders and continued on ahead.

They pressed forward blindly, shuffling along on the uneven, gravelly surface for what felt like an eternity. Finally, they came to a place where the light was brighter. To begin with, the mist hid the fact that they had actually passed behind the entire length of the fall and were coming out the other side. When Aaron realized where they were, he started looking for a way down and to their right but there was nowhere to go. They had come to a dead end. Brian joined him and started searching for another way out. Annie crawled along the base of the end wall. For a moment, Brian thought he'd lost her. Then he saw her poking her head out from a dark corner. He kept feeling around for handholds, but neither he nor Aaron were finding any.

Annie came back and hollered something but no one could hear her. She grabbed Brian's arm and tried to pull him but he was still searching for a way up. Finally, Annie let him go and grabbed Lia by the hand. A moment later, Lia returned and pulled both Brian and Aaron with her, pointing deeper into the rocks. They followed.

Sure enough, the little girl had found a crack which led up and to the right. She had no difficulty scrambling up and out. Lia followed, looking for the best way to help Mari through. That proved much more difficult, but with help, Mari was able to make it. Aaron himself found the crack a bit tight, but with a few contortions, he also was able to climb through the crack and get out.

Brian tried to force his way in afterward but his huge body simply wouldn't fit. He let out all his breath and still he couldn't squeeze in. The others were already somewhere outside, but he remained standing in the gap behind the Great Falls!

Something grabbed him from behind. Instinctively, Brian swung his arm and caught a goblin full in the face, knocking him off the shelf and into the plunging waterfall. The goblins were here! Frantically, he swung his great fists, blindly fending off several of the creatures without ever actually seeing them. One great big one slammed full into the gruffen's chest, smashing him back into the rock wall. Brian was cornered! He grabbed the goblin in a bear hug and crushed its ribcage. The he swung the gasping goblin in all directions, scattering his attackers in a wide arc until he finally flung the creature into the misty darkness. Cries and hollers from the mist told him the move had bought him a little time.

Quickly, he ran back to the end wall. He wedged one of his big arms into the crack and pulled himself up. Then he wedged the other one and pulled himself a little higher. From there on, he wedged and pulled, with only his great arms inside the crack and the rest of his body dangling outside, until he was able to get a foothold and clamber up where the others had gotten out.

No sooner had he done so than goblins came surging up the crack as well.

Brian kicked two of them off the shelf and squared off to face the next one. They could come through only one or two at a time, so he took them as they came, but he knew he couldn't hold off all of them.

Some well-aimed rocks from behind him felled the next two goblins. Aaron was yelling for him to join them. Frantically, Brian scrambled in the direction of Aaron's voice, almost losing his footing on the slick rocks. More goblins quickly surged into the crack.

Mari turned to see what was going on. The pain in her ankle almost dropped her to her knees. Lia grabbed her by the waist to steady her and Annie clung to her leg. To Mari's amazement, she felt a surge of power flow into her body from both of them. It almost made her dizzy.

"Hang on to me!" she shouted over the din. Lia and Annie held on tightly.

She faced the gap where Brian and Aaron heaved rocks at the rapidly emerging goblins.

"Don't let go," shouted Mari. "Whatever happens, don't let go!" Her face hardened into a mask of determination. With quick finger movements, using both hands, she wove a small pattern in the air in front of her. She concentrated, ignoring her pain as she increased the complexity of the pattern. Her lips moved but no one could hear her above the thundering waterfall. Brian and Aaron were being slowly beaten back toward her but she kept her concentration. She moved her hands faster, wider, faster, wider. The air crackled around her.

Annie and Lia dared not move. Both of them could feel energy surging through them and into Mari.

"FALL BACK!" shouted Mari in a voice louder than anyone could have expected.

She was forever grateful that Brian and Aaron obeyed without thinking.

Annie, Lia and Mari all jerked simultaneously as bolt of energy shot from Mari's hands toward the gap from which the enemy was now streaming unimpeded. The goblins who had just emerged were vaporized. The ground below rocked as if stricken by a heavy blow.

Brian turned just in time to see the crack they had just crawled through suddenly break wide open. A fifteen foot section of the second shelf cracked, shifted, and then collapsed, dumping goblins into the plunge pool as it fell.

When it landed at the bottom, the splash nearly emptied the plunge pool and the shock wave blasted all of them off their feet.

Brian stood to his feet. The place they had climbed up only moments ago was now a gaping hole. The goblins could follow them no further.

A horrible screech cut through the roar of the waterfall. Someone on the other side of the river was very angry but the smoke and spray were so thick no one could see who it was. No one doubted that it was the bird-man.

"Let's go! Let's go! Let's go!" shouted Aaron.

They groped their way along the steep wall, searching for yet another way down the rocks. The howling on the other side continued. It made Brian's fur bristle, drenched though he was. They forged ahead.

Halfway down from the top of the falls, they clambered westward over a ridge and came out where the southwind had ceased its insistent blowing. They had come out upon a wide field. Across from them, perhaps four hundred paces away, grew a dense forest of evergreens that marked the beginning of a row of foothills that stretched for miles to the north and south.

Brian thought hard. He remembered standing in the rain outside the cave over the Citadel, his arm completely healed. "Find the door in the brush..." the small man had said. The gruffen's weary body ached. That door could be anywhere in those trees.

Brian turned back to tell the others when he saw something that made his heart sink. Six eagles of enormous size were circling high above in the hazy sky.

"The Guard!" croaked the gruffen, grabbing Mari and hoisting her onto his back. "To the forest! Find a door!"

Then they were all off and running. Once they were off the ridge and on the open plain, they were completely exposed. To cross without being discovered was impossible, but cross they must and so they simply ran for the woods. They had not gone twenty or thirty paces when they heard the eagles cry. No one bothered to look; if the predators were going to attack, there would be little point.

The sun was on their backs now for the first time in days. They could see their own shadows at their feet. Any moment, they expected to be enveloped in the shade of gigantic wings and seized by sharp talons. They could hear the eagles screaming frantically above, but the attack was long in coming. Every pounding step they took brought them closer to the forest edge but the anticipation was dreadful.

"Hang on!" said Brian. When he felt Mari grab his fur in both hands, he dropped to all fours and shot across the field. In almost no time, he reached the forest edge. Once inside, he lay face down quickly.

"Roll off!" he yelled. "I'm getting Annie!"

Mari slid off into the underbrush and Brian galloped back out onto the field. Lia was several paces ahead of Aaron. Brian flew past her, stopped hard and grabbed Annie off of Aaron's back. He pounded along on two feet, carrying her in front of him as if that might shelter her from the danger overhead as they raced toward the shelter of the woods. They were almost afraid to hope. Yet they could see that in a few moments they might actually make it.

"Faster!" screeched a raspy voice over their heads. No one knew who shouted the order but somehow they all quickened their pace. Huge shadows now rippled across the grass all around them. The eagles screamed even louder. Annie's face was turned to the sky. Only she could see the eagle racing toward them.

"Look out!" she screamed. They scattered, but no one stopped until they had waded several paces into the dense woods. Brian flung a quick look over his shoulder and saw the eagle strike the bare ground some fifty feet to the south of them. It was burning! Stunned, he came to a stop and turned around. Another eagle came crashing out of the sky. It, too, was in flames!

"The door!" hollered Lia, somewhere off to his right. Turning to find her, Brian's sharp eye glimpsed a flash of iridescent blue up in the sky. Then he tripped and had to stagger forward to keep from falling. Wildly, he scrambled toward Lia's voice. Another eagle scream split the air. The flaming raptor crashed through the trees overhead, beak open and talons outstretched. With a sickening thud, it hit the ground just in front of Brian and Annie. The smell of burnt feathers and flesh singed the gruffen's nostrils. He skirted the dead eagle and ran toward a thick hedge in the midst of the woods. Part of the hedge swung open as if on hinges, revealing a dark interior. Aaron and Lia had already brought Mari inside. Brian set Annie on the ground and Lia scooped her up.

High above, a rasping cry ripped the air. Brian turned back through the trees to see a dragon falling limply from the sky across the field. Its blazing colors gleaming in the sun, it twisted slowly over as it plummeted toward the stony ground. All at once Brian heard a taut twanging sound a short distance away. A flash of light ripped through the trees and struck the dragon mid-fall. With a thrashing of scaly wings, the lizard righted itself just before it hit the ground. A second later, as the dragon swooped up and over the trees, Aaron grabbed Brian's hand and yanked him into the darkness of the hedge. The gruffen lost his balance and sat down hard. Somewhere behind and above him, it sounded like a heavy door slammed shut.

"Gasslic!" was the first thing Brian said when he got his wits about him.

"What?" came Mari's voice somewhere in front of him. They were in an underground passage. The floor below him was solid rock. The walls were hard dirt with roots of bushes and other plants sticking out on all sides. Looking up, he could see only pinpoints of light through the thick hedge.

"Quickly, we must go deeper," urged a voice that was not one of their own.

"Who speaks?" demanded Aaron.

"All in good time," insisted the Voice. "Go to the light."

"We go nowhere until we know who you are," Aaron returned.

"A friend," said the Voice. "You will be safer below. Please, go to the light."

"Any trickery and I will tear you apart myself," said Aaron.

Lia smiled in the darkness. She had little doubt he would do just that, if he could find where the voice was coming from. They could see a faint glow further down the passageway, but the voice didn't seem to come from there. Somehow, she didn't feel afraid. Everything felt very different in the tunnel, as if all danger had been left behind. For a moment, she wondered if they were falling under a spell as they had in the Citadel, but this didn't feel the same at all.

Up ahead, the passageway turned to the right. Aaron followed the wall to the corner and peeked around it. No one was there.

"All right," he said. "Where are you?"

"Here," answered the Voice. "Yes, I am invisible. Your questions will all be answered in due time. We must go deeper now."

The tunnel came to an end a few paces later where a small platform with benches and a railing was suspended over a hole or shaft from which emanated the light. There was a draft coming up through the shaft and a very different smell came with it. It smelled like dirt in the woods, but there was a different musty wetness to it that Brian hadn't smelled before.

"Please step onto the platform," said the Voice. Even in the light, they could not fix a spot from which the Voice came. Finally, tired and glad to be away from the danger above, they got onto the platform. Mari sat down and rested her ankle for the first time in a long time. Everyone grabbed onto something as the platform began to lower itself into the shaft.

Soon they were dropping at a dizzying rate. Then, just as quickly, they slowed down again and found themselves passing through the ceiling of a large cavern, deep beneath the surface. The platform settled to the ground between two glowing spheres some six feet in diameter, each set atop a stone pillar twenty feet high and four feet around. The spheres gave off a warm, golden light that shown on a barren hillside that sloped down and away. At the bottom of the hill to their left was a wide expanse of water, dark and quiet. Waves lapped gently at a strip of sandy beach, barely lit by the globes. By the sand, much to everyone's surprise, was a vale of green grass that led up a smaller hill on which stood a grove of trees that looked for all the world like it had grown in the blazing sunlight. The hill, the trees and the vale of grass were all inside a vast cavern whose ceiling was so high, the light of the globes never reached it. They got off the platform, somewhat bewildered. A steep path wound down to the water's edge directly to their left.

"Take this trail," came the Voice again. "Your immediate needs are many. In the grove is a house of rest where all may eat and be refreshed. The lady Mari will need attention. Lia, you will find the implements of the healing arts. Follow the path down and then go up to the house on the hill. The Master of the house will return soon. I leave you now, but I will never be far away."

"Wait!" shouted Brian. What was the use? There was no way of knowing if their invisible guide was still with them or not. Brian looked around, frustrated. Everyone was exhausted and Mari's ankle needed to be tended to right away. Wearily, he carried Annie down the trail toward the sandy beach.

When they reached the water, Aaron bent over, dipped a finger into it and smelled it.

"Brackish," he said, wiping his hand on his breeches.

"What?" asked Brian.

"There's salt in it," said Aaron. "I wonder where we are."

The lake in the cavern seemed very large; the far bank was lost in the darkness. The path they followed led them along the water's edge until it came directly across from the grove of trees. Near the grove stood a house. The windows glowed warmly, as if a fire had already been lit in the hearth. The path now passed through a large, open metal gate with hedges on either side. A three tiered fountain graced the small front yard, spilling water from its upper tiers to the pools beneath. The house itself looked small from the front, though it was two stories high. Rough-hewn logs held up the porch roof. A small window in the solid front door let out some of the inviting light.

CHAPTER 15

In the House of Ender

To the gruffen's relief, the gate did not clang shut magically behind them after they passed through. He had been half afraid that it might. Wearily, they climbed the steps to the house. Two large benches made of wooden slats set into tree stumps sat on the porch. Brian let Aaron open the door. There was no one inside, but food was simmering on the stove and the table was set for eight.

Aaron and Lia immediately laid Mari on a couch by the warm hearth. Annie pulled up a stool next to Mari's head and stayed close while Lia worked on the painful ankle. On the heavy mantle were the very things Lia needed for treatment, neatly arranged to one side. A poultice was already mixed and clean cloth strips were carefully laid out for a new splint.

"Obviously, someone is expecting us," said Aaron as he sat down in a comfortable chair. Had he not been so tired, he might have noticed that the clothes Owler had made for them were already beginning to dry.

"Many people," said Brian, indicating the eight place settings at the table.

"Well, yes, there is another on his way, I hope," said a woman's voice from the entry way.

Aaron stood up quickly and stepped in front of Mari as all turned to see who had spoken.

Into the firelight stepped a small woman with long, fine hair the color of wheat. She curtsied, almost embarrassedly. "Please sit, sit. Welcome, Brian and all," she said. Her smile was as warm as the hearth and any fears the company may have had melted away as she spoke. She did not seem particularly old, but there was something ancient and wise in her eyes.

Brian stared with amazement. He knew this woman! He had seen her in the Citadel tunnels. She was the queen he had met behind the statue in the hall.

"Are you the Mistress of this house?" asked Lia.

"Yes, my name is Calicia, and this is the Master of Cai-Amira," said the small woman, pointing to the door. "He is called 'Ender.'"

They heard footsteps on the porch and through the door stepped a very tall man with a great bow in his hand. Strapped to his back was a quiver of fine arrows fit for just such a bow. He nodded to the visitors. "Welcome," he said in a calm, quiet tone. "May our home be yours. Let us bring you something warm to drink." He looked around. "I can see you have availed yourselves of nothing yet."

"We've only just arrived," said Lia. "If you'll excuse me, I'll tend to Mari's ankle. Thank you for the supplies."

"Don't mention it," said Calicia, who was already pouring large mugs of something hot that had a most wonderful smell. They each accepted the drink gratefully.

Brian settled down onto the floor and took a careful sip of the hot liquid. It was thick and slightly sweet but not overly so. Its richness delighted the nose and the tongue and if not for that hint of sweetness, it might have been too strong to drink. The first swallow had a wonderful effect on the throat and belly and soon even Brian's wet fur began to dry.

The man went briefly into another room and returned without the bow and quiver.

Soon, Mari's ankle was secured in a sort of boot built from cotton and splints. Her pain had lessened considerably. Exhausted, she actually fell asleep as Lia was wrapping the splint. Calicia took Lia, Aaron and Annie upstairs to clean up. Brian just sat by the fire with his mug and let the steam from the drink soothe his face.

Ender settled into a large chair made from some reddish wood with deep burgundy upholstery. The legs were carved simply but elegantly and the back of the frame curved in an arc just over his head. It joined in the center with two oak leaves and two acorns. Next to the chair was a small table with two drawers, fashioned from the same wood as the chair. On its polished surface lay a great pipe, its bowl carved into no particular shape.

Ender opened the top drawer of the table and pulled out a pouch from which he filled the pipe carefully, tamping it down three times with a wooden stub. Then he came over to the fireplace. In a box to the left was a neat collection of thin wooden slivers. He held one of these to the flames until it caught fire. Then he lit the pipe with several strong draughts. A sweet smoke mingled with the smell of food and drink, masking a little the scent of wet gruffen fur.

When he sat back down once more, the man took a few puffs on the pipe and leaned back.

"Brian, I apologize for all the mystery. We have been racing against everything these months and have had to convey information quickly." The tall man drew another puff from his pipe before he continued. "As my wife, Calicia, may have told you, my name is Ender. When your friends have finished, we will eat and I shall tell you more about this conflict in which we find ourselves engaged. I expect our last guest to be here shortly. He knew no better how to find us than you did. The one who led you here will see to it that he arrives safely."

"Who was that?" queried Brian. "He knew who we were."

"He is a Sochhmahr and, as such, invisible," Ender said solemnly. "He has been entrusted to me for service and training. You will know him better soon."

Calicia had brought a clean garment for Mari whom she awakened gently. She had much more strength than one would expect of someone so small, for she was able to help Mari to her feet and bring her into another room to change.

"You said there was someone else," Brian prompted. "Who is he?"

"He has just arrived," answered Ender, rising from his chair and going to the door. No one had knocked, but when the tall man opened it, another man was coming up the steps. He was just as tall as the master of the house but more slender and wearing the colors of the deep woods.

"Welcome, sir, this is the place," Ender greeted him. "I am Ender, Master of Cai-Amira and this is Brian, whom you have met before."

Brian stood up, surprised. Owler had just walked through the door and was standing there with an astonished look on his face, shaking his host's outstretched hand. He looked at Brian and smiled broadly, then returned his eyes to the man before him.

"Did you say your name was Ender?" he asked. "I am honored and amazed. I never expected to meet you face to face." He bowed.

Ender laughed. "I feel the same, Owler. Come sit down," he said. "The others are all here. We shall have a small feast."

Owler sat in the chair he was offered. "My presence here baffles me," he said. "I would like to know how I ended up on the other side of the river and escaped the Guard."

"That I do not know, but we could ask the Great Master when we see him," said Ender, returning to his pipe. "I will be interested to hear that story myself. He obviously considers you as valuable to this endeavor as I do. I am glad to finally meet you, Owler. Calicia and I have been watching you for some time and are pleased to see you included in our company."

"The honor is mine," said Owler; "but I doubt my contribution shall add much to a company that includes Ender."

A moment later, Calicia emerged with Mari and seated her at the corner of the table so she could rest her foot on a stool. Annie, Lia and Aaron came downstairs in fresh clothes and all were surprised and thrilled to see Owler. After much passing of dishes from the kitchen and pouring of drinks, they all settled in to the wonderful task of eating.

There were two kinds of bread: sweet buns with butter and a very large, round loaf of sourdough. Corn and green beans waited, steaming in covered, earthen crocks. Next to Ender was a large, shallow pot covered with a great dome of a lid and containing a huge roast, marinating in its own juices and surrounded by hot potatoes. Of wine there was plenty and, for Annie, a delicious nectar, delightful to the tongue and wonderfully quenching.

Ender set the entire roast in front of Brian. "Please, eat!" he said, removing the lid.

The gruffen's stomach reminded him how much he loved good food and his eyes and nose confirmed that he was in the presence of it, but he hesitated.

"We expected a hungry gruffen," said Ender, grinning as he rose from the table. "Please, eat!" He returned from the kitchen with a second roast. "The rest of us can share this one," he said.

Brian smiled. Then he ate.

For awhile the dinner conversation consisted of little more than "ooh" and "aah" and "mmm." They ate their fill, including magnificent slices of apple pie, and then settled back in front of the hearth to enjoy hot cups of tea. Annie, sleepy and content, nestled in next to Mari on the large couch and was soon fast asleep.

Ender re-lit his pipe and sat back in his chair. "Would you like to tell your family story, Owler, or would you allow me?" he asked the tall man in green.

Owler laughed. "If you have a version, I prefer to hear that one!"

Ender began: "Let me introduce Franklin Thurmond Vasserman Everhabixortimus the Fourth, also known, for short, as Owler. I am happy to finally have this great grandson of a dear friend as a guest in my house."

Owler nodded, his eyes bright with interest as Ender continued:

* * *

If I first tell you of his great grandfather, the original "Owler," you will understand our present company better. I met him after a great battle with the Morve. My strength was drained and my powers were weak. I had assumed the form of an owl so I could escape and hide my whereabouts. However, I was soon too worn even to fly, and crashed into a tree. There I hung, one wing caught in the branches. I had no power left to return to my natural form and I was far from help, so I put myself to sleep.

Sometime later, I was awakened by the sound of movement in the branches. An owl can easily rotate its head, so naturally, I turned to see behind me. To my astonishment, I found myself looking into the eyes of a man who was also hanging upside down, just as I was. He had slung a length of rope between two trees and crawled across it to reach me as I was trapped in the outer branches.

He assured me in a quiet voice that he meant no harm as he lifted me up, taking the weight off of my injured wing. I did not complain.

"You must be the one!" he said. Then he tucked me snugly into his shirt and worked his way back along the rope until he could carry me down from the tree.

Back on the ground, he removed me from his shirt and expertly reset my wing. Then he tucked me back in, retrieved his rope and set off through the woods. He moved with remarkable grace and ease, and his footsteps were barely audible, even to my owl ears.

I was too tired and grateful to wonder where he was taking me. All he said over and over was, "This must be the one; this must be it."

We came to a hill, and he entered it somehow. I found myself inside his home underground. The dwelling was neither opulent or extravagant, but it was luxurious in its simplicity and functionality.

He took me directly to an upper level of the house and placed me in a large owl's nest built of sticks, straw and bits of soft cloth. He then showed me a small door to the outside. It was cleverly built, strung with pulleys and counter-weights, and was so light to the touch that an owl such as I could easily push it open or shut. The next night, when I gingerly ventured out, I discovered that the door was ingeniously disguised and hidden behind a thick hedge. It was virtually invisible.

The man spoke to me as though he expected me to understand, which I did. He said that when he was a small child, a wise man told him that someday he would free an owl with magical powers that would rid the land of the Morve.

*　*　*

At this point, Lia interrupted politely. "I beg your pardon, sir. You have mentioned the 'Morve' twice. What is it?"

Ender's face grew somber. "I am called Ender because I helped bring an end to an evil power that was known as the Morve, but the evil has not ended. The one who wields it is called Morvassus. He still lives and rules, though we do not know where. Even now we see evidence of his gathering strength. That is why we are here together, now." He took a deep breath and let it out. "But that matter is for later. For now, we rest and share a more pleasant tale."

He continued:

* * *

As a child, the man had been called "Owler" by the townspeople who laughed at him for attempting to communicate with any owl he could find. They thought him crazy. As he grew older, he and his wonderful wife, Deia, moved deep into the woods where owls were more likely to be found. For many years, he studied the owls, carefully nursing back to health every broken bird he discovered. None of them were "the one." However, when I did not struggle, he knew I was no ordinary owl.

Days passed, and still I did not recover. I was too weak to return to my natural form and I was deeply distressed, knowing that battles were still raging in the far hills. Finally, I scratched a message to my kind host.

"Find the Bow," I wrote. He and his wife asked many questions and I nodded or shook my feathered head until they understood. It was a dangerous task. He would have to find the place I had hidden it. The enemy would be watching. I scratched a crude map with as many details as I could manage. When he was sure he understood, he committed the map to memory, grabbed his cloak and his long knife, kissed his wife goodbye and left the house.

He was gone for weeks and I feared for his life every day. Deia treated me with great kindness. Never once did she question the mission on which I had sent her husband. One gray morning, he returned, tired and dirty but unscathed. He had the Bow with him. My estimation of his skills grew immensely!

"What now?" he asked me. Such resolve!

My strength was quickly failing but he needed rest. "Sleep," I scratched in the dust.

He collapsed into bed and slept. The next day, I weakly scratched one more message in the dust. The writing was barely legible but the meaning was clear. He must shoot me through the heart with an arrow from the Bow.

When he was certain of my request, he followed me outside. I stood motionless just a few feet away as he carefully placed an arrow on the string. Though his face was very sad, he kept his hands steady as he drew the Bow. With an almost imperceptible nod, he let the arrow fly.

It entered straight into my heart. Though I had fired the Bow many times, I had never expected to be the recipient of one of its arrows.

The effect was miraculous. Instantly, I was revived. To my great relief, I returned to human form once again. Though still weak, I could now regain my lost strength.

I spent many days with them, recuperating. The battle was not over. In time I left to find the Great Master.

When the threat of the Morve had ended and Morvassus disappeared, we learned of some magic residing in the Citadel. The great eagles of the Guard continued to fly abroad and return with food, but anyone who came close was captured and hauled away never to be seen again. The Great Master determined that no one would be better suited to watch the Citadel than Owler, so he sent me to charge him with that task.

I saw Owler and Deia only three times after that. I miss them still.

They had a son, cut of the same cloth as they. He was a marvelous fellow, full of energy. How he managed to find a wife that suited him, I do not know, but he married young and they lived a long and happy life together in the house in the hillside. Their son was another bright lad, quieter than his father, but even more of a woodsman. Our attentions were drawn elsewhere, so we did not see him grow, but when he had his own son, we were amazed that Owler the Fourth had skills that surpassed them all.

He has spent more hours near the Citadel than any of his forebears. His stealth and cunning render him almost invisible to the Guard. In fact, despite his own wizardry, the Great Master has had difficulty following Owler. However, time and again we have seen our friend discretely deter others from entering that dangerous place, and we are grateful for his service.

* * *

Ender nodded to Owler. "I spoke to your father only once," he said.

"He told me," said Owler. "Ever since that day, I have hoped to meet you."

"Unfortunately, it became too risky to make contact with you," said Ender. "However, we have kept an eye on you and, I must repeat, your skills surpass those of your sires."

"The honor goes to them, my teachers," said the woodsman with a bow of his head. He took a breath and smiled sheepishly. "Well," he said; "my estimation of myself has doubled, though I have done nothing but listen to our eloquent host. Would that all could hear their stories to the same effect!" He looked around the room. "Surely the others here have similar stories. I should like to hear them."

"Yes," said Aaron, grinning."I want to hear my own tale now!"

"The tales are only a glimmer, a reflection of the true stories," replied Ender. "None of us truly understands even his own history. Each sees only a part."

"Who is the Great Master?" asked Mari.

"My father," said Calicia. "Let me refill everyone's cup and we will move to the next subject, which is, unfortunately, not as pleasant."

CHAPTER 16

More Introductions

After everyone's tea was refilled, the room was quiet for a moment. Then Calicia spoke: "We have gathered here for a purpose. An evil is sweeping the world, and it must be stopped, but we cannot do it alone. We will go to Thihanan to meet my father, the Great Master. He has more instructions for us there."

"So you know about the King," said Aaron.

"The Birdman, yes," said Calicia; "but there are others also, some even more powerful and evil. In one way or another, each of you has already faced this force. Now we can band together to concert our strength. Your instincts and skill will serve all when the time comes."

"Aaron," she said, facing him. "You worry because you are not versed in magic, but your warrior mind sees things the others do not. Any weapon, no matter how crude, is most deadly in your hands. You are needed for what you already are, and your desire to learn makes you even more effective. Be glad, Aaron: the opportunities you crave are close by."

She turned to his wife. "Lia, you consider yourself the weakest link. You are not as crafty as your sister nor as powerful as your husband, but your heart is melded to theirs and you give them strength. You have always been a healer, and you shall continue to be so, but you are also now a warrior. Your grace and skill on both counts is needed among us all."

"Mari," said Calicia, turning her eyes to the older sister. "You are more of an asset than you know, and more of a sorceress than you dare to believe. You are the strongest in magic, and the most vulnerable. Consider this: there is no White Magic; there is no Dark Magic. Only magic itself remains. As a sword can kill friend or foe, so the spell can cause great good or great evil."

Mari looked down at the floor. "I do not know what to do with magic anymore," she said. "Sometimes it works; sometimes it fails altogether."

Lia leaned forward. "What happened at the Great Falls?" she asked. "I could feel something while you were casting that spell."

"That is exactly what I mean," said Mari. She explained how Lia and Annie had somehow given her the power to blast away the rocks at the Great Falls, cutting off the enemy. "When I hurt my ankle, I could do nothing magical to help myself, but when you and Annie supported me, I was able to cast an even greater spell. Now, once again, I feel powerless."

Calicia nodded. "Your heart is in pain," she said; "not just your body. Healing comes in waves. Your strength will return, and your understanding will increase as well. Here is the subtlety: your task is not to use only good magic, but to use magic for good."

Mari nodded but said nothing more.

Calicia smiled at Owler. "Owler, your woodsmanship is exquisite. May you be wary as the deer, patient as the mantis, deadly as the viper and silent as the owl. You are the least attached of all of us here. As such, you are the most free to choose your path. We will all benefit from your company. Do not worry that you have abandoned the Citadel. Your skills are much needed elsewhere."

"But it has been overrun!" Owler exclaimed. "This must be the most critical moment since my great-grandfather was charged with watching it!"

"My father made it very clear that you were to come with us, if at all possible," she replied, gently. "It was he who gave your ancestor his charge. Does his new directive not hold the same weight?"

Owler sat back. "It does," he said. "I will honor this new charge." He grinned. "Strangely, I look forward to it."

Ender smiled.

Calicia then turned her attention to Brian and Annie sitting by the fire. "This leaves the largest and the smallest, Annie and Brian. My father called these two 'the hinges on which swings the door of hope.' In fact, he said that without them the door is sealed." She stopped for a moment and looked around, and then sat back and folded her hands in her lap. "I wish I had more to say to both of you, but my father and I lost contact even as he spoke and I have not heard from him since. Of all of us here, you two are the most mysterious! Welcome, nonetheless. We look forward to learning more about you!"

Ender set down his pipe and leaned forward.

"You have met our other guest, though none of us can see him. He is a Sochhmahr, neither living nor dead. His power is strong but his scope is limited. His purpose here is to serve as best he can. He is to learn and to teach. Are you here, my friend?" Ender asked the air.

"I am," came a voice from the mantelpiece. "Have you need of me now?"

"Not at this moment," answered Ender, smiling. "But now that I think of it, you should choose a name by which we can address you."

"Considering my condition, would you not be better qualified to choose a name?" asked the spot.

"You are wise; choose for yourself," answered Ender.

There was a moment of silence and then the voice said: "Let me be known as 'Thoughtful.' I would appreciate such a name."

"Thoughtful it is, and well chosen," Ender smiled, settling back into his chair.

"May I make a request?" Thoughtful inquired.

"You may," nodded their host.

"I should like to be present when the lady Mari is instructed in the magical arts," said the invisible one.

Ender smiled. "My dear Thoughtful, indeed, your presence is required. The instruction of the lady will be your primary responsibility for several days hence. I wish to speak with you alone after the others have retired, but for now, go and prepare for your task."

Brian wondered how anyone would know if Thoughtful had left the room. He couldn't detect the being with any of his senses.

"Well, considering that most of us spent the last several days fleeing for our lives, I think sleep is the next order of business," said Calicia.

"How do you know when it's morning?" asked Aaron. "Aren't we inside a cave?"

"We are, but daybreak tomorrow will be a sight worth seeing," said Calicia. "You'll recognize it when you see it. If you are ready now, I can show you your quarters. We have special rooms for each of you."

"Wait," objected Brian; "you've talked about everyone but yourself."

"That can wait until after a good night's sleep," she said.

"But I reckon the afternoon is hardly over," said Aaron; "and I, for one, would like to hear your story."

The others agreed.

"We're not going to bed until we hear your story," said Annie.

Calicia looked at her husband. He shrugged good-naturedly. "There is only one child here," he said; "and she said she's not going to bed." He tapped out his pipe and set it down in its stand. "What do you know of the Citadel?" he asked.

"I told them what I learned from my fathers," said Owler; "but that may be legend for all I know."

"Let me review, then," said Ender. "You knew of the arrival of Nykos, as he was called then. You knew of the uprising, the creation of the Palace Guard, the division of the kingdom and the sequestering of the Northern Kingdom in the Citadel, correct?"

Owler nodded. "Yes, as I understood those events. I also spoke of Spakas' obsession with its emptiness, and of his demise, most likely at the hands of Korstad."

"Very well, then," said Ender. "To continue, the Citadel was built as a sanctuary in time of trouble and as the seat of government from which Nykos wished to bring lasting peace. It was also the center of the learning of magic. It was Nykos' intention that the Citadel would stand as a bastion for good. As you may have guessed by now: Nykos was the name by which the Great Master was called at that time.

"When Posaman, the last Northern king searched for him, the Great Master was many miles away in Thihanan. Fearing for his life and his kingdom, Posaman expanded his search far to the east and west. It was there he met Kafna, the beguiler, the sower of greed, a dealer in evil who sold magic for a price. Kafna was crafty, for he shrouded the true cost of his wares in a lie that convinced his victims that they were acting within their own sovereignty. Believing themselves in control they felt no fear, yet they became slaves to the magic they bought.

"Kafna learned of Posaman's fear of attack and sold him a powerful magic for protection. Had the king known his purchase would cost him and his people everything, he might have refused to buy, but in his fear, he bargained away their souls for security.

"The beguiler sold him a spell so complex and so dangerous that it eventually entrapped the one who cast it and everyone whom it affected. On that ill-fated night when Posaman returned to the Citadel, he began a series of irrevocable incantations. Each spell required that something precious be placed at risk. One break in the continuum and everything in jeopardy would perish. Such was the cost of creating the Palace Guard from nothing.

"The six eagles came from no egg and were sustained by the lives of the successive rulers themselves. In payment for their protection, the next rulers became eagles for a time after their death and served the Guard. Eventually, their eagle form also perished and their very souls were eaten by the Guard they served.

"When the Great Master learned of the assault by the Southern Kingdoms, he sent his daughter to aid Posaman, the Northern king. She arrived as a white dove."

Owler raised his eyebrows and glanced at Calicia. This was news.

"The king had herded the entire city into the Citadel until they could devise a way to regain their territory. When Calicia arrived, she discovered the magic behind the Citadel Guard and was appalled to find that Posaman had also set in motion a series of even more dangerous spells."

Ender sat back in his chair and shook his head. "They chose to accelerate their own time."

"They did what?" exclaimed Lia.

"They lived as children, grew to be adults, married, had children and grandchildren of their own and died, all within the space of a few days, generation after generation."

"That seems impossible," said Aaron.

Ender nodded. "Indeed," he said. "Calicia discovered that their days were filled with pleasure and their nights with great revelry, for it was required by the spell that no one feel pain or sorrow. Though their perceptions told them that generations had passed, in reality only a few days had slipped by. This was the most seductive lie of all because they never really lived; they had only the perception of living."

"But wait," interjected Mari. "Don't we believe that which we perceive, and doesn't that then become our experience? I believe I have eaten good food tonight. Even if it is not real food, I base my belief on the perception that my stomach feels full and my pallet is satisfied. I also have the memory of a marvelous meal, complete with dinner conversations. I have, for all practical purposes, eaten good food. So, even if you were to tell me that it was all a lie, I would still be unable to take another bite. My stomach would not accept it."

"True," Ender agreed. "If I were to suggest the knife would not cut you, you might still fear it because it appears to be sharp and your experience of sharp knife tells you that this one is likely to cut as well. However, if I convinced you my finger could shoot fire and kill anything within range, wouldn't it be tragic if you succumbed to an early death, believing I had killed you?"

"Yes, indeed," said Mari. "But the lives of those in the Citadel were lengthened because of their perception. They experienced a pleasurable, long life. Is that not a more humane fate? It is a gift, not a theft."

"Perhaps," said Ender. "But remember that the spell demanded that everything be pleasurable. This was the flaw that eventually swallowed each participant. No one was allowed to experience pain, sorrow, loss or disappointment. If anyone felt these things, he was attacked by the Palace Guard and devoured, for the spell for each person was contingent on continuing the spell for the next. So they danced and ate, creating festivity for festivity's sake, forcing themselves to believe they were happy. Generations grew and died this way, totally isolated from reality, never learning the pain, loss, grief or sorrow. They dared not face their fears or mourn the deaths of others. They perished in oblivion, never experiencing the fullness of life, only perceiving the passage of years and the appearance of events.

"You were there," he continued. "Do you remember the time you spent reveling about nothing? No. It was merely a sequence of events, a series of pictures, one after the other. For you, as for them, the meaning was removed and in its place was the perception. It was as if you lived only for the next dance, the next tempting bite of food. That foolish pleasure was the only reward for the acceleration of time. Eventually, the citizens of the Citadel were devoured by the very power they thought they controlled.

"A few managed to escape the Guard. Calicia helped them into the tunnels that had been carved in secret centuries before by her father. Some of those who escaped were already too old and perished in the tunnels. The magic had already progressed too far for them. Very few made it to the outside and died a natural death. When Spakas entered the Citadel, Calicia was the last person remaining within. The Guard had devoured all other survivors. The eagles also killed and devoured the king's searchers one by one, leaving no trace.

"Eventually, no one would enter the fortress, so Spakas took the only person who would follow: Korstad, the people called him. He was known better as Kafna. Calicia confronted them in the Chamber of Transformation where Brian found you. When Kafna discovered the power in the Chamber, he killed Spakas and claimed the throne. Then he offered Calicia a bargain, hoping to gain her power as a sorceress. She refused.

"His powers had grown mightily through the years and he began to weave the spell even more strongly. He nearly forced her under it but he, himself, was becoming enchanted even as he did so. Had he transformed her into an eagle with him on the platform, he might have absorbed her strength and taken control of the Citadel, but she took a thorn she kept hidden in her clothes and pricked herself. That deliberate choice to feel pain broke the spell at its crucial moment.

"Kafna transformed into an eagle but his new form was tortured, crippled and angry. The spell was broken in that moment. Its breaking was felt far away. Everything that had been placed at risk to maintain the magic was brought to ruin. Yet we know now that somewhere in the Citadel the magic remains. The Citadel Guard lives. Every month, it hunts again. Any who venture near have been captured, never to be seen again."

Owler had sat with his long legs crossed, listening intently as the tale was told. Now he leaned back. "That explains Brian's account of the continuing line of royal statues in the hall and the existence of other revelers—at least to a point. How fascinating!" he said.

"What do you make of the King and this bird-man?" asked Aaron.

"I have some thoughts," said Ender; "but they are mostly conjecture. We must confer with the Great Master in Thihanan. He knows far more about this than he has been able to tell me yet."

"For the time being, those dangers are behind us. Here on Cai-Amira we are safe from all of that," said Calicia. "Now, to bed with you all! Let me show you to your rooms."

Owler and Aaron carried Mari and they all went upstairs. At the top of the stairs was a simple hallway. The walls were paneled with wood and the floor was covered with a long rug woven in deep reds and browns, firm but soft underfoot. There were five rooms, two on either side of the hallway and one at the end.

The first room on the left was for Mari. Across the room from her large canopy bed was a smaller one for Annie. A door connected that room to the next where Lia and Aaron would sleep. They had a magnificent bed and a large bay window. Owler's room was the first door on the right. His bed was sturdy and simple. A table with two chairs sat in one corner next to a tall pine wardrobe. Owler smiled with recognition; it looked very much like his own room at home.

"And this is your room, Brian," said Calicia, opening the second door on the right. Brian chuckled with delight. There was no bed, no paneled walls, no lamp and no rug. In their place was stone and earth. A pile of firewood lay to one side and embers glowed from within a circle of stones. Just beyond that was a broad pile of straw and evergreen boughs with a tough blanket laid over it. A couple of blankets were stacked beside it.

"We thought you might feel more at home," said Calicia.

"I like it," said Brian. "It's good."

"I am glad," she said. "Goodnight."

With that, she shut the door and Brian lay down for the best night's sleep he had had in weeks.

* * *

"Thoughtful, eh?" chuckled Ender, leaning back in his chair. "A very good name indeed. What are you thinking now, my friend?"

"To be in this form is difficult," said the voice from the mantle. "Why is it necessary?"

"You are to learn to be effective yet unseen." answered Ender. "It is a harsh discipline but a wise one, I believe."

"If I must learn stealth—"

"I speak metaphorically," Ender interrupted, gently. "Your considerable power must be used without you getting in the way. So says the Great Master who rescued you. Therefore you have been made a Sochhmahr."

"How long will I remain thus?" asked Thoughtful after some time.

The man in the red chair shrugged. "Until the Great Master believes you have fulfilled your end of the bargain."

"Who is this Great Master?" Thoughtful wanted to know. "And what makes his judgment final?"

"The second answer is this: you owe him your life. The answer to the first question is more complex," said Ender. "In simple terms, he is Calicia's sire. His history goes back before the records were kept. He was called Nykos long before I was born. I have always referred to him as 'the Great Master.' Others call him Palanthar. It was he who first fought the Morve and who summoned me when he knew the Morve would grow beyond his ability to contain. I was his apprentice for many years. Now I see him when he sends me here or there on some task. We meet most often in Thihanan, which is where we will proceed tomorrow, but he does not live in any one place."

"And how did he bring me to you?" said Thoughtful.

Ender let out a puff of smoke. "I was above, looking for him in the valley. He had sent for us unexpectedly and was not here to receive us when we arrived. I waited for several days and had just begun to search for him when I saw him on the mountainside, struggling as if carrying a great weight.

"I felt a presence in the valley that I did not know so I proceeded with haste. I found the Great Master collapsed on a rock. He looked suddenly old; older than I had ever seen him look. His hands were torn and his eyes were unfocused and glassy. I was afraid, for I had never seen him so. I gave him a drink and he revived a little.

"Though I questioned him, he did not speak. I asked him if I should use the Bow, but he refused. Instead, he placed a small box of tarnished gold in my hand. Inside were ashes. When finally he spoke, he entrusted me with your care and told me to guard the ashes with my life. He did not say more. With great effort, he raised himself to his feet and, heedless of my objections, he disappeared. When we meet him in Thihanan, he will tell us more."

"What were the ashes?" asked Thoughtful.

"I do not know," shrugged Ender. "Again, he did not explain. I suspect they are somehow tied to his current state, and perhaps yours."

It was late and Ender's pipe had gone out again. "Goodnight," he said. "The lady Mari will be with you in the morning. She may not be an easy student. Prepare to be patient, but do not fail to be thorough."

Thoughtful assured him he would be ready. Ender went up the stairs to the master bedroom where Calicia lay waiting. She was still awake.

"He suffers under the discipline," she said.

"I think he will be the better for it." answered her husband. "I remember my own apprenticeship. Your father was no easier on me."

"True," Calicia acknowledged; "but you were young. He is older than you were."

"He may learn more quickly because he knows more already," said the other.

"Or he may refuse." Calicia sighed. "I worry about the little girl. There is something about her I cannot quite place. She is kin to none of them, though her attachment to the gruffen is strong. She took the hardest blow in the Citadel and was long in coming out of it. Somehow I doubt it was her youth that caused her to rankle under the enchantment so."

Ender lay still. Calicia turned her face to him. His eyes were closed and his breathing was even. He had fallen asleep. The lady smiled and rolled over. He hadn't slept for several days and she was glad to see him at peace.

"Sleep," she whispered. "Morning comes soon enough."

CHAPTER 17

The Circle of the Ancients

Brian awoke to the wonderful smell of breakfast cooking. It took him a moment or two to remember where he was. He heard someone call his name, so he got up and opened the door to his room. Bright sunlight streamed in through the downstairs windows. Everyone was heading down to see it.

"Good morning!" called Calicia. "It is a glorious sunrise and we have a feast to match!"

Annie came stamping up the stairs and grabbed Brian's hand. "Come look! We're about to come out!" she hollered.

Bewildered, the gruffen followed Annie downstairs and out into the yard. Now that he was outside, he had to sit down on the wooden bench. Looking up, he almost lost his balance and toppled over. The roof of the cave high overhead was sliding backwards with surprising speed. Ahead of them, the cave opened up to the east where the sun was just rising. Curious, Brian ran around to the side of the house and looked back into the cave. There was nothing but water where the hillside had been the night before. The glowing globes were very small, so far behind them that they were almost lost from view. In fact, they were surround on all sides by water. They were on a moving island: a small hill covered with trees and several acres of wooded flatland floating out to the open sea.

Brian had never been on a boat before and this was the first time he had experienced the sight of land slipping away. He steadied himself by holding onto the side of the house as they came sailing out from under the roof of the cave. Now, suddenly, he could see a line of mountains to the west and nothing but open sea in all other directions. He tried to catch his breath. The smells were so different: salty and fishy, but not like any salt or fish he had known before!

Ender opened the window of the kitchen. "You are safer than you think, Brian," he said. "This is Cai-Amira, one of the floating islands of the Ancients. The island guides itself and will bring us to a place called Thihanan, far across the sea. The island never sails through dangerous waters and there will always be earth under your feet. Enjoy it! This will be the best time any of us will have for many months, I should guess."

It took a little while for Brian to get used to the idea of racing across open water but hunger had a way of making him forget other things, especially when there was good food to be had. He ate honey and sweet cakes, ham and bacon, nut cakes and raisin cakes and something hot out of a large pot on the stove. It smelled of apples and cinnamon and was spooned like gruel into bowls but everyone said it tasted like pie.

Brian loved all the conversation. He laughed heartily at the jokes he actually understood. Most of the time, he was just happy that everyone was happy. Inside, however, he wondered about a few things. He knew he was different from the others. He wasn't funny or smart. To be sure, his life seemed have begun only a few months ago and he still hadn't sorted out what was going on. He decided it was better to enjoy the food than to think about it any longer, so he let it go and grabbed some more bacon.

After the meal, Thoughtful arrived and asked Mari to follow him.

"You'll have to go slowly," she said. "I'm not very fast with this cane."

"I will be patient," said Thoughtful from somewhere near the door. "This way please."

Mari got up from the table and took a few steps. She was indeed much better, able to walk on her own already. "Wait," she said, when she reached the door. "How am I supposed to follow you when I can't tell where you are?"

"I will have to lead you with my mellifluous voice," said her tutor. "Now we must go slowly to the other side of the hill and busy ourselves with dangerous matters."

Mari managed a smile. "Very well," she said. "As long as you use your mellifluous voice, it should be tolerable enough."

"I promise," said Thoughtful. He chatted with her pleasantly as they crossed the porch and left the yard.

Calicia asked Brian to stay behind and sent Annie off with Lia and Aaron to explore the island. Ender took Owler with him into another room.

The gruffen found himself sitting awkwardly at the table not knowing what to do as Calicia busied herself with cleaning up. Presently, Calicia wiped her hands on a towel and sat in a chair across the table from him.

"You seem troubled." she said kindly; "as if you no longer fit in your own fur."

"Maybe," replied the gruffen. "My fur is fine, but..." He frowned. "We met a dragon. He understands. Mostly, anyway. He knows who he is." He frowned again. "Not sure I do."

Calicia smiled and leaned on the table. "When I first saw you in the Citadel, I could see you were neither all gruffen or all man. When I actually met you in the tunnel and looked into your heart, I was astonished to find such a man and such a beast dwelling in the same body."

Brian sat back in the great chair they had set at the table for him. "Not much use," he said, bluntly. "You tell stories. I don't have any. You have Ender. They have each other. I'm...different. There's no one else."

He lapsed into silence. Calicia did not break it.

They say that gruffens never cry. Even the infants turn immediately from hurt to anger. They experience neither remorse nor grief. Pain is an enemy, but sorrow is a total stranger.

Whatever Brian was feeling, he fought to control it. His human heart felt the loneliness, but the gruffen in him reached for anger.

"Too bad there is no enemy," said Calicia quietly.

"Too bad," said Brian.

The lady rose from her chair and went to the door. "Come with me, Brian, I want to show you something."

Being outside cleared Brian's head a bit. The air was clear and the wind blew in the trees on the hill behind the house. Brian felt a little of his anger subside as Calicia took his hand and led him up the hill. At the very top of the hill was a ring of tall trees that stood so close together that they formed a near-solid wall.

Calicia took Brian around the outside a short distance, and then stepped between two of the tightly fit trunks. "In here," she said.

Brian could barely squeeze through. It seemed to him that the trees themselves let out a breath to allow him to pass.

Once inside the circle, he found himself standing on a grassy clearing about twenty paces across, surrounded by an opaque wall of leaves and tree trunks eighty to one hundred feet high. The wind was calm and the quiet was so deep that Brian could hear Calicia breathing.

She spoke in a calm, quiet voice as if her lips were right by his ear but he could hear her plainly. "This is one of the Circles of the Ancients. Here they would come when their thoughts were troubled, or they wished for wisdom. I come here when matters confuse me. I find that I understand them better."

"Don't want to understand," said Brian, letting go of her hand. His voice booming in the stillness. "I want to fight."

"For me, the Circle provides solitude and solemnity," said Calicia. "For you it may be quite different. I will leave you here alone. You are your own best teacher.

Be not afraid of anything you see. Face it and you will know it." She smiled at him kindly and then disappeared through the narrow gap in the tree trunks.

When she was gone, Brian stomped over to the gap in the trees, stopped, and then turned around and stomped back. A rumbling growl started deep in his chest. In the stillness of the Circle of the Ancients, it sounded like thunder. Every muscle began to tighten. His brow shoved down low over his eyes and he began to look about.

He found he was no longer alone in the Circle. A bent and withered figure in a hooded cloak of faded black was walking slowly around the edge of the clearing. He seemed to be muttering to himself. Then unexpectedly he turned toward the gruffen, pointed, and laughed.

Brian felt his face grow hot. "Who are you?" he growled. He could not see the man's face beneath the hood.

The man cackled. "Fool!" he said. "You dare not destroy me. I made you what you are, and I am the only one who can change you back. If I did, you would die. I know; I've done it with others. It is not a pleasant sight. Be glad I let you live! You were nothing but a stupid boy. Now you are a stupid beast, but that is only because of my favor. I am the King! Bow down, idiot, and thank me as you ought." A fleck of spittle shot from the hood in Brian's direction.

Brian roared. In a flash, he crossed the clearing and threw the small man to the ground. Then he grabbed the man's legs and swung him into the tree trunks, cracking both tree bark and bones. He flung the limp body across the clearing. It tumbled once and lay still. Brian went over to make sure it did not move. He nudged it with his huge foot, but it did not respond. Then he sat down a short distance from the little crumpled pile and breathed heavily through his flared nostrils. The pounding of his heart began to slow a little.

So it was done. There was no turning back.

For several minutes, Brian just sat and let his fur settle. Finally, he looked around.

He was not alone. A stooped, hooded figure was walking at the edge of the clearing. He wore only a faded black cloak. Brian started and looked to see if the King still lay dead. The crumpled body was there, just as he left it, but the figure across the way was clearly the same.

The figure turned toward Brian, pointed, and laughed again.

"Fool!" he crowed. "Twice fool! You kill me. It solves nothing! You should thank me. Indeed, you owe me for making your life so easy. Had I not intervened, you would have suffered with the rabble, your mind troubled by the pitiful thoughts of humans, your feeble body succumbing to some disease. Instead, I set you free from all their petty sorrows! You are long-lived and strong! Yet you feel cheated.

You didn't fit in then, and you don't fit in now. Oh, poor Brian P. Gruffenson! Kneel, creature! Bless me and beg my forgiveness!"

Brian leapt to his feet and charged across the clearing. His first bear-like slap caught the man square in the head, pitching the body sideways and dashing it to the ground. Brian grabbed it by the ankles and snapped it violently, shattering the vertebrae. Then with a yell, he whipped the body across the clearing. It landed with a dull thud and rolled several yards away.

This time he ran to it and kicked it over to see if it was really dead. There was no movement. Now there were two bodies lying in the clearing. Brian growled and looked around, fur bristling like the quills of a porcupine. He was still alone. He walked to the perimeter and searched the trees but he could find no exit. Circling the clearing several times, he still found nothing. He looked up. There was no way to climb out; the thin, poplar-like branches would not support his weight.

Brian turned around. A small hooded figure pointed and laughed at him, just as before.

"You're stuck here," said the King.

The gruffen lifted his hand to strike, then let it fall limp to his side.

"What's the use?" sneered the King. "You cannot destroy me. You cannot get out. Listen to me, Brian P. Gruffenson. You cannot change things. You must live with it. In magnanimity, I will grant you a choice. I will release you from your pain and all of these feelings will cease, or you can continue in your loneliness and awkwardness.You can have peace instead of turmoil, rest instead of strife. You can be content.

"The dog lies in the sun and wants for nothing. Its thoughts are not troubled. You can be the same. I offer you freedom. Relinquish your human soul. Your lot is not with men. What do they care about you? Let them go to their own doom. Peace, Brian, tranquility. Hope brings only anguish. Humanity is nothing but pain and suffering."

Brian sank to his knees, his shoulders bowed as if under a great weight.

"What do I do?" he groaned.

The King came over, slowly. The dark hood was now very close to Brian's face. The musty sweet smell that issued forth made breathing difficult. All became deathly quiet.

"I can relieve you of all pain," said the King in a still voice. "Let go your soul."

Brian crumpled sideways onto the grass. He closed his eyes like a dog in the sun.

"Let go your soul," said the King. "Be free. Let it go."

As if he were floating above the Circle, Brian looked down to see two creatures. On one side lay a gruffen, weakly gasping for air, its eyes closed. On the other side lay a man, quite still, barely breathing. A shadowy shape began to emerge between them. It turned toward the gruffen first, and then left it and flowed over the form of the man, starting at the feet and slowly working its way up. Brian could feel the movement like warm water spreading across his own flesh, even as he seemed to float above it all. The soothing warmth flowed around his feet and up his legs, but whatever it touched soon grew numb.

In the midst of this, Brian heard the voice of a woman weeping, the saddest sound he had ever heard. He saw a young woman bending over the figure of the man, her hair draped on his chest. Brian could see her tear-stained face, even though he was behind and above her. The flowing, black shadow crawling over the man spat like a cat and reached for the woman. She paid it no heed and did not shift her gaze from the man's face. Her hand was stroking his forehead. Brian could actually feel her caress.

Suddenly, he realized that he, himself, was lying back on the ground with the young woman bending over him. As she stroked his hair, he reached for her hand and his fingers touched something stuck in the hair behind his ear. It was the thorn from the Citadel!

The woman's image was growing faint, fading away. She was trying to say something but he couldn't hear her. Before she vanished, she held out her open palm, pleading with him. Then she was gone.

Brian's legs had gone completely numb, but somehow he forced himself to sit up. He found himself looking directly into the gaunt face of the King.

The black hood had been pulled back, exposing the King's burnt, hollow eye holes to the glaring sun. His mouth was quivering and a little spit dribbled from his lower lip. With trembling hands, he was coaxing the shadow higher and higher up Brian's quickly numbing body. In a moment, it would reach the gruffen's waist.

"Let it go," whispered, the King, breathing his sickly sweet breath into Brian's face. "Give me the thorn. No more pain."

Brian reached up and removed the thorn by his ear.

"Let it go," whispered the King. "Let it go." With one hand, he coaxed the shadow. With the other, he reached for the thorn in Brian's hand.

Without hesitation, Brian held up his own palm and drove the sharp thorn deeply into it. Pain seared up through his arm into his brain, flooding his entire body! The shock threw him to the ground.

The King let out a shriek and vanished in a wisp of smoke.

Brian quivered and shook on the grass, gasping for air, gurgling sounds choking in his throat. The pain rushed through him, banishing the numbness in his legs, burning through every pore in his thick hide. Slowly, very slowly, it bagan to subside. Eventually, it was isolated to his hand.

The gruffen rolled over and stared at his wounded palm. The long thorn was almost completely buried and he wasn't sure if he could get it out with his thick fingers.

"Oh, Brian!" said a kind whisper beside him. Calicia reached for the thorn and firmly pulled it from his palm. He bled immediately, but the relief was palpable. Calicia had him press his other thumb into the wound. "Hold that there," she said. "Let's get you back to the house."

Brian stood shakily to his feet. Calicia put her arm around his waist and led him from the Circle. To Brian's surprise, there was a gap wide enough for them to pass through together.

"That was hard," Brian said, when he could think straight again. "Very hard."

"Was it?" asked Calicia. "I saw nothing of what happened to you. I could not come in until the trees opened up. Were you harmed—other than your hand?"

"No," answered the gruffen.

"I would have been concerned if you were," mused Calicia. "I find it interesting that you have this wound."

Brian looked around as they walked through the woods back toward the house, acutely aware of everything around him: the way this particular branch moved in the breeze, the sound of the wind in the leaves, the smell of the earth as they took each step.

"This thorn," he said; "you know it, don't you?"

"Yes," said Calicia. "It's the one I gave you in the Citadel."

"Thank you," said Brian.

"You're very welcome," she said, hugging his waist. "Maybe when you're ready you can tell me what it was for."

They walked on in silence.

When they came out of the woods, Brian smelled food.

Some things never change, he thought. I'm hungry.

CHAPTER 18

The Conversation

few days passed. Brian's hand was almost back to normal, and Mari had healed to the point where she no longer needed the splint or the cane. On this particular afternoon, Annie and Lia were in the kitchen learning more about the healing arts from Calicia, and Aaron and Owler were off somewhere in the woods teaching each other their complementary skills.

At Ender's request, Brian went for a walk with him along the forward cliffs. Here the waves slipped sideways around the island as it parted them on its way through the sea. The salty smell of the sea and the vast, blue sky were now becoming more familiar to Brian. The awareness that he experienced after his time in the Circle of the Ancients was still with him. He had discovered that thinking didn't seem to hurt his head so much. This made him happy.

They saw Mari walking toward them, talking to the air over her right shoulder. Ender called out to her and she came over to greet them. Thoughtful was explaining some strange incantation he had been teaching her.

"I got it all wrong," said Mari; "but my sides still ache from laughing at my results." Her expression dimmed slightly, but then she smiled again. "It was good to laugh," she said.

Brian wondered why Mari looked younger. The sun shone on her warm skin and the breeze blew her gray-flecked waves of black hair around her shoulders. Her eyes seemed even more green. Maybe it was just his own heightened senses.

They parted and Brian continued on with Ender in silence. After an hour or so, they had walked almost the entire perimeter of the island and were now a good distance from the house. They had taken the long way around just to spend some time outside.

At this trailing edge of the island, the sand was flat and wide and the waves merged in a triangle of turbulence that left a wide wake behind them. Some fifty yards from the water's edge, with its back to the trees was a small, one-room cabin on stilts, with a balcony and many windows. A pile of firewood was neatly stacked under a lean-to just off to the side. They each took an armload up the ladder. Once inside, Ender lit a fire in the open stone fireplace in the middle of the cabin.

Ender pulled up a chair, Brian sat comfortably on the floor. Thus began the longest and strangest conversation Brian ever had.

* * *

Ender was a Tale Weaver. Most Tale Weavers could make their listeners see and hear the very things of which they spoke. When they described a river, the audience could almost splash their feet in the water and feel the cool wetness on their skin. Ender's skills far exceeded those of most Tale Weavers. He did not even need to speak; he could make the words of others come alive just by *listening* to them. When Ender asked probing questions about Brian's memories, Brian found himself being transported back in time to those very events.

It was like a dream. The scenery changed as he followed his train of thought; people wove in and out. Yet, just like real life, he could touch things and smell them. All of the emotions that went along with the memories felt real and immediate.

The cabin, the fire, and even Ender disappeared as Brian remembered being a young gruffen running through the forest. He remembered the day he found his cave, and what it looked like inside before he made it his own.

Ender probed further back and listened closely as everything Brian had forgotten since becoming a gruffen suddenly became real again.

As he saw and felt these things, Brian began to mutter.

Can't sleep here anymore. Lady chased me away.

Head hurts. Cold. Sitting behind a rock, licking crumbs from my fingers. So hungry. Big boys hit me. Took my bread. Have to steal again. What if they take that, too?

Girl just spit on me. Why? I didn't do anything.

He was a small boy again, struggling to survive in the village on his own.

Curious about how Brian had become a gruffen, Ender gently prodded the memories forward little by little.

There's a fire! I run to see. Someone is coming this way. I've seen him before. He's not very nice. He says to come with him so I'll be safe. I don't want to go.

Why? Why do I have to go? Why can't I stop? No! Ow! Leave me alone!

Brian's body grew rigid.

"What is he doing?" asked Ender. "Where are you? What do you see?"

Brian did not respond. His eyes were glazed over and he was hardly breathing.

Under his breath, Ender began to hum a low note that resounded through the room. Slowly, he reached out and waved his hand in front of Brian's eyes.

"Come back," he commanded softly. Then he waited.

The gruffen sat completely still..

"Come back, Brian," repeated the storyteller. Nothing changed.

"How did I lose him?" said Ender, but no one was listening.

* * *

The boy felt the cold hands on both sides of his head pressing inward as if they might crush his skull. Why couldn't he get away? He was usually so quick; it seemed so impossible that this young man could keep him fixed in place like that. Searing pain cut through his head as if the hands were driving a splintered stake from one hand to the other, right through his brain. It hurt so badly he couldn't breathe!

Finally, the hands let go, but still the boy couldn't move. He stayed standing like a statue as one of the cold hands touched his chest. The air crackled around him and he felt hot everywhere but where the hand was touching him. The boy tried to keep his eyes shut but he had to look. What was happening?

The young man was concentrating hard, but his face was fixed in a grin. His free hand was tracing a strange pattern in the air in front of the boy. Time seemed to slow. The boy's temperature shifted quickly from hot to cold and back again, back and forth with increasing speed. Still the boy couldn't breathe.

Suddenly, the young man's eyes snapped wide open.

At that moment, the boy felt a the sharp points of a thousand pins drive into his skin. Then the hot and cold stopped and he fell. He could see the smoky sky. He seemed to know when his body hit the cobblestones, but he felt no pain. All was numbness. He could hear nothing. He could see, but he could not understand.

The color of the young man's robes flashed before his eyes, but he no longer knew what it was. For a moment, he lay there, staring at the shifting smoke patterns in the sky.

Fire. Fear.

Then sensations began to flow back into his body, but they were almost incomprehensible in their intensity. The first thing he noticed was an acrid burnt smell that seemed to come from his own body. He felt the fur on the back of his neck start to stand on end. He discovered he could see little bits of floating debris in the smoke overhead. The pain in his skull began to permeate his whole body. He ached all over.

Slowly, he began to move. He could just roll over but he couldn't get to his feet.

He smelled someone coming close and the sound of footsteps reached his ears amidst all the other noises that had begun to crowd in on him. Two strong hands lifted him off the ground and helped him to his feet. He turned and looked into the face of an old man. He couldn't read the face! Was that expression anger, fear? He didn't know.

Run! He had to run! His muscles wouldn't wake up! The old man held him fast, no matter how hard he struggled to get away.

"Listen, young fellow," the old man was saying. "Your name is Brian P. Gruffenson! Remember that! Remember! Remember!"

Finally, the frantic youngster was able to break free, or the old man let him go. He dropped to all fours and raced down the street.

Run! Run! Run! Run! The gruffen ran as only gruffens can. In a few minutes, he had cleared the village and was heading full speed through the woods, following his nose. No humans. No fire. No burnt smell.

Run! Run! Run! Run!

* * *

Things began to blur. Brian couldn't see the woods anymore. He was no longer running. He was floating in the dark. Lights began to flash randomly, from different places, then all grew still and he found himself standing in a place he did not recognize, staring into a fire.

Many men and women were sitting in several rows around the fire, their faces illuminated by the flickering flames. It occurred to Brian that they were all very beautiful. One of the eldest, a man with long white hair and a short white beard, stood near Brian. He was speaking to the people in a language Brian did not understand. One term kept being repeated: "Valen dak-Lammethan." As the speaker went on, Brian saw people around the fire looking directly at him as if that term referred to Brian. The gathered company was apparently discussing him in front of his face.

As he looked at the people seated on either side of him, he realized they were winged like butterflies, but they kept their wings folded closed behind them, so Brian couldn't get a good look. Some stared at him, as if sizing him up. Yet their gaze held no prejudice. Finally, the elder took Brian by the hand and stepped forward, as if presenting him before the people. He made an announcement and waited for a response.

At first no one stirred. Then several moved aside as a young women came forward and spread her wings wide. They were deep blue with a curling gold pattern that was edged with a fiery orange-red as the blue trailed into indigo and then purple at the very edges. She had dark hair and, even in the firelight, her gossamer gown shown blue like the summer sky. Some of the older people around the fire caught their breath, as if choking back tears.

Brian stared. Where had he seen her before? He was sure he had never met anyone with wings, but why did she look so familiar?

"I will," she said. Or maybe she didn't speak. It just seemed to have been said.

The elder stood between them and looked at Brian. Reaching up and placing both hands on the gruffen's broad shoulders, he said: "Valen dak-Lammethan."

The fire was disappearing and the old man began to fade away.

Everything was going dark again!

Brian tried to say something but no sound came out. All was black again.

Then a little light began to glimmer somewhere nearby.

✳ ✳ ✳

Sounds began to enter his awareness. He could smell a wood fire, but this one was different. He was inside somewhere. A quiet rush of water was passing by somewhere outside, murmuring and whispering in the dark. The wind tapped a branch against the wall.

Brian looked up to see Ender watching him intently. They were both still sitting in the Watch House on Cai-Amira.

"Welcome back," said Ender, leaning back in his chair and letting out a deep breath.

"Is it night?" asked Brian looking out the window.

"It is the third hour of the night of the second day since we came here," said Ender. "Where did you go? For the last two days I could not reach you."

"Strange," said Brian. "Like dreams."

Ender nodded. "Most people feel like they've been dreaming in a conversation like this. I followed you most of the way in the beginning. How do you feel now?"

"Fine," said the gruffen. "How should I feel?"

"If you are well, that is good enough," said Ender. "I am curious, though, why I could not follow you. It was as if some other force took you away. I'm glad you seem to have come back no worse for the journey."

Brian noticed his stomach. "I'm hungry," he said.

"Glad to hear it. You should be," said Ender. "You haven't eaten in two days." He went to the larder and brought out smoked meats and cheese which he set on the small table. Then he brought out two cups and a jug of mead.

"I'm glad you're back," said the man, filling both glasses and setting one in front of Brian. "I find it fascinating that you were able to go back to your time as a little boy. Do you remember it now? I lost track of you just before you became a gruffen."

"If I talk, can I still eat?" asked Brian, a handful of meat held halfway to his mouth.

Ender laughed. "Yes, please eat. I will not weave your tale this time."

Brian stuffed the handful of meat in his great maw and then broke off a large piece of cheese to gnaw on at the same time. After a moment of chewing, he swallowed all of it, tossed the cup of mead down his gullet and grinned.

"Better," he said. "I can talk now." He grabbed a slightly less generous helping and popped it in his mouth.

"Tell me what happened when you became a gruffen," said Ender, refilling Brian's glass.

Brian related the story as best he could. Some parts of it were hard to describe but he seemed to have more words than before.

"You seem to be more comfortable with language," Ender remarked when he was done. "Do you notice a difference?"

Brian thought about it. "Yes," he said. "I remember how I used to talk."

"Interesting," said Ender.

The gruffen munched thoughtfully. "Gasslic knew," he said.

"Whom?" asked Ender.

"The dragon," Brian replied. "Knew who he was. Before, I mean."

"Ah, the dragon," said Ender. "The day I first saw him, he was a surprise to me! As you ran from the Citadel Guard, he defended you fearlessly, with utter disregard for his own safety. He would have fought to the death. Do you know where he came from?"

Brian nodded. "Underground. Deep cut. I'd been down there a few times. Always thought there was something down there. Never saw it until we hid from the King."

"You say he knew who he was 'before,'" said Ender. "What do you mean?"

The gruffen stuffed another mouthful of meat and cheese, chewed a bit and then said: "He used to be a trapper. Found a man. Very sick. Helped him get better. It was the King. Turned him into a dragon."

"He was turned into a dragon by the very person he nursed to health?" asked Ender.

Brian nodded, his great brow hanging low over his eyes. "Couldn't trap anymore. Couldn't be with people then. He stayed underground."

"That would explain why I never saw him before," said Ender. "I wonder what made him come out into the open."

"Gasslic tried to fly," said Brian; "but he crashed. Broke a wing. Said to leave him behind. Lia was upset. Didn't see him again until we were running. He burned the Guard in the sky. Then he fell. Someone shot him and he didn't die. He flew away." Brian looked out the window into the darkness. "Don't know what happened to him."

"I saw the dragon flying on the western side of the mountains," said Ender. "When I spoke to the Great Master, he did not know yet if the dragon was good or evil. When the Citadel Guard bore down on the six of you, the dragon came to your aid. The Guard was taken entirely by surprise and scattered. For a short time, he held the eagles at bay but the Guard soon recovered and their numbers were greater. They charged him. He sent several flaming to the ground. One of them finally struck him. That's why he was falling."

"Who shot him?" asked Brian. "And why didn't he die?"

"I shot him," said Ender; "but an arrow from that Bow does not kill; it revives. The magic in the Bow and its arrows is a powerful healer. I only hope the dragon escaped capture. I am surprised to hear that he lived underground all his life. I have seen a few dragons, but never one so swift."

Having devoured almost all the meat and cheese, Brian felt a lot better. He sucked on his teeth a bit and then asked: "How do you do that dream thing?"

Ender smiled. "What you experienced when you told your story?"

Brian nodded.

"I am both a Tale Weaver and a Thought Chaser," said Ender. "I have practiced the art of imagination and I have the gift of reading images in the minds of others so that they become real to both of us."

"You read me now?" asked Brian, wrinkling his face.

"No, not unless you allow it," he said. "On the other hand, once you begin to speak, you are open to me. Did you shut me out while we spoke?"

The gruffen looked puzzled. "No. But I went someplace else. Don't know where, or how I got there."

"I've been wondering about that," said Ender. "I couldn't follow you. Can you tell me what happened?"

Brian closed his eyes. "Don't know," he said. He tried to remember something about a fire and winged people. "Guess not," he shrugged.

Ender regarded him with interest. "Maybe later it will come to you," he said. "We've done enough for now."

"Could you always do this?" Brian asked.

"Weave tales?" asked Ender. "No, I learned that after many years." He sat back and re-lit his pipe. "Let me tell you my story," he said.

* * *

I was a huntsman's only child. My mother died in childbirth and I nearly died a year later when I was sick during an awful storm. I lay shivering with fever in the cabin where I had been conceived and born, on the same bed in which my mother had died. My father knelt by me and wept as torrents of rain dashed against the window of the tiny cabin. He had done his best for me, but he knew it was not enough. I was dying.

He barely heard the knock on the door. Being a kindly soul, my father opened the door. A thin old man came blowing in with the rain. My father leaned against the door to close it again as the old man shed his cloak and ran to the bed where I lay.

From his pack, the old man produced a vial of bright liquid. He asked my father for a cup of water and added one drop of the liquid to it. Then he sat me up and forced a little down my throat. I choked and coughed but enough of it went down to revive me. The rest of the mixture he soaked into a cloth. He bathed my head and chest with it. That night my father slept for the first time in a week. The old man stayed up with me, listening to my breath and bathing me with the elixir. The old man stayed for a few days until I regained my strength and was able to drink goat's milk. Then, one night after a long conversation with my father, the old man left.

As I grew up, my father told me I would one day be the apprentice of this Great Master. Though my father assured me it was a lofty destiny, I thought little of it. I was happy just to trap and hunt with my father. We lived alone in the woods and went to the village to sell skins and game. Some of the villagers told stories about someone named "Palanthar" which I soon discovered was another name for the Great Master. Not everyone had nice things to say.

I was nearly twenty four years old when I met the Great Master for the first time. I had been away for a week, hunting in the western mountains. When I returned to the house, my father told me my Master was soon to come for me. I had never seen my father so sad. I asked him if this Palanthar was a good man.

"He is a healer," he said; "and he is powerful. That is certain."

Still, I was apprehensive.

I could not sleep. For the next few nights, I sat outside on the chair we always kept by the front door. A strange haze had been hanging in the southern sky for the last several months. It had been looming larger every week. Now it had passed the rims of the nearer peaks and covered the sky over half the valley.

On the night of the full moon, I looked out across the dimly lit landscape, wondering about the haze. I saw a small, shadowy figure emerge from the woods. It moved slowly and deliberately along the path toward our house, as if every step were painful. The figure fit my father's description of Palanthar, though I saw no indication that this person was powerful in any way.

I grabbed my staff and walked a short way down the path from the house so I could be seen clearly in the moonlight. He continued trudging slowly forward.

When he was fifty paces away, I called out to him: "Halt and declare yourself!"

He stopped and raised his head, his hooded face hidden. "You would wield this staff against me?" he croaked in a weak voice.

"Only if necessary," I answered. "If you intend any harm, I would wield this and more."

"And would you pit your strength and courage against *anyone* who intended harm?" he asked.

"If they intended harm, I would," I said. The question made me wonder what the old man was thinking.

"What if you had nothing but your staff, would you weild it against an overwhelming evil?" asked the man.

I considered this. "I would do everything in my power to defend against it," I said; "even if I failed." I braced myself to fight.

The old man removed his hood and slowly straightened up. At his full height, he was still much shorter than I. Even in the moonlight, I could see the deep wrinkles in his face, especially around the eyes. He was beardless and completely bald save for a light fringe around the back of his scalp. His sharp nose and pointed mouth made him appear almost mouse-like.

"Then I have come to the right place." he said, smiling broadly. I was surprised that his voice conveyed such satisfaction. Then his face grew grave. "You have already seen our enemy. This," he said, pointing a bony finger toward the hazy circle around the moon; "is the Morve."

His words hissed and crackled in the air. My skin crawled and I felt a deep chill.

"This is an evil against which I can no longer fight alone," he said. "If you will join me, and wield your strength against the Morve, then you are truly a defender from harm." He paused. "Your life was saved for this reason, but the choice is yours. No one can force you."

I knew then that this was the Great Master. I nodded. "I will join you," I said. "Whatever strength I have, I will wield for the good of all." They were the words of a young man who knew very little what he was about to encounter, but I meant them.

He stretched out his right hand, palm down, his spread fingers aimed at me. "Wield it then!" he shouted.

I felt power shoot from his hand strike me in the chest but it did not fell me. Instead, a bolt of lightning blazed up from my staff toward the moon and blew a hole clear through the haze.

"This bodes well," murmured the old man. "Now perhaps we have a chance."

My arm was tight as steel and my hand clenched my staff painfully. I looked at the man in wonder.

He looked back and his face softened. "Well done," he said. "You are stronger than I had hoped."

"Are you the Great Master?" I asked when I found my voice again.

"I am Palanthar, your father's guest in a storm," he said. "Your father nearly lost you that night, but this new storm, will certainly take you from him. Go and say goodbye to him for you will not see him again for a long time, if ever."

I turned to go back to the house, but my father was already coming toward us. We spoke only a little. He was well prepared for this moment, but I wept in his arms. I had not known that I might not see him again.

Finally, he said: "I have something for you. Wait here."

He went back to the house and brought out a great Bow that I had never seen before. In the moonlight, I could see the fine wood, beautifully carved with runes and figures. It felt light but tightly sprung in my grip, and it fit my hand perfectly. He also gave me a quiver with fine arrows.

"Where did you get these?" I asked.

"I made them," he said. "I've known this day was coming. That's why I sent you away on the hunt. This is your bow, my son: The Bow of Ender. The Great Master has worked some of his own magic into it. May it sing for healing, not for harm."

Then he kissed me and I hugged him one more time. Turning away, I went back down the hill to my new master.

Palanthar raised his hand to salute my father and called out: "The huntsman keeps his word. May this cloud pass and never darken the hill of your home."

My father shook his head, saying, "My hill is darkened already. Be swift and dangerous. May you both keep it from swallowing us all in shadow." With that he returned to the house and I continued on with the Great Master. As we entered the woods, I looked over my shoulder. He was still standing tall on the hill, watching us go. Above him, the moon shone brightly through the hole blasted in the haze.

* * *

Brian set his empty cup on the table. "You learned from the Great Master then?"

"A great many things," replied Ender. "I knew nothing before I met him, or so it seems."

Brian grunted. "What about your father?" he asked.

Ender smiled. "In the last battle with the Morve, many heroes fell. Though it has been forgotten by some, that day lives on in tales and songs of many tongues. I was tending to the wounded when a small maiden begged me to come with her. I followed her away from my encampment to a fork in the road guarded by a stone tower. This bastion had been overrun by the enemy, but only after a brutal fight. The bravery of the tower guards had given us time and courage to regroup for what proved to be the decisive blow.

"High in the tower lay one of the guards, a tough old man now wounded beyond hope. I recognized him immediately. 'Alas!' I cried, 'to have come this far only to lose you!' The woman fell to her knees beside him and wept. He put his bloody arm around her and smiled.

"'Ender, my son,' he said with some effort. 'I hardly dared hope to see you again. You have done better than any had hoped. I am glad to have seen you at last.' His eyes went to the woman at his side. 'See to it that she is returned to her father with great honor. Look after her; she has been like a daughter to me. Tell the Great Master it was an even trade.' With that, he kissed her and I bent down and took him in my arms. There he died, and I cried bitter and grateful tears."

"Calicia?" Brian guessed.

"Yes," said Ender. "Unbeknownst to me, the Great Master had sent his own daughter to my father after I had gone with him. At that time, she was but a girl."

"I met the Great Master!" exclaimed Brian. "He healed my arm. He told me to find the door. His daughter met me in the tunnels."

Ender nodded. "That was he. I will tell you, the Great Master does not interfere when he can avoid it. Rarely does he show himself and speak face to face. He regards you very highly, Brian. We shall learn more when we reach Thihanan."

For a short time they continued talking but Brian was getting tired. He climbed the stairs to the loft and lay down to sleep while Ender sat thoughtfully by the smoldering fire. Outside, the waves rolled endlessly by.

* * *

Morning came with a shout. Owler's clear voice carried through the trees as he raced down the path, awakening the two in the Watch House.

Ender was out the door quickly. "What is it?" he asked as Owler broke through the underbrush at a dead run.

"Annie," gasped Owler. "Strange things are happening to her. We fear for her life. Come quickly!"

The news made Brian's fur stand on edge. Without waiting for Ender's response, he shot off through the woods directly toward the main house, whipping through the trees faster than the humans could follow. Ender and Owler came dashing along in his wake.

CHAPTER 19

Mari, Thoughtful and Annie

After Brian and Ender passed them on their way to the Watch House, Mari and Thoughtful walked on in silence awhile.

"What are you thinking?" asked her invisible companion.

Mari smiled. "I am curious about the look on Brian's face," she said.

"What sort of look was it?" queried Thoughtful.

"I am no judge of gruffen expression, but this is no ordinary gruffen," said Mari. "I felt there was more light in his eyes, as if someone had awakened in that massive body, someone more...human, perhaps."

"That would be most interesting," said Thoughtful. "I should think that the most wonderful thing in the world must be to see light in someone's eyes."

"The light of love shines the greatest in human eyes," said Mari. "I've seen it myself." Her face clouded over. "I miss it."

"I should think that you would often inspire such light, m'lady," said Thoughtful's quiet voice.

Mari did not respond right away. "I did, once," she said. "I wish he were here."

"Where is he now?" asked Thoughtful. "If you'll pardon me for prying."

Mari shook her head. "We lost him on the way here. He was defending us. I hoped we would find him again." She stopped. "At least his body, anyway."

"I am sorry," said Thoughtful, sadly. "He left behind a great joy."

"How so?" asked Mari, still lost in thought.

"I'm sure his time with you was of great value to him," said Thoughtful.

"Nice of you to say so," said Mari. "I sometimes feel like I gave him more trouble than..." Her voice trailed off.

"There is no telling now, I suppose," said Thoughtful.

There was a pause. Thoughtful spoke again: "My apologies. I've been insensitive."

"No, you're right," said Mari. "We do not know how we affect each other, sometimes...then it's too late."

They came to a flat stone near the beach that made a perfect bench. Mari sat down to rest. Her injured ankle was better but still tender. She dug the toes of her other foot into the warm sand. How different everything had become in the last few weeks. Somewhere, way off beyond the horizon, was her old life.

"He was a good man," said Mari. "Stubborn, and sometimes close-minded, but a good man."

"You loved him deeply," said Thoughtful.

"Yes," said Mari.

She crumpled onto the bench, buried her face in her hands and began to weep. Great rolling sobs rocked her shoulders and shook her whole body. Tears streamed down her face and through her hands. The sun shone, the wind stroked her hair, and the waves whispered to each other as they passed by but Mari noticed none of this.

Thoughtful remained quiet.

Sometime later, Mari finally sat up and rubbed her eyes. The wind had picked up a little.

"I must have fallen asleep," she mumbled, looking around. "Thoughtful?"

"You fell asleep," said the gentle voice not far away. "I hope it was some respite."

Mari sighed. "Some," she said. "It does help a little. I'm sorry you had to stay here through all that. You don't have to stay."

"It is not a burden," said Thoughtful. "Ah, I hear the little one coming, though. I leave you in her good hands. Shall I see you tomorrow?"

"Tomorrow, yes," said Mari. "Thank you."

Annie ran over to her. "There you are!" she said. "We're going to eat soon."

Mari hugged her and then stood back. "Are you getting bigger?" she asked. "I don't remember your clothes being too small."

"Really?" said Annie. "They do feel tight."

"What have you been up to today?" Mari asked, taking her hand as they made their way back to the house.

"Aaron and Lia and I have been exploring the island. Owler had a hundred questions for Calicia, so we went off on our own. Lia and Aaron went back but I wanted to go into the woods. I found this perfectly round clearing," she said. "It's surrounded by huge, leafy trees and it just seemed like a special place. I call it 'the Circle of the Ancients.'"

"What a remarkable name!" said Mari. "Did you come up with that by yourself."

"Uh-huh," said Annie. "I think it's magic."

"Really?" asked Mari. They came inside the house. "You should ask Calicia. I'm sure she knows about this place."

"Knows about what place?" asked Calicia from the kitchen.

"The clearing surrounded by trees," said Annie; "the Circle of the Ancients."

Calicia laughed. "How did you know what it's called?" she asked.

"I just made it up," said Annie.

"Fascinating! That's what I've always known it to be called," said Calicia, perplexed. She looked at the little girl. "Did you go inside?"

"Yes," said Annie.

"What did you find there?" asked Calicia. "You look different."

"Mari says I'm getting bigger or my clothes are shrinking." Annie said. Her tunic was beginning to pinch around her belly. "Anyway, I met an old man there who told me I would find a special tree in the woods with fruit on it just for me. So I went there and I found it! It was very good."

"A special tree?" said the lady of the house. "Where is it and what did it look like?"

"It had three branches and one piece of fruit, just low enough for me to reach it. Do you want to see it?" Annie offered.

"I would indeed," replied Calicia. "Right away!" She set everything aside and followed Annie out the door. Mari stayed behind since she couldn't keep up.

Annie took Calicia a short way into the woods where a small tree stood among the larger birch and alder. Its bark was a rough, ruddy brown, like cedar. Three trunks, joined at the base, spiraled upward for about a foot and a half. There they spun off in three different directions, branching out and upward into three different levels of leaves. The leaves were glossy and deep green. Each half of the leaf split into three points angling away from the stem. It held no fruit. In fact, the leaves were turning brown, as if Autumn had arrived for only this one tree.

"There was fruit on it when you found it?" Calicia asked the girl.

"The most delicious blue fruit!" Annie replied. "There was only one and the man told me to eat it all, so I didn't leave anything, not even the seeds. They were a little bitter, but I just chewed them up like he said. Ouch!" This last remark referred to the seam under her arm which felt terribly tight. Then it popped and split apart from the shoulder to the waist. "There, that's better," said Annie.

"We'll have to find something that fits you better," said Calicia. "I wish there was at least something left of the fruit. I have never seen this tree before!"

When they returned to the house, Annie said she was going upstairs to sleep because she was tired and didn't feel hungry anymore.

The others sat down to lunch but the conversation had a note of concern. Everyone agreed that Annie seemed to be growing right before their eyes.

"Could it be some magic from the Circle of the Ancients?" asked Mari. "She said it seemed magical."

"Oh, it is most definitely magical," said Calicia; "but I have never known it to cause a person harm. Brian wounded himself there, though, and said he had a difficult experience. Still, he seemed well when I found him. I'm surprised Annie found out about this tree, but I cannot imagine she could have been directed to harm herself."

"What exactly is the Circle of the Ancients?" asked Lia.

"It is a place where one meets one's own mind," Calicia explained. "Legend says that the Ancients used to communicate with each other from one Circle to another. This Circle is the last of its kind, as far as we know. I have experienced no outside influences. When I go inside, I sometimes find thoughts or feelings that I did not know I had—dreams, fears, or hidden desires—but the Circle magic works only when the occupant is alone. No one else can enter until the first person releases it. Once another person enters the Circle, the meeting with one's mind ceases. If Annie saw anyone in there, that person would be part of her own mind."

"Maybe she still suffers from the spell in the Citadel," suggested Lia. "She got the worst of it."

"No poison that I know of would cause this," Mari said. "I think it's magic of some sort. Perhaps the spell from the Citadel accelerates her growth like it accelerated time. The spell might affect a child differently than it affected us."

"True, but what of this strange tree suddenly appearing outside the Circle?" said Calicia. "I passed by that very spot only a few weeks ago and that tree was not there. How could any tree grow, mature, bear fruit and begin to wither in that short a time?"

"I should like to see this tree," said Owler. "Could you show me where it is?"

While Calicia led the others out to look at the tree, Mari gingerly climbed the stairs to check on Annie. She opened the door to their room and went in quietly. Annie was lying on her little bed. Her clothes seemed terribly tight. Her breathing was even and calm but her facial expressions kept changing, as if reacting to something in her sleep.

Mari decided to wake her so she could help her out of her uncomfortable clothes.

The little girl sat up sleepily and let Mari undress her. "Such a wonderful dream," she mumbled, her eyes still half closed. "Flying. Same as last night, but even better."

Mari helped Annie into one of Calicia's soft nightgowns and the little girl drifted immediately back to sleep. She had no fever. Her heart beat evenly, if slowly. Mari left her sleeping peacefully and went back downstairs to hear what they had to say about the tree.

CHAPTER 20

Thricewood

"I may have read about a tree like this in one of my father's old books," said Owler, coming in the door with the others. "He left me a great many books of lore, some from other lands and ancient times. I vaguely recall a tree with three of everything but I cannot remember where I read it or where it was from. Clearly, the tree is out of place on this island."

"It is definitely not native. If books will help, you are welcome to review ours," offered Calicia. "We keep this library for just such purposes."

Owler looked around the room and grinned. The walls were lined floor to ceiling with books. The smell of old leather, wood and parchment filled the air. The shelves were marked by subject and the books were arranged according to age. The woodsman easily found the section on exotic flora: six or seven venerable tomes on various types of plants.

"What luck!" he cried. "This may be a version of the one my father left me! Look, here is the chapter on fruit-bearing trees. And here...ah... no...wait, here it is. This sounds right:

> Thricewood or Trothianna, the tree of the Windborne. Extinct subtype of no known family. May be only legendary. Described as having three trunks entwined until knee height where they divide into three branches with six-pointed leaves. Fruit is said to be blue in color and bitter to the taste, possibly poisonous. Said to sprout only once every three hundred years and then to last only three months. The Legend of Eal-Ammeneth mentions the periodic appearance of such a tree in the garden of the same name.

"That is all the book says," Owler reported; "but there is something written with different ink in the margin. I'm afraid I do not recognize the rune."

"Excuse me. May I see it?" said Thoughtful's voice from the door of the library.

"Hello, friend," Mari said, warmly. "I was hoping you would help us. Do you know anything about this tree, or this rune?"

"I have no idea why, but I vaguely recall something about a tree with three of everything," he answered. "However, I do not know anything about the Legend of Eal-Ammeneth or its garden. Hmmm...I do not know this rune, but it appears similar to others I've seen. If so, it's an ancient tongue. If someone would help me sort through the books, I will to try to find it."

Mari volunteered. Lia and Calicia went to keep an eye on Annie. Aaron and Owler decided to resume their sparring, keeping an ear out for any new word. If Mari and Thoughtful found anything, Mari would let them know. If anything changed with Annie, Lia would alert the rest. Other than that, there was little else to do but wait.

* * *

The shelf labeled "Runes and Ancient Languages" consisted of quite a number of large volumes, several of them filled with loose sheets of parchment and cloth inserted between the worn and fragile pages.

"This will take days," groaned Mari.

"Then we begin at once," replied Thoughtful.

Mari carefully removed the first great book and set it on the reading table. The pages were dry and brittle; simply turning them risked tearing them. Elven runes of many ages and several translations of proper names and places covered the pages, all meticulously scripted by someone with very deliberate handwriting. Some of the chapters included maps and charts that told where the language was spoken. Most of these places were unknown to the two perusing the book so they moved on, chapter after chapter.

When they finished with that one, they knew no more than when they started. Mari set it carefully back on the shelf and they continued searching painstakingly through the next few books, finding a wealth of linguistic knowledge but nothing like the rune found in the plant book. Soon the sun was setting and they retired for supper with the others.

* * *

Annie was as hungry as a horse after her long nap.

"Doesn't seem to be hurting her appetite; that's well." said Lia. Both Aaron and Owler agreed that the girl looked taller and thicker than the day before. Annie herself seemed oblivious to all the fuss and was enjoying wearing Calicia's comfortable gowns. Even though she had slept through much of the day, she fell asleep on the couch shortly after supper. Aaron carried her up to the bed in the room she shared with Mari.

"I'm glad she is in with me," said Mari to Lia as they made their way upstairs. "I feel better having her nearby."

"Your ankle seems to be healing," said Lia.

Mari smiled. "So it is!" she said, surprised. "I've actually not noticed any pain for most of the evening. Perhaps the splint can be removed."

"Calicia's ointments must be very powerful," said her sister. "It's good to see you walking with some strength again."

Mari nodded. Perhaps having something important on which to focus was helping, too.

The night passed without incident. The island slipped through calm waters leaving a wide but gentle wake in its path. Off to the southeast, the anvil-topped clouds of a great storm towered high in the moonlight, but it was many miles away.

Mari awoke to see what she thought was Calicia standing in the room, looking out the window. Then she recognized the dark hair. It was actually Annie. The girl turned to greet her and Mari knew it was not an illusion: Annie was definitely taller, and her cheeks seemed fuller.

"Do you feel all right?" she asked the girl.

"I'm fine," said Annie. "A bit tired, maybe. I dreamt I was in the forest. I climbed trees all night."

Mari swung her legs over the side of the bed and stood up. Her ankle was still sore, but she could walk unaided. She dressed and the two of them went downstairs to help with breakfast.

When Thoughtful announced his presence shortly after the meal, he and Mari resumed their study of the books. The process continued to be tedious, but they kept at it. Just before noon, they found a series of runes similar to the one written in the margin.

"This one is almost identical," said Mari. "There are just as many strokes, though the ends seem to trail a bit longer here."

"Maybe it's just a different hand doing the writing," said Thoughtful. "I would suggest the rune is the same. Pity the definition of this rune is in yet another language neither of us knows."

They called the others. No one else recognized the other language either, so it was back to the other books of translation to decipher this new inscription. That process took the better part of the afternoon.

175

Meanwhile, Annie had spent most of the day inside, either napping or asking for something to eat. By evening she had become very quiet and slept even more.

Mari and Thoughtful were still deep in study when Lia came in looking very worried. "Have you learned anything?" she asked. "I think we should do something. She's changing before our eyes now."

Mari came out to look and was alarmed at the changes in Annie's appearance. The girl's face and hands had swelled up and she appeared to have grown taller still. Her skin was red and blotchy.

"When did this start?" asked Mari, aghast.

"Just now," said Calicia. "A few minutes ago, she seemed fine. Have you found anything?"

"We have narrowed the field to a specific language," said Thoughtful; "but we have not yet deciphered the text describing the rune."

Owler and Aaron came in from outside where they had been sparring in the dark. Both of them were drenched with perspiration and grinning. As soon as they saw Annie, though, their grins disappeared.

Thoughtful spoke up: "Owler, do you remember anything about the fruit being poisonous or tasting bad?"

"Yes," replied the tall woodsman, wiping his face on his sleeve. "The book said it had a bitter taste, but that would not agree with Annie's description."

"That's right!" exclaimed Mari. "She said it was the best fruit she had ever eaten. So far that is the only discrepancy."

"I am beginning to wonder if she is actually human," said Calicia. "The Elves and Dwarves have long since disappeared from North Agoria, but if she were descended from another race, she may react differently to such exotic fruit. What sort of language describes the rune?"

"It is a Dwarvish tongue, and very old for all we gather," Mari answered. "We only know for sure that the rune is ancient and was probably written by a dwarf or one well acquainted with dwarves."

Owler looked up from the towel. "I have always been interested in the languages of the dwarves. My great grandfather is said to have met one. I have never seen them, but I have a book of their runes. I may not be able to read the language, but I would love to have a look at what you've found."

He and Aaron went upstairs and the rest of them threw together a hasty dinner. Annie woke up in the midst of it and said she was hungry again.

"Are you feeling well?" asked Mari.

Annie smiled thinly. "I'm just going to eat something and go back to sleep," she said. She had some bread and a little cheese, and then lay down on the couch and fell asleep again.

The others quickly returned to the library to review the books spread all over the reading table. Each tome contained some clue about the language but none were actual translations. Mari and Thoughtful explained how they had come to this point and Owler immediately began to put some of the pieces together.

"So this whole family of runes appears to be labels or titles of one sort or another... yes, well... now this column refers to types of criminals, if I read it correctly. Notice how they all have these pointed tines angling up to the right. This column is of various...metals...or rather veins of ore, I guess. I have no idea what these are; there are some words I cannot make out in the explanation." Then he stopped.

"What does this colum refer to?" asked Mari, pointing to the one containing the rune they found.

"Well, I'm not certain this is the same rune," he said. "The bottom stroke goes only one direction, to the left." He went back to the original book. "This one extends the stroke farther to the left and leaves a short space on the right." He paused and looked from one to the other. "You probably already discussed this, but I think if it is simply another handwriting, then it may well be the same rune."

"Yes, but can you tell what the column refers to?" Mari persisted.

"Various levels of either danger or deadliness," said Owler quietly; "but I am not sure which direction to read the scale. It could be more and more dangerous as you progress to the bottom or less and less so."

"It seems that the more complicated the rune, the more intense the interpretation," said Thoughtful. "Look at the list of criminals. Owler, if this is Burglar and this here is Horse Thief and below it appears to be Murderer, the column reads top to bottom, correct?

"In which case, the rune we found must mean either 'highly dangerous' or 'deadly,'" said Mari. "It's bad either way."

"Perhaps, perhaps," said Owler. "But not all the columns are consistent. This one over here goes from more complex to less complex, top to bottom. Let's see what it is listing."

"If I'm not mistaken, it is grading levels of foolishness," Thoughtful grunted. "But is the most foolish on top or on the bottom?"

"If it is the level of stupidity, the least wise must be on the bottom," reasoned Mari. "Thus the runes are simpler. The ones closer to the top are symbolic of more intelligence and are thus, themselves, more complex."

Owler stood up from the table. "Then we have very bad news," he said. "The plant is poisonous."

"Then we must find a way to treat it," said Calicia.

Everyone began searching through the books of healing arts. At Thoughtful's suggestion, the books of legend were also consulted to see if there were any more references to the Garden of Eal-Ammoreth. "Perchance we may find what sort of garden it was and some clue as to the native country of such a tree," he said.

There were several false leads, diseases with similar symptoms and the like. Aaron didn't think he was much use researching books, so he stayed near Annie, tending the fire and keeping an eye on her. The changes seemed to have stopped for now. The swollen girl slept fitfully but did not awaken.

The night dragged on. It was nearly dawn when Aaron suddenly called the others. The girl was swelling up again, very quickly. By the time the others came in from the library, she had split the side seams on the dress and her bulging face was unrecognizable!

Mari tried to wake her. When the girl did finally come around, she began whimpering. She seemed to be trying to talk. Mari asked everyone to be quiet so they could hear. For awhile, they couldn't get her to say anything coherent but then she began to repeat something over and over.

"That sounds like 'cah no eh no pah lo pi tah no,'" said Owler. "Does that mean anything to anyone?"

Calicia blanched. "Run!" she shouted. "Owler, run quickly and fetch Ender! Tell him what she's saying!"

The woodsman did not hesitate; he shot from the room and out the door like a cat.

"What is it?" asked Mari, shaken.

"I've heard it before, but I can't remember what it means," Calicia answered. "Ender will know. It's in the language of the Ancients! Oh, I had no idea!"

"What?" asked Mari.

"She might be one of them!" said Calicia. "But how? I thought they had died out long ago!"

They cut the dress off of Annie but she did not awaken. As she swelled up even more, she could not lie flat. She lay on her side, curling slowly into a ball. Her back seemed to be swelling faster than her belly.

"She's getting very red," murmured Lia, feeling the girl's bulging back; "and hot also."

"I think she's getting a fever," said Mari, stroking the girl's hair.

Even as they spoke, the girl's breathing was getting slower and slower. Lia felt Annie's pulse and reported that it was also beginning to drop.

Annie's skin seemed tighter and hotter as the minutes slipped by but she began to shiver. She closed her eyes tightly and shrank away from the rising sun that peeked through the window. The women wrapped a blanket around her and moved her away from the light. This appeared to calm her. She had lost all consciousness by this time and responded only to touch. Still shivering, the poor child tugged at the blanket as if it were not wrapped around her tightly enough.

* * *

Brian barreled into the house with Ender and Owler hot on his heels. He stopped in shock when he saw the misshapen lump on the floor.

"Annie?" he asked, pointing. The others nodded.

"She said 'cahno ehno pahlopitahno,' correct?" asked Ender.

Calicia confirmed.

"Brian!" said Ender, quickly. "Bring Annie and follow me!" Without waiting for a response, he turned and rushed out of the house. Owler followed right behind.

The gruffen lifted the bulging girl in his arms and raced after the other two who were now heading deep into the woods. Ender began to look from tree to tree, inspecting each of the larger ones. Brian stayed close, his heart pounding. Annie seemed so hot in his hands!

"This one!" shouted Ender. "Up about fifty feet there is a brown, leathery sort of nest hanging from one of the branches. Remove the blanket, carry her up and place her in there naked. Do not disturb her once she is inside. Hurry! Owler, stay with me in case she falls."

Clutching Annie in one arm, Brian yanked himself up the tree, digging into the rough bark with his nails. He climbed out onto the limb, laid himself out along the branch and carefully slipped her into the opening on the side of the leathery looking bag. The bloated girl just fit into it.

"Let her be," said Ender from down below. "She will seal herself in."

Brian hung onto the branch and watched as the girl reached up and somehow drew the slit closed. A little liquid seeped out along the seam; it dried almost immediately.

Then all was still. Brian hardly dared to breathe.

"Now what?" he said, finally.

"Let's go back to the others and I will explain." Ender suggested, starting back toward the house.

"I don't want to go," said Brian.

"There is nothing you can do for her now, Brian," said Ender. "We'll come back soon and monitor her progress, but there is no point in close vigilance. She is beyond our help."

Slowly, Brian climbed back down the tree and headed back through the woods. When they passed the Thricewood tree, Ender shook his head in wonder. No one spoke a word until they met the others coming into the woods.

"Is she all right?" asked Calicia.

"She's up in the Chrysalis," said Ender. "That's the best we could do for her. The rest is up to nature."

"What's going on?" asked Lia.

Ender took a deep breath. "It's a long story."

"We're all ears," said Aaron.

When they met Mari at the edge of the woods, Ender began to explain as they returned to the house.

"The words she spoke were in the language of the Ancients," said Ender. "They meant 'bidden, hidden, resurrected,' loosely translated."

"This was when I knew she must be one of the Ancients," said Calicia. "I never suspected it until she spoke."

"Who are the Ancients?" asked Thoughtful's voice nearby.

"The Faeries," said Ender. "This island, Cai-Amira was originally theirs. Some of their magic still lives here. Its inherent navigational ability allows it to travel between South Agoria and Thihanan without a captain. It even steers clear of bad weather with no help from us."

"The Circle of the Ancients is another remnant of their magic," said Calicia.

"Do you know if she ate all the fruit from the tree?" asked Ender.

"She did," said Mari. "How did you know about the tree?"

"It's called a Trothianna," said Ender. "I never expected to find one on this island. It sprouts only when a female Faerie is nearby, and only when she has reached maturity."

"Wait," said Aaron. "So Annie is a Faerie?"

"Yes," said Ender. "The Trothianna would not have appeared for any other reason."

"And she has reached maturity?" asked Mari. "What does that mean?"

"That means she's probably twenty or thirty years old," said Ender. "For a Faerie, that would be late adolescence."

"Does the eating of the fruit cause the physical changes we saw?" asked Thoughtful.

"I believe so," said Ender. "If I recall correctly, female Faeries went into the Chrysalis and emerged as fully grown adults, much like the butterfly. The fruit is essential for the change to begin. Males matured differently."

"You say that as if they do not continue to do so," said Owler. "Are the Ancients extinct?"

"We thought they were," said Calicia. "I'm surprised to find one here, especially a young one. How she got here, I have no idea."

"Well it explains her precociousness," said Mari. "She never spoke of her parents, though. All she said was that she had been lost in the woods for a long, long time."

"That's all she said," Brian confirmed. His forehead wrinkled again. "She's not human?"

"No," said Ender. "How wonderfully fascinating!"

"Are you sure we can't help her?" asked Brian.

"Any interference now might disrupt the changes she must experience in the Chrysalis," said Ender. "We'll do well to leave her alone and have a good breakfast."

"I'm going back anyway," said Brian. "I won't touch her." With that, he turned and loped off into the woods again.

Ender watched him go, then he went into the house with the others.

* * *

Bran was glad to be out in the open air. It was another clear day. What he really wanted to do was to stay by the Chrysalis, but Ender had made it clear it was not to be disturbed so Brian promised himself he wouldn't touch it. The sun cast fingers of light down through the evergreens and deciduous trees, setting bright green leaves against deep shadows as he wound his way back toward the Chrysalis tree. The earth beneath his feet was alternately lush with mosses and blanketed with fragrant, dry needles, depending on whether there were pines or deciduous trees overhead.

He went straight back to the Chrysalis tree. He could barely see the Chrysalis between the branches. Resisting the urge to climb up for a closer look, he stared at it for awhile and then seated himself between a couple of massive roots at the base of the trunk. All was quiet. A little breeze stirred the upper branches. For a long time Brian sat there breathing in the rich smells. Every once in awhile he would lean back and look up at the motionless Chrysalis. Although nothing seemed to be happening, Brian felt like the air around him was poised expectantly.

After a long time, he heard an unusual rustle in the leaves overhead, as if an errant breath of wind had gone astray and gotten lost in the upper branches. It didn't last long. The gruffen's ears twitched this way and that, listening. He heard it again, a short distance away. Staring intently in that direction, he thought he could see the leaves moving. He smelled nothing out of the ordinary but his skin prickled and his fur stood up on edge. He caught sight of a flickering light—no, two of them. They converged on the Chrysalis tree, circled it once and then flitted through a break in the forest canopy. Brian jumped to his feet but they were already gone. The Chrysalis was undisturbed.

"Lightning birds," whispered Brian. He stood there a long time, ears twitching, nostrils wide, his sharp eyes searching the woods for any signs of more flickering lights. There were none. Restless now, he took one last look at the motionless Chrysalis and then set off quickly toward the Circle of the Ancients. As he passed by the Thricewood, he noticed that it had already withered away since earlier that morning. The little tree had dropped all its branches and the main trunk was rotting as if it had been dead for ages.

He came out of the woods, skirted the house and headed up to the top of the hill where the Circle stood. The trees weren't open in the same place he had entered before, so he walked around the perimeter looking for a place to get in. He couldn't find an opening anywhere. Maybe Calicia was inside, he thought. Still, just in case, he continued to circle around, looking for a way in. Finally, just ahead of him, the wall opened up. As he reached the opening, he felt a breeze blow by as two shimmering lights slipped between the tree trunks, lifted up into the air and shot off northward faster than any bird could possibly fly.

Brian's skin prickled again. Heart pounding, he peeked into the Circle but saw no one there. Apparently, someone—or something—had been in there or the Circle would have allowed him inside. He raced down the hill again, headed for the house.

* * *

Calicia sat by her husband on the porch, savoring the last sip of a cup of hot tea. She was exhausted from the long night but she wanted to know what had happened with Brian in the Watch House.

"Your timing was good," Ender said. "I think she got in soon enough."

"It was more risky than I realized, not calling you sooner," said Calicia. "I kept thinking we were looking for a poison of some sort."

"You did the best with the resources you had," said Ender. "I just happened to have read about the Trothianna out of curiosity many years ago. I'm still baffled by the presence of a Faerie, especially a young one."

Calicia agreed. "When we get to Thihanan, I'm going to ask Father what he knows. How could he not know they were still around, after all this time? And, if he knew, how could he not have told us?"

Ender smiled at her ruefully. "I have the same question," he said. "It will not go unanswered."

His wife leaned back, closed her eyes and changed the subject: "How was your conversation with Brian?"

"He learns quickly," said Ender. Then he frowned. "I lost him at one point. I could not follow his thoughts closely enough to catch him. It was as if he had left the Watch House or I had been shut out of his thoughts."

Calicia opened her eyes. "By what?"

"I don't know," he said.

"Was it evil?"

Ender shook his head. "Not evil, only different-- a different sort of magic perhaps. I sensed no malice but I could do nothing to re-enter his thoughts. Eventually, he came out of this trance state and was quite calm. He seemed unharmed."

"Perhaps it has to do with the gruffen himself," said Calicia.

"The Great Master did say that this was an unusual company. It is indeed."

"True," said Calicia. "We have never befriended a gruffen before. We have a wizard's bereaved wife, a warrior and his warrior wife who is also a healer, a remarkable woodsman, and, apparently, a newly matured Faerie." Her gaze drifted over to the woods. "I'm sure the gruffen will inform us if anything changes," she said. Tired, she took her leave and went inside to rest.

Ender sat back in his chair and looked out over the open sea. He had always loved this island. Many years ago, the Great Master had taken him down to the cave where the sea met the land in South Agoria. He watched in amazement as the small land mass drifted into a gentle and perfect fit in the bay. Palanthar had given him charge of this last of the Floating Islands of the Ancients. Since then, he had journeyed back and forth many times from the cave to Thihanan; the trips were always peaceful and quiet. This was the first time there had been any trouble.

Northward to his left, the sky was clear. To the south, another storm was brewing. The temperature had dropped a bit, and the wind had picked up. Still, it was, as always, a beautiful day on the island.

"Pardon the interruption," said Thoughtful's voice nearby. "I noticed a peculiar presence and I thought you'd like to know."

"Of course," said Ender.

"I cannot determine whether they are good or evil," said Thoughtful.

"'They'?" Ender raised an eyebrow. "More than one?"

"There appear to be at least two," Thoughtful answered. "They are impossible to contact although I was able to catch a glimpse of them, I think. They appeared as wisps of gossamer light. Almost as if the embers of a dwindling fire had sent up sparks shaped in nearly human form... quite extraordinary."

"I should wonder if you haven't just seen Faeries," said Ender, raising his eyebrows.

"Goodness!" exclaimed Thoughtful. "Such things do exist? But where would they have come from?"

"If they are anywhere, I expect they are North of Thihanan where the Great Master has forbidden me to go thus far," Ender replied. "But Faeries have not ventured this way in millennia. I wonder if the Chrysalis has something to do with this. Keep your eyes open, Thoughtful. They may return."

Brian came rushing down from the hill. "Lights!" he said. "By the tree and in the Circle!"

"They might be Faeries," said Ender.

"The lights?" asked Brian, bewildered.

"Somehow I remember that they change form," Ender replied. "We should study whatever we can find on them," he said, getting up. "Apparently, they're not just legendary."

Brian headed back out to the Chrysalis tree while the other two returned to the house and got out the books of lore again. Ender sifted through the endless pages, looking for any references to the Ancient Ones.

Hidden away behind a larger volume was a small book that Ender had forgotten was there. It was a collection of children's stories, bedtime tales about Faeries and their ways. They quickly perused the exquisitely written pages, some of them with beautiful illustrations. In the stories, the Faeries flew on magical wings and had wonderful adventures. In one story, the eldest brother could turn himself into a gossamer wisp of light.

"Apparently, not all of them can do it," said Thoughtful.

"Maybe this is what I am remembering," said Ender; "these children's stories. Still, I vaguely recall Palanthar saying that some of the Ancients could change form, but he never gave the impression that any remained. I have my suspicions, though. He was always very closed about anything north of Thihanan. If the Faeries are anywhere, they must be there."

"Perhaps we will find out when we make landfall," said Thoughtful.

"Yes," said Ender. "I have a growing list of questions for the Great Master."

The gentle tapping of raindrops on the window interrupted his thoughts. Ender stood up from the reading desk and went out the front door. Light rain fell as he crossed the yard and looked out through the gate. The eastern sky was filling up with dark clouds and the sun was now blocked from view overhead.

"Something troubles you," said Thoughtful.

"We have changed direction," Ender replied, pointing out to the choppy waves sweeping around the floating island. "We are heading directly into a storm. This is not normal. Most trips on the floating island avoid bad weather."

"What about the Chrysalis?" asked Thoughtful. "Can it withstand the rain? Will the child be all right?"

"There is nothing we can do while she is sequestered," Ender said, shaking his head; "but we should watch for her to come out. If her wings are anything like the butterfly wings we expect them to be, they should be kept dry. I hope she does not emerge in the middle of a storm."

"Brian is still watching, I assume," said Thoughtful.

"Yes," said Ender. "Maybe we can make a shelter for her in case she comes out."

The wind was picking up as Ender ran back into the house. Calicia was dressed and coming down the stairs. He told her of the visitors and the shift in direction. The others were awakened. Aaron and Owler left immediately to build a shelter close to the Chrysalis tree. The others returned to the library to see what the books might say about this new turn of events.

Ender was not optimistic. Never in his many years on the Cai-Amira had the island veered off its predestined course except to avoid bad weather. Now it was racing full speed into a storm whose winds were beginning to shake the house.

* * *

Brian had already begun to gather leafy branches and was building a shelter even before Owler and Aaron arrived. The three of them quickly erected a sturdy lean-to under the tree. The rain was coming down in sheets now, and they were soon soaked through. The shelter was large enough to fit Brian and one other, protected on three sides with tightly bound walls. A large pine bough was tied on as a sort of door.

"Go!" Brian shouted over the wind. "I'll stay here."

"If she's like the butterfly," Owler shouted back; "she'll probably not come out until the sun shines again."

Brian nodded and sat down in the shelter.

"Let us know if anything changes," bellowed Aaron.

Brian nodded again and waved them on.

The storm was getting worse.

CHAPTER 21

The Golrakken

"There is a ship in the distance," said Thoughtful. Hearing the edge of tension in that voice, Ender looked up from his book. "What kind of ship?" he asked.

"It is tall and dark," Thoughtful replied. "Its sails blow tattered in the wind but it is not driven by the tempest. It rides the waves like a wolf racing over a hill. It sails into the wind and is headed toward us at great speed."

Calicia caught her breath.

"Is there a crew aboard?" asked Ender, slowly rising to his feet.

"I see lights," said Thoughtful; "but I cannot see clearly enough to distinguish a crew."

Calicia and Ender exchanged glances.

"The Golrakken," said Ender. "If there are lights, there must be a crew. It has been too long for any fire to still be burning on board."

"How far away?" asked Aaron. "How long till they get here?"

"At this speed, I don't know," replied Thoughtful.

"Then we gird for battle," said Ender. "Thoughtful, keep watch on that ship and tell us where they intend to land, but whatever you do, I warn you, do not hail them or reply to any call from the ship!"

"Do we need Brian?" asked Owler.

"We need everyone," said Ender. "This is a dangerous enemy, in more ways than you can imagine. Thoughtful, please fetch Brian as well. Tell him he can do more good here than there. I adjure you, though: do not speak to anyone on the vessel."

"Understood," said Thoughtful. "I will speak to no one."

* * *

Brian shook himself outside but he still smelled like wet gruffen when he went inside the house. The others were gathered in the library.

"Stand clear of this space," said Calicia, indicating and area in the middle of the library floor.

They all watched as a sliding trapdoor revealed a secret room below. She lit a candle and they followed her down the ladder.

As Aaron looked around the room, he started to grin. Lining the walls were all manner of weapons, everything from pikes to axes, from rapiers to two-handed broadswords, all carefully oiled and maintained.

"Some of these could use some sharpening," said Ender. "They have not been needed for a long time."

Brian recognized Ender's Bow and wondered if it would be used again.

"The others may choose whatever suits them," said Ender to Brian; "but by order of the Great Master, this particular blade is for you." He handed the gruffen a long knife similar to the one Owler carried with him.

"I don't want a knife," Brian muttered. "Don't know how to fight with it."

"Be that as it may, accept it," Ender replied, adjusting the harness and strapping the sheath over Brian's massive shoulder. Amazingly, it fit. "The Great Master never gives unnecessary orders and he was very specific about this."

Brian took the knife out and looked it over. For some reason, his hand tingled slightly when he held it. He put it back in the sheath, and took it out and put it back a few more times. Eventually, he decided it wouldn't be a bother, slipped it back into its sheath and let it be.

Aaron selected a mail jerkin and shield that were both strong but surprisingly light. He chose a good belt and hung a hammer and two knives on it. Walking around the room, he handled several swords before he settled on a hand-and-a-half that he strapped onto his back.

"One more thing," he said. Striding purposefully across the room, he went straight to where a hefty axe leaned against the wall. He picked it up and flipped it over a couple of times in his hand. "This should do nicely," he said. Then he went over to see what Lia had chosen.

She had found a leather jerkin that fit her well. Her belt had an elegant long knife and a dagger. When Aaron came by, she was unsheathing a long, straight, two-edged sword that matched the dagger.

"Beautiful," said Aaron. "Good weight for you, too."

"Calicia says they're Elven," she told him.

He took the blade and bent it over his knee. "Excellent temper," he said, feeling the strength of its spring. "It's not steel, but it's good metal, whatever it is."

"It's a bit longer than I'm used to," said Lia, taking it back and checking the balance.

"A long reach is a good thing," said Aaron.

Mari picked out a slender rapier, though she said it was probably more for show. "I expect my hands to be too busy to use it much," she said.

Calicia donned her own hauberk which appeared to be the same Elven metal used in Lia's weapons. Her own sword was an ornate, curved affair that looked more looked more like a ceremonial weapon than a dealer of death, but she seemed quite capable of wielding it, despite her delicate frame.

Owler hand picked a selection of knives to add to his own belt and chose a sturdy hand-and-a-half sword similar to Aaron's but with a lighter blade.

Though these weapons were all well-oiled and cared for, everyone checked and re-checked them for damage and sharpness. Aaron found a sharpening stone and worked on a slight knick in the axe.

"This is no ordinary enemy approaching," said Ender. "I have fought no foe more dangerous than the Golrakken. They have not been seen for many years, and never have they been so bold as to approach Cai-Amira. Why they choose to now, I do not know.

"I will tell you more about them in a moment, but the first thing you need to know, the most important thing, is never to speak to them. You heard me warn Thoughtful and I warn you just the same. You must answer with action, not talk. If they engage your mind, they will turn your own soul against itself and draw it into their darkness with their twisted words. They will taunt, beguile, flatter or terrorize. Do not respond. Your only reply must be deadly force. Make no mistake. You cannot beat them with words. You will only destroy yourself. Am I clear?" He looked around the room, his eyes lingering on Brian; he wondered how much the gruffen understood. Everyone else nodded.

"The Golrakken are not truly alive, nor are they truly dead," Ender continued. "They were the favorites of the Dark Power and he gave them the ability to take over the bodies of those whose minds they can enslave. Thus, they live from body to body, casting aside the soul that lives inside and taking over. Not only can they prolong their own lives this way, but they can increase their numbers by twisting the souls of those whose bodies are not immediately needed. Many an army has been vanquished by changelings created within its own ranks.

"When the Morve was driven from South Agoria, the Golrakken leader, Karkaan, led his troops to the sea where they escaped on their Faerie ship. We pursued them to the coast, but a strange storm blew in suddenly and we did not put to sea. The storm lasted several days, and when it cleared, we searched several leagues out from the coast, but there was no sign of the ship. We wondered if the Golrakken ship had foundered. Apparently, it did not.

"Again, I warn you as I was warned," he said firmly. "Under no circumstances should you answer them. They will hurl invective at you; they will humiliate you and goad you. Avoid looking directly back at them, and by no means speak to them. If you do, your life is forfeit and you become the enemy."

Thoughtful's voice came from a corner of the room. "They will reach the island by nightfall."

"Not much time," said Ender. "Did you hear my discussion of the Golrakken?"

"I did," said Thoughtful.

"They are even more dangerous to you as you are in this state," said Ender. "They battle not only flesh and blood, but mind and spirit as well. If you had a body, you might find it easier not to respond to them. As a Sochhmahr, your thoughts may be open to them. Beware, Thoughtful! Guard your thoughts!"

Then he took his Bow, a quiver of arrows and a long, heavy sword. They all returned upstairs and Calicia concealed the entrance again.

Lia and Calicia made two kits with pouches of herbs and vials of whatever potions and salves they had on hand. Mari sat on the couch with her head in her hands, going over and over in her mind the things that she had been learning.

"What can we expect from these Golrakken?" asked Aaron. "How do they fight, and with what kinds of weapons?"

"The Golrakken fight like men when steel meets steel," replied Ender. "But they are even more dangerous before the fight begins. If they can engage the enemy in a verbal battle, they always win. No one can stand up to them. To open the mouth is to open the mind to them. It is a fatal mistake. As I have said, they are fiendishly clever and it is difficult to ignore them.

"Be prepared also for the first sight of them so you are not surprised. They are as ugly as death. Their flesh is gray and almost transparent, stretched tightly over their bony faces, barely covering their muscles. Their eyes are lidless and appear cracked and hollow until you see the baleful lights deep inside staring back at you, unblinking. Though their bodies seem wiry and ancient, they are strong and quick.

"Since they live in the realm of the spirit as much as the flesh, they see more than ordinary warriors and are impossible to ambush. Fight them head to head; it is the only way."

Aaron weighed his axe, switching it easily from his left hand to his right. "Conventional weapons, then," he said. "Do they use magic?"

"Not as wizards," said Ender. "Much of their power was given to them by the Morve, so their strength is more in the spiritual realm. They do not throw fire or cast spells. However, Karkaan, their leader, has long had designs to acquire such power. I believe Morvassus himself kept it from them, out of fear perhaps."

"Fear?" said Owler.

"They are a powerful race," said Ender. "Even the Morve cannot control them completely. A rebellion could be costly."

Day passed into night and still the Golrakken had not landed. Thoughtful reported that they had sailed further to the south and seemed to be coming around to attack the house directly.

"There is still powerful magic about this place," said Ender. "It may be that they are having trouble trying to advance against Cai-Amira." This was a small hope at best. The island's forward progress had ceased, but now they were a sitting target in the thrashing seas.

"Perhaps it will be too rough for them to land," offered Brian.

Calicia dashed his hopes. "It is still a Faerie ship, whatever they have made of it. It may land safely where another would founder."

It was dawn before Thoughtful came back with the news. The Golrakken had sailed around the island in the night and were about to land just north of the Watch House. "They intend to take the hill," Ender determined. "Bring the weapons and provisions. We have a much better chance in the Circle of the Ancients than we have here."

They gathered their gear and left the house. The rain had stopped and the wind had died. The smell of death hung in the air. All the grass had been battered into the mud by the heavy rains. The trees stood shorn of their weaker branches which lay tossed to the ground beside them. Calicia turned to look at the house and Ender put his arm around her as they climbed the hill.

"The dark ship has landed," announced Thoughtful.

The company had just reached the Circle of the Ancients when a lone call rose up from the beach below the hill. It was a loud, low, raspy voice that splintered the stillness. A deep chill fell upon all who heard it.

"Ehrmahann, son of Jarmahann, we know you are here!" it cried. "Surrender, and all who are with you will be spared. Fight, and this time you will surely die."

Ender motioned to the narrow opening to the Circle of the Ancients. "Go in," he said.

When they were all inside, Aaron and Owler stood on one side of the narrow opening to the trees. Brian and Ender stood to the other side. Ender already had an arrow on the string. Then everything stopped until the voice again cracked the silence.

"If you will not listen to counsel, then you will die," rasped the voice. The island was so quiet that they could hear the clinking of metal as the Golrakken moved up through the woods toward the hill.

"They are fanning out to surround the Circle," said Thoughtful in Ender's ear.

"How many?" asked Ender as he motioned to the others what was happening.

"I have not counted," said Thoughtful. "One moment."

The Sochhmahr rose up above the trees and floated there, trying to count the enemy. Everything about them was gray and black. The armor under their well-worn capes was dented and tarnished, but intact. Each Golrak wore a steel helm, some designed with gray horns or claws, some with sharp blades or spikes. The Golrakken faces were gray and almost skinless. Hollow, yellow eyes gleamed out from dark sockets. Jagged, ash-colored teeth stood on bony jaws; the lips stretched tightly in a permanent leer.

The tallest of the Golrakken strode confidently at the head of a short column of his fellows. In the center of his helm was a silver snake with crystal eyes and fangs. Thoughtful shuddered at the sight of him.

The Golrak fixed his eyes on Thoughtful and aimed a gloved finger directly at him. "Behold! A Sochhmahr! Hail, Doomed One!" he shrieked. "Do not think your form will spare you!" He beckoned. "Join me--or die; there is no other choice!"

To his horror, Thoughtful felt something inside him waver. He brushed it aside and returned quickly to the Circle. "They are now on all sides," he reported, his voice quavering; "thirty or forty of them. For some reason, they've kept their distance."

Before anyone could react, the trees of the Circle of the Ancients began to tremble. The leaves above shook and the trunks began to lean outward, pulled by some invisible force. Roots began tearing out of the earth, spraying dirt and rocks into the air. Their great weight crushed the other trees of the hill and they all came crashing to the ground, leaving the defenders completely exposed on the grassy hilltop.

Around the rim of the destruction stood the Golrakken. Their leader faced Ender fifty paces away and laughed. "You depend on the magic of the Ancients as defense against the Ancients themselves?" he mocked. "I, Karkaan, was here before you, Ehrmahann, and I will live on after you." He motioned towards the defenders. "These will die a horrible death or become my own, one way or the other. You, yourself will be killed; I have had enough of you. Your beloved Calicia may still serve me, though. We shall see. Your Sochhmahr, I will take as my own."

Aaron gripped his axe. Owler held a throwing knife in each hand. Everyone waited for Ender to make the first move as the enemy closed in.

With raspy, grating voices, the Golrakken called out to each of the defenders in turn, insulting them, threatening them, cajoling them. No one answered.

Brian noticed that no one addressed him directly, almost as if they hadn't noticed him. Also, the voices did not seem to bother him at all; his mind was clear.

Then, without a signal, the Golrakken surged over the fallen trees. For such decrepit-looking figures, they were surprisingly agile.

Ender's Bow sent out the first shot. It was aimed at the leader, Karkaan but another gray warrior threw himself in front and took the arrow in the chest. Karkaan plucked the arrow from the body, broke it over his knee and laughed. Ender was already firing on the others. He let three more arrows fly before he drew his sword and parried the first stroke that came his way. Calicia was at his back and her swift blade quickly cost one enemy his sword arm.

Mari, Aaron, Lia and Owler had already become separated from the lord and lady of the island. Aaron wielded his great axe one-handed as if it were pine and tin instead of oak and steel. He used both the blade and the blunt end, chopping off a helmet with the stroke and crushing a shield with the backswing. He stood a step away from the others so as to give himself room to swing, but the Golrakken could neither draw him away from the group nor drive in behind him. One Golrak dove for Aaron's legs only to slam into a shield. Still swinging his axe at the others, Aaron lifted the shield and kicked the helmet sideways, snapping the Golrak's neck.

Though Owler was not used to fighting in a group, he quickly adapted. The first Golrak made the mistake of charging him head-on and had a knife buried in his throat before he was even close. The others slowed and stepped over their dying comrade. Owler's hand-and-a-half sword proved as effective as Aaron's axe in keeping the Golrakken at bay. Still, the sheer numbers of them meant that every stroke had to count.

Lia's sword sang through the air. She had barely yanked her blade from the body of one soldier before she was parrying the strokes of two more. Her main concern was keeping them away from her older sister who stood behind her. Mari continued chanting, weaving patterns with her arms and hands, sending tongues of flame licking out over the enemy. The smell of burnt flesh hung pungent in the still air.

* * *

Karkaan stepped over his fallen soldiers as one steps over debris. He was confident Ender would fall sooner or later. He now had his eye on Mari, the fire-thrower, the sorceress. Surely this was the one he had been looking for. Her black hair whipped around her. As she flung her arms, shafts of flame blazed holes through bodies of the Golrakken. They shrieked and fell burning to the ground. The smoky stench singed the nose and eyes. Karkaan smiled and raised his hand. His forces pulled away from her and swarmed her three companions.

Karkaan watched the sorceress as she raised her arms to send a flame into his grinning face. He pulled his cape apart and opened his chest plate, exposing bare gray skin and releasing a smell like rotting flesh.

"Burn what you will," he cried. "It will not consume me. The fire you throw is nothing like the flame that already smolders in this chest. I give you another choice."

Mari's eyes grew wide and she fumbled her spell. Taking up the chant again, she started over.

Karkaan advanced slowly. "The power I will grant you is many times the strength you have already," he said in a voice that should have been too quiet to be heard. "You are a sorceress, a cunning woman. I can see that you know well the power of which I speak and have already wandered its borders. But now you shall have control. What you bid shall be done. These Golrakken will worship you and you shall be their queen. All will tremble at your approach. Come to me and accept my proposal. Or die by your own hand."

He came forward with one hand open and the other holding a cruel blade. His fingers gripped the sharp steel and he offered the carved handle to Mari.

Despite her horror, Mari found herself looking directly into his face. Her heart pounded fiercely and her shaking hands dropped the sword she had finally drawn. Strangely, now, she could no longer see the battlefield. Instead, she saw a vision of herself on a lofty and fearsome throne of gray stone. On her head was a crown of silver beset with crystalline tines that split the pale light drifting down from overhead. All around her the Golrakken stood at attention. Two of them bowed low before her; she pointed an accusing finger at one. He wailed and reeled backward, bursting into flame and collapsing in smoking ashes. The other rose and fell upon her feet. She touched his helm with her scepter. He jerked up and fell unconscious to the floor. At a motion from her hand, they carried him away while a beautiful but twisted maiden with dark skin came and washed Mari's feet.

When her vision returned to to the present, Mari found the handle of the knife was now very close. She had actually begun to reach out toward it.

Karkaan's grating voice seemed strangely soothing. "Come with me, Mari das-Karkaan."

"Leave her alone!" shouted a different voice at her shoulder. Too late did Thoughtful realize his error.

Karkaan's expression turned fierce. "Sochhmahr, gak bacchen tuk!" he spat. He reached out next to Mari's right ear and grabbed. Stepping back, the Golrak held his fist up near his face.

Mari, freed somewhat by the distraction, saw Holren's body materialize in Karkaan's grip. Her husband's ashen face was twisted in horror and rage. Karkaan had him in a stranglehold and had lifted him up off the ground. Holren struggled but could not pull away. The Golrak breathed into the man's face: a long exhalation of foul air. Holren's skin began to turn gray and tighten. His long nose shriveled back into his face and his lips peeled away like dry leaves near fire. His eyelids shrank back and his scalp shed all hair. His hands, still tugging at the hold on his throat, shriveled also and turned gray.

Mari cried out as Karkaan pressed his thumbnail against Holren's throat. Before he could pierce the air passage, Mari threw a blast of fire. Rocked by the explosion, Karkaan dropped Holren's limp body and stumbled back a few steps. Then he turned toward Mari with renewed interest. His gray skin was smoking, but she had not succeeded in stopping him. Frantically, she began a stronger spell.

At that moment, there came a sound no one expected. A voice began to sing, high and clear, sweet as birdsong and lyrical as wind in the leaves. The song sailed over the trees and up the hill, somehow audible over the clash of battle. The Golrakken suddenly pulled back and froze, looking fearfully toward the forest. The cloud cover was breaking at the other end of Cai-Amira. A flurry of lights came through the hole and flew across the treetops.

"To the ship!" cried Karkaan turning away from Mari. Instantly, the gray host abandoned the fight and ran for the woods, headed for the beach.

As they retreated, Mari dropped to the ground by Holren's violated body. He was now unrecognizable, but she knew she had seen him before the transformation.

"No!" she cried. "No, no, no!" She looked up as something approached.

Then something hard cuffed her on the side of the head and she knew no more.

* * *

"Let them go!" yelled Aaron as the fleeing Golrakken disappeared into the woods. The gray host would soon reach their landing boats and could not be pursued to their ship.

The flurry of lights had converged overhead. Now, instead of just one voice, a vast choir was singing, many voices calling to each other in intricate counter-melodies. In the middle of this unusual chorus, the original voice rose above them all, bell like and clear, wondrously strong. It sang a single note, long and steady, never wavering. Then all the voices converged on that same note and the lights descended into the forest on the other side of the island. The lights rose together as one flaming ball, lifted into the sky and were gone. Overhead, the sky was clearing.

Out on the open sea, tattered sails flying, the Golrakken ship sped away into the heart of the retreating storm.

Stunned, everyone on the hill looked around. Nearly a dozen Golrakken lay dead. Ashes and piles of burnt armor lay where Mari had blasted some of them into oblivion. The stench did not faze Aaron as he checked each body to be sure it was dead. Ever wary, he continued to scan the hillside and the edge of the forest.

"Where are Mari and Brian?" he hollered.

Ender was also working his way through the corpses. "Thoughtful!" he shouted. "Thoughtful, can you see them?"

There was no answer.

"Thoughtful!"

A gray figure on the ground groaned slightly. Owler was upon him in an instant, knife drawn. Aaron was right behind him.

"Stop!" shouted Ender. "We don't know who this is. Show his face!"

Owler rolled the body over and Ender knelt down beside it. The face was a thin veil of skin stretched over a bony skull. A faint, dry breath issued from the gaping mouth.

"Thoughtful," murmured Ender; "I can tell you are in there. What did you do? Did you speak to them? You must have. This is a bitter turn, Thoughtful. You deserved better."

The figure did not respond. With measured movements, Ender stood to his feet, took a white arrow from his quiver and shot the tortured body through the heart. The withered form convulsed once and then disappeared in a white mist.

"A Sochhmahr once again," said Ender. "May the Great Master grant you a third chance."

Owler looked up in wonder. "What did you just do?" he asked. "Was that monster our Thoughtful?"

"It was," said Ender.

Calicia pulled the white arrow from the ground and handed it back to Ender. "Magical instruments must be used against magical wounds," she said. "This was what the Bow does best. Thoughtful may possibly recover outside of that wretched body."

Aaron examined the ground. "Mari's footprints end here," he said. "They just stop."

Owler knelt beside him, checked the tracks, and looked back at Aaron. Their eyes met, but neither spoke. Owler looked away and stood up again.

Lia stifled a cry. "Could she have been transformed like Thoughtful?" she asked.

"It's possible," said Ender.

"Brian, too?" she asked.

Ender nodded.

They all checked the remaining bodies. None breathed. No more of Mari's footprints were found on the hill. They began a methodical search of the woods where the Golrakken had fled, and though they searched all the way to the beach, they found nothing. They branched out on either side and worked their way back, still searching but found no other recent tracks all the way back to the house. They fanned out across the hillside.

"Gruffen tracks!" shouted Owler. "He ran this way!" Everyone came running, but Owler was already racing for the woods.

The trail was lost for a moment over the fallen trees of the Circle, but Owler picked it up again on the other side. Calicia wept silently as she crawled over the beautiful giants that had stood so tall for so long, only to be torn from the earth and dashed on the ground. The gruffen tracks passed the Thricewood which had almost completely decayed by now.

"Golrakken tracks!" shouted Owler, drawing his sword.

Aaron already had his axe in both hands as he raced to catch up but there was no need for it. Near the lean-to they had built, they found the Golrak, its head nearly severed. The steel breastplate was sliced cleanly from the throat to the armpit. A clean puncture had been made straight through the armor and into the heart.

"How did that happen?" asked Lia.

Aaron shook his head. "What kind of knife cuts through armor like that?"

"The one Brian carries," Ender answered, thoughtfully. "But only under certain conditions."

Neither the knife nor the gruffen was there. In fact, neither was the Chrysalis tree. Here, at the edge of a wide circle of fresh, green grass, Brian's tracks ended.

The grass appeared to have been growing there all along, as if the Chrysalis tree had never existed. Annie had disappeared along with it, and no trace of remained.

"Brian!" bellowed Aaron. "Brian!" There was no answer.

"I believe the lights converged on this place," said Ender. "The lights and the singers seemed to be related."

"The first voice came from the woods," said Lia.

"Annie's, perhaps?" suggested Calicia. "The other voices came from outside."

"Were they spirits, ghosts maybe?" asked Owler, checking the surrounding area for more gruffen tracks. "The Golrakken retreated immediately. What did they fear?"

Ender thought for a moment. "Another clan of Faeries, perhaps. If they were Faeries, they were in a form I've never read of before. Perhaps they were looking for Annie."

"And then took her with them," said Owler. "Brian was clearly here but I see no indication that he left the area. Maybe they took him as well, but that does not explain the missing tree."

"Maybe it does," said Aaron, still looking for clues.

Calicia stepped into the grass circle and looked around. "This circle is the same size as the old Circle of the Ancients," she said.

"And look," said Owler. He pointed to a ring of saplings no taller than a span that ringed the perimeter. "These were not here when we arrived."

The tiny trees were growing before their eyes. Little leaves appeared at the tips of the slender branches.

"These are the same as those in the Circle of the Ancients!" said Calicia, gently touching the emerging leaves. The trees were halfway up to her knees now. "It's as if another Circle is growing right here!"

They spent hours searching before they all agreed that Annie, Brian and Mari were not on the island. By then, the trees surrounding the new circler were twenty feet high and their trunks were as thick as a man's thigh.

The sky had cleared and the wind had shifted when they came out of the forest and climbed once again to the top of the hill. The island had turned and was back on its northward course to Thihanan. Ender surveyed the damage and frowned. Many years would pass before Cai-Amira was pristine once again. The bald hill fringed by fallen trunks, its stately, ancient grove gone forever. He vowed they would build something good from the wood of those giants. Calicia smiled quietly and said nothing. She had hope that the new grove in the woods would be as beautiful as the last.

Aaron set about gathering the dead while Owler found a shovel and began digging a fire pit. Ender cut the smaller branches of the fallen trees for burning and Lia and Calicia hauled them over to the pit. The casualties of battle slowly burned away. Mercifully, a steady breeze blew the acrid smoke out to sea.

When darkness fell, they came again into the house and wearily trudged upstairs to clean themselves off. Of the nine souls that had begun the voyage, only five remained to see it through. The house seemed empty.

* * *

Lia and Aaron lay on their bed but neither spoke. Aaron lay quietly beside his wife, deliberately blocking out the horrors of the day. In time, he drifted off to sleep.

Outside, the moon danced on the water, but inside, memories and fragments of memories whispered in Lia's mind—laughter shared, childhood fights, secrets, glories and misunderstandings. A swirling collage of reminiscences enveloped her, taunting, pleading, tickling and prodding. Her quiet sobs woke Aaron. He held her until he felt her relax from exhaustion. When her breathing was even and quiet once more, he also slept.

CHAPTER 22

Annathía

Brian was surprised. The Golrakken treated him like nothing more than an obstacle, a large dog in their way; they just went around him. He reached out and grabbed one by the helm, twisted the Gray Warrior's neck and broke it with a whip of his arm. He knocked another one to the ground and crushed him underfoot. Rather than attacking him, though, the Golrakken just avoided him.

One particularly tall Golrak with a snake on his helm broke away from the group and moved quickly toward the woods on the far side of the hill. The fur on Brian's neck bristled; the Golrak was headed toward the Chrysalis tree! Brian had to fight his way through the gray throng to follow him. His heavy hands tossed them aside but by the time he reached the bottom of the hill, the Golrak with the snake helm had long since vanished into the woods.

Brian raced after the Golrak, dodging trees and blasting through the underbrush. The Gray Warrior's boot prints were easily tracked in the soft earth, and there was no mistaking the smell. Brian was very close to the lean-to when he came upon the Golrak from behind. He pounced. The Gray Warrior leapt sideways and Brian fell face down in the wet undergrowth. He rolled over quickly, to find the sharp tip of a Golrakken sword at his neck.

"Useless!" shouted the Golrak. "All that effort for nothing. You thought I wouldn't notice? No one minds you but me! Lazraak is not so careless." He stuck out his dark red tongue and licked his upper teeth wickedly. "What do you say to that? Talk to me, filthy dog. You know you can talk."

Brian lay on his back, tense, waiting, saying nothing.

"A gruffen with some sense! The better for sport, perhaps, but I have a more important prize. I need you for nothing, unless you would carry her for me when I claim her. Would you like that?"

The blade in Brian's grip caught the Golrak's eye. "A weapon?" he said, pressing the tip of his sword harder against Brian's throat. Then, suddenly, the Golrak sucked in a breath.

"The Dark Power will be mine!" he said. "None shall deny me! The Valenblade is found near a Chrysalis! Lazraak Snakehelm shall rule all!"

He looked back down at Brian.

"Beast," said the Golrak; "in your clumsy paws, the Valenblade is but a kitchen knife. In the hands of the Valen, it cuts through armor and stone. From you, I fear nothing."

Brian saw him shift his weight to strike. In a move that surprised both of them, the gruffen reached for the knife, knocking the sword away from his throat with the flat of it. Before the Golrak could thrust again Brian on his feet. Lazraak charged him, sword aimed at the gruffen's chest.

Brian dropped quickly, deflected the sword over his head and slammed his shoulder into the Golrak. Lazraak was thrown back but somehow kept his feet. Before he could bring his sword to the ready, though, Brian's long reach brought the long knife down. The blade found Golrak flesh at the base of Lazraak's neck and cut clean through the windpipe and spine, slicing through the collarbone and into the metal breastplate, all the way to the armpit. The Golrak pitched sideways and collapsed, his sword falling harmlessly to the ground.

Brian jumped on him, drove the blade into the Golrak's chest and pulled it back out. Lazraak Snakehelm did not move. Brian leapt to his feet and looked around quickly for more enemies. There were none. The stinking blood on the long knife sizzled, smoked, and then disappeared. Brian looked at the knife, puzzled. Then he looked back at the dead Golrak. The knife had cut through bone and armor as easily as it had cut through flesh.

A voice began singing in the tree above him. It was a beautiful sound: a single, long note, sweet and clear. It seemed to come from inside the Chrysalis. Heart pounding, Brian sheathed the knife and raced up the tree as quickly as his clawed hands could haul him. The fragrance of the bark was a welcome relief from the stench of the Golrakken blood. When he reached the branch where the Chrysalis hung, he stopped and held his breath. The Chrysalis was splitting from the top downward. The singing was indeed coming from inside. He wondered what had become of Annie, the swollen and disfigured little girl he had so gently placed in there not so long ago.

Suddenly, there were many voices, clear and strong like the first one, all singing different songs that blended together. The same flickering lights he had seen earlier appeared again, but there were so many they seemed to fill the forest. They flitted around the Chrysalis tree almost like hummingbirds. Brian squinted as the tree itself also began to light up.

Many voices were singing now. Brian kept his eyes on the Chrysalis which had split completely on one side and was opening wider. The inside was veiled by a thick, wet skin of some sort. The voice inside was growing stronger, singing over the top of all the others with its single, perfect note. A fine-boned hand reach out through the veil and pulled at it gently, revealing a brightness inside the dark brown sack. The flickering lights danced all around but Brian stared at the Chrysalis, transfixed. Slowly, a lithe young woman emerged, her dark, wet hair tumbling on her bare shoulders. She was clothed in a bright light which swirled about her as she climbed out of the open Chrysalis and easily pulled herself up onto the branch. From her back sprung two wings, damp and wrinkled, but of the same blue and gold Brian had seen in his vision in the Watch House. Though her mouth was not open, Brian could tell she was the one singing that long, sustained note.

She looked around, curiously, her eyes following one light and then another as if listening to some communication Brian couldn't hear. He felt himself being jostled from all sides, not roughly, but firmly. He hung onto the branch.

"Annie?" he croaked.

Instantly, she turned toward him and then, for the second time, he saw the most beautiful face he had ever seen. Her eyes fixed on him and the light about her gleamed furiously. She stood up and walked nimbly along the branch until she was right in front of him. Kneeling down, she took his rough hand in hers and turned it palm up. There was the thorn wound, still open in his leathery skin. With a smile of both discovery and recognition, she covered his palm with her other hand. Brian's senses tingled and his fur stood out all over.

"Annie?" he asked again.

She nodded, her eyes shining brightly. Then she sang out even stronger and all the voices converged on the one long note.

Brian felt suddenly weightless. He felt like he had been transformed into the light surrounding the tree. In fact, the tree underneath him also seemed to have turned into light. Its widespread, shallow roots pulled out of the ground, showering dirt everywhere and casting aside the little lean-to that had been built as a shelter. For a moment, Brian could see the ground below. Grass sprang up instantly in the circle of dirt left behind, leaving no evidence that a tree had ever grown there. Then the entire island seemed to suddenly shrink into the sea and he was surrounded by clouds and fog.

The winged maiden on the branch beside him finally stopped singing but she continued to hold his hand. He still had some difficulty thinking of her as Annie. All about them the song continued, a different tune now, with fewer parts but more voices on each countermelody. The maiden was getting dry now and the light around her body had become a sky blue dress of no particular design which seemed to flow about her. She squeezed his huge hand and smiled like the happiest woman in the world. Confused and disoriented as he was, Brian, himself, could not keep from smiling.

Then the lights swirled around them more closely. Annie turned this way and that following their movement. Brian watched, fascinated, as the lights approached her one by one, singing to her with crystalline voices. She nodded and laughed, her eyes dancing along with the music. If they were telling her something, the gruffen couldn't figure out what it was.

How long this went on, Brian couldn't tell. It was like a dream. He wondered if he would awaken to discover that all this was gone and he was actually somewhere deep in the snowy woods with no food and no firewood, wrinkling his nose at the smell of goblins on the march.

* * *

At some point, he realized he was sitting under a willow tree in the shade on a warm, sunny afternoon. He found himself looking out over a field of golden green grass toward another willow tree. More willow trees dotted the landscape further on. A quiet stream wound its way between all of them. As his eyes cleared, Brian could see rolling hills off in the distance. The jagged peaks of a mountain range, blue and hazy in the distance, marked the horizon.

He smelled food. It was unfamiliar food, but it sure smelled good.

"Brian P. Gruffenson! I thought you'd never wake up! Are you hungry yet or have you given up eating so you can sleep?" The words and the impish tone were very familiar, but the voice that delivered them was lower, and warm like the grass in the valley.

The gruffen rolled over quickly and found the winged maiden sitting in the shade beside him. He sat back away from her.

"It's just me, Brian," she said. "Annie."

"Maybe," stammered Brian. "I mean, maybe I met you. But how...could you be Annie?"

"I know," said Annie, looking down at her own body. "I look really different, even to myself. I'm still me, but I'm walking around in a big person's body. And I have wings! I don't know. It's strange. I don't even sound like me." She held out her hands to look at them. Then she shrugged. "I guess this is what Faeries look like when they grow up."

"Good, I guess," Brian said.

"They said my name is actually really long," she continued. "It's Annathía Something-or-Other das Lam...das Lammethan."

"Hard to say all that," said Brian.

She laughed, just like Annie would have laughed. Brian couldn't stop staring at her. She had the same mannerisms, even the same expressions, but she sure looked different. Somehow, though, she smelled the same, except for the wings. If he shut his eyes and didn't listen to her voice, this person really could be Annie.

She looked up and he recognized again the eyes of the woman he had seen in the Circle of the Ancients back on Cai-Amira.

He held up his hand and showed her the thorn wound in his palm. "Remember this?"

Her eyes widened and she nodded.

Brian's eyes grew bigger, too. "You do?"

"Yes," she said.

He could see her folded wings peeking out from behind her. They were nearly translucent and vibrant with color just like those he had seen on the woman in his vision in the Watch House. He did not mention it. He just sat there, saying nothing.

Annie was looking at the knife that Brian still had with him. "That knife makes me feel strange," she said.

"Strange how?" asked Brian.

"I don't know," she said. "Like I've seen it before."

"On the island," said Brian.

"No, before that," said Annie. Then she shrugged. "There's food if you're hungry," she reminded him. "No fish or nuts just yet, but I think you'll like the stuff the Lammethan eat." She opened a wicker basket full of fruit and bread, pulled out a skin poured a drink into a wide cup for him.

"Where are we? Where is everyone? How did we get here? Who are the 'lomm thon?'" he asked. The drink was sweet and good and he drained it all. He really was hungry now. She handed him a fruit and he popped the whole thing in his mouth. Oh, the food was very good!

"You eat and I'll try to explain," said Annie, laughing again. Over time, Annie's laugh had become Brian's favorite sound. He liked it now, too, even though it was lower pitched.

She continued. "I don't know much, but I asked a lot of questions. Here's what I figured out. Everyone else is still on Cai-Amira where we left them. The Golrakken (did I say it right?) left the floating island because the Faeries came, but the Faeries actually weren't there to get them, they were there to get me. Here's where I get confused."

She stopped, took a breath and let it out.

Brian popped another fruit in his mouth and kept eating.

"They say the Lammethan are my family, Brian," she said. "So I'm a Faerie, I guess. Makes sense, with these wings and everything." She looked back at them again, still fascinated. "They say I was born here. They also say that the Lammethan are only half of the Faeries that used to live here. The Golrakken used to be Faeries and they lived...out there." She pointed east.

Brian almost choked. "Golrakken live here?" he croaked.

"'Used to,'" she repeated. "Not anymore. I don't remember how all this goes. I think they said the Golrakken left a long time ago. Something awful happened and somehow they got turned into monsters."

"Hmph," grunted Brian. He swallowed his mouthful and stood up. "Got to go back to the island. Monsters might come back."

"We can't just go back," she answered.

"Why not?" growled the gruffen.

"The island is very far away," said Annie. "It was all they could do to carry us here."

"All who could do?" asked Brian.

"The Lammethan, the other Faeries," she explained. "I don't understand it all either but it took a lot of Faeries to get us here and they can't just take us back so easily. We can't get there by ourselves. And we have to talk to the High Council, whoever they are."

Brian sat down reluctantly. "Why talk? I don't understand the lights and how we got here." He frowned.

"Me either," said Annie; "but this is part of it. I want to show you something."

"What?" asked Brian.

"I'm not totally sure," said Annie, standing up. "Watch. I'm still learning this."

This was the first time he had seen her standing. Her wings were no longer folded out of the way. They were very much like butterfly wings, he decided, only much more blue than any butterfly he'd ever seen before.

She walked out into the sunlight and spread her wings fully. They were dazzling!

"Wait," she said. Holding her arms wide out to the sides, palms down, she threw back her head and suddenly vanished. In her place was a flickering light. The light came and sat beside Brian. In the shade, he could barely make out her shape. He could feel it when she touched him but if she spoke, it sounded to him only like some lovely song which he could not understand.

The tune shifted and Annie suddenly materialized again, sitting next to him. He sat back, amazed. "How do you do that?"

She shook her head. " I don't know; I just do it and it works—most of the time. They said that only the firstborn of the Lammethan can do it. I don't know why. They say they can fly very far and fast, and they can lift heavy things when they're like this. It just makes me tired." She leaned against the tree.

"Can't we go back if you're like that?" asked Brian.

"No. Not yet anyway," she replied. "Only the strongest ones can go that far."

"We should go," said Brian, wolfing down some bread. "Talk to the High Council."

"Yes, let's find out what they want and what we can do next," she said, rising.

Brian stuffed half a loaf of bread in his mouth and nodded. "Umph," he said, getting up.

Annie stood up to go with him. He was so big. Even though she was bigger now, he still seemed huge. She always felt safer next to him. He had used that massive body to protect her many times. Maybe she would get the chance to do the same for him. The thought made her smile. They stepped out into the sun and she admired his fur, dark brown with auburn hints. She felt more like herself now that he was with her. If he accepted her like this, she could get used to it more easily.

"You look at me funny," he said, catching her watching him.

"Because you *are* funny," she said.

He broke out laughing. "*You're* funny," he said.

She decided she loved his face the most, especially when he laughed.

She led him down a road toward a terraced city built around the base of a towering mass of stone rising a thousand feet high from its center. The city was walled by a ring of tall trees like the ones surrounding the Circle of the Ancients on Cai-Amira, only taller and much older. Where the road met the trees, a great stone gate had been set in the trunks. Its massive, iron doors were wide open. Standing on pedestals at either side of the gate were two Faerie sentries: a male and a female. With their wings folded out of sight they looked just like humans to Brian.

The man was dark haired. His white tunic was embroidered with golden thread which gleamed in the sunlight. His sword hilt was set with beautiful designs in gold, as were both his belt and scabbard. He stood at ease, keeping watch over the sunlit valley to the southeast.

The auburn-haired woman on the other side of the gate was similarly clothed. She wore a long knife at her side and carried a bow with a quiver of arrows. The bow was made of some pale yellow substance, almost white. She raised her hand as they approached the gate.

"Hale, Annathía Sayacia das-Lammethan," she called, spreading her iridescent wings and bowing in Faerie greeting. "Welcome again, Snowdaughter, and the same welcome to your friend."

"Thanks," answered Annie, bowing awkwardly back. "We're supposed to talk to the High Council. How do we find them?"

The male guard laughed heartily. "Right there," he said, pointing at the great stone tower that dominated the city. "You could fly there easily, but I will call someone to guide you. The streets can be confusing to someone on foot." He lifted a curved horn to his lips and blew a series of long and short notes. A reply sounded from the southern guard tower not far away.

"Please enter and wait in the shade," said the female guard. "Your escort will be with you shortly."

Brian and Annie passed between the massive gates and sat on a carved bench just inside the arch. Soon they saw a rider dressed in green galloping down the flagstone paved street. At the arch, he came to a clattering stop and dismounted.

Brian liked his face immediately. The rider was clean shaven except for a dark moustache that drooped slightly at the corners of his mouth. His long, dark brown hair was bound behind him, like a horse's tail, with three bindings. The uppermost binding at the nape of his neck was his only adornment: a golden clip with a green gem set in it. His weapons were plain and practical: a sword and a long-bladed knife.

His horse was chestnut with brown tack. A thick green blanket protected its back from the well oiled saddle.

The rider smiled, bowed to Annie. "I am Falnor, Captain of the Green Guard, the Eyes of the South, Servant of Raealann the Keeper of the Green Stone, at your service." He looked at Annie, then at Brian, and then up to the guards. "You called for a guide to the Shioroth. May I ask who needs one?"

The male guard laughed. "The lady can fly, but the gruffen cannot," he said. "They are to speak with the High Council."

Falnor raised a thick eyebrow. "The Council would speak with the beast? Why?"

The female guard nodded. "It is said he slew Lazraak Snakehelm. Besides, you have not noticed that he wears the Valenblade."

Seeing the knife at Brian's side, the captain bowed again. "I'm sorry, sir. I meant no disrespect. If the lady will ride, my horse, Janus, will carry her. I will walk next to you, sir, if I may. What is your name?"

"What?" asked Brian.

"Brian P. Gruffenson," said Annie. "Call him Brian."

"Well met, Brian," said the captain. "Now, to the High Council. It's a bit of a walk."

CHAPTER 23

The Shioroth

Falnor helped Annie into the saddle, took Janus' reins and walked beside Brian as they proceeded into the city. Since the man had no wings, Brian figured he must be human.

"What is this place?" asked Annie.

"The city is called 'the Shioroth,' but the name refers specifically to the central tower," said Falnor, pointing to the massive monolith. "Most of the buildings are made of stone quarried from the Shioroth itself. Some have suggested the streets were laid out by Faeries who thought the winding paths were pretty. Unfortunately, the rest of us who can't fly take a lot longer to get anywhere because of it."

Janus' hooves clacked on the paving stones past layer upon layer of houses and gardens as Falnor led them up the switchbacks. People came to their doorways, windows and balconies to see the Snowdaughter and the gruffen pass by. Little children, grinning and curious, hid behind rain barrels, pillars and mothers' skirts. Brian noticed that none of the children had wings.

"Four sentinel towers guard the Shioroth, one at each point of the compass. They are attached to the Shioroth itself with bridges," continued Falnor; "but the city's true protection is the wall of trees where we met."

"Like the ones on the island," said Brian. "They smell the same." Then his face grew somber.

Falnor watched him with interest. "Do they?" he asked. "It makes sense that a floating island would have magical trees."

"I hope it still does," said Brian.

The captain nodded.

"What else can you tell us?" asked Annie.

"Though Dwarves and Elves pass through on occasion, mostly Faeries live here, along with some Humans. Men of the Green Guard guard the South Gate."

They were now at the base of a high stone wall near one of the great sentinel towers. "This is the South Gate," said Falnor.

Two soldiers of the Green Guard saluted and opened the iron gates for them. Janus whinnied as one of the stable boys ran to meet them. The young fellow took the reins from the captain with a bow, stealing a wide-eyed glance at the Faerie and the huge gruffen. Falnor helped Annie dismount and entrusted Janus to the stable boy. Then he led Annie and Brian across the courtyard past a tiered fountain surrounded by flowers. Brian and Annie followed the captain up the stone steps around the sentinel tower and found themselves on a wide wall encircling the central monolith. Between the wall and the monolith was a wide, grassy garden, strewn with wildflowers. Trees of many varieties grew here and there, in copses or solitude. A quiet stream meandered toward a marshy pond where red wing blackbirds flitted and called among the cattails.

Brian drank in all the rich scents. What a wonderful place, he thought. He looked at the people walking about in the grass or sitting in conversation under the trees. Some folk were short and squat, as if someone had smashed full grown humans down to stumps. By a grove of elm trees stood a group of very elegant people, most of whom had golden hair, pointed ears, and skin so fair it seemed to glow even in the shade. Their quick, graceful gestures as they talked gave Brian the impression that they were swift and agile. Around the bend were several people with wings of various colors including the same deep blue to be found in Annie's.

"So many different people!" exclaimed Brian.

"Dwarves, Elves, Faeries...everybody!" whispered Annie, her eyes bright. "Aren't they great?"

Falnor smiled.

"Who is who?" asked Brian.

"The short ones are Dwarves: elbow high and wonderfully strong," said Falnor. "Elves are the tall, fair-skinned ones. Faeries have beautiful wings. Both Elves and Faeries tend to be slender, though there are exceptions. Humans are just simpler all around—no wings, no pointed ears—just plain folks of all sizes."

Brian turned and looked back across the terraced city to the tree wall. The sun was sliding westward across the fields of grass and rolling hills toward a range of mountains.

"Follow me, please," said Falnor, gesturing toward a guarded door that led into the South sentinel tower. Inside, to their left, the stairway spiraled upward. To their right, it spiraled downward. They descended to another door that opened out to the garden. From there, they followed a wide path which crossed the meandering stream on a stone bridge. Out of habit, Brian looked for fish. There were no fish, but there were frogs.

Their path led to the main entrance of the Shioroth, a grand archway sculpted overhead with a great many designs, figures and fanciful creatures. Huge wooden doors nearly a foot thick hung open, allowing them into the arch. The doors were deeply carved with grand landscapes. The iron bracing was cleverly worked into the designs.

Brian, Annie and Falnor entered a spacious hallway lit by tall, thin windows cut through the stone, and two large glowing globes that hung from the vaulted ceiling on golden chains. The three approached a set of double doors twenty feet high, carved elaborately from slabs of a rich, reddish wood. Two white-robed Faerie women bowed silently and easily opened the doors for them, revealing a vast chamber. Inside, several people were in deep conversation around a massive table. A few turned their heads as the visitors entered and then went back to their conversation.

"The High Council," said Falnor, quietly. "We'll wait here a moment."

Brian stopped and looked up at the shafts of light streaming through a large, intricately designed window high on the west wall. The place smelled of stone, wax and wood, cloth, leather, paper and ink, among other scents that Brian's nose did not recognize.

On a signal from the white-haired man at the head of the table, the three approached. Captain Falnor's boots echoed on the smooth marbled floor.

The captain bowed low and said: "Members of the High Council, I bring you the Snowdaughter, Annathía Sayacia das-Lammethan, and the gruffen, Brian P. Gruffenson." He bowed again, and, with a smile and a nod to Brian and Annie, stepped back a bit and stood by quietly. All eyes turned toward the pair before the Council.

The white haired man in the tall chair rose from his seat showing a glimpse of his deep indigo-colored wings as he stood. "Welcome to the High Council, Annathía and Brian. I am Rohidan Shahan dak-Lammethan of the White Stone, and this is my wife, Arienne. These," he said, nodding to his left, "are Raealann and his kin, Men of the Green Stone." Then he nodded toward the tall, pale-skinned people seated to his right. "And these are Hassila and her kin, Elven folk of the Blue Stone."

Annie bowed like she had seen Falnor do. Brian just nodded.

Rohidan sat down and looked at Annie with a smile. "They say you have many questions, my daughter. You may be candid here; there is nothing to fear. Ask what you will, and speak your mind as you wish."

Annie blushed. "You look familiar. Have I seen you before?"

"Indeed you have, my dear," acknowledged Rohidan to a chorus of delighted laughter; "and none too soon. We met on Cai-Amira, in the Mind Ring. Bless you for taking my advice and eating the Trothianna fruit. For many years we longed for your reappearance. We had almost given up hope of finding you, but our call was answered in a most unexpected way." He turned to the gruffen. "To you, sir, we are forever grateful."

Brian thought he also recognized Rohidan, but something more pressing troubled him. "Our friends need help," he said abruptly. "Will you help?"

Rohidan nodded. "We will help any friends of yours, but we must wait until the Floating Island lands at Thihanan. The Firstborn are exhausted from the long journey and the rest of us cannot fly such distances. Painful as it is, we must await your friends here."

"Golrakken!" Brian interjected. "They're still there!"

"We have been told that the Golrakken sailed away quickly when the Firstborn arrived. Chasing them is futile, and we can do nothing more against them from here." Rohidan raised an eyebrow. "If your friends are as brave as you, they will do well."

Brian's eyes went from face to face looking for help. The fair haired woman seated next to Rohidan smiled at him. He recognized her also from his vision in the Watch House.

"We will aid you any way we can," she assured him. "We owe you that for saving Annathía."

Brian thought for a moment. "All right," he said. "If you will help, that's good."

"We do have some questions for you, Mr. Gruffenson," said Rohidan. "Will you answer them?"

"Sure," Brian said.

"This knife you carry," the old Faerie began, indicating the blade strapped over Brian's shoulder; "how did it come to you?"

Brian nodded. "Ender gave it to me. Don't know where he got it." There was a murmur of voices at the name of Ender. "Said it was supposed to be mine. Don't know why."

"Did you use it to kill Lazraak Snakehelm?" asked the Elder.

"What?" said Brian.

"Did you kill Lazraak Snakehelm with this blade?"

"I killed someone. Don't know his name. Just killed him. He was after Annie," the gruffen replied.

"You used only this blade you wear?"

"To kill him?" asked Brian. So many questions!

"Yes, did you kill him with this blade?"

"Yes," said Brian, his great brow was wrinkled deeply. "Almost cut his head off, then stabbed him in the chest so he was dead."

Rohidan looked around at the others at the table. "One more question, my friend. When you killed the Golrak, did the blade strike flesh and bone, or was his armor pierced?"

Brian was confused. "It cut everything: metal, hide, bone. Everything."

The members of the gathered High Council murmured in low voices.

"A test," said Hassila, Queen of the Elves. "Thorval Lighthammer forged a test into the Valenblade. Let the gruffen perform the test."

The others agreed.

"If you would, Brian," said Rohidan; "Please drive the blade into the floor at your feet."

Brian looked at Annie. She shrugged.

"Why?" he asked.

"It is a test," said Rohidan. "If you would, please."

Without ceremony, Brian pulled out the knife, knelt down and drove the blade hilt deep into the marble floor. Several of the High Council gasped. Just as easily, he withdrew the knife and slipped it back in the sheath.

"It cuts everything," he said, simply.

"On the contrary," said the Elder Faerie. "Only in the hands of a true Valen does it cut everything." He bowed to Brian. "Please forgive the examination, sir Brian. We did not know who you were. Clearly, you are a Valen."

Brian's forehead wrinkled even more.

"You see the Golrakken are not truly dead when the body dies by the sword. Only the Valenblade can actually kill them, and only when wielded by a worthy Valen. Had his body been slain by another weapon, his spirit could have returned in another body, but the Valenblade in your hands destroyed him utterly. He no longer walks the earth. Lazraak is dead indeed."

"He seemed dead to me," said Brian.

A bench was brought for the guests and Rohidan asked them to sit down at the council table with the rest of them.

Then the Elder Faerie continued: "Lazraak was one of the most feared of the Golrakken. Second in command to Karkaan, he was at least as cruel. His misdeeds were legendary. Many years ago, Lazraak had led an army of Gray Warriors across the Abandoned Land, ransacking our outlying villages and homesteads. No one knew what became of those poor souls for none ever returned. Though more than a hundred years have passed since Snakehelm was last seen in North Agoria, news of his death has been long awaited."

Little of this made sense to Brian. Unfortunately, most of what followed was just as confusing.

"The knife you carry is called the Valenblade," Rohidan explained. "When the Faeries ventured south across the Savian Sea to live in this land, they were met by the Elves who already lived here. The Elven welcome was warm and sincere, and they were willing to share this great continent with us. The Elven people lived to the west, over the mountains. It was they who forged the Valenblade as a gift of friendship and solidarity. They gave it to the Golrakken, who were, at that time, much different from the gray horde against whom you fought. Indeed, the Golrakken were our most trusted allies, their veins filled with Faerie blood. They were wingless, but Faerie, nonetheless.

"Orkaan was kown as the Valen, Chief of Warriors and leader of the Golrakken, the warrior clan. My people were the Lammethan, the diplomats, led by Reidan, my forefather. Orkaan and Reidan were longtime friends. They were the Keepers of the Four Stones of the Shioroth, the heirlooms of our forefathers. The Golrakken kept the Red and Blue Stones. The Lammethan kept the White and Green Stones. Too adventurous to remain on the Old Continent, they gathered their people and set out in ships to find the origins of the Stones and, perhaps, a world of their own.

"Ancient history records how the Stones were cut from the top of the Shioroth, this very Tower, a pillar of rock that shot up from the earth long ago. Each of the four towers in the Uppermost Garden is at the terminus of a vein of rock. The Stones were given to the Faeries many thousands of years ago by the Stonecutter. They were entrusted for safekeeping as the Stonecutter fled from his brother.

"When the Faeries landed on this shore, they found the pillar of rock, and since others already lived nearby, they made peace with the Elves. As a token of trust, the Elves fashioned the Valenblade and, in exchange, the Golrakken gave them the Blue Stone. In time, Men from the south ventured northward and also made an alliance with the Faeries. They sent stone cutters, masons and sculptors, and carved the Shioroth and its four uppermost towers, and helped to build the city. In return, we gave to them the Green Stone and asked them to join the High Council.

"For twelve generations, peace reigned. The lands around us were kept clear of goblins, dragons, ogres and the like. The Valenblade was handed down from eldest son to eldest son, and with each passing, it was given more powers. When it came to Karkaan, his gaze drifted eastward, for a great power had been amassing there, and he wished to know it. From the Crimson Throne, he sought out Morvassus. Little did he know the power he had encountered. It called him, and he went to find it. Morvassus reforged the Valenblade and gave it the power to sunder the souls of Faeries. Karkaan never returned. Instead, he remained eastward, in the mountains. The Golrakken began to drift eastward to join him. We tried to restore our relationship, but we were rebuffed soundly. We had to resort to spies. When we discovered they were building an army against us, we fought them openly. The war lasted years and the battles were heart-breaking.

"The Golrakken changed. Their appearance grew more ghastly and grotesque. When the war came here, to the Shioroth, I wrested the Valenblade from Karkaan, but I could not kill him. Before we could finish the battle, Morvassus called the Golrakken away. They fled to the sea and over many decades, they turned into what they are now. We have handed down the Valenblade among the Lammethan ever since. Some were true Valens.

"Norhidan Nightwing, Annathía's father, was the last Valen to carry the Valenblade. He wielded it well, learning more than any others before him the extent of its powers. Not long after the Snowdaughter was born, he was drawn south and disappeared, the Valenblade went with him. We feared the worst: that he had been turned like the Golrakken. Though we still do not know what became of him and his beautiful wife..."

The old Faerie's voice trailed off and he paused for a moment. When he could continue, he said: "We are grateful that the Snowdaughter has returned safely. To find the Valenblade in the hands of a true Valen is more than we had hoped for."

Rohidan looked at the gruffen. "So now you, Brian, carry it to our halls once more," he said quietly. "No one will take it from you; it is not a thing to be taken. You may use it as you wish, only know this: it has the work of Morvassus in it and must be handled carefully."

Brian had almost fallen asleep during this story but now he felt his fur standing up on end. He stifled a growl.

Hassila the Elven queen said: "Tell us more about 'Ender,' Mr. Gruffenson."

Though her request was simple, Brian found himself stifling another growl.

"Will you help me if I do?" he asked.

"We expect to help," said Rohidan. "It all depends on who these people are. If we know them better, we will be better able to help."

Brian nodded, and, in very simple terms, told them about Ender and Calicia.

"They're good," he concluded. "I trust them."

Annie agreed.

"Besides," said Brian; "he's 'Ender' because he ended the bad...thing..."

"The Morve?" prompted Rohidan.

"That thing," said Brian.

"None of us has ever seen this Ender," said Raealann, the leader of the Men, and the Keeper of the Green Stone. "You say he lives on the floating island? It wanders the seas without a pilot."

The Elder Faerie shook his head. "Cai-Amira was abandoned when the Golrakken turned. We could not control it; it would not respond to the

Lammethan," he said. "But it was Palanthar who suggested I search for it from the White Tower, and because of him, I found it—and because of that," he added; "we found Annathía."

"Palanthar? You mean Ilstar, the wanderer?" said Raealann, the king of Men.

"Do not be so astonished," said the Elder. "If Ilstar trained the one who ended the Morve, there is far more to him than we know. Brian, do you know how Ender came to own the Valenblade?"

"Don't know," Brian answered. "Said the Great Master told him to give it to me."

"We should find Palanthar and speak with him. One way or another, we shall need them on our side," said Rohidan. His face clouded for a moment as he considered this. Then he looked up at the gruffen again and smiled. "Brian, you are welcome here. I am sorry you arrive at a time of turmoil. The winds whisper of war. Still, two lost treasures have returned: the Valenblade and the Snowdaughter. You are responsible for both. Our people have new hope. I thank you on behalf of the High Council for your candor today."

Brian just looked at him, quizzically.

"He's glad you told the truth," Annie whispered.

"Sure," stammered Brian. "Sure."

Arienne rose from her seat. "It has been a long day for these two. Let them rest. Brian, Annathía's kin shall provide for you. Young one, remind Shianna that you are all expected at the Tree for the evening meal. Tonight the Lammethan finally celebrate your return."

Brian followed Annie out of the council chamber into the hallway where they met Annie's aunt, Shianna. The Faerie was about the same height as her niece. By human reckoning, she was nearing her third century, but in Faerie years, she was only just past her prime. Brian was relieved that she was not as somber as almost everyone in the Council Chamber. She smiled and laughed easily as she led them out by the Westgate where they could see the Faerie dwellings that covered half the city. They followed Shianna down the winding streets until they arrived at the house where she and her husband, Erdan, lived. Shianna showed Annie to her room and then asked Brian if he would be comfortable using the bed in the guest room.

"Might break it," Brian said, hesitantly. "Stone is good."

Shianna laughed. "Please use the bed, or at least test it for us. Erdan would welcome any test of a bed he built!"

The gruffen ambled over to it and sat down gingerly. The bed was built well indeed and though it creaked a little, it did not give.

"It's good," said Brian with a grin. He had slept in very few beds but he was beginning to enjoy them.

Shianna showed Annie to her room next door and then headed off to prepare the evening meal.

Annie went to the west window and looked out. When she turned around again, Brian was standing just inside the door.

"What?" she asked.

"Don't know," Brian responded. He looked around for a bit and then said: "What if it's a dream? What if a fat little girl is dying in a dark sack? What if Golrakken are...what if all this—" he waved his arm at the room "What if all this is just a dream?" He slumped down, sat on the floor and leaned against the door frame.

"Maybe none of this is real," he said with a big sigh. "I should be in the woods. With animals." He leaned his head on a leathery hand.

Annie crossed her arms and leaned back against the window sill. "If you go to the woods, I'm going with you."

"Why bother?" asked Brian.

"It doesn't matter," said Annie. "I'm glad you're here. It is strange. Everybody's happy and they all say they're family, but I don't know anybody. Nobody but you, Brian."

Brian nodded his big, furry head. "Tired," he said.

"Me, too," said Annie. "I'm going to rest a little."

"Good," said Brian. With that, he stretched his thick legs out, right where he was by the door, and closed his eyes.

Annie came over and sat on his lap, leaning back on his big, furry chest. He wrapped one big arm around her and she turned so she could lay her head on his shoulder.

Brian took a deep breath and smelled her smell. It was a bit different, but it was still Annie. With that thought, he let himself drift into sleep.

215

CHAPTER 24

A Night of Celebration

Brian awoke lying on the floor by Annie's doorway. Annie was not around. He was disoriented for a moment before he remembered where he was. With a big yawn, he got up and went to the window. The sun had set but there was still a little light outside. Next to the house was a large, grassy area. Flames flickered on tall poles. Several long tables had been arranged to form three sides of a square. Shining lamps were placed in a row down the center of each table. The Faeries were gathering by a massive tree which stood behind the center table.

His sharp eyes noticed that a woman who had her back to him was unlike the others. She was fair haired and had no wings. She was very merry. Everyone who talked to her came away laughing. When she turned around, Brian recognized her as Arienne, the wife of Rohidan, whom he had seen at the High Council.

He heard movement in the hallway and turned to see Annie coming into the room. She looked even more different now. Her hair was threaded with gold and tiny jewels. She wore a new sky blue dress laced with gold. She sat down on the bed across from him and tucked her bare feet beneath her.

"We're the special guests tonight," she said, looking out the window at the preparations for the feast. "I'm glad you'll be with me. I have a lot of questions but I don't want to find out the answers all by myself. We're going to sit together."

"Good," said Brian.

Annie smiled. "Look at this pretty dress!" she said.

"Good," said Brian, not knowing what else to say.

Annie looked at him for a minute.

"What?" he asked.

"Wait right there," she said. "I have something I think you'll like."

She got up from the window seat and went to her room. When she returned, she had what looked like a stick with long, thin thorns stuck in it, all in a row.

"This is a comb," she said. "Now sit still."

Carefully, Annie combed the tangles out of the long hair on his head and combed his beard until it lay smooth on his chest. There were many snags, but Brian didn't flinch. Though he didn't usually like sitting still, he decided the comb felt nice so he let her finish..

When she was done, Annie stood back and beamed. "I've always wanted to do that!" she said. "I think you look very nice."

"Good," said Brian.

"And one more thing," continued the Faerie. "Rohidan says you're supposed to carry the Valenblade."

"Why?" Brian asked. "I just eat."

Annie handed him the knife belt. " It won't be in your way."

He shrugged, strapped it on over his shoulder.

In a few minutes, they were called out to the garden. A hundred Faeries turned to look as they passed through the gathering. The guests of honor were directed to the head table where Rohidan and Arienne stood waiting.

Arienne took Annie's hand in hers and introduced herself formally: "I am Arienne, the partner of Rohidan who is the Eldest of the Faeries and the Keeper of the White Stone. We request the pleasure of your company at table." Though her manner was formal, her expression was not, which made Brian feel more at ease. She took his arm and brought him to a very large chair near the center of the main table. Annie was seated to his left and Arienne sat down on his right.

The gruffen pointed a thick finger at Arienne's back. "No wings," he said. "Elf?"

Arienne smiled and winked. "Yes, an Elf among Faeries!"

When all were gathered, Rohidan stood up and everyone got quiet. "Tonight, we drink the long awaited cup," he said. "Our hope had nearly waned, yet, even as we despaired, the Lost One was already in the Chrysalis." He raised a goblet and all the Faeries raised theirs. "Tonight, we no longer pray for the return of the Snowdaughter. Tonight, we toast her arrival! To the return of Annathía Sayacia das-Lammethan! Our house is full again!"

There was a loud cheer and they all drank. Then came the food, more than one could possibly describe. While they ate, Arienne, chatted easily with Annie and Brian. From time to time Rohidan added a wry comment or two.

As his hunger waned, Brian settled back into his chair. No one seemed to care that he had devoured an entire chicken, bones and all. No one minded that he didn't understand half of what they said or did. The food was tasty and plentiful, the laughter was light, and he felt good in the company of so many well-wishers.

As the desserts were served, many Faeries came up to the head table to meet the guests of honor. Soon, Brian and Annie were thoroughly befuddled by all the names. A group of older men asked to see the Valenblade but when Brian offered to let them hold it, they merely bowed, smileed and told him it was not for their hands. The women were delighted to see Annie; a few of the matrons wept and kissed her. Shianna came and sat by her for some time while she talked with the others.

After awhile, they all left the tables and gathered on the other side of the tree where some of the men had lit a large fire. Many more winged folk were there.

"These Faeries are from all over the city," Arienne told Brian. "Every member of the Lammethan family is here tonight."

As they formed a semi-circle around the fire, Brian's heart began to pound. He knew this place! He had seen it before! He had no clue what it meant, but this scene was unfolding exactly as he saw it in the Watch House on Cai-Amira.

Rohidan, the Elder, stood before the fire and spoke again.

"Our guests of honor should know the full measure of our celebration tonight. They have not heard the tale of the Lost One. Tonight of all nights, one last time, a bard should sing the Song of the Snowdaughter."

Rohidan sat by Arienne as a minstrel stepped in front of the fire. To cheers and shouts of approval, the bard made a sweeping bow, and then took up an instrument with many strings. As he played, he sang with a most enchanting voice:

> On a day the world lay covered in snow, a daughter was born to Norhidan dak-Lammethan, Nightwing, son of Foridan, and to Veranna, great-granddaughter of Rohidan. She was called Annathía, "Snowdaughter," which in the ancient tongue also means "Last Child." She was, we knew, the last of our kind. Through Spring, Summer and Autumn, she flourished and grew in the Shioroth where she was born.
>
> The seers had long foretold that a child would be born in winter. And when this child was born, they said, the end of the age was nigh. That the child should be born a daughter was unexpected, but the Snowdaughter dazzled us all: by the time the snows reached the valley once more, Annathía was walking and talking
>
> A pair of years were lived in peace. Then from his seat on the Crimson Throne, Nightwing, our Valen, learned of magic further south, beyond the Forgotten Sea. This magic, so the Valen heard, would change the fate of all. His daughter need not be the last; the Faeries could continue. The three of them would venture south and bring this magic back. The Lammethan would begin anew, our children even stronger. So the Firstborn ferried them over sea, to

the Point of No Return. From there, the family flew alone. We sadly watched them sail away, their daughter held in arms of light, with hope in their hearts and no land in sight.

The years passed by and still the Valen and Veranna did not return. The Firstborn searched the waters, two by two and three by three. None but the swift and the strongest went; but none returned with news. Though several failed, and lives were lost, not one, it seemed, had found a trace of Norhidan Nightwing, Veranna and the Snowdaughter in any place.

Then Mohidan and Galidan flew, both swift and strong, to find the truth. When Mohidan returned—alas! —his feet touched on Thihanan's sands, and there he breathed his last. His right fist held the wedding rings of Nightwing and Veranna, and in his left was clenched a lock of our Snowdaughter's burnished hair. The mystery of their fate had died with Mohidan; we knew no more, and we were left in sorrow for tomorrow and tomorrow.

Do not give up, O Firstborn! We beg you search again! For all we have is mystery, and we must know the end. With you we sail the endless sky and watch with bated breath. For all we know today is hope, and all we fear is death.

Many in the gathered throng were weeping, for here the song usually ended. On this night, the bard struck another chord with renewed vigor and sang out a new verse, loud and clear:

The Shioroth awoke to flowers, with all the world in Spring. Our Arienne did meet the Wanderer in fields of green. He had a bit of news, he said, "Make haste, do not delay. The smell of Trothianna rides the wind from far away."

"For whom," she cried; "would Thricewood bloom, and where would it alight?"

"The Floating Island," said the man, and vanished from her sight.

So filled with hope, now Rohidan flew to the northern tower and sat upon the White Throne where he searched that very hour. Yes, Cai-Amira's magic lived, and there the Elder found the Snowdaughter, the Last Child, in a Mind Ring on a mound.

Then, out on the Forgotten Sea, Golrakken warriors sailed with Dragonhelm and Snakehelm on the winds that whipped and wailed. They landed on the island where they fought a battle royal while overhead and on the sea the skies and waters boiled. When

Snakehelm found the Chrysalis, our hopes might have been dashed, but Brian took the Valenblade and through the armor slashed. One cut, and that was all it took, blade had cut through Lazraak's soul, and tore it all asunder.

(Great cheers erupted at this point in the narrative and they had to be quieted before the singer could continue, but continue he did, with even greater fervor.)

The mighty blade of Norhidan, the Valenblade of old is with us now, and in this hand are legends yet untold. A single stroke from Gruffenson has made the Golrak bleed and with that stroke a thousand broken hearts have now been freed.

Shout, all who stand for freedom! Sing, all who strive for good! Let cheers and laughter fill the air from grasslands to the wood! The Valenblade returns once more! Our Snowdaughter is here! The Last Child is no longer lost! Sing out for all to hear!

With that, the Faeries were on their feet and in the air, shouting in approval. The cheering went on for several minutes. In the midst of it, Rohidan led Brian out in front of them all. The roar from the gathered throng was deafening.

Finally, Rohidan raised his hand and spoke in a strange tongue. Though Brian could not understand the words, he knew he was being discussed. This was the scene which he had envisioned in the Watch House. He watched now as everyone settled back to the ground. All faces became somber.

The Lammethan were deciding something. Several voiced opinions. The two strongest voices came from the eldest of the Firstborn. Then there was silence.

Rohidan smiled and nodded. "Then it is up to the Snowdaughter. Shianna has explained it to you, Annathía. What do you say?"

Annie stepped forward into the firelight.

"I will," said Annie. "He should be family. He's the best friend I ever had."

She turned back and ran to Brian, throwing her arms around him. He could feel that familiar ferocity in her hug, only stronger. This was the same little girl who gathered nuts and berries, the same little girl who slept so soundly in his lap those many nights huddled in the cave. Maybe she was bigger, and maybe she had wings now, but she was still the same! This really was Annie. Brian had never seen her so happy.

The Elder stood beside them and put his hand up on Brian's broad shoulder. In a loud voice, he announced: "Valen dak-Lammethan!"

Brian was utterly unprepared for what happened next. Another glorious shout arose from the Lammethan. He looked down at Annie in his arms. She just beamed back at him. "What are they saying?" he bellowed.

"They want you to join the family," she shouted back. "Do you want to?"

Brian thought for a moment. "Don't know family," he said. "What do you think?"

"I already said what I think," she replied. "You're my best friend. To me, that's as much family as anyone. Since you have the Valenblade, that makes you the Valen like my father was."

"What's the 'Valen?'" asked Brian. People were starting to calm down so he didn't have to shout.

"The Valen is the one who can use the knife like that. My father was the last one," she replied; "so I get to decide if you'll be the next Valen. If you say yes, you will be family and everything we have is yours."

"I don't need anything," said Brian. "What's the Valen do?"

"Helps the Faeries fight their enemies," she said.

"Many enemies?" asked Brian.

"I don't know," said Annie; "but you won't have to fight alone. All of them—all of *us*—will fight with you."

"OK. What if I don't?" said Brian.

Annie smiled. "Shianna said they'll always care for you," she said. "This is just a really close good friend, as if you were born from the same parents."

Brian took a deep breath. His brow wrinkled for a minute, then grew smooth.

"Good," he said. "Family then."

Turning to the crowd before the fire, Rohidan raised his voice again. "Listen, Lammethan, this is the declaration of Rohidan the Eldest: let the name of Brian P. Gruffenson be spoken with the highest honor, and may he be known from this day forward as Valen dak-Lammethan, Lord of Thains, Protector of the Lammethan. So says the Snowdaughter! So say we all!"

The Lammethan cheered again. Brian smiled and set Annie back on her feet.

Rohidan finally raised his hand for quiet and turned to Brian and Annie. "Dear children," he said. "Welcome to you both!"

Many musicians began to play and Brian was swept into a Faerie dance as someone took his hand and someone else took Annathía's. An average man would have tired quickly but Brian was strong and quick enough to keep up with the nimble Faeries. Though he never figured out the intricate dance, he was always being led or handed off to someone else so he was never lost or in the way. For a long time they swirled round and round, weaving their way out of one circle and into another. As the dance grew more lively, the circles began to leap and fly over and under each other, somehow always managing to weave in such a way that Brian and Arienne, the only two without wings, never had to fly. On it went for several hours, leaping and dancing in ever more marvelous patterns until Brian's head swam with the music.

Some time later, he and Annie retired from the dance, laughing and breathing hard. They found a comfortable spot near the grand tree. In a moment, Arienne came and sat with them to watch the Faerie dancers take to the air, the intricate patterns lit from below by the blazing firelight and lit from above by the spangled heavens.

CHAPTER 25

The Crimson Tower

When morning peeked over the hills, Brian was already awake and sitting by the window. He had risen with the first birdsong and was anxious for the rest of the world to wake up. As soon as the light touched the top of the wall of trees, he quietly went into Annie's room. She lay asleep on her bed, her hair loose to one side, one arm pointed languidly toward the window. He came to the edge of the bed and gently touched her serene face. She opened her eyes and smiled.

"Food," said Brian. "Smells good."

"Let's go get some," said Annie, rising. "You go ahead. I'll be there in a moment, but you have to promise to leave some for me."

"I promise," said Brian.

He followed his nose to the kitchen where Shianna was brewing some wonderful beverage and the aroma of a good breakfast filled the air. She smiled when she saw Brian.

"You are called to the Council again today," she said. "Rohidan asked me to bring you back to the Tower. There is much to discuss. He is pleased with what happened last night and looks forward to seeing you again."

"Good," said Brian. "Me, too."

After a delicious breakfast, the three set off for the central tower of the Shioroth. As they wound through the streets, the curious leaned out of their windows to catch a glimpse of the new Valen and the Snowdaughter.

Shianna explained to Brian and Annie the kind of council they were about to attend. All manner of folk would be represented.

"The leaders of each different kind of people sit at the table on great chairs, with their kin seated on benches behind them," Shianna explained as they walked up the winding streets. "You will recognize King Raealann who rules the Men of the Green Stone. Queen Hassila has brought a delegation of the Elves of the Blue Stone with her.

"Also present will be the Dwarves from the quarries and mines throughout the mountains that run between the plains and the vast desert to the west. Dwarves generally do not attend the Council, preferring to stay out of anything they believe does not concern them directly. They are self-governed but keep no strict boundaries except where veins of metal or rock are concerned. These they mark carefully and will guard fiercely, even from their own kind. We do not interfere with their internal affairs since they live peacefully on our borders and keep the mountain passes open and safe for friendly travel. They also provide (for a fair price) all the metal used by the neighboring countries. Dwarves live mostly underground but are remarkably clever in the woods, rivaling all but the Elves in stealth. The mountains are riddled with their tunnels and I am told that one can never tell when or where a Dwarf might suddenly appear. They are handy with the sword and prefer axes over bows and arrows. By the age of ten, a Dwarf boy is expected to split a sapling at twenty yards with an iron axe he forged himself."

Shianna's face clouded. "There is a reason why the Dwarves have come to the Council today. Recent tales of terror in the lower mines have reminded some elders of an ancient legend, so the heads of various Dwarven families have come to the Shioroth, both to tell their news and to seek wisdom from the learned ones.

"You shall also see three of the four remaining Small Giants. These are the last descendants of the Great Giants of the Carven Canyon where the Volgan River still cuts a frothing path through ancient layers of rock. They are taller than you, Brian, perhaps by a head, and have long gray hair and gray beards. They are known for both wisdom and strength. They may seem old, but they would still be a match for any of us in a fight. Rohidan sent Faerie couriers requesting their presence and I hear these three arrived early this morning after traveling nonstop on foot for two days."

Brian had difficulty following all this. So many people! Annie asked a lot of questions but Brian couldn't quite follow that either. Eventually, they came to the garden. Shianna bid them goodbye as they entered the Shioroth.

Brian and Annie were ushered directly into the Council Chambers where they were introduced to all of the people Shianna had just mentioned. It was a dizzying array of characters and Brian just tried to nod along as each person's name and title was given.

Finally, after everyone was seated, Rohidan addressed the High Council. "Much news has come to us in the last year," he said. "The most recent news seems to bring both hope and fear. The Snowdaughter has returned and brings with her the gruffen, Brian, a great surprise. The Valenblade which Nightwing took to the south accepts his wielding, so the Faeries have a new Valen.

"Brian drove the Valenblade through the heart of Lazraak Dragonhelm, so that story comes to a sad but final ending. From Brian's account, we also know that the Golrakken sail the Dorvan Sea. We also hear of a new threat from the land beyond: one who calls himself 'the King' and creates goblins from animals. He has amassed great strength and pursued Annathía and the Valen many miles.

"And I fear our most deadly enemy, Morvassus, rises again in the east."

During the discussion that followed, there was much recounting of lore, interrupted periodically by arguments around whether or not Morvassus could possibly still be alive. The Golrakken were discussed at length and much was made over the death of Lazraak. Brian tried to pay attention but by the time a rest was called at noon he was glad to take a short walk before he filled his gruffen stomach. All the talk was giving him a headache. The High Council met again after lunch but the talking went on and on. For the rest of the day, Brian struggled to keep from either falling asleep or bellowing out "*do* something!"

When the Council finally retired, Brian and Annie were shown to new quarters on the north side of the Tower. The gruffen was fidgety from having sat all day so he and Annie went out into the night to walk along the top of the inner wall that bordered the garden. As they passed the south end, they saw Captain Falnor in the yard below, talking to the horse master. The captain noticed them up on the wall, excused himself and came up to join them.

"Good evening, Snowdaughter and Valen!" said the captain with a bow.

Annie gave him a courtesy—something she vaguely remembered from childhood and had recently relearned to do. Brian just nodded.

"I enjoyed hearing the Faerie music from a distance last night," said Falnor. "Good that you had some cheer before today's Council meeting. Lots of talk."

"Very dull," said Brian.

Falnor smiled, knowingly. "They don't seem to do much do they? I also prefer action to talk. Trust me: once Rohidan is sure what is to be done, he will not waste time. I admire the Small Giants, though. Very wise and very patient but never slow. I have learned a lot from listening when they speak and watching when they act."

The three of them walked along the wall in the cool evening air, talking about this and that until Brian's headache finally went away. By the time Falnor escorted them to their quarters, the sky was a black blanket covered with scattered stars.

* * *

"Brian!" whispered Annie. "Wake up! Follow me—and bring the Valenblade."

Instantly awake, Brian grabbed the long knife and slipped the belt over his head. "Where are we going?" asked the gruffen.

"We're supposed to go to the top of the Shioroth and meet Rohidan and Arienne," said Annie, in a hushed voice. "I don't know why."

Brian's forehead wrinkled as he followed Annie outside to where Shianna stood waiting.

"In there," said Shianna, pointing to a place where several blocks of solid stone appeared to have slid out from the wall, allowing access to an empty chamber just large enough to fit four people. Brian and Annie stepped inside. Shianna did not follow.

"Are you coming?" asked Annie.

"No," said Shianna. "The Uppermost Garden is reserved for the Keepers of the Stones and the Valen." She stood back as the stone blocks resealed the outer wall of the chamber.

Brian smelled fresh air and looked up to see that chamber had no ceiling. Far above them, the shaft opened to the night sky. Slowly, the floor began to rise, lifting them up the shaft, very much like the platform that had lowered them into the cave when they went to Cai-Amira, except in the opposite direction. In a few moments, the platform came to a stop at the very top of the Shioroth. Here, far above the city, lay a wide ring of lush green grass surrounding a bubbling spring sixty paces in diameter.

At each point of the compass stood a tower, its base half in, half out of the water. Each door was set fifteen feet above the ground, facing inward toward the fountain. Rising from the green grass between the towers rose four footbridges just wide enough for two to walk abreast. They arched out over the water to a circular walkway elevated fifteen feet in the air and encircling the bubbling center of the pool. Like alternating spokes from the same wheel, four other footbridges led from the circular walkway to the doors of the four towers. There was no direct route to any tower; one would first have to climb a footbridge to the center of the pool, follow the circular walkway a short distance, and then turn and cross another footbridge to the tower door.

Three of the towers were the same size, but the northern tower was taller and proportionately larger in circumference than the others. Just under the spire of each tower was a cylindrical chamber surrounded by a narrow walkway rimmed with battlements. Each of those chambers was ringed with windows, evenly spaced. The windows of the eastern tower were dark, but those of the other three were lit softly from within. The western tower glowed blue, the southern tower glowed green and the chamber in the northern tower radiated white light.

Brian looked out across the plains to the distant mountains. From this high vantage point, he could see for many leagues by the light of the moon. Annie tugged on his arm. "We're supposed to go to the northern tower," she said.

They climbed to the circular walkway and crossed the footbridge and entered through a stone door that swung silently shut behind them. Brian's shoulders barely fit from wall to wall in the steep, narrow, circular stairway. The white light from the upper room grew as they reached the top. They entered directly into the room as if climbing up into an attic. Overhead, the ceiling rose nearly twenty feet into the point of the spire. The floor was of mostly white marble laced with veins of pale peach. Seams in the floor marked out curious designs that reminded Brian of the ones he had seen in the clearing of the King and in the banquet hall in the Citadel. The floor itself seemed to be the only light source in the room.

In the very center of the room stood a great throne made of the same marble as the floor and marvelously carved in a shape that reminded Brian of eagles. Two great wings reached upward to form the back, their tips almost touching twelve feet above the floor. The armrests were like twin eagles, their great clawed legs standing on the floor in front and their tails stretched out behind them to the floor, supporting the chair. Their outer wings swept back and outward.

Rohidan and Arienne were standing by the eastern windows and turned as Brian and Annie entered. Brian thought Arienne looked sad.

Rohidan gave Brian a tired smile. "Welcome, Valen dak-Lammethan," he said with a bow. "This is the Tower of the White Stone, the place where the Eldest of the Lammethan have sat for centuries and looked out across the land. When peace reigned, the Eldest could speak freely with other Faeries in the Mind Rings and follow the progress of the Floating Islands. Those days have mostly past."

He paused and shook his head. "I have sat on the White Throne tonight and what I have seen troubles me. The Golrakken muster for war. Morvassus has arisen anew and draws fell allies to himself. Other lands such as your own have fallen under domination. We may not survive the onslaught. The Valen's help will be of great comfort in our time of need."

Brian's forehead wrinkled again. "What can the Valen do that you can't?" he asked.

Rohidan looked again out of the eastern window and then turned back to Brian. "The Valen can do many things, Brian, but even if you do them, the war may still be lost. You have the Valenblade; that is a great power already. You are also a creature unlike any we've ever known. What you, personally, can and cannot do remains a mystery but I believe you are destined to walk a path not open to the rest of us."

Annie asked: "So what does he have to do? What can I do?"

Arienne took her hand and kissed it. "If you are anything like your mother, you will do what you believe is right and nothing will stop you. As for Brian, he can use the Valenblade as it was designed to be used.

"If Morvassus gathers strength, he will not be long coming to the Shioroth to seek the White Throne for himself. Should he find the Valenblade idle, he will take it. Then no one would survive, not even the Golrakken. He would enslave all of us. Under his power, we would become fearful, twisted, violent and hateful. The Golrakken are already twisted, but they still act on their own. Even that would be taken from them. All would do evil not for their own greed or pride but according to the whimsy of Morvassus."

Annie's mouth was open. "How do we fight him?"

"Many have asked that question," said Rohidan. "Not even the Small Giants have found the answer. Up till now, the questioners have all been Faeries, Elvenfolk, Men and Dwarves. No one like Brian has existed before. Our hope is that the Valen may ask the question and finally learn the answer."

"What answer?" asked Brian. "Don't know about the Valen or the knife. It killed an enemy. So? What difference does a gruffen make?"

"We don't know," said Arienne. "Our skills are not in matters of war. The Golrakken understood it far better. They were always the most battle ready."

The gruffen asked again: "So?"

Rohidan pointed out the windows to where the craggy outline of a jagged mountain range blocked out the stars on the eastern horizon. Directly southeast, ominously close, stood the darkened tower of the Crimson Stone, the ancient tower of the Golrakken. Brian looked down on its spire and battlements.

"From the Crimson Throne, the Valen may see as far as his eye wishes to roam. From there, Karkaan Dragonhelm, Valen dak-Golrakken, once surveyed this land, saw where troops were needed, and came to aid with swiftness and force. His son, Lazraak, would have succeeded him in time. The Golrakken were doomed when Karkaan gazed into the Morve, to the heart of Morvassus, and became converted. The Golrakken would have conquered us all had not the Valenblade fallen into our hands. Only then did we turn the tide."

The Elder Faerie turned his eyes to Brian. "Only the wielder of the Valenblade can sit upon the Crimson Throne and claim it. No one has been able to sit in the Crimson Tower since the departure of Norhidan, Annathía's father. Perhaps you may claim the throne as he did. Others have tried and failed. Some flew and some climbed the outside of the Crimson Tower only to fall lifeless from the battlements, as if rejected as intruders. None of them held the Valenblade. You do. It is the key to unlocking the Tower, and you must decide if you will attempt it."

"You take it," said Brian, pulling the knife from its sheath and holding it out.

Rohidan shook his head. "The Valenblade has come to you," he said. "I hold the White Stone. Its powers are weakened when the holder wields the weapons of war."

Brian turned the knife over in his hand. When he first saw it in the weapons room on Cai-Amira, it was just a knife. It cut more easily than any other knife, but that was all.

"Why me?" he asked, finally.

The Eldest shook his head again. "That is not the question. Rather ask what you will do with it."

Brian scowled. "I don't know. Cut things? Like what?"

"The secrets of its powers are hidden in the Crimson Tower. Once the Golrakken departed, Norhidan dared to enter and discover them. His strength was multiplied in the Crimson Tower and he learned the ways of war. We do not yet know why he went southward and was lost." Rohidan turned to Annie. She stood motionless. If she knew more, she offered nothing.

The Elder Faerie continued: "Riders of the Green Stone have been sent to Thihanan. Perhaps the Floating Island will arrive and the one you call Ender will tell us more."

"If he's still alive," said Brian, his fur bristling again.

"True," said Rohidan. "For now, the answers to most of our questions remain locked in the Crimson Tower."

Brian looked over at the dark spire. "So I go there to find out," he stated flatly. "If I don't come back, then what?"

"For that I do not have an answer," said Rohidan.

The gruffen snorted uncomfortably.

Arienne touched his shoulder. "We will not send you against your will."

The gruffen looked away from the eastern windows. "Maybe I die. Maybe I don't. Nobody knows."

He looked at the marble floor. The faces of his friends appeared and disappeared in the swirling patterns at his feet. He saw Aaron and Lia, Mari, Owler, Ender and Calicia. Suddenly, he remembered Holren falling from the rocks into the river, and the face of Karkaan as the great trees fell around the Circle of the Ancients. The fur on the back of his neck stood out like spikes now, and his face grew hot. The Valenblade was still in his hand. He could almost feel it piercing the armor of the Golrak at the foot of the Chrysalis tree.

"I'm going," he said. He turned abruptly and started down the stairs. Annie was behind him in a heartbeat, leaving Rohidan and Arienne in the White Tower.

Once outside, the two walked quickly around the circular walkway to the footbridge leading to the Crimson Tower. The moon shone on the dark battlements. In another hour it would be dawn. At the footbridge, Annie stopped Brian and threw her arms around his neck. He picked her up in a bear hug. She kissed his leathery cheek and buried her face in his beard. When he set her down, she stood back and let him pass over the bridge. At the door, he paused and looked at her once more, her wings shimmering in the moonlight, her hair blowing slightly in the cool breeze. Taking a deep breath, he turned away again.

The door to the Crimson Tower was fitted so perfectly that Brian could barely find its outline but the great, carved handle was obvious. He grabbed the handle and pulled but the door did not open. He pushed hard, but to no effect. He looked over his shoulder at Annie and then turned back to inspect the door handle. At the top of the handle was a cleft that looked like it might fit the blade of the long knife. The gruffen drew the Valenblade and carefully slipped it into the slot. It entered to the hilt and for a moment, it stuck fast. Brian pulled up on it sharply and could not release the blade. Then he pushed down on it and the door swung silently inward. He stepped inside. When the door was fully opened, the knife was released. Brian pulled it out and watched the door swing shut again, leaving him almost blind at the base of a dark stairwell.

The Valenblade gripped tightly in his hand, Brian climbed step by step around the inside of the tower until he came to the upper room. Moonlight drifted through the windows windows that ringed the chamber. In the center of the floor, lit by the setting moon, sat the Crimson Throne. It faced south like the White Throne. Like the Crimson Tower itself, the throne was cracked and broken in places, but also like the tower, it appeared quite solid. The back was sculpted in the shape of a mighty bird of prey, its head and beak forming a canopy over the seat. Each armrest was another wing, and under the seat, the talons were bared.

Unlike the throne rooms in the other towers, this one did not glow of its own accord. Brian approached the Crimson Throne, his pulse pounding, his right hand gripping the Valenblade. He thought he heard whispers wafting around the room, as if ghosts had been disturbed. His fur stood on end and his skin prickled. He didn't smell Dark Magic, but it was magic of some sort, that was certain. The whispers grew louder as he came closer to the throne. No one had sat here since Norhidan Nightwing—or if they had, they had not lived to tell of it.

Brian didn't think about it for long. In his mind, he kept the image of the Golrakken attacking his friends on the hill on Cai-Amira. He sat down hard on the marbled seat, his left hand on the armrest, his right still holding the Valenblade at the ready.

"I'm here," he said, as if someone needed to know.

The whispers stopped instantly. For a moment, all was still.

Then, a high, singing sound began, like the ringing of a bell long after it's been struck. It started quietly and began to grow. On the right hand armrest, a small slit was revealed, rimmed with red light, the same size as the slot on the door handle. For a moment, Brian just stared at it while the singing sound grew louder and louder. The light around the slot glowed brighter and the singing sound grew louder until it hurt Brian's ears. The light around the slot began to pulsate. Brian jammed the Valenblade into the slot. Instantly, the room went silent and the light went out.

Pain crept into Brian's back as if seeping from the chair itself. It worked its way up to his shoulders and down his arms and legs like a thousand tiny thorns threading through his fur and skin. The pain reached his chest and his heart seemed to tighten into a solid mass. His eyes grew wide and his mouth opened but no sound came out. He couldn't breathe!

The floor at the base of the throne began to turn a bright red. Soon, the entire throne was glowing like a hot coal. The light spread outward along the floor and up the walls until the whole room was filled with crimson light. The pain grew even more fierce. The Valenblade in Brian's grip was searing hot now but he could not let go. The knife had turned blood red where the blade met the hilt.

Brian's arms and legs were burning and his muscles were locked solid. Thunder like a roaring waterfall filled his ears. Pain saturated every muscle and bone. He could not pull the Valenblade out of the armrest. He could not move at all. His eyes saw only crimson fire. His heartbeat seemed to stop altogether.

All went black and quiet. The gruffen remained as still as the stone on which he sat.

* * *

The pain was gone. Everything was gone.

For what seemed like hours, Brian felt like a speck of life floating in a sea of darkness. Now and then, hazy forms appeared like scenes remembered in a dream, but he recognized none of them, and none lasted very long. They dissolved into vapor and blew away like wisps of steam.

Finally, one scene emerged and persisted. He found himself looking at two Dwarves emerging from a hidden tunnel into the cool light of dawn. Every glistening drop of dew was acutely visible. Every grain of dirt appeared clearly as a separate and individual particle. Brian stared.

"Well, it's morning," said the larger, apparently younger Dwarf.

"Yes," said the older Dwarf, with obvious annoyance. "The sun rises in the east and the moon sets in the west. That direction being east and the sun happening to rise just now, by very definition it is precisely morning."

"But this is surely a most *morning* sort of morning," remarked the first. "Don't you think so, Gavon?"

Gavon snorted. "You mean a 'mourning' sort of morning? Yes, there is plenty to mourn about with you tagging along. Otherwise, to answer you properly—as I'm sure I must or be plagued with the question until I do—no, I don't see it as 'more' of a morning than any other. Now enough of metaphysics or poetry or whatever this is and let's get on with it. No point in standing here discussing the time of day. There's work to be done."

"I don't see why you can't enjoy the day and travel at the same time," said the first. "I think it does one good to muse about the world one lives in."

"Fiven," growled the other; "your lungs are younger than mine and I did my share of musing long before you were born. Now leave me alone... and none of that infernal whistling either. I had to abide it all the way through the tunnel and it nearly drove me mad. If you must whistle, do it into your sleeve."

"You could let me walk in front for once," suggested Fiven.

"Last time you went in front, we got lost in the Iyalians. I will not go gallivanting all over the mountains today," said Gavon, with a grunt.

"That's hardly fair," Fiven protested. "That was six years ago."

"And we haven't gotten lost since," Gavon said, flatly. "Good reason to leave well enough alone."

They were going around the bend so Brian called to them quickly. "Where am I?"

They did not seem to hear him. He called again and received no response. They continued along the path and went over the ridge. Much to his surprise, they did not disappear, though. He could still see them as they traveled down the other side.

It was at this point that he realized that he was not out in the open air with the Dwarves, but actually still sitting on the Crimson Throne up in the tower. It was fully light by now. He was looking out the window, and his magically extended gaze had happened to fall on the two Dwarves emerging from their hole many miles away. If he wished, his eye could rove on and away, league after league.

He turned his head and the throne rotated in the same direction. Suddenly, he was looking into the land of the Elves. Unlike the Dwarves who seemed oblivious to him, a few of the older Elves actually paused as his gaze passed over them. Most seemed puzzled but some smiled as if touched by a long forgotten sensation. Brian's sight kept extending. He couldn't seem to maintain focus on anything very long.

At the western border of the Elven country, a range of jagged mountains rose sharply from the rolling foothills. Behind these, lay dry desert, cracked earth and sand with buttes, plateaus and tall towers of wind sculpted reddish stone. For miles and miles there wasn't a soul to be found. In some places, the dunes made vast undulating patterns clear across the horizon.

A thin plume of dust near one of the buttes caught the gruffen's eye and he found that if he stared harder, he could see it more closely. Suddenly, he realized he was looking at a rider on horseback. The rider was cloaked and turbaned in the same colors as the dusty rocks. His magnificent black horse was drenched with sweat but flew like the wind down the center of a dry lakebed between two plateaus.

As Brian focused on him, the rider pulled his mount up short and looked around, drawing a gleaming sword from a sheath hidden in his cloak. The rider turned his horse in a slow circle, looking intently in all directions, even overhead.

"Valen?" he asked, holding his weapon at the ready. "Valen dak-Lammethan?"

Assuming that like the Dwarves, the rider could not hear, Brian did not respond.

"Speak!" said the rider. "Declare yourself!"

"I'm Brian!" the gruffen answered, finally. He could see the rider's face clearly now. The man was fair-haired and red-bearded, but his skin was dark for having spent much time in the sun. He looked in Brian's direction, but seemed unable to focus on the gruffen.

"Who sits on the Crimson Throne?" he asked. "You are not Norhidan Nightwing."

"No, I'm not," said the gruffen, quietly. "I'm Brian P. Gruffenson. I have the Valenblade and they call me Valen."

"So Nightwing is gone. I feared as much," said the rider. "You don't sound like a Faerie or a Golrak, or a Human, Elf or Dwarf, for that matter. What are you, and how did you get the Valenblade?"

"I'm a gruffen. Long story," Brian returned. "Ender gave me the knife. I killed Lazraak with it on Cai-Amira. He was after Annie. She's here now. Everybody's happy about it. Sort of."

"What of Norhidan?" asked the rider.

"I don't know," said Brian. "Annie doesn't know either."

"Wait!" cried the rider. "You said 'Annie.' Do you mean Annathía!"

"That's her," said Brian.

"The Snowdaughter!" cried the man. "Is it true? Did you tell me Snakehelm is dead and the Snowdaughter lives?"

"She's here," said Brian; "and Lazraak is really dead. I used the knife."

"Does the Snowdaughter have her wings?" asked the man.

"Yes," said Brian.

With a shout, the rider threw his sword into the air and caught it again. "Then all is not lost and there is still some comfort in this world!" he said, fiercely.

"Who are you?" asked Brian.

"My apologies!" said the man. "I am Arvon Dustrider. Nightwing was my friend, and for many years I have hoped to hear that he, his wife and the Snowdaughter had returned. Is Veranna with you?"

"No," said Brian. "Don't know what happened to her."

Arvon Dustrider's face grew grave. "Then he did not find what he was looking for," he said. "But Annathía is well?"

"She's good," said Brian.

"Bring her here as soon as possible. I have an important gift for her, something from her father." Standing up in the saddle, he pointed off to the southeast toward a large, freestanding pillar of red sandstone, the tallest of many marching out from a steep escarpment that bordered the dunes. "Mark this place well in your mind. If you come soon, you will find me here. If you delay, I may not return for many days but you will be safe there if the Carthiss attacks. A warning: if you must travel at night, keep to the high plateaus. The Carthiss will not climb after you, for her soft belly cannot withstand the rocks, but she will swiftly overtake you on the flatland or the dunes. Come quickly, Brian, and bring the Snowdaughter with you."

"I will," said Brian.

The rider looked around, quizzically. "Sorry to have to ask this, but what is a gruffen? How shall I recognize you?"

Brian thought about it for a moment. "I'm a big, furry thing with four toes on each foot," he said.

"Amazing," said the rider. "I feel a great heart in you." He turned his horse again and called over his shoulder. "Forgive me, Valen; I must be off. I have far to go before nightfall. Come soon!" With that, he urged his steed forward and shot off toward the pillar with great speed.

Brian sat and watched the rider descend into a cleft in the rock. Then he surveyed the area and committed it to memory as he tried to bring his gaze slowly back to more immediate surroundings.

When he turned his head again, the throne shifted, throwing him off his bearings once more. His eyes ran swiftly over places for which he knew no names yet, over Pelnara, the land of Men, with its orchards and fields rich with fruit and grain, across the Everness river which was lined with beautiful trees and plied by boats sailing serenely between the towns on the banks. Beyond the coastal mountains, south and east of the delta where the Everness emptied into the Dorvan Sea, lay an unpopulated peninsula called Thihanan.

Brian's gaze was headed out into the open sea when it was unexpectedly diverted. He found himself staring into the eyes of a small man dressed in brown sitting on a boulder of quartzite on a grassy hillside. The man seemed very old and weary but his eyes were full of spirit.

"Welcome, Valen dak-Lammethan," he said. "And congratulations to you, Brian P. Gruffenson. Your awakening has exceeded all hopes."

Unlike Arvon Dustrider or the Elves, this man focused directly on Brian's face. He seemed so close that the gruffen was not sure whether they were in the Shioroth or if they were on the side of the hill by the sea as they spoke.

"I know you, don't I?" asked Brian.

"I am known as The Meddler to some, The Wanderer to others," he said. "You may call me Palanthar, or Ilstar, as some Pelnarans do."

"No, I know you. You're the Great Master," said Brian.

"I prefer Palanthar," said the Great Master. "I have news for you, and counsel if you will have it."

"I'll listen. You fixed my arm." The gruffen's brow lowered. "Maybe you know: what happened to everyone on the island?"

"Ah, the others are well! Cai-Amira returns to Thihanan. They will arrive in a few days," said Palanthar, smiling fondly. He motioned over the water. "Look, Brian; you will see."

Brian looked and saw the floating island still far out to sea. As his gaze drew closer, he could see the devastated hill behind the house where Aaron, Owler and Ender were cutting firewood. Lia was walking in the woods past the place where the Thricewood tree had completely withered away. Brian sought out the Chrysalis tree, but in its place, a ring of younger trees had formed a new Circle. Calicia sat inside it, eyes closed, head tilted back slightly as if breathing in the morning. Brian looked at her serene face and smiled to himself.

Startled, she opened her eyes and cried out. "Brian! Brian! Where are you? I know you're somewhere! How are you? Is Annie all right?"

The gruffen laughed out loud. "I'm fine. So's Annie. I'm glad you're safe!"

"Yes, but not all," said Calicia solemnly. "We believe Mari was captured by the Golrakken. Thoughtful was lost as well, or so we fear. Did you say Annie was safe?"

"She's safe." Brian's smile faded. "They got Mari? Where?" he asked.

"I wish we knew," came the reply. "When the singing host came, the Golrakken fled. She was not among us nor among the dead. They must have taken her aboard ship"

"Your father...Palanthar...he's in...Thi-ha-nan," Brian told her, struggling to remember the name. "I just saw him."

"Wonderful! Thank you for good news!" she said. "I am glad you are well, Brian. How did you find me?"

"I'm sitting in a tower," said Brian. "It's strange. I see anywhere. I'm going to look for Mari."

"Farewell, then," said Calicia. "Remember not to speak to the Golrakken! Be very careful!"

"I will," said Brian. As he looked away, his sight returned suddenly to Palanthar.

"From the Crimson Throne, you may find the lady Mari," said Palanthar; "but you will not be encouraged."

"I have to know," said Brian. "She needs help."

"I can show you where she is, but you cannot help her," said the small man. "Rescuing her is beyond my arts at this time. She is eastward, in the Golrakken ship, sailing to Uz-Ghemahl. They cannot be attacked at sea. When they make landfall and the ship is docked, there may be a way for someone to rescue her but the rescuer will be neither of us. Do you wish to see her anyway?"

"Yes," said Brian.

"Then look," said the Great Master; "but by no means speak, for it could cost you your life and you also endanger the lady and many others whose very souls depend on your silence."

"I won't talk," Brian promised.

Palanthar pointed further southeast. Brian looked there and could soon see the storm that enveloped the Golrakken vessel. His vision entered the storm and felt his skin crawl when he caught sight of the ghastly ship, its ragged, shredded sails flailing in the gale force winds as it sped up and down the massive waves. Brian's vision came in close and passed right through the blackened sides into the warship's dark interior. Timbers creaked and groaned as the ship rose and fell. Outside, the wind howled, but inside the air was deathly still. In each dimly lit chamber he saw the Golrakken, somehow uglier and more terrifying in their own world. Deep in the ship's belly, several sat huddled around a table playing some filthy game in which the winner drew a small cupful of blood from the worst of the losers and drank it lustily, tossing the dregs in the others' laughing faces. Further up, the officers conferred together in low tones. Brian could scarcely hear them, but he didn't like what he did hear.

Just below the main deck amidships, Brian found the captain's quarters. They were relatively spacious, but the once-exquisite woodwork of the Faerie craftsmen had long since decayed. Dust and rot had taken their toll; the magnificent cabinetry sagged and splintered. Mari sat in a dark chair, her arms and legs bound to it with tight cords. She appeared frozen, staring unseeingly at the wall. Though her hands were free, they gripped the armrests of the chair as if grasping tiny holds at the edge of a precipice. Brian thought she looked ill.

He felt his hackles rise as Karkaan Dragonhelm entered the chamber from Mari's left. She did not move. The Golrakken leader came close but she made no indication that she was aware of him, even when he stood directly between her and the wall. Her gaze never wavered, continuing to stare blindly forward.

"How long will you deny me?" crackled the voice of Karkaan. "How long will you deny yourself? I brought you out of the realm of fools into my world. That was my choice. Now you have a choice, dear girl: become my queen, or die in horror. You must choose. You cannot help but choose."

He opened his tattered cloak and brought out a wicked looking blade. Brian's skin prickled again but he said nothing.

Karkaan stepped to the side, bringing his face close to Mari's pale cheek. He held the knife blade before her eyes, twisting it side to side as one might hold a mirror.

"This knife marks your decision. Take it by the poisoned blade and you will cut yourself—a miserable waste, and a slow, painful death. Take it by the hilt and the Golrakken will exalt you above all others. They shall follow you helplessly, devotedly. You shall bathe in their blood. Only I will hold authority over you, and you shall come and go as you please. Hilt or blade, you must take it, my love. You will choose. Tell me, beautiful princess, which shall it be? I leave it here for you to decide."

As he laid the knife across her lap, Mari shuddered as if suddenly chilled. "Ah, so you recognize your opportunity," breathed the Golrak into her ear. "Do not disappoint me, my queen. The hilt is at your right hand. I eagerly await your decision. You must decide."

Brian's own hands gripped the Valenblade tightly.

Karkaan turned for a moment, as if sensing something. His burning eyes glanced around the room. "Who watches?" he said, warily. "I feel the Valenblade nearby. How can this be?" He looked around the room once more. "Bring it to me, fool!" he shouted, his voice grating on Brian's ears. "It belongs to me! You do not know what it can do to you."

Deliberately, Brian eased his grip on the knife and Karkaan stopped, listening intently.

"Ah, and it is lost again," muttered the Golrak under his breath. In a louder voice, he said: "When you tire of it, fool, return it to me. You will be glad to be rid of it."

Mari sat stoically, unmoved. Brian could watch no longer. He covered his eyes to shut out the sight. Almost immediately, he found himself back in the presence of Palanthar.

"You did well," said the Great Master. "There is nothing we can do for her while she is onboard ship. She will have to rely on her own resolve. I believe she has the strength. We shall see."

"What about the others?" asked Brian, feeling like he could breathe again.

"For now, entrust your companions to me," said Palanthar. "They will be coming to the High Council as soon as they arrive." He smiled. "You have met Arvon Dustrider?" he asked.

"Yes," said Brian. "He says he has something for Annie."

"He does," said the Great Master. "Go to him as he requested. This gift for the Snowdaughter intrigues me. I might guess what it is, but I do not know what it is for. Do not delay; whatever it is you may need it sooner rather than later. Tell Grisbane of the Small Giants that I have requested that he accompany you. Tell him to select an Elf to join you also. He will know which one. Now go, and blessings on you. I am pleased to see that my faith in you was well-placed."

With that, Brian's sight returned to his own immediate surroundings. The throne room glowed red even in the morning sun. As his vision returned to normal, Brian could see that the floor was set with patterns in shades of red, gray and black reminiscent of the designs in the upper room of the White Tower. He sat back gently in the stone seat. Finally, he could relax. His body ached, not the sort of ache that makes one want to lie down and sleep, more like the memory of hard labor after one has accomplished something difficult. It occurred to him that he was unafraid now. He lifted the Valenblade from its slot in the arm of the chair and his sight-magnification ceased completely. Turning his head no longer turned the throne. He took a deep breath and let it out again, slowly. Then he slid the Blade into its sheath and stood up.

He walked to the window and looked down on the sunlit Uppermost Garden.

"Everything all right?" called Annie from below, her blue wings twitching with worry.

"I'm fine," Brian shouted back. "I'm coming down."

He descended the spiral staircase as fast as his sore legs could carry him. When he got to the door, he inserted the Valenblade into an inner slot; the door opened easily. Annie flew to the footbridge and was upon him in an instant, wrapping her arms around his thick neck as soon as he stepped into the sunlight.

"You're back!" she said, burying her face in his fur. "You're back."

CHAPTER 26

Another Journey Begins

"What took so long?" asked Annie as Rohidan and Arienne joined them on the grass in the Uppermost Garden.

"I don't remember some parts," began the Valen; "but I could see forever and I looked all over." He recounted his meeting with Arvon Dustrider. Annie wondered aloud what gift could be so important. The gruffen also told of his visit with Palanthar and the discovery of Mari in the Golrakken ship. This news was greeted with dismay. Rohidan suggested they meet with the Council as soon as possible. The matter of the journey to the sandstone tower would be presented to Grisbane and the Elvenfolk and, if possible, they would set out before nightfall.

"First breakfast, then the Council," said Arienne.

Within the hour, the High Council was assembled again in the great hall. There was much talk and excitement about the light in the Crimson Tower. After the Elder Faerie brought everyone to order, Brian stumbled through another retelling of the events of the past few hours. All were silent as he described what he had seen. (He left out the episode with the Dwarves.) When he had delivered Palanthar's message to Grisbane, he finally sat down.

Standing to his full height, the Small Giant nodded to the gruffen and then spoke: "I have known Palanthar since I was young. He was never one to say more than necessary. Nor has he ever given me bad advice. If it he believes the Snowdaughter should be taken to the desert to meet this Arvon Dustrider, then I will go. As for an Elf to accompany us, I ask Eulian to lend her expertise."

This last drew an indignant cough from Hassila, the Elven queen and Keeper of the Blue Stone. She raised both royal eyebrows and glared at the Small Giant. "If you must cross the desert with an Elf, is not Thorval Lighthammer the obvious choice?" she said, coldly.

Directly behind the queen's chair stood a young Elven woman with blue gray eyes and loose hair the color of molten gold. Her face was solemn and kind.

"I will go," she said simply.

Hassila ignored her, keeping her eyes fixed on Grisbane. "Perhaps the Small Giant would reconsider," the queen prompted.

Grisbane was unmoved. "I have asked as I see fit. Besides, your majesty, the request was not put to you. She is of age."

Hassila glowered but said nothing.

Eulian put her hand on her mother's shoulder. "If we may have the stables of the Green Stone at our service, we shall return all the sooner," she said, nodding to the Pelnaran king.

"That you have as customary," said Raealann. "Take what you need from the stables. Captain Falnor will assist you."

The captain smiled and bowed slightly.

It was decided that they would leave as soon as possible. As the foursome followed Falnor toward the door, Eulian glanced over her shoulder and saw her mother watching her leave. The Elven princess smiled and nodded despite the obvious disapproval on the queen's face.

Falnor brought them to the stables by the Southgate and called to the horse master as they entered the long, beautiful hall that smelled of hay and horses. These stables housed the finest horses of their breeds, kept especially for the use of the Green Guard stationed at the Shioroth. This regiment of the Green Stone was an elite force of highly trained cavalry ready to ride at a moment's notice should the High Council require it. Falnor was their commander and one of their greatest horseman.

"By your leave," he said, walking away along the center aisle with the horse master. He returned, grinning a bit sheepishly. "Mr. Gruffenson," he said; "we're at a loss to find a suitable mount for you. Grisbane has ridden one of our great war horses, but...well, to be blunt, we would need a cart and a team to carry someone of your weight."

"Why?" asked Brian. "I'm not riding."

Falnor regarded him with a puzzled look. "That may slow the party somewhat."

"No, it won't," said Brian.

Annie laughed. "Don't worry about him. He'll keep up easily —and, in the woods, the horses won't be able to catch him."

"Indeed?" said Falnor, intrigued. "Now that is a chase I would very much like to try! That brings us to you, Snowdaughter. Will you ride?"

"I don't see why I would need to," she said. "I can fly, can't I?"

Eulian laid a hand on her shoulder. "It's a very long way," she said. "Even Faeries tire, but you can always ride with me when you wish to."

"That should work," said Falnor.

They had chosen a fine black horse for Eulian, but the chestnut mare in the next stall whinnied at her insistently. She went to it. The mare brought her head close to Eulian's face and nuzzled her shoulder. Falnor watched as the Elven princess patted the horse's muzzle and stroked its head.

"Pity," said the captain, smiling and shaking his head. "Arsha is neither patient nor kind. I'm the only rider she hasn't thrown. All she wants is her freedom. I'd gladly give it to her, but when speed is what I need, she's my first choice."

"She's fast?" asked Eulian, with a mischievous look in her eye.

The horse master laughed. "She must be saddled in the stall while she is still tied down, or she'll be out of sight before you shut the door." he said. "And she's nimble, too. Even so, I couldn't recommend her. She can be a lot of trouble."

Without asking, the Elven princess slipped inside the stall, leaving the gate unlatched. The horse master reached for the gate, but Falnor motioned for him to wait. The horse shivered as Eulian leapt lightly up on its back but it did not seem to mind at all. The Elf whispered something in the horse's ear as she leaned over its sleek neck. Gently, Arsha nudged the door open and walked out. Eulian spoke again to the mare, patted her on the neck and then dismounted. She slid her hand along its shoulder, patted its muzzle again and with the slight wave of the hand, she bid Arsha return to her stall. The mare obeyed calmly, actually shutting the gate again once inside.

"Arsha it is, then,"declared Falnor. "Remarkable!"

Eulian only smiled.

Next they were given tack for the long journey. Falnor insisted that they eat before they set off so they sat at the officers' table and enjoyed a meal together.

When they returned to the stables, the horses were saddled and ready. A great war horse some sixteen hands high had been brought for Grisbane. His name was Farax and he whinnied with recognition when the Small Giant came into view. Grisbane happily fed him a carrot he had brought from the kitchen.

Much to everyone's surprise, Arsha had allowed herself to be saddled and stood patiently awaiting the arrival of her new mistress. Falnor shook his head. "Believe no one who says Elves know nothing of horses," he said to the horse master.

Falnor rode with them through the city to see them off at the western gate.

The foursome set out across the wide valley Brian had seen from the Crimson Throne earlier that day. When they reached the open road, Brian dropped to all fours and, with an easy, loping gate, led the horses at a brisk pace. Annie flew just over his shoulder. They followed a straight path that rose and fell with the rolling of the landscape.

Periodically, they came across travelers on their way to the Shioroth on business. The few Dwarves nodded brusquely at the unusual company. The Elves they met bowed low before Eulian who always stopped to greet them, letting the others go on ahead. Arsha always caught up quickly, galloping smoothly and easily as if she bore no weight at all. Eulian declared her the best mount she had ever ridden.

Later in the afternoon, they came upon an elderly Elf walking alone down the road. He saw them a long way off and hailed them. When they came to a stop, Brian recognized him as one of the Elves he had seen from the tower that morning.

"Thorval Lighthammer!" cried Eulian as she leapt from her horse. She embraced the old fellow and he kissed her cheek.

"Where do you ride with such speed?" he asked, when she let him go; "and who carries the Valenblade? Do I sense that it is here?"

"Yes, it is here," said Eulian. She pointed to Brian. "Meet Brian P. Gruffenson, Valen dak–Lammethan," she announced. "Only a few hours ago he spoke to Palanthar from the Crimson Throne. We are going to the desert to meet someone named Arvon Dustrider. Do you know him?"

"I do," said Thorval. "Why are you going there?"

"He has a gift for the Snowdaughter," said Eulian.

"The Snowdaughter!" said the old Elf. "Is this you, my dearest Annathía?" he asked Annie.

"I guess," said Annie. "I'm still getting used to the idea."

Thorval Lighthammer smiled as if finally letting go of a great burden. "Oh, my dear girl! How wonderful to see you have arrived fully grown! What blessings abound! Long has the Valenblade been lost and long have we awaited word of the Snowdaughter. Much has happened since I left. I must soon be ready to die, now that these things both are before me." He searched her face. "Your father and mother are gone, I take it?"

"I don't really know," said Annie, awkwardly. "I hardly remember them."

The old Elf nodded. "Whatever their fate, they did what they thought best," he said. "Your return here is, perhaps, more than they might have hoped for."

He turned to Brian. "Valen, I felt your eye this morning. It made me glad that one with such a great heart sat in the Crimson Tower. In fact, I was coming to seek you and give you one piece of advice. The Valenblade you carry is powerful even beyond my knowledge, but this I know: it is dangerous. There is one against whom you must never unsheathe it unless you strike to kill. In the presence of Morvassus, be quick with the blade. He has turned it to his own designs once. Who knows what he can do with it now? In his presence, it may serve its master and not its wielder. Until you can kill him with it, keep it away from him."

"I will," nodded Brian. He looked at the knife strapped around his shoulder. This simple thing seemed to grow stranger every day.

"And as for you, Annathía Sayacia das-Lammethan," said the Elf to Annie; "may you not be only the last but also the first. Your coming brings the end of many things. Yet I still believe it is also the beginning of something new."

"It sounds so sad," said Annie.

"Not all is sadness," said Thorval. "There is always a new beginning."

"Tell me," said Eulian. "Who is Arvon Dustrider?"

Thorval smiled. "He will introduce himself. Treat him as my friend, dear Eulian."

"But you've never mentioned him," she said, one eyebrow raised slightly.

"True," said Thorval. "That time has come. Now go! If Palanthar sends you in haste, you should not delay."

After embracing him again, Eulian remounted Arsha and, with a wave, they set off again. The old Elf turned from his original path and followed their wake slowly westward.

"Shouldn't we have brought him with us?" asked Annie, flying just over Eulian's shoulder.

"He would not have come," the Elven princess responded. "Thorval Lighthammer would rather walk than ride any day, especially a day like this. No, his legs are stronger than they appear. I have spent many a long mile with him wondering when we were going to finally stop for the night. He showed me the ways of the desert when I was very young. My mother curses him for it every day." She picked up the pace.

They sped past houses that grew like scattered flowers along the road. Their course began to meander slightly as it came to the hill country. The land about them lay rich and green, much like Pelnara to the south, the land of Men. The road rose gradually as they wound around ever steeper hills. The sun was ahead of them now; the afternoon was waning. At the crest of a ridge, they paused to look out over a long valley that ran north and south. Dense forest covered the valley floor. Brian remembered seeing it from the Crimson Throne.

The forest was not yet entirely in shadow; the sun still cast golden rays across the western hills. At this point in early spring, the yellow green of the foliage shone brilliantly in the lowering sun. Here and there tall stands of dark evergreens stood out in stark contrast to the deciduous splendor.

In the center of the valley stood six giant redwoods circled so closely together as to appear from a distance as a single tree so tall that the upper branches seemed to be nearly level with the pass. The grove's edges were gilt with sunlight and it laid a long, cool shadow across the valley floor.

"Welcome to Val-Ellia," said Eulian with a sweep of her hand; "the City of the Elves. Here we will stay the night and prepare for the longer journey through the desert."

"There's no city," said Brian.

"You will see," the Elven princess replied as she led them down the hillside into the forest.

The road narrowed as it entered into a great forest. As they went deeper into the woods, the light of day grew dimmer and dimmer. Annie had to fly closer to the road to avoid the branches from all sides. Glad to be back in the woods again, Brian enjoyed the familiar sounds of squirrels, insects and birds, although he could not recognize some of the bird calls. His nose picked up what he now recognized as "Elf scent," and he noticed that the massive bases of some of the larger trees were neatly cleared of brush. If this was a city, Brian liked it very much. As they passed by, voices in the upper branches began to call out the return of Eulian and the arrival of Grisbane and "two others." Eulian's face was aglow with pleasure as they proceeded at a canter down the path, she and Brian in front, and Annie flying beside the Small Giant behind.

The road brought them to a wide clearing, in the middle of which stood the towering redwoods they had seen from the pass. The trees seemed even more enormous up close. Their massive trunks rose up into the twilight sky, and Brian could see that their bark actually merged in various places. Most of the foliage was concentrated in the uppermost third of the trees, so the impression was of a mighty tower wrapped in green mist at its height.

Somewhere in those heights, a trumpet blew. Brian watched in wonder as a section of the trunk closest to them slid toward them and then rose upward, revealing a courtyard in the midst of the redwoods. Elven soldiers lined the walls of the tunnel through the trunk, standing at attention as Eulian rode into the courtyard with her companions. When the company was well inside, the great wooden gate lowered, sealing the entrance behind them.

A tall, Elf came into the courtyard to greet them, a handsome fellow with a distinct resemblance to Eulian. A blue stone clasped his fine Elven cloak at the shoulder. Eulian introduced him as her younger brother, Thadris, who was in charge while the queen was away at the High Council. After he had made everyone's acquaintance, Thadris bade them all a hearty welcome. "And a welcome even to you, dear girl," he said to his sister. "I'm glad you're back. You leave me no end of trouble when you go."

"Yes, well we are leaving again tomorrow, continuing westward," she replied; "so whatever trouble you have now will continue."

"Tomorrow? Westward? Not to visit the Dwarves, of course," he said, rolling his eyes. "No, I doubt you will stop before you have sand under hoof."

"Indeed," said Eulian.

"I suppose it can't be helped," said Thadris. "If only Mother knew—"

"She knows," said Eulian.

"Does she?" asked Thadris, raising an eyebrow. "And she approved, no doubt?"

"I didn't say she approved," said Eulian.

"No, you didn't," said Thadris. "But then, again, what's new? Thorval Lighthammer was not available?"

"His services were not requested," said Eulian. "Mine were, and I agreed."

"Wholeheartedly, I'm certain," said her brother. He turned to the others. "Pardon the family jousting, my friends. While I cannot imagine why you must trudge through the dust of a rain-forsaken desert, at least you will have the second best guide with you, and your chances of returning unscathed are actually rather high."

"What?" asked Brian.

Thadris grinned, glanced at his sister once and said, "Simply put: Eulian will get you back alive. Of that, I have no doubt. I went there with her once, and while I would not choose to go again, no one dares speak ill of her skill in my hearing."

Very few Elves would speak ill of Eulian. Though her love of the desert was baffling to her people, she was much respected and well loved. Hassila was the queen but in many ways her daughter had more influence. The young generation of Elven maidens was strong, independent and self-assured, less likely to follow tradition and authority unquestioningly. Years later, it would be said that Elven life was simpler before Eulian went to the desert, but all would agree the change was for the better.

The palace of the Elves was built directly out of and into the trunks of the redwoods surrounding the courtyard where the party now stood. There were many levels with many rooms, all with windows or balconies facing inward. From the center of the courtyard, one could look up and see the sky unobstructed by either branches or roof, and all around the inside of the cylinder were walls of living wood and bark.

Thadris and Eulian led them inside. As they climbed the steep stairs, Brian was amazed at how vines and branches had been made to grow into walls and floors. Elven woodwork blended in so seamlessly that it was difficult to tell where the plants left off and the cabinetry began.

About halfway up, they came upon a place where large sections of the inner walls, hinged by some ingenious design, were being lowered down into the center of the cylinder where they met to form a grand floor a hundred feet in diameter.

Thadris explained that their banquet that night was to be held on this floor, out in the open air with the stars overhead.

Annie caught Brian's eye and shook her head in wonder. Brian grinned back.

"Pardon me. I have some business to attend to," said Eulian; "but I leave you with the Master Chef who will do you no end of good!" She disappeared with her brother as an unusually portly Elf entered from the adjoining kitchen to greet them with a delightfully graceful bow.

"Bostler, Master Chef at your serv—my dearest Grisbane!" he interrupted himself with a cry; "had I known you were coming I would have been better prepared! Oh, it's madness to put on a banquet on such short notice—not that I ever tire of it mind you, but they must at least *try* to give me time to prepare for *such* an appreciative pallet as yours!" He quickly turned back to the kitchen, calling out to them over his shoulder, "I don't suppose it's terribly polite, but if you want to eat properly tonight, you'll have to settle for tea and a biscuit or two in the scullery with me while I work. My, but it is good to see you again, Mr. Grisbane! And who are your companions today?"

"These are Brian P. Gruffenson and Annie. I think you will find Mr. Gruffenson's appetite rivals my own, Master Bostler," chuckled Grisbane.

"What now? 'Gruffenson,' you say? Good heavens, what sort of name is that?" blurted Bostler, not looking up from the potatoes he chopped vigorously. "Aren't there enough malcontents about without naming (what is he, a bear?) anything else after them?"

A low laugh rumbled in Grisbane's chest. "He is a gruffen, Master Bostler, and his title is Valen dak-Lammethan."

The Master Chef dropped his knife. "Oh lordy mercy I've cut myself!" he exclaimed in shock. "Haven't done that since before I was an apprentice. Well never mind that, I do beg your gracious pardon, Mr. ...Mr. Gruffenson, yes... I never, well rather I... I mean to say, I simply didn't expect you to be more than a large pet. No, no, now I've only gone and made it worse. Now Mr. Grisbane, you must apologize for me; I am doing a terrible job of it on my own."

"It's fine," said Brian with a laugh. "Sorry about your finger."

Bostler stopped for just a moment and gaped in astonishment. "Well I never—I—thank you very much!" said the befuddled Chef. Then he slipped away between the quickly weaving cooks and returned with a rag around his wounded finger.

With a grand flourish, he shoveled the potatoes into an iron pot that one of his many assistants brought him. Reaching up to a cabinet, he fetched a tray with all manner of pastries and cakes.

"I fear this meager assortment is all I have at the moment and I haven't anything proper to serve to drink with them," he complained. "You will have to make do with water. It's good water, as water goes. I'm sure Mr. Grisbane can expound upon the virtues of our drinking water, although it isn't nearly as good as the beer we make with it, but that will have to wait till dinner, don't you know. Now help yourselves and I will try to see what disaster has gone on behind my back while we've been talking." He vanished into the well organized mayhem behind him as they settled in to enjoy their repast.

Just as quickly, he was back. "Well I must say I am blessed to have this crew working for me. Can't ask them to do something half the time because they've already begun. I'm sure I don't know why I worry about them anymore. Habit, I guess, silly really. Oh, but I'm being rude again! My dear Faerie, I haven't seen such a young Faerie in this palace since, oh it must be going on twenty five years when Veranna (bless her soul) came to visit that last spring before... well, those were happier times for all of us I'm sure. Heavens, I'm still being rude! Has anyone mentioned your name, dear? I don't think I'm old enough to have missed it yet."

Grisbane chuckled again and said, "Master Bostler, this is Annathía, the very Snowdaughter you saw last."

"And I'm so pleased to—mercy me! I'm glad I hadn't a knife in my hand this time, I would have caused my own demise!" crowed the chef with wide eyes. "I should have recognized the wing colors, shouldn't I? How perfectly mindless of me! The Snowdaughter, indeed! Well, now. Well, well, well, well, well! Let me look at you! I haven't seen you since the year you were born!"

Annie stood and hugged him which prompted a sharp whimper from the portly chef. When he stood back, his eyes were brim full.

"Do pardon my tears. Your mother was a dear friend of mine and I have missed her terribly since she went away. And I thought—" He caught himself. "I thought I would never see her beautiful baby...and, of all the miracles...but, I guess this means your mother...won't be back now, will she. Oh, I'm sorry, dear. This must be so much harder for you than it is for me," he said to Annie.

"I'm all right," said Annie. "I don't actually remember her."

"Oh dear," said Bostler. "Oh dear oh dear oh dear." He looked at Grisbane helplessly, mutely shook his head and then excused himself from the kitchen to regain his composure.

When the chef came back, red-faced and smiling despite himself, he actually took off his apron and led them to one of the tables set up for the banquet. They talked about this and that and Bostler asked Grisbane many questions about the goings on at the High Council. He also gave them bits of news he had gathered. Apparently, the Dwarves in the western mountains had encountered a poisonous smoke in some of their deepest tunnels. Also, the Carthiss had been seen as close as the dunes by the Lake of Salt, and could be seen moving about even at twilight or dawn.

"If this continues, it won't be safe even in the daytime, they say," muttered Bostler, sullenly. "It makes it hard to get salt anymore. I daren't send anyone to the lake. Young Barker barely escaped with his life just last month and none of the boys would try it after that. I'm about ready to go myself, if I have to. I hate how bland everything tastes without it and the Dwarves charge you an arm and a leg for the gritty stuff they carve out of their mines. I haven't the patience to dissolve it, pan out the silt, re-crystallize it and grind it again. Pelnaran cooks are using sea salt from the Dorvan but it's even more expensive and I think it tastes like seaweed. Don't you? No, nothing but Lake Salt for me. Maybe you could bring some back with you! No, no, that's ridiculous! You have far too many other things to worry about besides salt. Forget it. Put it out of your mind."

Soon, Eulian and Thadris returned to show them where they would sleep that night. For an hour or so they sat on a balcony overlooking the banquet hall as the stars came out to spangle the sky. While they were waiting, Grisbane asked Eulian to educate them on the perils of desert travel.

As familiar as she was with the desert, she believed the place Brian described was further west than she had ever gone. The main concern during the day was water, of course. Eulian could lead them from water source to water source for most of the way. Once they were beyond her normal range, she knew how to look for hidden oases. Most likely, Arvon Dustrider had a water source nearby, so they should be able to resupply there for part of the return journey.

The other danger, which Eulian assured them was far more deadly, was the Carthiss. For centuries beyond memory the Carthiss had roamed the desert badlands, hunting in the moonlight or burrowing into the dunes. Always assumed to be female, though no one had proof, she was a magical creature, an ancient monster that had somehow long outlived her summoner and now prowled the night, preying upon anything traveling in the desert.

The Carthiss was a hundred feet long and might be described as a cross between a scorpion and a lizard. Six of her eight legs moved her swiftly across the sand, as fast as a horse could gallop. Her two forelegs ended in massive scorpion-like pincers, and her long tail ended in three, curved, poisoned spikes nearly six feet long that delivered a devastating poison. Legend said that if the spikes didn't kill you, the sting was so terrible you would be glad to be eaten.

The head of the Carthiss was short and lizard-like, with two main eyes that moved independently. Like the scorpion, she also had six tiny, lateral eyes, positioned on either side of her forehead, allowing her to see a wide view at all times. Like a snake, she had heat sensing pits in the front of her snout. It was said that her long, black, forked tongue could smell as well as taste. Her ears appeared to be little more than indentations but she could hear a mouse scrabbling on the sand a league away. Seven horns protruded backwards from her forehead across the top of her skull, providing protection for the breathing hole in the middle of her crown. The airhole was always sealed unless she was actually breathing.

"How do we stay away from her?" asked Brian.

"She avoids high, hard ground," said Eulian. "Her belly is soft and vulnerable and her legs are not strong enough to carry her whole weight for very long. We will follow a trail of scattered buttes during the day and we will take shelter on top of one every night. We will never be more than a half day's journey from one to the next."

"Why doesn't she move around in the daytime?" asked Annie.

"She turns to stone when sunlight strikes her," said Eulian. "It does not kill her. She merely returns to her usual form the following night, but she does not like the touch of the sun. Usually, she will burrow into the sand before dawn and not come out again until after sunset. She also moves somewhat more slowly during the full moon. However, if the rumors are true, we cannot count on her to burrow at dawn. We should stay on high ground until the sun shines on the sands."

By this time, Bostler's crew had set the tables and Brian could hear music being played. Elegantly dressed Elves converged on the banquet hall under the stars. Brian and Annie followed their hosts and Grisbane into the hall where they sat at the table with Eulian and Thadris as guests of honor. The Elves toasted them with much fine drink and regaled them with songs and dances far into the night. They went tirelessly on and on as the moon crept across the starry sky. At some point, the others tottered off to bed and drifted into slumber.

* * *

As Eulian mounted her horse early the next morning, her younger brother was uncharacteristically quiet.

"What is it?" she asked.

Thadris shook his head. "You've done this a hundred times, I know. Still...it's dangerous. Somehow today it seems even more so."

Eulian leaned down from the saddle and looked him in the eye. "If I don't come back, brother," she said, gravely; "you can have my room."

Her brother grinned inspite of himself. "I should take it now," he said. "You hardly use it for a closet anymore." He patted her horse's flank. "Open the gates!" he called. "They'll need all the daylight they can get!"

The company rode out from Val-Ellia and turned swiftly down the road through the forest. From time to time an Elf would seem to materialize suddenly out of the forest only to wave at them passing by and vanish once again. Eulian always waved back, and she greeted many by name.

The way grew steeper and the road wound this way and that as it crossed a stream here, and a drainage there. An hour later, they broke out of the trees and began to climb in earnest. The Western Mountains were the last ramparts before the vast desert.

Eulian called to Brian who was out front again racing along easily on all fours at the head of the company. "The trail is this steep for most of the way, but it gets even steeper in spots," she said. "Will you keep us at this pace?"

Brian looked over his shoulder but didn't slow down. "This is go all day speed," he said. "Too slow?"

"No!" Eulian called back. "Not at all!"

"Remarkable," she said to Grisbane riding beside her. "At this pace, we'll clear the pass and reach the sands in three days."

"Amazing what the great Farax can do," said Grisbane, patting the neck of his massive horse. "I've taken this route many times on foot but this is my first time on horseback. If the weather stays clear, it will be a much shorter trip."

Once the switch-back road crested the pass on the first ridge, they could see several more steep ridges marching into the distance.

The road split at the pass. The main road turned south to Pelnara, the land of Men, following the mountains as they turned eastward two days' journey away. The other road was much less traveled and wound along at the base of the cliffs that blocked their progress westward. Here they had to go mostly single file. Periodically, rockfall obscured the path completely. They slowed to allow the horses to pick their way more carefully. Brian found it rather leisurely.

Bringing up the rear, Grisbane began to sing one of his favorite songs:

When in March, with melting snow
Green of grass and rushing stream
Up the winding path I go
Watching in a waking dream
Lost is what I long to be
Ere I lose what I might see

When in April, sky of blue
Road a-winding 'round the hill
Rimmed with blooms of every hue
Leading me where'er it will
Here I walk and there I roam
Ever farther from my home

When in May, the sun astride

The border twixt the afternoon
And twilight of the eventide
Then will I await the moon
Rising like the flaxen swan
Born to fly until the dawn

When in June, the evening waits
Long until the day shall wane
Then may I behold the gates
Beckoning to rest my cane
By the mantle by the fire
Only then shall I retire

"I can't decide if it's a happy song or a sad song," said Annie up above, flying near Brian.

"Then it's a good one," replied the Small Giant.

"I don't understand why he stops in the midst of summer, the best time for traveling the high country," mused Eulian.

"Perhaps he has reached his destination," countered Grisbane. "One who keeps on after having arrived will never rest. Without rest there is no strength."

"Sing another one," said Annie.

Grisbane thought a moment, and then cleared his throat, but before he could begin, a rough and hearty voice halfway up the hill interrupted him, bellowing with raucous insistence:

Buckle and harness
Blanket and saddle
Horses and riders and travelers fair
Gruffen and Giant
Princess and Faerie
Where is your errand and what seek you there?
Welcome you could be
Wisdom it would be:
Halt and be questioned or fight if you dare.

Brian stood up, fir bristling.

"Dwarves," said Grisbane. "They mean no harm unless you actually do fight."

Eulian stood in the saddle and called out. "Hail, Korban, sentinel of the western pass! These are with me, or I with them, rather. Come be acquainted."

An old Dwarf appeared on a rock outcrop just above their heads, axe in hand. "Korban, at your service, Princess of the Elves," he said grandly, doffing his deep green hood and bowing. "May I inquire as to your business, or is secrecy required? I see you do not travel with the Old One this time. Too bad; I could use his counsel. But I know none of your companions, other than Grisbane. He knows me not, but I know him." He winked.

"I am quite flattered," began Grisbane, but Korban cut him off.

"Oh, I wouldn't be flattered if you intended stealth," said the Dwarf. "You can be heard for miles, clumping along with stones for feet and braying with a veritable trumpet of a voice."

"If I had *intended* stealth—" the Small Giant began again.

"A jest, dear sir!" interrupted the Dwarf again, bowing low. "Since I have successfully offended you, and that was my purpose, I desist. Your singing is actually famous in these parts. Many of us eagerly await your every passage. You have quite an audience. We know most of your songs by heart and we sing our children to sleep with them. Please, be flattered as you were. You quite deserve it."

Grisbane smiled and nodded with a twinkle in his eye. "May I say—and without interruption, please—that I have never been so humiliated and so praised so quickly by anyone as stumpy as yourself," he said.

"Stumpy' says he—'stumpy,' indeed!" The Dwarf stopped himself mid-outburst and let out a great guffaw. "Ah! Well done!" he crowed. "A fine play! Oh, this is a good day! That it is!"

When he settled down, Korban asked again to be introduced to the rest of them and was delighted to know that Brian was not a massive squirrel that had lost its tail and that Annie would not wither in the sun.

"We've heard rumors of trouble, Korban; what is it?" asked Eulian.

The Dwarf grew suddenly serious. "A deadly smoke seeps up from the deep," he said. "A team including two of my own broke through the ceiling of an open channel deeper down, releasing some sort of smoke, they said. Three of them died right there. The few who escaped described the smoke as a living thing that pursued them. They suffered the most maddening fear. The smoke appears to be moving through the tunnels now. Fear precedes it, a fear that cannot be ignored. We shall be driven from here entirely if we cannot find a way to dispel it or seal it out."

"When did you find it?" asked Grisbane.

"Three weeks ago. A crew had spent all month digging through the strangest mineral," explained the Dwarf, leaning on his axe. "The stone is a brilliant black and very hard. They had cut several feet into the stratum when they felt stale air escape from a hidden chamber below. Then the fear came upon them all, even those far away from the hole. They say that when the smoke seeped out, those working nearest the hole died horribly. Those who escaped will not return to the lower levels." He shook his ruddy head.

Grisbane rubbed his chin. "Many years ago, I heard stories about the Necrowights. It was said that their breath was poison and their smoke-like bodies were like fear itself. They were said to have come from the blood of a battle long past, washed underground by the rains. I assumed they were legend. We must ask Palanthar when we see him again."

The Dwarf nodded gravely. "If you learn anything, tell us."

"We will," said Eulian. "For now, we are heading to the desert in search of a man named Arvon Dustrider. Do you know him?"

Korban shook his head again. "I've not heard of him. You should know that the Carthiss has been prowling the edge of the badlands," he said. "She has even been spotted roving about at dawn. You will need more than courage if you will face her in her own lands."

"We do not intend to face her," Eulian assured him.

Korban said he would send word to the other sentinels that they were passing through. They bid him farewell and good luck. He wished them the same. Then he turned and slipped away between the rocks.

CHAPTER 27

The House of Stoneboots

The terrain became even steeper as the road turned westward again and threaded the pass. The day was so grand and the sun on the mountains so spectacular, Annie flew higher to get a better view as the path worked its way through the crags. She drank it all in: the smells and the light on the rocks and evergreens. They stopped for a meal early in the afternoon and let their mounts rest for over an hour near a thin stream which was lined with plants the horses were happy to eat.

Not much further, the trail was hardly more than a scratch in the rocks.

"The main Dwarf holes are behind us," said Eulian. "From here, few but the sentries travel very often. Every once in awhile Bostler sends someone for salt."

The air grew colder as they climbed higher. Later, as the sun dipped behind the ridges that crisscrossed in front of them, Eulian wrapped a cloak around her shoulders and suggested they look for a place to spend the night.

Grisbane had been humming along behind and now he called out to Eulian. "If I may suggest it," he said; "there is place hereabouts where we may find a friend or two and spend the night."

Eulian hesitated a minute, then turned and called back, "Can we afford the lost sleep?"

The Small Giant laughed. "I think the company is just as refreshing!" he answered. "I have never slept less than in the house of Rummel Stoneboots, and I have never left any home with more vigor. I think it will serve us well to pay Master Stoneboots a visit."

"You may be right," said Eulian. "I've been thinking about this all afternoon, but whenever I went there, I was always with Thorval. I was not sure if I should just appear unexpectedly."

"Ah," said Grisbane; "but no visit to the house of Stoneboots is entirely unexpected, and no one is unwelcome. Of course, *finding* it is a matter of luck. Either way, once you've been to the house of Stoneboots, there is always a bed for you there."

"Who is Stoneboots?" asked Brian.

Before Grisbane could answer Eulian cried out happily and pointed to the ridge where the sun had just set. Waving from the crest was a powerful, man-shaped figure who stood twice as tall as the fir trees on the rocky slopes below. He wore a great green cloak with its hood thrown back, allowing his thick silver hair and beard to fly loose in the wind. He descended the steep incline swiftly, almost at a run, but he seemed to wade through the rocks rather than stepping over or between them. He left no wake, passing through the crags like a ghost.

When he arrived, he had somehow diminished in stature until he was about the size of a Small Giant. His ancient face was deeply lined and his hands were especially wrinkled, but he stood tall and strong like a man in his prime. His rich beard of white and silver almost covered the front of his broad chest. His thick mustache curved over his wide grin and his deep-set blue eyes twinkled brightly.

"Well now this is an unusual company, if I do say so!" he crowed. "Two legends, royalty and the world's largest traveling musician!"

Grisbane guffawed. "I have already been insulted for that once today," he said.

"Then Korban must be the sentinel at the First Outpost," nodded Rummel. "He has the sharpest tongue ever wielded in fun. But did he also tell you how much they enjoy your recitals?"

"Yes, much to my relief," said Grisbane.

"You will be pleased to know that I have prepared for your arrival and that July awaits us on the step. I have been told to bring you by the shortest route, so, if you don't mind..." With that, he walked over to each of the horses and stroked their necks as he whispered something that made their ears prick up. "Here we go!" he bellowed and suddenly grew very large. "I'll be back for the rest of you in a wink!" he said. "July wishes to speak to the princess, she says." Thus, he scooped up the Elven maiden, horse and all, growing to even more immense proportions as he did so. With a single bound, he was suddenly on the other side of the slope.

Brian and Annie stood dumb with amazement.

Grisbane laughed merrily. "I have sat on his shoulder as he strode over hill and valley from here to the Dorvan Sea," he said. "I have been awakened from a sound sleep in the middle of the night to find myself cradled in his forearm as he bore me to who knows where. Tonight, we would have ridden another hour had he not intercepted us, even if we had taken the shortcut. As it is, he should be returning for us soon."

"Who is he?" asked Annie.

"Maybe once someone knew, but not anymore," said Grisbane. "Rummel Stoneboots has been here since time immemorial. Some tales say that he sprang fully formed from the hills themselves. I've asked him about that. He says it's as good an explanation as any. His wife, July, is equally shy about her origins. She calls herself the sister of the mountains. She has silver hair that tumbles about her shoulders and down her back like a waterfall. In Spring, her dress is the color of every bloom in the mountains. In Summer, it is as green as fresh grass, and in the Fall, it turns red, orange and yellow with the leaves, but in Winter, it is brilliant, sparkling white, like new-fallen snow.

"They live in the heart of the western range," he continued. "The Dwarves revere them. Indeed, sometimes if a young Dwarf is careless in his digging or disturbs an underground stream unnecessarily, July might appear as if from nowhere and teach him better. No one was anyone confronted by her who did not mend his ways, for she is always kind, and her plea is so compelling."

"Do the Elves or the Faeries know them?" asked Annie.

"They generally do not get involved in matters beyond their mountains. Of the Elvenfolk, Thorval Lighthammer is well acquainted with them, but the Faeries have little discourse with them. The grandfather of Raealann of the Green Stone consulted Rummel on occasion, but Raealann was never introduced. Since Stoneboots rarely ventured south, the Men of the Green Stone let him be."

After a few minutes, Rummel returned, his huge shadow stretching across the rocky ridge. Begging Grisbane's pardon, he plucked Brian and Annie off the ground and set them both on his right shoulder. "You will have to hold on to my hair, Brian; and you, my dear, may hold on to him," he instructed. Off they went, up the side of the hill, down the other slope and then swiftly across the steep valley between the ridges. With a sharp turn, he leapt to the top of another peak and stepped across to the opposite side.

"We shall go for a jaunt at Grisbane's expense," he said with a laugh. "You must see the sunset from the Twins. It should be well worth the wait tonight."

Below them, Brian could see a cabin in a grassy clearing on a steep slope. A stream splashed past it on its way to the river in the valley. Arsha, Eulian's mount, was already grazing peacefully. She looked up and whinnied when she recognized Rummel.

With wondrous speed, Rummel swept past the cabin, now leaping across the mountains, range after range. He waded through dense forests and crossed rivers without leaving the hint of a wake. He tread on loose rocks and dirt without dislodging a single stone or causing a slide. In fact, though he seemed so obviously solid, obstacles appeared to pass through him and out the other side unharmed. It all took place at such exhilarating speed that Brian and Annie found it difficult to observe.

In no time, they were taken to the very crest of the Western Mountains. The Twins were two matching peaks of a mighty mountain that was always capped with brilliant snow. Rummel climbed to the top of the Southern Twin, which also stood slightly further west of the Northern Twin. Just below the summit was a level place that was a natural windbreak. There was just enough room for them to move around comfortably. The Giant set them down. Out of the wind, it was warmer than Brian expected up at this altitude, but Annie was still cold.

"You have Brian to keep you warm," said Rummel. "Don't let her get chilled, my boy."

Brian stood close behind her and wrapped his huge, furry arms around her. Annie smiled and snuggled in.

Rummel pointed out and named the snow capped peaks that could be seen from their lofty vantage point. North of them was the jagged crest of Issle. Further west was Orivel and the glaciated series of peaks known as The Hannadain. South and west stood Urzian, a wisp of steam rising lazily from its ice rimmed crater. Rummel named many others that Brian knew he could never pronounce.

"Well, those are the ones you can see from up here," he said. "You stand among some of the grandest nobility to be found anywhere, good company with whom to watch a sunset. I'll be back for you before it gets too dark."

Then with a wave and a laugh, he flung himself off the cliff and tumbled backward down the snowy mountain until he got his feet and strode off again to fetch Grisbane. Not a track was left in the snow behind him.

Annie and Brian stood still for a long time, looking silently across the vast landscape. The sun sank slowly down, turning the snow around them to gold and their shadows to deepest blue. The valleys grew misty and were soon lost in the deepening shadows cast by the stark outline of ridge after ridge. A few high clouds gleamed in a sky that faded from gold to pale yellow, then into a deep blue as twilight crept in stealthily from the east.

Content in Brian's arms, Annie watched the sun sink below the edge of the snowy sea of mountains and mist. She turned her face up toward him and smiled again. He smiled back, his eyes crinkling at the edges like they always did.

"I am glad you're here," she said quietly, looking back out over the mountains. "It's beautiful, but it would be lonely without you."

Brian grunted thoughtfully. "Pretty," he said. "Better with you here."

They said no more until the sun disappeared and they could see Rummel running across the mountaintops to reach them. The stars were coming out as he set them again on his shoulder and headed for the cabin on the side of the hill. By the time they saw the smoke from the chimney, the sky was full of heavenly lights.

July welcomed them in at the door with hot mugs of something sweet to drink. The latecomers found places to sit near a fireplace that was so huge, Brian could have stood in it upright. A mighty mantle framed the fireplace, its shelf supported by carved oaken mountain lion heads on either side. Each piece of furniture in the house of Stoneboots was unique, and none looked out of place. The chair in which the Small Giant sat was just his size and appeared to be made of old driftwood riddled with river rocks worn to a gleaming polish. Eulian's chair looked like a tree growing right out of the floor. Its branches spread around and behind her to support her back and around the sides so she could rest her arms.

Brian found a chair of granite cushioned with live grass, both solid and comfortable when he sat down. Next to it was a delicate seat of alabaster, cut with careful attention to the faint swirls of color in the white stone. Its shape followed the veins of the stone and it fit Annie perfectly. The silky seat cushion was embroidered in the same colors as her wings.

July and Rummel brought out a large board full of things to eat and drink and set it on a low table near the fire. The company helped themselves to whatever looked good to each, and settled back into their chairs to eat and talk of merry things. After dinner, came wonderful drinks and more delightful conversation. At some point, July asked Grisbane for a song and he sang several before they let him sit down again.

Then Eulian was called upon. She told the story of the building of Val-Ellia, the Elven castle. Her tale described the battle for the woods in which Tisphial the Reckless drove back an army with but a sword and a firebrand. The company enjoyed her skill with a tale and cajoled her into telling several short stories (particularly short for Elves, but medium length to everyone else). Some of the stories were very sad but some had her audience roaring with laughter. Often she had to wait for quiet before she could continue.

When she was done, Brian was afraid he would be called upon next. To his relief, July turned to Annie.

"My dear girl, would you dance for us?" she asked. "It has been too long since a Faerie danced in the house of Stoneboots."

Annie nodded and stood up. Then she hesitated, giggled, and said: "I have no idea what to do!"

"Whatever you feel the music suggests," said Rummel as he handed Grisbane a long, thin bow and a strange five-stringed instrument. The Small Giant held the neck of it in his left hand close to his cheek, and stood the large hollow end on the floor. Then his face lit up as Rummel brought out a similar instrument for himself. They took a moment to bring the instruments into tune and then Grisbane began a soft melodic line that rose and fell in a soothing pattern. Rummel joined in with a countermelody that was slightly more rhythmic and complex.

It reminded Annie of wind in the trees and running water and she let these thoughts flow through her movements in the firelight. As she danced, the roof and walls of the house began to fade away. In a moment, the musician, the dancer and the audience were all out on the hillside under the stars. Annie flew up and around with the music, following its melody for a moment and then playing with the idea on her own. Rummel and Grisbane wove in new musical themes inspired by the dance.

The tune grew gradually more lively and the audience watched as, from a flying leap, Annie would stop midair and flip lightly over to touch down again simply by extending her wings. She flew straight upward, wings a blur of blue, and then dropped, flaring at the last second to land lightly on one foot. Her timing is uncanny; she never missed a beat, no matter how complex the rhythm.

Finally, the song wound down to a close and Annie landed in a curtsey to much applause.

Grisbane looked at Rummel with astonishment. "Never have I played so well," he said, almost breathless.

Rummel nodded. "Our dancer required it," he said, beaming.

July turned to Brian. "What would you like to do on such a night?" she asked him.

"Don't know," he said. "I hunt, get wood, eat, sleep. Not much else."

"But even before you met all of us, surely there was something you did simply for the joy of it," July insisted gently. "When the stars are out and the night is clear, what was it you love most to do?"

A boyish smile lit up Brian's face. "I run. Fast. In the woods. In the dark. With the stars."

"Then run you should," declared the lady of the house; " and we will go with you."

"How?" asked Brian.

"Don't worry about that," said Rummel. "We'll manage."

Brian looked around at the beckoning rocks and trees. A moment later, he leapt from his chair and flew with gruffen speed into the forest. Surprisingly, he could still hear the laughter of his companions. They sounded far away but when he stopped suddenly and turned to look, he was astonished to find them sitting on his shoulder, much as he and Annie had ridden on Rummel's. Brian had not grown at all; somehow, they had shrunk.

"Run, Brian!" crowed Rummel, close to his ear.

So Brian ran, down on all fours, dodging in and out of trees, scrambling over rocks and fallen logs and racing through the stream in a headlong rush. He could hear Eulian's tiny voice shouting with delight as he burst almost silently through the underbrush. The muted thud of his feet startled a bobcat and spooked two deer who barely had time to get out of the way. He climbed up out of the woods and fairly flew up the rocks and back down the steep embankments. With powerful arms and sure feet, he hoisted himself onto ledges and leapt over boulders. His nostrils flared and his eyes opened wide. Such a night! Finally, tired and elated, he looped back and brought them all to where the house had magically reappeared under the stars.

The others tumbled off his back as they returned to their normal size, laughing with joy.

"Mr. Gruffenson," gasped Eulian, as they came in through the front door of the cabin; "I have ridden swift horses and run with the fastest Elves, but never have I been on such a ride!"

Annie laughed. "Last time we went flying through the forest, he was carrying me and rolled me in the snow!"

Brian laughed and collapsed into his stone chair. He had never had so much fun in one night.

"Well, now we have heard or seen something special from nearly everyone," said Rummel. "The hour is late and we should retire." There were groans of disapproval.

"We are children being sent to bed!" Eulian protested.

"But now it is my turn," said July; "and I wish you all sweet dreams." With that, she showed them to the next room where a bed was already made for each of them.

"My bed is always here!" said Eulian. "Thorval's is not, but there are three others, tonight."

"Of course," said Rummel. "You expected us to make the rest of them pile in with you?"

"But why does everything fit us just right?" asked Annie.

Rummel Stoneboots smiled. "Nothing you see here is permanent. If we chose to make it permanent, it could be, in a way, but we prefer to form what we need when we need it. Even we, July and I, are not constant. We are of the mountain, the air, the water. What you see as flesh and bones comes from the earth. Our bodies change to suit our needs and the surroundings. That is why we never leave a footprint.

"The cabin is formed the same way. When we knew you were coming, we made your furniture and adjusted the house accordingly. Look, there is Thorval's bed, just as you are used to seeing it."

The company looked over to where a new bed had suddenly appeared in a comfortable niche that had not been there moments before. Eulian gasped in recognition. "So you rearrange matter to create these things?" she asked. "And you rearranged us so we could ride on Brian's shoulder."

"Simply put, yes," their host acknowledged. "Not many know what we do. Grisbane, Thorval and a few of the Dwarves are aware but it is best kept a secret. Kindly keep it to yourselves."

When they were all settled into bed, July put out the lamp and then kissed each one goodnight. They fell into deep sleep as she kissed them.

She came to Brian last. When she reached his bedside, she paused a moment and touched his chest with her hand. "Deep in your great heart lies a great soul," she said. "Welcome back to the world of men, Brian. Rest and dream."

Before he could reply, she kissed his cheek and he slept.

In his dream, he found himself alone in the early afternoon. Tall pines and fir trees stood all about him, a light breeze whispering among their branches. Warm sunlight filtered through the canopy, dappling the soft, dry needles at Brian's feet. The fragrance of evergreen filled the air. He walked among the silent tree trunks for some time with no particular place to go. Eventually, he came upon a little brook burbling along a winding course through the woods. He followed it until it came out of the forest and emptied into a calm sea. A pebbly beach stretched expansively on either side, ending in a massive outcrop far off to his left and curving away out of sight behind the forest to his right. The pebbles rattled against each other as gentle waves washed in and receded. Sea birds called to each other here and there across the sky.

The sun-bleached trunk of a huge pine lay on the beach. All that remained of its once massive root system was a single crooked finger now pointing skyward. Brian went over and sat on the polished wood, enjoying the sounds. Hours crept by as the waves went in and out, and the sun drifted further out to sea. The wind picked up a little and ruffled the gruffen's hair and fur. The setting sun slowly turned both the sea and the sky to a deep gold.

At some point, Brian looked up to see a Faerie coming around the outcrop in the distance. She started walking down the beach toward him. Though she was still a long way off, he knew it was Annie. Her face was turned toward the setting sun, and her dark hair blew loosely in the breeze. Her filmy Faerie dress flowed about her, and her outstretched wings waved with every breath of wind. Brian thought to call out, but the evening was so peaceful and calm that he chose not to. If this was all a dream, it was very real. As far as he could tell, Annie was truly coming toward him, walking barefoot at the edge of the water in this wonderful place.

He watched as she turned her head and saw him sitting on the log. For a moment she walked on, staring curiously. She waved tentatively. He waved and she opened her wings and flew to him. Landing on the log beside him, she said, "I didn't think I would see anyone else in this dream! I was missing you, and that was kind of sweet, but there you were on the beach. This is better. I like my dream."

"Thought it was my dream," said Brian. "Good either way."

They walked along the by the waves as the sun sank into the sea and the world was swallowed in a cool darkness lit by countless stars. When the half moon rose up from behind the trees, Brian stretched out on the cool grass and Annie laid her head on his arm and looked up at the stars. For a long time they talked about everything and nothing at all. After a long silence, Brian noticed that Annie had fallen asleep. For a long time he lay there, happily listening to her breathing. Then, finally, he also drifted off to sleep.

CHAPTER 28

Through the Pass

Brian awoke to the voices of Rummel Stoneboots and Grisbane singing somewhere outside:

> Come wash your face
> And scrub your nose
> And splash the water with your toes!
> Then leap into the lily pond
> And bathe among the froggies!
> I do declare
> The lily fair
> Has not a rival to compare,
> So dive right in with croak and fin!
> Let all be soaked and soggy!

Eulian and Annie were laughing and July was calling for Brian to come out to the pond for a bath. They were down the hill in a wide pool that was fed by a stream that spilled over a rocky shelf. He trotted out the front door and went down to join them.

"One must leap into the pond from as great a height as possible," Rummel informed him with mock seriousness, pointing to the top of the small waterfall. "The water is plenty deep and we expect you to do your best to empty as much of it as you can."

Everyone cleared the area in the center. Apparently, Grisbane and Rummel had already made quite a contest out of water displacement and they challenged the gruffen to outdo them. Brian was eager to try once he understood the game. He climbed up on the overhanging rock and leapt off, curling into a tight ball. He hit the water with an impact that stung severely. Indeed, the plunge pool was very deep. He thrashed around until he came to the surface again, sputtering and paddling off to the edge where he could get some footing.

"Now that one beats all!" howled Grisbane, his hair matted down over his ears. He pointed at Rummel who was shaking water from his beard. "Don't you change size and put us at a handicap, Rumme. Brian wins!"

Rummel cheerfully conceded defeat. After a bit more splashing around, they all headed back to the cabin for some dry clothes while Brian simply stood off to the side and shook himself until his fur stuck out all over.

Breakfast was jolly and plentiful, but then, as always at the house of Stoneboots, they were reluctant to leave. After many good-byes, the entire company was shuttled off on Rummel's shoulders. He left them further down the trail than he had found them. "It makes up for the time lost over breakfast," he said. They bid him farewell and sent their thanks back to his wife. Then in a bound, he headed across the mountains, waving over his shoulder as he sped away.

"Such a welcome," said Eulian.

"Yes, they feel like family, don't they," said Grisbane.

"Indeed," said the Elven princess; "one that knows me better than my own."

The day was as beautiful as the sunrise had promised, and the trail was easily followed. Wherever the way grew wide enough, they took off at a gallop, as much for the fun of it as for the speed. Brian was always in the lead, and the horses rarely caught him before the trail narrowed again. By mid morning, they slowed as they began the steep climb toward the continental divide.

Their path led up switchback after rocky switchback

"Kaliff's Cleft," said Grisbane, pointing to what looked like a thin, vertical crack in a massive buttress that joined two towering peaks.

"This was always the most dangerous part," said Eulian to Grisbane. "But you and I are the only ones at risk here."

Grisbane laughed. Indeed, Brian easily scrambled along the trail, and Annie merely flew to the next point and waited for everyone to get there. Thanks to the good horses, they expected to be well on the other side of the Cleft by nightfall. Lesser mounts would have found the going treacherous but the horses of the Green Stone were well-trained, confident and sure-footed.

When they reached the snow line, they were still a thousand feet below the pass. Some two hundred feet below the cleft, Grisbane and Eulian stopped everyone.

"Why?" asked Brian.

"I can't make out the trail under the snowdrifts," said Annie.

"I remember this view of the pass," said Eulian; "but I'm trying to remember exactly how goes from here. There are a couple of hidden drop-offs which would be even more treacherous with the snow."

The Small Giant nodded. "From this point, it makes two more switchbacks: one short and steep, and one longer and more gradual. The short one should take us south until the pass is out of sight. Then the longer one traverses to the right along the cliff base. The pass itself is entered with a sharp left turn."

"I remember the left turn," said Eulian. "But we could be five feet high or low from the trail and never find the switchbacks."

"True," said Grisbane. "The tricky portion is a blind turn. If we miss it, we could get in trouble quickly."

"Maybe I can find it," said Annie.

"I don't know if I could describe it for you," said Grisbane. "I think I'll recognize it when I see it, though."

"Me, too," said Eulian; "even in the snow. I did not expect the snowpack to be this deep so late in the year."

"Claws," said Brian, showing them his hands and feet. "I got claws. I'll carry someone. Find the trail from the top."

Grisbane liked the idea and Eulian agreed to ride. The gruffen knelt down to let her climb onto his back.

"I'm much heavier today than I was last night on your shoulder," she said apologetically.

"Too bad we're not going for another run," he replied.

They climbed slowly up the ice covered slope. When they had gone about ten feet, Eulian pointed out part of the trail. They followed this southward and upward until they could no longer see Grisbane and the horses. They had come to a place where the cliff dropped away sharply for thousands of feet on the left side and rose in a near vertical wall to the right.

"There's got to be a turn here somewhere that the horses can take safely," said Eulian.

But when they looked around, there was nowhere else to go.

"Up here," said Anni, pointing to an outcrop about thirty feet over their heads. "I think you're too low."

Brian carried Eulian carefully back the way they came and started hunting around for the trail again.

"If you can get here, it seems big enough for a horse to turn around," Annie said.

Eulian decided that they must have been one switchback too low. An hour of careful searching revealed a likely path. Brian took Eulian back to her horse, and then he and Annie retraced the path to mark it well. Once they were all underway again it was not such a great matter to reach the pass.

Kaliff's Cleft was, indeed, merely a crack in the wall. Icy rock stood several hundred feet high on either side of the crevice which was just wide enough for

Grisbane to pass through comfortably on his great horse. The cleft was about two hundred paces long and had been cut nearly level hundreds of years ago by the Dwarves when it was the main route connecting two great families. The riders dismounted once more and Brian and Grisbane went in first to clear a small rock fall that the horses would have trouble getting over. Then they led their horses through, single file as Annie flew over the top of the buttress.

It was mid afternoon when they emerged to meet Annie on the other side of the pass. From here on, the snow was not as deep and the trail was clearly visible. Lunch had been postponed in order to get through the pass, so they paused to eat and feed the horses some mash provided by Rummel and July. Then, much more relaxed, they wound their way down the mountain.

They were out of the snow and into the twisted junipers as the sun was setting. Grisbane knew of a windbreak on the east side of a ridge that served well as a bivouac. They headed for a pile of boulders on the further slope. Although it was drier on the western side of the divide, it was also colder, and soon all but Brian felt the chill. Annie also had to wear a heavy cloak so she now rode behind Eulian. They arrived at the windbreak as darkness fell. After rubbing down the horses, they made a quick fire for a hot meal and then huddled together and slept.

Just before dawn, Brian awoke to the sound of the horses shuffling fretfully. He sat up slowly, his nose and ears scanning the night air. He thought he could hear galloping hoof beats but they were hard to pick out amidst the general nervousness of the horses nearby. He stared hard into the night but nothing moved in the shadows. A moment later, he could smell something he didn't like. He couldn't make out what it was, though. He kept very still for some time, all senses alert, but he heard no more. The horses calmed down and returned to grazing. Finally, Brian lay back down beside Annie and drifted off to sleep.

* * *

The mind that commanded the Twin stretched farther, farther.
No, he could no longer sense his rider.
Pity, he thought. I might have learned something.
He leaned back in the darkness and let out a long, slow, hissing breath.

* * *

As they prepared to depart the next day, Brian mentioned the disturbance in the night. No one else had noticed it. They searched the area.

"Mountain lion," said Eulian.

"Hmph," said Brian. "Downwind. Maybe that was it."

They set out on the trail and passed over to the other side of the ridge. The sky was again clear and blue. As they descended further, the air got warmer. Grisbane began singing again. His songs wove in and out of old legends some of which Eulian knew, but most of which were foreign to all of them. The songs told of heroes and villains, lovers and lost ones. It was a pleasant way to pass the time as they went on and on, league after league.

Brian brought them to a halt. He could see clear tracks on the dusty path. Another horseman had been this way recently, apparently in a hurry. Eulian dismounted to take a look.

"These marks," she said. "Men of the Green Stone do not notch their horseshoes in the rear like this." She pointed to the distinct cut at the back of one of the prints.

"Does everyone give horses shoes?" asked Annie.

"Only Men," the Small Giant answered. "What is one rider doing out here alone?"

"A scout, perhaps, or a messenger," suggested the Elven Princess. "But why?"

Brian put his nose to the tracks and snorted.

"Horse," he said, flatly. "Not happy."

"What tells you that?" asked Grisbane.

"Smelly," said Brian.

"Lots of things are smelly," said Annie; "including you sometimes!"

Eulian stifled a guffaw.

Brian just nodded. "This one's not happy," he said.

"The rider is going the same direction we are," said Grisbane. "I wonder where he's headed. The main road leads to the desert, but there are other routes through the mountains. We should see if his tracks diverge."

"I'll watch," said Brian.

The company rode on without incident. Stopping for lunch, they rested the horses and sat on the rocks, glad for the warmth of the sun. A few wispy clouds brushed a few streaks high in the blue, and the good weather steadfastly refused to leave.

Within an hour, they had passed all the known turnoffs to other places. Any travelers this far along intended to reach the desert. Most were headed for the salt lake on the edge of the mountains. Very few ventured into the desert itself. Even fewer returned.

Brian stood up and announced that there were no more horse tracks. He could not determine where the rider had gone. There seemed to be no further trace of it. He checked back along the trail but there was no indication of its passage there. They moved on.

As the afternoon waned and the trail smoothed out, they made good time, passing the place where Grisbane usually spent the second night on the western side of the mountains. A few hours further on, they decided to make camp before they lost daylight. They chose a flat spot a short way up from the trail. It was more exposed than they would have liked, but it was a safer place to sleep than down on the trail where there was no room to move.

Not far from their camp, Annie happened upon the concealed entrance to a Dwarf tunnel. The door was actually a large boulder, pinned and counterbalanced so it could be swung aside with very little effort. She called the others who came to investigate. There appeared to be no one inside.

Suddenly, a rock flew out of the entrance, whizzing by at ear level.

"Halt!" shouted someone in the darkness.

Somebody was indeed home.

"Who goes there?" shouted the voice inside the tunnel.

Grisbane answered in a loud, calm voice: "Grisbane, the Small Giant; Eulian, Princess of the Elves; Annathía, the Snowdaughter; and Brian, the Valen dak-Lammethan."

"Grisbane Goldenthroat, from the sounds of it," answered the voice from within the tunnel. "I am glad it's you."

Coming into the light was one of the wiriest Dwarves any of them had ever seen. Though he was well muscled by any standard, he was remarkably lean for a Dwarf. He seemed younger than Korban, clearly in the prime of manhood. His sparse red beard tapered to a ragged blonde point at the juncture of his angular collarbone. Unlike most Dwarves, he kept his hair close-cropped, and, from the looks of it, he cut it himself with a razor-sharp knife. His deep-set green eyes seemed to smile even when he was serious.

"Roggin, at your service," he said with a bow. "I had heard you were passing by, but I did not expect anyone on my doorstep. There's a strange rider about, so I've been cautious. Pardon the rude welcome."

Eulian waved it off. "No offense taken. We found tracks and followed them for some distance before they disappeared," she said. "It could have been your strange rider."

"Are there tracks nearby?" asked the wiry Dwarf. "I'd like to see them."

"We haven't seen any in the last hour," Grisbane said. "Perhaps he took another path."

Roggin motioned down the tunnel. "I would be happy to have you stay with me, if you don't mind stooping low for a few hundred feet," he suggested. "It's no luxury, but it is warm and I find it comfortable."

"Thank you kindly, Mr. Roggin," said the Small Giant. "We have two horses that should not be left unattended. Brian and I will stay and watch if the princess and Annathía wish to accept your invitation."

Roggin eyed the gruffen curiously and then looked back at Grisbane. "You said the Valen was with you. Is he with the horses?"

"He's right here," Grisbane replied. "Roggin, this is Brian P. Gruffenson, Valen dak–Lammethan."

"Pleased to meet you," said the astonished Dwarf; "and I beg your pardon!"

"It's okay," said Brian. "Bostler thought I was a big pet."

"Pet indeed!" Roggin laughed, his green eyes lighting up even more.

Brian liked him.

"Well," said Roggin; "no one needs to sleep outside with the horses, pet or not! There is a place we use as a corral when someone comes out to gather salt. Your mounts will be safe there."

He came out of the tunnel and led them around to what appeared to be a random row of boulders. The Dwarf pressed on one of them and it swung inward to reveal a grassy hollow where the two horses could graze comfortably.

"How many times have I passed by here and never seen your corral?" exclaimed Grisbane. "We will gladly accept your hospitality." They led the horses into the hollow and removed their saddles, blankets and halters. Then they rubbed down the tired animals and followed Roggin out of the "gate" back to the tunnel.

All remaining daylight was sealed out as Roggin closed the entrance. In a moment, they heard him strike his tinderbox and they all blinked as he lit a torch. Brian and the Small Giant had to crawl on hands and knees but Annie and Eulian were able to manage without stooping too much. The watchman's quarters were surprisingly grand with a high vaulted ceiling so even Brian and Grisbane could stand up straight and walk about. Roggin insisted that they share some hot food that was cooling in a big pot by the hearth.

"But you could live on this for a week!" said Grisbane.

"I can get more," said Roggin. "Other than the rare occasions when a party on horseback comes to gather salt, I rarely have company at this post. I'll not miss the chance to serve a good meal to friends."

Brian particularly enjoyed the simple, hearty fare. When they were done, the pot was empty and everyone was satisfied. Roggin left for a moment and returned with a tray full of large mugs filled with beer drafted from a keg that was kept cold in a deep cellar. They spent a happy hour together talking of this and that, each of them sitting in a chair or on the floor.

After that, they pulled out the extra blankets (two each, of course: one for the body and one for the legs) and all lay down for a welcome sleep.

269

* * *

Brian awoke to the smell of food cooking and for a moment was not sure where he was. When he sat up, he awakened Annie lying next to him. She rolled over and smiled. Roggin was cooking something over the coals. The whole room was filled with the fragrance of breakfast.With a dash of this and a pinch of that, Roggin had made a delicious gruel out of oats, wheat and barley. It was lightly sweetened and deftly spiced. To his credit, the Dwarf had again made enough for all of them to eat their fill with none left over: a masterpiece of appetite estimation.

They did not tarry long. The sun was just rising when they went to retrieve their horses. Roggin opened the gate to an empty corral. The saddles and blankets lay where they had stashed them, but their mounts and the halters had disappeared. The Dwarf stood in the center of the hollow and looked around, dismayed.

"No animal has ever been stolen from here before," he said. " I would have guarded them myself." He paused. "I have treasure of my own and I will repay you, but that will not bring your horses back."

Grisbane shook his head. "We are responsible for our own mounts and we chose to place them within these walls," he said. "We will track them down."

"I'll go with you," said Roggin. "I know these hills well."

Brian already had his nose to the ground near a telltale hoof print. "Smelly horse," he said. "Same one." The tracks led downhill to the main trail.

It was clear already that the horses were being led parallel to the path. The rest of the party could not keep up with Brian, so they decided to go back to the trail and let him follow the markings while Annie flew overhead and kept them in contact.

Judging from the hoof prints, the horses were traveling fast, but it was hard to tell when they had been stolen. After two hours at a rapid pace, the searchers on the ground paused for a rest.

Annie sailed up on the currents to have a look around. Her friends looked like small dots in the clearing and she wished she had Brian's sharp eyesight. Off to the west, she could see the desert stretching out into the dusty horizon. Parts of the path were hidden from view so she flew along the westward route for awhile until she was sure she had gotten a good look several miles ahead. There was nothing to be seen.

On the way back, flying very low this time, she caught sight of three horses. A dark figure rode one of them. They were following a steep-sided rift perpendicular to the main trail, heading south. She quickly flew back to the others.

"We're in luck," said Roggin. "They're heading directly toward a tunnel opening and there's a shortcut from here. If we move quickly, we should be able to catch him." He looked at Brian and the Small Giant towering over him.

"Don't worry," he said. "The ceiling is high enough."

They scrambled up the hill to another ingeniously hidden entrance. After the company crawled along for several yards, Roggin lit a torch, illuminating a long passageway leading south. They set off at a run.

Roggin Steelsmith knew this place like his own smell. It had been his grandfather's responsibility to guard this sector, and the charge had been handed down to him through his father, so Roggin had essentially grown up here. Since he was unmarried, he spent all his time in these deep chambers and tunnels, sometimes remaining behind to explore even when his cousin Scoggin came to relieve him periodically.

The passageways had been cut by his ancestors, the great Steelsmith Dwarves. They, and their kin the Goldsmiths, had also cut Kaliff's Cleft to provide common access through the western mountains. The Steelsmiths had sculpted beautiful pillars and elaborate doorways in their network of tunnels. Now, sadly, only the watchmen wandered these routes. They had been abandoned centuries ago. Folk tales spoke of a great evil lurking beneath the ancient floors but Roggin considered them to be scary stories told to wide-eyed children by irresponsible adults.

The company ran on southward through several branching corridors until everyone but Roggin was completely lost. Suddenly, the wiry Dwarf turned westward through a large doorway leading to another long hall.

"We are very close," he said, huffing and puffing.

Roggin had been running full speed the whole time. His heart was pounding so loudly in his ears that he couldn't hear much else. Around another corner along the left side wall, he could see a series of stone steps leading up to the thin splinter of light that indicated the hidden exit. He set the torch in a sconce by the wall, climbed the steps and peered through the crack to get used to the light. Once his eyes adjusted, he readied his knife, opened the door and looked around. There was no sign of the dark rider or the horses. If the horses had already passed, they would still be close by. He listened hard. There was no sound.

He was about to say something to the others below when he was suddenly gripped by fear! Why, he could not imagine, but it hardly mattered. Something behind him was debilitatingly frightening. Every fiber of his body screamed at him to break out of the tunnel and run for his life. Instead, he turned and looked back down the stairs. He could see nothing in the darkness below.

"Who's there?" he hissed. No answer.

Heart pounding, he closed the tunnel entrance, dropped to the floor and shielded his eyes from the torchlight. He called again, a little louder. Still no answer. The fear grew stronger as he forced himself to go all the way back down the stairs. His left hand retrieved the torch from the sconce and his right hand gripped his knife.

Then the stench hit him. Such a smell! It was an awful reek, thick with death and rot. It almost felled him with its intensity. He reeled back, and then, gathering his courage, he shot around the corner and stabbed fiercely into the air. He struck nothing. A dark shape, huge and powerful, suddenly appeared and roughly scooped him up. The torch was knocked from his hand and his knife arm was pinned to his side. His captor was running off with him!

Roggin struggled but he could not free himself. The reeking stench swirled about as the sound of running footsteps pounded in his head. After awhile, the awful smell faded and the pace slowed. He realized suddenly that the strong arm that was carrying him belonged to Brian. The smell was gone and the fear had eased when they finally stopped to rest.

Then, he heard Annie's voice, Grisbane's and Eulian's. The Small Giant had Roggin's torch.

"What happened?" gasped Roggin.

"Don't know," said Brian. "Something bad!"

"That seems like the smoke they found in the deep eastern mines," Roggin said; "but we're not that deep here. The smoke must be rising."

It did seem like the same thing Korban had described two days before. "Why didn't Rummel or July mention it when we were there?" Annie asked aloud.

The Dwarf's eyes widened. "You were in the house of Stoneboots!" he exclaimed. "I have met the Lady July, only once." He stopped.

"Where are we?" asked Eulian.

Roggin took a good look around before he answered. "We're a long way from that exit. We've gone east and south," he said. "I can get us out of here by another route but we'll have to hurry, or we may have lost your horses for good."

"One thing at a time," said Grisbane. "Lead on."

CHAPTER 29

The Necrowights

For a thousand years, the Necrowights had festered in their prison beneath the western mountains. Only once, when the Steelsmiths built their vast halls, had the Smoking Death nearly escaped. July intervened and warned the Dwarves to stop digging there, but that was long ago, and much had transpired in the depths since the Necrowights' capture. They had not lain idle. The evil that consumed them had grown more fetid and vile, and they had heard a call—their Master's call—something they had not heard for a millennium. Though they wished to answer, they could not yet escape.

Many hundreds of them had found the breech that had recently been cut. They seeped through various cracks, roaming the Dwarvish tunnels as they searched for the source of the call, two now roamed the halls of the Steelsmiths. In torchlight, they appeared as a black fog drifting along the floor of the tunnel, following the footsteps of the Faerie.

The Necrowights had not always been evil. Once they were winged and glorious, but the Dark Master had seduced them with the promise of power. They fought for him, and many died, but true to his promise, the Dark Master had converted their blood into the amorphous form they now took. Those who had not been seduced by the Dark Master were jealously destroyed by those who had. Their being still boiled at the betrayal. Here, after a thousand hateful years, they had come across another winged one and the old anger burned again. She must be destroyed.

* * *

Roggin led his companions northward, and they kept on determinedly until they came to a great pile of rubble blocking their path.

"This was not here last month," Roggin exclaimed. "I saw no weakness then, but the cavern roof has collapsed!" They doubled back several hundred yards before the Dwarf found an alternate route.

After another exhausting hour of running down corridors, they stopped to rest. They had come into the circular atrium of a vast hall. On either side, stone staircases curved upward toward a second floor, Another set of stairs vanished out of sight from there. The high ceilings lay far beyond the reach of torchlight. Annie crossed over to the foot of the stairs and sat down wearily.

"This is the Great Hall of the Steelsmiths," said Roggin. "It rises up three stories before the domed ceiling even begins. I've spent many hours in this hall, going into the many rooms that line the great walkways. I like to think of it as the palace of my kinsmen, but they loved the deeper levels and may have built something even more grand further down. I haven't been able to get away from my post long enough to explore much of the next two levels. This is the largest chamber so far."

"The workmanship is impressive," said Eulian; "though I admit I would appreciate it more above ground."

No one said anything but they all noticed the same thing at the same time: the fear they had encountered farther back in the tunnels. Everyone scattered. In the torchlight, they could actually see smoke streaming along the floor, licking at the dusty imprints Annie's feet had left on the paving stones. It rushed toward her and she flew blindly into the air, smashing against an overhanging balcony. Her wings fluttered wildly but she could not keep herself from crashing onto the stone steps halfway up the stairs.

Brian dropped to all fours and shot across the room at full speed. The others came from all sides.

Annie turned fiercely to face the smoke that was roiling up the stairs toward her. Her damaged wing angled awkwardly behind her. Brian charged up the steps, eyes wide and heart pounding. The fear made him gag. He was almost to the trailing edge of the smoke, but he could see the vapor closing in on Annie. He dove forward and grabbed at the smoke with both hands, grasping nothing. Instantly, his hands and arms felt like they were freezing and burning at the same time. He roared and grabbed again. It was useless! There was nothing to grab!

"The Blade!" shouted Grisbane, who had just reached the bottom of the stairs. "Use the Blade!"

Desperately, Brian yanked the long knife from its sheath and slashed through the smoke. He felt the knife slice into the stone steps. A nasty shriek went up, tearing at his ears as some of the smoke disappeared. There was still some left!

It whirled about and wrapped around Brian's leg, climbing quickly toward his chest. The gruffen howled in pain. He stabbed at the smoke with the Valenblade, slicing through a bit of fur on his own thigh. Another shriek split the air.

Then all was quiet. The smoke had vanished.

Every muscle in Brian's body began to seize. He doubled over, curled into a knot, and tumbled down the steps. Grisbane stopped him and carefully slid him to the stone floor.

The others were already on their way. Roggin held the torch as Grisbane rolled Brian over and quickly found the wound from the Valenblade. It was only a scratch, very clean. Grisbane tore his shirt to bind the wound.

Eulian headed up the stairs to Annie.

The Faerie was crouched against the curved stone wall, bleeding from her shoulder and the back of her head. "Is he all right? Is it gone?" she asked.

Eulian nodded. "I think Brian killed it."

"What happened? Did it hurt him?" asked Annie. She stood up, wincing and gasping. Her wing hung uselessly from her back.

"I don't know," said Eulian. "But you're wounded, too. Go slowly. Grisbane will do his best."

Annie said nothing, but she let Eulian help her descend the stairs to where Brian lay twisted and paralyzed. Roggin and the Small Giant were rubbing his limbs briskly and trying to straighten them.

"No!" cried Annie, kneeling beside the gruffen. Brian's eyes were looking at her but he couldn't say anything.

Suddenly, a rumble rippled through the mountain like far off thunder that grew closer and closer. Centuries old dust drifted down into the light of their torches. The company huddled together and Grisbane put a great arm out to either side, shielding them as best he could with his large body. The roar grew louder and soon, it was upon them. In a shower of dust, a massive figure rose from the floor of the hall as if from a pool of water. The shape of a head appeared first and then the huge body thrust its way upward. The mouth was open and a horrendous growl issued from it. Its shoulders filled the hall and when its arms were free, the creature leaned over at the waist, its legs still under the floor.

"Rummel!" shouted Grisbane. "Rummel Stoneboots!"

Rummel's face was grave with anger and concern. He shrank to a more manageable size as he emerged completely from the floor. Kneeling beside Brian, he put his hands on both sides of the gruffen's head. Slowly, Brian began to relax. The strain left his frozen limbs and the light came back into his eyes.

"Tell me what happened," said Rummel, quietly. Grisbane told him how they had come upon the smoke in the tunnels, and how Brian had attacked it.

Rummel shook his head sadly. "How did you get rid of it?" he asked.

"Brian cut into the smoke with the Valenblade and the smoke disappeared," said Grisbane.

"Indeed?" said Rummel. "That is good to know."

After awhile, Brian was able to sit up again and Rummel turned his attention to Annie. Taking the Faerie in his arms, he held her close as he tended to her cuts and her bruised and bent wing. She bit her lip and trembled as his hands straightened her wing and then slowly worked it back into shape. Amazingly, the pain disappeared as he worked. When he was done, Annie kissed his great cheek, thanked him, and sat back next to Brian who was still groggy.

Roggin stepped forward and stood before Rummel Stoneboots, his eyes wide with awe. "Honored to meet you, sir," he said with a bow.

Rummel let go a warm, booming laugh."Roggin Steelsmith, the one-time chisel vandal!" he said. "Good to make your acquaintance finally. You may not know this, but July checks up on you from time to time to see how you're getting on. She says you have done well."

"If I may, sir," said Roggin. "I need your help."

Rummel smiled broadly. "Of course. How may I help you?"

Roggin took a breath. "Their horses were stolen from my corral," he said. "We were searching for them when we were attacked. Would you help us find them again?"

Stoneboots laughed again. "My dear Roggin, you will not rest until those poor beasts are found! I can help. We can make up for the lost time, too. First, we should leave here and take to the open air."

Brian got shakily to his feet and they all followed Rummel out of the Great Hall. Not much further on, Stoneboots turned abruptly toward the solid wall of rock. Much to Roggin's astonishment, the wall opened like liquid displaced by a glass bowl. Rummel stepped inside and the rest of them entered after him. They walked on, upward and westward in a bubble of air passing through layer upon layer of stone, the way closing behind them as they went. The Dwarf marveled as they burrowed through granite and quartz and vein after vein of metal and precious stones. Rummel halted and easily scooped a shining bit of metal out of the wall with his fingertip. As they continued walking, he rolled it between his fingers until it formed a perfect little sphere. Then he turned and handed it to the Dwarf.

"This is cold forged steel," said Stoneboots; "a token of friendship, and a souvenir from this trip through your beloved mountains."

The Dwarf accepted it, speechless with wonder. He held it in his fist for awhile before putting it deep into his pocket.

In a moment, they broke out into the noonday sun. They were in the bottom of a steep walled ravine. Here the creek widened into a pool before it slipped over a rocky ledge and plunged out of sight to their right. To Roggin's relief, the missing horses were grazing comfortably, enjoying a patch of green grass nearby. There was a third horse as well, a great black beast. As soon as they arrived, the black horse panicked and bolted, splashing through the water and leaping wildly over the fall. Stoneboots disappeared. The others calmed their mounts and waited until Rummel returned, climbing up the waterfall. He held a horseshoe in one hand.

"Senseless waste of a good animal," he growled, showing them the shoe. "I don't know what they did to the poor thing."

"Dead?" asked Annie.

Rummel nodded. "At least now it is at peace."

"This must be the mount we were tracking," said Eulian, pointing to the three notches cut in the shoe.

"But where is the rider?" Grisbane asked.

"Below!" shouted Rummel, suddenly. "Brian, Grisbane! With me!"

He grabbed the two and plunged into the earth. It swallowed them and left the others standing there, dumbfounded.

"Now what?" said Eulian, drawing her sword. Roggin unsheathed his short blade and they surveyed the landscape warily. The horses returned to their grazing. Nothing else moved.

Not much later, Rummel reappeared with Brian and Grisbane.

"Found him," grunted Brian.

"Who was he?" the Dwarf asked

"Black Warrior," said Grisbane, with a grave face.

Eulian blanched. "I thought they were legend," she said.

"No," said Rummel, shaking his head. "Morvassus must have sent him, perhaps to summon the Necrowights. I doubt he came just to steal your horses. I don't know if he delivered his message. But you can put your weapons away; the danger is past."

"What happened to the horse?" asked Annie. "I didn't see it at the bottom of the fall."

"It was already dying when we found it," Stoneboots replied. "The creature perished as all Black Warriors' mounts do: it vanished to nothing. Magic transforms them and magic destroys them. Some can be restored; this one could not."

"Sad," said the Faerie.

The Lord of the Mountains looked about at his companions. They were tired and dirty. "Come," he said. "I will take you to the edge of the desert."

"I'll go back to the outpost," said Roggin.

"No," said Rummel. "For now, you come, too. It will be faster."

He grew large again and Roggin followed, amazed, as they all climbed onto Stoneboots' shoulders. Then Rummel gently picked up a horse in each hand and carried them all to the border of the desert. They were back on the ground with in the space of an hour. Stoneboots bid everyone a safe journey and strode off over the hills with Roggin waving from his shoulder.

Since they had to follow a set path each day to avoid the Carthiss, they would not start across the desert until the next morning. To begin the journey now would leave them stranded on the sand at nightfall when the Carthiss was out. Setting up camp did not take long; for the remainder of the afternoon, they rested.

When night fell, Grisbane took the first watch and the others stretched out under the blanket of stars. The temperature dropped quickly at night, but they drew their cloaks about them and soon all but the Small Giant were fast asleep.

Eulian woke Brian for the third watch. The moon was high, three quarters full, and the hills about them were lit by its glow. Brian sat in the cold night air and mulled over the events of the day before. His thoughts turned to the blade sheathed next to his chest. It certainly had unusual powers if it could kill smoke. And what of the Black Warrior? Rummel had opened the wall beside the soldier and completely surprised him but the Lord of the Mountains would not attack the Black Warrior himself. One stroke of the Valenblade was all it took. Strange.

The night rolled on. Somewhere, far away in the darkness, the Carthiss let loose a rattling howl that drifted across the cold sand, bounced off the cliffs and sailed over the hills, finally reaching the ears of the gruffen sitting on a rock. Brian's ears pricked up at the sound, but it felt nothing like the horror of the Necrowights. It was more like hearing wolves on distant hills. For now, Brian knew they were safe from the Carthiss, but the howling reminded him that tomorrow they were going directly into her territory.

CHAPTER 30

Thihanan

The sun had not yet risen on Cai-Amira, when Lia awakened and could not go back to sleep. She slipped out of bed and dressed, eager to get out of the house. Wandering aimlessly in the woods, she passed by the spot where the Trothianna tree had been. She could see hardly any remnants of the little tree. She thought of Annie and the gruffen. Then she felt the tightening in her throat again as the image of her sister came to mind. She choked out a sob and tried to compose herself. As she wiped her eyes, she heard Calicia say her name quietly behind her. When she turned, she saw her friend had also been crying.

"Sometimes it helps," said Calicia.

Lia sank to the ground and let the tears flow. Calicia sat down beside her, and for a long time they wept and hugged each other, wept and sat numbly looking about. Then, Calicia took Lia's hand and helped her to her feet. They walked together through the forest until they came to where the tree of the Chrysalis had stood. The new ring of trees was even taller and thicker than the night before. Lia did not wish to enter so Calicia kissed her, found the opening and went in.

The long rays of the rising sun filtered through the light fog that had formed in the woods. Lia wandered about slowly, taking it all in. Being in the kind of place her sister had always loved assuaged the loneliness somewhat.

After about an hour, Lia turned back toward the house when she heard Calicia calling behind her. She whirled about. Calicia was radiant and could hardly contain herself.

"I've seen Brian!" she cried. "Annie is well. He says he spoke to my father who awaits us in Thihanan."

"What? How? Did he say anything about Mari?" Lia asked urgently.

"No. He didn't know she was gone," said Calicia. "I told him our suspicions."

"At least two are safe, then," said Lia both relieved and disappointed.

They went back to the house where the men had just sat down to breakfast. Calicia broke the news.

Ender sat back, amazed. "Brian? Brian spoke to you in the Circle?"

"Yes!" she said. "I could not quite see where he was and I did not speak to him long; he seemed to have pressing business, but I noticed he still held the long knife," she said. "No word of Mari."

Still, this news gave everyone more energy. After breakfast, they went back to cleaning up the wreckage on the hillside. The men hewed the branches off the fallen trees and dragged all the lumber with chains, ropes and pulleys to a flat area behind the house. There they were stacked for cutting and drying. Ender had no immediate plans for the wood, but Owler was full of ideas.

"If ever you decide you can spare some of this, do let me know," he said enthusiastically. "I have never seen such wonderful grain."

Lia and Calicia chopped off the smaller branches and piled them up to burn. The thicker limbs were stacked by the logs and all the rest of the bracken was thrown into the fire. That evening, as the sun went down, the fire crackled and smoked. It filled the cool air with a wonderful smell. Calicia made a special tea and they all sat on the log bench outside the house to watch the daylight fade. The day's work had exorcised some of their pain.

Tired, they bid each other good night and fell asleep almost as soon as their heads hit the pillow.

Morning came again and they spent another day working with the fallen trees. Keeping busy seemed to be the best antidote for sadness. By the time evening rolled around again, they were all glad to stop and rest. After dinner, Lia collapsed lazily on the couch and Ender lit his pipe for the first time in days. Judging from the position of the stars that night, he reckoned they were within a half day's sailing of Thihanan. He was anxious to meet with the Great Master again. There were so many questions.

* * *

Their packs, weapons and provisions ready and waiting, they spent the last morning at sea roaming the island together, taking in the good weather and relaxing. The coast of Thihanan was a dark line on the horizon, growing thicker by the hour. They were entering the bay even before lunchtime and Ender called everyone together to watch the docking. "The island has done this for centuries and nary a dish is knocked from the cupboard when it slides into shore." he said.

This time was no exception. The coastlines of the two landmasses lined up perfectly as the island slipped into place, leaving not a trace of beach when it came to a stop. Grass met grass just as it did on the other shore in the cave. In a few minutes, the waves settled and the sea flowed around it, as if it had always been there.

Ender led them off the island and up the hill, where they found Palanthar sitting on a boulder of quartzite. The Great Master's eyes were closed, and he appeared to be lost in meditation.

"Master, we have finally arrived," said Ender.

Palanthar looked up slowly as if roused from sleep and sat a moment before he rose and greeted Ender with an embrace. He was a remarkably small man, tiny next to Ender, Owler and Aaron. Still, his lithe hands, lean muscles and easy movements gave the impression that he could spring like a cat whenever he wanted to. Great joy and great sorrow had both etched lines around his eyes and mouth. Aaron, Lia and Owler liked him instantly.

Calicia wrapped him in her arms and delightedly kissed his wrinkled face. He laughed merrily. For a moment, he would not let her go. Then he released her and turned to the rest of the company.

"This was not such a peaceful journey," he said, looking from one to the other. "I have seen much and we must speak of it all in due time, but for now, let us continue northward."

"Sir," Lia began, as they turned to follow the coastline. "Do you know what happened to my sister, Mari?"

Palanthar looked at her and gave a sigh. "I know some," he said. "She was captured by the Golrakken, and she is alive but she is not within reach."

"Where?" asked Lia. "We will go there anyway."

"You cannot attack the Golrakken at sea," said Palanthar gently; "and few have ever returned from their island outpost alive."

"Then we die trying," said Aaron, flatly.

Palanthar shook his head. "She is strong. Fulfill this mission on which you find yourselves now, and you will be helping her more than you can imagine."

"Is that all?" asked Aaron. "No disrespect, sir, but it's not much to go on."

"My apologies for the cryptic answer," said Palanthar; "but the only chance your Mari has lies in your doing your part."

"So, what are we to do next?" asked Lia.

"Pelnara, the Land of Men, lies to the north of us," said the Great Master. "Beyond is the Shioroth, the City of the Faeries. There you must meet with the High Council."

"What will they do to help us?" asked Aaron.

"Actually," said Palanthar; "it is you who must help them."

"'The City of the Faeries' you say?" said Owler. "We will meet Faeries?"

"You will," said Palanthar, smiling.

"I suppose next we'll be meeting Dwarves, Elves and who knows what," said Aaron.

"You will," said Palanthar again. Aaron could only shake his head in wonder.

After each had eaten his fill, they set off northeastward along the coast. The warm sun, the cool breeze and the sounds of the waves rolling in made for pleasant walking on the soft sand. The party separated naturally into three pairs: Owler and Aaron set a light, steady pace up front; Calicia and Lia came next, and Ender and Palanthar lagged a bit further behind so they could talk in private.

"Why did you leave me so suddenly in the valley?" asked Ender. "I need a lot of information from you. Things are changing rapidly and I want your perspective."

The Great Master nodded at him solemnly and said nothing for a time. Finally, he spoke. "I have watched you for many years, Ehrmahann. I have seen you exercise great judgment with admirable skill. You have wisdom and authority, and your heart is without guile or malice. These things I have known about you for a long time. What you cannot know is the joy I carry with me each day knowing that you are strong and sure." He paused. "This is late in coming," he said; "but as of today, I am no longer your master."

"I don't understand," said Ender.

"I am no longer the Stonekeeper: you are. As of today, I bequeath the Midnight Stone to you," said Palanthar. Without breaking stride, he reached into his robe and drew out a small, round stone of true Black. No light reflected from the opacity of its sphere. He handed it to Ender.

As the stone touched Ender's hand, his vision became dark and strange, but he became acutely aware of the life within everything. He could see it emanating from the sand under their feet. He could see shellfish below the surface, crabs behind the rocks, even the tiny life forms in the sea. Every blade of grass on the hill stood out in sharp relief. He calmed himself and his vision became less chaotic.

Ender had carried the Midnight Stone only once before, after Palanthar was nearly killed in battle. The Great Master had entrusted the Stone to his apprentice for safekeeping until he, himself, was well enough to carry it again. Its powers were vast and mysterious. The Midnight Stone gave the Great Master the ability to travel without a body. It was a source of seemingly endless magical wonders. Unbeknownst to the High Council, it was the greatest of the Stones of the Shioroth.

* * *

It was one of two.

Its Twin was far away in the East, in the land of dread, the land of the lost ones: the land of Morvoth. Deep in the darkness of the Dark Magic, Morvassus sat with the marble sized sphere of Black in his hand, rolling it around between his fingers. It tingled on his skin. Something was happening to its counterpart and the Blind Menace pressed the Stone into his remaining eye socket to see. He let out a low growl as his will to observe was thwarted. Removing the Twin from his eye, Morvassus stood up and stepped away from his throne. He motioned to his captain.

"Send for Karkaan," he said, his breath hissing and crackling. The captain snapped a salute and left the throne room. Morvassus stood for a moment, fingering the Twin in his shiny black hand. Then he returned to his throne and sat down, slowly. The time was drawing near. Things were converging. He now had allies in places he had long needed them. If his plan was executed as formed in his mind, there would be few to fight and little chance of failure. Yet that was thinking too far ahead. He needed more information. There would be time enough to begin the subversion.

* * *

Ender slipped the Midnight Stone into a pocket and immediately his normal sight returned. "I did not expect this," he said quietly.

"I have awaited this day a long time," the Great Master responded. "I would have given it to you when you found me in the valley, but I had lost it. To my joy, it had not been discovered and I retrieved it without a struggle."

"Lost it!" gasped Ender. "How?"

"It has a mind of its own, my son. Never forget that." Palanthar stared straight ahead. "I do not even remember losing it."

"But if you had lost it, how could you travel like you do?" Ender asked, bewildered. "You have always said that without the Stone you were only a mortal."

Palanthar laughed. "True! The Stonekeeper must choose between submission to either greed or mercy. I chose mercy, and for that, the Stonecutter, Dain himself, sustained me. Even now I am sustained by him."

Ender's eyes studied the small man walking beside him on the sand. He could not remember how long it had been since he had seen the old man so serene or his stride so light. It was as if the weight of the world had finally slid from his shoulders and he weighed nothing at all.

The Great Master took a deep breath. "I have told you this many times: if you use the powers of the Midnight Stone for mercy, you strengthen both the Stone and yourself. If you show strength only, it will feed the Twin, and in time you, yourself, may be subverted." He looked his son-in-law square in the eyes. "I have learned to eschew violence until there is no other solution," he said. "The desire to use it is strong and the risk to your soul is great."

Ender said nothing, pondering what had just been entrusted to him. Things were changing. He hoped he could keep up.

CHAPTER 31

The Golden Box

In the wee hours of the morning, Ender felt something touch his sleeve. He was instantly awake. Moving only his head, he looked around. There was no one else about. His companions were all sound asleep. Who could have touched him? Ender stood silently to his feet and wrapped his cloak about him. With a chill of excitement, he reached for the Midnight Stone in his pocket. As his fingers touched it, his vision became dark again, but in a moment, he could see everything clearly. He scanned the area.

Down the beach, about a hundred paces away, stood a tall robed figure. As Ender looked, the figure raised its hand in greeting.

"Hale, Ehrmahann Ender, son of Jarmahann," called a voice inside Ender's own head.

The voice felt familiar, though Ender was almost sure he had never heard it before. He searched his instincts for misgivings and found none. Something about the man on the beach imbued everything with a sense of peace. Ender left the others and approached him.

"What is your name?" asked Ender. "You obviously know mine."

"Dain," said the man.

Ender raised his eyebrows. "Dain! The Stonecutter! Am I truly speaking to you, or is this some trick of the Midnight Stone?"

Dain smiled. "It is no trick."

"What do you want?" asked Ender.

"Just listen, Stonekeeper," said Dain. "Let me first remind you of the story of the Midnight Stone. Efrihel, my brother, and I discovered the Four Stones of the Shioroth: White, Green, Blue and Crimson. We cut them one by one, but the Midnight Stone would not be cut like the others. It was but a spot of black embedded in the rock and it would not be dislodged, no matter how we carved around it. Finally, I spoke to it directly. I called to it, and it leapt from the heart of the Shioroth into my hand. It was instantly clear that the Midnight Stone had powers far greater than the other four. It was also wild, with a will of its own. I kept it hidden and dared not bring it out into the open, for I hardly knew how to control it.

"Its ruin was brought on by greed. Efrihel desired the Stone. I was afraid to share it with him because I did not trust his impetuous nature. In time, he found it, and hoping to keep it from me, he cursed it, but the curse did not work as he expected. I called to the Midnight Stone once again, and despite the curse, the Stone would not reject the one who called to it from the beginning. It split into the Twins. Now there were two Midnight Stones, each equally powerful and equally desirous of being rejoined. Efrihel fled with his prize and I guarded the Stone you carry now. My brother has always sought it, hoping to reunite the Twins for himself, and someday they will be joined again, for they cannot be denied forever. Because of this, neither the Midnight Stone nor its Twin is safe to its keeper."

"Where is Efrihel now?" asked Ender. "Have I met him before?"

Dain looked at him sadly. "You have. In fact, you wounded him once, very deeply," he said; "but Morvassus is not dead. The Morve lives on in Morvoth. He gathers strength. He hoped my banishment would free the Midnight Stone, but Palanthar was able to carry it for me and prevent him from uniting the Twins. Yet even the Great Master could not battle the Morve alone so I sent him to find you. Now the task is yours alone: carry the Stone so that it may once again be whole. It must happen in your hands."

"What of the Great Master?" he asked. "Is he not more experienced and better qualified?"

"The Great Master is already gone," Dain stated quietly. "The day he sent you the Sochmahr was the day he died. When you found him on the plains, he was no longer counted among the living."

Ender turned to see the sleeping figure of Palanthar on the hill. "Then who sleeps there and walks with us?"

"It is he," replied Dain. "It was granted him to remain among the living for a time. You were at sea and the Golrakken were too close for us to risk the transfer of the Stone. Now that you are here and the Stone is safely in your hands, he will pass on from this life to the next."

Turning again, Ender saw Calicia rise and go to her father. He started after her.

"Give them a moment," said Dain quietly.

Ender stopped and watched, tears streaming down his face, as Calicia knelt beside her father, cradled his head on her lap and kissed his face. Then she gently laid him back down. Slowly, the body faded from view until there was only a shadow, and then only the light of the stars on the grass where he had lain.

Calicia stood and came over to her husband. He hugged her tightly, feeling her shaking body as she wept silently. They held each other for a long time.

Finally, Calicia pulled away and looked up into his face. She was smiling through the tears. "He called to me before he left," she said. "He would not leave without saying farewell." She turned to Dain who bowed slightly. "Bless you for caring for my father. I am glad to finally meet the master of whom he was so fond."

"This is the last time you will see either of us," said Dain kindly. "We cannot help you in the presence of Morvassus. There only the living may find victory. That makes your task both easier and more difficult. Before the Stones of the Shioroth may again dwell in peace, Morvassus must be destroyed. This will break the curse. When the Twins reunite, the one who holds the unified Midnight Stone must use it for mercy only, or the horror that will follow will make the Morve pale in comparison."

The Stonecutter pointed at Ender's cloak. "In there," he said solemnly; "you have a box."

Ender reached into the cloak and brought out a tiny golden box.

"Do not open it here. The ashes inside are Palanthar's," Dain continued. "They are your receipt for the price he paid for the life of Holren. Go into Morvoth and pour them into the Fountain by the Great Gates of Ulvanoth. Then will the Sochhmahr be restored."

Ender raised his eyebrows in surprise. "The Golrakken curse failed?"

"Your Bow did its work well," nodded Dain. "His soul was still alive."

He told the full story behind the bargain for the wizard's life, the encounter with the King and the deal Dain and Palanthar struck with him. Ender and Calicia were astounded. "And where is the Sochhmahr now?" asked Ender.

Dain smiled. "He is with me. He learns very quickly. Woe to any who provoke the wrath of Holren Avan-Ihlac, the Fire-bringer. Only remember, when you reach Morvoth, spill the ashes into the Fountain behind the Great Gates of Ulvanoth. There the oath will be fulfilled and the sorcerer may become himself again."

"Dare I carry the Midnight Stone into Morvoth?" Ender searched the face of Dain for an answer.

"A wise question," nodded the other. "I would not send you there if I feared you would fail. You are ready to carry the Stone. Lead your company to the Shioroth," he continued. "They play their own parts in this matter. When you arrive at the Tower, speak to Rohidan and the High Council without delay, but reveal the Midnight Stone to no one. Take a scouting party into Morvoth to learn the strength of your enemy. You will learn your own strength there as well."

He turned to Calicia. "Dearest Calicia," he said; "no father was more proud of his daughter than Palanthar. Your responsibilities and your temptations increase now that your husband is the Stonekeeper, but you are ready. This journey to Morvoth is not for you, however. You are needed elsewhere. That will become clear when you speak to the High Council."

The lady looked at him, troubled, but Dain smiled again. "Ehrmahann is stronger than you know—stronger than he, himself, knows. Such strengths must be divided among the needy. Has it not always been so?"

Calicia nodded. "But I grow weary of it," she sighed.

Dain looked eastward. "The time draws near," he said. "If you succeed, you may live the rest of your lives in peace. If you fail..." His voice trailed off. "You must not fail."

The Stonecutter put his hands on their shoulders and looked from one to the other. "Go to the Shioroth. Speak to the High Council. Then survey the enemy and pour the ashes into the Fountain of Ulvanoth."

Ender placed the golden box back in his cloak. "Must the story of the Sochhmahr remain a secret?" he asked. "His kin have endured terrible grief. This news would give them hope."

"You are free from the earlier promise," answered the Stonecutter. "And give this message to them: 'The time is upon us. Each must do as each has learned, to the best of his abilities. Take heart. The world is changing and the form it will take has not yet been determined. Let each one take care to influence it for the good of all.'

"Now go back and sleep. You will need the rest for the journey and the diplomacy you must exhibit when you reach the Shioroth. Bless you, Ehrmahann Ender. May your thoughts be wise and your words and deeds likewise."

With that, Dain left their sight and they were alone on the beach. They went back and lay down together beside their friends who still slept on the grass. Despite their strong emotions, they were soon deep in dreamless slumber. The stars continued wheeling slowly overhead. All was once again quiet save for the waves on the sand.

* * *

Aaron rolled over and sat up. The rising sun had not yet warmed the dew laden grass around him. For a groggy moment, he wasn't sure where he was. Lia stirred beside him as he pieced his thoughts together. They had landed at Thihanan and traveled a half day's journey up the beach. Aaron stood and took in his surroundings. They had camped in the grass beneath the low hills that ran along the coast. He saw Ender, Calicia and Owler sleeping nearby. The old man was missing.

"The Great Master is gone," said Calicia just behind him.

She sounded so final. "Gone?" whispered Aaron. "Dead, you mean?"

"Yes," she answered. "We said goodbye to him last night."

Lia and Owler awoke and they all sat quietly as Ender explained in detail, leaving out the details about the Midnight Stone.

"We are grateful to have walked with him for a time, and for the chance to say goodbye. I am also instructed to tell you some very good news. You remember Thoughtful. I have a tale to tell of him. It's a long one, but it has a good ending."

They ate breakfast as they walked, and Ender related the story Dain had told him concerning the purchase of the wizard.

* * *

The company was on the run from the Citadel, pursued by the King's minions. As Holren cast his own spell, he took the full force of the Birdman's fury and was knocked off the cliff. He hit the water hard and sank beneath, but much to his surprise, he soon found himself bobbing on the surface, gasping for air. For a long time, he tumbled down the surging rapids, smashing up against the rocks along with the rest of the floating debris. Finally, he came to a place where the water became deeper and smoother. Exhausted, he swam blindly across the current in the dark of night, hoping to make the shore.

Something bumped him from below. He could see nothing in the blackness, so he kept swimming. It bumped him again. This time more sharply. He kicked at it but hit nothing.

Then the water began to swirl around him. Faster and faster it went. Thrashing wildly, he struggled to get out of the vortex that was sucking him under. Something huge seized him by the waist and threw into the air. For a few seconds, he was flying, then falling. He plunged back into the river. He swam but had no clue where to go. It didn't matter. Once again, he was yanked out of the water and sent flying, this time even higher. Taking a breath, he desperately gathered strength and flung fire at the boiling river beneath him. For a split second, he got a glimpse of his attacker.

It was Wofrung. The long, sinuous body was not covered in scales but a smooth, glossy skin, mottled gray and black like a salamander's. making him almost invisible in the depths. Rising up from the water, dominating Holren's view was Wofrung's long, narrow head as it opened its toothy mouth. The forked tongue lapped at the fire like a snake testing the air for signs of warmth. Its eyes were thin slits of bright white on either side of its head. Its nostrils were a series of great gashes on either side of its snout which opened and shut with each hissing breath.

The monster had already eaten his fill that day, so this was merely play. The fire aggravated the creature, and he beat the man sorely for it, batting him about on the water for a long time, nearly drowning him one minute, holding him up in the air until he breathed again, only to toss him back into the river once more. Finally, Holren was thrown senseless onto the river bank where he lay as one dead. Wofrung, no longer interested, let him be.

The wizard awoke to a steady drizzle. It seemed to be nighttime, but he had no idea where he was or how long he had lain there. Everything hurt. Somehow he figured out that he was on the sandy bank of a river. He opened his eyes and would have screamed if he'd had the strength.

Wofrung was rising out of the river, eyes glowing, mouth opening in a leering grin. Holren tried to move, but could not manage even to shift his broken body. The monster in the water seemed to be waiting, watching. Through the pain, Holren felt a strange cold starting at the back of his neck and spreading down his spine until it flowed into every part of his body. He felt himself being flipped over onto his back. Everything went black as a suffocating hand closed around his mouth and nose. Mercifully, he lost consciousness again.

When he awoke again, the pain was no less intense. He felt frozen and on fire at the same time.

"A stroke of fortune," said a thin, harsh voice. "My former master falls into my hands."

Holren could hear his captor breathing, but he could see nothing. They appeared to be in some dark place underground. His body lay rigid on its back, frozen at attention.

"You have Elven blood in your veins, even if it is not pure," said the voice. "I think you may serve me well. I need your skill with the White Magic but you must be brought under the will of the Dark Magic if you are to serve any purpose at all."

A sickly light began to glow about the place. Holren could see his captor now for the first time, and at once wished he had never laid eyes on him.

"I am the King," said the black figure.

The King's new form was even more horrible than the monster Brian saw in the clearing. Since entering the Citadel the King had changed his shape into a grotesque amalgamation of man, a predatory bird, and something altogether different. His mouth was a long, brittle beak, cracked and splintered. His skull was horned with three sharp curving spikes of black bone. But his eyes were hollow, and naught but a dull glow showed where there should have been iris and pupil. He turned to the wizard and brought both hands down toward Holren's face.

"By necessity, old master," said the King; "you will be transmutated into something more useful. Will you yield willingly, or must it be forced upon you? Either way suits me fine. I am not picky."

Hard, gnarled fingers touched the frozen skin of the sorcerer. They burned on his face. Darkness issued from them like smoke, wrapping around his head and seeping in through his skin, slipping into his eyes, nose and mouth. His mind struggled to resist it.

"Ah, some sport, perhaps," said the King. "Good then." His amused chuckle rattled off of the bare stone walls. His fingers pressed inward toward the wizard's skull, intensifying the already unbearable pain. The sorcerer's body began to change. The pungent odor of his own flesh transforming filled his lungs. Slowly, the monster lifted him off the stones by his head, causing searing pain in every part of Holren's body.

Then suddenly, the wizard fell back to the floor. An explosion and a flash of brilliant white sent the King crashing against the wall. Holren lay motionless, still frozen stiff.

"Mine!" howled the King. "He is mine now. I took him from Wofrung, myself!"

A shock of energy rippled through the air. Holren jerked once and blacked out.

* * *

Palanthar faced the monster. Pointing at Holren's warped, half transmutated body, he said: "I am taking him with me."

"On whose authority, Meddlesome One?" taunted the King. "I claimed him first. He is mine and I shall make him a worthy opponent for you."

Palanthar motioned to his right. "Behold: the Stonecutter!"

The King shrank back as Dain appeared beside Palanthar. Holren's warped, half transmutated body lay on the floor before them.

"The Stonecutter? You may have authority with some, but power? No," said the King. "You are not of this world. You cannot touch me on this plane."

"True," said Dain; "but the Great Master has power on this plane, and he can act for me. Give him the sorcerer."

"'Great Master'—fah! He is no threat; I can kill him myself," the King growled. "All I need is the right moment."

"You overestimate yourself still," Dain replied.

"Not this time." The monster's face split into a grin. "Have you not heard? The Citadel is mine, and all the magic in it."

Dain was unmoved. "Neither of you would survive a direct confrontation."

The King knelt down and spread his arms over Holren's frozen form. He fixed a blind eye on Palanthar and then turned to the Stonecutter.

"A bargain then," he hissed. "If this miserable wizard means so much to you, let us exchange. A sorcerer for a Meddler, I call it fair: one you prize for one I hate. Take the poor fellow now and be gone, but leave me the Meddler."

Dain and Palanthar kept one eye on the Birdman while they conferred together.

"I am old," said Palanthar; "and my young friend is ready. We may yet save this one. What can this Birdman do to me that I cannot bear?"

"He means to transmutate you, subjugate you. Would you endure that?" Dain asked.

"Only let me pass on my charge and I will go to this Birdman."

"You shall pass it on then." Dain looked at the small man with joy and sadness. To the King he said: "One more errand he must attend to and then he is yours. He shall return to you when he is finished. In trade, we will take the sorcerer."

"An idiot's bargain!" sneered the King. "Give me the Meddler now, and I will release your precious sorcerer."

Dain nodded.

"No tricks," said the King.

"None," said Palanthar, stepping forward.

"Poor choice," said the King, lifting the wizard up from the ground. As he hurled the broken body toward them, he shrieked a curse. Instantly, both Holren and Palanthar burst into flame!

The Great Master crumpled to the floor, fire consuming his skin. Holren lay in a burning heap, his flesh peeling back like dry bark on a fireplace log. He was beyond repair.

"You will not deny me justice," said Dain. He placed his hand over the face of the wizard and began to chant quietly.

"That sorcerer is useless to you, old fool," spat the King; "and this one will not trouble me again." Stretching out his knotted arms, the King brought all his power to bear on Palanthar. The Great Master's body was reduced to smoking ashes within seconds. The monster grinned, eyes glowing with satisfaction. He turned to the Stonecutter across the room and laughed again.

Dain only smiled. "Your choices conflict. I have the sorcerer. You would have had the mightiest warrior in your hands. Your former master becomes a Sochhmahr even as we speak, as a murdered innocent should be. I can do that from this plane for you have sent him here."

"The 'Great Master' is dead," spat the King. "I care nothing for the Sochhmahr."

"No," said Dain. "Palanthar you have forfeited. He is not yet defeated and he will rest indeed only when he has fulfilled his errand. So justice decrees, and so it shall be."

As he spoke, Holren vanished. The King could only stand by as Dain knelt by the small pile of ashes on the stony ground. The Stonecutter took a tiny golden box from his cloak and filled it with the ashes. Then, raising his hand, he called out and Palanthar reappeared, looking a little bewildered.

The King howled with rage. "This is not justice!" he cried. "The terms of the exchange said he was mine!"

"And you have done with him exactly as you wished," replied Dain, evenly. "Your claim on him is fulfilled. Now I may do with him as I choose, for he is in my plane. Only for a short time will he remain in this body. Then he will cease to live here, exactly as you have chosen. Mark your choice well."

"No matter," muttered the King. "He is dead nonetheless. Even you cannot maintain him forever."

Dain said nothing. With a wave of his hand, he and Palanthar both disappeared, leaving the Birdman alone in the cave.

* * *

Though Ender recounted this tale for the company, he said nothing of the Midnight Stone. For the time being, that was best kept secret.

CHAPTER 32

Arrivals and More Departures

Everyone was encouraged that the wizard was still alive but the details were confusing. Ender answered as many questions as he could. Then, for the next several hours, they reviewed the various threats that had presented themselves—the increase in goblins, their larger size, the change of the King into this new bridman, the return of the Golrakken. Perhaps the High Council would have information that might prove useful. One way or another, they would need allies to combat the rising menace.

Continuing up the coast, they came to the wide delta where the river Everness emptied into the sea. There they turned north, following the river into the land of Pelnara. It was a beautiful place. Tall trees lined the broad banks. An hour after they joined the river, the company came upon the beginnings of the road. It was hardly more than a trail, wide enough for two to pass abreast, but not enough for a carriage or wagon. There were no dwellings this far south. Most likely, only hunters used this road. Owler figured it had been several weeks since the last person passed that way.

"And it hasn't rained much since then," he added.

The company kept a good steady pace the whole afternoon; the weather was good and the air was warm but not hot. When night fell, they stopped under a grove of trees just off the river bank. After supper, they set a watch and drifted off to sleep.

The next day brought blue sky with scattered clouds. Farther from the open sea, the road grew wider and small trails branched off of it into the eastern hills. As the company went further and further upstream, the river became narrower and deeper. At this point, there were a few scattered dwellings along the river, all of them on the far bank, beyond hailing distance. A horseman heading south along the west bank turned tail and rode quickly back northward when he saw them.

A few hours later, the road came out into a wider plain. In a small bay in a quiet bend of the river lay a small town. known to the locals as Freshwater, the last harbor on the Everness. While they were still some distance away, a soldier dressed all in green rode out from the gates to meet them.

Ender called everyone to a halt. They gathered loosely together.

"Twenty archers," said Owler, nodding toward the fields around them.

"No need to engage," said Ender.

The rider pulled up short about forty paces away. "Hale, travelers," he called, raising his right hand, his eyes scanning the group. "You come from Thihanan?"

"We do," answered Ender. "Who asks?"

"Falnor, Captain of the Green Stone," said the rider; "Are you Palanthar, also called Ilstar?"

"I am not," replied Ender. "Neither are any of these with me. Do you seek him?"

"The High Council wanted to speak with him," the captain responded. "Do you know him?"

"I know him well. He was my master," said Ender.

The captain raised an eyebrow. "And who are you?"

"I am called Ender'" replied the Stonekeeper.

"Well met, Ender," said Captain Falnor. "Would you tell me where your master is now?"

Ender bowed slightly. "You will not find the Great Master on this plane. He is dead."

"How did he die?" pressed Falnor.

"I would wish to speak of this and many other things with the High Council," Ender answered. "Such matters are best not discussed in an open field within range of twenty archers. Will you show us the way to the Shioroth?"

Falnor shifted in his saddle and was silent a moment. Then he said: "I was sent to find Palanthar and you say he is dead. I have heard of Ender, but I have no proof that you are he. And I know nothing of the rest of you, all of whom are well armed. That axe, in particular, would not be allowed into the council chambers." He nodded respectfully at Aaron.

Ender smiled "All good points. However, if you will not help us, we will simply find it ourselves. We believe the High Council will benefit from our presence. If you believe caution is necessary, then escort us with armed guards, if you like, but let not caution cause any more delay."

"If you will be brought to the council chambers as prisoners," said Falnor, "then I will take you there directly."

Aaron held his tongue.

"You may keep our weapons safe for the journey, but we will not be bound as criminals," said Ender calmly.

"Fair enough," said Falnor. He shouted, and the company was quickly surrounded by twenty men in green. "Take their weapons, but do not harm them."

Aaron quietly handed over his axe, his sword, his knife, his other knife, and his dagger. Ender's Bow was the object of much interest; no one had seen anything like it. The soldier who bore it was an honest looking fellow who took it almost apologetically. He wore it on his back, along with the quiver of arrows. The others' weapons were distributed as well.

Then the five were escorted into town. People lined the streets to see whom the Green Guard had been sent to find. Horses were procured from the constabulary for each of the prisoners and soon, they were off again at a brisk pace.

By dusk, they were within two days' ride of the Shioroth. Rather than stop and rest, Falnor brought them to another stable of the Green Stone where they changed horses and continued riding into the night. Around midnight, they headed through the hills in a more northerly route.

Aaron kept an ear cocked to the two soldiers behind him who had struck up a conversation. Apparently, they would eventually meet not only Faeries, but Dwarves and Elves when they arrived at their destination. Even more interesting was their mention of a large, furry beast that Aaron was sure was Brian. They kept referring to him as "the Valen" which seemed to be some sort of Faerie title. The soldiers mentioned one Faerie called the "Snowdaughter" who was the talk of the town

"Makes me wish I was a Faerie myself," sighed one.

"You can't be serious," countered the other.

"I'm quite serious."

The second one laughed and shook his head. "No thanks!" he said. "Not for me. I don't want to turn thirty years old and be just out of childhood! Can you imagine fifteen more years of growing stumpy wings and shedding them every spring like antlers? I'm thirty seven and I have a wife and six kids already. I'll be a human any day."

"Sure," said the first. "But when you're a hundred and hobbling about with a cane, I'd be in the prime of life. But don't worry, I'd still fly over to see you, even if you were old and decrepit!"

"Old and decrepit, perhaps," nodded the elder. "But at least I would have heirs and grandchildren and great-grandchildren. She's the last of them, you know."

The subject ended there and Aaron wondered what they meant. He guessed that the "Snowdaughter" might be Annie, but he couldn't figure out how everything fit together. He puzzled over it a little while and then let it go. He'd find out soon enough.

As the sun came up, they found themselves on the vast plain between Pelnara and the Shioroth.

"From here, we still cannot see the central tower of the city," said Captain Falnor. "It is unmistakable, though."

Not long afterward, Owler looked up to see three Faeries, winging their way southward, their bright wings gleaming in the morning sun. "Marvelous," he said.

Aaron could only shake his head.

They stopped and let the horses graze while everyone got something to eat; they had not rested since noon the day before. When they resumed their journey, Ender rode beside Captain Falnor, asking about the customs of the Men of the Green Stone in Pelnara. He also was curious about the landscape. While the captain clearly knew the land well, Ender noticed that he judiciously avoided revealing any details an enemy commander would want to know in a strange country, all without appearing rude or even suspicious of the question being asked.

By noon, everyone was exhausted. They gathered by a grove of cottonwoods near a creek and Falnor called a rest during the heat of the day. They would continue on that night. Once the horses were curried and watered, the riders grouped into a circle around their charges and settled down to sleep.

Ender, however, did not sleep. He sat on the grass and gazed eastward. The Midnight Stone tingled in his pocket, even though he wasn't in direct contact with it. Ender knew it longed for the Twin. He could sense it every time he thought about the Morve. The Stonekeeper felt uneasy about his own mixed emotions. Palanthar was right: the Stone had a mind of its own. He could feel its desire urging him to reunite the Stone. It was an animal-like craving, as persistent and insistant as hunger. If he let it, he knew it would grow until he could think of nothing else.

An anger as fierce as the hunger rose up from his gut. Part of him wanted to destroy the Stones and all they stood for. The anger and the hunger raged hot and cold within him, each trying to consume the other, but he knew the conflict had no end. It would continue whether he thought about it or not.

"Very well," he decided; "then I'll not think of it any more." Remarkably, the confusion and frustration faded. It was still there but the need to resolve it was gone and he was no longer attached to it. Relieved, he lay down and considered how to approach the High Council.

Four hours after they had stopped to rest, Falnor roused them again and they rode out the last of the daylight. They were traveling on wider roads with more traffic. Passersby, both Men and Elves, eyed the procession curiously. Rumors of evil had reached everyone's ears so the sight of a company surrounded by guards on their way to the Shioroth brought with it a certain fear.

Late that night, they caught their first glimpse of the Shioroth, the great stone monolith in very center of the city. A white light shone from the highest tower on its crown. Ender felt the Stone tingling in his pocket again as the light flickered.

Better not to use it, he thought. Already it interferes. For a moment, he wondered if it could give him away. He put the thought aside.

"Is the tower called the Shioroth, or is that the name of the city?" asked Lia.

"We refer to either one as the Shioroth," said Falnor. "It can be confusing, I know. We're just used to it."

They entered the city by the Southgate and wound their way through the streets to the outer wall of the Tower where the Men of the Green Guard were housed. Falnor's men ushered the company in to a small room by the mess hall and Falnor ordered food for them and for his men.

"I will ask Lord Rohidan, the Elder of the High Council, what to do next," said Falnor, bowing. "Do you have a request?"

"I would meet tonight, as soon as possible." answered Ender.

"I will let him know," said the captain. "Please, eat, and rest here while I go." He called for fresh guards and then departed for the High Council.

Lia was glad for the chance to sit on a stationary object. She turned to her husband who was looking around the room. "What are you grinning at?" she asked.

"Look at how they have set themselves and us," he said.

Lia glanced around. Ender's company had been seated at a corner table, away from the door, with their backs to windowless walls. Between them and the door stood four guards, well rested and fully armed. Just outside the door stood six more. Beyond them, the twenty who had just arrived sat facing the room which held the company, not staring at their food like unwary civilians, but still paying attention, even as they ate.

"I like these Men of the Green Stone," said Aaron.

They had just finished eating when Falnor returned.

"Rohidan will see you now if you are ready," he announced. Dismissing the guards from the door, he ordered one of his men to fetch the weapons taken from the company. "You are guests here now," he explained, as he handed Ender his Bow. "We are cautious these days. Please do not consider it an affront."

"To the contrary," Ender replied. "I appreciate your situation and you have our respect. I am interested in continuing our conversation."

"I'd like that," said Falnor. "May the High Council judge well."

He led them up the stairs and over the wall along the same path Brian and Annathía had followed five days before, through the arched door, and into the council chambers.

At this late hour, there were only four at the council table: Raealann, King of Men; Hassila, Queen of the Elves; and Rohidan and Arienne. Falnor bowed and asked to be dismissed, but Raealann bade him stay.

Rohidan looked at the company seated before him. His eyes met Ender's and he searched them for a time, saying nothing. Finally, he spoke: "Captain Falnor tells us Palanthar is dead and that you have taken his place," he said.

Ender nodded. "My master asked me to carry on in his stead."

"When and how did he die?" the Faeries asked.

"He was killed not long ago by a monster who calls himself the King," Ender responded.

"Where did this take place and how do you know?" the Elder continued, leaning forward on the table. "Were there witnesses?"

Aaron looked at Ender. The Stonekeeper did not waver.

"I have only my word," said Ender; "so please hear it all and then judge as you will."

The Tale Weaver began his tale. All present in the chambers soon found themselves in the room with the King and the Great Master as the battle for Holren unfolded. They saw the treachery of the King and the death of Palanthar. When Ender was done, they were once again in the council chambers.

Rohidan pondered what he had just seen. Then he leaned over to Arienne and whispered something. She nodded and he turned back to Ender: "You are a Tale Weaver with great skill and we have heard your story clearly. My wife, Arrienne, is a Thought Chaser. I suggest we put you to the test. If what you are saying is true, there is nothing to hide."

"True, but the Thought Chaser is as yet unknown to me," replied Ender carefully. "Until I know her better, I must respectfully decline such a test."

Rohidan smiled and sat back down in his chair. "A fair answer," he said. "For now, we take you at your word. It seems we have mutual enemies and your urgent request underscores our sense that the time for confronting them is near."

"It is," said Ender. "First, we should all hear who and what we are facing."

Aaron and Owler reported the rise of the King and his goblin minions. Owler described the Citadel and its guard of eagles. Several listened with raised eyebrows as he spoke of the bluffs and the hidden fortress inside.

Then the council members spoke, each in turn. In the south, the Men of Pelnara had seen the Golrakken storm cloud even from their short ventures into the Dorvan Sea. To the east, beyond the Volgan River, Rohidan had seen a veil of darkness falling over the Abandoned Land, the ancient home of the Golrakken.

Ogres and goblins had been seen in the foothills beyond the river. In the western desert, the Carthiss was becoming more and more bold. Hassila, the Elven Queen and Keeper of the Blue Stone, told of a smoke-like fear terrorizing the Dwarves in the Tyrian mountains. It seemed to have seeped up from their deepest tunnels. She knew no more about it than that, though.

"Enough for one night," said Rohidan when all had spoken. "The solution will become more clear when we've all had some rest. Let us convene with the rest of the High Council tomorrow. We will need our wits about us to sort wisdom from folly."

They left the chambers and the company was led to the guest quarters where Annie and Brian had slept before going up to the high towers. Each couple had a comfortable room and Owler had a place of his own.

* * *

Calicia looked out the window at the moonlit garden with its winding stream. She wondered what the world would be like next year at this time. For now, everything seemed peaceful and calm. She sighed and went to bed. Her husband, weary of all the responsibility, had barely kissed her goodnight before he fell asleep.

She rested her hand on his chest, which rose and fell with his even breathing. He hadn't bothered to undress. She lay close to him and suddenly noticed that she could feel the tiny lump of the Midnight Stone in his pocket pressing against her thigh. The sensation was unmistakable. Her fingertips tingled and her heart raced just being near it.

Her father had never allowed her that close to the Stone. "It's an insidious thing," he used to say. "You may not realize you are being taken in until it's too late. I was trained carefully for years before I was allowed to carry it."

His words were true. The deep magic of the Midnight Stone quickly washed her father's warning from her thoughts. She felt awfully curious. It seemed like a simple thing to take out the Stone and have a look at it. She would just slip it back in Ender's pocket when she was done.

Weariness had abandoned her. Wide eyed, she reached down and caressed the little lump under her fingertips, feeling its smooth roundness through the pocket. More than once, she thought she heard her husband stir, but he was sound asleep. Still she fingered the tingling marble of Black. Under the power of the Stone, she couldn't decide why she shouldn't take it out. She trembled slightly. She pinched the garment under the Midnight Stone to see its shape in the cloth.

"I am his wife," she reasoned with herself, toying now with the edge of his pocket. "We can share it. Tonight, it shall be mine. Tomorrow, I will leave it to him." Her hand was shaking as she started to slip her fingers into the pocket. Slowly, she came closer to the Stone. Ender did not stir. Calicia began to worry about awakening him, she was shivering so. The Stone drew her inexorably.

"I will not claim it," she insisted; "I will only borrow it."

She never got the chance. Ender rolled over suddenly and she nearly caught her fingers in his pocket before she could pull her hand away. He was awake and heading for the window, but he shot her a look of fear, worry and disappointment. She buried her face in the pillow.

"Something's out there," he said, turning to the window. He drew the Midnight Stone from his pocket and peered out into the darkness. He could see a winged shape sailing high in the night sky, its massive claws carrying what looked like a man. Ender felt a chill slide down his back. "A dragon!" he said. "With a Black Warrior."

The dragon swooped low over the western fields and deposited the Black Warrior in the shadow of a grove some distance west of the city. Then it lifted back up into the sky and flew back eastward at tremendous speed.

Suddenly, several of the flying lights they had seen on Cai-Amira appeared. They chased the retreating dragon away but did not intercept it.

Holding the Midnight Stone, Ender could see the Black Warrior on the ground slipping between the trees. He could still see the Warrior's shimmering aura moving inside the grove. Ender remembered why the Black Warriors had an aura unlike that of any Faerie, Elf or Man: they were only half alive. Morvassus had created them himself.

Suddenly, the flickering shape of the Black Warrior disappeared. Ender couldn't see it anymore amidst the auras of the living plants. Puzzled, he stood back and listened. All was very quiet. He thought of alerting the guards but already two Faeries were flying over the tree wall, swords drawn and ready.

For a moment, he struggled with himself. Should he become invisible and fly to the grove to see for himself? Palanthar had traveled this way often, but was it wise in this case? He watched as the Faeries searched the area. They weren't looking in the right place. The Black Warrior was gone. The two Faeries returned alone.

Ender stared into the night, searching for movement. There was none.

"I'm going to have a look," he said to Calicia, without even a glance over his shoulder.

He felt disoriented as soon as he decided to fly. He could not feel his own physical body. He felt no wind as he sailed over the wall and across the field into the grove, passing through the tree branches without disturbing a leaf. It was as if he was not there at all.

Struggling to keep control, he searched the grove from all angles and found no trace of the Black Warrior. The soldier's tracks led into the grove, but then they stopped. The Warrior had covered his tracks completely and though Ender could see remnants of the aura, he could not track the Black Warrior any further. Perhaps there was a deeper magic at work, one that obscured the Warrior's passage. There was only one place such magic could have originated. If it was close, this was not the time to confront it. Ender flew back to the Shioroth. He had already used more magic than he had originally intended. Besides, he was finding it difficult to direct the Stone. That was enough.

When he returned to the room, it took him a minute before he felt reoriented. He looked over to see his wife lying on the bed, trembling. Her life force was still strong, but the aura around her was jagged and torn. She was crying silently. Quietly, he put the Midnight Stone back in his poket and knelt down by the bed.

"Calicia," he whispered. " Do not be so surprised. It is a terrifying magic."

She nodded miserably. "I nearly had it," she said. "I almost touched it."

"You are very strong," replied her husband. "I was trained for years before I was allowed to hold it and I remember what it was like in the early days. There is nothing to be ashamed of."

She closed her eyes and cried bitterly. Ender sat down beside her, stroking her hair.

"When my father kept the Stone, it did not affect me like this," she said.

"He kept it more skillfully than I," said her husband. "I am still learning."

Calicia wept again, this time giving it full rein. Ender lay beside her and held her until she cried herself to sleep. Then he lay awake for a long time, thinking about the reemergence of his old enemy.

*　*　*

Deep in the darkness of Uzzim-Khail, Morvassus stood and peered blindly into the pool before the massive throne. Though he could see nothing, he could sense many things. Something was afoot in the Shioroth. Slowly, he placed the round marble of terminal Black, into his empty eye socket. The pain was excruciating, but the effect was worth it. In the flickering images within the pool, he could make out the shape of the dragon winging its way westward.

"Havvac has proven a fine friend," he hissed, piercing the silence in the huge chamber. He raised a slender, powerful hand and rubbed the back of his neck, wiping away a small trickle of fluid. "Send the crow to Akka-Illin and inform the Interrogator that the dragon is to be rewarded."

"Yes, m'lord," answered a Black Warrior standing almost invisibly in the darkness of the throne room.

Morvassus removed the Twin from his eye socket and faced the Black Warrior. "Remind Jehzik that he is being watched, Captain. I will have no more of his foolishness. One more attempt to impede my wishes, and he will wish I had destroyed him. Is that understood?"

"Yes, m'lord," nodded the Warrior. "Should he return here once he has completed his task?"

The Morve sat down on the cold stone throne. He smiled. "Yes, let him come and serve me awhile. That will make an impression on him. Tell him I wish to see him immediately after he has spoken to the Interrogator."

The captain bowed and turned hastily away. Striding across the length of the chamber, he left through the single door opposite the throne. Quickly, he walked crossed the long, open chamber beyond, and wound his way up the many steps leading to the world above. Finally, at the end of a long hallway, he came to the western door. He stepped out onto the wall and let his eyes get accustomed to the starlight.

An unusually large crow was perched on the battlements, tearing at a piece of gristle. Jehzik choked down a bloody strand and didn't bother to look up. "What now, Captain?" he spat.

"Fly to Akka-Illin and inform the Interrogator that the dragon is to be rewarded," replied the Warrior.

"Let Morvassus send his own messages," croaked Jehzik. "I am weary of playing courier for him and I have no desire to see that ghoul again..."

"Silence, idiot!" barked the captain. "When you have delivered the message, you will return here to serve the Dark Master."

Jehzik stopped pecking at the meat and looked up sideways, his glistening eye searching the face of the Black Warrior for signs of his master's presence. "And if I do not?"

"You will," responded the other. "Foolishness will not be tolerated. You have been warned. Now go! You have eaten more than you're worth."

The crow flicked the bloody scrap onto the Warrior's boots. "I can't stomach it anyway," he croaked. Heedless of the curses hurled behind him, Jehzik lifted off into the cold air and sailed over the tortured peaks of the Orryx, faster than any crow should be able to fly, faster even than a falcon in a steep dive. All the while, he muttered under his breath. Slavery hung about him like a heavy chain, but he could only curse the magic that bound him.

He flew on.

* * *

The council chamber was a-buzz with talk of the dragon.

"A horrible creature, but magnificent," muttered a Faerie who had witnessed the arrival. "I've never seen anything so huge. It dropped down to the field and then rose again with a great straining of wings. You wouldn't expect something so massive could stay in the air like that. Then it was gone, lost in the stars. The Firstborn chased it across the Volgan River but it did not even look back."

Ender watched everyone carefully, listening to the conversations. Apparently, no one else had seen the dragon's cargo. The Faeries reported finding nothing. The Black Warrior had come and gone unnoticed. To Ender's relief, no one mentioned his own movements that night.

Rohidan brought the Council to order.

"More evil is afoot," he began. "Rumors of danger persist on all sides. A dread power rises in the east and a darkness covers everything beyond the Abandoned Land. A dragon flies across our fields like some carrion harbinger. Our guests tell us of a Birdman King with armies of goblins heading north across the lower continent. In the west, a death-smoke seeps into the Dwarvish tunnels, killing with fear. And the Golrakken have attacked the lost island of Cai-Amira while it was at sea.

"But the Snowdaughter has returned to North Agoria. She brings with her the gruffen, Brian, slayer of Lazraak Dragonhelm. And Brian carries the Valenblade which was lost when Norhidan Nightwing flew south.

"So, everything converges on the Shioroth."

The Elder Faerie sat down. "We are here to consider what to do next," he said simply.

"Until we know the strength and purpose of the enemy, we cannot properly prepare for battle," said Ender at last. "Are these forces gathering to the Morve? Does the King bring his goblins and do the Golrakken bring their swords to the same place? Will Morvassus raise up his Black Warriors again and lead them all here? If not here, where?" He sat forward in his chair and looked across at the others around the table. "We need answers. I have an errand to fulfill at the Fountain of the Great Gates of Ulvanoth. Since I must go there, let a few warriors, strong, skilled and stealthy, go with me to spy out the forces and determine what sort of battle can be expected."

There was a gasp of surprise. No one had dared to make the journey to the Great Gates since long before the fall of the Golrakken. The Fountain there held some mysterious power. A few Faeries remembered the tales of valiant warriors bathing in its waters and vanishing. It was said that their voices were heard for centuries thereafter, but they were never seen again.

"Very few would dare such a venture," said Raealann with a bit of a chuckle; "fewer still might return."

"Then those are the ones I need," answered Ender.

"And will you cross the Abandoned Land and stroll into Uzzim-Khail so many sightseers?" asked Raealann.

"Do you wish to tour the place yourself?" Ender asked.

Unbeknownst to Ender, King Raealann's great grandfather had died in a foray very much like the one Ender now proposed. Raealann's sires were still remembered as the mightiest of the Pelnaran kings, but Raealann's own father had not followed that path, and neither had he. Despite his warrior heritage, Raealann's skill was administration. His wisdom and foresight had brought them through the Great Drought with food enough for all. During his reign, the land of Men had prospered. Indeed, though, as he aged, King Raealann grew less and less like his ancient forebears. He became ponderous, slow to move. He rarely traveled. He preferred the palace in Pelnara.

Raealann returned Ender's even stare. "The acceptance of a suicidal challenge has no value," he said. "Let those who have the stomach for such risks take them as they will. I see no purpose."

Captain Falnor's brown eyes lit up. "I accept that as permission to volunteer, my lord," he said, standing to his feet. "I am one of the few who has returned alive. If Ender will accept my services as a spy, a warrior and a scout, I would gladly render them."

Raealann turned and looked at the commander of his elite troops. "You've come back alive more times than anyone else," he said, gravely. "Why risk it again?"

"I believe the information will serve us," said Falnor; "and my skills and knowledge of the land will be necessary."

"You can't bring him back," said Raealann. "No point in getting yourself killed, too."

Captain Falnor shook his head. "I do not expect to fail, my lord."

"No one does," said the King of Pelnara. "We will have your successor chosen before you leave." With a slow nod, he leaned back in his chair and folded his hands on his lap. His dark look remained.

Ender nodded. "Offer accepted," he replied. "This should be a small company, but I would take with me two more."

Aaron could feel Lia's eyes on him. He looked up and she gave him a subtle nod. Why did that make his heart sink?

Once again, he saw the beautiful girl laughing at him from behind the barn. The game of hide and seek was only half serious. She fully intended for him to find her. When he did, she went running down the path to the woods.

Aaron carried that memory deep in his heart. He could always bring up the image of her as she turned to look over her shoulder, eyes bright, hair sweeping around her neck, the sunlight from a thousand wildflowers reflected on her face—young, beautiful, carefree and in love.

He looked at her now. She was not a girl anymore, nor was she carefree; but she was still beautiful. And she was still in love.

So was he. The world was different, but they were still together. He knew they were both ready.

"I'm in," he said.

"And I," Lia chimed in quickly.

"So our company is complete," Ender said with a grateful smile.

"Yes," said Aaron; "I know we have an errand there, but before we go, wouldn't it make more sense to scout the enemy from the air? People with wings could fly there and back quickly, staying well out of arrow range." He looked around the room.

Rohidan nodded. "An honest question," he said. "The Abandoned Land holds a curse which the Faeries cannot easily counter. This Dark Magic has no effect on Men or Elves, but it drains the energy of any Faerie who dares come within reach. We have flown across the Volgan River only to sink to the ground on the far side. The longer a Faerie remains there, the weaker he becomes. Some have died before they could reach the bridge on foot."

"Fair enough," said Aaron. "I just thought I'd mention it."

"When you see the Abandoned Land, you'll see what the curse has done to the land itself," said Arienne. "Even the plants are twisted and grotesque."

Ender continued: "Now, what of the smoke in the tunnels of the western mountains? What do the Dwarves need?"

A grizzled old Dwarf stood on his seat at the end of the table. "For those who don't know, I am Yorgun Steelsmith, Chief of the Dwarves. We have discovered a danger unlike any other, a deadly smoke whose first weapon is a sickening fear and whose death blow is but a touch. Steel, fire and water cannot stop it." Here he paused a moment."We Dwarves have never burdened our allies and we will deal with this alone, if need be," he said; "but if there is a magic that can vanquish this Death Smoke, I will lead the magician into the tunnels."

"Tell us more about this Death Smoke," said Hassila.

"I have seen it only from a distance, in torchlight," said Yorgun. "It writhes along the floor like a living fog. I will not recount the fear for you. I am loathe to remember it. Those who have been touched by the smoke die a thousand deaths before their bodies succumb to a freezing cold. The smell is foul and rank. Its only warning is the fear that precedes it, and that can cause even the strongest to quail. That is all I know."

Rohidan shook his head. "This tale is told by no coward," he said.

Calicia rose and faced the Dwarves. "I will go," she said. "My magic may be exactly what you need."

The elder Dwarf bowed to Calicia. "My dear lady," he said; "what sort of magic do you have that might help us? I mean no disrespect, but it will take an unusual magician to kill this enemy which we cannot even fight."

"Fighting is not the solution," she said. "There is a presence that dispels this kind of evil. I have brought it elsewhere; I can bring it here."

"If what you say is true, we thank you," said Yorgun. For a moment he looked as if he meant to continue, then he simply sat down. Calicia also bowed and sat down.

Owler stood. "I will join you," he announced. "I have no magic, but I would consider it an honor to lend support."

"I will speak on his behalf," said Calicia. "He has already faced the Golrakken in battle. His eyes are keen and his blade is sharp, but it is the strength of his heart and the clarity of his mind that will serve us best here."

"Then he is welcome," said Yorgun.

Ender surveyed the faces of the High Council. "Unless anyone knows of another threat, I say we leave as soon as we can be ready," he said. "May we return soon with news, good or bad."

Once again, the company was divided.

* * *

Calicia and Owler joined Yorgun and his companions as they gathered supplies to bring back to the hills. The Dwarves had brought metal and salt to exchange for grain, leather and other goods. Many Dwarves had come with Yorgun, nearly two dozen in all, and eventually they all introduced themselves. Owler proved to have an uncanny ability to remember their names and keep them straight. As they packed to go, messages arrived at the Shioroth telling of more encounters with the Death Smoke. The sense of urgency was palpable. Yorgun kept everyone's tempers in check as they worked quickly to complete their preparations. Any delivery that was delayed was summarily canceled. Even so, the Dwarves knew they would be working through the night.

Ender, Lia and Aaron spent hours with Captain Falnor, going over the maps and books of lore, exchanging freely now everything they knew about the dangers in the east. Then they went to the stables of the Green Stone to find suitable mounts.

That evening, the entire High Council gathered to eat together and wish the two companies well. Though the food and drink were fine, and songs were sung in honor of those about to go forth, but it was a relatively somber affair and the companies excused themselves early to get some rest.

Ender and Calicia went down into the garden and walked in the starlight for a long time. With whispered words and gentle touches, they said their good-byes.

* * *

Daylight was just creeping through the windows as the company ate breakfast in the mess hall of the Green Stone. Arienne and Rohidan had come to see them off. Raealann had already gone southward on business at home. Hassila intended to return to Val-Ellia that very day, so she and her company would ride with the Dwarves. Within the hour, they were saddled and ready.

Yorgun and his weary fellows met them in the courtyard in front of the stables. The Men of the Green Stone kept sturdy ponies and mules for the Dwarves who had no use for them underground. One of the stable boys was sent with the Dwarves to bring the animals back. When the tunnel dwellers required them again, they would send a message by homing pigeon asking for them. It was a convenient relationship. The Dwarves were spared the bother of keeping horses. In return, they fashioned the fine metal tack fittings for the Men of the Green Stone.

Calicia and Owler mounted excellent steeds that were saddled in leather trimmed with Dwarvish silver. Ender handed his wife a small vial with a clear liquid inside. She looked at him quizzically.

"You leave this with me?" she asked. "Will you not need it?"

"I have other magic," he replied. "This is what it was meant for."

"May we use it well," said Calicia. She leaned over and kissed him.

Then, with Yorgun in the lead, their procession headed toward the Westgate. Owler looked back once and waved. Aaron raised his axe in reply. In a few moments they were lost from view down the winding streets.

CHAPTER 33

The Carven Canyon

Falnor expected to overtake Thisvane and Gullen, the cousins of Grisbane, along the way as they journeyed eastward. The Small Giants had set out for their home by the Volgan River two days prior. Their long legs could carry them very fast so the five travelers would not likely meet them for yet another day and a half on horseback.

"Courage and good fortune to you," said Rohidan to Ender as the Stonekeeper tightened the belly strap of his saddle. "May you return swiftly and safely."

"Thank you," said Ender.

Rohidan shook his hand and left to speak to the prince and Falnor.

As he was about to mount, Ender felt a tap on the shoulder. He turned to see Arienne.

She lowered her voice so only he could hear. "I did not chase your thoughts," she said; "but I can see that Ilstar did not depart without an heir. May your use of the Midnight Stone be prudent. You carry my best hopes with you."

If Ender felt a flicker of surprise he did not show it.

Arienne continued. "I have told no one, not even my husband. Some doubt its existence. It is not for me to expose. Do not fear my intentions, Stonekeeper. I know better than to overstep you."

Ender took her hand. "Then it will be much easier for me when I return," he whispered. "I do not yet know when this should be revealed."

She smiled, squeezed his hand firmly and bade him well. Ender put his boot in the stirrup and swung himself up into the saddle.

"Lead the way!" he shouted to Falnor.

The captain turned his horse smartly and, with a rumble of hooves, the five riders left the courtyard. They rode out through the the Eastgate, out of the shadows of the tree wall that surrounded the city and straight into the morning sunlight.

For many miles the wide, ancient highway between the Shioroth and Morvoth ran straight and flat across the fields of the Lammethan. Beyond the hills which rippled along the horizon lay the Carven Canyon cut by the Volgan River. Long ago, a mighty bridge had been built across the canyon beyond which the highway continued through the lands of the Golrakken. In centuries past, when the Golrakken and the Lammethan were allies and friends, the road on both sides of the bridge had been well kept and well traveled. Now everything east of the Volgan lay in decay.

Between the river and the mountains of the Mirrak-Haas lay a desolate landscape. Once it had been a beautiful country. The Lammethan had settled in the Shioroth, and the Golrakken, the other great clan of the Faeries, had chosen the rich land east of the Carven Canyon as their home. The Lammethan were traders and city dwellers, but their cousins the Golrakken were more self-sufficient and liked open spaces for their farmlands and herds. They built no great cities, only small towns and isolated houses surrounded by open hills and groves of trees.

When Morvassus turned the Golrakken to himself, the Lammethan banished them across the river. The Golrakken continued moving south and eastward, leaving their dwellings behind. In less than a year, the land lay empty. From then on, they were known only as the Abandoned Lands. The Dark Magic that had destroyed the Golrakken hung over the land for centuries, spoiling even the trees and once-fertile farmlands. Now the place belonged to roving gangs of goblins and the odd ogre or troll.

The Small Giants guarded the bridge over the Volgan River. Grisbane and his kin were more than capable of keeping the only bridge from evil hands. Grisbane, the eldest, traveled often, roaming the land for months or even years at a time. roamed the land. The other five preferred their life by the bridge. No menace ever successfully crossed the bridge; few bothered to try. If goblins or ogres ventured down to the southern fords when the water was low, they might venture into the pasture lands of the Men of Pelnara. Then the Green Stone would send troops to route them. Such sorties were always led by Captain Falnor.

As the sun climbed higher, the company slowed to a walk to rest the horses. Falnor took the opportunity to continue the conversation he had begun with Ender on their journey to the Shioroth. This time, he gave clear descriptions of the Pelnaran landscape and laid out various possible routes through the Abandoned Land. He also said he knew of at least one dragon in the mountains beyond.

"Probably the fellow that paid us a visit last night," said Aaron. "Not something I want to meet if I can help it. Is it allied with Morvassus?"

"We've seen signs of it, but never laid eyes on it," answered Falnor. "If you believe the stories, dragons are selfish, independent and not easily charmed."

"Our legends say the same," said Lia; "but everything we've heard of Morvassus tells me he would be no ordinary enchanter."

"True," said Falnor. "Regardless, I find myself keeping an eye skyward."

Aaron grunted. "Me, too. Tell me," he said; "how does a tree wall serve to guard the city? Couldn't you just burn it, or climb over it?"

Falnor laughed. "I'd like to see you try," he said. "It's one of the first things children learn, usually by having someone dare them. The Faerie wall cannot be climbed. The branches come off in your hands, and there never seems to be any fewer of them. Axes bounce off and fire simply fails to catch."

"Magic," said Lia. "What sustains it?"

"The Shioroth itself," said the captain. "As I understand it, the life force of the wall is linked to the bedrock beneath it."

"So the gates are the weakest link, as always," said Aaron.

Falnor nodded. "The gates are built from stone cut from the central monolith and are supported by the same magic that sustains the wall," he said. "The gates join seamlessly with the trees; you couldn't slip a dagger between them. The doors, on the other hand, are vulnerable, just like any other doors. They can be barricaded, but that's all."

Shadows were lengthening as the road led from the flatland to more rolling hills. Here and there stood a stone chimney or a crumbling rock wall, the only evidence that people had ever lived here. When the Golrakken turned, Falnor told the others, everyone living along the great highway on this side of the Volgan River had fled to the Shioroth.

At dusk, they arrived at a spring-fed pool surrounded by oaks and cottonwoods. The company dismounted and led the horses to Falnor's favorite bivouac overlooking the pool from a knoll which provided the best view of the surrounding hills. Here they took the saddles from their mounts and led the horses to the water.

Lia noticed two sets of very large footprints at the edge of the pool.

"Thisvane and Gullen," she said.

Falnor knelt down and took a look. "A few hours ago," he said. "Small Giants are amazing. They walk at a Man's running pace, and they can keep it up for days."

Though they kept a watch, the night passed without incident.

Before dawn, they rekindled the fire and cooked a hot breakfast. They would not eat so well once they crossed the river, so they made the most of it.

They saddled up again and left the spring behind them. Further into the hills, the dirt became sandy and red. The highway wound its way eastward, narrowing and becoming more overgrown.

When they were not galloping along, they talked about the fighting tactics of goblins, trolls, and ogres. Aaron's teaching echoed in her head: "Get it in your head. Then get it in your body. Then forget it and fight."

As Falnor discussed the near-sightedness of trolls, Lia watched her husband's face. She had seen that look many times. His eyes were focused on the horizon, but his cheeks and his mouth twitched slightly. He was practicing each move in his head.

I'll never master the art at his level, she thought. She took a deep breath and let it out.

Aaron pulled his horse closer to her. "Lia, how many Golrakken did you face on Cai-Amira?" he asked quietly, looking straight ahead.

"Three."

"Were you wounded?"

"No."

"How many Golrakken did you kill?" he asked.

"Three."

"Including that one on my blind side."

"Yes," she said.

"Thanks again for that."

"You're welcome."

They rode on in silence for awhile.

About an hour and a half past noon, Ender spied the two Small Giants some distance ahead. "They're running," he said.

"That would explain why we're catching up with them so late in the day," said Falnor.

"Yes," the Stonekeeper confirmed. "They're in a great hurry!"

"Let's find out why!" said Falnor, spurring his horse forward.

The riders thundered over the old road toward the Small Giants. Soon it was obvious that the Small Giants were indeed running at full speed. Thisvane, the younger one, was half a mile ahead of the elder Gullen. Falnor brought the company alongside Gullen.

"What's the hurry?" asked the captain.

The Small Giant was breathing hard but he slowed only a little to talk. "Trouble," he said. "At the bridge. The vultures brought this message: 'Make haste. Black Warriors. Defgar hurt.' We'd seen them in the distance before. They had not approached the bridge until now. Go! I will come as soon as I can." He set off again at a run with his long, loping gait.

They caught up with Thisvane and passed him. Leaving the Small Giants behind, Falnor led the company up the road that now began to zigzag up the steep sides of basalt cliffs. Darkness was gathering when they broke out onto a high plateau where they could ride much faster. They rounded a butte and could finally see the bridge which looked like a sliver of white slung across the canyon and suspended between two great towers. The canyon was so deep that they could not see the river from where they were.

Spurring their horses onward, they raced ahead, weapons drawn and ready, but they slowed as they approached the span. All was quiet; the entire area was deserted.

"It's either the wrong bridge, or the fight is somewhere else," said Aaron.

"This is the only bridge," said Falnor, looking down at the ground. "I see no disturbance here. We should find out how it went with the Small Giants."

A loud voice bellowed out from somewhere near the bridge: "Halt! Who rides?"

"Falnor of the Green Stone," hollered the captain; "and three others who come as friends."

"Come! And bring whatever help you have," the other voice called back.

A Small Giant came up to the rim of the canyon and greeted them wearily. "Nosgun," he said introducing himself with a slight bow. "We kept the bridge this time, but we have no idea how many Black Warriors there are nor when they might appear next. Is there a healer among you? Defgar is badly wounded."

"Take me to him," said Lia.

Nosgun led the company to the south side of the bridge and down a short distance to a wide ledge. The Small Giant opened a massive door revealing a cave opening large enough for him to step inside without ducking. Falnor saw to the horses as the rest went inside and Nosgun returned to his watch post, above.

Off to the right, a short distance from the entrance, Aaron, Lia and Ender came upon a large room lit by oil lamps where they found Defgar lying on a rough wooden bed. He was cut badly just below the ribs. The rags stuffed into the wound dripped with blood.

Lia crossed to him quickly and opened a small pouch she had brought from her saddlebags. "How was he wounded?" she asked.

"Sword cut," said Rifgar sitting near his brother's feet. "We forced a confrontation at the eastern end of the bridge to keep them from taking it. They attacked all together. We were hard pressed, but our pikes repelled them. They turned to smoke when pierced, even the horses! Those behind simply rode through the smoke and continued the attack. One of them flung an axe and wounded Defgar, but then they suddenly wheeled and rode away as if called by some silent command."

Lia removed the bloody rags and trickled a strong smelling liquid directly into the wound. Defgar, flinched as the cut began to foam, but he kept silent.

"Let it out," said Lia. "You may as well."

Defgar began to moan.

"Better," said Lia. "This next will hurt even worse. I expect to be deafened." She poured some white powder into her hand and pressed it into the foaming gash, holding it there with her hand. Defgar did not disappoint. His roar filled the room .

Gently, deliberately, Lia cleaned the wound again and applied the powder until the bleeding stopped. Then she called for fresh strips of cloth and bound his midsection while Rifgar and the others helped Defgar sit. As the pain subsided, Defgar began to breathe more easily. Great tears rolled down his leathery cheeks and he smiled through them at Lia. She smiled back and asked Rifgar for a small cup of water. She stirred several drops of a sweet smelling essence into the water and gave the cup to Defgar.

"Oh," he said as he handed the cup back. "That's good. Very good." They helped him lie back down again so he could rest. Soon he was asleep, his massive chest rising and falling peacefully.

"He looks much better," said Rifgar. "Our thanks."

* * *

All this time, Ender had sat by Defgar's bed, watching Lia's actions closely. Hidden in his clasped hands was the Midnight Stone. He could actually see the Dark Magic coursing through the Small Giant's body like a shadow. In his mind's eye, Ender reached out and grasped the shadow which writhed and fought like a cat caught by the tail. He pulled and pulled again until he gathered it all into a swirling ball. Then he imagined compressing it into a tiny mass, but it would not go away. For a moment, anger rose in him and violent thoughts flickered in his mind. The seething ball grew even more agitated, growing stronger, not weaker. He calmed himself and imagined that he simply opened his hand and told the shadow to leave. It grew still. He continued this until the shadow finally dissipated into nothing.

Then, as Lia was wrapping the wounds with clean bandages, Ender focused the Midnight Stone on the torn tissues and the bleeding, knitting things back together. When it was over, he slipped the Midnight Stone back into his pocket and took a deep breath. He felt tired, but happy that he had used the Stone for good.

* * *

Nosgun came in from outside and sat by Defgar while Rifgar took his turn at the watch. The company was invited to help themselves from the larder which held bread, dried fruit and cheese, a fine meal before they settled in for the night. Lia asked to be awakened should Defgar's condition change. Then she lay down beside her husband and slept.

When morning broke, they were treated to fresh broiled fish. Defgar was still asleep but he looked much better. Lia checked the bandages and let him lie. Thisvane and Gullen had arrived sometime during the night and were glad to see their cousin was recovering so well.

While they ate, Ender wondered aloud why the Black Warriors had fled.

"I doubt they were afraid of us," said Rifgar.

"No, something happened," said Nosgun. "It was as if they were called away."

"Then perhaps this was only a show of strength, or even decoy," suggested Aaron. "Perhaps the real mission was elsewhere."

"They'll be back," said Falnor. "The fords are far south of us. If the Shioroth is the goal, the bridge is the best route. If they take it, they have unrestricted access to the west."

"We'll secure the bridge," said Thisvane with a grunt; "but I don't think we should cross it again. Let them come to us."

"We should move quickly," said Ender.

Lia left instructions behind for the further treatment of Defgar's wound.

As the Small Giants gathered at the bridge to see them off, Rifgar presented Lia with a small gift. "This is an Elven ring," he said. "It was forged long before the Faeries came, a gift to my grandmother who saved the life of an Elf, just as you saved my brother's. We have held it for hundreds of years, but we all agree it should go to you."

"Thank you," said Lia. "I don't know what to say."

"Wear it and it will bring light in darkness—but to your eyes only—and it will make your enemy's footsteps easier to hear," said Gullen. "If it is taken from you, call for it. Somehow, it always finds its way back."

Lia bowed in the saddle and took their hands. "May Defgar be well and on his feet when we return!" she said. Then they turned eastward and sped across the bridge.

CHAPTER 34

The Forest of Irslaak

For the first hour as they followed the highway, they could see the retreating hoof prints of the Black Warriors. Then the trail veered off the road and headed southward.

"That might mean they're heading for the fords," said Falnor.

"Is there a safer route than the road?" asked Aaron.

"This open stretch is the safest place to cover distance at speed," said the captain. "Later on, the road gets dangerous. We'll veer off and cut through the forest."

They raced forward at a gallop. Behind them, across the river, the land lay green and lush. On this side, it was all dry dust and scruffy grasses. Barren hills rolled away as far as the eye could see. The riders stopped for a short rest at midday beneath the shade of a few scrub oaks growing beside a meager spring. If anyone else had stopped here, they had left no sign.

Falnor dipped his finger into the water and sniffed at it. "Still good," he said. They watered the horses and drank some themselves.

As the afternoon wore on, the hills ahead became more pronounced. Falnor led the group through a maze of drainages and up onto higher and higher ridges. By now, they were beyond the reach of any help.

Dusk was turning to night when they came to the edge of a wood.

"This is the Forest of Irslaak," said Falnor. "It becomes dense very quickly. Ten years ago, we stumbled upon a shortcut through it. If we had known about it sooner, we might have saved a few brave souls."

Lia noticed his tone. "Good friends of yours?" she asked.

"Yes," said the captain; "including the king's son, Prince Gaealann."

"That explains his exchange with you," said Lia.

Falnor nodded. "We've never seen a goblin in these woods. They give it a wide berth."

"Why?" asked Aaron.

"We don't know," said Falnor. "Something about the area bothers them. While the forest is very dense and dark, we've never experienced anything strange. I've used this shortcut three times and seen neither tracks nor scat. Nothing. I usually wait till daylight, though. It takes most of the day to get through."

"I bet the view is good from up there," said Aaron, pointing to a low rise nearby. "I assume we camp there tonight."

"We do," said Falnor.

*　*　*

Ender took the second watch. Gazing out toward the lowlands. He saw nothing in the pale starlight. The silent hills rolled on. Making a wide circle, Ender walked to the back of the camp where the woods marched eastward in ever more tightly crowded ranks. No night birds sang. The only sound was from the crickets, and even they seemed muted and secretive within the stillness of the trees.

The Stonekeeper reached into his pocket and touched the Stone. Again his eyes saw the strange eminence of light from the life around him, but there was nothing out of the ordinary other than the lack of animal life. There were no birds, no raccoons, squirrels or mice, only insects and plants, for all he could tell. The woods, however, seemed particularly vibrant. Each type of tree had its own distinct aura. For some time, he stood and watched as their life force seemed to change color, shifting slowly from one hue to the next with no particular order or pattern. He slipped his hand back out of his pocket and resumed the watch with his normal sight. Using the Midnight Stone left him feeling unusually tired.

*　*　*

At dawn, Falnor led them around the border of the forest until they came upon a stream which they could follow into the dense woods. They had not gone far before the canopy overhead became so thick that the pinholes of sunlight peeking through looked like stars in the night sky. Everything else was dark and dusky and cloaked in the rich scent of mosses, dead leaves and rotting wood.

Judging time was difficult with no light. The stream bubbled on interminably. They rode deeper into the forest, not stopping to eat.

Something about this place made Ender's skin prickle. He slipped his hand into his pocket and touched the Midnight Stone. Ah! With his enhanced vision, the trees took on a completely different look. They were tall, sleeping monsters with many arms, some of which ended in sharp, twisted claws. Their ugly faces appeared serene, though, quiet for now. He wondered what would happen if they were to awaken.

"You said it takes all day to get through the wood?" Ender asked Falnor, almost in a whisper.

"All day," replied the captain. "It's hard to go much faster here."

"Is it always this dark?" Ender asked.

"No," said Falnor. "This feels different. I don't know how to describe it."

They continued on along the stream's stony banks. In places where the creek grew wide and gravelly, they picked up the pace a little. Still, the further they went in, the darker it became.

Ender rode in the back, behind Lia. He could see movement behind them once they had passed. There wasn't a breath of wind, but now the branches shivered slightly as if caught by a breeze. Slowly, gradually, the trees turned as if to watch the company following the stream.

"What is it?" Lia whispered over her shoulder. "I have the Elven ring on, but I'm wondering if I'm seeing things. The trees seem to move on their own."

"They seem to be awakening," said Ender.

Aaron reached for his axe.

"No sharp objects," said Ender. "We mean no harm."

"Unless harm comes to us," said Aaron, placing his hand on his thigh.

A whisper rose up along the banks, like leaves rustling in the stillness.

"By my reckoning, we should come upon a great tree soon," said Falnor. "After that, we should be almost through the wood."

They rode on in silence. The movement along the banks became more and more obvious. The trees bent and spoke to each other in whispers low and strange. They reached over the riders' heads or pointed at the intruders, but they did not touch the riders or the horses.

Then, in the darkness, the horses suddenly stopped of their own accord. Directly ahead of them, in a broad, low island in the middle of the stream, stood a fir tree so massive that thirty men clasping each other's outstretched hands could not have encircled its girth. The waters flowed around its mighty roots on either side.

"This is the great tree," said Falnor, quietly.

Ender moved to the front. The whispering on the banks increased excitedly and then abruptly ceased.

"We request safe passage," Ender said aloud, his hand still holding the Midnight Stone. He watched as, some distance up the trunk, two eyes opened slowly.

"Who travels through the Forest of Irslaak without my leave?" said a voice that rumbled down from the crown high above.

"It speaks!" whispered Falnor. He patted his horse to calm it.

"We mean no harm," said Ender. "Let us pass and we promise no disturbance."

"What is your quest?" queried the tree. "None enter here without cause. None leave here without our approval. You will tell me the reason for your journey or you will continue no further. So says Irslaak Deeproot."

Ender bowed in the saddle. "Well met, Irslaak Deeproot. I acknowledge your wish to hear our quest, but our errand does not concern these woods and we promise to leave the forest as it was before we came. You will recognize one of us who has brought others here before and caused you no harm."

Irslaak shook needles all about them as he bent his branches downward. "Yes, but he did not bring with him the magic you carry. That is a power too great to ignore. You will not leave until you tell me your errand. I will judge whether or not it concerns these woods. Those who enter the Forest of Irslask are under my domain. Those who ignore my authority do not survive. Neither will you, magic or no. Disclose your mission or stay where you are until we bid you leave."

Ender sat quietly, weighing his choices. "This much I will tell you," he said. "We are friends from the Shioroth out on reconnaissance. Enemies approach our borders and we wish to know their strength and numbers."

"And which are we?" asked the tree. "Friend or enemy?"

"Which relationship do you prefer?" asked Ender quietly. "We can be strong allies or deadly foes."

Irslaak laughed, scattering a light shower of needles around them. "Deadly foes? How would you fight us? And what can you offer us as allies? Our cause benefits nothing from your skills and our soil would benefit little from your decaying bodies. How do you propose that this relationship be mutually beneficial?"

"I know nothing of your cause," said Ender. "If you will explain, I may answer your question."

"No, no," laughed Irslaak once again. "You are hoping I will provide you with air enough to breathe. I await your answer. I have plenty of time."

"Then I offer no answer," said Ender. "I have answered your first question already. You have not answered mine. We have no desire to hew a path through your ranks, but we will not be barred by those who will not respect us or accept the hand of friendship. Speak now, Irslaak Deeproot."

The great tree stood in silence as the woods around the company leaned inward, their branches coming very close. The riders would have to defend themselves from all sides in the darkness. Aaron had one hand on his axe, but the branches of some of these trees were as thick as the trunks of some of the oaks at home. It would take a long time to hack one off.

"Our cause is the protection of the forest," said Irslaak. "That is all."

"To that end, we have no quarrel," said Ender.

"I have told you my name, but you have not told me yours," said the tree, thoughtfully.

"I am Ehrmahann Jarmahann," said Ender.

The tree shook its head. "You have another name, no?"

"To some," the Stonekeeper replied. He could see Irslaak's eyes studying him carefully.

"Tell me your other name, for I can see inside your palm," said the tree, solemnly.

Lia turned to look at Ender. I wonder what he means by that, she thought.

"I am also called Ender," said the Stonekeeper.

The forest denizens whispered among themselves and leaves and branches rustled all around. Irslaak Deeproot's voice came from deep beneath the ground: "I have heard your name before. A great master gave you that name, did he not?"

"He did," said Ender.

"And he is no longer with us, I presume," said Irslaak.

"Sadly, that is true," said Ender.

"Now I know who you are and why you carry the magic," said the tree. "Well met, Ender. We will indeed make a most dangerous and welcome alliance. You and your company may pass." Irslaak fell silent as the trees around them backed away to give them room. Then he said: "We will not speak of this meeting. There is much afoot that endangers us all. If you pass through here again, do not fail to tell me what you find."

Ender bowed. "Thank you. If we return this way, we will speak again. At your request, we will say nothing of this meeting."

Irslaak raised himself up to his full height and all the trees parted their upper branches to allow the moonlight to peek through.

"With your permission," said Ender.

One by one, the company rode quietly past the massive tree. When they were on the other side of it, Ender turned and raised his hand. "May neither blade nor fire trouble the Forest of Irslaak," he said. Irslaak bowed slightly in return, and then the company continued on upstream.

The trees along the sides of the brook watched them pass, drawing back as they approached. Further on, the trees seemed less and less awake, but every once in awhile a name was whispered among the branches.

"Ehrmahann...Jarmahann...Ender..."

CHAPTER 35

Choices

The next morning dawned gloomy and dim. The way had grown steeper and now the company came to a sharp bend which led to a cascade on their right.

"Here we leave the stream," said Falnor. "Now I know why the goblins leave this place alone."

Ender nodded. "There is great magic in those woods. I'm glad to have met Irslaak Deeproot."

"Your reputation precedes you, Ender," said Falnor. "I look forward to learning the story behind it."

"Someday," said Ender. "It's not a tale to be told in this country."

They left the woods and turned north, diagonally ascending the ridge in front of them. There was no trail, so the horses had to find their own way. These mountains were not as formidable as the Mirrak-Haas that divided the Abandoned Lands of the Golrakken and the realm of Morvoth. They would travel five days more before they would reach the foothills of that mighty range.

At the top of the climb, they found themselves on a wide, sloping plateau that fanned out at the feet of the mountains. They continued eastward now with all speed, letting the horses run while the way was smooth. At midday, they came to a butte standing alone on the plains. At its summit stood the remains of a tower.

"This is Vis-Hulak, the Watchtower," said Falnor as he scanned the ground for tracks. There were none. "It used to be much taller. From here, the Golrakken could see all the way to the Shioroth. Men of the Green Stone tore it down for fear that it might be used again after the land was abandoned, but the butte is still a good lookout. From here, we can see if anyone else is about."

They road up a winding path to the top. A great deal of rubble lay strewn about the base of a fifty foot wide structure which still stood thirty feet tall. Stairs wound up the outside. Ender dismounted and worked his way across the rubble until he could scale the steps. Falnor was right behind him. They found a flat spot on the broken wall and looked around.

The view westward into the land of the Faeries was blocked by edge of the far plateau, but it was unbroken north and south across the sloping grasslands. To the east, the outline of the Mirrak-Haas cut a jagged horizon. The air was clear except for a thin plume of dust rising from the foothills some distance to the south of them. Ender put his hand in his pocket and looked hard at the base of the dust cloud. With the Stone in his fingers, he could make out fifty black horsemen riding westward at full speed.

Ender felt the power of the Stone burning in his hand. Fifty horsemen could be wiped out in a heartbeat should he so choose! His head swam and his vision grew hazy as he envisioned himself sweeping down upon the Black Warriors and destroying them before they even knew he was there. The Midnight Stone seemed to want only to be wielded; it cared nothing for the consequences. The mere thought of violence unleashed a bloodlust made Ender shiver with excitement. Shutting his eyes, he forced his fingers to open and let the Midnight Stone fall to the bottom of his pocket. As his normal vision returned, he wondered why the Stone did not inspire good as easily as it inspired violence.

"What do you see?" asked Aaron, below.

"Black Warriors," Ender replied. "North of us. Fifty on horseback heading west."

"Yes, I see the plume now," said Falnor. "Why would they be this far north?"

"Time to be careful of our own dust," said Aaron.

"Agreed," said Falnor, coming back down the steps

They descended from the butte quickly and set off at a swift but more measured pace.

By nightfall, they were due south of the plume of dust. They could see it dissipate as the Black Warriors apparently stopped for the night. They decided to put some distance between them and their enemy under cover of darkness when they could ride with more speed. Tired though they were, they pressed on and in several hours covered more distance than they had all day.

The next morning, they awoke to dense fog.

"Well, we won't be easily seen," said Falnor to Aaron as they saddled up.

"Harder on guards and easier on spies," said Aaron.

"Thank goodness we're spies," said Lia, looking around. "Sure is hard to get my bearings, though."

"Lucky for us, if we just keep going up slope, we won't get lost," said the captain as he led them up the gentle climb.

With Falnor in the lead, they set off again, climbing gently, keeping an ear out for unexpected company. The fog burned off by late morning and the day warmed up quickly. They doffed their cloaks, happy to let everything dry off. The Black Warriors' plume of dust drifted off far to the northwest. Eventually, they could see it no longer.

Around noon, Falnor said: "This section is very dry at this time of year. There is an ancient watering hole by the road before we get into the passes. The horses should be watered, fed and rested before we head into the mountains. The highway is the shortest route."

"How far are we from the road?" asked Aaron.

"Not more than half an hour's ride over these hills," said Falnor.

Night was falling by the time they came to the well. Just off the highway was a deep depression cut many years ago by the road builders. The profusion of hoof prints indicated that the Black Warriors had been here a day or two earlier. Lia wore her Elven ring and reported no sound of the enemy. Still, they approached the well cautiously. No one was down there.

Aaron and Lia kept watch above while Ender and Falnor descended to fill their skins and water their horses. They were all back up and moving again soon. When it was too dark to ride, they made camp on the backside of a low hill.

Once again, they awoke to fog. As soon as it was light, they mounted up and set off again.

When the fog burned away again, the spy party found themselves in ever more hilly countryside. High clouds drifting in from the east brought some relief from the sun. The Mirrak-Haas, the westernmost mountains of Morvoth could now be seen, their summits cloaked in heavy clouds.

"What more can you tell me about the Black Warriors?" Falnor asked Ender. "We have seen them only a few times, never up close. What are they?"

"They are changelings, not unlike the Golrakken," Ender replied. "Morvassus conquered many peoples in those days and planted the souls of the fiercest into bodies he created himself. They are powerful and dangerous for they have their wits about them. Their minds are not controlled by Morvassus directly, but they are utterly loyal to him. Any good in their hearts seems to have died with their original bodies."

"So are they dead?" Falnor queried.

"Half dead," said Ender. "What lives is only the shadow of what was, but it is a dreadful shadow, empowered by the Morve."

"There seem to be hundreds of them," said Falnor.

"He had more than a hundred with him when he fled the southern continent. I don't know if he could have created more of them since we defeated him there," Ender said. "Our victory was by a thread. Now we face him again on another front. This time we must prevail."

They grew more and more wary as they drove deeper into the Abandoned Land, staying within sight of the road, but not daring to leave tracks on it. Only the hoof prints of the Black Warriors gave any indication of life ranging across these hills. The company saw neither troll nor goblin. That night, they continued on for several miles before they set a watch and slept fitfully. Lia awakened once or twice, thinking she had heard something. Eventually, she removed the ring so she could get some sleep.

Morning broke on the third day since they had left the Forest of Irslaak. The now familiar fog shrouded their passage as they began to climb and descend ever steeper hills. Still, they were making good time.

"These are only the foothills of the Mirrak-Haas," said Falnor. "The actual ascent will begin within the next day or so."

The large, heavy prints of Ogres and a smattering of goblin tracks scattered across the hillside were the first indications of life in the wild the company had seen, but they saw no sign of the track makers themselves.

"This place is more abandoned than usual," the captain said. "These tracks are old. The most recent tracks generally seem to be going west, but we've come across no enemies so far."

The hills steepened and the company climbed up out of the fog before the day was warm enough to dissipate it. Just before noon, they came upon a deep ravines that had to be crossed before they could ascend to the divide. The road was the only safe way down.

"I dislike this part," said Falnor; "but there's no way around it."

He led them down the switchbacks. They could see a bridge that was still in good repair. The road was clear and the bridge was not guarded, but there were thick woods on the far side.

"Lia, do you hear anything?" asked Ender, casually slipping his hand into his pocket.

"Nothing," she answered. "No, wait! I'm not wearing the ring! I took it off—"

Before she could finish, the whole place erupted with shrieking and howling. Goblins, too many to count, swarmed down the road behind them cutting off any retreat.

"No better way but through!" yelled Aaron, spurring his horse toward the bridge.

Another wave of goblins surged out of the forest into the bright sunlight and poured across the bridge. The company was surrounded and completely outnumbered. Falnor's sharp blade cut a bloody swath through the crowd as he urged his horse forward. Lia cut the hands off of an attacker who had seized her horse by the reins, taking the goblin's head off with the backswing. Aaron swung his axe in tight arcs, hacking through flesh and bone. Falnor took a bite in the leg but quickly sliced off the biter's face.

Ender already had the Stone in his hands. He felt his fear shift to anger. Everything seemed to get smaller and he found himself towering above the fray. He had grown to the size of a giant sequoia.

Seething, he waved his huge arm at the goblins swarming the company. The creatures burst into flame! With another wave, he sent the whole burning mass of them squalling and yowling into the abyss. Hundreds of goblins were still emerging from the woods. The Stonekeeper roared, leaned down, reached over and swept them all into the ravine.

"Go!" he roared at the remaining goblins in the woods.

They fled in terror, all but one great brute of a fellow who stood alone on the bridge and glared at Ender.

"Who are you?" demanded the goblin; "and why do you trespass on the land of Nog, King of the Goblins?"

Ender's mind reeled. The bloodlust of the Stone was screaming through his whole gigantic body. He calmed himself and the temptation slowly waned.

"Neither we nor our business is any concern of yours," responded the Stonekeeper. "If we are attacked again, however, we will defend ourselves." He steadied himself. "Go," he said from his lofty height. "Trouble us no more. Safe passage is all we ask."

The goblin stood for a moment. "Leave mine alone and we'll leave yours alone," he growled.

"Agreed," said Ender.

The great goblin turned and walked back into the forest.

The Stonekeeper could see the auras of the creatures fleeing through the woods. "Lia," he said. "Can you hear them now?"

Still breathing hard, Lia put her ring on her finger and listened. "They are retreating. I hear no other threat."

"Agreed," said Ender, stepping across the ravine. "There is a protected spot up here on top of the ridge. Can you make it?"

"We will," said Aaron. His axe still at the ready, he moved forward across the bridge.

Falnor took the reins of Ender's horse and led it up the road, Lia close behind him.

Ender stepped onto the ridge, shrank back to normal size and returned the Stone to his pocket. Once the energy of the Stone left him, he felt dizzy and weak. He stood there dazedly, waiting for the others to come. When they arrived, he took the Midnight Stone from his pocket and checked the area again. He could sense nothing amiss. Quickly, he surveyed his companions' injuries with his enhanced sight.

Lia's horse had been caught between Aaron's and Ender's so she had escaped relatively unscathed. Her husband was not so lucky. A rusty goblin blade had caught him just below the kneecap, exposing the bone. Falnor's bite was already festering and he had received several cuts on that side. The horses were also suffering, though they bore it well.

Ender helped Aaron off his horse. Lia was quickly at his side with her oils. She had just started working on the knee when Ender gently touched her hand. Eyes wide, she gasped as she felt the energy flowing from him.

"Let me help," he said.

She nodded and leaned back out of the way.

The Stonekeeper ran his fingers over Aaron's wounded knee. The blood stopped flowing and the skin sealed over.

"Amazing," said Lia. "Please continue! I will tend to Falnor."

Moments later, Aaron had barely a mark on him.

"Even the pain is gone!" he said.

The Stonekeeper went to Falnor next and repeated the process until all the gashes were closed. Then he tended to Lia.

"I did not know you were such a healer," said Lia, watching him carefully. "Your magic works almost instantly."

Ender nodded.

"Then why did you let me tend to Defgar?" she asked. "Why didn't you do it yourself?"

"Your methods work," he replied. "I tended to a different part of his injuries and aided your efforts."

Finally, Ender turned his attention to the horses, wiping away their cuts and soothing their bruises. When he was finished, he stood up. "News will travel swiftly," he said.

"I didn't like the looks of that big fellow," said Aaron. "Wish we had finished him off when we had the chance."

Ender nodded but said nothing.

They rode quickly, meeting with no further resistance. By evening, they had reached the forested lower slopes of the Mirrak-Haas where they left the road and covered their tracks. No one spoke. Falnor led them to a place with a natural cave and a patch of decent grass for the horses. Lia took the first watch and the rest of them went inside and tried to get some sleep.

* * *

In the middle of the night, Ender lay in the cave, wide awake. He came out of the cave and found Falnor atop a tall boulder near the horses, eyes slowly scanning the area.

"It's not time to change the watch," said the captain.

"No, but I can't sleep," said Ender sitting on one of the rocks below. "You might as well get some rest."

"I'm not sure I can sleep either," said Falnor. He came down from the boulder and sat next to Ender. "Clearly, you hold a magic like few have ever seen. Tell me, why didn't you kill the goblin king?"

Ender took a deep breath and let it out. "By the time he appeared, the enemy had been routed. More bloodshed would have simply been more bloodshed."

"But he lived to fight another day," said Falnor. "Why risk the chance that he will regroup and attack again somewhere else?"

"Violence feeds on itself," said Ender. "In this case, it was feeding me. I was the most violent one there."

"You were provoked," said Falnor. "You were defending yourself and your friends."

"Up till then, yes," said Ender. "That attack had been rebuffed at great loss of life. Further violence would have simply fed the bloodlust. I had the upper hand. It was up to me to end the cycle."

The captain thought for a moment. "The risk of vengeance remains," he said. "One final blow would have ended the cycle completely."

"Perhaps," said Ender. "At what cost?"

"Nothing," said Falnor; "a few goblins."

"Not nothing," said Ender. "I have no fondness for goblins either, but killing is hard on the soul. Everything we do affects us in one way or another."

"That I do know," said Falnor.

"And we are not the only ones affected," Ender replied.

"Agreed." The captain sat quietly. "You showed remarkable restraint in the heat of battle."

"That is what the Great Master Palanthar taught me," said Ender.

"I look forward to that tale," said Falnor.

"Let's get through this first," said the Stonekeeper.

"Fair enough," said Falnor. With that, he took his leave and went in to get some rest.

When the captain was gone, Ender stood up and looked around. The forest provided good cover but it also blocked the view of the road. His strength had returned now that he had not touched the Midnight Stone for several hours. Curious, he brought out the Stone and thought about what the view was like from a sturdy fork in the tallest tree. Perhaps he should fly there.

He almost cried out as, once again, everything changed. One moment, he was standing by the rock; the next moment, there was a brief burning sensation and he was hurtling through the air. He stopped abruptly at the fork in the tree and turned to look back at the cave. A thin puff of smoke drifted placidly away from the ground below.

Ender tried to grab hold of the tree and discovered his hand was immaterial. He was not actually sitting on the branches either; he was floating just above them. In fact, he had no body at all.

I'm like a Sochhmahr, he thought. It was a strange sensation. He could sense that his being had physical boundaries but they were vague and amorphous. His invisible hands flowed like oil through water yet they touched nothing corporeal. The Midnight Stone was the only palpable object.

What if I want to materialize? thought Ender.

As soon as he fixed on the thought, it was done. He found himself sitting in the fork, instantly aware of his body weight as if he had been floating in a pool which had suddenly drained away. His hands were visible again. With a thought, he could turn invisible again.

Thought is action, he reminded himself. Action without intention was folly.

Ender looked across the tree tops to the highway. All was still. Though he would have preferred to keep watch from this spot, he would cause undue alarm if anyone awoke to find him gone. He decided to go back to the rock and braced himself for the heat flash. If he concentrated, he could control his speed, and if he wished, he could change direction simply by choosing. Before he landed, he experimented a little. The sensation was very much like swimming without moving his arms and legs, but there was no danger of crashing into anything. Objects passing through him caused only a minor disturbance, like a ripple in the pool.

I'm sensing their life, not their substance, thought the Stonekeeper.

Soon, he was sitting back on the rock. What a marvelous way to travel! The hours went quietly. The sky was growing slowly lighter when he heard horses on the highway. Lia came out of the cave, sword drawn.

"Black Warriors?" she whispered.

"Yes," said Ender. "Keep watch. I'm going to disappear for a minute." Then, with a puff of smoke, he was gone.

Lia jumped back a step and spun around, sword ready. He had utterly disappeared. If she hadn't just spoken to him, she would have wondered if he had been there at all.

* * *

Invisible now, Ender deposited himself high in a tree next to the road. A platoon of thirty Black Warriors was riding double file down from the pass. At the head of the line, not more than fifty paces from Ender's hiding place, rode the lieutenant and the standard bearer.

Up from the valley below came a lone goblin in great haste, wildly waving its arms. Ender watched as it raced up the hill to meet the Black Warriors. The Warriors stopped below Ender's tree as the exhausted goblin tried to catch his breath.

"Speak, goblin. Speak up and get out of the way," barked the lieutenant.

The creature nodded and gasped. "Enemies... attacked Nog... many killed... a huge man and some on horse—"

STOP!

It had been only a thought in Ender's head, but it silenced the goblin instantly.

"Speak up! What's wrong with you?" snapped the lieutenant. "Who attacked?" The leader stopped suddenly and looked more intently at the goblin. The messenger was choking. Quickly, the Warrior stood in the saddle and looked around as if searching for someone. "My lord?" he called out sharply.

By the time Ender cleared his thoughts, the goblin had collapsed in a heap. The Stonekeeper was aghast. He had not meant to kill it.

The lieutenant sat back down in his saddle.

"Did you feel the Master's hand?" he said to the standard bearer.

"I thought so, sir," said the other. "But why would he stop the creature mid-report?"

"It must have been a liar and a meddler," growled the lieutenant. "Onward!" he shouted to his troops. They trampled over the dead goblin.

When they were gone, Ender sat in the tree and looked at the flesh splattered on the road. The dilemma of the Stone rolled over and over in his head. It was an effective defense, but it could so easily turn deadly. He could have merely rendered the goblin mute. He could have caused him to forget. Instead, he thoughtlessly throttled the fellow and killed him. The Great Master's warning against violence thundered again in his head.

The ache in the pit of his stomach was nothing compared to the exhilarating power that surged through his whole body. He forced himself to relax. In a few moments, the ache and the rush both subsided.

He dared not attempt to bring the goblin back to life; a mistake could have dire consequences. Ruefully, he incinerated the remains. The grisly pile burned quickly and left only a blackened patch on the road. Even this he restored so that all that remained were the hoof prints of the Black Warriors. Then he returned to the cave.

Lia nearly ran him through with her sword before she realized who he was. "You should announce yourself somehow," she said. "I heard a goblin speak. What stopped him?"

"I did," Ender replied, flatly. Again, the use of the Stone left him feeling nauseated and weary.

Lia nodded. "Good, then we have not been discovered."

They went inside and roused the others. Foregoing the last hour of sleep, they saddled up the horses and headed toward the pass.

CHAPTER 36

Akka-Illin

Formidable peaks towered above them, ominously watching their progress as if already aware of the spies in their midst. Aaron rode as rear guard. Lia kept her ears open and her ring on her finger. They urged their horses forward, intent on making it through the pass before sunrise.

"There is an abandoned fortress on the other side of the pass," said Falnor to Ender. "Akka-Illin used to be a Golrakken stronghold, but it's been empty for years."

Other than a few short stretches where rockfall had covered the road, their path was mostly clear. The company made excellent speed up the steep ascent. They began to wind their way between the peaks, deep in shadow. The predawn light barely lit the floor of the high walled cleft so the company let the horses find their way at their own pace. The road turned sharply many times, making it impossible to see what lay around the bend.

They came to a wider section of the cleft. Ahead of them, two towers guarded the exit from the pass. The battlements were crumbling and all that remained of the gates were the twisted, rusting bolts that had once secured the hinges.

"Not much farther to the fortress," said Falnor.

"Stop," said Lia, quietly. "Footsteps. I can't tell how far away. Two on foot."

Everyone paused and listened.

"I'll climb up and have a look," said Falnor, pointing up the cliff wall.

"No," said Ender. "Let me do it. I'll be right back." Then he vanished in a puff of smoke.

"Invisible even," muttered Falnor, leading his horse and Ender's to the deeper darkness on one side of the gate. Aaron and Lia quietly moved to the shadows on the other side with their horses.

Almost immediately, Lia signaled that two Black Warriors were coming up the road on foot. In a minute, they could all hear the footsteps and clinking metal. The foursome in the shadows readied themselves but the footsteps stopped before the warriors reached the gate. Aaron had his sword in one hand and a long dagger in the other. Lia stood back far enough to let him swing freely, her sword held in both hands. On the far side, Falnor stood ready.

Not long afterward, the footsteps resumed, but this time they were moving away. A moment later, Lia signaled that they were beyond even her enhanced hearing.

"I don't like it," whispered Aaron. "They must have seen something."

Lia nodded. They waited in silence but there were no more footsteps. Still Ender did not return.

Suddenly, Lia gasped. "Horses!" She hissed. "Moving fast!"

No sooner had they mounted up when they heard a crackling roar from above. A massive shape darkened the sky.

"Dragon!" hissed Falnor.

Even as they turned their horses, the dragon landed on the cliff, cutting off their retreat with a blast of fire. Lia's mount reared. Hoof beats thundered toward them from the east side. Wheeling back around to face their attackers, the company could see there was nowhere to go.

The dragon on the cliff leaned down and sent another searing flame licking across the rocks.

"No more, Havvac!" shouted the Black Warrior captain. "The Interrogator wants prisoners!"

The dragon ceased spewing fire and merely hissed at them.

"Off your mounts, and surrender your weapons," barked the Black Warrior.

The company knew better than to resist now. If they killed half a dozen, they still didn't stand a chance.

"Where is the fourth rider?" asked the Black Warrior captain, pointing to Ender's empty saddle.

No one replied.

"No matter," said the officer. "The Interrogator will drag the answer out of you."

Black Warriors disarmed the company, bound their hands behind them tightly and led them and their horses through the ruined gates. Behind them, they heard the heavy whoosh of wings as the dragon flew off. They turned northward and headed down an incline to the fortress Falnor had mentioned. The fort was obviously no longer empty: its towers stood black against the dawn, but the gates and several windows were lit from within. The portcullis was raised with much grinding and clanking, and the prisoners were ushered into the mouth of the stronghold.

They entered a large courtyard paved and walled in stone. Fires burning in stone pits lit the walls and glinted off the armor and weapons. Aaron noted two pairs of guards at the portcullis. Watchmen patrolled the high battlements on the wall above the courtyard. Besides the main gate, there appeared to be no other exit.

Several Black Warriors dismounted and led the prisoners through a small, heavy door on the far side of the courtyard. Torches lit a short hallway that ended in a dark stairway leading steeply downward. Down they went into the dank darkness.

"Say goodbye to daylight," grunted their captor. "Next time you see it, I doubt it will mean much to you."

The stairs led down to a low-ceilinged corridor. There was no further way forward. To their right, there were six cells, sealed by heavy steel doors. To their left was an empty hallway with a large wooden doorway at the end. One of their escort, a particularly large soldier, pulled out a ring of keys and unlocked one of the cells. The Black Warriors shoved the prisoners inside, slammed the door shut and rammed the bolt in place.

The big turnkey set the lock. "A word of advice," he said, through a slit in the window. "When you meet the Interrogator, tell him what he wants to know. You'll thank me for it."

Some of the soldiers laughed as they left.

"Turn around," said Falnor to Aaron. Immediately, he went to work on Aaron's bindings.

"Impressive knots," he whispered. "Were you able to keep one hand stiff?"

"No," said Aaron. "Were you?"

Falnor grunted. "They're good. I'll just have to be persistent. Hold still."

Still wearing her ring, Lia looked around the room for some sign of structural weakness. The walls that weren't solid stone cut from the bedrock were well masoned, their individual stone blocks set tightly together. The ring the Small Giants had given her allowed her to see better in the dark but she saw no indication of a likely escape route.

Soon, they heard muffled voices in the hallway, shuffling feet, and another large door opening and closing.

Not much later, several soldiers arrived with a great clanking of steel. The prisoners flattened themselves against the wall on either side of the cell door. The lock was undone and the bolt slammed aside. The metal door was yanked wide open but no one came through. The prisoners could see the long shadows of swords and spears cast on the floor of the cell.

"Send out the woman!" barked a soldier.

The prisoners did not respond.

"There are ten of us out here, fully armed," said the soldier. "Send out the woman."

"I'll go," said Aaron, calmly.

"You have not been sent for," said the soldier. "The Interrogator will see the woman. Send her out, or we smoke you out."

Lia stepped into the doorway. A guard grabbed her and pulled her through. The door was slammed shut again and quickly bolted. She could hear Aaron grunt as his shoulder hit the door. The big turnkey locked the cell and stood aside.

There were, indeed, ten heavily armed guards surrounding Lia. Two of them took her roughly by the arms as they marched her down the hallway. At the end, they opened the door, pushed her through the door and bolted it shut again. They seemed to be in a hurry to get it done.

When she had her balance again, Lia looked around. She was in a wide, bare stone chamber. In the middle of the floor was a pool of water which appeared to be lit from within, providing the only light in the room. She felt a strong compulsion to look into the pool but forced herself to look elsewhere. On the far side of the pool sat a stone seat with a high back, a simple, bare design that matched the sparseness of the room. Save for these two things, the hall was completely empty. Even wearing the ring, she could not see into the dark corners of the hall, but she could barely make out the back wall on which the throne cast a tall shadow. She took a few steps to her left and pressed her back to the wall so she could keep an eye on both the door and the pool.

For quite some time, she stood there, her eyes shifting from the pool to the throne to the door, just waiting. Time dragged on. The only noise in the room was her own breath and the pounding of her heart. She kept wanting to check her weapons but, of course, they were gone and her hands were bound. The combination of monotony and anticipation played tricks. One minute she thought she saw movement, but then she could see nothing, even in the half-light of the pool.

Finally, she heard a rustling sound and almost jumped in surprise. The throne was occupied! A gaunt, robed figure sat hunched over in the chair, staring at her silently. He seemed twisted, and deathly old. If he had ever grown hair, it was all gone now, including his eyebrows. Deep lines creased his pale, hawk-like face as he smiled. Lia felt as if her whole being was invaded by the gaze from his sunken eyes. She half expected him to be able to feel her heartbeat and taste her breath, even from a distance.

The gaunt figure leaned sideways in the throne and beckoned to her with a withered hand. His movements were measured, slow, disciplined.

Lia stood with her back to the wall, unmoving.

He beckoned again. "Come," he said in a voice that both hissed like stones rubbing together.

To Lia's horror, she felt her feet move. She could not stop them! Step by step, she came to the edge of the pool, facing the hooded figure seated on the other side.

"Come around and stand here," hissed the Interrogator, pointing to the floor directly at his feet.

Despite herself, Lia obeyed. Soon she was standing just in front of him. Everything inside her shivered.

"Very pretty," said the Interrogator. "I doubt Akka-Illin has ever had such a lovely visitor."

Lia said nothing.

"Turn around," said the Interrogator.

Heart pounding she willed her body to stop, but she could not resist. She turned away from the stone seat. She heard the rustling of robes and shuddered as a bony hand slid upward along the outside of her right hip, found her arm and lightly traced the edge of her forearm down to her bound wrists. She held her breath, frozen stiff.

"Ah, you brought me a gift," he said. "Relax your hand, my dear. Let me see it."

The grip she had held so tightly suddenly became impossible to sustain. Weakly, both hands opened. She felt the thin fingers caress her palm and then gently grasp the ring, slipping it it easily from her hand.

The Interrogator leaned back in his throne behind her. "Very nice," he said.

Lia breathed again, her mind searching for some way to free her body. Though his hand was no longer there, she could still feel the energy of his touch.

"Now," said the Interrogator. "Kneel and look into the pool."

Lia sank to her knees and found herself staring into the pool. Its light was dazzling now. It burned into her brain and hurt her eyes, but she could not shut them.

"Show me all that you see," he whispered slowly. "Who are you? Where are you from? Whom are you with, and why are you here? What else might you tell me that I may find useful? Show me all. Show me...show me..."

As if a fog were burning off, the water cleared and she could see fragmented, dreamlike images floating inside the pool. They were from her own past, real and treasured memories of times when life was simple. There were scenes of herself as a child with her sister, playing in the woods. Her mother and father appeared, so clearly that she wept when she saw them. Then there was Aaron, young and strong, riding past her home as she peered out the window, hoping he would stop in on his way back from the village.

All these things flashed by in moments. Every once in awhile, the story would be interrupted by the image of her interrogator. His thin-lipped grin leered at her through her own memories. Nothing she did could stop the pool from revealing her childhood hopes, her youthful joys and sorrows. She could neither hasten or delay the rush of memories; she was merely the source from which the pool drew its images.

"Yes," said the Interrogator behind her, his voice ripe with satisfaction. "How lovely. Show me more."

The scenes were becoming more recent; soon the Interrogator would see information she did not want to reveal. Her body ached. She could not shut her eyes. She fought to rise but an invisible weight on her head pressed down, down, down, harder and harder until her face almost touched the water. Her struggling seemed to have slowed the process somewhat, but the stream of images continued inexorably toward the revelation of the company, their identities and their plans. She focused all her mind on breaking free.

It worked! Somehow, Lia rolled sideways and wrenched her face away from the pool. She lay there, twisted and exhausted, her head at the edge of the water. The Interrogator rose up from his seat and glowered over her.

"You will not impede the questioning!" he warned. Kneeling down, he reached toward her face with one hand. Covering her eyes with his palm, he pressed his thumb and middle finger into her temples. The shock that ripped through her jerked every muscle in her body. He let go. When he took his hand away, she could see only blackness.

"Now," he hissed; "we will return to the pool and continue our interrogation."

Lia felt her body roll over and fold itself again before the pool. Though now she could not actually see the pool, the images began again in her head, displaying the unfolding story of how the company had formed. So far, the tale had not reached the point where the gruffen appeared, but soon all their allies and their plans would be revealed. Lia struggled to think of something else but every attempt at resistance caused severe pain. Still, she kept on struggling.

Without warning, everything went completely dark. The images stopped and Lia heard the Interrogator choke out a strangled cry. There was a heavy splash.

Lia recoiled from the stinging spray. Though she could hardly move, she still tried to crawl away from the pool on her knees. Powerful arms grabbed her firmly around the waist and picked her up off the floor. She was too weak to fight.

"Be quiet, Lia, we have yet to free the others," a voice she knew murmured in her ear. "We must be silent as snakes. I'm sorry I could not come sooner. For now, rest, sleep."

Lia lost consciousness and went completely limp.

CHAPTER 37

The Pull

Leaving the others in their saddles, Ender vanished in a puff of smoke. He lifted high into the sky, intending only to get a better look at their surroundings. To his dismay, the fortress on the other side of the pass was occupied. Rising higher, he looked eastward toward the Mountains of the Orryx. Here and there in the valleys he saw various gatherings of both goblins and Black Warriors, hundreds of troops, all told. He also saw clumps of ogres and trolls ranging throughout the valley, all apparently converging on Akka-Illin.

Further south, he saw a great army of Black Warriors heading away from him toward the Great Gates of Ulvanoth, precisely where he had to deliver the ashes in the golden box. His enhanced sight gazed further and saw an even larger army of goblins coming up towards the Gates from the south. At their head, they carried small, withered man seated on a litter. A powerful darkness swirled about him. Up from the southeastern coast rode a contingency of Golrakken on fearsome horses, heading toward the Mountains of the Orryx, presumably to join Morvassus in the fortress of Uzzim-Khail. The mountains around the Dark Lord's stronghold were veiled in some way; Ender could not see inside.

The sheer numbers of the enemy made Ender doubly glad he had made this sortie alone. He considered his options. Now that he had used the Stone to this extent, there seemed to be no point in conventional travel. He must immediately fly to the Great Gates of Ulvanoth, pour the contents of the golden box into the fountain and return to his friends. Somehow, he would manage to get them all back out of there.

As soon as he decided this, he shot through the sky, almost instantly arriving at the gates. He felt like he had been shoved through a thick wall. Energy swirled all around him, and he felt utterly exposed. Holding the Stone seemed to draw the energy toward him. He put the Stone back in his pocket and returned to his physical form but he could still sense seeker spells flailing about all around him. From where he lay, he could see the rising dust from the approaching armies both north and south. He lay still, looking up at the mighty stonework of the gates, trying to get his breath, gathering strength enough to stand.

The fountain was about a hundred paces from the gates themselves. It had been built over a natural spring more than a thousand years ago. Its main basin was thirty feet across and four feet deep. The torch-like top towered fifty feet high, spilling water down its sides to fill ever larger basins until it finally filled the base. When Ender had first seen it, the fountain was alabaster white; now it looked very different. All but the rim and the outer wall had turned from fine alabaster to some strange, silvery metal.

Ender rolled over and painfully got to his feet, staggering the hundred paces to the fountain. Leaning heavily on the outer wall, he reached into his cloak and brought out the golden box. He opened the lid and poured the ashes into the water. Much to his surprise, they did not float on top; instead, they turned to flecks of silver and quickly sank beneath the surface. Then, within a few seconds, they simply vanished.

He stood staring into the pool for a moment, and though he did notice a slight increase in the energy around him, that seemed to be the only change. He set his intention to fly more slowly back to Akka-Illin. Then he reached into his pocket and took out the Midnight Stone.

"ONE!"

The word screamed in his mind. A darkness black as pitch engulfed him and for a moment, he could see nothing. All he knew was that he was moving rapidly, drawn by an inexorable force, like one magnet racing toward another.

"ONE!"

Ender's mind reeled as he struggled to regain control of his thoughts. His vision cleared, found himself soaring eastward with dizzying speed, sailing over the valley and over the jagged crags of the Mountains of the Orryx. The fountain at the Great Gates was quickly lost in the distance behind him.

"ONE!"

The Midnight Stone itself was in control, but he could feel another force, just as strong, just as hungry. He struggled to control the Stone in his hand, but he could slow his progress only a little. He couldn't seem to make himself stop or turn back.

As he was flung over another knife-edged summit, the Dark Lord's fortress came into view. Like fingers from a menacing hand thrust up from the mountains, its towers and spires jabbed skyward, black as night. It had been a long time since

Ender had driven the wounded Morvassus into Uzzim-Khail. Clearly what had been begun as a place of exile had now become a stronghold. The magic that once banished Morvassus had been absorbed, twisted, and expanded.

Ender drew his thoughts back to himself. He must get grounded. Concentrating, slowing his heartbeat, he finally slowed his progress and began to drop slowly from his great height. The pull remained strong, but he was better able to manage it. His arc brought him ever closer to the dark towers of Uzzim-Khail. He must land soon.

Quiet. Slow. Peace.

He continued to focus.

"Release!" insisted a voice in his head. Ender let the thought pass. It was not his own.

"Bring us together!" spoke the voice again, almost pleading. It was a lovely thought, full of warmth and peace. He could be rid of the responsibility, free of the conflicting emotions and strain. Again, he noticed it and let it go.

"Join us!" said the voice, stronger now, but just as sweet. The pull was so strong.

Ender focused on the ground. His pace was finally slowing. Down he came, down through cold air, down to the ground. Somehow he managed to land on the castle's outermost wall. As soon as he touched down, he deliberately placed the Stone in his pocket. Its will continued to call to him, but the pull was not as strong as when he held it. He made his way silently along the rim of the fortress until he found a corner in which to hide.

A crow landed on the wall some distance away and squawked loudly. Ender froze as a soldier stepped out from nearby guard tower.

"What's your message, crow?" asked the soldier, gruffly.

"A tidbit, a morsel, and most probably a nugget of great worth to your Master," spat the crow.

"Your Master as well, remember? Out with it then, or there will be no morsels for you," the soldier retorted.

"Well, I have been conveying the Master's will to his favorite lieutenant: Kafna the Interrogator," said Jehzik.

"That is no news," said the soldier. "You waste my time."

The crow cocked his head and continued. "The news is that Kafna has kept the Master's messages to himself all this time, ordering his troops to his own ends. I learned this when the commander of of the Black Warriors in Akka-Illin accused me of keeping silent for my own gain." The bird crowed with indignation. "The Interrogator had not passed on what I had so dutifully reported. So I am here to ensure the Dark Master knows I have not left him uninformed even when his allies prove to be traitors."

"Don't congratulate yourself just yet," the soldier said with a laugh. "I doubt your life will be worth much when you call the Interrogator a traitor."

"You will not be laughing when you hear the rest of my message," said the crow. "A mighty sorcerer has ridden from the Shioroth, through the Abandoned Land and into the Mirrak-Haas without a scratch. Nog could not detain him. A platoon of your own kind, watchful though they are, passed him by without blinking. As we speak, he and a small company have ascended into the pass and approach Akka-Illin."

"How many?" queried the soldier.

"No more banter," said the crow, tersely. "The Interrogator wished to keep this information to himself. Will you also? Take me to Morvassus. My neck is at stake already."

"We shall see what the Master makes of your news," said the soldier as he opened the door and entered with the crow.

Ender took a deep breath and released his fears. For now, the most important thing was to bring himself back into full mastery of the Midnight Stone. If he could do some good deed with it, he could strengthen its independence from the Twin and counter the effects of the darkness that seemed to permeate the air in this place. He focused on his present position, letting all dread and worry go. He could help his friends only when he, himself, was grounded, solid and strong.

If Ender could sway the Midnight Stone to do good here in Uzzim-Khail it would deal a heavy blow to the user of the Twin. If he failed, he might find himself facing Morvassus directly. Right now, he didn't feel strong enough to survive that. Either way, the Dark Lord would soon know there was a new Stonekeeper.

For several minutes, Ender crouched in the corner, focusing his mind, managing the pain that coursed through every fiber of his being.

A noise in the guard tower caught his attention. Ender leaned slowly forward to peer around the stonework. The tower door was roughly kicked open and an ogre ducked out, stepping onto the battlements. It carried two broken and bloodied creatures, one large, one small, grasping them firmly by the ankles like slaughtered chickens. One was the soldier Ender had seen when he first arrived. The other was the crow. They were still alive, but just barely. Apparently, neither had survived the meeting unscathed.

With a grunt, the ogre flung the two creatures over the wall like so much trash, then simply turned back and ducked inside again. Ender heard the discarded bodies tumble down. He dared a peek over the battlements. In the gathering dawn, he could see the drifting smoke left behind by the disintegration of the Black Warrior's body. There would be no carcass. The crow, however, was somehow still in one piece. It had come to rest on a thin ledge several hundred feet below. Ender knew he couldn't possibly climb down to it safely on his own, but here was his opportunity to heal. He would have to risk using the Midnight Stone to help him climb down, but he dared not fly again, not yet. For now, he must remain grounded. He set his intention, took a deep breath and let it out, then slipped his hand into his pocket and grasped the Stone.

Instantly, he could feel the pull of the Twin and the chaotic power of the Morve swirling about him. He ignored it and concentrated on climbing down the wall. Despite its raw desire for reunion, the Midnight Stone helped him cling to the fine finger holds and toeholds. From the base of the wall, he descended the sheer cliff another hundred feet to where the crow lay smashed against the talus. An aura still emanated around the animal. Mixed with that aura was another life force that Ender did not recognize. Whatever magic had been used on this bird to allow it to talk was beyond Ender's understanding, but he could heal the body. He knelt down beside the bloody bird and worked slowly, methodically, holding the Midnight Stone over the stricken crow. It took all his concentration to set the bones back into place, restore the joints, and knit the sinews over them.

"Wasssssssted! Uselesssssss! Ssssssstop!" the air itself seemed to be hissing all around him. "Ssssssstonekeeperhhhhh! Foolishhhhhhhh Ssssssstonekeeperhhhhhhhh! RELEASSSSSSSSE!"

Ender could feel the Midnight Stone being pulled toward the dark fortress, but he continued to move it slowly over the crow, concentrating on reviving the internal organs, covering the muscles with skin, mending the feathers, healing the eyes. His hands trembled as the voices around him became louder, harsher and more insistent. They began to wail, first with pain, then with anger. Still, he was able to slowly stop the bleeding. Flesh and new feathers were beginning to emerge where once had been only carnage. The more he worked, the calmer he became and the stronger he felt. The voices turned from a cries to shrieks, but Ender's hands no longer trembled.

The crow stared at him fixedly and began to twitch this way and that, trying to flex its newly reformed wings. Then it turned its head jerkily to all sides, taking in where it was.

"Be free," said Ender. "You may go."

The crow staggered to its feet, gave out a full-throated croak, and with swiftly beating wings flew off westward over the Mountains of the Orryx.

The Dark Lord was moving. Ender could feel him within the tower. For a moment, the pull of the Twin was lessened.

Run, thought the Stonekeeper. He had friends to attend to, and he had been gone a long time. Keeping his connection to the ground, he ran as fast as a falcon could dive, down the slope, away from the dark fortress. The air screamed around him but he continued to run, turning up toward the snowline. His feet left no marks but he could feel the earth power beneath him as he charged up the mountains. Now he grew large, wading through the snowfields like Rummel Stoneboots. He crossed one range and then another, the pull of the Twin becoming less and less with every league, every step.

Finally, when he was sure he was clear, he took to the air and shot off westward like a streak of lightning.

* * *

Deep in Uzzim-Khail, Morvassus lay crumpled at the base of the stone wall. The Black Warriors stood at attention, still at their posts, not daring to move. Slowly, the Dark Lord raised himself to a kneeling position and leaned on his hands, his breath hissing in and out as he labored for air. Once more, he focused on the stream of power rising up from the pool in the center of the throne room. With practiced mental rituals, he reestablished his connection to that stream. The power at the base of Uzzim-Khail was both his prison and his source of strength, the reason that he was able to control the Twin. This was the first time that connection had been damaged, but it was the first time that the Midnight Stone had ever come so close. Never had he experienced the raw power of the Twin's desire for reunification. It had wrenched him from his throne, flung him against the wall and nearly crushed him with its lust for union. Centuries of careful practice had kept him grounded in this place, allowing him to extend his power out into the world while minimizing the risks. Yet the Twin's attraction to the Midnight Stone had nearly broken his hold.

He searched the Mountains of the Orryx and sent his feelers out to the high valley beyond but he could find only the trace of the Stonekeeper's passage. He knew that aura, though. Something had changed. Palanthar no longer held the Midnight Stone. Somehow, it had gone to Ermahann.

"Ender," he said, standing up and slowly making his way back to the pool. "He has ended nothing. It is only beginning."

Sitting down on his throne once again, he focused on that central stream, aligning himself with it, and it with himself. He would deal with Kafna later, when he had more strength.

* * *

Ender laid Lia down gently near the door. For a moment, he remained on all fours, trying to breathe, trying to manage the pain that continued to wrack his body. The fight with the Interrogator had been brief, but it had taken even more of his already-sapped strength. Still, there was much to do. Holding the Stone in his hand, he shut his eyes, imagining the visage of the Interrogator. As he focused, his beard slowly disappeared. His face turned pale and his skin shriveled. His eyes sank back in his head and his nose grew thin and sharp. His lips creased markedly, and great lines appeared around his eyes, on his forehead, on his neck and on his hands. His lean, tall body shrank and bent with age. A dark robe covered him, shrouding his face with a hood.

He went to the door. The Stone unlocked it easily.

The big turnkey stood stiffly at attention. Stepping through the door, the Stonekeeper motioned inside toward the woman on the floor.

"Lock her up," he said. "She's not much use at the moment. Take care not to harm her, though. I like this one."

The guard quickly stepped inside to gather up the woman and then led the way back down the hall. Ender followed a few steps behind.

"Shall I call for reinforcements, my lord?" asked the turnkey as they reached the cell.

"Do you need reinforcements, coward? Open it," Ender hissed.

The turnkey set Lia on the floor and reached for his keys to unlock the door. As he did so, Ender reached over and touched the turnkey behind the neck. The big fellow dropped to the stone floor, unconscious.

Returning to his own form, Ender unlocked the cell door and unbolted it.

"It's Ender," he said quietly, in his own voice. "Your bindings are off. I'm opening the door."

For a moment, the door stood ajar but nothing happened. Suddenly, Aaron leapt through the opening. In an instant, he had pulled the dagger from the fallen turnkey's belt and brought it to Ender's throat.

"Don't move," he hissed as Falnor drew the turnkey's sword and quickly slit the soldier's neck.

The captain stepped back in alarm as the body dissipated into smoke and disappeared! He turned his weapon on Ender, eyes wide. "Who are you, really?" he said in a hoarse whisper.

"I'm Ender. Let me take care of Lia," said the Stonekeeper, pointing to the woman lying limp by the door.

Keeping the blade at Ender's throat, Aaron quickly looked over at Lia. "Her hands are unbound, just like ours," he said. He turned back to face Ender. "What happened to you? How did you get here? What about the Interrogator? Didn't I just hear him?" It was as much a challenge as anything.

Ender shook his head. "I mimicked his shape and voice," he said. Wearily, he pointed back at Lia. "Let me take care of her. I'll have to tell the rest later. Right now she needs help and we need to get out of here. I cannot sustain this effort for long."

With Aaron's dagger still at his neck, Ender knelt slowly to the floor and gently touched Lia's face. He found the slight impressions the Interrogator had made on her temples. From his pocket, he removed the Midnight Stone and held it in front of her closed eyes. Lia did not respond. Holding the Stone in his left hand, he put his right hand over her eyes and placed his thumb and middle finger in the impressions left by the Interrogator. Lia's body stiffened and then relaxed. When he let go, she sat up and rubbed her eyes.

"Is he gone?" she asked Ender, looking around in the torchlight.

"Yes," said Ender.

"How did you get here?" she asked.

"There's a back entrance to the room with the pool," he said. "We can get out that way without passing the guards."

"I don't want to go in there if we can help it," said Lia, getting to her feet.

"We won't linger," promised Ender. "How do you feel?"

"Tired and sore, but I'm all right," she said. "Thank you." She looked at his face. "How are you? You look exhausted."

Ender smiled wanly. "We should go."

Aaron did not take the dagger from Ender's throat. "Get us out of here. Then I'll let you go."

Ender stood up slowly and led them down the hallway. When they got to the door, Lia hesitated before she went in. She gave the pool a wide berth.

Suddenly, she stopped. "My ring! Come to me!" she whispered. With the singing of metal, the shiny circlet splashed up out of the water, arced through the air and landed in her open hand. The others stood amazed as she slipped it back on her finger.

"That's better!" she said. "It didn't belong to him."

"The door is here," said Ender leading them behind the stone chair. He pushed against the wall and it swung open silently.

They entered a laboratory cluttered with instruments of magic and science, many covered with a thick layer of dust and dirt like abandoned toys. Books of lore and magic were piled here and there in disarray. Strange looking talismans were scattered throughout. The room itself seemed to be aware of their presence. Everyone's skin prickled as they passed through.

At the other end of the room was another hidden door. Ender searched the wall until he found the latch that released it from the inside. It opened into a dark tunnel, tall enough for them to walk upright but only wide enough for them to pass through one at a time. Ender led the way, Aaron's dagger at his throat.

In single file, one hand on the shoulder of the person in front of them, they went the length of the tunnel. Ender pushed on the trap door at the end and they came out into a juniper thicket. The sun was just now rising on the Mirrak-Haas.

"All right," hissed Aaron. "You got us out. Still, how do we know you're Ender?"

Ender turned to Falnor. "You asked me to tell you something," he said. "I told you 'Let's get through this first.'"

"True," said the captain.

The Stonekeeper thought for a moment. "Aaron, you and I were alone in the kitchen in the house on Cai-Amira one morning, before anyone else was awake. You asked me what I was called as a child. I said 'Stinky.'"

"Yes, you did," said Aaron. "What was my reaction?"

"You almost sprayed tea all over the table," said Ender.

Aaron nodded and eased the blade away from Ender's neck. "Good to have you back. Now, if we can just get our horses and weapons, we'll be fine," he whispered.

Ender nodded. "Wait here," he said. "I will return with them soon."

"No disrespect, sir," said Falnor; "but the last time you said to wait, we got captured."

Ender smiled ruefully. "I have learned a few things since then," he said. With that, he went back into the laboratory and sealed the wall behind him.

"He looks exhausted," said Aaron. "Whatever he's up to, it's costing him."

Falnor nodded. "Did you see what he had in his hand?"

Aaron shook his head. "I didn't get a good look at it. He seemed to be holding something small."

Lia shrugged. "All I can say is that we wouldn't be standing here now if not for him."

* * *

Back in the interrogation room, Ender shriveled once again into the misshapen form of the Interrogator. He ventured out into the hallway and down the corridor where he quietly closed and locked the cell door before heading up the stairs. When he reached the top, he came upon another guard who snapped to attention immediately at the sight of him.

"Where are the prisoners' weapons?" hissed Ender.

"In the weapons room, sir!" answered the soldier quickly.

"Why were they not brought to me as I requested?" shrieked the Stonekeeper.

"Sir, I had no such orders!" stammered the guard.

"Fool! You let a sorcerer's weapons lie among common steel? Fetch them at once and bring them to me at the stables—and tell the commander to meet me there with a full report," said Ender.

The soldier took off at a run and Ender let the Stone guide him to the stables. The Black Warriors generally kept their distance. Whoever this Interrogator was, he inspired a great deal of fear. Still, he noticed a certain confusion in the faces of those who stood stiffly at attention as he passed by.

The company's horses were stabled amongst the other mounts, but their auras were distinctly different. The horses of the enemy ate, stamped and whinnied like other horses, but they seemed both fearful and more dangerous. Their life force appeared jagged and chaotic to Ender's eyes. He glanced around the stable but the company's tack was nowhere in sight.

In a moment, the officer who had captured the prisoners entered the stables.

"You keep these toys to yourself?" Ender accused him in the scraping voice of the Interrogator.

The commander looked at him skeptically. "You never asked, Kafna," he said. "If you had wanted them, you would have asked for them. The Dark Lord has ordered us to obey you, but when you fail to command, we do as we see fit. Our allegiance is to Morvassus." The captain leaned in toward Ender. "His power is near," he said in a harsh whisper heavy with both fear and devotion. "You must have noticed it. We all have. Do not think that your designs are secret."

Ender let his own misshapen face sneer back. "If you're not afraid," he hissed, "we will ride to Uzzim-Khail and deliver these toys personally. Your own designs are not unknown to me, Commander."

The commander laughed. "Good, then! I will deliver your treacherous head myself and we will see what he thinks of me then. I have kept him apprised of all your comings and goings. He is not the friend you think he is."

"Bah!" scoffed Ender. "Friendship is not what I seek. Gather fifty of your best and equip them for battle. Then let us ride to Uzzim-Khail and we shall see who delivers whose treacherous head."

"What sort of idiocy are you suggesting?" spat the commander.

"It is not a suggestion," said Ender, evenly. "Have the weapons brought to me and go gather your men."

The commander did not move.

Ender pointed a bony finger toward the door. "You have your orders, commander, and you are duty bound to follow them. You have two hours. Now go!"

Without a word, the commander turned on his heel and stomped off.

Ender ordered that the horses be readied. A few minutes later, the weapons were brought and the horses were saddled. Ender made a show of inspecting the fittings. The guards stood by.

"Leave me," hissed Ender. "I don't need you rabble standing around." The soldiers quickly left.

Ender stumbled into an empty horse stall and leaned against the wall. For a moment, he shut his eyes and focused on breathing, but he knew he had to move quickly. Concentrating once again, he began to change his shape. His hands and face filled out. He stood taller, straighter and stronger. No longer was he pale, withered and bent. The robe was replaced by dark armor. In a moment, he was the very image of the Black Warrior commander. He climbed into the saddle and waved the Stone over the horses. Now there appeared to be a Black Warrior riding each one.

"Come," he whispered into the horses' thoughts. "Follow my lead."

Then he wheeled around and led them into the courtyard.

"Open the gates!" he ordered in the commander's voice. The portcullis was raised and the horses passed underneath it at a full gallop.

As it shut behind them, Ender quickly led the horses away from the fortress, down to a deep drainage which he followed back toward his friends' hiding place. He put the Midnight Stone back into his pocket and turned back into his own form. The illusion of the other riders also vanished.

Without warning, his strength simply left him and he slumped over in the saddle. The use of the Stone had drained him more than he had ever realized was possible.

"You're hurt!" Lia whispered when he found them.

Ender shook his head. "Exhausted, but not wounded," he said. "My errand is done. I have seen the enemy amassing. We should go back, but not the way we came."

Falnor nodded. "We can go around the mountains to the south and cross into Pelnara at the fords," he said, mounting up.

"Keep to the hills," said Ender. "Two armies fill the valley."

"We will," said Falnor.

"Are you sure you're all right?" asked Aaron.

"One more thing," said Ender, summoning his physical strength. "I am going to cast an illusion, but I can't keep it up for long. We will look like Black Warriors to each other and to the outside world."

He took the Midnight Stone in hand and instantly felt the pull of the Twin. The pain grew worse. Energy swirled about everywhere. Flickers of lightning crossed the great valley at odd angles, as if magic were charging the air. Focusing on his intention, he waved the Stone at each of his companions. Though they did not truly change shape, their forms turned dark and they appeared to wear the armor of the Black Warriors.

"Now, speed at all cost!" said Ender.

"Follow me!" said Falnor, wheeling around and setting off down the drainage from which Ender had come. They raced down to the road and galloped away as fast as the horses could carry them.

Once they were out of sight, Ender slipped the Stone back into his pocket. Instantly, the illusion vanished and the pull of the Twin lessened, but the pain and weariness were even worse. He could hardly keep focused on the road ahead.

Not much later, Falnor led the company off the main road onto a less-traveled track that wound up into the mountains. They kept on, mercilessly. Ender rode in the middle with the captain up front and Lia and Aaron bringing up the rear. Once or twice he thought he fell asleep only to awaken and find himself following the two horsemen around some obstacle or up a detour to avoid some enemy. All the while, he concentrated on keeping himself upright in the saddle.

* * *

"Drink this," said Lia.

Ender felt a liquid touch his lips. He was so thirsty. The taste was bitter and sweet. He let it slide down his tongue and into his throat.

"Good," said Lia. "Can you eat?"

Ender shook his head. "We need to keep moving," he croaked.

"Not now," said Lia. "You nearly fell from your horse. Rest. We'll keep watch."

Despite himself, Ender lost consciousness and slept

* * *

Falnor came back down from the outcrop. "Lia is right," he said. "Goblins everywhere. They're building a bridge." He looked somber. "None of ours have come to stop them."

"Is this the only crossing?" asked Aaron.

Falnor shook his head. "We've had no rain for almost a week, and the flow is low, especially for this time of year," he said. "We might be able to safely cross the upper shallows without having to swim."

"How far is it from here?" asked Lia.

"It's still within sight of the fords," said Falnor. "On foot, it would take them several minutes to get us within bow range. The ravine on this side should be dry. That will give us cover until we're ready to cross. By the time they see us and reach the banks, we would be across the first gravel bar. The trees will give us some cover from arrow fire."

"Can we wait until dark?" asked Aaron.

"Maybe," the captain replied. "The Volgan is at its lowest in the late afternoon. If we wait too long, the horses will have to swim the section after the last gravel bar. If we go during the lowest flow, we'll have the sun full in our faces as we cross."

"So will they," said Aaron. "If we have to turn and fight, we'll have the advantage."

"Let's go somewhere we can rest until then," said Lia.

Falnor nodded and mounted up again. "We'll backtrack to the spur and follow it to the ravine."

* * *

Though he was fully aware of his surroundings, Ender felt like he had spent all his physical strength just staying on his horse for the last few hours. Before she had gone on watch, Lia had given him some more water mixed with that elixir that had dulled the pain, but it was the weakness that concerned him most. The Midnight Stone could not help him recover his strength. Now he lay in the shadows of the ravine listening to Aaron and Falnor talking in low tones.

"It would sure be easier if we had Ender's wizardry again," said Falnor; "but I'm sure if he could do something, he would have by now. I'm concerned that the Faerie curse may have something to do with his condition."

But I'm not a Faerie, thought Ender. I have no Faerie blood. Why would it affect me and not affect the other humans with me?

"If so, we need to get him out of here now," said Falnor.

Ender could see Aaron watching him.

"There's been no change," said Aaron. "Strange stuff affects wizards. They can do amazing things but when they're in trouble, everyone's in trouble."

Exactly, thought Ender.

"A young boy once asked me what humans were good for," said Falnor.

"Really?" asked Aaron.

"He had gone on and on about how Faeries fly," said Falnor. "He talked about the Elves' amazing eyesight and woodsmanship. He said he felt inferior."

"What did you say?" asked Aaron.

"I told him I would have to think about it and come back later," said Falnor.

Aaron snorted. "Did you?"

Falnor smiled. "A few days later, I just took him to see Jerrod."

"Who's Jerrod?"

"Our stable dog," said Falnor. "You probably saw him, the black and white mutt with three legs. We just watched him work for awhile."

"What did the boy think of that?" asked Aaron.

"At first he thought I was showing him some lame animal until I pointed out how Jerrod can herd a sixteen-hand warhorse back into its stall," said Falnor. "Even the cats leave him alone. Jerrod does everything a normal dog does, and more—with one less leg."

Aaron grunted. "Good dog."

"I told the boy that Jerrod never thought of himself as inferior," said Falnor; "not to the horses, the dogs, or even to us."

Aaron nodded. "Did the boy appreciate that?"

Falnor raised an eyebrow. "He said he still wished he could fly."

Aaron chuckled. "That would come in handy just now."

Lying on the ground, Ender could see Falnor glance back at him and then turn back to Aaron.

"I wish we had some way to revive him," said the captain. "Whatever his powers are, we could use them."

"We'll just have to do this with three legs," said Aaron.

Just then, Lia came down from the lookout point. "We need to go now!" she said. "A large contingent of goblins is crossing the river. It took me a minute before I realized they weren't just going to work on the bridge. They'll be on the other side in a few minutes."

Aaron and Falnor helped Ender back up onto his horse.

"Can you sit?" asked Lia.

Ender nodded, but he wasn't doing too well keeping upright.

They came racing out from the ravine, as fast as they could with Ender unable to ride properly. As soon as the horses' hooves hit the water, a cry went up downstream. The company had already been spotted!

"Follow me!" said Falnor, spurring his horse forward across the rocky shallows.

Aaron took a quick look over his left shoulder. Goblins were swarming up from the bridge on the east side of the river. He looked across to the west bank where the contingent of goblins Lia had warned them about was just emerging from the water. They were turning northward to intercept the riders upstream.

It was an uphill climb for the goblins, but the humans were slow in crossing the river.

The rush of water across the rocky shallows drowned out clattering sound of arrows falling short on the rocks behind them. About a third of the way across the shallows, the horses clambered out of the water and onto the gravelly banks of a long, slender island. Falnor led them around the line of trees and then turned a short distance upstream to the best place to cross. Between the island and the western bank lay two more thin gravel bars. Between them, the water flowed a bit deeper and faster.

Falnor urged his mount into the first crossing. Aaron kept his horse on the downstream side of Ender's. Lia followed right behind.

To the south, they could see the mass of goblins racing up the relatively flat land toward them. The goblins would have to climb a short, steep rise in the ground, but that obstacle was all that stood between them and the humans crossing the river. A quick visual estimation was all it took to see that the company would have a pitched battle on their hands once they reached the other side.

They climbed out onto the gravel bar and immediately entered the last crossing. This time the horses had to swim through a swift current. Aaron's and Ender's horses were having difficulty staying together. Aaron's mount found its footing and unexpectedly surged ahead. Ender's horse twisted about in the swirling current. Lia urged her horse forward to catch Ender, but somehow the Stonekeeper stayed in the saddle.

The goblin horde was scrambling over the rise, firing arrows as they came, but they seemed to be shooting at something else. Aaron looked northward to see a dark shape winging its way toward them at great speed. It screamed out of the sky with a shriek and a roar that sent shivers through everyone who heard it.

Fire rained down from the heavens and goblins scattered everywhere as a brilliant flash of blue and gold sailed over the company's heads. It seared the front ranks of the goblins, wheeled back into the sky and dove quickly back down, lighting the brush on fire all around them. Blocked by a wall of flames, the goblins stopped advancing and turned to flee. The dragon cut off their path to the river, and then continued on southward.

In the fracas, the company reached the other side and picked up speed as they headed for the safety of the hill country.

"Northwest!" shouted Falnor in the lead. "Follow me!"

They hadn't gone far when the dragon returned and swooped down toward them.

"Take him! Take him!" Aaron bellowed, waving toward Ender slumped over in the saddle. "Northwest! Northwest!"

The dragon snatched Ender from his horse and sailed off over the hills.

"We know this one!" yelled Aaron to an astonished Falnor.

"I sure hope so!" yelled the captain. Quickly seizing the reins of Ender's horse, he took off at a gallop for the hills.

* * *

"Does this hurt?" asked Lia, applying ointment to a spot where an arrow had punctured the leathery wing.

"Only a little," said the dragon.

"He would be better at this if he were well enough," said Lia, pointing at Ender who still slept in the shade.

"Who isssssss he?" asked Gasslic.

"His name is Ender," said Aaron. "We don't know much about him, but he is a powerful friend."

"Ender?" said Gasslic. "Then he issssssss a mossssst powerful friend indeed!"

"You know him?" asked Aaron.

"I know of him," said Gasslic. "I sssssssspoke with the Great Massssssster. It wasssssss he who sssssssssssent me to the Great Fallssssssss to find you."

Ender sat up slowly as Falnor came back from tending to the horses.

"You look better," said the captain.

"Considerably better," said Ender. He took a deep breath and shook his head slowly. "I owe all of you my life."

"We owe that to the dragon," said Falnor.

Ender nodded. "I have not yet made your acquaintance, though I recognize you from an earlier encounter," said the Stonekeeper.

"I recognized the arrowsssssss," said Gasslic, nodding toward Ender's quiver. "One of them ssssaved me."

"That wasn't the first time you've held off an enemy," said Aaron. "You certainly know when to suddenly appear."

"The Great Massssssster told me how to use the high wind currents to fly north," said the dragon. "It wasssssss a long journey. Once I sssssssaw land again, I sssssssspent sssseveral dayssssss ressssting. Not knowing where to go, I wandered around until I met a crow named Jehzik who told me hissss sssstory. An amazzzzzing bird. He sssssssaid sssssssomeone had healed him and ssssssset him free from yearsssss of bondage. When he heard my tale, he urged me to come to the river where he sssssaid the goblinssssss might be waiting for you. It turnsssss out he wasssss right. Sssssso we have Jehzick to thank, really."

"I'm glad to hear the crow remains free," said Ender.

"When did you meet this crow?" asked Lia.

"When I got pulled away from Akka Illin," said Ender.

"You got 'pulled away?'" asked Falnor.

"It's a long story," said Ender; "but if we are safe here, I think it's time you heard it."

"First, what of the goblin bridge?" Falnor asked the dragon.

"I burned it," said Gasslic. "They will have difficulty rebuilding it, but that may be only a ssssmall ssssetback. There are otherssss on the move in the eassssssst who do not sssssssscatter sssssso easssssssily."

"If the bridge is burned and the forces there are decimated, we are safe for tonight," said the captain; "but I want to get back to Pelnara soon. If they do not know of this danger at our borders, then it's high time they learned." He sat down by Ender. "But, please, your tale."

Ender recounted the experience of being dragged away from Akka-Illin and landing in Uzzim-Khail, including the depositing of the ashes in the Fountain at the Great Gates, leaving out no details this time.

"So using the Midnight Stone drains you physically?" asked Aaron.

"Yes," said Ender. "I am not as experienced as the Great Master. He warned me that training alone could never be enough. Now I know why. I also know how careful I must be in the eastern lands where the Twin resides."

Falnor shook his head. "News of this Midnight Stone will not be well received in Pelnara," he said.

Ender agreed. "For now, it is best kept secret," he said.

"In the meantime," said Falnor; "we have our reconnaissance, and that is what is expected of us."

They talked for another hour as Ender and Gasslic described all they had seen from the air. Gasslic gave them detailed accounts of the King's movements and some idea of his expanded powers as the Birdman. Gasslic was also able to tell them where the goblins were stationed in the regions around the Citadel. Apparently, the King had no intention of leaving the southern lands empty; most likely, he would return there once again.

* * *

Ender awoke in the middle of the night, suddenly restless. His strength had returned. The weariness of the last few days had finally worn off and he felt eager to move. Experimentally, he slipped his hand into his pocket and touched the Midnight Stone. The pull of the Twin was almost nonexistant. He stood up quietly and walked out to where the dragon lay quietly.

"I'm not assssleep," said Gasslic.

"I wondered," said Ender. He looked out at the stars. "It's a nice night to be awake."

"Indeed," said Gasslic. He lay silently for a moment. Then he lifted his head. "Sssssssomething issss bothering you."

"My wife is investigating a danger in the west," said Ender.

"Do the othersssss know of thissss?" asked Gasslic.

"Yes," said Ender. "Once we speak to the High Council, I will go to join her."

"The information is eassssily delivered by the other three," said the dragon.

Ender nodded. "That is true."

Neither of them said anything for a few moments.

"I will tell them you've gone," said Gasslic.

"Thank you," said Ender.

CHAPTER 38

The End of the Sochhmahr

Mari sat stiffly on the throne of the Golrakken queen. A shaft of dusty light fell from the ventilation grate high above and gleamed back at her from the shiny blade in her lap. All else was darkness.

The Golrakken maidens had dressed her in black and gray. On her head they had placed a crown with six sharp spikes radiating from a circlet of silver. On her arm they placed an amulet shaped like a winding dragon with a crimson stone for an eye. Around her neck Karkaan himself had affixed a fine, shining chain with a circular metal pendant that rested against her skin, just above her cleavage.

Each day, Karkaan had stood before her and reiterated his charge to her: take the knife by the handle and rule, or take it by the poisoned blade and die. Each time, she held her tongue, stayed her hand, forced herself not to respond. She could feel the spell he wrapped around her; it moved constantly, its cold, numbing tentacles reaching deep inside her, seeking a hold. Though she dared not sleep, sometimes she awoke with a start, her face mere inches from the sharp blade in her lap.

When the sconces were lit at night, she could see the honor guard of the Golrakken lining the walls, spears and swords at the ready, waiting for either her command or her demise.

Once more, a Golrakken maiden entered with food. She was tall and wiry like the rest of the Golrakken, and her face was just as tight and twisted. She climbed the three steps to the dais and set the food on a stand beside the throne, exactly where the last meal had sat untouched until they had taken it away. Then she stood directly before Mari, just out of reach.

"Why do you not eat, O 'Great Queen of the Golrakken?'" she mocked.

Mari did not respond.

"Perhaps you are not what Karkaan thinks you are," rasped the maiden. "You do not look like one of the Lammethan. Where are your lovely wings? Or did you cut them off to look more like us?"

The maiden leaned in, close enough to kiss the woman on the throne. "If you are so powerful," she whispered; "use the knife in your lap to cut out my tongue. I think you will not."

Mari did nothing.

"The mighty Karkaan Dragonhelm made a mistake bringing you here," whispered the maiden, her breath rank in Mari's face. "You have done nothing to prove your worth."

"Enough!" barked the captain of the honor guard. "Dragonhelm has chosen this one over you. Perhaps he is no longer pleased with you. I've half a mind to silence you myself!"

"'Tis true," spat the maiden. "You do have but half a mind." She stood back, waved her hand dismissively at Mari and turned away. "Where is the mighty Dragonhelm now?" she asked.

"He leads the army to Morvoth," said the captain.

"The Dark Master calls," said the maiden; "and the dogs come yowling."

"Watch your mouth, or he'll come back to find his mistress needs a new body," the captain snarled.

"Not likely," said the maiden. "There's not a one of you here who could touch me."

"Don't try us," said the captain.

The Golrakken maiden turned back to the throne, spat at Mari's feet and left the room.

* * *

Thoughtful looked down in shock to see his hands, his beard, and his own booted feet. He could feel the wind about him.

"What is this?" he asked. His tutor was nowhere to be seen.

"You have been redeemed, Holren," answered the voice of Dain. "Ender is at the Fountain of Ulvanoth where the price for your life was to be spilled. Now you are free to go."

"Go where? What am I?" Holren stammered, incredulous. "A moment ago, I was a Sochhmahr. Do I have a body? Is this real?"

"This is very real," said Dain; "though it is not like what you have known before. You are Holren Avan-Ihlac. You have a second chance. You have studied well, Holren. I am glad to have taught you. There is someone with whom you need to reconcile."

"My wife," said Holren.

"Indeed," said the Stonecutter. With great detail, he described where she was and what had become of her. "Her strength is waning. I am sending you to the Golrakken to bring her back."

"I will go," replied the sorcerer. "I will not make the same mistakes again."

"I believe you," said Dain. "Go north, directly to the sea. When you reach it, help will find you and take you to them. Pay his price. He asks very little."

Dain's voice had faded to nothing with this last instruction.

Holren looked about him. The sky was blue, the air was brisk and the wind ruffled his gray beard. He was alive! He could see, smell, touch, taste!

With a shout, he ran like the wind toward the sea. To the birds overhead, he looked like a streak of gray racing over the hills. For two days and two nights he ran, league upon league without tiring, over the fields flung far beyond the Citadel, up into the coastal mountains and down to the edge of the Dorvan Sea.

At dawn on the third day, he reached the sands by the Dorvan Sea. The sky was heavy with clouds, but the sea was calm. He knew that somewhere far out in the salty waters, myriad islands lay scattered. In one of them, Mari sat frozen on a throne. Despite his speed on land, Holren could not imagine how he would find the island, nor how he might traverse the sea. He wandered the shore, sizing up the trees to see if he might make a boat. A few hours later, an aged, dilapidated sailboat appeared around a promontory to the east. Holren stopped to look. The craft was slowly—one might say reluctantly—navigating the shoreline.

"Hail, wizard!" shouted the pilot who looked as ragged as his craft. Most of his face was covered by beard, dusty brown and streaked with silver. His shaggy hair hung stuck out in all directions and covered his shoulders. By all indications, the captain had not been groomed since before the boat was built. He wore no shirt, and his tattered breeches hung on his body wearily, perhaps wistfully dreaming of a retirement that would never come.

"You know who I am?" asked Holren.

"I know! I know! I know folks, many folks," said the sailor with a skittering laugh. He hopped out of the boat and splashed his way to the shore, dragging his sagging craft behind him. Holren walked out into the waters and helped him bring the boat ashore. It creaked and groaned at having to support its own weight, but grudgingly obliged and did not fall to pieces when it was beached.

"You, me fine sir, will be needin'..." the bristly one's voice trailed off as he peered intently at Holren's face as if looking for something stuck in his eye. "A BOAT!" he said, suddenly.

The wizard took a step back. "And who are you?" he asked.

"I am Nibbitz!" said the other, doffing an imaginary hat. "This is the Invincible, my sturdy ship!" He slapped the boat's gunwale. The craft gave a dull groan and shed a few bits of rotted wood somewhere. "If ye need to get from here to there, she'll do it."

The sorcerer eyed the boat. "Do you know how to get to the island of the Golrakken?" he asked, getting right to the point.

"Well that'll be depending on which one," said the sailor. "There are many islands out there, many islands on which the uglies eat and sleep."

"Then, where is their ship anchored?" asked Holren.

"Ah, directly into the bowels of it, then!" Nibbitz gave a low whistle. "Aye, the very guts! Well, it's going to cost ye," he said. "I'll need a certain item stolen from me many years ago by the ugliest of them, aye, the ugliest." He raised his eyebrow and looked at Holren strangely. "I want me compass back."

"And what is remarkable about this instrument so that I may find it and bring it to you?" the wizard asked.

"Now there's a question I can and cannot answer," returned his odd companion. "I won't describe the design—ye wouldn't have time to study it anyway—but it's round, and it's THIS big, and it hangs on a chain that cannot be broken." He made a circle with his thumb and middle finger. "And if ye sing this little song in its presence, it will fly to ye so fast, ye best beware of being struck in the head with it. The ditty goes like this:

> Nibbitz set sail
> But to no avail
> For want of a proper direction.
> He needs to find north
> Before he sets forth
> And gets lost with a reddened complexion."

Nibbitz remained motionless, staring at the wizard.

"You cannot be serious," said Holren.

"Then neither can you!" crowed the sailer. "If ye wish to be taken to the uglies, ye pay the price. All I can say is, do as ye wish. If ye go with me, I'll take ye. But I leave ye there if ye don't fetch me compass!"

"Then teach me the ditty and I will find your compass," said Holren, laughing.

They shoved the creaking boat back out into the water, climbed aboard and sang the silly little song at the top of their lungs, over and over, until the sorcerer had it memorized. Though the wind was calm, the sails were full, as if the will of the pilot filled them. Soon they were sailing out among the islands. Slipping between the many half hidden protrusions of rock, the boat plied a haphazard path through the maze. The sky grew darker and the seas grew rougher.

After awhile, Nibbitz grew quiet and wouldn't sing or even smile. They were now beneath the storm. The blackened sky gave no rain but the wind had picked up. The seas roiled and boiled beneath them. The Invincible groaned along, tacking first one way and then another, somehow avoiding half-hidden rocks that suddenly protruded in the trough after a wave had passed. They were making their way slowly toward the largest of the many islands, circling away from the entrance to its narrow bay.

Finally, Nibbits spoke. "This is the place!" he called over the rush of the wind. "I've not been here in many a decade. I do not wish to come again. Go now, wizard, and bring back ye prize! But remember me payment, or ye won't find me when ye need me!"

Holren nodded. Nibbitz brought the Invincible dangerously close to a narrow, rocky beach and the wizard jumped out. Holren waded onto the beach and then searched the steep sides of the ancient volcano for some way up. Dain had told him where to find the outside entrance to the stronghold, but it took the wizard some time to get to the top of the cliff. Once on top, he looked around and saw steam rising from the ground off to his right, a wisp of vapor quickly blown away by the wind.

It came from a cavity about ten feet in diameter and four feet deep. In the center of the indentation was a square, wrought iron grate with nasty spikes. Slowly, crawling on his belly over the rocks and dirt, he crept down to the grate. He cast two quick spells: one to turn his own image the same color as the cloudy sky, another to erase any shadow he might cast, rendering him essentially invisible to anyone below. Then he cast two more, enhancing his sight and hearing. Avoiding the spikes as he eased out over the grate, he stared hard into the dim depths. He could barely make out the form of a pale, darkly clad woman with a silver crown seated on a throne almost a hundred feet below. On her lap lay a long, shiny knife.

Holren looked around the room. The walls were lined with Golrakken soldiers. There seemed to be female Golrakken as well, wretched creatures in garb as ghoulish and ugly as that of the soldiers. They stood silently by, as if in attendance.

One of the maidens did not stand silently like the others. She paced back and forth before the pale woman seated on the throne.

"O Queen," she said, mockingly; "you are weak and weary. It is time to choose. You cannot refuse your destiny. What is the point of waiting? Take the knife and slay yourself, or rule and slay us all—else we die of boredom!" She laughed, a wild, feral sort of sound.

Holren kept quiet, noting shape and dimensions of the room, the exits, the placement of soldiers. None of his observations were encouraging.

"If the queen cannot decide," continued the maiden below, pacing slowly in front of the throne and addressing the whole room; "someone here should decide for her."

No one answered.

"If anyone should decide, that would be me," hissed the maiden.

"Beware the wrath of Karkaan!" barked an authoritative voice.

"I do not fear Dragonhelm," said the maiden. "I have survived his wrath before. But you, Captain, might be wise to fear it if you threaten me again. He has gone to Morvoth and left her here. Perhaps this new queen bores him. I say we dispatch her now."

"Interfere and die," spat the captain. "I will kill you myself."

"Do not threaten me, Captain, ere I take the knife by the hilt!" The maiden turned and climbed the three steps to the dais. For a moment, she hesitated, then she darted in to seize the knife on Mari's lap.

Suddenly, Mari unglued her hand from the arm of the throne. Both of them seized the knife by the hilt.

"No!" screamed Mari, her voice shrill and harsh. "It's mine! It was given to me!" The Golrakken soldiers stirred about but no one interfered. Mari rose in her seat as they grappled with the knife.

"It should have been mine to begin with," growled the Golrakken woman. She pushed the tip of the blade toward Mari's breast.

"You have no claim! Let go!" ordered Mari, strong and sure. "I may spare you if do."

"You will kill me like I will kill you when I have the knife," the other retorted through gritted teeth. "If you do not escape me now, you will never escape."

Though her grip did not change, Mari's voice and demeanor turned soft, silken and seductive. "No, no, my dear," she said. "It is not right that you should die. You are strong and beautiful, lithe and lovely. You should stand proudly by my side when I come to power." The Golrakken maiden said nothing, but the words clearly made her pause. "Let me make of you what you wished to be in the first place. You will be cherished, worshipped. Any mate you desire shall be yours, even Karkaan when you like. I, myself, ask only that you come to me once a day and do my bidding. You shall have my protection from all who would cause you harm. What do you say, my precious?"

The other woman stared, transfixed.

Holren watched, horrified, as Mari gained control of the knife. As she did so, he could see magic pouring from the knife like a cold, blue light, sliding over her hands, up her arms and across her shoulders. Soon it was enveloping her head, rippling like lightning around the spikes of her crown and pouring down over her body. Very slowly, the other woman was relaxing, her muscles growing soft and pliable as Mari's body grew tense and taut. Holren could hear Mari's sweet voice still persuading the Golrakken maiden to yield, to give in, to succumb. The Golrakken maiden sank to her knees, staring up at Mari. Holren watched the Golrakken maiden's jaw slacken until her mouth hung open. The wild eyes glazed over and she allowed her fingers to be pried off the knife. She stood back and bowed before Mari, who now held the knife over her head in triumph. Blue luminescence now covered Mari's entire body.

"Bow to the queen!" said Mari, in a voice that Holren shuddered to hear.

All the Golrakken fell to the floor before her. Even Holren trembled.

Mari threw her head back and looked directly upward, arms spread wide. Holren felt his skin turn cold. Her face was beginning to change! Her skin was turning gray and her lips were growing darker. Her mouth opened and she began to laugh and cry out all at once. Her voice became raspy and shrill as it filled the room. She threw her arms wide and howled, sending the blue light rippling around the room.

Just then, Holren noticed the amulet between her breasts, an ornate disk of some silvery metal hanging on a chain far too strong for such a pendant. While her voice rang throughout the room, Holren discarded his cloaking spells and, with magical strength, tore the spiked grate from the vent and tossed it aside. As he leapt into the hole, he sang loudly over Mari's shrieking:

> Nibbitz set sail
> But to no avail
> For lack of a proper direction!
> He needs to find North
> Before he sets forth
> And gets lost with a reddened complexion!

He landed just in front of the throne and rolled to a stop at the edge of the dais. As he had hoped, the amulet flew toward him, its unbreakable chain yanking Mari off her feet and dashing her to the floor. The knife was knocked from her hand and she was dragged toward Holren. No sooner was the compass in his grasp than Holren found himself struggling against his enraged wife. She screamed and pushed against him, desperately trying to get back to the knife. He fought hard to keep her. The Golrakken maiden stood up dazed and bewildered; she did not see the knife on the floor. Mari shrieked and flung herself at it, nearly bringing her husband down with her. The chain around her neck cut off her breath and she choked.

Gasping and coughing, she pulled at the chain, finally turning to look at her attacker.

"Mari," he said. "Come back."

When her eyes met his, the blue light around her faltered. "Help me," she gasped.

Suddenly, the Golrakken in the room seemed to come back to life.

Holren kept a firm hold on the chain as he scooped her up and turned toward the door. Mari dared not look away from his face. "Ashkan, esso himinovak!" hissed Holren, invoking a confusion spell.

With a crash, the doors opposite the throne flew open. Into the room rushed the Golrakken horde. Holren pushed through the surging crowd, out into the dark corridor. The gray host forced them against the wall as they plunged past. The wizard pulled Mari into the refuge of a doorway only to have it burst open behind him and shove him back into the hallway. More Golrakken entered the fracas.

He continued forcing his way down the hall when another door opened beside him and someone pushed him inside. He fell to the floor and nearly landed on top of Mari. Releasing her, he rolled over and leapt back to his feet. His assailant bolted the door and turned around, keeping close to the door as if afraid of getting too close to him. The wizard was astonished. It was a young woman. From her dress, she appeared to be the Golrakken maiden who had challenged Mari, but her face was no longer a tight mask of gray skin. Instead, it was a rich, warm black. Her brow was smooth and her eyes were dark and bright. Her cheeks were fine, her lips were full, and her hair was black and shiny, not gray and scraggly as before.

She pointed to Mari on the floor. Then she beckoned frantically to Holren to follow her.

Holren did not move. The last phrase of a fire spell was on the tip of his tongue but he did not utter it.

"Please!" she pleaded. "Escape!" She shut her mouth quickly and clamped a trembling hand over her lips, eyes wide.

Holren nodded and picked up Mari again as if she weighed nothing at all. His wife clung to him, still shaking, but the blue light seemed to have left her completely.

The dark maiden opened the door and led them back into the hallway. No one was around. They could hear the Golrakken throng fighting it out in the throne room. Holren followed as the maiden ran full speed down one hallway and then another until they came to a rancid kitchen. She went straight for a stinking pile of refuse and turned the crusty handle of a rusted steel door beside it. The door opened into a shaft, slick with slime, that emptied into the sea.

She waved to Holren to follow and and dove inside.

Holren did not hesitate. Stuffing Mari into the malodorous shaft, he dove in behind her, yelling the spell to make heavy things float. One after the other, the three splashed into the salty foam.

Overhead, the sky boiled and thundered. Wind and rain pelted them from above. Foamy waves churned around them, crashing into showers of spray on the rocks behind them. Desperately swimming away from the sharp cliffs, Holren shouted, "Nibbitz! Nibbitz!"

The dark maiden fought through the foam to find him. She grabbed onto Mari and helped Holren swim with her away from the rocks. Another wave drove them back. Light as driftwood, they floated on top of it. As the water drained away for the next wave, they swam as hard as they could with the current. Another wave rose before them and they crested it only to tumble down the other side in front of yet another.

"Nibbitz!" bellowed the sorcerer. "Nibbitz!" As they crested the wave, he could see the tiny boat lashed by the rain, its sails ragged and torn. Against all odds, it was making its way toward them.

"The compass!" hollered Nibbitz.

"Here!" Holren shouted.

"Hang on to the chain!" Nibbitz called back. Then in a wild frenzy, he bellowed out his silly song, as fast and as loudly as he could.

"Nibbitz set sail but to no avail..." sang Nibbitz.

"Hold onto the chain!" cried Holren. The dark maiden grasped the chain around Mari's neck, clinging to Mari's waist with her other arm.

"For want of a proper direction!"

"Quickly!" called Holren. He slipped under Mari wrapped his right arm around her, grabbing the amulet with that hand. With his other arm, he tried to keep both their heads out of the water.

"He needs to find north before he sets forth..." warbled Nibbitz.

Everyone held on tight.

"And gets lost with a reddened complexion!"

As Nibbitz finished, the three were dragged roughly across the waves toward the Invincible. The compass pulled them up the sides of the creaking boat and into the raggedy captain's hand. With surprising strength, Nibbitz hauled Mari into the boat. Holren lost his grip and fell back into the sea. Nibbitz reached over the side and pulled the dark maiden aboard. Holren found a handhold in the gaps in the planks on the side of the boat. He grabbed on and pulled himself out of the water. Amazingly, nothing came off in his hands. Nibbitz got a hold of him and hoisted him over the gunwale. The wizard landed hard on the deck of the Invincible.

"Get us out of here, Captain!" he said from the floor, rain beating down on his face.

"Aye, we shall! That we shall!" cried Nibbitz. The Invincible careened away from the island. The black cliffs vanished behind sheets of heavy rain. Holren gathered Mari into his arms. The black maiden huddled in the bow of the boat, shivering. Up one wave and down the other they went. Before they came out from under the storm, Mari lost consciousness.

When things had finally calmed a bit, Nibbitz leaned back on the tiller and cocked a crazy eye at the dark maiden. "Aye, here's a surprise!" he said to Holren. "Found an extra passenger did ye?"

"She helped us escape," said Holren.

"Did ye?" said Nibbitz, staring at the maiden with renewed interest. "That beats all." He turned back to Holren. "So, then...where would ye go now?"

"Thihanan," said Holren.

"A much nicer destination," said the pilot. He squatted down on the deck to be eye level with Tania. "And where do ye wish to go?"

The black skinned maiden's lip quivered and she shook her head.

"No speak?" asked Nibbitz.

The maiden shook her head again.

"Ah, I understand," said Nibbitz, sitting back again at the tiller. "Then ye can choose when we get there. Good?"

The black maiden nodded.

Nibbitz turned the Invincible due west and they sailed into ever calmer seas. When the sky cleared, they were watching the sun go down. Nibbitz opened a large trunk in the middle of the boat and brought out some salted meat and fish. Even the dark maiden ate some. It was a little hard to chew, but everyone was glad for some food. Mari came to and was able to eat a little, but when she finished, she fell asleep. Holren was glad to see her resting.

The night passed silently save for the lapping of salt water on the sides of the creaking boat. Exhausted, Holren was snoring within an hour of sundown.

The dark maiden remained huddled silently at the bow of the ship.

"Ye be needing some reassurance, maybe," said Nibbitz from his post back at the tiller.

The black woman looked back at him, startled.

"Ye seem to be holding up pretty well, for all ye been through," he said

She searched his face in the moonlight, saying nothing.

"I'd ask who ye are, but ye may not remember," Nibbitz said with a shrug. "How ye made it out alive, I daren't guess. Ye must be more than mere mortal to have escaped like that."

The dark maiden took a breath and then caught herself. She shook her head.

"It's all right," said Nibbitz. "Ye can talk safely now. No words ensnare ye here. That's all gone and done with."

She remained silent.

"You are in good company," said Nibbitz. "At least I consider m'self good company. Now, ye probably wonder what ye are--now that the nightmare is over, that is. A fine question to be sure. Good place to start. Now, I don't know who ye were before the uglies, but I can tell ye what ye were on the island, if ye got the stomach for it."

She nodded.

"A brave girl!" he said. "All right, it's like this: when the uglies get their voice in ye ears, and you find y'self answerin' back, there are two choices. Either ye kill y'self, or ye become one of 'em. Now the first option is the smart one, if ye have sense at all—only most of us don't. The second one is what usually happens. Still, some of us have survived it somehow. Stubborn, I guess. In any case, most have their bodies taken by an ugly and their souls die.

"Now, the likes of y'self and me, we must have be too ornery to simply hand the body over. Aye, we took on their ugliness instead, living like an ugly until someone came along to break the spell. I was freed by Dain himself, many years ago. Been prowling these waters ever since. Aint seen no one come out of there alive until y'self and that pair over there. Ye must be something special, if I can say that without flattering m'self too much."

The dark maiden nodded.

"One of these days, you'll see that ye can use your voice again," said Nibbitz. "When ye do, we'll be glad to know who ye are."

The maiden smiled.

"Aye, that's better," said Nibbitz. "Now ye be gettin' some sleep. I reckon you need it."

The dark maiden smiled again, curled up in the bow of the boat and was soon fast asleep.

The gaunt sailor chuckled, patted the gunwale fondly. "Steer y'self for awhile, m'lady," he said to the boat. Then he reached down to where the compass lay against his scrawny chest. Slowly, he released the latch and opened it. Light illuminated his face with star-like brilliance. He peered into it and smiled warmly.

"Hello, my dear," he said.

CHAPTER 39

Travels in the Land of Men

Mari awoke to the sound of two men talking. She rubbed her eyes and rolled over. How long had she been asleep?

"Well, here is where I say goodbye," said a voice she did not recognize.

"I am grateful," she heard Thoughtful say.

She was lying on the grass by the Watch House on Cai-Amira, or so she thought, but when she looked eastward, she could see the sand stretching on for miles. The waves were lapping quietly on the beach, not streaming out behind them in the wake of the island. Confused, she sat up. Someone steadied her as she almost collapsed again.

"Thoughtful?" called Mari, disoriented.

Then she heard a laugh she had not heard in years—a big, booming laugh that brought back days of bright sunshine and cool rain, walks in the woods, a warm hand on her face and two very blue eyes that twinkled with mischief. She shut her eyes tightly, afraid to look.

"Thoughtful, indeed!" said the voice. "Open your eyes and let me see you." Two strong arms turned her gently.

Mari hardly dared to look. When she opened her eyes, she saw her husband's face, but it was not the same. Gone was the sunken look he had worn for the last fifty years. Gone was the underlying tension of worry. This was the Holren she remembered before Taron Kaiss, before the rift between them. He was no younger; if anything, he seemed even older now, but time seemed not to have worn him down.

Overcome, Mari buried her face in his lap and cried openly. As she wept, she felt strength returning to her legs and arms. Her head began to clear and when at last she had finished, she was relaxed and tired. Something deep inside had been washed away.

"Weren't you dead?" she asked, when she could speak again.

"It's a bit confusing," said Holren. "Someday I'll tell you. For now, we should head north."

"Where are we? Where are the others?"

Holren took a deep breath. "We are on Thihanan. We'll go to the High Council at the Shioroth. Don't ask me: I don't know more about it than you, nor do I know what has happened to anyone else."

Mari nodded and looked around. For the first time, she noticed a dark skinned young woman dressed in gray rags sitting quietly some distance away.

"Hello," said Mari. "Do I know you?"

The maiden smiled and shook her head.

"This young woman helped us escape," said Holren. "However, she has not yet told us her name."

"Tania," said the black skinned maiden.

"Well met, Tania," said Mari. "I'm sorry that I do not remember much of what has happened recently."

Tania shrugged. "I hardly remember it either," she said, shaking her head.

"I am glad to hear you have found your voice," said Holren. "You are welcome with us. We should gather some supplies and then I think we should be going." He helped Mari to her feet. "First, let's get the two of you some proper clothes."

They walked slowly up the hill, past the empty circle where the old Mind Ring had stood. For a second, Mari paused and then, thinking better of it, kept going. They entered the empty house and went upstairs to find suitable clothing. The dress Owler had made for Mari was stored in the upstairs bedroom where she and Annie had slept. While she doffed the black Golrakken dress, Holren and Tania went into the other rooms to see if they could find something to replace her rags.

"Could I wear these?" she asked when they found a pair of breeches and a shirt in Owler's room.

"As you wish," said Holren; "if they suit you better."

He went back to his wife as Tania shrugged off the rags. Blissfully, she pulled on the breeches and shirt, rolling up the legs and sleeves until they exposed her feet and hands. The clothes hung rather loosely on her frame, but felt so much more comfortable. A belt tied around her waist outside the shirt made it appear to fit her better. This settled, they gathered food for the trip and found a pack for each of them.

Holren opened the door to the weapons room.

Mari looked at him quizzically. "Please, no weapons," she said. "I want nothing to do with knives. I will use the skills you taught me."

"Very well," said Holren. He and Tania went below as Mari took the old clothes outside to burn them.

Holren tried several weapons before selecting a long sword for himself and strapping it onto his back.

Tania's attention was drawn immediately to a small bow in the corner. Beside it lay a quiver of arrows too short to be used on any other.

"These are mine!" she said, astonished.

"How is that possible?" asked Holren.

"I don't know," she said; "but I know this bow." She picked it up and tested the tension, releasing the string with an authoritative twang. The weapon fit her hand perfectly. With natural ease, she slung the quiver onto her back. Drawing an arrow, she looked it over carefully. "These are mine," she said again, full of wonder.

"So it appears," said Holren. "Is there anything else you should take with you?"

Tania slipped the bow behind her with the quiver. Looking around, she selected a long dagger and a light sword which she fitted to her sling with baldrics.

When they returned, Mari was standing at the doorway. Her strength had fully returned and she was anxious to go. With a final farewell to the house, they set off down the sandy beach toward Pelnara.

The day was clear and the wind blew in the trees to their right as they traced the steps, now long since washed away by the tides, where six others of their company had traveled some weeks before. Holren, full of vigor, could have maintained a tremendous pace if his wife and their dark young companion could have kept up. As it was, he found the traveling very pleasant. Before darkness fell, they chose a comfortable place to sleep.

On the third day from Cai-Amira, they came across travelers on their way into the town of Freshwater from the outlying farms. Tania was the object of much attention, whether the passersby meant to stare or not. If she took notice of it, she paid it no mind.

Sometime after noon, they saw the rising dust of ten horses galloping down the road toward them. On each steed rode a soldier bristling with weaponry. The wizard guided his companions off the road and waited for the riders to pass. They did not. Surrounding the threesome, the green-garbed cavalry eyed them suspiciously with drawn swords.

"Who are you and where do you come from?" demanded their captain.

"I am Holren. This is my wife, Mari, and our friend Tania," explained the sorcerer calmly. "We come from Thihanan."

"More trouble from the peninsula," grumbled one of the soldiers. "It should be hacked off and cast it into the sea."

"Silence!" ordered the captain, a surly character, if a little over-groomed, with shining black hair and a great ebony moustache that curled at the ends. "I am Captain Achor of the Green Stone and I command you in the name of the King of Pelnara to state your business."

"We seek our friends who should have passed this way some days ago," said Holren.

"Did these friends include one called Ender?" queried the captain, leaning toward them with one eyebrow raised significantly.

"They did," answered the wizard, bemused but unperturbed.

"Then I wonder why he didn't mention you would be coming along later," countered Captain Achor, settling back into his saddle as if he had just scored a major point. The other soldiers laughed and nodded at their captain. He winked back.

"No one expects the dead to be coming along later," the wizard responded, just loudly enough to be heard over the laughter which then stopped.

"Yes," said the captain, scowling once again through his curled moustache. "Well...are you dead?"

"Not by all indications, no."

"Then why would they think you were dead?" asked Captain Achor.

"Because we were lost in battle against the Golrakken, of whom you might have some knowledge," the sorcerer said.

The captain was silent for a moment and then reeled back, laughing. "And you expect me to believe that an old man, his wife and a darkling girl in men's breeches escaped from the Golrakken?" He hooted as if it were a marvelous joke. A few of the men chortled but none actually laughed out loud.

Mari held her tongue.

"We are bound for the Shioroth, which I believe is north of us still," said Holren. "We intend to pass peacefully. What is the harm in that, Captain Achor?"

The swaggering captain thought for a moment and then said: "Come with me to Pellían and speak first to Realann King. We shall let him decide what is to become of you. First, you will have to relinquish your weapons."

"We agree to meet with your king, but we shall remain as we are," said Holren. "Besides, These are the least of our weapons. Beware that you do not induce us to use the ones you cannot take from us."

"I have no reason to believe anything you say, stranger," retorted the captain. "Come! We waste time."

The sound of hoof beats made the captain turn.

"A rider!" called one of the men. "One of the Green Guard!"

"Not what we need just now," muttered the captain under his breath.

"Captain Achor?" shouted the rider.

"Responding!" called the captain. "And who hails me?"

"Falnor of the High Council!" returned the other. "I am looking for travelers."

"We have found them," said Achor. "You may announce it when you return."

Falnor shook his head. "Release these three at once, by order of the High Council."

"I have no reason to release these dangerous criminals into your hands," said Achor.

"My orders are from the High Council," said Falnor. "And I will need horses for them to ride, for we require speed."

"Then you should have brought mounts," said Achor. "Poor planning on your part is not my concern."

"Perhaps," said Falnor; "but my report to the king will include several counts of insubordination, obstruction of duties and failure to serve in the best interest of the alliance."

"You wouldn't," said Achor.

"I would," said the other.

Captain Achor pointed to three of his men who obediently dismounted. Achor pointed at three others who accepted their comarades as passengers.

"I will make my own report," said Achor. "Watch your back, Falnor. I question your allegiance, and I will make my reasons clear to the king."

"I expect no less," said Falnor.

Wheeling about, Captain Achor led his company off at a gallop.

When the dust had settled, Falnor invited the three to mount up.

"I beg your pardon on behalf of one who does not know how," he said. "I am Captain Falnor of the Green Stone. Welcome to Pelnara, where we are more civilized than we initially appear."

"We are Holren, Mari and Tania," said the wizard.

"I had hoped to meet two of you," said the captain. "I was not expecting a third, but she is welcome."

Tania nodded.

"Do you have word of Aaron, Lia, Owler, Ender—"

Falnor interrupted him with a merry laugh and a raised hand. "I do indeed!" he said. "They are well, very well. In fact, I will tell you of several adventures while we ride."

* * *

"Well, at least they drew us a map," said Aaron rather glumly as he plodded along beside Lia in the hot sun. They were two days' walk from Pellían and not yet far enough away for Aaron. "I've been better treated by beggars, thieves and mercenaries."

Lia smiled ruefully and shook her head. "I doubt the days will go any better for Falnor, judging from the mood of his king. How will the High Council receive us without the captain? Besides, most of our strategic information is second-hand."

Aaron grunted. They walked on through the green fields of Pelnara, following the main road that led to the Shioroth. All about them lay rolling hills and tall grass, quite a contrast to the vast dryness of the Abandoned Land. Lia was delighted to find a small pond as the sun was beginning to sink, and she convinced her husband to stop early and bathe in it before dusk. The cool water washed away some of the gruffness in Aaron's voice. They ate the food that Falnor had provided for them (despite the king's stinginess). Then, lying under the trees with the night wind whispering through the leafy branches, they slept.

* * *

The sky was barely light when Lia rolled over and smelled the wonderful scent of roasting rabbit. Aaron squatted by the circle of rocks over which he turned a large hare on a spit.

"You've been busy," said his wife as she found one of the water skins and offered him a drink.

He smiled and accepted it. "A rabbit already in a snare makes any fool a crafty hunter. We get breakfast and the farmer keeps his vegetables."

"Not all his vegetables, I see," said Lia, looking at the little pile of carrots.

Aaron shrugged. "It's less than the rabbit would have spoiled," he said. "You might clean those, if you don't feel too guilty."

Lia washed the carrots and then came over to sit beside him. They munched in happy silence until the cooking was done.

Back on the road, they met few travelers. It was easy to dismiss the ignominy they had endured in the court of the Pelnaran king out here where the air was cool and fresh.

An hour after lunch they heard horses behind them and moved off the road to get out of the way.

"That one looks like Falnor," said Aaron.

"Yes, but who—" Lia was suddenly speechless.

"Impossible," said Aaron.

Suddenly, they both took off at a run back down the road toward the riders. In a moment, the sounds of shouts and tears and laughter rang out as the reunion brought everything else to a halt. Everyone talked at once. Eventually, everyone mounted up again, Mari and Holren on his horse, Aaron and Lia on Mari's mount.

"Our apologies for not asking sooner, who is the lovely lady?" asked Lia when they were all situated.

Holren introduced Tania and briefly retold the story of the rescue.

Aaron shook his head in amazement. "Who would've guessed?" he said.

"How accurate have been any of our guesses?" said the wizard.

"So, Captain, why did King Realann let you leave?" asked Aaron. "He seemed keen on keeping you in Pelnara, despite your duties at the Shioroth."

"Perhaps he had a change of heart," said Falnor. "I had stated my case well, so when I learned that I was released to go, I asked no questions. When the messenger arrived from Captain Achor telling of your friends' arrival, I sent word to the King that I would escort them to the Shioroth myself."

"He was more than just cool to us," said Aaron. "I wondered if he trusted us at all."

"I am puzzled," Falnor responded. "To be honest, the King has become rather inscrutable. He has grown cold in recent years. I can no longer read his face."

The conversation shifted again to all that had transpired while the two couples were apart. Falnor listened carefully and marked down the details in his mind. He watched Tania's face during the more detailed recounting of the escape from the lair of the Golrakken. The dark maiden kept silent, her face a solemn mask.

They rode until dark. Holren started a cozy fire, and they sat around for another hour before the conversation finally wound down and they settled in for the night. The captain took the first watch.

* * *

The chill of the night was upon them when Falnor heard someone stir. Tania was sitting up under the cloak she had borrowed from the house on Cai-Amira. The captain walked around the fire and knelt down beside her.

"You cannot sleep?" he asked quietly.

"I cannot keep from dreaming," she said.

"Sometimes when I am troubled, the same happens to me," Falnor offered.

For a long time, she sat with her head in her hands. Falnor sat nearby but did not break the silence.

When she looked up again, her eyes were dry. Her dark skin reflected a little of the light of the campfire. She turned and looked him in the eyes for a moment; then she looked away again.

"I have dreams of brutality without remorse," she said quietly. "I don't do it, but I stand by and watch. Somewhere, a small voice cries out in anguish, powerless to put an end to my own complicity." She looked over at Mari. "That one resisted until the end."

Falnor's brow furrowed and he sat for some time without responding. Tania stared into the fire and did not move. Then the captain stood up.

"Come with me," said Falnor. "I think a brisk walk is in order."

"No thank you," said Tania.

"It's just a suggestion," said the captain; "but I think you should accept it."

Tania looked at him sideways. "If I accept, what is required of me?"

"A brisk walk," he said.

She rose and covered her shoulders with the cloak. They set off into the field at a fairly good pace. Falnor turned them in a wide circle so they could keep an eye on the camp. In time, as she breathed deeply of the moist, cold air, Tania began to relax. The walked around and around in silence.

The captain glanced over at her periodically. Her dark skin was striking and her eyes seemed all the brighter for it. Her hair, black and coarse, was hastily pulled back into a thick braid and tied at the end with a piece of rough twine. Falnor stopped and Tania turned to find him staring at her.

"What?" she asked.

"I have something you could use," he said. "If I may see your braid, please."

She looked at him quizically and turned her back to him.

"This was thrown together in haste," observed the captain.

"I was escaping by sea, captain, not attending a meeting of state," she said.

"We of the Green Stone are fully trained in the proper care of long hair," said Falnor.

"So it seems," said the dark maiden.

"If I may, I would like to fix yours," he said.

"Proceed," she said, the hint of a smile in her voice.

He took out his knife and carefully cut the tough thread. Her black mane unraveled in his hands. Gently, he untangled her hair with his fingers. Then he braided it, a little at a time, starting at the crown and adding more with each strand until he came to the nape of her neck. From there, he finished the braid as normal. Leaving a span's length unbraided at the bottom, he affixed a simple, elegant clip carved from the wood of the walnut tree.

He laid the end of the braid on her shoulder and she lifted it up to look at it in the firelight. Her hands held the clip close to her face in the dark, turning it side to side and feeling it with her fingers.

"It's nice," she said, finally looking up.

"I made it when I was a lad," said Falnor. "I've kept it as a spare but never used it. It's yours if you'll take it."

"Thank you," she said. For a moment, she looked down. Then she let a smile play about her lips. "Do Pelnaran men all braid the women's hair?"

"We do," said Falnor. "In Pelnara, it is the custom for companions to braid one another's hair, even comrades in arms—"

"Of course," said Tania. "Again, thank you."

Falnor nodded.

"I think I will try to sleep again," she said. Flashing him a brief smile. "I feel better."

They returned to the fire. Falnor stoked it and awoke Aaron for the next watch. Then he lay down a short distance from Tania and waited until he heard her breathing evenly. Then he, too went to sleep.

When Tania awoke in the middle of the night, she saw him still there. Holding her braid, she curled up under the cloak allowed the sound of his breathing to lull her to sleep again.

CHAPTER 40

The Carthiss

The sun in the east of the wakening sky
Transforms it from blackness and dark
To a red, and a gold, and a lightening blue
An ever-more glorious, luminous hue
'Til finally the glistening white of the dew
Hears a song in the voice of the lark.
To-whay, to-whillow
To-whit, to-why
The sun in the east of the sky
To-whay, to-whillow
To-whit, to whay
The lark, as it welcomes the day.

Despite the early hour, no larks were being awakened by Grisbane's resonant singing. The company had been crossing the desert for four days and only twice had they heard or seen the Carthiss. Perhaps it was hunting for better prey, thought Brian, eating a little breakfast. Eulian and Grisbane were saddling their horses.

They set off again with the sun at their backs and their long shadows riding ahead of them. Eulian took the lead, as she had since Rummel had brought them to the edge of the desert. They would ride almost all day on the butte they had scaled the night before. Depending on how quickly they covered ground, the would either remain on the same butte that night or ride hard to reach the next high plateau before dusk.

Brian was tired of the dust and heat, but they would travel several more days before they came to the Sandstone Tower and Arvon Dustrider. Annie was bearing up well, though the heat did tire her over time. During the hottest part of the day, she rode with Eulian. Grisbane looked dried out and more wrinkled than ever, but nothing seemed to rumple his disposition.

They moved swiftly over the red rocks and stopped only to rest the horses and get them a drink. They were not likely to run out of water if they could keep to the current pace and schedule, but they rationed it even more sparingly than the food. Brian had never been so thirsty. His thick coat of heavy fur was matted down and oily with perspiration and dust. Nothing sounded better than a dip in a cold, rushing river.

They arrived at the edge of the butte before the afternoon was half over. Eulian found the best path down the cliffs and within an hour or so they were racing across the rolling dunes toward the next high plateau. Strong though the horses were, they soon slowed to a canter in the hot sun. The Elven Princess urged them on as the sunset grew red on the western horizon. The distance between the riders and the next plateau did not appear too far, but they did not seem to be getting any closer. They pushed forward, listening for the howl of the Carthiss. A thin strip of fading blue on the horizon was all that remained of daylight when they reached the bottom of the cliff.

"Can the horses scale this in the dark?" asked Annie.

"We haven't much choice," said Eulian. Quickly, she brought them around the north side of the butte where she expected to find the rise she usually took to the top. But there was no place to climb; the usual path was destroyed as if a great fist had pounded it to rubble.

"This is the only way up that I know of," she said.

"I'll go have a look," said Annie, lifting off into the air.

The rest continued around the butte looking for any path that might lead upward. Eulian attempted a few possible routes, only to turn back when they became too steep to climb. The last glimmer of blue had faded into darkness and they found it difficult to see anything in the remaining twilight.

Annie continued flying around the cliffs, unsure if she could recognize a proper route if she saw one. She rose higher to get another perspective. Looking out across the dunes, she could just make out a moving shape on the sand many miles away

"The Carthiss!" she shouted.

Flying very close to the towering rocks, she finally came upon a place where she thought the horses might make it to the top. In a flash, she returned to her friends and told them where they it was.

"But it's closer to the Carthiss," she said.

"Go!" said Eulian. "Lead on!"

Brian raced off around the butte behind Annie. Eulian and Grisbane followed at a full gallop.

The Snowdaughter sailed up and disappeared over the plateau. As Brian came around the west side, he saw the shadow racing across the desert, up over one dune, down again, up and over the next, its tremendous length spanning several dunes at once. The path Annie had found was obvious. The gruffen clambered easily up the treacherous rocks, knowing that it would be much more difficult for the horses. Any boulders in the way, he wrenched off the path and sent tumbling down the side of the cliff.

"It's here!" Eulian cried out. "Go! Go! Go!"

Brian whirled around to look. Below him on the sand some distance from the butte, a massive black serpentine shape was writhing and twisting, slashing its tail and striking with its head at a flickering light that darted in and out. The Carthiss reared up on her four back legs and swung her pincers as if fending off a large insect. For a few seconds, Brian watched, transfixed, while Annie's light form wove in and around the Carthiss, somehow staying just out of reach. He heard hoof beats behind him and saw Eulian's horse coming up the rock. Quickly, the gruffen raced on ahead, continuing to clear the way.

The climb was taking so long! Brian reached the top of the butte and could do nothing more than watch as the Carthiss suddenly gave up on catching the Faerie and dropped to the sand, headed for the butte. The gruffen reached down and grabbed a loose rock, heaving it at the advancing beast. It landed far short. He raced along the rim, hoping to get closer. The horses were still climbing, somehow strong enough and brave enough to continue forward despite the howling behind them.

Brian heaved another rock. It glanced harmlessly off the scaly hide. Then he saw something that made him gasp. The flickering light had landed on the monster's back, just behind the head. The Carthiss stopped suddenly, planting six legs into the ground and whipping its tail up to strike, its huge pincers snapping at either side of its head.

"No!" bellowed Brian, launching another rock which glanced harmlessly off a pincer.

The Carthiss writhed desperately, its stinging tail spines raking across the back of its neck, shoulders shivering and its head thrashing side to side. In all the dust, Brian couldn't see Annie anymore. He dared not throw another rock.

Then, suddenly, it was deathly quiet. Brian stared from the rim of the cliff as the cloud of dust began to drift away. Nothing moved below.

Eulian and Grisbane finally reached the top of the cliff, dismounted and led their horses to safety in the middle of the butte.

"Where's Annie?" yelled Grisbane.

"Down there," yelled Brian, pointing toward the Carthiss."

Throwing their cloaks over their horses' heads, Eulian and Grisbane came running to where Brian stood watching. No one spoke.

Down below, the Carthiss lay silently poised, still as stone. Her tail was raised to strike. Her head rested on the sand and six of her eight legs were braced to allow her to move quickly in any direction. Her foreclaws remained open and motionless on either side of her head. The two main eyes roved around and around. One of them fixed on the three on the cliff, but the monster did not move.

"There!" Brian hissed.

A flicker of light flashed momentarily on the very crown of the Carthiss, silhouetting the seven horns that rose from the monster's scalp.

"She's in there!" said Eulian.

The light flickered once more and then went out.

All was silence.

"What can we do?" asked Brian.

"Nothing," said Eulian, grimly. "If she's still there in the morning, we can get to her then."

Brian grunted.

Eulian and Grisbane, in turn, went to care for their mounts before settling in next to Brian to watch.

None of them slept.

* * *

Annie crouched in the shelter of the great horns on the back of the Carthiss' head, clinging desperately to the longest horn in the center. She kept one leg jammed into the breathing hole on the monster's crown. Though she had been holding this position for hours, she dared not move, not yet. The Carthiss had begun to burrow into the ground, perhaps to scare her off with the threat of burying her alive. Shoving her foot in deeper had made the monster stop again, half-submerged in the sand. It had sneezed out great blasts of air, but she still hung on. The Faerie's muscles ached but she did not let go. Air continued to flow in and out of the breathing hole around her leg, sucking her toward it one moment, and forcing out a rank exhalation the next.

The sun's rays had reached the tiny figures of her friends up on the butte. Brian was pacing back and forth. She lowered her eyes. Better to wait than to watch the slow progress of the sunrise illuminating the red cliffs. Now that there was some light, she could see more clearly where she was. She was surprised to note that the airhole itself was rimmed with what looked like a pattern of scars.

As the sun rose, the Carthiss' breathing became more agitated. She began to shift her great body again, settling her hindquarters a little deeper into the sand. Her spiked tail was already lowered and buried, but the she did not lower her head any further.

Annie twisted hard, but she could not force the airhole to open more. Great gasps and wheezes issued raggedly from the monster. The great legs shuffled deeper under the sand. The Faerie hung on. The cliff in front of her was now lit by the sun. The monster beneath her shivered as the tip of its longest horn pierced the the broad shaft of light that slowly lowered itself toward the sand. Three quick blasts through the airhole almost blew Annie out of position. Finally, the first rays of sun lit Annie's face. The great horn in her hands turned to stone. Below her, she could feel the beast trembling. As light poured over the horizon, the gargantuan lungs slowed more and more. The Carthiss' body was turning to stone quickly now. It seemed that the only area that was still flesh and blood was the airhole. The muscles around Annie's leg began to grow hard. Quickly, she pulled her leg from the airhole before it also turned to stone. The trembling stopped. Everything was still.

Suddenly, a great, furry mass scrambled up onto the stone back of the Carthiss.

"You made it," said Brian.

CHAPTER 41

Arvon Dustrider

"Looks like the man I saw," said Brian, squinting at the figure riding toward them.

"I'm looking forward to meeting this Dustrider," said Grisbane.

"We must be close to the sandstone tower, then," said Eulian, looking around. "I don't see any sign of it from here. It must be along the base of the mountains beyond."

Annie flew up higher and came back down. "Yes, there's something northwest of us that looks like it could be the tower," she said.

In a few minutes, the rider raised a hand in greeting. They greeted him back.

"You have come!" shouted the man when he was within hailing distance. He slowed his magnificent bay horse and came to a stop in front of them. "Arvon Dustrider," he said, his green eyes almost glowing in his angular, darkly freckled, red-bearded face. He was dressed in loose-fitting clothing the color of the sand. A turban kept the sun off his head. The wrinkles around his eyes spoke of years of harsh weather, but he seemed to be full of the energy of youth.

He saw the knife slung around Brian's shoulder and cocked an eyebrow. "You are the Valen I spoke to?"

"That's me," said Brian. "Brian."

"Your description was accurate," said Arvon. "I'm sorry, remind me again,...what are you?"

"Gruffen," said Brian.

Arvon nodded. "A gruffen," he repeated. "Well met, Brian." He looked up at Annie who had settled on the back of Eulian's horse. For a moment, he seemed not even to breathe. Then he said, "The Snowdaughter, I presume."

"I'm Annie," said the Faerie, looking at him curiously.

"The Snowdaughter," said Grisbane. "Annathía Sayacia das-Lammethan."

"Well met, Annathía," said Dustrider, bowing low in the saddle. "Your father was a friend of mine."

Annie looked at him even more curiously. "You don't seem that old," she said.

Arvon laughed. "A high compliment for a small blessing," he said.

"I am Grisbane, one of the Small Giants," said Grisbane; "and this is Eulian, daughter of the Elven Queen, Hassila."

"Well met, Grisbane and Eulian. An Elven princess rides in the desert?" said Arvon. "This is a strange company indeed. I have known only one other Elf, and I owe him a debt of gratitude that I repay every day. You must know Thorval Lighthammer."

Eulian's eyes widened with surprise. "My mentor," she said.

"Indeed?" said Arvon. "That would explain your being here. I fully expected *him* to bring the Snowdaughter. No one else travels so deeply into the land of the Carthiss."

Eulian nodded. "I have spent weeks in this desert with Thorval Lighthammer, though we never ventured so far in this direction," she said. "I find that curious."

"So do I," said Arvon with a nod. He glanced around. "You will understand the need for us to keep moving," he continued. "The horses will not have to ride hard from here. We are headed just over the dunes, a few hours more." He indicated his saddlebags. "I have water. Do you need it?"

"We have plenty," said Grisbane. "Eulian has made sure we stayed well-supplied."

"Excellent," said Arvon, regarding the Elven princess with increasing respect. "Then we'll be off." He turned his mount and headed back the way he had come.

"How did you know to look for us?" asked Grisbane.

"Nothing raises dust like two horses and a... a gruffen," said Arvon. "Besides, that glint of airborne blue had to be a Faerie." He turned and nodded to Annie. She smiled back over Eulian's shoulder.

Arvon looked down at Brian who loped along easily beside the horses. "Gruffens do not tire?" he asked.

"I do," said Brian. "More when it's hot."

"Then you must be able to cover amazing distances when it's cool," said Arvon. "Only certain horses will endure desert travel."

"These were chosen specifically for this journey," said Eulian. "How did you find this magnificent animal?"

Arvon smiled under his red moustache. "I am lucky to have access to a herd of wild horses wily enough to avoid the Carthiss." He patted his horse's neck. "I have had this mare for six years. She was sired by my last mount."

They worked their way up the drainages to the base of the Sandstone Tower as the sun was setting. The monolithic spire stood a thousand feet over their heads. Millennia of strong winds and blowing sand had carved away all the softer rock around it, leaving only the hardest stone. In the sunset, it burned like an ember in the fire.

Eulian shook her head in wonder. Finally, she thought; the end of the dunes. She wondered again why Thorval had never brought her here.

Arvon brought them to a halt and everyone dismounted. At the base of an outcrop preceding the tower was a steel door, very hot from its exposure to the sun. Arvon spoke to the door in a strange tongue and it opened slowly. The entrance to the underground cave was wide enough to admit even the mounts of the Small Giant and the Dustrider. Inside it was much cooler. They climbed several sloping tunnels lined with lamps that gave off only a little light. Inside, the air was much cooler. They followed several halls, some with doors on either side, some without.

After climbing what felt like a series of switchbacking ramps, they came into a place where the air was fresh. A warm breeze blew in from an opening in the wall. Much to their surprise, they found themselves looking out on a vertical drop of almost a hundred yards to the dunes below. They could see the sky, now studded with brilliant stars, stretching out over the sand for hundreds of leagues.

"Here we can leave the horses," said their host. "They have food and water." Removing the blankets from their mounts, they gave the animals a complete grooming and then followed Arvon through a wooden door.

The chamber into which it led opened out onto a sort of porch. The gurgling of running water played its rhythms in this room as well.

"Where does the water come from?" asked Eulian.

"The sandstone releases it constantly," said Arvon. "This dwelling was carved to make good use of it."

Seeping from the wall on one side, the water flowed down channels in the walls into several of the rooms past which their host brought them. One room had its own waterfall in the corner, splashing into a pool deep enough to stand in.

The women were given some privacy so that they could take full advantage of the bath. They emerged wet, happy and blanketed.

"I'll go last," Brian said. "Better that way." Grisbane and Arvon laughed and agreed.

By the time they were finished, Eulian and Annie had raided the pantry and set out a simple meal.

"I am being served in my own house!" Arvon exclaimed. "I will not complain but I oblige you to let me prepare breakfast tomorrow."

They sat down around the massive table and ate ravenously, happy to have such good food and drink after days in the heat and dryness. Arvon asked many questions and entertained them with many stories. Their laughter rippled into every corner of the room. A couple of times, Brian had to stop chewing to make sure he did not choke with laughter. Finally, they finished the meal and were shown where they could lie down for the night.

"I have a gift for you, Snowdaughter," said Arvon; "but such a gift is best received in daylight. Rest tonight. Tomorrow will bring what it will bring. Good night."

They all lay down on soft blankets and fell asleep.

* * *

Eulian awoke restless. A little light came from the hallway in the great room where they had spent the evening. Pulling on her cloak, she walked out into the larger room and looked around. The fire still smouldered in the hearth but she saw no one. A wide door opened out onto the balcony. Her bare feet made no sound as she crossed the sandstone floor, went outside and leaned out over the balcony wall that surrounded the porch. The wind, blowing along the rock wall played with locks of her hair that had slipped free of her braid. From here, she could see across the wide expanse of sand. Never had she imagined such a place existed.

Far off in the distance, the Carthiss wailed. The princess shivered.

"Was that shiver from the cold or from the Carthiss?" asked Arvon's voice behind her.

"The cold," she replied; "but the thing does give me the chills sometimes."

"There is a certain thrill to being so close to danger," said the Dustrider, joining her. "I have faced the Carthiss many times; it's never a pleasant experience, but there is something about the contest that I find invigorating. I wonder if the difference is in how you respond to your fear."

She looked at him quizzically. "How do you respond?"

Arvon laughed quietly. "It scares the sweat off of me every time I see the thing," he said; "but I know the fear well and am not afraid of feeling it anymore. When I become afraid of fear, then I will die."

Eulian studied his face as he looked out over the sand.

He continued: "It is a strange relationship. The Carthiss has kept me alive these many years. I am sharp and strong because of the creature. If I should drop my guard for a moment, the Carthiss is there to remind me of my mortality. No enemy could be more dangerous. Nor for me is any foe so necessary. I live because it thrives, and I'll mourn its death like no other. Yet in many ways, a great evil will be destroyed when it finally dies."

He stood there for awhile, staring out at the sands, and then turned to look at his guest. The Elven princess looked back, smiled and looked away again. Arvon chuckled. "You have a surprisingly dark complexion for a royal Elf," he said.

Eulian nodded. "Most of my people are fair-skinned and love the woods, but I have been a child of the desert and the mountains. Thorval showed me the places where the Carthiss cannot climb. For some reason, he never brought me this far west, and though you clearly know him, I was told nothing about you. Why would that be?"

"He kept you a secret, too," Arvon observed. "He said nothing about a royal Elven apprentice."

Eulian turned and looked at him. Though she could not see the green of his eyes, they glinted sharply all the same.

He smiled briefly and looked back out over the desert. "There," he said, pointing to a dark shape slithering across the dunes.

"Does she come all the way here?" asked Eulian.

"No," said Arvon. "She does not like having the water table so close." They watched the dark shape awhile. "How is it that an Elven princess is allowed on this sort of adventure?"

"My mother is not pleased that I love the desert," Eulian replied. "She knows I am different. My brother is more to her liking. I'm the rebellious one, as she sees it. We've come to the point where she knows there's not much she can do about it."

"Somehow that does not surprise me," said Arvon. "How did you become an apprentice under Thorval Lighthammer?"

"He was a great friend of my father's," said Eulian; "but my mother still resents him for taking me away from her after my father died."

"I should think so," said Arvon. "Besides, those who do business with Palanthar rarely receive much respect, it seems."

"Thorval never mentions him in front of my mother," Eulian said. "I have heard him called Ilstar or 'the wanderer.' Brian and Annie call him the Great Master. I have not met him. Who is he?"

"An enigma to me," said Dustrider. "I always called him Palanthar. He appears unannounced and I could never track him. Once, I caught him arriving in a cloud of smoke and I laughed at all my attempts to follow him. Several times, he has come to my aid, though he seems rather frail and heaven knows how old. He taught me how to approach and escape from the Carthiss."

"Annie found the one place she could not be attacked," said Eulian. "She hid near an airhole under the spiked crown."

Arvon turned in surprise. "Where did she learn that?"

"She just stumbled upon it," said Eulian. "She had the presence of mind to wait until dawn."

"That is truly amazing," said her host. "I was fortunate to be taught by one who could take the shape of the Carthiss so I could practice. The beast, herself, grants no second chances."

The monster's howl wafted toward them on the wind.

They stood in silence for quite some time until Eulian felt herself grow tired. "Thank you for the company," she said, yawning.

"Likewise," said her host. "Rest well."

She bid him goodnight and returned to her blankets where she fell immediately into dreaming.

* * *

She was running across the sand in the dark. The dunes exploded beneath her feet. The Carthiss loomed up all around her, encircling her with its massive body. Clawed arms reached for her and crushed her pelvis. She screamed as the gaping mouth closed over her.

Again, she was running across the sands. Again the dunes exploded beneath her feet. As the Carthiss swirled around her, she ran quickly to get out of reach of the pincers. A whip of the tail sent her flipping through the air, back toward the grasping pincers and gaping mouth.

Once again, she was running across the sands. Once more, the dunes erupted and the Carthiss spun about to find her. She ran alongside it, trying to stay close. From out of the sky, the tail spikes stabbed downward, directly into her skull and shoulders. Pain seared through her entire being as her muscles seized and she fell to the sand in convulsions. A clawed pincer crushed her ribcage as it yanked her up and tossed her into the open mouth.

Yet again, she ran across the sands in the dark. She knew the dunes would erupt any moment and the Carthiss would arrive. Poised, she stopped and waited, looking for that telltale shifting of the sands. There! She ran to it, arriving just as the behemoth rose, scrambling to keep her feet, she raced toward the spikes that were always the first to appear from the wave-like dunes. Seizing the largest one, she pulled herself under their protective cage. Below her, the airhole blasted sand and rank breath nearly blinded her. Quickly, she shoved a foot into the hole.

Instantly, the Carthiss stopped moving, tail in strike position, six legs braced, pincers poised to grasp anything that might emerge from the airhole.

Eulian looked down. Dangling from her belt was a water skin and a sharp knife. She twisted about until she could brace herself inside the cage of horns. Her hands now free, she untied the skin and unsheathed the knife.

She drove the knife into the hide that rimmed the airhole. The monster stopped breathing and lay perfectly still. Withdrawing the blade, she filled the water skin with the blood of the Carthiss. The wound closed when the skin was full.

Breathing hard, Eulian looked around. The monster was nowhere in sight.

She was sitting on the sand beside a wooden chair and table that were partially buried in the dunes. On the table stood a strange looking contraption. Its metal levers and gears, brass cylinders and glass tubes were all coated with dust and sand. A long, sharp needle was affixed to the end of one of the tubes, parallel to the table's surface, aiming at the wooden chair. On either side of the device stood a three-legged glass bowl large enough to hold the entire contents of the water skin she held in her hand. A glass tube at the base of one bowl led to the brass cylinder. Another glass tube led from a second, smaller cylinder to a second long needle also aiming at the wooden chair. The bowl on that side was fed by a tube coming from this smaller cylinder.

She looked up to see July, the wife of Rummel Stoneboots, standing before her.

"Will you?" asked the Lady of the Mountains.

"I don't understand!" cried Eulian. "I don't understand!"

"Now I will tell you," said July.

CHAPTER 42

The Gift and the Exchange

nnie awoke the next morning with a sense of anticipation. As she came into the sitting room, she saw Brian sitting by the table speaking with Arvon. Dawn had just broken, and Eulian and Grisbane were still asleep. The Snowdaughter sat down by the gruffen.

"I have waited for this day for many years," said Arvon. "I am glad to finally fulfill my oath to your father."

"Can you tell me about him?" asked the Faerie. "You were his friend."

Arvon smiled at her sadly. "I was, though that was not well known. I spoke to him just before he went south. He had Thorval Lighthammer bring this to me. Dear girl, your father believed he had found a magic which would keep you from being the very last Faerie. He would never have gone—and he certainly would never have taken you with him—without a clear, solid reason. Sadly, I believe he was tricked."

Arvon studied Annie as if searching for the answer to some troubling question. Then he smiled and sat back. "How they perished and you survived is a mystery. It would not surprise me to learn that Palanthar had a hand in it. It might explain also the reappearance of the Valenblade."

"What can this knife do?" asked Brian. "Nobody knows."

"It is the key to the Crimson Tower," said Arvon. "Of course, you know that already. All I know is that it is apparently impossible to destroy and that it was of Elven craftsmanship. Thorval Lighthammer was sorely distressed when it was lost, but he would not say why. 'An Elvish matter,' he said; and that was all. I don't know why the wise ones are so tight-lipped. I learned early on never to press Thorval for information."

"It only brings out the curmudgeon in him," said Eulian as she and Grisbane came in from the other room. Arvon rose from the table and brought out food that smelled just wonderful. In a moment, they were toasting the Snowdaughter with hot drinks. There were breads, heavier than the normal sort yet full of flavor and of a wonderful texture. A rather plain, gritty-looking gruel actually had a very enticing aroma and tasted as good.

The sun was streaming in from the porch when Arvon bade them sit in the larger room while he went elsewhere to fetch the gift for the Snowdaughter. When he came back, he held a tiny bag made of soft, dark cloth, bound at the top with fine golden thread. He stood for a moment in front of her and looked at the object as if reluctant to part with it, but in the end, he smiled quietly and gave it to her. Annie felt its light weight as she carefully untied the string. A flash of reflected light caught her eye as she looked inside. She turned the bag upside down over her palm and out fell a delicate ring.

It seemed to be made of bright silver, but it was surprisingly light. It was wrought in a stylized representation of Faeries' wings, four of them, arranged symmetrically like a butterfly's with the larger wings on top and the smaller ones below. In the center of each wing, tiny chips of clear crystal were clustered together to form a snowflake. Each snowflake was unique. The ring caught the light from the window and sent it splashing out across the walls and ceiling like tiny sparks.

"The Ring of the Snowdaughter," said Arvon, letting out a deep breath.

"What do I do with it?" asked Annie.

"That I don't know," said the Dustrider. "I have kept it for thirty years at your father's request. It kept alive my hope for you."

Arvon settled back in his chair. Annie looked at the delicate ring and then at the Dustrider. She searched his eyes as if somewhere in there she might see a glimpse of her father. Finally, she asked, "But what is it for? You told Brian I might need it."

Arvon sat up as if brought back from sleep and leaned forward toward her. "I'm sorry; I honestly don't know what it is for. I was instructed to give it to you immediately should you return. For me it has been the symbol of your father's love for you and also a bit of a puzzle. There is some power in it, I can sense it, but I am not the one to discover it. Your father made it himself the day you were born. I believe he had the help of someone else. We should consult with Palanthar or perhaps Thorval Lighthammer."

"That would make sense," said Eulian. "The Valen would likely have consulted with him on such a thing. Thorval Lighthammer is the one who forged the Valenblade."

"He and others," said Arvon.

"Others, yes," said Eulian. "That was later." She looked over at their host with great interest. What did he actually know?

Brian shrugged. "If we're done here, I say we go back."

"The Snowdaughter has not put on the ring yet," said Arvon. "I should like to see what happens when she does, if you don't mind."

Annie looked down at the ring in her hand. It seemed almost alive, as if it might lift off and fly away any moment. Carefully, she put it on the ring finger of her right hand and was surprised to find it fit perfectly. Though the metal felt cool on her finger, nothing visible happened. Her arm grew unexpectedly tense and then relaxed. They all sat there gazing intently at the ring, but after a few minutes, it seemed obvious that nothing else was happening.

"That was anti-climactic!" said Grisbane when everyone decided to breathe again.

Annie sighed and leaned back in the chair. The conversation took a new turn and the Small Giant asked Arvon what he might know about the trouble in the mountains of the Dwarves.

"They die when the Valenblade cuts them," said Brian.

"Does anything else affect them?" queried Arvon.

"No," said Grisbane; "and Rummel Stoneboots cannot see them."

Arvon pondered this. "Then they must be of the dead, as the legends say. I wonder if their appearance has anything to do with the Carthiss' odd behavior. She has been more willing to come out of the sand when the sky is still light at dusk and she waits until the last minute before dawn. She seems restless and has grown gaunt even though there is plenty of food available. I'm afraid she is losing her appetite."

"She seemed aggressive enough when we found her," said Eulian. "I would say even more so."

"But she does not eat," said Arvon. "From your story, I would say she was not interested in food when she attacked you. Had she been hungry, she would have ignored the Faerie as a mere nuisance." He turned to Annie. "No offense to the Snowdaughter; I think your action was brave and brilliant. I'm just surprised she focused on you as long as she did."

Grisbane rubbed his chin. "But what connection do you draw between the tunnel smoke and the odd behavior of the Carthiss?"

"If they are the Necrowights, they have the power to take control of such a creature," said the Dustrider. "I have read the legends of the black smoke that brings fear. They subdued and controlled the Carthiss once before, nearly killing her just to extend their reach. To deploy her among the living is to unleash death itself. She is, by nature, a wild being, yet it is her very wildness that makes her predictable. To thrive is her only motivation; she feed herself, protects herself and guards her territory. Nothing else matters. No living thing I know of can kill her. Only the Necrowights held the power of death over her. She obeyed them just to stay alive."

"She couldn't leave the desert, though, could she?" asked Grisbane. "Doesn't her softer belly keep her from leaving the sands?"

Arvon nodded. "It does—or, rather, it used to. She seems to be willing to venture outside her normal range. I don't know where or why. I know her old boundaries well and I have tracked her for many years, but in the last two seasons, she has become impossible to follow. All her tracks lead eastward and then she disappears without a trace. I believe she may have found softer rock beneath the sandstone and is tunneling underground."

Eulian's eyes were locked on the Dustrider. "We should find out," she said. "I shudder to think what she would do in the thrall of this death smoke."

"So do I," said Arvon. "If these are the Necrowights, the fury of Morvassus drives and sustains them. Though they were separated from him long ago, the fact that they remain active suggests they have lost none of their vigor."

Grisbane sat back. "If you expect to follow the Carthiss into the deep, you will need Brian's help. The Valenblade was our only defense against them."

Arvon Dustrider looked at the sandstone floor. "My desire to save the Carthiss may taint my judgment. If she is conquered, she will surely die." He paused. "And that is unacceptable."

With that, he excused himself and left the room. His guests looked at each other questioningly.

Eulian spoke first. "Which threat do we address?" she asked.

"We cannot go back through the desert to the mountains without crossing the path of at least two of the perils," said Grisbane. "Let us take them one at a time."

Brian grunted. "Over the sand or under? Both, maybe."

"If there are new tunnels, how do we find them?" countered Eulian.

"We would have to follow the Carthiss," said Grisbane. "You mentioned an area of softer stone close to the Salt Lake. Perhaps the Carthiss finds the carving easier there. We could survey it on the way by."

They discussed this for some time. When they ran out of answers, Arvon still had not returned. Outside, the world had grown dark. Thunder rolled in the distance.

"Good we're not out there," said Brian, getting up to look outside.

"That's strange," said Annie.

"What?" asked Brian.

"The ring on my finger seems to move when you move," she said.

Brian walked closer to her and then further away. "Does it move?" he asked.

"A little," said Annie. "It's like it knows where you are."
"Strainge," said Brian.

* * *

By late afternoon, the storm outside was at full strength, battering the sandstone tower with wind and rain. Inside, everything remained dry.

Eulian wandered along the dark corridors, peering through the doorways. Some rooms were empty, or had but a table and chair. Others were well-furnished sitting rooms, or sleeping quarters complete with bed and bath. There were also full suites in which a guest could live quite comfortably. A few chambers had shelves lined with books bound in leather and wood.

It was in one of these libraries that she found their host stretched out face down on a rug that covered almost the entire floor. His lanky frame seemed to fit into the intricate designs and patterns, as if he and the rug had been woven together as one piece. Eulian walked over and knelt down a few feet from his head. He was breathing, but it seemed to take a long time for his back to rise and fall with each breath.

If he was sleeping, Eulian thought, he certainly looked more peaceful than when she had last seen him. She knelt there quietly for a moment. He did not stir. Glancing around the room, she noticed an open book on the reading table. Curious, she got up and went over to have a look. The page to which it was opened was entitled The Last Chapter, written in a strong but graceful hand. The chapter was only a few paragraphs in length. The rest of the book was blank.

From all indications, this was Arvon's own writing. There was an inkwell on the table; a dark quill pen lay beside it. Glancing back at the book, Eulian was startled to see her own name. She turned away quickly, found a chair and sat down. For a moment, she thought about what took a deep breath. As she let it out, Arvon rolled over onto his back and looked up.

"Hello," he said. His eyes went to the open book on the reading table.

"Hello," said Eulian; "and yes, but I stopped reading when I saw my name."

He sat up and regarded her awhile, silently. She studied his face as he studied hers.

Dropping his eyes back to the designs on the rug, he pointed to a particular spot and said: "That's me as a young lad playing on the dunes."

Eulian looked. Sure enough, there was the depiction of a young boy running full speed across the blowing sands. The image was so clear, she could see the delight in his face and almost hear his breathing as he raced. Following the design, she saw an older Arvon sitting in the dwelling where now he lived. Further on there were other scenes, several of them involving a small, frail-looking old man. Winding in and out of this tapestry—sometimes hidden, sometimes obvious—was a lizard-like form with eight legs.

"The Carthiss appears in every frame after a certain point," said the Elven princess.

Arvon smiled ruefully. "The Carthiss and I are irrevocably linked," he said. "That is why I can never leave this place." He looked around at the pattern in the rug. "And that is why the Carthiss must not be controlled again. It must remain wild and free if I am to stay alive."

Eulian leaned forward on the table and looked him full in the face. "That is where I can help," she said.

"Help?" Arvon looked at her quizzically. "Say more."

"It is not yet time for you to die," she replied. "I spoke to July in the house of Stoneboots. She told me why you cannot leave the desert."

"Then Rummel knows more than I thought," said Arvon.

"What matters is this," she continued. "Though the Carthiss may die, you must not."

"To destroy her is to doom me," said the Dustrider. "I am linked with her; I live because she lives. If she dies, I would not be far behind her."

Eulian stood up and offered him her hand. "Show me where you make the exchange," she said.

Arvon's face turned pale. "You know?"

She nodded. "July explained it to me."

Arvon Dustrider got up from the floor and went to the bookshelves. He removed a particular volume and immediately set it back. Then he removed a second book from another shelf, moved the adjacent book into the empty space, removed a fourth book from yet another shelf and placed it into the space just opened, finally placing the second book into the slot vacated by the fourth book. The bookcase opened like a door, revealing another chamber behind it in which stood a table and what looked like a simple rocking chair.

Eulian caught her breath. On the table was the device she had seen in her dream, complete with its system of metal levers and gears, brass cylinders and glass tubes. Attached to the device via another tube was a glass bowl large enough to hold the contents of a water skin. A long shaft coming up through a hole in the table connected the extended foot of the rocking chair to a lever on the device.

"Each new moon I come here to replenish my blood with that of the Carthiss. If I fail to do so, I will die within seven days. The blood of the Carthiss has run in my veins too long for me to survive without the transfusion. I have gone as long as six days without it. I could never go the seventh." Arvon leaned against the table and looked up at Eulian. His green eyes were dark. "It's been four days. I must go tonight."

"In this weather?" asked Eulian.

"I have tarried too long already," said Arvon. "I don't have a choice."

Eulian approached the table solemnly. "I know how this works," she said. "You extract the blood from the rim of the airhole. You attract her by stepping on the dunes where you know she is hiding, climbing on her back as she rises from the sands. Then you crawl behind the horns protecting her airhole, driving your leg into it to force her to freeze. Then, just as the dawn turns her to stone, you drive a blade into the rim of her breathing hole and extract the blood."

"How do you know all this?" asked Arvon. "Not even the lady July has ever heard this from me."

"I dreamt of it all night," she said. "I was killed many times before I learned it properly. It was not something I would choose to experience again, though."

Arvon looked at her, speechless.

"How fresh must the blood be for it to be useful?" she asked.

"Not more than two days old," he said. "If she is too far away, I risk not making it back here in time for the transfusion." He motioned toward the chair and the device on the table.

"That is why you need the Carthiss to be wild and free," she said. "Your life depends on her predictability."

"Exactly," said Arvon; "and her recent erratic behavior makes this all the more risky."

"The lady July told me you did not always need the monster," said Eulian, quietly.

He nodded.

Eulian pointed back to the pattern woven on the carpet. "She said you were tricked. The story on the rug bears that out."

"Yes," said Arvon; "but that is long past. I live with what I am."

Eulian looked him in the eye. "There is a way to break this cycle," she said.

"If there is, I don't know of it," said Arvon.

"My blood in place of the blood of the Carthiss," said Eulian.

Arvon looked at the chair and the device. "Will it work?" he asked. "How does the lady July know such a transfusion will be successful?"

"She said it was the only way," answered Eulian.

"Why you?" he asked.

"She said that any Elf blood would work," said Eulian; "but not every Elf would survive it."

"And you would survive it?" asked Arvon.

"I believe I will," she replied.

"What if you don't?" he said.

"Then I will have made my choice," she said.

He said nothing for a moment. "What if it doesn't work?" he said.

"Then you live as you did until you can no longer do so," she said. "That is the risk."

"My risk is far less than yours," he said.

"I disagree," said Eulian. "The fate is the same."

Arvon sat down in the chair, staring at the floor. Then he looked up. "Come," he said. "Let's see what the rug has woven. Perhaps it tells us something."

"The rug weaves itself?" asked Eulian.

"Yes," said Arvon as they went back into the sitting room. "It weaves the future, just a little ahead of the present."

They both stopped at the edge where an image was already emerging. Eulian suppressed a shiver as she saw herself seated on the wooden rocking chair, arm outstretched, head bowed as the glass bowl filled with blood.

"My choice is clear," she said.

"Wait," said the Dustrider. "I want to see the next part."

A new image began to evolve. This time, Arvon was seated in the chair, receiving blood from the other glass bowl.

"Your choice is clear, too," said Eulian.

"What choice?" asked Grisbane from the doorway. He stepped into the room. Brian and Annie were close behind him.

Arvon looked up and took a deep breath. "Let me start from the beginning," he said.

Outside, the storm continued to rage, its fierce winds eerily reminiscent of the howl of the Carthiss.

* * *

"It's almost full," said Arvon quietly.

Eulian took a breath and tried to hold it in. Her grip was weak on his hand.

"Help me move," she said. "I can't..." Her voice trailed off.

Gently, Grisbane kept the chair rocking for her, back and forth, back and forth, moving the lever that turned the gears. Blood pumped out of her arm and flowed through the glass tube into the receiving bowl.

Eulian could no longer hold up her head. Her eyes fluttered shut and she slipped sideways only to pull herself upright once again. Still the pump continued on, drawing the blood out of her as she grew more and more pale. Arvon slowly kneaded her limp hand. She roused herself again and tried to push. When she let go, her eyes rolled back into her head and she slumped over unconscious.

"That's enough," said Arvon, holding her upright in the chair. "I've done with this much before."

Grisbane shook his head and kept the chair moving. "She made us promise to fill it all the way," he said. "If we stop too soon, she risks all this for nothing."

Arvon nodded.

When the bowl was full, Arvon pulled Eulian's arm back, withdrawing the long needle from her vein. Annie wrapped a clean rag around it and pressed her thumb against the puncture as Arvon instructed. Arvon disconnected the shaft under the table and Grisbane pulled the chair back. Carefully, Brian gathered the Elven princess into his arms and carried her into the other room. Annie had laid out a blanket on the carpet. Arvon instructed her to be laid by the hearth with her feet slightly raised.

"When she awakens," he said. "Make sure she has something to drink."

"Your turn," said Grisbane. "Annie will watch over Eulian."

Arvon went back to the secret room and stared at the machine on the table for a moment. Then, methodically, he disconnected the fittings and carried the bowl of Eulian's lifeblood around to the other side of the table where he carefully poured every drop into the other glass bowl. Then he set the empty bowl down and adjusted the glass tubes on the receiving side of the table so that the needle no longer pointed toward the chair. Finally, he settled into the chair, moved it back into position and reconnected the shaft to the rocker.

Grisbane put a hand on his shoulder. "What you do now is no less brave," he said. "We're all with you."

Arvon smiled briefly but said nothing. Slowly reaching forward, he slid his hand under the remaining long needle, palm up, so that the sharp point entered into his forearm. Once it was firmly inside, he began to rock the chair back and forth, back and forth.

Not long after the blood began to flow into his arm, Arvon began to sweat. He kept rocking. A few moments later, his hands began to tremble. By the time a quarter of the bowl had been drained, he was soaked with perspiration and shaking uncontrollably. Arvon groaned as the needle began to pull free.

"Please," he said to Grisbane; "keep my hand still so my arm does not move."

The Small Giant put both of his big hands around Arvon's and held it firmly against the table.

Arvon's breath came in ragged gasps. Brian had to move the chair to keep the pump going. The Dustrider's face contorted first one way and then another as pain seared through his body. When the last drops finally entered his arm through the needle, Grisbane helped Arvon draw his shaking arm back from the needle. Annie wrapped a rag around Arvon's forearm and he clutched it savagely as Brian and Grisbane pulled his convulsing body out of the chair. They took him into the other room and laid him down some distance from Eulian as he thrashed about, wailing in a high pitched scream eerily reminiscent of the howl of the Carthiss.

* * *

Eulian opened her eyes and looked around. A low fire in the hearth cast a warm light around the room. The storm no longer blew outside.

"Hello," said Grisbane's rumbling voice nearby.

She turned to see him sitting cross-legged nearby. He stood up and brought over a small cup.

"Can you sit up?" he asked.

"With some help, maybe," she said.

He helped her sit up and lean against the wall. "Drink this if you can," he said.

"In a moment," she said; "once the room stops spinning. How is Arvon?"

"Better," Grisbane replied, pointing to a sleeping figure on the floor. "This morning, he was able to stand up and walk around a little. He's not left this room."

"This morning?" asked Eulian. "How long have I been asleep?"

"Four days," he said. "You opened your eyes a few times, but not for long."

The figure on the floor sat up slowly. "You're awake!" he said. "How are you?"

"Weak," said Eulian.

Arvon crawled over and sat beside her.

Grisbane handed her the cup. "Can you drink now?"

She obliged. The drink tingled on the way down and took away some of the weariness.

"How about you?" she asked Arvon. "Any ill effects?"

"Besides the fever and the severe pain, no," he said.

Eulian laughed. "Good," she said. "You made it to the eighth day then."

"I did." The Dustrider took her hand in his and looked her in the eyes. "Thank you," he said.

She smiled. "You're welcome."

"Next new moon, I will thank you again," he said, letting go of her hand and resting against the wall.

She took another sip from the cup. "In person?" she asked.

He thought for a moment. "Yes."

"I look forward to it," she replied.

Arvon smiled. Neither of them spoke for some time.

Eulian pointed to the rug. "There's more," she said.

"Yes," said Arvon. "The Carthiss is no longer part of the pattern, and the design appears to be complete. I often wondered how it would end. I had no idea it would be this way."

* * *

Eulian looked out across the desert from the open porch. After the storm, color had sprung up everywhere. Great swaths of gold, blue and green washed over places that had seemed completely devoid of life only a few days before.

"This is my favorite time of year here," said Arvon beside her; "but I don't think I've ever seen it so lush."

"You should see it in the woods," said the Elven maiden.

Arvon smiled. "I should."

"Are you well enough to travel?" asked Eulian.

"I should ask you the same," said Arvon.

"I think we're both ready," she replied. "My restlessness has long since overcome my desire to rest."

Arvon laughed. "I think Brian will be the most pleased."

"Lucky for him, he's had the whole mountain to roam."

"Yes, but he will be glad to get out of this dryness," said Arvon. "I think it's time for me to do a bit of exploring in lusher climes, myself."

* * *

"Clear evidence of digging," said Arvon, pointing out the massive parallel scrapes in the stone. "Those claw marks are hers."

"What is she digging for?" asked Annie. "What would she want that's down there?"

"Good question," said Arvon. "Everything she needs is on the surface. She might dig when she has an animal trapped in soft sandstone. These cuts seem to have no purpose, just like the other ones."

Grisbane squinted up at the seemingly random scrapes. "It's as if she is testing the rock for softness."

Eulian looked around at the lengthening shadows. "We should get to higher ground," she said.

"There's a good place not far from here," said the Dustrider. "We can continue to track the Carthiss from there tomorrow. I'm curious about the rest of this series of canyons." He steered them back toward the dunes while Annie flew up to take a look around.

"I can see the Carthiss!" shouted Annie from high overhead.

"In the daylight?" said Eulian.

Annie called back. "She's not moving. She must be stone."

"Where?" asked Arvon, urging his horse forward.

"On top of the dunes by another cliff," said Annie, dropping back down a bit. "She looks like she was hunting something and just froze like that. I'm going to go see if she's really turned to stone."

"Careful," said Brian.

"It shouldn't matter in broad daylight," said Arvon; "but what doesn't make sense to me is that she would be hunting at dawn and get caught out in the open like that."

As the Faerie flew off, the others came around the corner and saw the sunlit Carthiss, poised as if to strike with her tail arched, foreclaws raised and mouth open wide, still as a statue.

"That's not a hunting stance," said Arvon. "That's a fighting position."

"But if she was defending herself, why didn't she burrow into the sand?" asked Eulian. "The sun would have touched her tail first, so why did she leave it raised?"

"Unless she was already paralyzed before the sun rose," said Grisbane.

"Precisely," said Arvon. "Her first defense is to bury herself. Whatever she was defending against must have been in the sand."

"Or under her," said Eulian.

Annie returned. "She's completely turned to stone," she said.

"This I want to see," said Arvon, urging his horse forward.

Brian raced on ahead, Annie just above him. When they arrived, the gruffen gave the creature a wide berth, but he needn't have done so; the creature was, indeed, turned to stone. The Carthiss cast its still shadow on the shifting sand.

"She was digging over there," said Annie, pointing to a gaping hole in the cliff.

"That's large enough for her to fit inside," said Eulian. "It would seem that she's tunneling somewhere."

The Dustrider eyed the opening. "Big enough to get in, but she would have to back out. She would also move very slowly since her usual swimming motion will not work." He scanned the area. "This place was flooded," he said.

Grisbane nodded. "That storm we had last week, perhaps."

Arvon looked back at the Carthiss. "If she's been standing here that long..." he said, his voice trailing off.

Eulian glanced around. "We should get to the safe place, even so," she said.

"True," said Arvon, wheeling his horse about. "That's it, just up there. We'll be able to watch the Carthiss tonight to see if she changes."

They gathered at the edge of the cliff as the sun set. Even in the twilight, they could clearly see the outline of the Carthiss. She did not move. Darkness finally hid her from view, but there was no sound.

The others lay down to rest while Arvon and Eulian sat at the cliff edge and talked. When the moon came up, they could once again see the still, ghostly shape on the sand.

Brian awoke before dawn to the sound of Arvon and Eulian saddling their horses. He got up and ambled over to the cliff edge. The Carthiss was still there.

"You going down?" he asked the Dustrider.

Arvon nodded.

"I'll go, too," said Brian.

"We'll be right behind you," said Grisbane, getting up.

Annie came over and stood with Brian. "She hasn't moved all night," she said. Without another word, she shifted to light form and shot off toward the sand.

Brian yelled, but she was already there. A second later, she appeared on the creature's crown by the airhole. The light had still not touched the raised tail. Grisbane, Arvon and Eulian came running over only to see Annie walking slowly down the massive spine of the Carthiss. The Faerie took off again and returned to the others.

"She's stone," she said, soberly, just as the light touched the top of the arched tail. "She's completely turned to stone."

Arvon nodded. "We suspect she got caught inside the tunnel during a flash flood and could barely back out fast enough," he said. "When she did, the sand was saturated. Dawn must have arisen suddenly, perhaps a break in the clouds. It was either turn to stone or drown."

By the time the sun came up, they were back on the dunes. The massive stone shape of the Carthiss towered over them. Arvon dismounted and approached it solemnly. Then, he deftly climbed up one leg and stepped onto its back.

"She's gone," he said, slowly walking down the length of the mighty spine to where the tail curved upward. He returned to the airhole and stood there looking at it for a moment before he knelt down and ran his hand along the edge of it. The airhole was open; windblown sand had already begun to collect inside.

After he climbed down again, he patted the stone pincer and came back to the others, his face wet with tears. No one said anything until he had mounted up.

"The end of her long, healthy life," he said; "and the beginning of a life for me, without her." He nodded to Eulian. "My thanks, once again, for the blood that flows through my veins."

Her voice trembled as she spoke. "You're most welcome," she said.

The Dustrider looked up at the stone visage one more time. Then he turned his face eastward. "Something in my heart wants to see the forest," he said. "Lead on, Eulian. I want to see where my new kinsmen live."

CHAPTER 43

Into the Tunnels

"It's a pity you can't stay another day, Owler," said Thadris, popping another tart into his mouth. "Val-Ellia is going to be dull without you."

"Val-Ellia is marvelous," said the woodsman as he sat back in his kitchen chair. "The Elves have been so kind, and your Chief Cook is as good a historian as he is a baker!"

Bostler had just breezed off elsewhere after having finished a long-winded explanation of how the Elvin palace was built (including who hired whom for what, and who else was really the better designer).

"You have many admirers here," said Thadris; "but it's not just your woodsmanship—though that is impressive enough. You fit in our hearts, my friend. You're a leaf from the same vine."

"Or, in our case, two nuts from the same squirrel cache," said Owler.

Thadris laughed out loud. "You see what I mean? Boring!" He leaned forward. "I have a challenge for us: when you can come back and stay awhile, I think we should have a contest."

"Of what sort?" asked Olwer, grinning.

"We should be blindfolded and taken out in opposite directions and then released to see who can track down the other first."

"Too easy," said Owler.

"Why?"

"Because you know these woods like I know mine," said the woodsman.

"That should give me the advantage," said the prince.

"Yes, except that all I would need to do is find a hidey hole and wait until your official duties draged you back here."

"A time limit, then," suggested Thadris.

"Underground," said Owler.

"Done!" said the prince.

Owler raised an eyebrow. "A brave choice for an Elf! If the Dwarves will allow it, I accept the challenge."

Thadris stood up. "That will be great sport! Don't you forget."

"I will not forget," said Owler. "In fact, I'll be studying the tunnels for the next several days."

Thadris nodded, more somber now. "We should see to whatever Yorgun still needs," he said.

"Agreed." Owler rose from his chair.

"The tarts! You've been at the tarts!" cried Bostler, as he burst into the kitchen. "Oh, I knew I should have made another batch. You might as well finish these!"

"We left at least fifty!" said Thadris.

"Forty seven!" countered the Chief Cook. "There were only fifty to begin with."

Thadris shook his head. "I can never get away with anything around here," he said to Owler. Turning back to Bostler, he said: "Breakfast will be early tomorrow."

Bostler wiped his hands on his apron. "I'll be sure we have something available—something hearty, of course, not just the usual. Now I know Mr. Yorgun and his crew must be simply itching to face death in the tunnels, but I'm glad they'll be here for two more meals. I can't imagine attempting such a dangerous task on an empty stomach," he said, looking around distractedly. "Rittur? Rittur! Where is the dough you promised me—? Oh! Never mind; it's right here on the counter. Thank goodness for such a staff! Couldn't boil an egg without them. Now, if you'll excuse me, I have a dinner to put on and breakfast will be early, don't you know...!" He bowed low and hastened away to some other part of the kitchen, wiping his hands on his apron shouting encouragement to his staff. They paid him no mind and continued working as quickly and efficiently as ever.

As they left the kitchen, they met Hassila.

"Mother, that look means bad news," said Thadris.

"Yorgun has word from his furthest outpost," said the Elven Queen. "There has been another attack by the Black Smoke."

"We're on our way," said Thadris. He led Owler quickly around the inside of the tree palace, toward the Dwarves' guest quarters. "What will you do when you find this smoke?" he asked, half under his breath.

"I don't know," said Owler. "We need to know where it comes from and how to seal it off. At this point, I hope we can simply outmaneuver it somehow."

Thadris knocked on a door.

"Enter," said a gruff voice within.

They came inside to find Yorgunsitting with a, wiry younger Dwarf.

"Mr. Roggin here has been to the house of Stoneboots," Yorgun informed them, offering two full-sized chairs nearby.

They listened with great interest to Roggin's story.

"You say it disappeared when the Valenblade cut through it?" asked Yorgun when the tale was finished.

"With a shriek that almost shredded one's ears," said Roggin.

Yorgun shook his head. "So we don't know if the blade destroyed it or just drove it away," he said. "We will face it, whatever it is."

"I will take you there," said Roggin. "I know those tunnels well."

"Spoken like a true Steelsmith, Mr. Roggin," said Yorgun. "A Steelsmith indeed."

Roggin nodded solemnly. "When do we leave?" he asked.

* * *

Early the next day, Owler bid Bostler and Thadris goodbye and was over-laden with good wishes as he left. Two Elves of the Blue Stone were assigned to go along until they reached the closest Dwarven outpost. Their task was to return the horses to the Shioroth.

To keep their spirits up, the Dwarves kept the conversation light. The younger Dwarves plagued Roggin with questions about Rummel Stoneboots, but Yorgun gave him a wink and shook his head, so Roggin merely laughed and shrugged them off. When they realized they could not cajole him into doling out any information, they lapsed into a sullen silence.

"Let's have a riddle," called Yorgun. "There will be time enough for dullness later."

"I've got one!" yelled someone in the middle of the group. "Two of me rule one of you! Who are we?"

"They're in your hands and and under your backside!" yelled another, immediately. "Reins and a horse! Somebody come up with a better one!"

That set them off. From then on, almost all the way to the first outpost, there was a boisterous competition which no one appeared to win but everyone seemed to enjoy.

Owler set aside the dread of what was coming and immersed his senses in his surroundings, basking in the warm air and the lushness of the woods. The sunlight falling through the tall evergreens set the new leaves of the lower canopy glowing with a brilliant green. The company approached the entrance to the mountain pass in a long train, single file with Yorgun in the lead. Roggin, Owler, and Calicia followed, with the rest of the merry band trailing out behind. The two Elves brought up the rear, a short distance back.

By mid-afternoon, they had come to the first outpost. Much to Yorgun's relief, Korban confirmed that there was no new word of the Black Smoke. The Dwarves unloaded the pack horses and entrusted them to the Elves who said their goodbyes and rode back eastward. Then each Dwarf heaved a load onto his back and they proceeded down the large, dark tunnel into the heart of the mountain.

They met many Dwarves along the route to the Great Hall. Yorgun made Roggin walk up front with him. Word had traveled quickly and the wiry Dwarf was being hailed as something of a hero. Roggin just nodded and answered questions when he could, shouldering his load and moving forward like all the rest of the Dwarves in the company behind him.

Owler fell back a bit and asked some of the others about the newcomer.

"Ah, he's an odd one, that!" said a grizzled elder Dwarf. "Pretty much a hermit, really. Stays in the westernmost outpost for months at a time. Wanders the empty tunnels on his own."

"And he's got short hair!" said another.

"I noticed," said Owler. "What does that say about him?"

"Just that he's an odd one, that," said the first Dwarf; "but he's a Steelsmith, all the same. You can see that in his eyes."

Owler was intrigued. "What is it in his eyes that tells you he's a Steelsmith?"

"A little bit more fire than we're used to," said the elder Dwarf; "like he's forged a little differently than the rest of us. Reminds one of Yorgun, himself, in younger days, I say."

"Hot tempered?" asked Owler.

"Nay," said another. "Just a better temper. He'll do the right thing, no matter how hard it is; you can count on it. I think the greatest Steelsmiths were born that way."

"Aye, and the greatest Goldsmiths may melt more quickly in the heat, but their hearts are purified by it," said yet another.

"Ah, Gankin, the Goldsmiths are all worth their weight in copper," said another. There were guffaws all around.

Gankin shook his head. "Spoken like a true Leadbottom," he said.

The continued through the cavernous tunnel for three solid hours. Along the way, most of the Dwarves were dispatched elsewhere with their various loads. The remainder of the company entered the Great Hall of the Dwarves.

The arched roof of the Great Hall soared high above them, barely reached by the light of the many torches that lined the walls. A vast display of shields, axes and swords of Dwarvish proportions were hung as if in tribute to the cunning and creativity of the great smiths. Owler learned that each item had a history and a legend that was maintained by the bards and storytellers. Behind the heavy wood and metal throne hung a banner of fine linen through which were woven the names and accomplishments of generations of Dwarven chiefs. It was a lengthy list that ended with the name of Yorgun Steelsmith.

Two long, low tables were brought in and set with food. Chairs were placed around them and larger chairs were brought in for the guests. Calicia and Owler sat on Yorgun's right; Roggin was directed to sit on his left. When all was ready, the elders of the clans entered the Hall and sat down at the tables.

Yorgun stood and addressed them without preamble.

"We are beset with our most fearsome enemy since the Great Dragon," he said. "Whether we face this fear or turn and flee, our lives will never be as before. I say we face it. We will learn what it is, what it can and cannot do, and with courage and cunning, we will find a way to drive out this menace so that our children and our children's children may live in these mountains which have always been our home."

There were murmurs of agreement.

Yorgun continued: "No one thinks properly on an empty stomach. When the meal is over, we will address the issue at hand. First, we eat." He sat down, raised a glass and took a great quaff of ale. The rest did the same. Then the food was brought out and everyone fell to, heartily.

"Do you think this Rummel Stoneboots will assist us?" asked Owler.

"The Lord of the Mountains does as he deems best," replied Yorgun. "I have not been so bold as to ask him for anything yet. Roggin, here, seems to have more pluck than the rest of us. Surely, Stoneboots knows our peril. He was quick to the rescue when the others were in danger."

"Not exactly, sir," objected Roggin. "Stoneboots appeared only after the smoking death had been killed or driven away by the Valen. He told us nothing about the enemy."

"Did you inquire of him?" asked Calicia.

"Yes,"said Roggin. "He did not speculate as to what they were, but he seemed troubled that he was not aware of them before we were."

There was deep concern at this news.

"If he can't sense this smoke, it must be magical indeed," said Yorgun. "Let us leave this subject for now. We'll think better after we eat."

When they had eaten their fill, several of the elder Dwarves stood and offered suggestions of possible approaches to the problem. No idea was wasted, no plan thrown out until it had been heard. When all was said, Yorgun sat silently on his throne and rubbed his bearded chin.

"It appears we have no other choice than to close up the deepest of the tunnels," he said. "Any passages that have been compromised must be sealed off, regardless of their value. For now, we must barricade ourselves against further attack."

All sat solemnly still. Finally, Calicia stood.

"I ask permission to seek out this enemy and discover its weaknesses," she said. There was a gasp from the Dwarves in attendance. "I have with me a vial of pure Jalice," she continued, holding up the crystalline container. "One drop can dispel much evil. It has served in many wars already."

Owler stood as well. "I will go as well," he said.

"And I," said Roggin, standing up on the other side of Yorgun.

Calicia smiled and nodded. "If the Chief of the Dwarves will allow, I would like very much for Roggin to serve as guide."

Yorgun nodded in reply. "We are astounded again by your offer," he said. "It is not the custom of the Dwarves to let others walk into harm on our behalf. Both Roggin Steelsmith and I will go."

There were cries of objection from all sides.

"I will not be excluded," said Yorgun. The elders grew quiet. "On this occasion, however, let Roggin lead us through the western tunnels. He knows them better than anyone. I go as a warrior, no more."

"You are decided, then," said a white-bearded elder Dwarf.

"I am, Murdun," said Yorgun.

"Then you have our blessing," said Murdun.

There was a moment of silence and then the Dwarves stood together and toasted everyone with a solemn blessing:

> May axe be swift and sword be sharp;
> May feet run swiftly on the stone;
> May knife and dagger find their mark
> Till peace is once again enthroned.

* * *

Dawn was announced by torchlight, which gave the "overlanders" the feeling of having slept through an entire day, only to wake up the next night. They were treated to a hearty breakfast without much pomp, other than the presence of several elders who mumbled and nodded to each other with grave expressions.

Yorgun, himself, did not look as if he were marching out to face death. He ate well and carried on a lively conversation with Owler, who plagued him with questions as usual. After breakfast, they took their weapons and provisions and set off westward on the path to Roggin's outpost.

Much to Owler's delight, Roggin and the Chief of the Dwarves detailed the history of the tunnels for their companions as they went. The histories were interrupted periodically as Dwarves stopped to speak with the company and wish them well. Yorgun seemed to know most of them by name and shook their hands warmly when they greeted him. This made the going rather slow, but after several miles and a short lunch, they saw fewer and fewer of the small folk.

That night was spent in an ancient chamber that had once been a fine stateroom. An underground waterway had long ago cut through the wall and now ran across the floor. They bathed their faces and hands in it before settling down to sleep. Owler took the first watch and Calicia the second, but the night passed without incident.

When Roggin woke them all the next day, they continued westward through the mountain. As they drew further and further away from the dwellings of the Dwarves, they began to search the small passages that joined on to the main way. Careful inspection revealed no evidence of anything amiss. It was mid-afternoon when they came to Roggin's outpost and were greeted by his cousin, Scoggin, who was relieved at the sight of them.

"Nothing to report," said Scoggin, shaking their hands vigorously. "But the suspense is enough to give you the jitters. Sleep is almost impossible for fear of waking up to the smell!"

Yorgun released him to return to his family and he quickly gathered his things and left.

After he was gone, Roggin fixed them a good meal and they ate it with no pretense of haste.

"Is it very far to the outside of the mountain?" asked Calicia.

"A bit of fresh air for the overlanders would be wise," said Yorgun. "We should have a look outside before the day wanes."

They left the table and followed the Dwarves to Roggin's hidden door. They emerged from the ancient passage into a cool evening breeze. Owler climbed a tall rock and turned to watch the sunset. The sky was a golden orange in the west where the sun was melting into the horizon behind the mountains. The deep blue and purple shadows of their steep sides looked cold and hard beneath the fire on their sun-ward ramparts. Owler felt a chill breeze blow by and the sky grew slowly darker. When daylight gave way to starlight, Owler climbed down from the rock and followed the others back into the mountain.

They talked for awhile, each with a mug of beer, before they settled down for the night. Owler asked for the first watch. As the others slept, he took a lamp and explored some of the closer tunnels, never straying far from his companions. He found it all very fascinating: the carvings on the walls, the tunnel engineering. In most of the passageways, he had to stoop to avoid hitting the ceiling. Eventually, he returned to the dwelling and looked through some of Roggin's books until it was time to wake his host for the second watch.

* * *

"It's sweet," said Owler, swirling the drink around in his mouth before swallowing the last of it.

"I wouldn't say 'sweet,'" said Yorgun. "'Rich' is a better word."

"Jalice tastes different to everyone," said Calicia.

"I was going to say 'spicy,'" said Roggin. He looked at his empty cup. "In any case, it's very good."

"What does it do?" asked Owler.

"Primarily, it strengthens what you already have," said Calicia. "It also wards away evil. Dark magic is more easily withstood."

"And a drop is all it takes," mused Yorgun. "Amazing. How long does it last?"

"No one knows for sure," said Calicia. "My father recommended a drop a day."

With Roggin in front, they headed for the corridor where he had first come in contact with the smoke. The going was tedious and tense, but they kept on, methodically checking each side passage as they went by. Finally, they reached the chamber where Rummel Stoneboots had come up through the floor. There was no sign of his having been there at all, however: no hole in the floor through which he had entered or in the wall through which they had left. The company did see ample evidence of the fight, including dusty footprints, broken stone and a trail of dried gruffen blood. Their hearts pounding, they searched every room.

After carefully combing the chamber and finding no new clues, they now followed the tracks of hurrying feet down the halls to the place where the foul-smelling creatures had surprised the company. The wiry young Dwarf doggedly led them down the dark passage.

"You're sweating, my son," said Yorgun, sword drawn, tramping along beside Roggin.

"Yes, sir," said Roggin.

"No more than I am, Mr. Steelsmith," said the Chief Dwarf.

"I'm sweating a lot more inside," Roggin replied.

Yorgun chuckled darkly. "As am I," he said. "That makes you the braver one."

Roggin kept his eyes on the receding tracks in the dust. "How is that, sir?"

"You have faced this before," said Yorgun; "and still you continue on."

Roggin nodded and said nothing.

"This is the place," said Roggin quietly, as they came to the narrow slit of light that heralded the great outside. "Last time I was here, I thought we'd lost everyone."

Yorgun went to the opening and pushed aside the stones that obscured the sun, letting in a virtual waterfall of light. Calicia took a quick look back over her shoulder and then followed the Chief of the Dwarves out into the open air. The others, glad for the chance to breathe freely once again, did likewise. Warily, Roggin stayed inside to keep watch.

"I doubt we will find them topside," he hissed from inside the cave. "It is more likely that our trail has been discovered and the creatures await us in ambush."

Calicia nodded. "We should search until we know where they are."

They all filed back underground. Yorgun shut the stone and they waited until their eyes grew accustomed to the darkness before they moved on. Roggin sniffed the air as he walked, straining for any trace of the pungent scent, but despite their fears, they found no indication of the presence of the smoky death.

"Enough for one day," said Yorgun, exhaling slowly. "We should get some rest and continue tomorrow."

They all agreed. Though they set a watch, no one slept well.

Over the next several days, they passed back and forth, threading through every passage and tunnel. Day after day of tense exploration became day after day of tedium. They found absolutely nothing at all. Their best efforts would not reveal any access point where the smoke could have come in, nor where the enemy was now gathered. Further and further they went, searching the tunnels in ever wider circles, all to no avail. They spent several days in the uncharted and even unfinished passages, fully expecting any moment to be engulfed in deadly smoke. Finally, they returned to the outpost, weary, disheartened and frustrated.

"It is time we paid a visit to Rummel Stoneboots," said the Chief of the Dwarves, leaning back in his chair with a hot mug of tea.

"Why is that?" asked Calicia.

"He may have an option we had not considered," Yorgun replied. "He may also have news we have not heard; his senses are much keener and deeper than ours. He knows the breath of every tree in the hills. In any case, there is nothing better than an evening spent in the house of Stoneboots to clear the head and give one a fresh perspective—something I surely need right now."

That night, in the relative safety of the outpost, they slept heavily.

The following day, they packed some food and left the tunnels by the main entrance. It was a glorious morning and they were all in better spirits now that they were out of the tunnels. Roggin led them over the hill on a cleverly disguised trail. They followed this for most of the day

The sun was sinking low when Yorgun stopped everyone, stepped off the path and headed directly uphill to the summit. When he came back, he was grinning broadly.

"Follow me," he said. "This will be worth it."

At the top of the hill, they descended into a shallow depression that split the summit lengthwise for about five hundred paces. Two rocks, about four feet tall and a dark blue-gray, stood conspicuously like short pillars in the middle of a circular patch of lush, green grass. Yorgun approached the stones and took out his blade. Grasping the knife by the steel, he tapped the handle on one of the stones three times, quickly. After a short pause, he tapped the other stone, slowly, five times. Then he tapped the first one, even more slowly, four times.

With a broad grin, sheathed his knife and promptly flopped down in the lush grass.

"Nothing left to do but wait," he said. They all looked at each other, amused, and stretched out on the grass beside him.

The few clouds in the sky grew stark against the darkening blue above them. No one spoke. It was a lovely stillness, broken only by the whisper of the breeze that stirred as evening drew near.

They lay there for some time, one or another of them sitting up periodically to look around. Yorgun fell to snoring. As the stars were just peeking out, a big, booming laugh reached them from a long, long way away. They heard it again, this time, much closer. Only then did the Chief Dwarf sit up and look around. His face broke into a broad grin.

"Rummel!" shouted Roggin as the mighty head appeared above the hill to the south and east of them.

"Roggin Steelsmith!" bellowed the huge man as he crested the hill. "Hello! Hello! And hello, to the rest of you, Yorgun, Calicia and one whose name is, if I am not mistaken, Franklin Thurmond Vasserman Everhabixortimus the Fourth! Welcome to you all!"

They all stared with amazement as he took a step toward them, shrinking smaller as he came closer. When he reached the standing stones, he was only a little taller than Owler.

"How do you do?" he said with a deep bow. "I am here to bring you to our home to restore what needs restoration. The Lady of the Mountain awaits! Permit me to assist you. You'll need a ride."

With no further warning, he knelt on the ground and grew suddenly large again, beckoning to them to climb up his arm onto his shoulder. Owler laughed in surprise and scrambled up. The rest of them clambered aboard behind him.

Rummel made sure everyone had hold of his long hair, and then he stood all the way up and waded straight through the summit to the other side. Up and down they raced in the gathering darkness, lit only by the last glimmer of sunset.

Looking back behind them, Owler wondered if it was a trick of the light, or if indeed Rummel's feet never actually disturbed the ground beneath them. Several times, he ran down slopes of loose shale, never sliding an inch. The huge man's strides were light as the gait of a deer, not heavy and thundering. The cold air in their faces added to the sheer thrill of the journey. When finally they came to a cabin on the side of the hill, they were all laughing and out of breath.

Rummel shrank down to a more manageable size and herded them all into the house like a father gathering his children.

Roggin had hardly gotten to the door when he found himself swept into a hug by the Lady July.

"My dear Roggin!" she exclaimed. "So good to have you here, finally!"

Yorgun clasped her hands and held them to his face. She kissed him on the forehead and brought him inside. Owler and Calicia were welcomed just as warmly.

When they were all inside, July motioned toward the table where a sumptuous feast was already laid. Steaming mugs of something wonderful were set by plates and silver utensils. There were seven chairs, only six of which were empty. A tall, handsome man was standing up from the seventh chair.

"Ender!" shrieked Calicia, flying across the room and into his arms. She pressed her face into his chest, drinking in the smell of him. Then she pulled back. "Are you really here?" she gasped.

"I am," he said, smiling back at her; "and so are you!"

CHAPTER 44

Rummel Again Plays Host

Everyone was introduced, each found food that appealed to each, and they all sat in their various places. Owler's chair seemed to grow out of the floor like a bush with thick branches covered with soft needles similar to pine. Roggin's chair was formed of stone with veins of iron marbled throughout. Yorgun sat in a mighty chair shaped like his throne, only smaller and more intricately designed. Rummel and July sat down also in their great chairs, each a mountain complete with snow, trees and waterfall.

Ender was prevailed upon to tell the story of what had happened since they last parted. Sparing them the details, he related the meeting with the Small Giants, the attack at the Northern Bridge before the Mirrak-Haas, and the subsequent journey toMorvoth.

Calicia noticed he did not conceal his use of the Midnight Stone. What she did not know was just how close he felt he had come to being swept away by it.

When the meal was over, Yorgun cleared his throat and stood solemnly on his seat to address the group.

Before he could utter a word, Rummel broke in: "There is plenty of time for business, dear Yorgun. Tonight, other activities are required."

Yorgun, bowed and started to sit back down.

"Oh, don't sit down yet," said Stoneboots, with a laugh. "Let's make good use of your nearly wasted breath. Everybody stand up!" They did so, and, with a wave of his hand, their chairs simply disappeared and reappeared around the hearth. He brought out his instrument and waited, poised. "Give us a poem, a ditty, a jig, my good man. We need to dance tonight," he said.

The Chief of the Dwarves bowed his head to think. Then a broad smile crept over his grizzled face. Tapping his foot, set a proper rhythm and then launched into a rollicking jig, half sung, half spoken.

> Yo he ho
> A-rocking go
> A-jingle, a-tingle, a-flocking go!
> Hard to the left!
> Hard to the right--
> A wiggle and a giggle and a nibble and a bite!
> Leaping to the window,
> Lunging to the rug,
> A-tripping and a-flipping and a-zipping like a bug,
> Up against the wall now,
> Flying down the hall now,
> Under tables, over chairs,
> through the kitchen, up the stairs,
> on the floor and in the air,
> it really doesn't matter where
> as long as it will take a lot of energy to get you there!

By the time he had gotten halfway through the first verse and was making up the second, they were all racing about the house like children who have just been told that nothing will break and no one will be upset if they make a mess. The beauty of it was that there was, indeed, nothing breakable and no mess to be made. Somehow they were able to dance on any level surface at all, including the table, never once upsetting anything or knocking something out of place. The dance turned into a mad game of tag with the entire group zooming about in all different directions, narrowly missing each other in an effort to get away from whomever was currently "it." All the while, the song churned along as Yorgun made each verse more raucous than the last. Finally, they all collapsed into their chairs, holding their aching sides and laughing so hard that tears rolled down their cheeks.

"Does this always happen here?" asked Roggin, when he had caught his breath.

"Not every time," said Yorgun. "Next time you might be the one to bring a song."

"I couldn't possibly!" said the younger Dwarf.

Yorgun's eyes twinkled. "In this house, you find skills you didn't know you had," he said.

After they had gotten something to drink and were once again seated, July suggested that Calicia sing for them. Ender smiled at his wife and nodded, expectantly. She stood in the center of the circle and looked at the floor for a moment, taking a deep breath and letting it out. Then, she looked up at everyone and began. The melody wafted through the air as if on wings of its own. Her voice was clear and sweet, with a hint of deeper tone only brought to the fore when the melody required it.

The song told of a traveler, lost in the mountains but unafraid because she is surrounded by beauty and majesty. Her heart is torn between finding the lost path and longing to remain in this beautiful place for the rest of her days. The music led the hearer up out of a valley and over the ridge. There the traveler sees for the first time that all along she has been moving parallel to the path she had thought was lost. She discovers that she need only scale the ridge to find this beautiful place again. It had always been there; she had merely been unaware.

As she sang, Calicia's face shone as if lit by the morning sun. When she was done, everyone waited in silence, waiting for the final notes to float off into memory. Quietly, she turned and took her seat with the others. Her audience burst into enthusiastic applause and she was obliged to stand again and take a bow. Ender leaned over and kissed her on the cheek; his eyes bright with delight.

"Roggin Steelsmith," said Rummel. "What would you do for us next?"

"Me?" said Roggin.

"You're the only Roggin Steelsmith here," said Yorgun, looking around.

"I just know history," said the younger Dwarf, running a hand through his close-cropped hair.

"History it is, then," said Rummel. "What shall we hear tonight?"

Roggin thought for a bit. "Stoggle Steelsmith and the Great Dragon," he said.

"Oh, now this I want to hear," said Owler, leaning forward.

Roggin started a bit shakily but was soon fully engrossed in this age-old tale from the annals of the Steelsmiths. He described the Great Dragon in vivid detail, down to his broken claws and ragged wings. He introduced them to the legendary Stoggle Steelsmith who forged thirty axes before he had one he knew would slay the dragon. Roggin took everyone into the cave and made them wait with bated breath as Stoggle Steelsmith found a crack in the rock where he could hide. The final fiery battle was fierce and frantic, ending in the death of the monster who had caused the deaths of so many others. When Roggin sat down, he was breathless and soaked with sweat. So were most of the others!

Ender stood up and applauded. "Well told! Well told!" he said.

Rummel grinned at the young Dwarf. "That is high praise, my boy. Ender is, himself, a Tale Weaver!" he said.

Roggin turned a deep red and bowed very low.

Owler was next. He stood in the center of the room, slowly turning, looking around at this and that as if weighing his choices. He caught a twinkle in they eye of Lady July. She nodded almost imperceptibly, as if she knew what he was thinking. Suddenly, he dropped to a crouch and called for lots of noise. This was provided by all who could clap, sing, shout, or play an instrument. When it rose to a fever pitch, he leapt right over his own chair and proceeded to bring from the table all manner of silverware, goblets and plates, some still nearly full of food.

They all watched in astonishment as he began either to balance them one on top of the other, or juggle them. As smooth as silk, he could slip a platter full of meat up on top of an already teetering stack of dishes without endangering a drip of gravy. Then, with one hand, he kept several miscellaneous utensils up in the air at once (including one or two sharp knives) while quickly grabbing a bite to eat or tossing a biscuit to an unsuspecting member of the enraptured audience. This grew more and more complicated until he was balancing a stack of plates on his head, juggling a knife, fork and spoon with one hand and three crystal goblets with the other while weaving his way in and out between various pieces of furniture—all this while sipping water from a glass held tightly in his teeth. In the end, he returned each object to its original place on the table without missing a beat.

Finally, he took a deep bow, somersaulted over the back of his chair and collapsed into his seat. Everyone else cheered and hollered.

When things finally quieted down a bit, Owler clapped a hand to his forehead and exclaimed, "If I had been polite at all, I would have washed them before I finished!" This brought hoots of laughter from Rummel who assured him it was entirely unnecessary.

Ender was the last to entertain that evening. He told the story of two ancient, wrinkled tortoises. Though both were terribly slow, they had argued for centuries about which of them was the fastest. At long last, they finally agreed to a race that would settle the feud once and for all. Choosing a starting point, they set off, making up the rules along the way. This was simple enough. They were well matched in speed and although their pace was frantic (for ancient, slow, arguing tortoises), they could still carry on arguing.

Eventually, they got to arguing about where they should place the finish line. Neither would agree to any spot the other one chose. This went on for days, both of them trudging along side by side disagreeing about where to end the race. It seemed that there would be no answer to this problem, but they did eventually decide, after about a week, that the fastest one should be allowed to decide the finish line. Of course, neither could outpace the other, so the finish line was nowhere to be seen.

The tortoises began to tire. They had been a week and a half without food, running as fast as tortoises can run. They had come far from the water in which they were used to living and were very thirsty and dry. Still, neither of them was willing to turn back for fear that the other would declare the place the finish line and claim the victory, so on they went, shoulder to shoulder, each one hoping the other would give up first. Off to their left was a pool of clear water surrounded by muddy banks and reeds and grasses, but neither of them would turn.

They were about to drop when along came a great vulture. The huge bird landed in the dust by the tortoises and asked them what they were doing all the way out there in the desert. They told him of their wager and he laughed a great cackling vulture laugh. This made the tortoises very angry and they picked up the pace a little. The vulture hopped alongside them.

"I'll tell you something," said the carrion bird. "It doesn't matter to me which of you is the fastest. By tomorrow evening, you'll both be fit for my supper. I sincerely doubt the winner will have gone much farther once I have finished off the loser."

This made the tortoises even angrier and they pressed on harder than ever. The vulture flew a short distance ahead and waited for them until they came near. Then he flew a little further on, all the while eyeing them hungrily.

When the vulture was still some way off, one of the tortoises suddenly turned toward the water. "The water is the finish line and I'm in front!" he shouted over his shoulder as his competitor forged ahead.

Suddenly realizing the rules had changed again, the other tortoise tried to make the turn. Too late did he realize that his wobbly limbs had run out of strength! He collapsed in the dust. He drew his legs and head into his shell, but he soon perished out the hot sun.

The vulture ate the tortoise as he had predicted. When he was done, he went over to check on the "winner." Also as predicted, the other tortoise hadn't gone far; he never made it to the water.

The vulture, on the other hand, got two good meals and lived for many years thereafter.

This tale was received with much laughter. The hour was late and July announced that it was time for bed. The guests all insisted that they would help clean up first, but when they turned to look, the table was already clean. July showed them to their beds in the other room and wished them all sweet dreams, one by one.

Roggin was the last to be bid good night. July knelt by his bed and smiled at him. "You have much to do, Mr. Steelsmith," she said; "but you are well able to do it. I have had my eye on you since you were very small—before we met, actually."

"Then you remember the incident with the chisel, don't you?" asked Roggin.

July smiled and closed her eyes. "Of course I do," she said. When she opened her eyes again, he saw only kindness in them. "I have also seen what you have become since, and for that I am grateful."

"Why?" asked Roggin.

"Because the time is coming when you are needed most," she said.

"What do you mean?" asked Roggin. On the one hand, he was genuinely curious, but on the other hand, he simply did not want her to say good night and leave just yet.

"Do you have the steel Rummel gave to you?" asked July.

He rummaged in his pocket and brought out the perfect metal ball.

"May I hold it?" she asked. He handed it to her and she rolled it between her open palms. It began to glow as if being melted down again, but it did not lose its shape. She stopped rolling it and the glow faded slowly away. When it was no longer glowing, she handed it back to him and asked him to look into it. He could see the room in which he and his companions lay. If he concentrated on any one of them, he could see that person clearly, just by staring harder.

"If you wish to find someone, rub the marble between your palms as I have done and look deeply into it. You will see your friends wherever they are. It may help you know where to look."

He put it back in his pocket and she leaned over and kissed him on the cheek. "Good night, Roggin Steelsmith," she said. "Trust your dreams."

* * *

The stone ceiling arched high overhead, its intricate carvings lit by a hundred torches lining the walls of the Great Hall of the Steelsmiths. Massive columns rose solemnly from the floor to the dizzying heights above. On the polished granite floor, tables and chairs had been arranged. Glittering candelabras graced every table, casting warm light on platters and great, shining steel bowls filled with fine food and ale. The smells filled Roggin's nose. Moving between the tables were many, many Dwarves, all dressed in their finest. Happy conversation filled the room as fathers walked arm-in-arm with their daughters and mothers with their sons.

"May I take your arm?" asked a lovely voice just behind him.

Roggin wheeled around. "Mother!" he cried.

"Good to see you tonight, son," she said, taking his offered elbow. "The Steelsmiths have been looking forward to seeing you, too."

"I'm hardly dressed for it," said Roggin.

"You wear your father's jerkin," said his mother. "He would deem that worthy enough."

He looked down to see that he was dressed in the shining metallic threads of the Steelsmiths. The last time he had seen his father wear this was on his funeral pyre.

"Mother," said Roggin. "Why—I mean, how are you here? You look so young! If you are here...then...is Father here?"

"Right here," said an older Dwarf who was almost as wiry as Roggin and wearing the same jerkin. "And your grandfather is here as well." Behind him stood another, even older Dwarf wearing the same colors.

Grandfather strode directly to Roggin, took him by both shoulders and stared him straight in the eye. Then he looked back at his own son. "You're right," he said. "It's a good face."

"It's an even stronger heart," said Roggin's mother.

"Yes," said Grandfather, giving Roggin a good, solid shake; "and there's a backbone to go with it."

Roggin smiled. "Grandfather, I never met you," he said.

"More's the pity," said Grandfather; "but at least we get to now."

"How is this possible?" asked Roggin.

His mother squeezed his arm. "The Lady July."

"Enough talk," said Roggin's father. "The Steelsmiths have gathered. Stoggle has called for order."

"Stoggle Steelsmith?" asked Roggin.

Grandfather grinned. "Aye, the old fellow has expressed some curiosity about you."

"How could the legendary Stoggle Steelsmith know anything about me?" asked Roggin as his father and mother steered him between the tables toward the center of the room.

"Word gets around, boy," said Grandfather.

Roggin found himself standing alone in the center of the Great Hall of the Steelsmiths, surrounded by banquet tables at which sat hundreds of Dwarves dressed in all their family finery.

On a simple wooden throne, directly in front of Roggin, sat a Dwarf dressed in a hooded cloak which covered most of his ragged leather armor. His breeches appeared to have been repaired numerous times and his boots were nearly worn through. His tough, wrinkled left hand rested on the heel of the haft of an upended axe. The simple, single-bladed weapon with its head on the floor was in far better shape than the rest of his gear.

"So this is Roggin Steelsmith," said the Dwarf on the throne, drawing back his hood.

Roggin gasped. If he looked into a glass a hundred years hence, he would expect to see this craggy visage staring back at him. The silver hair was close cropped, somewhat haphazardly, as if cut by his own hand with a razor-sharp knife. The sparse, white beard tapered down to a ragged sort of point at his collarbone. The intensely green eyes focused clearly on Roggin.

"Don't look so surprised, lad," said the Dwarf. "You're bone of my bone, flesh of my flesh, though a thousand years lie between us. I'm glad to see the Steelsmith vein continues."

"You're Stoggle Steelsmith, then," said Roggin; "the slayer of the Great Dragon."

"The tale grows old," said Stoggle. "Had you been in my place, you would have done the same."

"I should like to think I'd try," said Roggin.

"You'll get your chance," said Stoggle. He stood up and looked around the room. "Where's that scamp Yorgun?"

"On my way," said Yorgun.

Stoggle Steelsmith smiled grimly as the Chief of the Dwarves approached the center of the hall. "Are you sure you want to do this?" he asked.

"I am," said Yorgun.

"The we shall begin," said Stoggle.

A loud roar outside the hall startled everyone from their seats. Roggin's hand went immediately to his hip, but he discovered he wasn't wearing a sword.

"Grandfather!" he hollered. "Give me your sword!"

Grandfather shrugged. "I haven't got one."

"Father!" shouted Roggin. "A weapon! A knife, anything!"

"Sorry, son," said his father, stepping back.

The roar outside grew louder. Flames swept through the huge doors into the Great Hall of the Steelsmiths. The scent of burning raiment and flesh soon followed. Dwarves were falling left and right, some already charred beyond recognition, some still on fire. Tables were overturned as people panicked, desperately fleeing the flames that swept through the doors.

Roggin turned to Yorgun and Stoggle Steelsmith. "I don't have a weapon!" he shouted.

Neither of them responded.

In through the huge doors came the snout, then the crown and then the long, snaking neck of the Great Dragon. The beast turned its head to one side and snapped at a crowd of Dwarves, catching several in its sharp teeth, cutting them in half with a single bite. Streaming blood, it licked its scaly chops as it turned the other way, snapping at the fleeing Dwarves on that side. Several more were summarily beheaded. The Great Dragon swallowed them down like morsels, opened its mouth again and spewed flames across the banquet hall, setting the tables on fire.

Roggin saw a few of the elder Dwarves, all dressed in their finery, moving in toward the Great Dragon their ceremonial swords drawn. He turned once again toward Stoggle Steelsmith. "They'll be killed," he yelled above the din.

Stoggle nodded slowly.

The younger Dwarf felt his cheeks burn. Holding out his hand, he bellowed: "Give me that!"

Stoggle hefted his axe off the floor and jammed the haft into Roggin's hand. Roggin wheeled around.

The Great Dragon was halfway into the room now. Smoke, ashes and the pungent smell of burnt flesh choked the hall.

Roggin stuffed the axe into his belt and raced for one of the huge central columns that supported the high ceiling. Grasping for handholds and footholds, he climbed quickly. The dragon was still coming into the room. Every turn of its reptilian head brought death to a dozen Dwarves. The roar of its fiery breath shook Roggin's chest even as he climbed.

About fifty feet up the column, Roggin came to an overhanging ledge that blocked any upward progress. He could not reach out far enough to get a grip on it. Pulling the axe from his belt, he extended his reach and caught the rim. As he swung out over the open space, he hooked his leg around the arm that held the axe, hanging upside down as he reached up with his other leg to hook his heel on the ledge. When he found purchase, he hauled himself up until he could roll onto the narrow shelf.

All hell had broken loose below. The dragon was in the center of the room now, thrashing the floor with its tail. The smoke was getting thicker, but Roggin could always find the fiery mouth. Flames shot across the room, answered by cries of agony. The Great Dragon swung its head this way and that, raking the room with fire. As it swung close to the column, Roggin jumped onto the monster's massive crown.

He hit hard, lost his footing, and jammed his axe into the scaly scalp. It caught just enough to keep him from being tossed off. The Great Dragon roared, spewing hot flames and swinging its head about. Roggin's axe began to tear free. He seized one of the many spines on the dragon's brow, but he could not hang on for long. The dragon twisted its neck and Roggin felt himself slipping off the side of the brow. He hooked his leg on the root of the dragon's ear and somehow swung himself inside. The sweltering heat all around him singed his skin but he was able to brace himself as the beast waggled its head violently. A huge claw reached in but Roggin burrowed deeper, getting hotter still as he scrambled away from it. The heat burned his lungs.

He braced his shoulders against the ear canal and swung the axe hard, burying its blade into the wall. The roar that erupted from the dragon shook him to the core but he yanked the axe out and swung again. Scalding blood spewed out, drenching him and searing his hands and arms. Still he kept swinging. The dragon slammed its head against something, almost dislodging Roggin, but he continued to hack a ragged hole. He could see nothing. He could hear nothing. Everything was pain, but he swung again and again, hoping his strength would not wain too soon. The canal grew slimy and he could not hold his position. He slipped and scrambled even deeper into the spiraling canal, still swinging, cutting his way through a drum-like skin and continuing to hack. Everything had gone black. He was running out of air. Still, his arms brought the axe to bear again, again, again. The hot chamber into which he had crammed himself was being flung about. Finally, he could hang on no longer and he felt himself sliding out through the hot, blood-slickened canal, dragging the axe to try to slow his exit. He landed on stone paving and, for a moment, everything went black.

When he came to, all was quiet. Flickering flames still licked at the charred remains of fine banquet tables. Blackened bodies lay strewn about the floor, some of them still holding their ceremonial swords. Roggin's entire being felt like it was still burning, but he forced himself to turn around. Behind him, the massive hulk of the Great Dragon blocked his view of the rest of the room. It was not moving.

The wiry Dwarf dragged himself up off the floor. At his feet, in a pool of dragon blood, lay the axe of Stoggle Steelsmith. Weakly, he picked it up.

"Congratulations, lad," said Stoggle. "Well played. You slew the Great Dragon."

"For what?" asked Roggin, looking at the destruction all around them.

"For your own sake," said Stoggle; "and for everyone's." As he spoke, the lights returned to the Great Hall of the Dwarves. Once again the vast room was filled with a great feast. Generation upon generation of Dwarves, all dressed in their finest, began to cheer.

Roggin felt the pain slip away. When he looked down again, his father's jerkin was shining and clean; there was not a drop of blood on it. He spun around. The dragon was gone.

"Now, if you'll excuse me," said Stoggle, as the cheers finally died down; "someone here insisted on having a few moments with you before you leave."

Roggin looked up to see his mother, her eyes brimming with tears. He took her arm. Then he turned back to Stoggle Steelsmith. "Your axe, sir," he said, holding it out. "I borrowed it."

"Good choice," said Stoggle, taking the weapon back. "It's done this before."

"Come," said Roggin's mother, steering him away from the center of the hall. "Just walk with me awhile and tell me how you are. Are you getting enough to eat? You look a bit thin. You really need a wife, dear. Are you ever going to get married?"

"Mother, I have no idea!" he said, rolling his eyes.

Just then, he looked up to see a Dwarf maiden passing by the open doors to the Great Hall. Even from this distance, her beauty was obvious. She stopped and looked inside, caught his eye and then quickly hurried on her way.

"Maybe someday," said Roggin.

His mother's eyes twinkled. "She looks like a fine lass," she said.

"Mother, I don't even know her," said Roggin. "I've never seen her before."

"Well then," said his mother; "you keep an eye out for that one."

* * *

"I'm glad you're here," said Yorgun.

Stoggle Steelsmith set his flagon of ale on the table and clapped a hand on his great, great, great, great, great, great grandson's shoulder. "So am I," he said. "The ale is good. You should invite me more often."

The Chief of the Dwarves laughed. "I had nothing to do with that, and you know it," he said.

"Indeed," said Stoggle. "The Lady July weaves these dreams. We merely appear when needed." He looked hard at Yorgun. "Talk to me, lad," he said. "Why did you need me here tonight?"

"I wanted to see him tested properly," said Yorgun.

Stoggle nodded. "And you wanted it to be a real test, with a real dragon."

"Yes," said Yorgun, taking another swig of ale; "and not just any dragon. You were the only one who actually knew the Great Dragon well enough to make this a proper test."

"Glad to oblige," said Stoggle Steelsmith. "I wish I'd been as quick as this young fellow when I fought it."

"Really?" said Yorgun. "We were always told you dispatched it by splitting its skull with a few quick blows to the crown."

Stoggle guffawed and slapped the table. "More than a few quick blows," he said. "If the beast hadn't first slammed its own head on the wall, I'd never have finished him off."

"You're too humble," said Yorgun.

Stoggle snorted. "Not hardly, but I'll tell my mother you said so." He looked around the Great Hall. "This is how I remember it," he said. "Just like this. Are you going to have it restored finally?"

"I'm two hundred and thirty years old," said Yorgun; "and we have war on the horizon. If I make it through this, I'll be glad for a few years' peace before I join you."

"Hmm," said Stoggle. "Maybe our young friend will do something about it."

"I believe he might," said Yorgun.

* * *

Calicia found herself lying out in the sun on a grassy hill. Her husband was stretched out beside her. He looked so peaceful, she wondered if he was asleep, but then he rolled over to face her.

"Hello," he said, smiling. "Now we have time to talk."

"I suppose we do," said Calicia; "but this is only a dream."

"No ordinary dream, though," her husband replied. "This is a dream from July Stoneboots. You are not alone. I am here with you, and you are here with me. You could wake me and ask me, but I will simply tell you not to have bothered."

"Really!" she said. "What a marvelous thought! Well, remind me tomorrow when we wake up that I laughed and tossed a dandilion when you said that!" She plucked a nearby yellow tuft and deftly flicked it onto his chest.

He laughed and brushed it off.

Calicia sat up and looked around. "Shall we loll about on the grass, or shall we go for a walk by the river?"

"Walk by the river," he said, standing up and reaching for her hand.

She let him help her up and took his arm while they strolled to the river bank. How amazing, she thought; I can see his face, feel him breathing, even smell him.

As they walked, he told her everything that had happened in the east, filling in the gaps she had suspected were there when he related his tale earlier that night. Somehow, in this landscape, in the realm of pleasant dreams, the amassing of evil forces did not seem so frightening. Even the Midnight Stone, still in his pocket, was not a thing of power.

Calicia told him of their exploration of the tunnels and he sympathized with their frustration. They did not dwell on it long.

They continued on beside the quietly rolling river for miles, speaking of anything or nothing as the mood struck them. Time did not seem to pass, nor did the sun sink to the west as they walked. They grew tired, the contented sort of tired one feels after a leisurely afternoon stroll.

Near a bend in the river, a shade tree grew, standing alone on a carpet of cool grass surrounded on three sides by the sharp curve in the slow-moving water. At the base of the tree, they lay down again and rested, he with his head on her lap and she with her hand on his chest. They lay there forever it seemed, watching the breeze ruffle the green leaves overhead, listening to the birds flying from from bank to bank over the water. Neither one noticed when the other peacefully drifted off to sleep.

CHAPTER 45

Necrowights

Calicia awoke to the smell of breakfast. It took her a minute to remember where she was. Rolling over, she felt Ender's back next to her in the bed and nudged him gently.

"You laughed and tossed a dandelion," he said with a grin.

Calicia gasped. "I did, didn't I!"

Yorgun was in the other room extolling the virtues of hot coffee. Apparently, everyone else was already up.

Ender and Calicia came out to join the rest. When the meal was finished, the guests rose again to help with the cleaning up, but Rummel insisted that they not trouble themselves and, with a wave of the hand, he cleared the table! All evidence of the meal simply disappeared.

"How do you do that?" asked Owler.

"It's quite simple," said Rummel. "Everything here is made from the stuff of the mountain beneath us. We rearrange it to suit our needs. Just now, I simply returned what we did not use to its source."

They left the table for the hearth and sat again in their chairs, which were now drawn into a circle.

When Yorgun had described their search in detail, he asked Rummel what he thought.

For a long time, Rummel said nothing, only sat with his chin in his hand, staring straight ahead, deep in thought. Presently, he cleared his throat.

"It seems the ancient menace is out," he said, finally. "How the Necrowights have eluded us, I do not know, and that troubles me."

"Can you not sense them?" asked Yorgun.

Rummel shook his head. "And I do not know why," he said.

"But you knew we were under attack from the smoke when you came to us in the Great Hall, didn't you?" asked Roggin.

The grand old fellow looked at him sadly. "No, I did not know what had attacked you," he said. "I could tell that you had come in contact with some deep magic, but I saw the cut and thought Brian's wound was from the Valenblade. I have never been certain which side of the world could depend on that weapon. I have many questions, too, Roggin, and few answers."

"From all I can tell, the Valenblade either killed the smoke or sent it away," said Roggin. "All Brian had to do was cut them with it. Their screams were horrific."

Stoneboots raised his eyebrows. "Is that so?" he asked. "It is said that the Sochhmahrim can be destroyed by the Valenblade. I would not be surprised if this power over the Faeries carries over against other forms of life. How was Brian wounded in the leg?"

"He grazed it with the knife as he struck at the smoke," replied the Dwarf.

"So the deeper trauma may have been from the Necrowights themselves," said Rummel; "not the Valenblade, as I assumed."

"Still, this blade becomes more mysterious by the hour," said Ender. "The Great Master brought it to me but did not tell me where he got it, what it was, or why I should keep it for a strange visitor. Brian refused it, to begin with, only taking it when I insisted, but it seems to function as if it were meant for his hand."

"There is more magic about it than I can decipher," said Stoneboots. "Back to our main concern, though: all evidence indicates that the Necrowights are loose. The smoke is only their latest form. Long ago, they were proud warriors, but the Dark Master brought them under his spell and they fought for him against the Stonecutter and against me."

He told them the full tale of how the warriors were beaten back by the Stonecutter in a pitched battle in which every last one of that great clan fought to the death. However, Morvassus had already charmed them. No sooner had Dain cut them all down than they returned as smoke-bodied ghosts, more dangerous than before. Dain enlisted the Lord of the Mountains to make a hole for them where they could be trapped forever. Dain lured them into the deep with the Midnight Stone and Rummel sealed their fate.

"I, myself, encased them in the rocks, never to set them free, or so I thought," said Rummel. "Their power must have increased somehow, for they can hide themselves from us."

"We know every weed that sprouts on the hills," said the Lady July; "but neither of us can sense the Necrowights. We do not know when this changed."

"Somehow the barrier has been breeched and they have kept hidden from me," said Stoneboots. He turned to Yorgun. "My dear friend, I fear we have failed you utterly."

The Chief of the Dwarves shook his head. "No, my dear Rummel," he said. "It is we who have brought this threat back out into the world. We delved too deep without consulting you."

"We would have stopped you," said July; "had we known they were just below you. We cannot see them."

"If the smoke has escaped," said Yorgun; "there is really no way of gathering it together and sealing it up again. Closing the tunnels is pointless. Still, there has been no word of them now for days. We found no trace of them when we scoured the tunnels—not even the scent of them. Wherever they are, they are hidden away again."

Rummel rubbed his eyes and then turned to Ender.

"You hold the Midnight Stone," he said, quietly. "I assume Palanthar entrusted it to you."

"He did," said Ender. He drew the black marble from his pocket.

"What is it?" asked Owler. "It makes my skin prickle."

"As well it should," said Rummel. "There is more magic in that small, black marble than any number of wizards could hope to wield. It is the Stone that Dain, himself, cut from the center of the Shioroth, but it is one of two identical twins. Morvassus split the Stone, and the Twin has the same strength."

"Where is the Twin?" asked Roggin.

"In Morvoth," said Ender. "The Great Master charged me with reuniting the Stones, but he said it must happen in the hands of one who will not wield it for power's sake alone."

"But the Midnight Stone can be wielded, can it not?" asked Yorgun.

Ender nodded. "It can, but that is more difficult than one might think."

"Even so," said the Chief of the Dwarves; "it may be the only way to rid us of the Necrowights. If the Stonecutter drove them into their prison, perhaps the Midnight Stone can force them to return and our good Mr. Stoneboots can encase them once more. As the wielder of the Stone, you must carry some authority over them."

"A risky endeavor," said Rummel. "The Midnight Stone and the Twin are of the same power. I expect the Necrowights will follow whichever Stone will lead them, but the wielder would have to be very strong to control their magic. Dain himself was a mighty sorcerer. He knew the power of the Stone intimately and wielded it with that knowledge. Our friend here will find the Necrowights are significantly more difficult to manage."

"We need to find them first," said Calicia, gently.

Owler spoke up. "I've been listening to the history and I wonder now that if the Necrowights are aligned with the East, they may have simply gone there as have all the other forces that are gathering."

"A distinct possibility," said Rummel.

Ender nodded. "I've been thinking the same. I recommend that I search for them, alone, using the Midnight Stone."

No one said anything for several minutes as each one silently considered the alternatives.

"I see no other way," said Ender. "Any other option is either a waste of time or reckless endangerment."

"Agreed," said Rummel.

Yorgun's jaw tightened and then relaxed. "How will you do this?" he asked.

"With the Stone, I can travel where you cannot," said Ender. "If the Necrowights are there, the Stone will draw them to itself, I believe. If they are not there, I would be the only one who could be sure."

"Again, I agree," said Rummel. July nodded as well.

"What if you do find them?" asked Calicia.

"I cannot help you seal them in again," said Rummel. "I cannot imprison what I cannot sense."

"True," said Ender. "If I cannot contain them, I will banish them."

"Can't you just destroy them?" asked Roggin.

"No," said Ender. "Such an act plays into the hands of darkness. I cannot take that risk. If I can remove them, I will, but I will not destroy them."

Yorgun shook his head. "That I cannot agree with," he said. "They must be destroyed."

"Once the Midnight Stone begins to destroy," said Ender; "the wielder finds it difficult to stop. The distance between thought and action becomes shorter and shorter. The danger is that the destructive tendency will overcome the wielder; that has always been the greatest risk in using the Stone."

"You seem strong enough to manage it," said Yorgun.

"That is what turned Morvassus into who he is," said Ender. "I have suffered already from the power of the Midnight Stone battling lesser foes. From what I hear, this is an even greater foe."

"So the risk is greater," said Yorgun. "I mean no disrespect."

"None taken," said Ender. "Yes, the risk is greater."

"Understood," said Yorgun. "If we are agreed that you should go alone, is there anything we can do to assist you?"

Ender thought a moment. "No," he said. "And I will not keep us waiting. I will meet you at the Shioroth."

With that, he vanished.

* * *

Ender pursued the smoky throng through the cracks in the rocks. They were a cloud of wraiths before him, racing forward at great speed. He had cast a net behind them that they could not penetrate, but he could not seem to gather them all together, so he kept driving them forward.

They slipped through a thin crack and suddenly entered a vast cavern with many pools of still water separated only by dirt paths just wide enough for a horse to pass. The Necrowights fanned out across the waters and turned to face the Stonekeeper as his presence entered the chamber.

Then a voice whispered in a foul tongue. "What is it you want from us that we may satisfy your quest? What must we do for the Midnight Stone?" The voice came from nowhere in particular. It seemed as though all the beings spoke together through the one voice.

"I want nothing from you," said Ender, surprised that he could not only understand the language, but that he could speak it also.

"Surely you desire something," whispered the voice again. "One with such power must always have designs. Our strength is great, and we know what we do. We have always obeyed the Stone. We must obey the Stone. What, then, does the Stonekeeper wish?"

Ender seemed to have drawn closer to them. His body began to expand to fill the cavern. As it did so, he could feel the Necrowights coming into direct contact with him, their own smoke-like bodies merging with his, as if now they were a part of him.

They began to move about slowly, seeping into every empty space. Ender felt like he had become more space than body. The intrusion filled him with a deep chill. Instinctively, he held grasped the Stone more tightly, even though he had no hands with which to grasp it. The smoke roved about relentlessly within him, as a poison permeates the blood and the blood travels throughout the body.

Ender said nothing.

"No need to speak," said the voice, somewhere near where his heart should be.

The smoke had now infiltrated his entire being and he felt deathly cold. His very soul seemed to be encased in a block of ice. His thoughts stumbled and faltered. He felt his grip on the Midnight Stone begin to weaken as the cold crept into his mind. The deeper the cold crept, the more numb and frozen he felt.

"Now, Stonekeeper," hissed the voice, directly into his thoughts; "you have a choice. You must decide what it is you want. If you do not choose, you are unfit to carry the Stone and we may rid you of it. If you choose ill, we may kill you for it. Know now that you cannot destroy us; we were formed by one stronger than you. Know also that we can destroy you if you prove unworthy of the Stone."

Ender strained to control his thoughts as the cold reached the Midnight Stone itself. The small marble of darkness that he had guarded so carefully now felt very light, as if someone else also held it.

"I am not willing..." he began, but a sharp stab of freezing pain shot through him.

"We have no interest in what you are *not* willing to do," spat the voice in his head. "Tell us what you *will* do—or is that too much to ask?"

The pain shot through him again. The Stonekeeper tightened his grip on the Midnight Stone, but it made no difference.

"How tightly you hold the Stone proves nothing," hissed the voice. "We wonder more about the strength of your mind, but we will test the body, nonetheless."

Cold and searing pain wracked Ender's expanded body but he could not move. The Necrowights were everywhere at once, their frenzied motion starkly contrasting with his petrified form. They were turning his mind to stone, it seemed. He could not muster the wits to fight them. In a moment, the Midnight Stone would be easily lifted from him and he would be left powerless. Desperately, he tried to hold on.

"Do something soon, Stonekeeper, or you will perish," sneered the voice. "Command us, if you can. Fight us if you dare. You cannot survive much longer."

Forcing himself to speak, Ender said: "You may not remove the Stone."

It seemed to him like a pitiful proclamation, but it had an immediate effect on the Necrowights. They stopped their movement and waited.

The cold was almost unbearable, but Ender willed himself to speak again. "What I will do with the Stone is none of your concern." With every word, it became easier to speak. "If I wish to reunite it with the Twin, I will do so in my own hands." The cold began to recede from his heart. His will entwined around the Stone once again.

Ender could feel his body begin to consolidate. The Necrowights bled from him rapidly as he grew smaller and smaller. The voice was no longer breathing in his mind, and his heart began to warm again.

"I will choose what I will chose when I choose to do so," he said, finally. "No one tells me when to decide. That is for me alone, and I say that as long as the Midnight Stone remains in my keeping, it will serve the greater good. Now hear and obey: leave these lands and return to your master. You shall not stop until you have passed beyond the Mirrak-Haas. You shall touch nothing on your way. Now GO!"

With a great howling, the Necrowights gathered together and flew directly toward him. Ender stood his ground. They did not touch him as they swept past and continued eastward through the tunnels. They were under orders from the Midnight Stone and they would obey. Down the passages they flew, screaming and wailing, with Ender close behind. Suddenly, they broke out into daylight.

The Necrowights billowed out from a small grove of trees like thick smoke, swarming toward the tree wall that surrounded the Shioroth with a great shrieking and wailing. Ender emerged behind them, driving them forward, but they sped directly toward the city.

South of the Shioroth, a lone runner approached with magical speed. Holren's white beard streamed out behind him as he rushed through the grass toward the smoke. Before the Necrowights could reach the tree wall, the wizard plunged into their midst with an explosion that shook the earth. The wraiths whirled about in chaos. Another blast sent them fleeing eastward like wisps of foul-smelling smoke running through the grass.

Ender and Holren pursued the wraiths beyond the city, chasing them through the fields and across the hills. They came to the Bridge over the Carven Canyon when the sun was high. There the Necrowights quickly crossed and disappeared into the Abandoned Land, their speed increasing as they drew closer to Morvoth.

As the Stonekeeper and the wizard came to a stop at the Bridge, the Small Giants emerged from below.

"Necrowights!" said Thisvane. "How did they ever break loose?"

"This bodes very ill," growled Rifgar. He pointed to Ender's hand. "I see from what you carry that you have news."

"The Midnight Stone," acknowledged the Stonekeeper. He held it up for them to see.

"Then Palanthar has passed on," Gullen said, solemnly.

"Would that he were with us still," Ender replied.

"Who is your friend?" asked Gullen. "It seems the Necrowights run from him as well."

"This is Holren Avan-Ihlac, the Firebringer," said Ender. "I know of no one else who has entered the realm of the Golrakken and rescued a friend."

"The mark of the Stonecutter is on you, Holren," said Thisvane, with a bow of the head. "It's good to know a wizard of such strength, especially now. We have seen patrols of Black Warriors at a distance every night for several days. When you did not return this way, Ender, we feared the worst. We are glad to see you safe, but where will you go from here? War is brewing; we can smell it."

"Courage, then," Ender replied. "Those of us who remain must gather to the Shioroth. I will return there and confer with the others."

"As will I," said Holren.

"What of the Midnight Stone?" said Rifgar. "What do the others say?"

"Not all of them yet know that it exists," said Ender. "There may be conflict when they learn the truth. What do you say?"

Thisvane looked at him hard. "Did Palanthar give you the Stone of his own free will?"

"He did," answered Ender.

Thisvane studied his face carefully and nodded his great head. "Then tell the Shioroth that we guard the Bridge against all who speak ill of Ender Stonekeeper."

"I take great heart in that," said Ender. "Send word if help is needed at the Bridge."

*   *   *

"Something approaches, m'Lord," rasped the Gray Warrior.

Karkaan turned his dragon-helmed head to look westward. A smoky shadow was streaming down the mountainside.

"It has the mark of Morvassus on it," said Karkaan.

"It does, m'Lord," replied the lieutenant. "Shall we address it directly?"

"We may not have a choice," said Karkaan. "It comes our way."

The smoke slipped down the talus slope and fanned out across the dry meadow before coming to a halt in front of the Golrakken army.

"What are you?" asked Karkaan.

The Necrowights moved like a low fog across the ground, shifting but not advancing or retreating.

"We would ask the same," they said.

"Then we are even," said Karkaan, the permanent leer on his face betraying nothing.

"We serve the Midnight Stone," said the smoke. "Whom do you serve?"

Karkaan shifted easily in his saddle. "We serve the Dark Master," he said. "May the Stone reunite in his hands."

"Then we are agreed. There is a warrior who holds the Other," they hissed. "He is not the Stonecutter. He pursued us here, but he did not cross the river."

"Where are you going?" asked Karkaan.

"To the Dark Master," hissed the smoke. "We must. Why are you out here in the dry lands?"

"We are taking over a stronghold," said Karkaan. "The Dark Master's request."

The black smoke swirled along the ground. "Your magic is strong," it said; "but do not think that ours is any less."

"We bring no challenge," said Karkaan. "Follow the Dark Master and we shall all be the stronger for it."

"Agreed," said the smoke. "We depart now."

"Begone then," said the Golrak.

With that, the smoke swept away eastward, quickly abandoning them.

The Golrakken army watched them go.

"Will they be a threat?" asked the lieutenant.

"I think not," said Karkaan. "They need nothing from us, nor we from them. Onward!"

The grey company continued forward toward Akka-Illin.

CHAPTER 46

Through the Mountains

"He found them," said the Lady July.

"And he drives them eastward," said Rummel, sitting back in his chair.

It had been a long wait.

"How can you tell?" asked Calicia.

Rummel smiled. "We can sense the Stonekeeper," he said; "even if we cannot sense the Necrowights themselves."

"Is he in trouble?" asked Calicia.

"Not that I can tell," said Rummel, looking to his wife.

She shook her head. "He has overcome whatever trouble may have been," said July.

"There was some trouble then," pressed Calicia.

"It seems so, but only for a moment," said July. "Your husband is very strong."

Calicia nodded and looked down at her hands in her lap.

Yorgun took a deep breath and let it out. "We are grateful for his help," he said. "The Dwarves will stand by the Stonekeeper and the Lady Calicia, wherever we can."

"Thank you," said Calicia.

"Roggin," said Yorgun; "we should see to our people. The Dwarves should know who is responsible for their protection."

"Good," said Rummel. "I will carry you two to the Great Hall."

"Will the Lady Calicia and Owler accompany us?" asked Yorgun.

"If that is best," said Calicia.

"I recommend that you do," said Rummel. "I also suggest that we venture eastward toward the Shioroth by nightfall. It has been many centuries since I stepped outside this range. I think it's time I paid the Elves and the Faeries a personal visit."

Once outside, he grew large and bent down to allow everyone to climb up onto his shoulders. Then, with great, loping strides, he cleared the ridge and set off for the entrance to the Dwarf tunnels.

* * *

The arrows came quickly, one after the other but none landed. Rummel simply raised a hand and absorbed them.

"This is Yorgun, Chief of the Dwarves, with Roggin Steelsmith," bellowed Yorgun from Rummel's massive shoulder. "Jorfen, Gluckburn, lower your bows. If you fire again, somebody might get hurt."

"Yes sir," said the two dumbfounded Dwarf guards, aiming downward and slowly releasing the tension on their bowstrings. "We didn't see you, sir."

"Anybody hurt?" asked one of the them.

"Not this time," said Rummel. "Oh, and you'll need these for later." He held out his hand and let seven arrows slide to the ground in front of the guards.

"One more," said Owler, tossing another arrow onto the pile at their feet.

"Is this...are you...I mean...is it really...?" stammered the other guard.

"Yes, Jorfen," said Yorgun. "This is Rummel Stoneboots, Lord of the Mountains. With us are the Lady Calicia and Owler, of whom you have already heard."

Both guards dropped to one knee and bowed. "Our apologies!" said Gluckburn.

"No apology needed," said Rummel. "Please stand up, brave soldiers! I am pleased to see that nothing approaches the Dwarves without a challenge!"

"Indeed," said Yorgun. "Now, Rummel, if you will let us down, we will go in." As Rummel bent down, Yorgun called to the guards. "Let the elders convene! We have news, and counsel must be taken. Send word!"

Gluckburn called for a runner. When the young fellow arrived, he took one look at Rummel Stoneboots and stopped to stare with his mouth wide open. Gluckburn had to tell him the message three times before he actually understood and ran off down the tunnels.

Then the guards bowed very low and stepped aside to let them pass. Rummel shrank to a size that would allow him to walk upright in the tunnel and followed Roggin inside. They walked quickly to the Great Hall. Those who saw them pass fell in behind them, whispering among themselves. Soon a great crowd was with them. Hushed, they entered the throne room where all the seats stood empty.

Yorgun strode directly to his throne and directed the others to sit, with Roggin on his left and Calicia at his right hand. The crowd entered with them and lined the walls as the elders came in and found their own places around the table.

Once they were all assembled, the Chief of the Dwarves stood up and motioned for silence. The crowd fell silent. Yorgun made brief introductions. Though even the crowd lining the walls seemed to know who all the guests were, there were still gasps around the room as Rummel was formally announced.

"We have news, both good and bad," said Yorgun, sitting back down. "First, the smoking menace is gone, but it was not cleared by any of us here." He nodded to Calicia on his right. "The Lady Calicia is here representing her husband, Ender, who single-handedly swept the death smoke from our mountains."

There was a great murmuring around the room.

"What was it?" asked Murdun, the next eldest of the Dwarves. "Some say it was wraiths."

"It was," said Yorgun. "They were Necrowights, sealed in the depths by Rummel and Dain, the Stonecutter, ages ago. Our deep digging freed them from their prison. Ender sent them away."

"Where have they gone?" asked someone else.

"How do we know they're all gone?" called another

"What happened to them? Why weren't they destroyed?" said yet another.

Yorgun raised his hand for silence.

"If I may speak," said Rummel.

Yorgun nodded.

Rummel stood up in the throne room, towering over everyone. "Ender carries the Midnight Stone," he said. "Some of you have heard the legends. They are true. The Stonecutter cut one black stone from the center of the Shioroth. It rules over all. Dain handed it down to Palanthar, whom some of you know. Palanthar has handed it down to Ender. When Ender ordered the Necrowights from the tunnels, they had no choice but to obey and flee."

He let that sink in a moment.

"You may note that Ender did not destroy the wraiths," he continued. "Only the Stonekeeper knows the risks that come with the wielding of such power. This was not the time."

"How could it not be the time?" asked another of the elders.

Yorgun addressed this himself. "I asked the same thing," he said. "The time for such destruction must be prepared for carefully. He who holds the Midnight Stone must be clear on what should and should not be done. We can suggest, but we cannot advise. We haven't the experience nor the responsibility."

"What if they come back?" asked another of the elders.

"They have other obligations," said Yorgun.

"They are beholden to Morvassus and will serve him," added Rummel. "That's where they have gone."

"Yes, but all the worse if they come back then, eh?" shouted someone from the crowd.

"My husband risked a great deal to rid you of them," said Calicia, quietly. "He would not make it easy for them to return."

Yorgun stood up and looked slowly around the room. "Let me make this clear," he said. "This company set forth a week ago to find an enemy which no known weapon could kill. We risked our lives searching day after day, but to no avail. A great master wizard has come to our aid and singlehandedly removed this threat. For that, we should all be grateful." He glared at the others. "And that is the GOOD news!" he said. "I told you there was bad news. There is war afoot on a much larger scale, and the Dwarves cannot just bury themselves in the mountains and wait it out. We have allies. We have friends. We are one of the many peoples who inhabit this world and all are under threat from Morvoth. Already someone has come to our aid. The Dwarves must cast their lot with the West, or the East will overtake us, sooner or later."

"So you are commiting us to war," said Murdun.

"War does not wait on commitments," said Yorgun; "but we need to know how we will defend ourselves and to whom we are allied." He looked around the room again. "And I want to know who of my people will come with me to the Shioroth to meet the enemy."

Roggin stood to his feet. "I will go," he said.

"Good," said Yorgun. "I needed a strong commander. Who else?"

"Myself," said Rummel. The crowd grew hushed. The Lord of the Mountains continued. "Whatever we can do to protect the good people who live on our mountains, my wife and I will do. This is no time for mere heroics: even I am not safe from the enemy, but if ever the Dwarves needed to muster their strength, now is the time."

One by one and two by two, the Dwarves came forward, some of them rough, hardened tunnel carvers, tough in body and soul; some young and strong, all of them with eyes clear and heads held high. Each of them nodded to Rummel as they passed and came to stand beside Roggin and Yorgun.

"Very well," said Yorgun. "Those who do not fight in the fields of the Shioroth will strengthen our position here. Those of you who stand with us, collect your gear. We march within the day. Spread the word throughout the tunnels: Roggin Steelsmith gathers an army. Let all who will fight for our allies come to him here. For now, the council is dismissed."

There was a great murmuring of voices as the Dwarves left the hall.

Roggin turned to Yorgun and looked at him curiously.

Yorgun caught his eye. "You're wondering why I made you the commander," he surmised.

"Exactly," said Roggin.

"I needed someone who would take the weapon from the hands of a legend when the need required it," said the Chief of the Dwarves.

Roggin's eyebrow wrinkled.

"Yes," said Yorgun. "That dream was not yours alone. I watched you slay the Great Dragon with Stoggle Steelsmith's own axe. That's when I knew I had found my commander." He chuckled at Roggin's bewildered look. "Don't be so surprised, lad. That's how the Lady July works her magic. Two may dream together, if that is what is needed."

"I had no idea," said Roggin.

Yorgun clapped him on the back. "For now, Commander, I suggest you concentrate on the ordering of your troops. Find your leaders and let them choose their companies. Those who are not chosen by others, keep as your own command."

"My friends," said Rummel Stoneboots; "I must go. Keep your lines of communication open to Pellían, Val Ellia and the Shioroth. I will take our companions eastward and will meet you there, but I will come quickly if you require me."

He took young Roggin's hand and shook it firmly. "Best of luck, Roggin," he said. With that, he began to grow. "Come with me," he said to Owler and Calicia. "We have friends to meet, and a long journey eastward thereafter." After they climbed onto his shoulders, he simply turned and disappeared with them into the wall.

* * *

"Horses!" said Owler, standing on Rummel's massive shoulder and pointing to the dunes; "and I see Brian on the ground beside them."

"And a Faerie flying nearby!" shouted Calicia happily.

"I see three horses," said Owler. "A Small Giant, an Elf maiden and a man."

"Grisbane, and Eulian I know," said Rummel. "I look forward to meeting this third rider." Within two strides, he was standing in front of them. Two of the horses whinnied with recognition and the third stood proudly by, alert but unafraid.

"Hale, Rummel!" shouted Grisbane. "And whom do you have with you?"

"Owler and Calicia!" cried Annie, flying up to greet them. "It's me! Annie!"

"Annie! A Faerie indeed!" said Calicia. "Oh, you beautiful girl! I am so glad to see you well!"

Rummel lowered himself so his passengers could dismount. "And you must be Arvon Dustrider," he said.

"I am," said Arvon, his face lit with wonder. "You must be Rummel Stoneboots!"

Rummel nodded. "It is good to finally meet you," he said. "You are well, I hope?"

"Better than ever," said Arvon. "Good enough to venture out of the desert."

"This is good," said Rummel. "So the Carthiss is no longer needed?"

Arvon shook his head. "No longer needed. Sadly, though, she no longer lives."

Rummel looked puzzled. "How so?"

"Something seems to have paralyzed her, and the sun caught her fully exposed," said Arvon. "She is only stone now."

"A strange time is this when all things are changing," said Rummel. "I also am going eastward for the first time in a long time."

"Do you have news from the tunnels?" asked Eulian.

"Yes," said Rummel. "The black smoke has been routed."

Grisbane let out a sigh of relief. "What was it?" he asked.

"They were Necrowights, wraiths from a battle long ago," said Rummel. "The tale is long. Ender, the husband of Calicia here, drove them from the mountains and sent them eastward."

"Eastward?" exclaimed Eulian. "Why?"

"That is another long explanation," said Calicia. "We are going to meet Ender at the Shioroth."

"Will you come with us?" asked Rummel. "All of your help is needed. War is brewing, and it will soon cross the Volgan River. We cannot avoid it for long."

"We can meet you there in a few days," said Grisbane. "These horses have ridden hard."

"Then let me carry them," said Rummel. "I'm sure the Men of the Green Stone will be happy to have them back. Arvon, shall I carry your mount as well?"

Arvon patted his horse on the neck. "No," he said. "I think not. This fine mare can freely roam now. This desert is her home." He dismounted, pulled the blankets from her back and gently lifted the halter from her head. The mare whinnied and nuzzled him.

"Go home," he said, patting her on the head. The horse would not turn to go. Arvon gave her a solid slap on the flank but she still refused to go.

"Do you like it here?" he asked. She simply waited. "Then do as you wish," he said. "Thank you for your service." He rubbed her side and nodded to Rummel. "I'm ready."

"Then we will go," said Rummel. He stooped low and they climbed up onto his shoulders. Without another word, he fairly flew toward the hills, leaving the mare to graze on the scrub at the edge of the dunes.

Soon, Rummel had grown to such a size that his head was level with the highest summits. He raced furiously through mountains. Peaks of hard granite and ice rose before them and slipped behind them just as quickly. Valleys opened up beneath them only to become hills and mountains once again. They crossed great rivers known only to the Lord and Lady of the Mountain and strode through forests where no footprint had ever fallen.

When they came to Val-Ellia, Rummel did not wait for a greeting. Instead, he peered directly down into the open top of the Elven palace and called loudly for the Queen of the Elves. Several attendants went scurrying to find her while Bostler came running out of the kitchen to see what all the fuss was about.

"You should announce yourself with proper decorum!" scolded the Chief Cook, shaking a wooden spoon at the Lord of the Mountains. "On the other hand, if you came by more often than once in a lifetime, you wouldn't need to." He stepped aside as Hassila entered.

The Queen of the Elves did not seem pleased to have been summoned. She dismissed her Chief Cook. "Back to the kitchen with you" she said. Turning to Stoneboots, she said: "Now, what is this about?"

"I bring you good news and bad," said Stoneboots.

"I will have the bad news first," said Hassila. "Tell me."

"The Necrowights have been released," Rummel growled.

"That bodes evil," the Queen answered. "Is there more?"

"Have you felt their passage here?" asked Stoneboots.

"We felt nothing," said the Queen.

"Then, of ill tidings, that is all," said Rummel. "Let it be also known that the Carthiss is dead and I bring your daughter with me alive and well."

Eulian waved from the giant's shoulder but her mother took no notice.

"Sorry for the lack of ceremony, but I must be quick," said Rummel. "I am looking for Thorval Lighthammer. Is he here?"

"No," replied Hassila; "and I do not pretend to know where he may be."

Rummel nodded. "If you find him, let him know I wish to see him. He is sorely needed. Time is on the march; the Blue Stone must march as well. Eastward, great evil amasses. Gather your strength and come quickly, Hassila! We will meet you at the Shioroth. For now, Eulian rides with me. Farewell!" With that, he was off.

"You played that one rather deftly," said Eulian from his shoulder as Rummel waded through the lush forests.

"Good," Stoneboots responded. "They will march all the faster knowing you are already there."

"I don't know," said Eulian. "Something strange is going on down there. Did you feel it?"

Rummel frowned. "Yes," he said; "but I cannot imagine what it is. Your brother is not there."

"Perhaps he is on patrol," said Eulian.

Rummel did not break stride. "Perhaps so," he said. "There are Elves in the woods hereabouts." He squinted into the distance. "Look. Do you see that?"

"See what?" asked Grisbane.

"It's like a blue sheen across the sky," said Rummel. "Ah, we have passed through it." He stopped and looked back. "From this side, I cannot see it," he said. "Hmm...that gives me one more question for Thorval Lighthammer when we find him."

He waded through the forests, up over the next ridge and into the valley beyond.

CHAPTER 47

The White Stone, the Green Guard and the Crimson Tower

The sun was setting behind the Western Mountains. Far in the distance, the Shioroth cast a long shadow toward Ender and Holren as they returned from the Volgan River. They did not run now; both of them felt the need for quiet and rest.

Up from the south flew a huge, bat-winged creature, its long neck stretching out ahead and its sinuous tail trailing out behind. With a rush of scaly wings, the indigo dragon landed in the field, a short distance away from the two travelers.

"Gasslic!" called Holren. "What a fantastic surprise!"

"Holren?" hissed the dragon. "Sssssso good to sssssssee you! I thought you were gone!"

"So did I," said the wizard; "but we both seem stronger than ever!"

"Yesssssss," said Gasslic. "Sssssso it sssssssseemsssss!"

"Glad to see you," said Ender.

"Then you will be doubly glad," said the dragon, crouching to allow a passenger to climb down. "I bring Thorval Lighthammer."

The old Elf bowed and shook their hands. "Well met, if not too late," he said. "Had I been more free at home, we might have known each other sooner."

"Pleased to make your acquaintance, no matter how late," said Ender.

"I will come straight to the point," said Thorval. "The time has come to reveal the Midnight Stone."

"It seems the thing is not so secret after all," said Ender.

"The dragon said nothing," replied Thorval. "I even asked him outright, but he would not tell me, so there has been no betrayal. I have long known of its existence, though I did not know its whereabouts until we landed just now. When I discovered the Great Master was not in Thihanan, I feared the Stone had been lost. I am certain I was not the only one looking for it."

"Indeed," said Ender. "Arienne, already knew."

"Is that so?" Thorval rubbed his chin. "Good, then. Our position is stronger." The Elf gazed off into the distance at the black darkness that clouded the eastern sky.

"If the Great Master did not reveal the Stone years ago, what do we gain by revealing it now?" asked Ender.

Thorval grinned in a pained sort of way. "Despite my constant nagging, Palanthar refused to reveal the Midnight Stone. He wished for North Agoria to run its own affairs without it. The other Stones must submit to its authority. As long as the power was balanced on this side of Thihanan, he said he would rather 'meddle' than rule. His subtle influence was enough to maintain that balance."

Thorval paused for a moment and looked south toward Thihanan. "He was right, perhaps, for his time, but we are already at war, whether we know it or not, and we can no longer simply meddle." He looked hard at Ender. "The Midnight Stone must be reconciled," he said. "It must happen in your hands. That is the only way to defeat Morvassus. If you do not try, we perish. The Golrakken will triumph over the Shioroth and Black Warriors will rule Pelnara. The Dwarves will fall to the sword or to the Necrowights. Not an Elf will remain in Val-Ellia; goblins will fester and rot in the forests. Utter calamity shall befall us all if you stand back. The Stonekeeper must act, and Palanthar has passed that responsibility on to you, Ender."

Ender said nothing. Bringing the Midnight Stone out of his pocket, he felt its magic surge through his body once more. On the one hand, it promised him more power than he could possibly need to complete this task. On the other hand, he knew it cared nothing for him or those he loved.

"There is no certainty of success," he said.

"Indeed," said Thorval. "Still, if the Stonekeeper does not take the lead, the power of the Midnight Stone only weakens the efforts of the others."

"Does it indeed?" Ender raised his eyebrows.

"It does already, by its mere presence," answered Thorval. "The Midnight Stone rules all, even if the Stonekeeper chooses not to act. The other Stones may challenge, but they cannot overrule it."

As Ender held the Stone he could feel the faint pull of the Twin, even this far from Morvoth. "The Dark Master succumbed," he said. "If I fail, the Stone will reconcile itself not in my hands, but in the darkness of Uzzim-Khail."

"It is the curse of experience to know what there is to fear," said Thorval.

"Can we help in any way?" asked Holren. "There must be something we can do."

Thorval nodded. "Our unity provides the best support. The more we can unite behind the Stonekeeper, with our hearts strong and our intentions clear, the stronger he will be. Arienne das-Lammethan will be with us, and I believe her trust in her husband is well founded. Rohidan will not stand in the way of the greater good. Arvon Dustrider will rally to us, if he can be freed, and I trust in the wisdom of Grisbane and the other Small Giants. The keepers of the other Stones must see for themselves and choose. Be bold, Stonekeeper. There is no turning back."

"I suggest, though, that when you reveal the Stone, my presence would be more disruptive than helpful," said Holren.

"Most likely so," said Thorval.

"I will return to my wife, then," said Holren. "You can find us with the Men of the Green Stone."

Ender nodded his head. "Let us go, then, and be done with it."

"Farewell, Stonekeeper," said Holren. "I will await your call." He set off westward into the last rays of the sunset.

Gasslic allowed Thorval to climb aboard his back once more and they lifted off into the cool air, further away from the Abandoned Land, away from the dark cloud of the Morve, toward the uncertain strength of the Shioroth. Holding the Midnight Stone, Ender flew along easily beside them. Below, they could see the shadowy shape of Holren running through the fields.

* * *

The city lay in troubled sleep under the watchful light that glowed in the throne room of the White Tower in the Uppermost Garden. The light flickered feebly, wavering on the brink of extinguishment, but then recovered.

"He struggles with the White Stone," said Thorval Lighthammer, over the muffled beating of the dragon's mighty wings.

They landed on the wall that ringed the circle of grass surrounding the pool. A woman approached them from where she had stood hidden behind the White Tower.

"I am glad you have returned," said Arienne, bowing to them as Thorval dropped down to the cool grass and Ender materialized beside him. "It is time."

Gasslic reached his long neck over to the Stonekeeper's ear and whispered something to him. Ender nodded, and, with a graceful dive, the dragon launched itself from the Tower and sailed off across the fields to the north.

"Should the High Council convene?" asked Ender.

"No," said Arienne. "By then it may be too late. Falnor brings news of strange behavior by the Pelnaran King. From his report, Raealann's allegiance to us seems to be vacillating. I have wondered about this, myself, recently. I have reason to believe that Hassila is yet on our side, but I doubt she will welcome the arrival of an even higher authority. Her obligation to the White Stone is fulfilled grudgingly even now."

"Let the wisdom of Rohidan lead the way once again," said Thorval. "If he accepts the Stonekeeper, the rest must choose either to align themselves or break completely. Such is the obligation of the Stones."

As they spoke, the light in the White Tower flickered and went out. They waited in silence for several minutes before the door at the base of the tower opened. Rohidan stood in the doorway, his wrinkled wings hanging wearily behind him. He held the stone door open with a trembling hand, steadying himself against the frame. Then, carefully, he stepped out onto the bridge and walked the catwalk to the center and down again to join them. As he did so, he seemed to slowly gather strength.

"You have something to tell me," he said, quietly, as he stepped down onto the grass.

"I hold the Midnight Stone," answered Ender; "the one that was cut from the center of the Shioroth by Dain, himself. It was passed down to me by the Great Master, Palanthar, whom you may know carried it for many centuries. I do not come as a usurper, only to lead. If we act together, we are stronger."

The elder Faerie nodded. "I had suspected as much. My control over the White Stone always faltered when Palanthar was near, and my ability to wield the White Stone has waned considerably since you came from Thihanan. It takes all my strength now to hold it and make it do my bidding. What are your intentions, Ender, Keeper of the Midnight Stone?" He took a shuddering breath and let it out.

"The Midnight Stone I carry has a twin," said Ender. "That Stone is of equal strength, and it lies in Morvoth, in the hands of the Dark Master himself. I intend to reconcile the two in my hands, finally stripping Morvassus of his power."

Rohidan looked deeply into the face of the Stonekeeper. "So the power I felt in the presence of your former master was indeed similar to the one that rises in the East," Rohidan observed. "Answer me this: why will you now do what he would not?"

"Until now, the threat from Morvoth has remained dormant," said Ender.

Thorval continued the explanation. "The Great Master did not want to interfere in North Agoria, as long as the powers already in our hands kept it at bay. We cannot survive alone now. The Midnight Stone must lead. It was cut from the Shioroth before ever the White, Crimson, Green or Blue were carved. Its authority is over all."

"I have long wondered about this," said the Elder Faerie; "but I am curious why we did not have this discussion before. I did not know you knew so much about it. Did you know all this, my dear?" he asked his wife.

"I had suspicions, as we all did," said his wife; "but I was not clear concerning the powers of the Midnight Stone. Palanthar did not explain them to me."

"Nor to me," said Thorval Lighthammer. "I knew only that its authority was supreme." He turned to Ender. "The time has come for openness. Tell us what we need to know."

Ender looked from one face to the other. "Its power is nearly instantaneous," he said. "Thought becomes reality very quickly. When it does violence, it incites even more violence. When it does good, it acquiesces to the will of the one who wields it. I find that using it to heal allows me to more easily manage my thoughts. The discipline required to wield it properly can be exhausting. I have had to use it for both defense and healing. The former is dangerous; the latter, miraculous.

"But it has one intention of its own," the Stonekeeper continued. "It wishes to be reunited with the Twin. Nothing else matters more to the Stone itself."

"By supporting the Stonekeeper, we strengthen both him and ourselves," said Lighthammer. "The proper order of things will be established, and we can move forward." He nodded toward Rohidan. "You, yourself, said the White Stone becomes unmanageable in the presence of the Midnight Stone."

The Elder Faerie nodded. "I understand," he said. Reaching into his robes, he brought out the White Stone and held it out in his open palm. He stared at the glowing stone as one might stare at an old friend who is soon to leave for places unknown. Then, suddenly, almost violently, he flung it straight up into the air high. Like a shooting star, it blazed forth in the waning twilight.

"Choose!" shouted Rohidan. The stone exploded with a blinding flash and a sharp crack that ricocheted off the distant mountains. Then all was quiet.

Rohidan took a deep breath and straightened his shoulders. No longer did he seem gaunt and weary. "It has chosen," he said; "and so have I: the White Stone will lead no more."

Arienne gasped. "Is it gone?" she asked.

Ender shook his head. "What was his by right has not abandoned him," he said.

The elder Faerie opened his palm. The White Stone appeared in it, intact.

"It is the same," he acknowledged. Once again it glowed in his hand. "You did not take it from me by force; nor would you acquire it as the opportunist. Lead on, Stonekeeper. May wisdom guide your every move."

"Let us pool our wisdom," Ender responded, with a deep sigh. "We will need every bit of it we can muster."

* * *

The Necrowights swirled about the throne of the Dark Master. "What is the will of the Stonekeeper?" they hissed.

Morvassus stood up from the throne and stepped to the edge of the pool. "You would follow me?" he asked.

"Of course!" hissed the swirling smoke. "We have always followed you."

The Dark Master smiled. "Such loyalty should be rewarded," he said.

"Yes!" whispered the Necrowights.

"You should serve no longer," said the Dark Master.

"But we serve YOU, m'lord," hissed the smoke.

"Long enough," said Morvassus. "You should no longer serve me, you should become me."

The smoke swirled in agitation. "How can this be, m'lord?"

"It is a simple thing," said Morvassus. "Release your power and meld with me. It is but a matter of will." He held out the Twin.

The smoke thrashed about chaotically. "Does the Dark Master will it?" it asked.

"I do," said Morvassus.

"Yes!" shrieked the Necrowights.

Morvassus held the Twin to his chest. One by one, the Necrowights separated themselves from the swirling cloud of smoke and entered Morvassus' chest through the dark stone in his hand. The smoke slowly diminished as each of the wights melded with its master. Each transaction gave the Dark Master a great jolt of energy. With a rush and a roar, the last of them entered through the Twin.

The Dark Master dropped to one knee and held his face close to the pool in front of him, drawing up even more power from the unfathomable depths. Once more, he stood to his feet.

"Captain!" he called.

The officer entered the room and snapped to attention. "Yes, m'lord."

"Prepare for departure," said Morvassus.

* * *

Falnor came in from the stables and sat down heavily on a chair by the table in his quarters. Aaron was there waiting for him.

"*Still* no word from Pellían," said the captain, as if saying it with the proper incredulity might render it false.

The truth of the matter remained: no contingent had been sent from the Green Stone. Worse yet, there were rumors of trouble in Pelnara.

"One more day, and I will take ten riders with me to see what has become of the Birdman," said the captain.

"What difference does one more day make?" asked Aaron, bluntly.

"Kirin here, sir, with official word from the king!" said a young officer outside.

"Finally!" said Falnor, standing up and heading for the door. "What is it?"

Kirin, his young face blazing with controlled fury, stepped smartly to the side and made room for the mustachioed captain who brushed past him, followed by two remarkably burly soldiers.

"The boot is on the other foot, Falnor," said Captain Achor, twirling the curled ends of his moustache. "The king has written his orders." He tossed a rolled parchment onto the map table. "Read it for yourself; I've already seen it. His Majesty conferred with me before he sealed it."

The seal was clearly stamped with the imprint of the king's ring. Falnor broke it and opened the scroll. He scowled. "The king authorized this?" he said. "It makes no sense. It doesn't even sound like him."

"Temper, temper, Falnor," said Achor. "Not very flattering is it? If you had left the prisoners in my hands, this might not have happened, but no, you had it your way. 'Direct insolence and blatant misuse of power,' I believe it says. That is treason, Falnor. You leave in one hour. I, myself, will choose a horse for you. I wouldn't want you to take anything important from this honorable edifice."

"What does the letter say?" growled Aaron, still sitting down.

"Shut up," snapped Achor. "I'll deal with you later."

"Rude," said Aaron. "What does it say?"

"You can tell him," said Falnor.

"Tell him yourself; I no longer answer to you," said Achor. "One hour!" With that, he turned on his heel and left the room with his men.

The young officer stayed behind. "He already told me, sir," fumed Kirin. "They have no right."

"Indeed they have," said Falnor, dropping the parchment on the table and sitting down on his bunk. "I have been stripped of rank and have been ordered to report immediately for duty in the king's stables as a tack steward."

"For relieving that ass of his 'prisoners?'" Aaron grunted. "The king must be out of his mind, pardon me for saying so. Did he give the orders himself?"

"That is his seal," nodded Falnor. "What I find strange is the language. It sounds like Achor, not the king—and Achor has been given charge in my stead. For some reason, we are all to return to Pellían. Something is afoot, and I don't like it."

"Speaking for myself, sir, and I might speak for many others also, I will not follow this Achor anywhere. If you are to be tack steward, then I would rather be your stable boy than a commander under Achor."

"That's kind of you, Kirin, but I would watch what you say from now on," said Falnor, quietly. "Your duty lies with the Green Guard; is that clear?"

"Yes sir," said Kirin. "Permission to be dismissed, sir."

"Granted," said Falnor.

The young officer turned and left the captain's quarters.

"What will you do now?" asked Aaron.

"This morning, I would have been able to answer that; at the moment, I am not sure." Falnor returned to the map table and scanned the positions he and Aaron had marked. "The danger is here at hand and I have trouble at home. Perhaps the king has decided that the Green Stone has fulfilled its obligation to the Shioroth and he wants to gather his forces home. Or perhaps he is bewitched and no longer does what he does of his own accord."

"A bit drastic, but it could well be either," said Mari coming to the open door. "I detect trickery. Captain Achor is not telling us everything."

"M'lady, if you can discern something I cannot, I would appreciate all the information you can give," Falnor replied.

"I asked him if the king was well, and he lied to me," said the sorceress. "What the truth is, I do not know, but the king is not well at all, even in the estimation of the belligerent captain."

"Achor will die if he has done anything to harm King Realann!" hissed Falnor.

"I do not think what ails the king is the captain's doing," Mari continued; "but there is indeed something amiss in Pelnara."

Falnor turned quickly and motioned for Aaron and Mari to follow. "I need your help," he said, strapping on his sword. "If there is trickery, the men should not suffer for it. Achor will be gathering them even now!"

They flew across the yard toward the soldiers' quarters where they could hear the voice of Captain Achor calling for all men to gather to Pelnara to protect their families and their king. The three entered the rear of the room and were immediately intercepted by ten swordsmen of the contingent from Pellían.

"Do not listen to him!" shouted Achor. "Our king has stripped him of his rank for insubordination. The same could happen to you!"

Falnor spoke quietly, only loudly enough to be heard. "The Pelnarans have always been free men," he said. "Even the king is subject to the law. The men of the Green Guard are chosen for their wisdom and good sense, none of which changes simply because their circumstances have changed."

"Silence!" barked Captain Achor. He yelled at the gathered soldiers: "Pay him no heed! He is a tack steward, nothing more!"

"Every Pelnaran tack steward has the right to be heard," Falnor returned, evenly. "Let those who must choose know their choices."

"There are no choices," said Achor, his voice rising. "Orders are orders, and these come from the king himself, sealed with his ring!"

"Tell me then," countered Falnor. "Is the king alive and well on the throne in Pellían? We have a Truthsayer here. Tell the men what you have to say in her presence."

Achor turned red and cast a glance at Mari staring at him from across the room. "I answer no questions from a tack steward."

"Lieutenant Kirin here, sir!" shouted Kirin standing to his feet. "A question, then, from an officer of the Green Stone to his superior, as allowed by law: Is King Raealann alive and well on the throne in Pellían?"

Achor glared at the young officer. "Fool!" he said. "You play a dangerous game!"

"The question stands, sir," said Kirin. "We await your answer."

The captain turned away. "He is as he has...always..." his voice trailed off. Mari's eyes bored into him. "I say... the king..." He looked up to face Mari and stopped short.

The soldiers looked from the captain to Mari, to Falnor, to Kirin, back to the captain. Achor was beginning to mumble something about a window and blindness. Mari did not let him free of her gaze.

"I repeat, sir," said Kirin. "Is King Raealann alive and well on the throne in Pellían?"

"He is... ill," said captain Achor. He tore his eyes away from Mari's gaze and angrily drew his sword. "I won't say it! You can't make me say it!"

"Say what?" asked Kirin, his hand on his own sword hilt. "Why will you not say if he is on the throne? You deceive, Captain! For that, I defy you!"

Achor's eyes burned. "Clear the room!" he shouted. "Those who obey the king's orders will follow me now!" He stared at the floor as he strode to the door.

Falnor, Aaron and Mari stood aside. The men who had come with Achor fell in line. The Men of the Green Guard watched but did not move.

Achor turned once more to face the room. "May the wrath of the king fall upon this company until none are left alive!" Motioning to his men to follow him, he left quickly for the stables.

Falnor waited until they were out of the room before he drew his sword. "Kirin, Norsen!" he called. "Make sure they leave emptyhanded!" The two officers brushed past him and hurried toward the stables.

"The Men of the Green Guard must choose," said Falnor to his men. "You are free to go and take care of your own in Pelnara. Those who remain here must realize that some may call us traitors. I believe the war has already begun. The Shioroth has always been our duty. Those who choose to stay with me here will defend this city under the direction of Ender Stonekeeper. Join me, if you will. Leave as you see fit."

Several of the men stood and took their leave. Falnor assured them they would have horses and whatever supplies they needed.

In the end, thirty men chose to remain at the Shioroth, including Lieutenant Kirin, Dorsen the Horsemaster, and his brother Norsen. Falnor drafted a letter to be sent with those going to Pellían, explaining their actions and appealing to the king and all Pelnarans for understanding.

"I doubt it will be read by many," said Falnor; "but I hope there are some with open eyes who know what is really going on in the castle."

✳ ✳ ✳

Brian and Annie walked in the Uppermost Garden of the Tower on a night with no stars. The growing blackness had blocked out both sun and moon since the day they returned from the desert.

"What are we waiting for?" grumbled Brian.

"I don't know," said Annie. "What would you do if you didn't wait?"

"Don't know," grunted the gruffen. "Anything."

They continued on around the perimeter of the grass, pausing to look across the valley to the east. Brian sniffed the air and stopped.

"What is it?" asked Annie, finally.

"Can't tell," he answered. "Wind smells different. Like death, but more spicy."

"Is it the Necrowights?" asked the Faerie.

"No, that's thicker. This is—don't know. Sharper." The gruffen growled and turned to go up the bridge over the center pool. He had not gone into the Crimson Tower since he had returned to the Shioroth.

"We should tell Ender," said the Faerie, standing on the grass.

"I want to see," he said.

He opened the door using the Valenblade and climbed the dark, spiraling staircase, feeling his way with a hand on the wall. The throne room at the top was

452

just as dark. He found his way to the throne and sat down, slipping the Blade into the slot in the armrest. Once again, the room glowed red, but this time it did not cause him any pain.

"Welcome, Valen-dak-Lammethan," whispered a voice that seemed to come from the room itself.

Brian looked out the windows. As he sat on the throne, everything outside appeared to be lit by a crimson moon. He could easily make out the trees and grasses on the hills and plains of the Abandoned Land to the east.

Dark figures roved across the fields. He stared deeper. Now he could see men on horseback, hundreds of them, riding in companies of forty and fifty each. They were spread out across the land in strategic positions along the Carven Canyon. As yet, none of them were within sight of the bridge that crossed the Volgan.

Brian looked further south and saw a familiar sight: goblins. All along the banks of the lower Volgan, the forests were thick with them. A large contingency of them was crossing a wooden bridge that had been built across the river. Leading the way, was a small man whom Brian recognized immediately. Taron Kaiss stopped in his tracks and Brian looked away quickly, hoping he had not been discovered.

Just west of the new bridge, Brian saw a battalion of men riding toward the Volgan river from Pelnara. At their head rode Captain Achor. Brian wondered if the captain knew the vast numbers of goblins he was riding to face.

Looking further east, Brian followed the line of the mountains up until his eyes lit on a dark fortress. Its highest tower appeared to have been recently repaired.

"MINE!" rasped a razor-sharp voice.

Brian found himself staring directly into the face of Karkaan Dragonhelm.

"What beast is this who sits on the Crimson Throne?" shrieked the Golrakken leader. "You are not fit to wield the Blade! Tell me, fool: how did it come to you? Did you slay Lazraak? SPEAK!"

Quickly, Brian yanked the Valenblade from the armrest and stood up from the Crimson Throne. The room went instantly dark. Fumbling around in the blackness, he found the wall and leaned against it awhile. Then he made his way over to the staircase and followed it downward, his heart still pounding in his chest.

Annie met him at bridge. "Thank goodness you're back," she said in a whisper. "What happened? My skin has been crawling ever since you went up there. What did you see?"

"They're everywhere," said Brian. "Everywhere. I think they saw me."

"Who?" said Annie, eyes wide.

"Golrakken," said Brian.

"Now we really need to tell Ender," said Annie.

They entered the moving chamber and were lowered down into the Shioroth. When the doors opened, they went quickly to the room where Ender and Calicia were staying, they were surprised to find quite a crowd already there.

"Everyone else seems to be here, too," said Annie.

"Good," said Brian.

Ender sat in the middle with Calicia. Mari and Holren sat beside Lia and Aaron, who was saying something to Owler. To their left, Falnor stood beside Tania and Arienne. On the other side, Rohidan conferred with Grisbane, and Arvon and Eulian spoke quietly with Rummel Stoneboots.

"We were going to send for you," said Ender, as Brian and Annie came into the room. "The principal players are all here. As usual, more is accomplished after the council than in the meeting itself." He looked at Brian's face. "You have bad news," he said. "Tell us."

Brian nodded. "I was in the tower," he said.

Everyone grew quiet.

"Go on," said Ender.

Brian recounted his experience on the Crimson Throne.

"Karkaan spoke to you directly," said Ender. "Where was he?"

"Somewhere on horseback," said Brian. "Not far from the river."

"They're in the Abandoned Lands," said Falnor. "They must be on their way here."

"Did you sense the Necrowights?" asked Ender

"No," said Brian.

"Good," said Ender. "We should not expose ourselves further."

"I agree," said Rohidan. "We will not enter the Towers."

"I wonder what Achor thinks he is doing leading a single battalion eastward with no support," said Falnor.

"What does he know about the Birdman?" said Holren.

"Nothing," said Falnor. "What I know, I learned from you."

"The Tree Wall will protect the Shioroth from the Golrakken," said Rohidan. "It has rejected them before."

"Their threat is not just from outside the city," said Mari. "Simply answering them is enough to turn one of us into one of them."

"Agreed. The Valenblade is the only true defense against them," said Rohidan.

"Just me and a knife," said Brian. "No good."

"From what you say, there are now two bridges across the Volgan River," said Grisbane. "I suggest we fortify the northern bridge where my kinsmen stand guard. The Valen and the Valenblade will be most useful there where the battle is contained. We Small Giants are capable of fighting off the Black Warriors, at least for now, but we will need his help against an attack by the Golrakken."

Falnor agreed. "If the enemy already crosses the southern fords at the new bridge, we must depend on my own kinsmen to hold them back. Achor may be overwhelmed, but many Men can still be mustered. I agree with Grisbane: the Golrakken must not be allowed to cross from the north."

Ender nodded. "Brian, will you help defend the bridge?"

The gruffen nodded. "Better than sitting," he said.

"I will go, too," said Annie.

"What will you do, Snowdaughter?" asked Rohidan, kindly.

"Whatever I can," said Annie, her face getting hot; "just like everyone else."

"Fair enough," said Ender.

"Can we go?" asked Brian.

Grisbane stood, towering over the others. "If the Stonekeeper has no more for us, we should join my kin immediately," he said.

"Agreed," said Ender.

"Tell Dorsen you are to be granted a horse," said Falnor. "You need speed."

"Thank you," said Grisbane. "We will send the mount home when we arrive."

The Small Giant, the Faerie and the gruffen left the room and headed quickly down the darkened hallway.

"Annie," said Grisbane.

"Yes?"

"We welcome anyone brave enough to fly in the face of the Carthiss to save her friends," he said.

CHAPTER 48

Beyond the Bridge

Morning thunder rolled through the cave of the Small Giants like a lion on the prowl. The sky outside was a dark gray, and the clouds swirled and churned. Lightning struck the peaks of the Mirrak-Haas, barely visible across the Abandoned Land. The air itself seemed to tingle.

Grisbane stood in the mouth of the cave and shielded his eyes from the bits of windblown rock and dust that whipped down the canyon. "Another torturous day," he growled. Even though they had arrived late the night before, he was already up. Sleep had not been easy.

A cry from Gullen at the lookout brought everyone racing up the path, weapons at the ready. Two hundred Black Warriors, were riding over the hills toward the bridge over the Volgan River.

Grisbane and his fellows were equipped with great clubs covered with steel and spikes. Brian had the Valenblade. Annie carried a sharp Faerie sword which suited her better, a gift to Grisbane from the Shioroth many years ago.

On the other side, astride their dreadful horses, the Black Warriors bristled with weapons. When all the riders were arrayed on the eastern edge of the Carven Canyon, one of them raised a horn to his lips and blew a blast: two notes that cut through the rush of the storm and the roar of the river below. Five riders came forward onto the bridge itself.

"Halt!" bellowed Grisbane from the other side. "None set foot on this bridge without our leave."

The party on the bridge stopped; one of them rode forward a pace.

"We are the soldiers of Morvassus himself!" he shouted. "The Dark Master sends us to the Shioroth. Surrender or die!"

"We choose neither," hollered Grisbane. "Many of you have fallen trying to cross. You will not pass!"

"One hour!" responded the Warrior. "Then we destroy you!" He turned and rode back with the other four.

"Now we wait," said Grisbane, as the five on the bridge returned to their troops.

"Just wait?" Brian queried.

"There must be two hundred of them," said Defgar. "Let them come to us."

They stood in the darkness of the stormy morning, speaking together in hushed voices.

The Black Warriors stood motionless, like statues carved from onyx, their wet armor gleaming in the harsh lightning that stabbed its crooked fingers into the Mirrak-Haas. For an hour, they stood this way, neither side making a move. The storm tapered off, the wind died down and a light drizzle set in.

At the end of the hour, the trumpet blew again. Then it became deathly quiet.

Once again the riders came, slowly, like cats approaching wary prey. They paused at the threshold of the bridge and the captain of the Black Warriors raised his spear. "What is your decision?" he called.

"We propose a sport," answered Grisbane.

Laughter rippled through the ranks of the Black Warriors.

"We expect little sport from you," said the other. "But tell me: what game do you propose?"

"Seven of us against seven of you," suggested the Small Giant. "Is that not fair?"

More laughter rippled through the ranks.

"You are no diplomat," said the Black Warrior captain; "and I am no fool, but I will gladly keep my reserves fresh while we dispatch you with only a few. I will send seven at a time, but if one of you should fall, it will be seven on six. If you are so confident, that should not concern you."

"We will meet your seven mid-span," shouted Grisbane.

"This had better work," said Rifgar, as they started across the bridge. "If we destroy them all, we will each have killed thirty horses and thirty men."

Seven Black Warriors selected by the captain rode to meet them. There was just enough room on the Bridge for them to ride abreast. When they came to the middle, they stopped.

Defgar reached the first of the riders, knocked the warrior's spear aside and crushed the horse's head with a backswing that was astonishingly quick. The dead animal fell sideways into the horse beside it, dropping both riders to the ground. The other horses spooked. Brian grabbed one mount by the bridle and pulled its head down so forcefully that the soldier on its back came pitching over top of it and fell into the Valenblade. Both horse and rider exploded into smoke and disappeared.

"It works!" yelled Brian. He swung at another horse. It, too, died instantly.

Rifgar and Thisvane knocked two more riders into the canyon. Grisbane pounded horse after rider against the stone pavement. Annie attacked from the air, darting in with lightning strokes, forcing the enemy to defend itself from above and below.

Still, every time a rider fell and vanished in a cloud of smoke, another rode up to take his place. Each time, the replacements seemed stronger and more skilled.

Brian was having more than his share of good luck. Though the Valenblade was shorter by far than the weapons of the Black Warriors, it cut through iron, wood and steel with ease. Brian hacked his way through, killing mounts and riders equally.

Still, the Small Giants were being pushed back across the bridge.

Suddenly, the army of Black Warriors surged onto the bridge in full force.

"Retreat!" cried Grisbane over the noise. "Retreat!"

The Small Giants turned and fled. Grisbane reached the threshold first, yanked open a small stone hatchway and reached inside.

"Wait!" bellowed Rifgar, pointing at the gruffen who continued to cut a smoking path through the Black Warriors. Grisbane froze.

"Brian!" yelled Annie. She could not get close. Arrows had begun to fly from across the river. Everyone hollered at Brian but he could not hear them.

All at once, a shout went up from the throng on the bridge and the Black Warriors scattered, racing eastward and westward. A dark shape swooped low over the bridge, knocking several riders into the canyon. The huge dragon seized Brian and soared skyward on thundering wings, dragging the gruffen eastward with it.

Annie felt the Ring of the Snowdaughter move on her finger. Her eyes followed a glint of steel arcing into the Carven Canyon below the departing dragon. The Valenblade was falling! Without thinking, she dropped her sword, changed to light form and raced after the Valenlade, catching it just before it was lost in the rushing river. She pulled up sharply and raced after the dark, winged shadow. A swarm of arrows surged behind her but fell harmlessly away.

Rifgar watched in horror. There was nothing he could do for either the Faerie or the gruffen. He turned and ran full speed from the bridge. "PULL!" he bellowed.

Grisbane hauled on an iron lever and dove to join the other Small Giants behind a low wall a few paces back from the cliff edge. Rifgar piled in behind him.

The Small Giants had guarded this bridge for centuries, but they had built a secret device as a last resort. Grisbane's pull set in motion a series of irrevocable actions.

An explosion severed the bridge from the western cliffs. Stones crumbled beneath the foremost Black Warriors, who plunged into the abyss. The remaining forces turned and retreated across the bridge at a gallop.

A second explosion rocked the pair of towers supporting the western half of the span. Then, with another explosion, the eastern towers also shuddered like ancient trees hewn by some gargantuan axe. The roadway beneath the Black Warriors buckled and began to fall. Yet another explosion blasted away the last part of the span on the east side. Horses, riders and weapons rained into the canyon along with the massive stonework as the shattered bridge fell thundering into the Volgan River.

* * *

Annie slowed from light speed and spread her wings to stay airborne. The dragon carrying Brian was getting away. She couldn't keep up. Every bone in her body ached and her muscles seemed to be losing strength even as she flew. Gusts of wind tossed her about, lifting her up into the sky only to drop out from under her or fling her sideways. Rain stung her face and pelted her wings. She struggled forward, aiming for the saddle between two peaks where she had last seen the dragon. As she rose on the updraft just before the saddle, she realized she hadn't the strength to clear the ridge. How could she be so exhausted? She dropped to the ground by a rocky outcrop, folded her weary wings and crawled under a boulder to get out of the rain, dragging the Valenblade in with her.

She grasped the knife with both hands to keep the sharp blade away from her. As she did so, the Ring of the Snowdaughter came in direct contact with the Valenblade's metal guard.

Blue lightning flashed out from between her hands. A jolt of energy bolted up through her arms and shot out from her feet, her back and from the top of her head. Blinding pain coursed through her veins. She could see nothing but a brilliant red. She did not let go.

For a long time, she lay shivering under the rock, breathing in shuddering, shallow gasps, her hands glued to the Valenblade, her eyes staring blindly forward.

The rain poured down incessantly, little streams running in rivulets past the rocky shelter. Annie saw none of it.

* * *

The Golrakken leader's eyes searched the increasingly stormy sky. Several days had gone by since he had sent the dragon off in search of the great furry beast that he now knew held the Valenblade. Karkaan's hands itched at the thought of finally holding that mighty blade in his hands once more. The treasure he had promised the dragon would be paid from the avaricious accumulations of Kafna, the Interrogator, the one whom Karkaan Dragonhelm had replaced as lord of Akka-Illin.

The Black Warriors had not welcomed the arrival of the Golrakken, but they were under orders from Uzzim-Khail and they would obey once again. Karkaan had barely settled into his new command at Akka-Illin, though, when he and his Golrakken were ordered westward. The Black Warriors were also sent, but on a different mission. Karkaan was pleased that his army also had the use of the Black Warriors' horses. The animals were fast and aggressive, much to his liking.

Dragonhelm searched the sky again. Rain had begun to fall. No matter, he thought. He might soon have the Valenblade in his own hands. A little leverage of his own against Morvassus would give the Golrakken a much needed advantage.

* * *

Brian clawed and bit, but the dragon did not loosen its grip. The gruffen figured he would be free by now if he hadn't lost his grip on the Valenblade.

Free or dead, he thought, considering the height at which they flew. For some reason, the dragon had not simply crushed him.

Maybe he wants to eat me, thought Brian. That seemed unlikely. The dragon had come from nowhere and scooped him off the bridge, not caring at all what happened to the Black Warriors. There seemed to be no reason for flying all that way just to pick up a furry meal to be eaten elsewhere.

The dragon continued to fly through the rain, ignoring the struggles of the gruffen in his grip.

* * *

The Dark Master rolled the Twin in his fingers. If Karkaan was using the dragon to his own ends, it would be a simple matter of redirection to determine what those ends might be.

"Come, Havvac," he said, sending his voice out across the land at a pitch that only the dragon could hear. "Whatever prize you have found, bring it to me. Whatever price you've been offered, I double it. Whatever punishment you have been threatened with...I double that as well."

* * *

Annie awoke to utter darkness. The rain had stopped. She lay there, trying to piece together where she was and how she got there. She remembered fighting the Black Warriors on the bridge, but what had she been using as a weapon? Ah, the Faerie sword, yes, but where was that sword now? One hand rested on the wet, gravelly ground. The other held the handle of a knife that seemed too big for her to wield comfortably.

The Valenblade!

She searched her memory until she remembered Brian dropping the Valenblade. Where was he? The dragon had snatched him from the bridge and she had given chase. She did not remember catching the dragon. Why had she stopped? Eventually, she recalled the debilitating weariness that had forced her to the ground.

She wriggled free from the position into which she had wedged herself under the rock. The strange weariness was gone, but every fiber in her body ached. She could see nothing. Cautiously, she crawled out, listening. She heard nothing but the runoff from the rain splashing over the rocks on its way downhill.

Lightning flashed off in the distance, giving her a brief glimpse of the jagged summits around her. The air felt cold. She had no idea where she was. She stared into the inky blackness but could see nothing more.

Switching the Valenblade to her other hand, she gasped as she felt the ring on her finger touch the metal guard. Everything became suddenly brighter, as if the full moon had just come out. She looked up at the sky and saw only clouds, but even they were more visible than a moment ago.

Startled, Annie stared around her, trying not to make any noise, even with her quickened breathing. Her eye noticed a twisted tree. To her alarm, it instantly seemed to come very close. She could see every crease in the twisted trunk, every broken twig on its tortured branches. Moving her gaze from one side to the other made her dizzy. She braced herself against the rock and stared straight ahead. Now the rocky slopes across from her filled her vision, every rock, every pebble standing out in sharp detail. Shifting the blade to her other hand again, Annie found herself in total darkness once more.

Experimentally, she touched the ring to the guard again. The "moonlight" view returned and she could see everything as if it were up close. Slowly, she lifted her gaze to the summit of one of the far peaks. Much to her surprise, she could also see across to the other side of it. To Annie, it felt like flying while sitting still. She could allow her vision to go off into the distance without actually moving from this spot.

This seems like what Brian described about the Crimson Throne, she thought.

She worked her newly acquired vision outward until she could see the saddle in the mountains where the dragon had disappeared with Brian. Random searching in different directions revealed scattered bands of goblins but no dragons. Most of the area was rugged, mountainous and utterly unpopulated. How would she find a gruffen in all this?

She decided to see if she could at least determine where she was. Making sure she kept the ring in metal-to-metal contact with the Valenblade, she looked back in the direction from which she had come, hoping to find the Volgan River. She had been scouting for some time when she came across a group of Black Warriors on horseback. The sight of them gave her the chills but they did not seem to notice her. She looked past them until she saw another group of Black Warriors coming a different direction some distance away, following a river downstream. The river looked large enough to be the Volgan. Further downstream, she saw a vast number of goblins encamped by a wooden bridge. The Black Warriors appeared to be heading for the bridge.

Moving her gaze upstream, Annie recognized the spot where the old bridge had spanned the Carven Canyon, but there was no bridge. She could see the two roads leading to the ancient crossing, one coming from the Abandoned Land, the other from the Shioroth. They were no longer connected. Two ruined gates stood across from each other on either side of the chasm, and four broken pillars jutted up out of the river below. These, and some new rapids surging over the rubble, were the only remaining evidence of that great stone bridge.

Annie's throat tightened. How had this happened? Where were the Small Giants? They were nowhere near the old bridge. She almost made herself sick again searching for them. Slowing her movements, she looked down the road and found them all heading for the Shioroth. From the speed at which they walked, she surmised that they had survived the battle intact. She almost called out to them but then realized they wouldn't be able to hear her. Taking a deep breath, the Faerie allowed her gaze to return to her immediate surroundings. Nothing had changed. She was still alone, wet and cold.

Resting for a moment, she looked around her for a better place to sit. Finding Brian was going to be a long, methodical search. She might as well be comfortable.

* * *

Brian lay quietly in the dragon's talons, biding his time. All attempts to free himself had proven futile. For now, he decided to rest until a better opportunity presented itself. He looked down toward the swiftly moving ground, hoping to get some idea of where he was. As they cleared a particularly high pass, he could just make out the movements of gray-cloaked riders on horseback below: Golrakken!

The rider in the lead called out with a rasping, crackling voice, barely audible over the storm. The dragon turned and circled back, losing altitude. Every bristle of fur on Brian's body stood on end. As the dragon passed over the Golrakken leader again, the rasping voice below called out a second time. The dragon circled around once more as the voice continued to call. Brian couldn't make out the words, but he didn't need to. The dragon flared, its great wings billowing with air.

Just as the great winged beast seemed about to touch down in front of the Golrakken army, Brian felt a deathly chill. The dragon responded immediately, thundering back into the air again, turning into the wind and beating its massive wings to gain altitude. Brian's heart was in his throat as the dragon strained upward. They caught an updraft and circled back overhead. The dragon turned again, hunting for another updraft. They lifted higher, further away from the Golrakken army.

The rasping voice of Karkaan was all but lost to the wind as the dragon climbed up into the cloud base. Then, once more, Brian's captor turned eastward and continued threading its way among the craggy mountains. Daylight was almost gone and the tips of the jagged peaks were lost behind the thick veil of the darkening storm. Still the dragon pressed forward, ever closer to the ground as the clouds drew ever lower. At one point they passed over a wide valley cut through by a river only to climb back up into the mountains again. Perhaps it was the gathering darkness, but this range seemed even more jagged than the one before. Buffeted by treacherous winds, the dragon flew on, slipping between sheer cliffs, dropping over impossible precipices only to rise up and barely clear the next narrow saddle.

Suddenly, up ahead loomed a dark shape that looked for all the world like some massive hand had thrust itself up from the ground and frozen there, all fingers pointing skyward. Brian's skin crawled: this place was prickling with Dark Magic. The closer they came, the worse he felt. The dragon was struggling to manage the wind. It lifted up into the undersides of the clouds, twisting to avoid a sheer cliff on their right side. Then it banked hard left, its leathery wings deafening Brian as they filled with air one moment and were emptied of it the next. The dragon brought them around to the lowest, flattest portion of the wall, just over what looked like the entrance to the mighty fortress.

With great difficulty, the scaly beast landed on the battlements. Its wings continued to beat, countering the powerful winds that thrashed the fortress. Brian looked frantically in all directions. Black Warriors appeared to be guarding the walls; he could not guess how many. Some were not far from where the dragon had just landed. The gruffen could see almost nothing in the shadowy depths inside the castle walls.

The dragon let out a roar, sending flames licking into the sky. Black Warriors approached tentatively from the nearby guard tower. As they did so, the dragon brought its prize down to the wall.

As soon as Brian felt the talons loosen, he went limp and slipped from the dragon's grasp. Black Warriors blocked the way forward so he scrambled back between the legs of the dragon. He headed directly for the outer battlements but the dragon's massive tail forced him back. The dragon roared again, its fiery breath giving Brian a very quick view of the castle. Quickly, he covered the distance between the dragon's body and one of the great towers. Two guards stepped through the doorway and cut off his route to the outside once again. Not pausing for a second, he clambered over the battlements and clung to the stonework of the wall. He began to move sideways along the base of the battlements, his sharp claws finding purchase where others could not, but there was no way out. All routes to the outside were blocked by the enemy. His only path was upward. Scrambling desperately, he scaled the tower itself. Arrows whizzed up toward him, casting sparks as they glanced off the stones.

The dragon roared again, twisting its long neck, looking about for its escaped prize. Black Warriors shouted over the din. Brian found a thin catwalk leading from one tower to another and quickly pulled himself onto it. Feeling his way along, he followed it to the taller tower, resuming his climb, clawing around almost blindly to the far side to get some masonry between him and the enemy. He came upon a high bridge and pulled himself onto it. For a moment, he crouched there, panting, listening to the chaos on the battlements below.

The clap of thundering wings told him that the dragon had taken off again. He couldn't stay out on the bridge. He followed the bridge across a great abyss to yet another tower. He could smell Black Warriors inside but one glance over his shoulder told him he dared not go back. The dragon was circling, looking for him, though it was having difficulty in the turbulence. Once again the gruffen started up the stonework, avoiding the yawning windows and lookout points—anything that smelled faintly of Black Warriors. The dragon continued to circle the fortress. Brian knew he couldn't stay outside in the wind and rain. Finding another bridge that had no scent to it, he climbed onto it and fairly ran across to the massive central tower of the dark fortress. There was no sign or scent of the enemy around the open doorway on the other side. Brian stepped into the entrance and shoved his back against the interior wall, not daring to look outside.

The wind grew worse. Eventually, the dragon stopped circling. Brian hunkered down inside the tower wondering where he was and what to do next.

* * *

"I have ordered the men to search the upper towers, m'lord," said the Black Warrior captain.

"No need," said Morvassus. "Call them back. Whatever Karkaan wanted from this thing, I suspect he already has it. The beast itself is of no consequence." He stood up from the throne and knelt down once again before the pool at his feet. "Are preparations complete?" he asked.

"Yes, m'lord," said the captain. "The men await your orders."

"It's time, Captain," said Morvassus. "We leave within the hour."

"Yes, m'lord," snapped the captain. He turned on his heel and strode quickly from the room.

The Dark Lord heard him send the orders.

"Finally," he said to himself, drawing in a bit more strength from the pool; "I have the power to leave this prison once and for all."

CHAPTER 49

Movements

"Captain Achor called for a parley?" asked Falnor. The day outside was gloomy and foreboding, but this news was blacker still. Ender, Holren and several others sat nearby, listening.

"Not a parley," said the exhausted young soldier. "It was as if they had already expected to meet."

Falnor nodded. "Where were you when this meeting took place, Gerran?"

"On our side of the river, not far from Fahrnam Wood," said Gerran. "There were about fifty goblins, tall and fierce-looking, but I thought we had a fair chance of taking them if things got ugly. Captain Achor talked with the little blind fellow in private for some time. At sunset, he came back and ordered us to escort the goblin army to Pellían."

"Why?" asked Falnor.

"He didn't say, sir," said Gerran; "but I looked around and no one seemed bothered by it. The strange thing is, the blind man kept talking as the two armies came together, and soon it all seemed to make sense. It's hard to explain, sir. He just kept telling us that we were allies, that we needed each other. I almost believed it, myself."

"Then what happened?"

Gerran scratched his head. "The little blind man and Captain Achor toasted the new alliance. Then the blind fellow made some rambling speech about loyalty and honor while they started passing around bottles of some goblin drink. I didn't drink it, myself, but everyone started carrying on like it was a celebration. Then things got ugly."

Falnor simply nodded.

Gerran continued. "Next thing I knew, drunken soldiers were being hewn down. Some of us still had our wits, and at first we fought hard but it was clear there was nothing to do but retreat. No one sounded the call. A few of us escaped to the forest as it got dark."

"What of Captain Achor?" asked Falnor.

"I don't know, sir," said the soldier. "I caught only a glimpse of him during the fight. Later on, in the woods, I found two more who also escaped. We circled back after dark to see what had become of the rest of the battalion." He stopped for a moment and rubbed his eyes. "We were hidden in the trees some distance away and couldn't see or hear very well, but—well, I had to come to warn you," he said. "The blind fellow was nowhere to be seen, but this tall bird-headed man which I hadn't seen before seemed to be in charge. The goblins were afraid of him."

"We know of this Birdman," said Ender. "Any details you can give us will be appreciated."

Gerran took a breath and blinked a few times before he went on. "All of our men who were still alive were bound and sitting on the ground, surrounded by goblins. The Birdman lit the grass around him on fire somehow but it didn't spread. He stood in the middle of this burned out circle and called out something I couldn't understand. The goblins dragged one of the bound men into the burnt circle. Then this strange light appeared in front of the Birdman. It changed color several times. I had to squint to keep from being blinded so I couldn't see our man." He stopped again.

"Go on," said Falnor.

"Yes sir," said Gerran. "Well, I couldn't see, but I could hear. The man was screaming, sir, like he was being burned alive." The soldier was sweating heavily, just telling the story. "Then, well, I don't know, sir. It just looked like the Birdman drove his hand into the man's chest. The light got so bright I had to shut my eyes."

"Did he kill the prisoner?" asked Falnor, quietly.

Gerran shook his head. "I don't know" he said. "The worst thing was that the man's screams were changing. It made all my hair stand on end."

"How did it change?" asked the captain, glancing over at Holren and Mari who looked on gravely

"It went from being a scream of pain to a wild shriek that wasn't even human," said the young soldier; "and then it was became a howl which dropped down, deeper and deeper until it was a roar, like an angry bear. When I forced my eyes open again, I couldn't see our man on the ground anymore. Instead, there was this taller man-shaped thing with no hair or beard, just standing there, its long arms outstretched, roaring at the sky. Maybe I was just unable to see, but it seemed like our man had been changed into this roaring thing. The rest of our men tried to get to their feet but the goblins kept them down. The Birdman was laughing."

Gerran took a shuddering breath and forced himself to go on. "The Birdman said something and one of the biggest goblins stepped into the circle. The tall, hairless man was even larger than that goblin, almost the size of a Small Giant. At another word, the goblin charged the tall, hairless man." Gerran's eyes grew wide. "They fought hand to hand, no weapons. For a short while, it seemed like an even contest, but then suddenly the goblin was dead. The Birdman just laughed again as the tall, hairless man picked up the body and tossed it away like a rag.

"Worse yet," he said; "the tall, hairless man went over and dragged another one of our men over to the circle and the lights changed. The whole thing happened all over again. The screaming still haunts me, sir. When it was done there were two of these tall men. We couldn't watch anymore, and sneaked away while we still had a chance. Three of us weren't enough to help the others, sir. There were just too many of the enemy."

"I believe you," said the captain. "Did you send word to King Raealann?"

"We did our best, sir. When we got to the road, we found an even bigger army ahead of us, heading for the city. My two companions went to Pellían by another route and I came here to warn the Shioroth. I do not know if they made it."

Falnor stood up and clapped a hand on Gerran's shoulder. "We thank you very much for your service and your speed," he said. "You go get some rest."

Gerran saluted and left the room.

Falnor turned to the others. "My heart aches for Pellían," he said. "This act of treason is more than I expected from Achor. What do you make of this news?"

Holren spoke first: "This reminds me of what Brian said the King was doing in the valley, only back then the monster was making goblins out of animals. Now, as the Birdman, he makes some human-like creature out of people. I can hardly imagine what he has made out of a sentient being."

"Gerran said the creature killed a large goblin with its bare hands," said Falnor.

"That would be only the most obvious of its abilities, I expect," said Holren.

"How soon could the Birdman's army arrive here?" asked Aaron.

"Even if the goblins are fast on foot, it would take them at least three days," Falnor replied. "Gerran is our fastest runner and he can cover the distance in two days. If the Birdman's army intends to take Pellían first, that will add even more time, of course."

"His army grows stronger with every captive he takes," said Ender.

"And slower, I hope," said Aaron. "Captain, with your help, I would like to take a good look at the battlefield and our defenses before he gets here."

Falnor nodded. "Let's go now."

* * *

Brian awoke with a start and looked around him in the dull darkness, his nose searching for strange scents, his ears listening for footsteps. No one was there. His hiding place in the high tower was apparently still a secret.

Dawn had not penetrated the heavy overcast, but the wind and rain had stopped.

A great horn blasted two long notes, making every hair on Brian's furry body stand on end. Daring to get closer to the doorway, he peeked out over the edge of the catwalk that had led him to this great central tower. Far, far below, the cranking of heavy chains and the grinding of massive machinery announced the opening of the solid iron gates. Brian could see dark shapes filling the courtyard and he could hear the clanking of weapons and armor.

The army was on the move as soon as the gates were open. Like a dark river, the army of Black Warriors rode out onto the steep road that led westward from the fortress. Brian squatted down and watched row after row of footsoldiers passed through the gates, down the steep road. After a long time, the river of soldiers crossed the valley and followed the road up the far ridge.

Brian's stomach growled. He was thirsty, too, but he had no idea where to find food or water. Somehow he had get down from here and escape. Maybe it would be easier with all the activity going on below, but where would he go?

The horn blew again, this time a single, long note, and Brian felt the presence of Dark Magic. His skin prickled as if stung by a thousand nettles, and his heart was pounding. Quickly, he ducked back inside and tried not to pant too loudly. His ears and nose were on full alert, but he could smell nothing close by. A shout rose up from below. Despite himself, Brian looked out over the edge and saw what looked like a swirling ball of black smoke that seemed to be carried on the back of some huge four-legged beast that Brian did not recognize. Surrounded on all sides by Black Warriors, the swirling cloud exited through the gates. Once again, the army roared. Spears and swords clattered against shields in a great cacophony of sound. The horn blew loudly and the mass of Black Warriors began to chant in a strange tongue as the army proceeded westward. Still more riders and footsoldiers poured through the gates.

Brian stared, mesmerized, until the last of the Black Warriors left the fortress. Another horn sounded three short blasts outside the walls. Then, with another great clanking of chains and machinery, the gates finally closed. For a long time, Brian crouched there, looking below for signs of movement in the fortress, and looking up to watch the dark army disappear marching westward. Once the beast with the dark cloud on its back had clambered out of sight over the pass, Brian's skin finally stopped stinging. His ears strained to hear any sound. The acrid smell of Black Warriors remained, but he could see no movement in the courtyard. The fortress seemed deserted. Had the great gates closed on their own?

The day wore on and the rain began again, washing away some of the smell. Brian hunkered down inside the tower. He would wait until dark to see if any lights burned in the tower windows as they had the previous night.

* * *

Annie blinked and looked around, wondering what time of day it was. The sky was so dark that even midday had felt like dusk, so she couldn't be sure. She must have fallen asleep. The rain was picking up again. She climbed down from her lookout perch and crawled back under the huge boulder. Once underneath, she stared out at the stony landscape. A dark flicker of movement caught her eye. She froze. Then, slowly, she moved her hand along the Valenblade until the Ring of the Snowdaughter touched the metal knife guard and her vision grew sharp. She looked hard at the moving object. To her relief, it was just a crow. Still, it was a very large crow.

Just then, the bird cocked one eye in her direction and seemed to stare right back at her. Annie hardly dared to breathe. She just kept staring back at the crow until it finally looked away and flew off. Before she could breathe a sigh of relief, it had circled around and landed not far from her sheltering rock.

It cocked its head and fixed her with its dark eye again. "What is a Faerie doing all the way out here in the Mirrak-Haas?" it croaked.

Annie gasped in surprise. It talked!

"I've been watching you since you got here yesterday," said the crow. "I thought your kind withered and died after a couple of hours out here, but you've been here almost a whole day and you're still moving."

Annie nodded but didn't say anything.

"My name's Jehzik," said the crow, bobbing its head in a nervous approximation of a bow. "I'm guessing you're aligned with the Healer since you're a Faerie—or at least I hope you are."

"Who's 'the Healer?'" asked Annie.

"Ah, the rival of the Dark Master, that's who!" cackled Jehzik. "The Healer's got a Stone of his own, he does! Put me back together after they tore me apart. Amazing! I was a pile of bones and guts when he got to me, but look at me now! You know him?"

"Yes," said Annie. "We know him as Ender."

"'Ender,' eh? Good name. But that doesn't explain why you carry the Deadly Weapon." The crow nodded at the Valenblade in Annie's hand and shook out its feathers. "Do you mind if I get in out of the rain?" he asked.

"How do I know you're not serving the Dark Master?" asked Annie.

Jehzik shrugged his black wings. "You don't, I guess," he said. "I don't know how you could. But it hardly matters. If you needed to get away from me, you could just do that flickering light thing and off you'd go. Besides, I'm not stupid enough to get too close to the Deadly Weapon." He shook out his feathers again.

"Come in then," said Annie, moving aside a bit.

"Thanks," said the crow, hopping under the rock with her but keeping a respectful distance.

"You don't like the knife, do you," said Annie.

"No," said Jehzik.

"Why do you call it the 'Deadly Weapon?'" Annie asked.

Jehzik stopped. "You don't know?" he sputtered, incredulous. "Unbelievable! You carry it and you don't know?"

"I know it's the Valenblade," said Annie. "I know it can kill Golrakken and Necrowights. It cuts stone and steel as easily as it cuts fruit or wood when the Valen uses it."

"Is that all?" prompted the crow. "Really, is that all you know about it? Blathermick! We're worse off than I thought." The black bird looked about furtively. "It is the only weapon that has ever wounded the Master of Uzzim-Khail, Morvassus himself. With any luck, it might actually kill him off. You could do that, you know."

"That's not why I'm here," said Annie.

"Probably not," said Jehzik. "But there's always the chance..." He cocked his head sideways until it was almost upside down. "How in the world did you end up with it anyway? Morvoth and the Golrakken have been searching for it forever, but here it is, in the hands of a Faerie—and a girl at that."

"I'm trying to get it back to Brian," said Annie. "He's the Valen and he's supposed to have it."

"Who's Brian?" asked the crow.

"He's a gruffen and he's my friend," said Annie.

"What's a gruffen?" asked Jehzik.

"He's a big, furry person," said Annie. "A dragon carried him off and I'm trying to find him."

"That furball is the Valen?" exclaimed the crow. "Now I've heard everything!"

"What furball?" asked Annie.

471

"The one the dragon was carrying, like you said," replied Jehzik. "I saw the dragon hauling something. I just didn't know what it was. Then you showed up."

"Did you see where the dragon went?"

"No," said Jehzik; "but I can guess. It's got to be one of two places, and you're not going to like either one."

"I don't care," said Annie. "I just need to find him and get us both back to the Shioroth."

"How are you going to get him there, carry him?" asked Jehzik.

"I don't know if I can," said Annie. "He'll have to run for it. I just want to help."

"'Run for it?' You have no idea where in the craw you are, do you?" sputtered Jehzik. "It would take days to get back to the Shioroth on foot."

"Brian is very fast," said Annie.

"No, no, you're not listening," said Jehzik. "Even if he was just over the ridge, he'd have to cross the Mirrak-Haas, pick his way past a whole army of Black Warriors heading west, and then fight through a few bands of goblins, only to get stuck at the Carven Canyon. The bridge is gone, you know."

Annie's face fell. "It's really gone then?"

"Destroyed," said Jehzik. "Hardly a stone left standing. Not that it will matter in a few days. It just delayed things a bit. The Black Warriors have headed south to where the the goblins have built a new bridge."

"How do you know all this?" asked Annie.

The bird cocked his head again and shook more water out of his feathers. "I get around, and I keep my eyes open," he said. "It's what I'm good at. Now that I'm free, I'm not exactly sure what to do with myself, though."

"Why is that?" asked Annie.

The crow shrugged. "I don't know. It's been a long time since I was around ordinary people. I hardly remember what it's like." He fell silent for a moment, still eyeing the Valenblade. "Something about the Deadly Weapon must have changed," he said, finally.

"How so?" asked Annie.

"I don't know," said Jehzik. "It doesn't give me the same sense that I get from the Golrakken or the Dark Master. I've lived so long near Dark Magic that I can easily recognize its presence. The Deadly Weapon doesn't have that kind of darkness in it."

"How do you know it's the Deadly Weapon, then?" asked Annie.

"You, yourself, said it was the Valenblade, but I would recognize it anywhere," said Jehzik. "Karkaan Dragonhelm was obsessed with it. Depictions of it are carved into the walls of the Golrakken ship. The Dark Master impressed the image of it into my mind—not something one gets rid of easily." He shook his head violently. "And now I've found it but I don't have to say a word to him about it!" He looked back at Annie. "You couldn't understand what it means to be free of that curse."

"No," said Annie.

"I was a slave to the Dark Master until he finally grew tired of me and cast me away to die. Somehow, the Healer gave me back my life and my freedom."

"I'm glad for you," Annie said. She took a deep breath, looked out at the rain and then looked back at the crow. "Would you help me find Brian?"

Jehzik hesitated a moment. Then he nodded. "I'm pretty sure I know where the old dragon took the furball—"

"The gruffen, you mean."

"—the gruffen, yes. But like I said: you're not going to like it."

"Just tell me where," said Annie.

"If the Golrakken wanted him, he's been dropped off at Akka-Illin," said Jehzik. "That place is swarming with the enemy, but it's not far from here, 'as the crow flies,' you know—but that's the same for you, now that I think of it."

"You said there was another place he might be," said Annie.

"The other one's worse. Uzzim-Khail," said the crow; "the Dark Master's own fortress, deep in the mountains of the Oryxx. You'll know it when you see it: looks like a hand shoved up out of the ground and froze there"

"How fast can you fly there?" asked Annie.

"Faster than you'd expect," said the crow. "It's one small advantage of having been enchanted, the only one I actually like." He fixed his dark eye on her. "You're sure you're okay? I've not seen a Faerie who can still breathe after being here very long."

"I'm fine," said Annie, not sure if it was actually true. "You lead, but if you're taking me to a trap, you'll meet the Deadly Weapon, understand?"

Jehzik nodded. "Don't worry," he said. "I was happy to be out of that place and I wouldn't take you anywhere near it if I didn't believe in you. Besides, I'd hate to see you just waste away out here. One question, though: what are we going to do when we find Furball?"

"Brian," said Annie. "His name is Brian."

"Brian, then," said the crow. "Still, what do you have in mind?"

"I don't know," said Annie. "We'll find out when we get there. Let's go."

* * *

Aaron, Lia and Owler rode back from the low rise to join the others as the setting sun cast long shadows eastward.

"The view is good from there, like you said," Aaron said. "I have a better idea of how the enemy could use the drainage beyond."

"Most of that area is visible from the Southgate towers," said Falnor.

"Good," said Aaron. "I'm just glad to know there's nowhere else they can hide out there."

"Elves," said Owler.

"What?" said Aaron.

"Elves," Owler repeated. "Approaching from the eastern woods."

Aaron twisted around to follow his gaze. "I don't see them yet," he said; "but that shouldn't surprise me."

Lia grinned and turned her horse toward the woods.

In a few moments, a company of well-armed Elves emerged onto the fields with Eulian's brother in the lead.

"Welcome, Thadris!" shouted Captain Falnor as the survey party rode up to meet them. "Thank you for coming so quickly. We can use all the help you can bring."

"Fifty of our finest archers," said the Elven prince; "and a hundred more who are experts with sword and shield."

"Come," said Falnor. "We will ride with you to the Westgate."

Thadris ordered the Elven company foreward and then stepped aside to have a word with his sister. When the prince rejoined his company, Eulian rode back with the rest of the survey party, her face was grave. Arvon gave her a questioning look but she did not volunteer anything.

Once the Elves were inside the quarters of the Blue Stone, Thadris turned once again to his sister. "Let me ride behind you," he said. "We should speak with Arienne."

"Agreed," said Eulian, giving her brother a stirrup and a hand up. "Please excuse us," she said to the others and took off at a gallop out of the courtyard and up the cobbled street.

* * *

The smell of Black Warrior was strong but it wasn't fresh. Even so, Brian sniffed the air constantly for any shift in the scent. Darkness had fallen hours ago, but no lights flickered in any of the windows. The gruffen made his way down the inside of the massive central tower one flight of steps at a time, checking every doorway before he passed it. Periodically, he looked out a window into the blackness. The fortress seemed abandoned.

He had come down a considerable distance when he realized he had no way to open the gates. For that matter, he wasn't sure if he could even find his way out in the dark. He stopped just inside a large doorway that led to the outside. Nothing on the wind gave any indication that there was life below. Cautiously, he stepped out. He could see nothing in the darkness. Going back inside, he slumped down against the wall to wait till dawn.

* * *

Without warning, the crow dipped low and skimmed the rocky slope, coming to a quick stop behind a large boulder. Annie landed beside him and changed back from light form.

"Why did you stop?" she asked. "We just started."

"Golrakken!" hissed Jehzik, jerking his head several times to indicate down-slope. "They're still some distance off, but they're coming this way."

"Are we close to Akka-Illin?" asked Annie.

"Not really," said Jehzik. "That's why I didn't expect them. If I'd known they were on the move, I wouldn't have come this way."

"Let me take a look," said Annie.

"Don't go down there!" croaked Jehzik. "If they see you, we're in big trouble."

"I'm not going down there," she said. Touching her ring to the Valenblade, she peered around the boulder and down the hill. The sight of the Golrakken made her catch her breath.

"What are you doing?!" hissed the crow.

"I can see far like this," said Annie in a hushed voice.

"But you're holding the Valenblade!" hissed Jehzik. "It will give you away! That's what they're looking for!"

Annie ignored him. Her heart pounded as she searched the gray ranks for the auburn hair of the gruffen. He was nowhere to be found. No one was carrying a sack big enough to haul him. No horse had a rider his size. She deliberately avoided looking directly at Karkaan Dragonhelm, but no one seemed to notice her. Finally, she turned around and sat down with her back to the boulder. "I don't think they've got him," she said.

"You can see that?" asked Jehzik.

"Yes," she replied. "But I'm not very good with this far-sighted thing."

The crow peeked around the boulder. "If we stay here, you won't need to be far-sighted to see them!" he said. "We've got to get out of here, but I don't think you can move without them spotting you." He looked at her strangely. "No one noticed you just now?" he asked.

Annie shook her head. Her heart was drumming loudly in her ears. "If we go up high enough, will we be safe?" she asked.

Jehzik shrugged. "I don't know," he said. "I can stay here. They'll not see me in the rocks, but I don't know where you can be safe—especially with that knife in your hands."

"Then I'd better go," said Annie.

Without another word, she changed back into light form and shot up into the clouds. A cry went up from the Golrakken on the ground. Without intending to, she took a breath to reply. Shutting her mouth, she focused on climbing higher. Still the voices called to her. Her throat worked, but she clamped her tongue between her teeth and dared not even breathe, climbing higher and higher until she could no longer hear their rasping voices. Finally, she let out a scream of relief.

The winds blew strongly at that altitude, and even in light form, she found it difficult to keep a straight path. She fought her way through the turbulence in the darkness, trying to keep what she thought was an eastward bearing. If she didn't drop down out of the gusting winds, she would tire soon. When she came out of the clouds, she had no idea where she was, or where anyone else was either, for that matter.

* * *

Jehzik peeked out from behind the rocks as the Golrakken warriors approached.

Bless the Faerie for not responding, he thought. His heart had quailed when he heard their calls to the flickering light that had shot skyward as they reached the base of the rocky hill.

"How is it that a Firstborn survives out here?" he heard one of them ask.

"Something strange about that one," said Karkaan Dragonhelm at the head of the group. "Our calls had no effect."

"Still, I wonder why a single Faerie would be out here at all," said the first. "If it's a scout, we have been discovered."

"No matter," spat Karkaan. "Whatever preparations they are making, a few days' notice will not serve them any better. The force that rises against them is far too great for the united armies of the Shioroth to withstand."

"With or without the Valenblade," continued another.

Karkaan grunted. "Fool of a dragon," he growled. "Whatever he had with him was good for nothing. If Morvassus wants it, he can have it."

"If the beast didn't have the Valenblade, it must still be in the hands of someone in the Shioroth," said the other.

"And we will take it back when we take the city," said Karkaan. "We have rivals, my brothers. The Black Warriors consider themselves the Dark Master's pets, but they cannot wield the Valenblade."

"What about this Birdman?" asked another. "His powers are still unknown."

"True," said Karkaan. "Forward, Golrakken! We will do well to arrive sooner rather than later."

The crow remained motionless, nestled between the rocks, as the parade of gray warriors rode past. He didn't hazard a look until the sound of Golrakken horses had faded away. By that time, the gray army had moved up the hill and were rounding a bend in the trail. They would soon be out of sight.

Jehzik hunkered back down under the rock, out of the steady rain. So, the gruffen wasn't with the gray ones. Karkaan had confirmed his suspicions about where the dragon had gone, so now he knew where to look for the furball, but where would he find the Faerie? He had seen no sign of her since she escaped.

The thought of flying back to Uzzim-Khail turned his stomach. Even so, he remembered the Healer. If Annie and the furball were friends of the Healer, then he would do all he could to help them. Despite his nausea, he shook out his feathers, hopped out into the open and took off.

He winged his way across the landscape with preternatural speed, his sharp eyes searching in all directions. With any luck, he would find her again. Actually, it might take a lot more luck this time.

* * *

Brian waited until the dawn's dim light allowed him to make out distinct shapes. He peered out of the doorway and surveyed his surroundings. Just in front of him lay a circular landing which was part of a wide stone bridge that curved around the inside of the fortress. He had seen this bridge from above. It seemed to connected all of the main towers. No one was in sight. The fortress was dark and quiet, as it had been all night.

On all fours, he scuttled over to the low wall that rimmed the landing. From here, he could see the solid iron gates, and the battlements that lined the outermost wall. Still there was no movement. The massive gates were shut. He watched for some time but saw no evidence that the guard towers were occupied as they had been when the dragon lost hold of him on the wall night before last.

His eyes followed the line of the stone bridge all the way to the first tower and looked until he found the route he had climbed that night. He could probably climb down the same route and get back on the outer wall. Once there, though, he wasn't sure where he could go. A drop from the wall to the road would probably be fatal. He would have to go inside the guard tower and try to find another exit from the fortress.

His stomach growled and he shoved away thoughts of food.

No more waiting, he decided. Quickly, he loped along the wide bridge until he came to the first tower. Scrambling back out on his earlier escape route, he clawed his way down to the perimeter wall. Without hesitation, he raced silently to the guard tower.

There, he stopped and listened, sniffing the air. The stench here was distinctly different. He remembered it from a couple of nights ago, but he had been very busy then, hardly able to log all the different smells that assaulted his nose on his arrival. It wasn't goblin or Black Warrior; of that, he was certain. He thought he might have gotten a whiff of it when the gates were opened the previous day. As he listened, he could make out a slow, rhythmic, hollow whooshing sound. Something big was breathing down inside the tower.

Brian looked over the edge of the battlements on the outside. There appeared to be no safe way to climb down. The overhang had no handholds. He would simply fall from that point. The battlements on the inside proved to be no easier. There was no ramp or stairway from the top of the wall to the lower level inside. The only route up or down was apparently through the guard tower.

A great, guttural roar from down below made Brian drop to a crouch. His fur stood on end. It stopped just as suddenly. Brian waited. Once again, something fierce roared down below, filling the stone tower with sound. Then, once again, the roaring stopped. Brian stayed in his crouch, every muscle poised, waiting for the next sound. Sure enough, there it came again. If it was a bear or a mountain lion, it was a huge one. The roaring continued, starting and stopping, then starting again, in a predictable rhythm.

When the roar began again, the gruffen stepped into the tower and took several steps down the stairs, stopping just as the roaring ceased. He waited a little longer. When the next roar happened, he ran quickly down the steps to the next level. The stench burned the inside of his nose and made breathing difficult, but he simply stood still and waited until the roar started again.

Then he peered over the edge into the empty space that had now opened up in the center of the tower and found himself looking down on a massive, lumpy shape the same color as the stone walls. The roar reverberated through the chamber, shaking Brian's bones, but now the source of the noise and the stench was clear. There was a troll below, and it was snoring.

Standing vertically, side by side in front of the sleeping troll, were two massive wood and iron wheels. Steps and handles had been built into them, large enough for the huge creature to grasp and climb. Attached to each of these wheels was a complicated system of machinery which Brian guessed made the noise he had heard when the gates were opened and closed.

The deafening roar continued. Brian moved with every inhalation and waited through the quieter exhalation. Bit by bit, he was able to get down the stairs, past the troll and out the door to the stone courtyard just behind the gates. The rain started up again. Other than patter of raindrops and the raucous noise in the guard tower, everything else was still. Brian scanned the rest of the fortress for guards, but saw none. He searched the wall on either side of the tower for any sign of a smaller door, a side gate, anything. He found nothing. Keeping one eye out for enemies, he tried his strength against the great iron gates. They wouldn't budge.

Rain fell steadily as Brian went to the other guard tower. Judging from the smell, there was no troll in this one. It proved to be vacant. He hunted around for a door there as well but couldn't find one. Climbing up to the top of the tower, he searched for a way down from the wall on that side also. Again, there was none. Apparently, the only way in or out of the fortress was through the massive iron gates.

Brian sat in the guard tower looking at the rain falling outside. It didn't take him long to figure out what he had to do. He went back to the first tower where the sleeping troll was still snoring.

The gruffen studied the mechanism for a long time but he couldn't figure out how it worked. The only thing that seemed obvious was that the wheels were intended to turn when the troll moved them, and that turning worked the rest of the machinery. The huge handles were too big for Brian to grab but he thought that maybe if he stood on one of the steps, his weight might be enough to move one of the wheels.

He waited for another great snore and then quickly moved into position. At the next roar, he stepped on the first step of the wheel on the left. Nothing happened. He stepped off when the roar stopped and waited. At the next snore, he jumped on the first step. Nothing happened. He tried this several times, jumping higher and higher but to no avail. Giving up on this wheel, he got into position in front of the one on the right and tried jumping on its steps. Nothing happened there either. Frustrated, he climbed up onto the wheel and looked all over for something that might be stuck, keeping it from moving, but he didn't find anything.

Finally, he climbed back down. He was about to inspect the wheel on the left when the troll flopped over and woke up.

"WHAT ARE YOU DOING HERE?" bellowed the huge creature, staring wide-eyed at the gruffen. His great bulk blocked the door.

"Trying to get out!" Brian yelled, backing up a few steps.

"WHY ARE YOU STILL HERE?" hollered the troll, his forehead all wrinkled up. He banged his fists on the floor. "EVERYONE IS SUPPOSED TO BE OUT!"

"I'm trying!" shouted Brian. "How do I get out?"

"THROUGH THE GATE!" bellowed the troll. "LIKE EVERYBODY ELSE!"

"Well, open it up, then!" shouted Brian.

"YOU'RE NOT SUPPOSED TO BE HERE!" howled the troll.

"So let me out!" shouted Brian.

The troll slumped down and thought about it. "THREE BLASTS MEANS SHUT THE GATE!" he said.

"I need you to open the gate!" yelled Brian. "I need to get out!"

The troll's head lolled from side to side. "YOU'RE STILL HERE!" he wailed.

"Open the gate!" Brian hollered, waving his arms. "And get out of the way!"

"OH!" yelled the troll, getting to his feet. "I'LL OPEN THE GATE THEN!" The huge fellow lumbered over to one of the wheels and started climbing up the steps.

As soon as the troll was clear, Brian raced through the door and ran to the great gates. He heard the great machinery clunk once, then again, but the gates did not move.

"Open the gates!" he bellowed at the guard tower.

"IT'S NOT WORKING!" came the answer.

Brian banged on the gates. The machinery clunked again but still the gates wouldn't open. The gruffen stood there in the rain, heart racing. "Try the other wheel!" he yelled.

"OH! THAT'S RIGHT!" hollered the troll from inside the guard tower.

The great machinery clunked heavily, the wood creaked, and metal ground against metal as, link by link, the chains and wheels began to open the massive iron gates.

As soon as there was enough space to squeeze through, Brian was out the gates and down on all fours, racing down the steep road. He left the main path and cut directly up the hill toward the pass, due east.

Back in the guard tower, the troll felt the mechanism come to a halt. "IT'S OPEN!" he bellowed. "ARE YOU OUT?" He listened for a reply. "ARE YOU OUT YET?" The big, lumpy fellow listened hard. Finally, he got down on hands and knees and looked through the tiny door through which he could never leave. There didn't seem to be anyone there. "SHOULD I SHUT THE GATES?" he asked.

By that time, Brian was too far away to answer.

CHAPTER 50

Hassila

It was already the second watch of the night when Rohidan landed in the courtyard of the Westgate. The Elven soldiers on guard snapped to attention.

"Where is Rummel?" asked the Elder Faerie.

"We have not seen him today, m'lord," answered one of the guards. The others nodded in confirmation.

"Have you seen the Lady Arienne?" asked Rohidan.

"No sir."

"I haven't seen her since I spoke to her this evening," said Thadris, coming out of the officers' quarters. "She was looking for Rummel Stoneboots."

"So I heard," said Rohidan. "She was last seen with Stoneboots shortly after dark." The Elder Faerie fingered the White Stone in his hand and turned quickly away. "Excuse me," he said.

"Of course," said Thadris.

Rohidan spread his deep blue wings and sailed upward toward the city's central monolith, higher and higher until he reached the Uppermost Garden. He had not sat on the White Throne since Ender had returned to the Shioroth, but now he touched down at the entrance to the White Tower and quickly opened the door. His feet whispered against the spiraling steps of white stone that led to the throne room. The soft glow of the marbled floor and walls welcomed him into the pinnacle of the White Tower. Trembling, he sat on the throne and turned westward.

His eyesight dimmed, as if he had grown suddenly old, but as he focused, he was able to make out shapes and colors. With the Midnight Stone preoccupied elsewhere, the White Stone seemed more free to work on its own. Staring hard, Rohidan searched the western hills and forests until he saw the unmistakable shape of Rummel Stoneboots sweeping through the trees. The Lord of the Mountains was headed straight toward Val-Ellia. On his shoulders sat Arienne, the Elven Queen of the Faeries.

Rohidan let out a sigh. If he flew quickly, he might catch them before they reached the Elven palace, but what would he say?

Suddenly, they vanished completely, mid-stride. Rohidan took in a sharp breath and stared harder but he could see nothing beyond their last step. It was as if he could see only so far. An invisible wall impaired his ability to see further. Slowly, he sat back in the throne, keeping his eyes fixed on the spot where Rummel and Arienne had disappeared.

Thadris had spoken of changes in Val-Ellia. Somehow, the Blue Stone had gone wrong. Those who came with Thadris were apparently the few remaining who had not fallen under the spell of fear coming from within the palace. Eulian had dragged details from her brother during the night and had brought the news to Rohidan and Ender as quickly as she could find them. It was clear now that Arienne had gone to confront Hassila personally, and Rummel had gone with her, leaving the Shioroth without his considerable resources. Rohidan sat on the White Throne staring woodenly out the window.

According to Thadris, a few days before Rummel had stopped briefly in Val-Ellia with Eulian and the others on his shoulders, Hassila had decreed that no one was to venture outside the forest on penalty of death. Thadris argued fiercely against this, but she would not renounce her decree. Things came to a head when a young couple violated this order, and the Queen had them brought before her. Taking the Blue Stone in hand, she struck and killed them herself. News of the execution spread rapidly. Thadris secretly fled the palace, taking his most trusted troops with him to the Shioroth.

Now Arienne and Rummel had gone to face the Queen, and some shield was keeping Rohidan from seeing into the Elven lands. The Elder Faerie finally closed his eyes and sat back. There was nothing he could do from here.

* * *

Arienne dropped off of Rummel's shoulder and landed lightly on the ground outside Val-Ellia. The tall trees that formed the Elven Palace towered over her head in the darkness.

"We passed through some sort of shield," said Stoneboots quietly. "I do not know what kind it was, but I do not like it at all."

"There is something terribly wrong here," whispered Arienne. "Where is everyone? The woods seem deserted."

She walked around outside the mighty tree palace until she came to the ancient hidden entrance. A few times before, she had let herself in through that doorway, but never before had she felt such dread about doing so. To her surprise, the door would not yield to her touch.

"I cannot get in," she said, incredulous. "Something else holds the door shut."

"I could set you inside," said Rummel.

"I don't know if that would be safe," said Arienne. "Whatever is going on here, I would rather not just appear in the middle of it."

Rummel grew taller and peered over the wall. Very quietly, he reached in and drew out a portly Elf dressed all in white. Stoneboots placed the trembling fellow on the ground next to Arienne and shrank back to normal size.

Bostler's voice was a hoarse whisper. "Well, well, WELL!" he scolded Rummel. "It's about time you came back! Didn't I tell you it wouldn't be long before all this got out of hand?"

"You did," acknowledged the Lord of the Mountains; "but we have been preoccupied with a coming war. Now tell us what has gotten out of hand."

"I will, I will! I do beg your pardon, your ladyship; I'm still a little shaky, what with all that's going on these days." Bostler looked around. "I could get killed for telling you this, you know," he hissed.

"We shall see to it that you don't," said Arienne. "Now, please tell me what is the matter."

"The Queen has gone mad, completely mad, if you don't mind my saying so," said Bostler. "Somehow she found out this morning that Thadris, her very own son, had gone off with all of her strongest and brightest. She was livid. I had brought down her breakfast: a wonderful plate of eggs, toast, two kinds of jelly, a bit of my special garlic cheese and a drink so warm and wonderful you must certainly try it sometime—but she hardly touched it! In any case, she stays in the wine cellar all day now; did I tell you that? The wine cellar! I couldn't guess what it is she does down there, but she's not depleting the supply. Couldn't smell a drop on her."

"How often do you see her?" asked Arienne.

"Twice a day," he replied. "She refuses visitors (not that anyone would want to visit) and I am the only one allowed to bring her meals and I must leave them by the door at the bottom of the stairs. Going down there gives me hives anymore, but of course she can't go without food, and it's the only good thing I can do for her these days—at least that's something—only now she won't eat. I've gotten a glimpse of her a few times. She looks worse every day." Bostler lowered his voice. "I tell you, some terrible thing is happening in that wine cellar."

"What do you think it is?" asked Rummel.

"Most of what I know I have learned with my nose and ears because she won't open the door, at least not much." The Master Chef frowned. "There's something or someone else down there with her, I am certain. Every once in a while, I hear his voice. It would unnerve a Small Giant: raspy, grating, and full of awful insinuations. She talks to him—or it, whatever it is."

"What do they discuss?" inquired Arienne.

"I can only catch a word or two at a time from the raspy one," Bostler, scratching his head. "And I can never make out what he says. I'm certain he said 'yes' once, but I didn't hear the question, so that's no good at all, is it."

"Does she let you in the door?" Arienne wanted to know.

"She hasn't, and I doubt she ever will, though I did get a quick peek inside yesterday when I brought her supper," he added. "Odd thing, this: there appears to be a large puddle on the floor! It doesn't seem to have reached the wine casks—at least as far as I can tell, but, like I said, I had only a quick peek."

Arienne looked at him quizzically. "What does Thorval Lighthammer say about all this?" she whispered.

"Nothing, or everything," scowled the cook. "He faced her alone after Thadris refused to kill the poor dears who had left the woods. Did you hear? They had gone out for a picnic! A picnic, mind you, and she..." he stopped, red faced, eyes bulging. "In any case, Thorval showed up not long afterward and gave her his opinion, full force, and you know how he is! Followed her all through the palace. I could hear them arguing all the way from the kitchen.

"It was beginning to unnerve me, especially when they came charging through my kitchen, heading for the wine cellar, still fighting it out. I decided to risk my neck and go down there with a hot drink and a tart. Sometimes that's all it takes to bring the Queen around when she gets in her moods. You remember that, don't you, how she's always been fond of my tarts. Of course, I didn't know then that she had executed anyone or I would never have dared approach her—I'm such an awful coward, you know!—but I arrived just in time to see her fling the door open, toss Thorval inside, and storm in after him. Correct me if I am mistaken, but I don't recall ever seeing anyone—besides, perhaps, Lord Stoneboots here—who can toss around Thorval Lighthammer. In any case, no one has come out of there since. I'm afraid something has happened to him."

"Do you think he might be the raspy-voiced one?" asked Rummel.

"No, no, no—and that's what bothers me!" said Bostler. "No, I think he is held captive down there...or dead."

"But it remains to be proven either way," said Arienne. "I will speak to the Queen."

"Oh, my lady, you take your life in your hands!" protested the chief cook.

"Now is the time for courage," said Rummel.

"Then put me back in the kitchen," said Bostler. "I'll make a fresh batch of tarts and you can bring a bit of that drink I was telling you about. It might put her in a better mood. If nothing else, have some yourself, and I'll have some with you. It will calm your nerves, or at least it will calm mine!"

"No time for that," said Arienne. "Rummel, please get us to the wine cellar straight away."

Rummel nodded. Growing once again to his gargantuan height, he let Bostler and Arienne climb onto his palm. Carefully, he stepped into the center of the palace. As he shrank down to fit inside, he deposited the cook and Arienne in the courtyard.

"This way," said Bostler, hurrying off toward the kitchen. "Oh, why do I bother saying such things! You know the way."

They passed through the kitchen and came to the trap door to the underground wine cellar. Bostler stayed behind as the other two proceeded down the flagstone treads, which had been worn smooth by many centuries of footsteps. At the bottom of the stairs, they came to the heavy door that sealed off the wine cellar. The cool and damp of the earthen cellar mixed with a hot smell neither of them could identify.

Arienne knocked. "Hassila, open up! It is Arienne," she called.

There was no answer. Arienne knocked again.

Slowly the door opened and Hassila appeared, hair disheveled and robes a rumpled mess.

"I knew you would come eventually," she said, in a tired but perfectly normal voice. "What is it you want? I am very busy."

"We were concerned for your safety. The Elves gather to the Shioroth. Your son and daughter await you there. Come," said Arienne, reaching for her hand.

Hassila stepped back quickly.

"You left Val-Ellia long ago, Arienne. I will not abandon it as you have done," replied the Elven queen. "You and your dear friend Thorval left Badris in the desert to die, and die he did."

"Badris! You still blame us for that? We could do nothing for him. We never saw him alive. He was dead long before ever we arrived; that was obvious to all who were there. We did not abandon him, and I have not abandoned Val-Ellia." Arienne calmed herself before she spoke again. "You must come with us. Val-Ellia is no longer safe. You cannot stay here."

The Keeper of the Blue Stone stood unmoved. "That much is true," she said. "Val-Ellia is no longer safe. Yet I alone have remained to fend for our people. First my daughter, and now my son and the best of our breed have deserted Val-Ellia for the Shioroth. Now here you come for my own flesh and blood. No, Arienne! You would have the Elves fade into your Faerie family and desert everything we love. You rejected Val-Ellia, but I will not spit in the face of the Elves, not like Arienne."

"Hassila, listen to me," pleaded Arienne. "Goblins approach from the south, along with some new sort of warriors we can hardly imagine. The Golrakken have mustered once again, and Black Warriors from Morvoth itself—"

"Enough!" shouted the Elven queen. "Your troubles do not concern me. Val-Ellia will stand. Did you not notice the shield surrounding my kingdom? You passed through only because I allowed it. I will not leave. Here the Elves remain, to live or to die."

"Where is Thorval Lighthammer?" asked Arienne.

"Gone!" said Hassila. "I know not and I care not where!"

"We'll find him later," said Arienne.

"I don't think so!" said Hassila in a sing-song sort of voice.

"Come," said Arienne again, holding out her hand. "We need to get you out of here. Come with us to the Shioroth. It is safer there, at least for now."

The Elven queen shrank away, her eyes wide. Her smile turned to a grimace. "No, Arienne!" she hissed. "It is you who must return to the Elves, back here, where you belong. For though you may not act the part, Elf you are, Elf you have always been, and here you will stay."

"My place is beside my husband," replied Arienne, bristling.

Hassila's face grew red. "As was mine, Arienne! Badris will be avenged. His blood cries out for yours and he will have it."

"You are mad, Hassila," said Arienne. "Your fear and sadness have driven you out of your mind."

"You call me mad," spat the Elven queen. "Mad? Mad? No. For once I have my wits about me. I see you for who you are: a traitor, a weaver of evil. You will surely pay, Arienne!"

"Where is the Blue Stone?" asked Arienne, calmly.

"Ha!" laughed the other. "There! See? Now you would rob me!"

"You forfeit the right to carry it. When I entrusted the Blue Stone to Badris, he swore to use it to protect the Elves in my absence," Arienne said. "You have already killed two of your own people with it."

"They abandoned Val-Ellia!" screeched Hassila. "They paid the price for treason!"

"If you will not fulfill the duty of the Keeper, I will lead the Elves once again, myself." She held out her hand. "Give it back to me!"

"Never, Arienne. Better thrown away than returned to your traitorous hands!" Hassila flung the stone into the broad puddle of water on the floor behind her.

"Foolish girl!" cried Arienne, pushing past her.

"Wait!" said Rummel. "That's no puddle!"

As Arienne brushed past, Hassila seized her and shoved her into the pool. Rummel reached for Arienne, but as she hit the wet floor, she vanished, swallowed up in a muted splash. Rummel's hand hit the water and simply bounced off. He tried again, but could not penetrate the surface. He might just as well have been a mere human pounding on solid ice.

Hassila laughed and whirled about, waving her arms. "Ha ha, Stoneboots!" she cackled. "You cannot get in can you? One got away this time, eh? What a pity! She'll not be back, I'll wager.

> Gone below, is Arienne!
> Ne'er will she be back again!
> Such the fate of every fool
> Who ventures near the silver pool!

The bedraggled Elven Queen danced wildly around the puddle. "Aye, wouldn't you like a trip into the pool, Mr. Stoneboots? Too bad, too bad! He won't have the likes of you roaming around down there. Oh, so sad for Mr. Stoneboots!" She watched with glee from the other side of the cellar as he tried in vain to step into the water.

"Where has she gone?" said Rummel.

"I wouldn't know, I wouldn't know," cackled the Elf. "Gone they are, far away."

"Who are 'they?'" Stoneboots growled.

"Ah, yes! Thorval Hammerhead, Arienne the Falsefaerie, gone they are, far away," crowed the queen, still dancing. "He'll eat them, maybe, I don't know. Says he wants them. Says he might come back again if I will go with him."

"Who says this?" glowered Rummel, coming across the pool to face her.

She cowered in a corner, laughing nervously. "Oh, you wouldn't hurt me! Couldn't do that! No, not Rummel Mr. Stoneboots! I know you better than that, dearie. You cannot hurt a soul. Your body would crumble—your hands, to dust. I wouldn't threaten me, sir. You'll lose your life if you do and that would be terrible, a terrible thing now, wouldn't it?"

"You haven't answered my question, madam. Of whom do you sing so carelessly?" Rummel stood over her, his arms folded across his chest.

"Oh, don't you see?" she whimpered. "He's going to come back. I told you he was not gone forever. He's coming back. I've been waiting for him all this time, and he'll be back. Soon, he says. Soon!"

Puzzled, Stoneboots looked into her twisted face. "Badris?" he queried.

She nodded, eyes wide open like a little girl awaiting a much-anticipated present.

Almost as soon as he said it, Rummel knew the answer. Badris, last King of the Elves, had died before Thadris, was born. He had gone on a sojourn into the western desert just before the queen discovered she was with child. He never returned. Grisbane, Arienne and Thorval Lighthammer had found the king's remains only after weeks of searching. They brought back his wedding ring, his dagger and the Blue Stone.

"Your husband is gone, Hassila," said the Lord of the Mountains.

The Elven queen drew herself up to her full height and spat at him. "I will not listen to you any longer, fool. Now leave before he comes and destroys you where you stand!" She flailed her arms as if warding off a swarm of bees.

Rummel turned away from her in sadness and frustration. Kneeling down, he pressed his hand hard onto the glass-like surface of the pool. Still it would not yield to him; he could not penetrate it.

"Leave it alone!" shrieked the queen. "Get away!" She screamed in fear and drew back against the wall.

Rummel stepped back toward the door. Out of the pool rose a figure seemingly formed from some sort of dark metal, hands held forward as if reaching for something. The face was immediately recognizable. Stoneboots froze. Arienne das-Lammethan was dead. Before he could react, the statue slipped back beneath the surface leaving hardly a ripple as it sank.

Another face showed itself in the pool.

"Well done," said a raspy voice wafting up from the pond. "You fulfilled your promise. Come meet your beloved."

"Hassila!" shouted Stoneboots, but the Elven queen had already stepped into the pool. For a brief moment, he saw her expression change from madness to simple fear. Then she was swallowed by the pool.

Once more, Rummel slammed his hand on the surface of the water. It would not give. He pounded on it but it remained impenetrable.

Stoneboots stood up in the wine cellar and let out a roar of anger. The ceiling shook above him and wine casks rattled against the wall. Bostler came bursting through the doorway, several of his trusty staff with him, armed with swords. Rummel quickly blocked their way to the pool.

"Lord Stoneboots!" shouted Bostler. "Where are they?"

Rummel pointed to the pool. "In there! I cannot reach them."

"The Blue Stone?" asked Bostler.

"Gone as well," said Rummel. He looked around. "Some magic lives here. We must leave this place. Gather everyone and bring them to the palace gates. We will meet outside."

Huffing and puffing, Bostler led the way back up the long staircase to the palace, gasping out orders with every step.

Rummel was last to leave. He stood by the pool and slowly waved his great hands around the room. The dirt walls crystallized to solid obsidian. He backed out of the room and, with a last, sad look into the wine cellar, he sealed the entrance with the same solid black stone. Then he seemed to melt into the floor. A moment later, he returned, rising up through the staircase.

"Strange," he muttered to himself. "I find no evidence of this pool. None at all." Slowly, he turned and walked back up the stairs to the kitchen.

By early afternoon, nearly seven hundred Elves were gathered in the wide clearing. Bostler ordered the gates to be shut. Everyone watched as their beloved tree palace was closed and sealed.

Stoneboots sent Bostler and his staff westward into the mountains with the children and their mothers. They were to retreat to the caves and remain there until sent for. The rest, about two hundred fully armed men and women followed as Rummel opened up the ground and led them into the tunnels beneath the forests and hills. They would have to move quickly.

CHAPTER 51

Defiled

"I don't see them, sir!" shouted the guard in the tower on the other side of the Southgate.

"You will!" shouted Owler. He raced down the stone steps of the guard tower, taking three at a time. When he reached the battlements on the wall, he ran a few paces and leapt over the inside parapet to land halfway down the stairs on the lower landing. Two more leaps of the same height and he hit the ground, cat-like, already running.

"What news?" yelled Falnor, coming out of the officers' quarters.

"They're here!" said Owler, not slacking his pace.

"Archers up!" shouted the captain. "To arms!"

Owler swung himself onto the bare back of a stallion, seized its mane and went racing up the cobblestones toward the inner wall of the Shioroth. When he reached the inner garden, he dismounted and sprinted straight for the chambers of the High Council. As he burst into the room, everyone turned to look.

"The Birdman is here," he said; "and he's brought an army."

Outside, the rays of sun that had pierced the overcast for a moment faded and disappeared as the clouds closed in overhead once more.

* * *

The longbowman shook his head. "They're out of range, sir. No point in wasting arrows."

"Hold your fire!" shouted Captain Falnor. "Bows down!"

The archers on the battlements lowered their arrow tips and released the tension on their bowstrings.

The noisy horde outside spread slowly across the field in front of them like molasses oozing from a broken jug. Trolls and ogres lumbered among innumerable goblins of all sizes. The Birdman made his way slowly to the front, flanked on both sides by tall, lanky but well-muscled figures with long arms. They were almost as tall as the trolls. The goblins shrank back from them in fear.

"Surgoths," said Ender, shaking his head. "I was afraid of this."

Holren raised his eyebrows. "Then the legends were true."

"They certainly are now," said Ender.

"They've got prisoners," said Owler.

The goblin shouts grew louder as the Birdman came to the front lines and surveyed the empty fields at the Shioroth. He spread his arms and the goblins pulled back to form a half-circle about forty paces wide with the Birdman in the center and the rest of the army stretched out to either side. Turning his back to the Shioroth, the Birdman motioned to the Surgoths who opened a path in the middle of the semi-circle. Through this path, the goblins brought the prisoners, a stream of reluctant men, women and children with their hands bound behind them. The goblins hauled them to the front and lined them up between the Birdman's army and the Shioroth.

"A coward's defense," said Aaron.

"Effective nonetheless," said Falnor, through gritted teeth.

"If these are Surgoths," said Holren; "their hide is impervious to steel."

"Then what's their weakness?" asked Aaron.

"Only the eyes are vulnerable," Holren replied.

"With conventional weapons, that is correct," said Ender, still looking out to the fields. "They can be killed by magic, though. A fire hot enough will also destroy them."

"Pass the word," said Falnor to the soldiers down the row. "Aim for the eyes."

The parade of prisoners continued until it stretched across the field, shielding the entire width of the goblin army. When they were all in place, the Birdman turned around again to face the Shioroth.

"Hail, you who are about to fall!" he cried, his razor-sharp voice cutting through the distance between them. "Recognize anyone you know?"

No one responded.

"Good!" said the Birdman. "Keep your eyes fixed on me." He turned back to the prisoners within the semicircle and pointed at their feet. Flames leapt up in front of the startled captives as the Birdman turned slowly, burning a complete circle around himself. The goblins kept the prisoners from backing away. The flames did not spread outward; they burned inward toward the center of the circle until the Birdman stepped across them into the charred grasses and the fire burned itself out.

Then the Birdman sat down cross-legged in the center of the smoking circle with his back to the Shioroth. "Bring me a prisoner!" he cried, loudly enough for the audience at the Southgate to hear.

Two goblins dragged a struggling young woman from the line of prisoners

"Sarah!" gasped one of the archers.

"Steady!" called Falnor.

The goblins bound her feet and forced her to the ground in front of the Birdman, out of sight of the watchers on the battlements at the Southgate.

"May I fire, sir!" hissed the archer who had cried out. "It's my Sarah, sir."

"Steady, Rinard," said Falnor. "They're out of range, even for you."

The archer nodded and lowered his bow.

A strange light was glowing in front of the Birdman. It started out blue, then changed to red, then white, then green. Some of the prisoners in the semi-circle tried to turn away but the goblins forced them to stand and face the Birdman. The light began changing colors even more rapidly, faster and faster until it began to pulsate with a chaotic rhythm.

The Birdman began to howl. It started off as a wail, then turned to a shriek and a scream as the light pulsated more and more. Then, with a flash of brilliant white, the light ceased altogether.

"No," said Rinard. "Oh, no, no, no!"

Standing up in front of the Birdman was a Surgoth. It raised its arms to the sky and let out a roar.

Rinard, the archer, looked over at Falnor in anguish. The captain shook his head.

Down on the field, the Birdman stood and turned toward the Shioroth. "Behold!" he crowed, pointing at his creation. "This is what becomes of your kin!"

The Surgoth opened its mouth and howled. The goblin horde roared in approval, drowning out the wailing of the captives. As the Surgoth bellowed again, its head jerked backward. It stumbled a few steps, buckled in half and crashed to the ground at the edge of the burnt circle.

The Birdman strode over to examine his fallen creation. Reaching down, he plucked an arrow out of its eye.

Falnor turned to Rinard who looked back in astonishment and shook his head.

"Up there," said Owler, aiming his chin at the part of the tree wall closest to the battlements. Perched up in the high branches was a dark-skinned young woman wearing the uniform of the Green Stone. A shout went up from the Shioroth as the Birdman ordered his army to fall back.

Slowly, the vast horde retreated, leaving the Birdman standing in his burnt circle. When he ordered them to stop, he turned back to the Shioroth.

"A lucky shot!" he crowed. "No matter. There are many others, as you can see, and I have all day. Every time you see the lights, know that another one of your own has become one of mine. Soon you will face them in battle, and they will destroy you!" He strode back to where his army had reformed. Turning slowly, he burned a new circle in the grass. In a moment, he was sitting down and calling for another prisoner.

No one on the wall dared watch as the lights began to change again.

Falnor caught Tania's eye. She shook her head and climbed down from the tree wall. As she passed behind Rinard, she laid a hand on his shoulder.

Wide-eyed and choking, he grasped her hand with his own. "Thank you," he said.

Tania nodded and returned to Falnor's side.

The captain stared at her for a moment and then said: "You climbed the tree wall."

"Yes?" said Tania.

"No one's ever done that before," he said.

"Why not?" asked Tania.

The flashing lights in the field continued.

"The magic of the tree wall does not allow it," said Falnor. He turned quickly. "Beldar! See if you can climb the tree wall!" he ordered.

"Sir?"

"Just try it," said Falnor.

"Yes, Captain."

The young man grabbed the lowest branches and pulled hard. His hands slipped off. No matter how hard he tried, he could not get a grip.

"Would you climb that again, please?" asked Falnor.

"I will," said Tania. Ignoring the lights in the field, she focused on crossing the battlements to get to the tree. Just as she was about to climb, the pulsing in the field stopped and the Birdman let out another howl. She grabbed the first branch and swung herself up. Branch after branch, she climbed until she reached the highest possible perch. Looking back down at Falnor on the battlements, she nodded.

Before she climbed down, the lights had begun again, to the wailing of the captives on the front line.

* * *

Rummel stopped, bringing almost two hundred fully armed Elves to a stop with him.

"I don't like the feel of that," he said.

"Of what, Lord Stoneboots?" asked the eldest Elf.

Rummel shook his head and remained still, listening. He put his hand up on the ceiling of the sort of bubble or moving cave in which they were traveling underground. Then he pulled it away quickly, as if it were too hot to touch.

"That," he said.

"What is it?" asked the elder.

"A powerful force has encamped on the fields of the Shioroth," said Stoneboots. "There are many goblins, trolls and ogres, along with something else which I do not recognize."

The Elves exchanged glances and murmured amongst themselves.

"Come," said Stoneboots. "We need to move carefully now."

He led them forward again, peering upward as if searching for something. Every few steps, he would wince.

"Does something hurt you?" asked the elder.

"They defile the ground with every footfall," said Rummel. "I cannot touch their poison. We must find a safe route back to the surface."

A moment later, he stopped again. He turned to face the Elves. "They have prisoners," he said.

No sooner had he said this then he let out a sharp cry and buckled to the floor, shaking. Everyone else had felt it, too. The air in their moving chamber prickled.

"What happened?" someone asked.

Rummel crouched on his toes, his hands poised above the floor in case he should lose his balance. "Wait," he said. "It seems to be passing." When he could stand again, he said: "We must help. Now is when we are most needed."

"We are with you, Lord Rummel," said the elder.

* * *

The Birdman felt around in the mess of flesh in his lap. "A waste," he said, shaking the blood from his hands. Focusing his power, he incinerated the remains. The pungent smoke drifted away. "Bring me another," he called; "a stronger one." He looked around the half-circle of prisoners. Some of them had

495

fainted. Others were on their knees, sobbing. Some stood woodenly, staring at the ground.

The goblins seized a young man and hauled him into the charred circle. They bound the prisoner's feet and forced him to the ground in front of the Birdman. As they hastily retreated, the young fellow tried desperately to wriggle away after them. The Birdman calmly reached out and pulled him back.

"Don't worry," croaked the Birdman, turning the young man over to face him. "It will all be over soon enough, one way or the other."

The prisoner froze.

The Birdman began to weave his hands in a fixed pattern, changing the motions slightly with each repetition. The prisoner lay transfixed. He could not look away as the lights began their cycle of changing colors. The young man's body twisted and squirmed as its shape elongated. His shoulders broadened and his arms lengthened. Though his eyes remained unchanged, still staring at the Birdman, his hair fell off little by little and blew away. As the lights changed more rapidly, the young man's forehead grew thick and bony. His cheekbones became more solid and his jaw grew heavy. Wrinkles appeared in his skin and cracks split across his face. The tips of his ears grew pointed and the edges became ragged and irregular. His mouth began to open, revealing teeth that had grown uneven and sharp. The muscles in his neck bulged and his chest expanded.

Still, his eyes did not change. They stared out in anguish from his ever more grotesque face as his hands and feet grew great knuckles and claws. The flashing lights burned into those staring eyes, searing deep into the body. Light began to show in the cracks in the skin. The eyes themselves now burned with the same light; no longer did they stare. As the light pulsed stronger and the Birdman's roar turned to a shriek, the body lying before the Birdman broke its bonds as if they were made of straw. It spread out on the charred grass and shook violently with the pulsing light. Then the light went out and the Surgoth stood slowly to its feet, a roar rising in its throat.

"Yes," said the Birdman. "Let it out."

The Surgoth howled at the darkened sky.

"Good," said the Birdman. "Go join your fellows and await my orders."

At that instant, the earth began to rumble. A cry went up from the goblin army. The ground behind the Birdman was rising quickly. The Birdman got to his feet and turned around. The goblins pulled back in alarm as the rising ground burst a seam and opened up.

A gargantuan hand emerged from the ground at one end of the long front line of the goblin army. Another hand emerged at the other end. Between them rose a massive head and shoulders, lifting the field as if it were a thick blanket.

The goblins abandoned the prisoners and scattered. The prisoners quailed, their arms still tied behind them.

Out from under the outstretched arms of Rummel Stoneboots raced the Elves. They went straight for the prisoners.

"Let none escape!" shouted the Birdman, sending a blast of fire down the length of one row of prisoners, knocking them down and burning some of them. Several Elves grabbed the frightened captives and rolled them on the ground to put out the flames. Then they pulled them to their feet and hauled them off toward Rummel's outstretched arms.

The Birdman sent another blast of fire down the other side, dropping many of the Elves as they tried to reach the prisoners, who had now begun to run toward Rummel.

"Fools!" shrieked the Birdman at his cowering goblin army. "The giant cannot harm you! Take back the prisoners and bring me more!"

He turned back to face the Elven attackers and quickly waved aside an arrow that had been aimed at his head. "Surgoths! Forward!" he commanded.

With a roar, the great brutes strode into action. The first one to reach a prisoner wrenched the poor woman from the arms of her Elven rescuer and tossed her aside. The Elf recovered his balance in time to face the enemy but his sword merely glanced off the monster's hide. The Surgoth swung his long arm and cuffed the Elf sharply on the side of the head, knocking him clean off his feet. The woman captive came to her senses and struggled upright just in time to see the Surgoth fall on the stunned Elf, grab his head and snap it sideways. Choking back her horror, she stumbled toward the huge giant under the blanket of earth. She had gotten only a few paces when she felt strong hands grasp her by the shoulders and lift her off the ground. Struggle though she might, she could not break loose from the Surgoth's powerful grip. A moment later, the monster dropped her on a growing pile of those who could not escape.

"To me!" bellowed Rummel. "To me!"

Goblins surged over the front lines, chasing the stragglers. Many of the Elves had already gone underground. Those who had not yet made it were having difficulty helping the freed prisoners to cover the distance back to where Rummel was slowly closing the gap in the earth.

"Quickly!" urged Rummel.

"Kill none of them!" screamed the Birdman, his rasping voice cutting through the chaos. "I want them alive!"

The Surgoths were converging on those remaining above ground. Two Elves were overcome as they tried to help their fallen friends. A group of prisoners struggling forward on their own were dashed to the ground. A few more were able to get under Rummel's outspread arms before he bowed his head and drew his hands back into the earth. With a great rumble, the ground closed up again.

Seeing the Southgate ahead, two young men, their hands still bound behind them, ran for all they were worth toward the Shioroth.

"After them!" screeched the Birdman. "Those are strong ones! Bring them to me!"

Three Surgoths dropped the prisoners they were carrying and pounded across the field toward the two men. Despite their bonds, the men were quickly covering the distance but the Surgoths were faster. One in particular was outracing its fellows. Within a few moments, it would have them in reach. Its clawed hands grasped for them but then its legs faltered and it stumbled a few paces. After staggering a few more, the monster collapsed face forward into the ground and lay still.

The two young men did not slacken their pace for a moment, driving steadily toward the Southgate. Another of the Surgoths behind them was felled, a small, distinctive green arrow driven straight into its eye. The third monster shielded its face with its great forearm, still running to catch the two young men. The goblin army came surging across the fields behind them.

Just in front of the two young men, the ground simply gave way. Both men fell into the hole that opened up in front of them. Just as quickly, the ground closed up again, leaving the Surgoth and the goblin army with no one to catch.

Arrows began to fly from the battlements on the Southgate. Goblins fell by the dozens. The Birdman called a retreat and the goblins obeyed. The Surgoths simply turned their backs and walked back to pick up the recaptured prisoners, impervious to the waves of arrows coming from the Shioroth.

* * *

Ender knelt down by a sturdy, middle-aged Pelnaran woman as she lay in the infirmary of the Green Stone. Holding the Midnight Stone in his hand, he surveyed her body, noting the deep claw marks in her back, the bruises on her arms and legs, the places where her hair had been torn out. As she lay there unconscious, Ender could see the damage that had been done to her soul. Until this was resolved, her physical injuries would have to wait. He poured healing light into her troubled heart. Slowly, the tangled mess began to dissolve. He remained there until it had washed away. Then he focused on her external wounds, closing the cuts, easing away the bruises.

When he finished, he stood up and took another deep breath. There were many wounded already. He had found their inner wounds to be particularly confounding. Whatever horrors the Birdman and his army had inflicted, they were proving difficult to erase.

"It's spreading," said Rummel.

"I thought so," said Ender, slipping the Midnight Stone back into his pocket. "The Stone takes all my concentration to control."

"The Dwarves are on their way," said Rummel. "I cannot go deep enough to bring them in as I did the Elves. The ground is completely defiled outside."

"Then we must find another way," said Ender. "When do you expect them?"

"That is difficult to tell," said Rummel. "My senses no longer extend beyond the tree wall."

"Are Falnor and Thadris aware?"

"They are," said Rummel. "Thadris has gathered the Elves by the Westgate. Falnor commands his troops at the Southgate. When the Dwarves arrive, we hope to be able to protect their entrance from the Western woods."

Aaron and Owler came in the doorway.

"We have another option," said Aaron. "I don't think we have much of a chance bringing in the Dwarves through the Westgate. It's too close to the Surgoths and the goblin archers would have them within range fairly quickly."

"What do you suggest?" said Rummel.

"The enemy has set up camp in the south," said Aaron. "If the Dwarves keep to the woods and move north to come in through the Northgate, they should be out of range long enough to cover the extra distance."

"But Yorgun knows nothing of this," said Rummel.

"Set up a distraction. I can slip into the woods unnoticed," said Owler.

Rummel winced.

"Another one," said Ender.

"Yes," said Rummel. "The extent of their power spreads with the creation of every Surgoth."

Owler looked from one to the other. "I suggest we move now. I can hide in the woods as long as is necessary, but if Yorgun and Roggin are here soon, we will have no choice but to risk the Westgate."

"Agreed," said Aaron.

"Do as you say," said Ender. "I have an idea. Owler, where will you exit for the Western wood?"

"The shortest distance is from the Westgate," said Owler.

"When you see smoke, it will be time to go," said Ender. "Come, Aaron. I want Mari and Holren's help with this."

* * *

Tania stood on the battlements beside Falnor and tried not to focus too much on the transformations that continued across the fields. The lights had been flickering and flashing without pause.

"We have company," she said as Holren and Mari came out of the guard tower door, followed by Ender.

"So we do," said Falnor.

"Warn your men," said Ender. "We are going to be making a lot of noise and light."

"Send the word," said the captain. "Stand by!"

The three wizards aligned themselves in the center of the battlements. The Birdman was busy with yet another transmutation. The lights continued to flash as always.

With a nod, Ender brought out the Midnight Stone.

A great wailing sound began off to the east, seemingly somewhere in the heavy overcast. It grew louder and louder until the goblin army turned to look at the bright orange light that came screaming out of the clouds. The huge fireball scattered the goblin army. Even the Surgoths stood back as it came crashing down in front of them, spreading fire across the entire front line, just in front of the remaining prisoners. A wide swath of grass leapt into flame.

The Birdman tossed aside his ruined creation and turned toward the Shioroth. Another flaming ball was hurtling toward him from the east. The Birdman reached back and then shoved his hand forward toward the fireball. His own flaming mass headed upward on a collision course with the one coming from the sky. They met in midair and exploded in a blinding flash that showered flaming bits across the field, lighting the grass on fire.

Still another flaming ball came screaming out of the eastern sky. Shrieking in anger, the Birdman immediately sent another ball of flames to meet it. As the molten fire rained down, more fireballs began to fall, this time behind the line of prisoners that had been made to stand in front of the goblin army. These were much smaller fireworks but they still scattered the goblin troops.

"Surgoths! Seize the prisoners!" cried the Birdman. "Spread them out. Hold them up for all to see!"

The Surgoths obeyed, grabbing the captives and carrying them back in amongst the rest of the army, holding them high in the air so that they could be seen from the Shioroth. As the Birdman expected, the fireballs stopped falling.

Smoke filled the air between the Southgate and the goblin encampment. The Birdman stepped back into his circle and faced the Shioroth. Slowly, at first, then faster and faster, he wove his arms in a complex pattern. A thin, purple wall of fog began to form in the air in front the goblin army. It swirled like a sheen of oil on water, semi-solid in one place, only to slip away and reform elsewhere.

* * *

"He creates a shield," said Holren.

Ender nodded, his eyes focused on the Birdman and his hand holding the Midnight Stone at arm's length. "I am impeding him," said the Stonekeeper; "but there is another great power impeding me. The pull of the Twin is very strong."

"Understood," said Holren. He and Mari both began to weave their own shield spells, raising a green-tinged wall of light about halfway across the field, just at the edge of the purple fog. The wall grew higher and the Birdman directed his own shield to match it. Sparks flew between the swirling fog and the wall of light. Wherever the fog was strongest, the green light increased to match it and the fog swirled away to another place where the green light was weaker.

"He's turning away," said Falnor.

The purple fog continued to swirl against the green wall of light as the Birdman returned to his burnt out circle and sat down once again to call for yet another prisoner.

"The spells are in place," said Holren, ceasing the weaving of his arms and hands. "The shields will counteract each other as long as they both exist."

Mari leaned on the parapet. "That takes a significant amount of strength to maintain," she said.

Ender nodded. "It does," he acknowledged. "I can impede his magic only if I continue to focus on it."

"At this point, we have a draw," said Holren. "I hope it was long enough for Owler."

* * *

"More sorcery," said Roggin, holding his hand up to halt the Dwarf company as the sky beyond the forest canopy lit up again.

"The battle has begun without us," said Yorgun.

"I'm going to take a look," said Roggin. He turned to the Dwarves nearby. "I need a volunteer to go with me."

"I'll go," said one of the taller Dwarves.

"Polfern, is it?" asked Roggin, looking up at the long face with the dark beard and dark eyes.

"Fleetfoot Polfern, at your service," said the tall one.

"Good," said Roggin. "I'm hoping we won't need speed, but it can't hurt."

They set off ahead, keeping watch on all sides as they cut quickly and silently through the forest. The constantly changing lights made Roggin's cropped hair stand on end. As they came closer to the edge of the wood, they moved carefully through the underbrush from tree to tree, working toward a spot where they could see better.

A muffled grunt beside him made Roggin turn around. His sword tip was smoothly, almost silently moved away by Polfern's sword.

"Roggin!" hissed the shadowy figure aiming Polfern's sword at Roggin and holding a knife at Polfern's throat. "It's Owler!"

Roggin lowered his blade and Owler swung Polfern's sword around to hand it back to its owner, grip first. "My apologies, sir," he whispered. "Roggin and I know each other better, so there was less chance that he might try to take my head off."

Polfern put his dagger away and took his main weapon back. "Understandable," he said. "I would have if I could have."

"What are you doing here?" asked Roggin. "What is happening on the fields?"

"Come see," said Owler. He led them to a great tree behind which they could all hide.

Roggin's eyes grew large.

"What is that thing?" asked Polfern.

"What's he doing?" asked Roggin.

"The Birdman is creating Surgoths," said Owler. "He's making them out of Pelnaran captives. These monsters are larger than humans and their only weak point is their eyes. Elsewhere, they're impervious to steel, but they can be burned."

"Hard for a Dwarf to reach that high," said Roggin. He looked at the Westgate across from their position. "It will be a sprint to the finish."

"We have another option. How many are with you?" asked Owler.

"Two hundred and fifty," said Roggin; "armed and ready. It's been a long march, but we expected that."

"If we exit the forest north of the city wall, near that massive pine, the Lammethan will be waiting for us at the Northgate where we can get in safely," said Owler.

"That will give us a little more room," said Roggin. "Let's get back and get moving."

As they turned to retrace their steps, Owler stopped them and they all dropped low. Several figures were moving through the undergrowth just inside the edge of the woods, coming from the south.

"Goblins," said Owler. "Fifteen." He tapped Roggin on the shoulder. "Go! Don't wait for me!"

With that, he turned and ducked into the undergrowth, heading deeper into the woods. Finding a moss-covered mass of boulders, he climbed up the backside and perched near the top where he could get a good look.

The goblins were traveling quickly but not particularly quietly, moving through the woods in a loose group, swords drawn. Each one had a bow and a quiver of arrows. Owler figured they intended to watch the main road and ambush any help arriving from the west. They would probably just inflict some damage and quickly retreat to sound the alarm.

He drew two small daggers and waited, keeping his eye on a tall goblin on the far side of the group. When they were just parallel to him, he sent one dagger flying. The tall goblin went down with a piece of sharp metal embedded in his temple. Another dagger took out the shorter goblin just behind him. A guttural shout from one of the goblins nearby brought the rest of them to a halt. All goblin eyes turned to see. Before they could react, another goblin right in the midst of them took a dagger to the nape of the neck and dropped like a felled tree, face down. The remaining dozen goblins clumped close together, looking frantically in all directions. Three of them had arrows on the string and the rest had their swords drawn. Owler launched several small rocks in various directions and quickly climbed down, purposely dislodging a great deal of moss.

"Take cover!" shouted the goblin leader. "Over there!"

Owler shot away from the boulders, zig-zagging through the underbrush. After leaving behind several deliberate misdirections, he found a hard patch of ground and took off northward at a dead run.

* * *

"Scurvy bastards were just here!" hissed one of the goblins, pointing to the broken moss scraped off the backside of the boulders.

"How many?" asked the leader.

"Don't know," said the first. "Looks like three or four."

"Tracks!" said another. "Human...Elf maybe."

"I say we hunt him down and kill the rest of them," said the first.

"And run into another ambush!" said the leader. "Stupid idea."

They waited, listening, sniffing the air, looking for anything that moved.

Finally, the leader grunted. "All right, you rats. Arrows on the string. Let's go."

* * *

Calicia saw Ender making his way down the steps from the Southgate, one hand against the stone wall as if to steady himself. Quickly, she ran up to meet him.

"You're injured," she said.

He smiled reassuringly. "No," he replied; "just hurting."

She shook her head. "Not so," she said, pointing to his left ear.

He reached up and wiped away some of the blood trickling down his neck. "Ah," he said. "The strain of using the Midnight Stone is becoming painful."

Calicia took his arm and helped him down the last of the steps, steering him to a bench where they could sit a moment. She opened a small pouch at her side and took out a vial.

"You gave me this," she said. "I think you need a drop of it now."

Her husband nodded. "Just a drop," he said. "There may soon be many others who need it."

Calicia opened the vial and dropped a single drip on his tongue. Putting the stopper back on the vial, she said. "That should make a significant difference."

No sooner had she said so than Ender leaned forward as if to retch. She clutched him tightly to keep him from pitching off the bench. He stared blindly at the ground, convulsing randomly, his body heaving. Even through his tunic, she could feel a certain tingling sensation when she touched him. When the convulsions lessened, she reached up to wipe the hair back from his face. Touching his skin sent a shock through her that made her dizzy. Quickly, she pulled her hand back.

In a few minutes, Ender was able to sit up again. His eyes were still somewhat glassy.

"What happened?" asked Calicia when his breathing was more normal.

"The Jalice," said Ender. "I think its magic and that of the Midnight Stone do not mix well."

"How do you feel now?" asked Calicia.

"No worse than before," said Ender; "but no better."

Calicia nodded. The strongest cure had failed.

* * *

Roggin peered out from behind the tall pine. On the south side of the Shioroth, the lights continued to change colors, reflecting off the low clouds and casting the great central monolith of the city as an ominous silhouette. He could see the gleaming helmets of the Lammethan on the battlements of the Northgate. The low, grassy rise ahead was all that stood between him and the safety of the Northgate. Still, it was more than half a league away, and two hundred and fifty Dwarves would need a considerable amount of time to cover that distance on foot. Looking south, he could see nothing moving in the relatively narrow gap between the Shioroth's outer wall and the western woods. Turning back to his fellows, he whistled three times.

The first group of ten Dwarves charged ahead with Yorgun in the lead. They had not gotten far when a goblin cry went up from the woods. Roggin waited for a count of twenty and whistled again. The second group of ten charged after the first. The wiry Dwarf kept his eye on the western edge of the Shioroth's tree wall as he counted to twenty again. Time after time, he continued to count to twenty and send out another group. Still no goblins appeared.

Group after group emerged from the woods and raced toward the Northgate as fast as their Dwarven legs could carry them. Roggin's heart pounded. There was still no sign of the enemy. Finally, he gave the signal to his own group, the last of them. On his whistle, they all surged forward, their feet pounding the tall grass on their way up the hill. The long, tense wait in the woods had made Roggin's legs feel stiff and sore but he raced ahead anyway, quickly outstripping the rest of his group of ten. He slowed to keep pace with them, shouting encouragement to the slower runners toward the back.

They had climbed half of the low rise when Roggin glanced to his right and saw arrows flying. Around the corner, closing at tremendous speed were ten huge, dark figures, such as Roggin had never seen before. They seemed overly tall and top-heavy and appeared to have some sort of shield on their heads.

"Run!" yelled Roggin. Some of his group were not keeping up well. He urged the faster ones forward and fell back to join the slower ones. When he turned his head to his right again, he got a better look at the top-heavy creatures. They seemed to have strange arms wrapped around their waists.

Whatever they were, they could run alarmingly fast and they cared nothing for the rain of arrows coming from the Westgate battlements. Another quick glance told Roggin he had misinterpreted: each of the tall creatures had a goblin riding on its back. The goblins were holding a shield over the taller one's head with one hand and clutching a bow in the other as they hung on to their mounts.

"Surgoths!" he yelled. "Goblin archers!"

Roggin's group had covered perhaps a third of the distance to the Northgate when the arrows began to fly toward them. The Surgoths had taken the shields from their goblin riders and held them high to protect the archers. This slowed the tall monsters a little, but not much.

"Keep moving!" called Roggin. "Don't stop!"

At first, the arrows fell short. The Dwarves pounded forward. Soon, arrows were thudding into their shields. Two Dwarves in the group ahead of Roggins fell. The roar of the Surgoths rang out across the field. Ahead, Roggin could see that more than half of the Dwarven company had made it to safety. Clearly, the rest of them would have to stand and fight.

"Halt!" he cried over the howls of the goblins and the roaring of the advancing Surgoths.

The Dwarves closest to him stopped immediately and formed circles, swords and axes out. The goblins dismounted from the backs of the Surgoths and dropped to the ground, firing arrows at the legs of the Dwarves as the tall monsters surged forward.

Roggin marveled at the sight of these hairless, man-shaped, long-armed creatures whose swarthy skin glistened darkly. "The eyes!" he yelled. "Go for the eyes!"

The goblins shrieked and called to their comrades but Roggin had no time to guess why; the Surgoths were upon them, crashing through the armed Dwarven circles, swinging great iron cudgels. Dwarves fell beneath the heavy blows. Some would not rise again.

Roggin swung his sword at the first monster to break into his group, but the sharp edge merely bounced off the tough hide. As the Surgoth turned on him, he ducked and rolled out of the way. A goblin arrow thumped into the ground where he had been standing. The Surgoth vented its wrath on the skull of one of Roggin's companions who fell to the ground.

Roggin scrambled upright and jammed his shield into the path of a Surgoth hand reaching to grab another Dwarf who had been knocked down in the fray. The Surgoth seized the shield and yanked Roggin off his feet, flinging him and his shield a short distance away. The wiry Dwarf caught a glimpse of flickering lights and fluttering wings as he rolled over to get up again. He dodged one goblin sword stroke and parried another and another, finally getting enough room to take a full swing with his blade. The goblin went down, one knee cut out from under it. Roggin bashed the wounded creature's sword tip aside with one stroke and severed the goblin's neck with the next. He looked up to see where the others were.

Bright lights were flickering all around. He couldn't make out what they were, but some of them seemed to be attacking the Surgoths. One of the tall monsters had somehow taken an arrow in the face; it crumpled to the ground. Another was covering its face with one arm and fending off a barrage of blows with the other. The Dwarves at its knees were pounding it with axes, and though they made no cuts, they were able to bring it down.

Roggin raced over to an older Dwarf who was trying to crawl to the Northgate, two goblin arrows lodged in his leg. Before he could get there, three flickering lights converged on the old fellow, surrounding him and lifting him up into the air. A goblin arrow pierced one of the flickering lights. To Roggin's amazement, an older Faerie man materialized where the light had been. Another goblin arrow found its mark and the Elder Faerie fell from the sky. The flickering lights sank lower to the ground with their Dwarf cargo until another flickering light came to help. Roggin heard a bow twang higher above him and looked up to see a female Faerie archer draw another arrow from her quiver, twisting sideways to avoid a goblin projectile.

"Run!" she yelled at Roggin. "We'll hold off the rest of them!"

"To the gates!" hollered Roggin. "To the gates!"

Every Dwarf who could run fled for the Northgate. Faeries traded arrows with the goblins. Several Surgoths continued forward, chasing down the Dwarves. Roggin looked about to see if any who had fallen were still moving. A goblin arrow struck his shield, splintering off a bit near his face. There was no more time. He turned back toward the Northgate and ran for it. Not far ahead of him, a dark Surgoth had caught up with a pair of fleeing Dwarves and reached down to seize them. It knocked one over and grabbed the other by the neck, lifting it clear off the ground. Roggin plowed into the back of its knees, shield first. The Surgoth stumbled and dragged its Dwarf captive down with it. Roggin got kicked out of the way but he was back in a second, hammering at the back of the Surgoth's neck with repeated blows.

The Surgoth rolled over on its back and reached for Roggin's sword with its free hand. For the first time, Roggin got a look at the thing's face. It seemed to have only a dim glow in the dark holes where the eyes should have been. The mouth split into a jagged-toothed grin as the monster grabbed Roggin's sharp blade barehanded. Roggin yanked on his weapon but could not pull it away as the Surgoth jammed its shining tip between the captured Dwarf's helmet and shoulder armor and jerked it sideways. Roggin let go of his own blade and dove for his companion's weapon, wrenching it away from the dead hand. The Surgoth let go of the dead Dwarf and grabbed Roggin by the leg.

Someone else stabbed hard with a Dwarven sword, driving the sharp tip in deep, just under the Surgoth's heavy brow. The Surgoth went limp.

"Let's go!" said Owler, leaving Roggin's blade in the Surgoth's head and grabbing his friend by the sleeve.

Roggin hauled his leg free and ran for all he was worth. The woodsman kept pace with him.

A firestorm of Faerie arrows covered their entrance into the Northgate. As soon as they were inside, the gates were slammed shut and barred, but there was no longer any need. The remaining Surgoths had hauled up the few goblins that were still alive and were now racing away into the western woods.

Owler slipped his own sword back into its sheath. "Good to see you, my friend," he said.

"Good to see you!" answered Roggin, breathless.

High overhead, Faerie archers returned to the Shioroth, some of them carrying the wounded or dead.

* * *

"Open the gates!" called a deep voice from below, breaking the stillness of the second watch.

"Open the gates!" called the Lammethan guard in the watchtower, recognizing the voice immediately.

Grisbane, Thisvane, Defgar, Rifgar and Gullen slipped between the gates and nearly collapsed once inside.

"What news?" asked a Faerie messenger.

"Tell Ender, Falnor and Rohidan that the bridge is gone," said Grisbane between breaths. "Black Warriors attacked. Brian taken eastward by a dragon. Annie followed." He stopped to get some air. "We've seen neither of them since. Came straight here."

He swallowed, dry-mouthed and looked down at the messenger. "Black Warriors here yet?" he asked.

"No," said the messenger.

"They will be soon."

"Anything else?" asked the messenger.

Grisbane bent down to rest his hands on his knees and shook his head.

"Do you need food?" asked one of the Lammethan soldiers as the messenger flew away.

"No," said Defgar. "Water and rest." Grisbane and the others nodded.

CHAPTER 52

The Stage is Set

Falnor stood outside in the courtyard of the Green Stone, watching the constantly changing lights in the southern fields. The howling and shrieking that followed every creation of a Surgoth made it difficult to sleep. This news from the Small Giants was grave. The Valen and the Snowdaughter were missing. A dragon was on the loose. Black Warriors had forced the destruction of the bridge and would be arriving soon.

He went back inside, determined to get at least a little rest. Candlelight seeped out from under the door to Tania's quarters. He walked over and gently rapped on the door. He heard her gasp inside.

"It's Captain Falnor," he said. "Is there any trouble?"

"Come in," she said.

He opened the door to find the dark young woman huddled in the far corner of her room, her arms around her knees. He looked quickly around the room, his hand going instinctively to his dagger, but she waved him off.

"Come in," she repeated, resting her forehead on her knees so her face was hidden.

Falnor entered. There was no one else in the room.

"What is the matter?" he asked.

She shook her head without looking up, her tousled, black hair rocking from side to side. "Please," she said. "Shut the door and just sit with me a moment."

He did so, crossing his legs and settling down with his back against the wall, about arm's reach from her. For some time, they remained like that,

"They are close," said Tania, finally. "I can feel them."

"The Golrakken?" asked Falnor.

"Their minds are constantly probing, and they consume everything within reach," she said. "I am afraid."

"They are not here yet," said Falnor.

"You cannot know how dangerous they are until—" She caught herself. For a few seconds her body shook silently.

Falnor reached out and placed a firm hand on her shoulder. She nodded, her face still hidden behind her knees.

"You must remember," she said weakly. "I was one of them." She shook silently again.

"There are times," she said, her voice trembling; "when it still seems to attract me, to draw me back in."

"I understand their magic is very powerful," he said, sitting back against the wall.

Tania lifted her face and looked at him. Her deep green eyes were swollen and red-rimmed. "I failed once. What if I fail again? They are not even here yet and still I hear them calling me back into that living death. I hated it then. I hate it now. But something inside me still wants to return to it."

Falnor nodded. "Can I do anything for you?" he asked.

She studied him a moment. "Yes," she said, reaching for his hand. "I understand that among the Men of the Green Stone, comrades in arms will braid each others' hair."

"We do," said Falnor.

Tania managed a meager smile. "Would the captain kindly braid my hair?"

"Certainly," said Falnor. "Turn around and I will see what can be done."

Instead, she curled up on the floor at his feet and rested her head on his knee. Falnor spread her thick, black hair across his lap and gently began to work out the tangles.

* * *

"I do not like the looks of this," said the Golrakken lieutenant, his hollow eyes roving back and forth across the southern fields in the dull gray dawn. "There are thousands of them. And he has more of the tall ones with him. Where does he find them?"

The light pattern sped up once more and the Birdman in the southern fields leaned back and howled as the light finally went out.

"He's making them," said Dragonhelm, leaning forward in the saddle. "Watch."

Another Surgoth stood up and roared in front of the Birdman.

"Indeed," said the lieutenant. "Can they be turned?"

"I think not," said Karkaan; "no more than those goblins he made earlier." He looked off at the Shioroth. "Captain, lead the men to the Eastgate," he said to another officer nearby. "Set up ranks just outside of arrow range." Turning back to his lieutenant, he said: "Let us go see what this Birdman has to say."

* * *

"Your lordship, the Golrakken leader would speak," said the goblin messenger to the Birdman once the lights and the roaring had come to a stop. The newest Surgoth looked at him disinterestedly and walked back to join the dozens of other dark-skinned, hairless monsters that now stood in loose groups throughout the encampment.

"Blindfold the remaining prisoners and block their ears," said the Birdman to one of the larger goblins. "Take them out of sight."

"I need six Surgoths!" he called. "Come." The closest half dozen of the monsters strode to his side. "Now," he said to the messenger. "I will meet this Golrakken leader away from the rest of the troops."

The goblin messenger flinched just a little as the Birdman laid a bony, clawed hand on his shoulder.

"Lead me to him," said the Birdman.

The messenger steered the Birdman through the maze of goblin platoons. The six Surgoths followed just behind him.

"Stop here," said the Birdman, quietly, squeezing the messenger's shoulder when they had walked a few paces away from the encampment. The Golrakken leader and his lieutenant were still a short distance away.

"Hail, Golrakken!" croaked the Birdman. "I see that some of us are slower to arrive than others."

"Hail, Birdman," returned Karkaan. "All things in good time. What are your intentions? Are you following orders as directed by the Dark Master?"

The Birdman croaked a little and fixed them with a blind eye. "We can all feel the influence of the Dark Master even here, can't we," he said. "I have fulfilled the orders as I have seen fit. I'm sure you intend to do the same."

"Indeed," said Karkaan. "However, I notice that you build your army even as the rest of us arrive according to plan."

"All the better to execute the plan," said the Birdman. "You would do the same, given the opportunity."

"Of course," said Karkaan. "I also notice you were careful to put away your spoils before we came too close."

"No need to subject them to unnecessary influence," said the Birdman. "I'm sure you understand. Now, to let you know what has been done in your absence, we already infiltrated the woods to the west and we hold the southern fields secure."

"I sense a shield," said Karkaan. "How far does it extend?"

"Only to the point where we now stand," said the Birdman; "but the greater magic is deeper in the earth itself. It now laps at the roots of the tree wall."

"Understood," said Dragonhelm. "That will make our task that much easier. When the time comes to attack, the signs will be obvious. Do we have your agreement that the attack will be simultaneous, as decreed by the Dark Master?"

The Birdman nodded. "And do we have yours?"

Karkaan nodded.

The Birdman stood silent a moment. Then he said: "Your answer, Golrak."

Karkann leaned forward and chuckled, a sound like gravel in a barrel. "I gave you the same answer you gave me, Birdman."

The Birdman nodded. "Very well," he said. "I await the signal to attack. Keep your men outside the shield and nothing will befall them."

"What would you do to a Golrak?" asked Karkaan. "Not even the Black Warriors can touch us without consequence. Nothing kills us. We come back in another body—and there will be plenty of fodder for the Golrakken as the day unfolds."

"I have magic of which you do not know, Dragonhelm," said the Birdman. With that, he turned and had his messenger lead him back to his army.

The Golrakken turned their horses and headed for the eastern fields.

"Mere threats?" asked the lieutenant.

"Not likely," said Karkaan. "But we cannot tell either way, which is what he intends, I'm sure. In the meantime, let us see if we can take the Eastgate without a fight."

* * *

"Under NO circumstances will any of us respond!" shouted Thadris. "There is nothing to discuss. Your life depends on your silence!"

The hundreds of Elven and Faeirie troops that had mustered to the Eastgate nodded fervently.

Arrayed across the eastern fields was a line of a hundred Golrakken.

"Is there anything we can do?" asked Calicia, looking up at her husband as the troops lined up on the battlements and took their stations on either side of the street leading up to the Eastgate.

"This time, yes," said Ender.

To Calicia, he seemed paler than the day before. He was more stooped, his voice was a little softer, and the creases around his eyes seemed a little deeper. She knew he had not slept in days.

"Good," she said, trying to sound cheerful.

He smiled down at her, put his arm around her thin shoulders and gave them a squeeze. Then he picked up his bow, slung his quiver over his shoulder and left to join the archers on the battlements. Calicia returned to care for those in the infirmary.

The clouds that had covered the sky for the last several days were darker than ever. Though it was mid-morning, a pall had settled over the Shioroth. In the distance, lightning flashed, sending long peals of thunder rolling across the flatlands. The wind had grown cold. Bits of stinging rain sputtered out of the black sky.

The Golrakken leader stood up in his saddle. He appeared to be saying something. He stopped. No one on the walls said a word. He appeared to say something once again, this time a longer harangue. The Elves on the wall looked at each other.

"No need for us to have to hear him," said Ender, quietly. "Just do not respond in any way. Let him speak if he likes."

Now more and more of the Golrakken were yelling and gesticulating at the company guarding the Eastgate. None of their efforts made any sound.

One of the younger Elves snickered.

"Beware," said Thadris loudly. "We are blessed not to have to listen to the Golrakken, but we are no less vulnerable. Each one of you is needed to fight when the time comes but we cannot risk having anyone respond and betray us all. Sober yourself or be dismissed!"

"Yessir," came the reply.

This went on for well over an hour. Several times, the Golrakken regrouped, spoke amongst themselves and then tried again.

Ender continued to hold the Midnight Stone. The pull of the Twin was constant now. He wondered how close Morvassus must be for the pull to be so strong. He had kept himself grounded by standing on the solid stone, and he had kept the Midnight Stone busy with protective or healing tasks. Still, the control he had over the Stone felt like it was weakening. As foolish as Ender knew it was, the urge to fly off and find the Twin was urgent and unrelenting. He wiped away a little fresh blood that had oozed from his ear and focused on maintaining the shield of silence that blocked out the harsh Golrakken voices.

*　*　*

Just before midday, Rohidan flew to the Eastgate.

"The Black Warriors are in sight," he said.

"How many?" asked Thadris.

"Thousands," said the Elder Faerie; "all on horseback."

"I assume they will secure the fields by the Northgate," said Thadris.

"As do I," said Rohidan. "The Small Giants and the Dwarves have reinforced the defenses on that side."

"They're here," said Ender, pointing at a dark line of horses approaching from the southeast, already heading northward behind the Golrakken. Two of the Gray Warriors were riding swiftly to meet the arriving army.

The Midnight Stone in his hand seemed even more alive in the presence of this new force. From what Ender could tell, the stronger the connection of the army to Morvassus, the more the Twin's power played on the Midnight Stone. He returned his concentration to maintaining the silence spell.

The defenders on the Eastgate watched as the two Golrakken returned and the long line of Black Warrior cavalry spread out around the Shioroth.

"Ender!" came a booming call. Taking a deep breath, Ender turned to see Rummel Stoneboots standing a short way up the street leading to the Eastgate.

"The defilment has crept past the tree wall!" said Rummel. "The trees are dying!"

Ender turned his attention to the ground beneath them. Perhaps it was the Midnight Stone's attunement to the darker magic that allowed him to sense it now. Still maintaining the silence, Ender thought about counteracting the spreading menace below. At first nothing happened. Then, the more he thought about it, the more he could feel the deep magic under their feet. The more he could feel it, the more difficult it was to control the Midnight Stone. The resonance of the Stone and the deep magic was stronger than his small spell of silence.

Quickly, he broke into his thoughts about the encroaching defilement, focusing once again on the silence. While he felt better, doubt had set in about his ability to protect the Shioroth. The pain in his head was spreading slowly throughout his body.

"I cannot stop the spread," said Ender to Rummel. "Are all the elderly and infirm in the central garden?"

"Yes," said Stoneboots. "Your wife is there, tending to the injured. I will inform the Southgate and then go to the central garden see what comfort I may give."

Ender only nodded.

"I will return to the Northgate," said Rohidan.

"May the gates hold as they always have," said Thadris.

Rohidan flew off, skimming the rooftops on his way to the Northgate.

Not much later, the Black Warriors had formed a solid line cutting off the Shioroth from the north. The city was surrounded.

* * *

"What do you make of it?" asked Owler.

Captain Falnor swallowed hard and set his jaw. "This changes everything," he said. He had taken them a short distance back from the Southgate so they could confer in privacy.

"The Circle of the Ancients collapsed outward on Cai-Amira," said Owler. "That seemed to be the doing of the Golrakken."

"Were that to happen here, we would be completely exposed," said Falnor. "Do we fall back now? Rummel said the trees were dying, but they may still be intact otherwise. They are very dense. Even if the branches no longer repel climbers, they still offer some protection."

"Yes, but that's only a matter of time," said Owler. He looked back toward the Southgate. "They have no siege engines. No one is building ladders. Nothing about their behavior suggests that they expect to have to scale the wall."

"We can pull back to the inner garden," said Falnor. "Lerran!" he called to a Faerie courier. "This is important. How you deliver this message will mean the difference between determined action and panic when it is received. Spread the word that the tree wall is compromised and that we are to defend it like we would any strong wooden wall. Do you understand?"

The courier repeated the message back to the captain and was coached again to ensure he had it right. Then off he went.

"Ah," said Owler. "Better to tell them now, from an authority, than for the rumor to spread."

CHAPTER 53

The Mountains of the Oryxx

The gruffen raced across the barren landscape, crossing over the trail time and again as he cut across the switchbacks. The heavy rain that had been falling most of the morning had finally tapered off. Not that it mattered; Brian was already soaked to the hide. Running hard was the best way to stay warm. He charged over an icy pass and dug his claws in to control his descent down the other side. Back on the rocks, he loped along swiftly. His pace would have exhausted a horse but the gruffen could keep it up hour after hour.

Stopping by a stony brook, he took a good look in all directions before he stuffed his face in the water and got a quick drink. The taste was acrid, but it was better than nothing. It was odd to be so wet and so thirsty at the same time, he thought.

His inner sense of direction kept him going due west. When he had to divert his route to avoid a particularly dangerous cliff or skirt a body of water, he always continued westward afterward, not correcting to the north or south, regardless of how far out of the way he had gone to avoid the obstacle. By now he had gotten completely away from the main trail, which made him actually quite happy, since it reduced his chances of running into the Black Warriors.

Descending the back slope of a high pass, he came to a stop at the edge of a deep ravine, a great crack in the rocky landscape. From where he stood, he could see no easy way down, and no obvious route back up the other side. Down the slope a good distance to his left, the ravine appeared to end in an even steeper gully. Brian decided to take his chances uphill. Moving quickly, he followed the edge of the ravine, keeping an eye out for a place where he could cross.

After a long time, the sides of the ravine seemed to be coming closer together, but they were steeper and more sheer than ever. He kept moving, checking every so often to confirm that there was really no way down. The ravine wasn't as deep here, but a fall would still be fatal. A short distance further up, he came upon a place where a section of the cliff on this side had broken off and fallen in. A great block of rock had lodged itself partway down the ravine, connecting one wall to the other. The wall on this side where the rock had come loose seemed to be down-climbable. In the dim light, the far side seemed almost smooth. There didn't appear to be a lot of holds. Brian went a short distance further, took another look at it and decided to try it. At worst, he would simply have to climb up the same side and try again elsewhere.

He backed into the break and started down. The rock must have fallen relatively recently because much of the rock on this side was still loose. He tested every hold, breaking apart any bits that were not solid. The last few feet to the bridging block was a steep, short slope of loose scree. He half walked, half slid down to the great chunk of stone in the middle of the ravine.

The upper, exposed side of the rock was sharp and angular, like a steep ridge line leading up to the far wall. The climb looked much steeper from here than it had appeared from up above. Below, the narrow ravine continued to drop into darkness.

Brian straddled the angled edge of the rock, inching his way up, digging his claws in anywhere he could find a crack and taking advantage of every available bump. About three quarters of the way up, he came to a great crack in the rock that allowed him to get a good grip with both hands. He pulled and scrambled up beyond it so he could get his foot in the crack.

Finally able to rest a moment, he studied the far wall.

It still appeared featureless and smooth. His eyes roved across the cliff face, looking for any cracks that might be useful. The most obvious crack was off to the right, too far to reach from the rock which he straddled now. His foot was getting sore jammed in that crack, so he pulled it out and set it a little higher, still studying the wall. No new, promising holds presented themselves. He decided to get closer to see what he could find.

He moved his weight forward and instantly felt the shift. With what sounded like crackling thunder, the rock on which he had been sitting began to crumble. Chunks of it fell off into the ravine. Brian scrambled forward toward the solid wall. Bits of rubble began to slide off left and right. When he reached the cliff face, Brian dislodged a large boulder and almost tumbled down after it. The entire bridge was starting to slide into the deep, rolling slowly to the left as it broke apart, exposing a flake of rock. Brian got a hand on the upper edge of the flake as the bridge collapsed underneath him. Without a foothold, he swung wildly to the side, hanging on for dear life.

As he swung back the other direction, dust came blasting up out of the deep crevice below, blinding him before he had a chance to shut his eyes. Choking, he felt around for another handhold, still unable to find a good foothold. He blinked frantically, but the stinging dust clouded everything. Blindly, he felt his way to the right, following the upper edge of the flake.

It seemed like forever before he could get a hand inside the vertical crack he had seen earlier. With a great deal of effort, hand over hand, he pulled himself up high enough to get a foot on the top of the flake. Finally, he was able to get a hand free and rub the dust out of his eyes. He looked back at where the bridge had been. Some scree on the other side of the ravine slid off and showered down into the crevice. Taking a deep breath, he exhaled heavily, took a look up the crack and started to climb out.

* * *

The crow flew fast and high across the wide valley, scanning in all directions. He wasn't entirely sure what he might find. Would she be on the ground, wings folded? If so, he might as well be hunting for a human. Would she be in the air, wings spread? Would she be in that flickering light form used by the Firstborn? He might never see her, she was so fast. She could be above him, below him, to one side or the other.

Once more, he muttered to himself. Why hadn't he taken a different route in the first place? Of course, he handn't counted on the Golrakken being on the move, but then, when the time came to hide, he picked the spot that was most dangerous for her. If he had led her back up over the ridge, they might have gotten away undetected, or at least made enough distance to avoid capture.

Jehzik flew on, his bright eyes still searching. She could be anywhere.

* * *

Annie crossed over the wide valley and took a look at the mighty peaks ahead of her. She was pretty sure she was still heading due east. Coming in for a landing on a high outcrop, she took a look around. The rain was falling harder now. Soaked to the skin, she sat down, folded her wings behind her and touched the Ring of the Snowdaughter to the metal part of the Valenblade. Her extended sight allowed her to see far down the valley. Objects once again appeared to be very close. The face she saw next gave her such a fright, she almost dropped the Valenblade. She quickly looked away but the memory of it lingered.

The skin was dark as night. One eye appeared to have been burned away long ago, but sinews and flesh had grown over it, burrowing into the bony cheek below like tree roots seeking nourishment. The nose also seemed to have been burned away, but it had only shriveled back and cracked. The mouth seemed somehow blacker even than the black skin. The sharp, uneven teeth were also completely black.

What made her skin crawl was the brief glimpse she had gotten of the other eye. Deep in a hole where the eye should have been there lay a small marble of shiny black. She found herself breathing hard, trying to look around, to fill her vision with something other than the sight of that vast empty space with its compelling black stone.

Unfortunately, there was nothing else to look at besides the monochromatic landscape under a heavy veil of rain. As uncomfortable as she was, Annie dared to bring the ring back in contact with the Valenblade. She had to find Brian.

A cold half hour of searching with the dizzying extended vision turned up nothing. Finally, she plucked up the courage to look back where she had seen the black face. She recognized the dark figure immediately, though it seemed to be surrounded by some kind of dark smoke. The rest of the riders in the massive army were Black Warriors. She searched rank after rank, wondering if Brian was being held among them. The search was exhausting, but she did not stop until she was certain he was not there. Wearily, she turned her gaze further eastward.

Following the trail left behind the army, she traced their path back through the mountains. It was tedious going, following every turn of the road and checking along both sides. Hoofprints were everywhere, but she saw nothing with four clawed toes. The Faerie allowed her vision to rise higher, like she was flying over the road. This way she was able to move more quickly, as it were. The beaten tracks led back through several passes, finally coming to a stop at a dark fortress that looked like a hand had thrust itself up from the ground and frozen there. She knew that description. This had to be the other fortress where Jehzik had said Brian was probably taken. She was a good distance to the north of it. If she changed to light form, she could be there in a few hours.

She brought her sight back to her immediate surroundings and rubbed her eyes. When she opened them again, she gasped as a huge, moving object closed in on her, swallowing her into darkness and sweeping her off the boulder.

"Got it!" said a deep, muffled voice.

"What is it? Is it good to eat?" asked another, deeper, muffled voice.

"I don't know," said the first voice.

Annie felt around for the Valenblade. She must have set it down. Frantically, she kicked and pushed on the walls surrounding her. They gave way just a little but would not move.

"Tickly!" said the first big muffled voice.

Annie changed into light form and pushed hard, bouncing around inside her prison chamber.

"Ooh! Very tickly!" said the first big muffled voice again.

"Squish it and see if it stops," said the second, deeper voice.

"No!" said the first one.

Annie felt herself being moved very quickly a great distance and then coming to a stop. She braced herself against one corner of her prison and stayed very still.

"There, it stopped," said the first big voice.

The Faerie felt her chamber being moved again, this time more slowly.

"Let's have a look," said the deeper voice.

"What if it gets out?" asked the first voice.

"Just clap it and it won't get away," said the deeper voice.

"I'll just shake it first and see if it moves," said the first voice.

"Good idea," said the second voice.

Eyes wide, Annie braced herself again and hung on while the chamber moved violently one direction and then the other.

"Shaky, shaky, upsy-downsy!" sang the first voice. "Twisty, twisty, round-and-roundsy!"

Annie tried to keep from getting jarred loose as the chamber rolled this way and that. This made her even more dizzy than the extended sight. When she was pretty sure it finally stopped, she stayed very, very still. The chamber still seemed to be moving, but she thought it might just be her dizziness.

Everything outside was quiet.

"Now, let's have a look-see," said the deeper voice.

"A little look, a little see," said the first voice. "A little bitty lookee-see."

A bit of light came into the chamber.

"Open up already!" said the deeper voice.

Immediately, the light was doused by something in the way.

"I can't see anything," said the first voice.

"Why not?" asked the deeper voice.

"Too dark," said the first voice.

The bit of light got brighter again.

"Lemme look," said the deeper voice.

Annie was starting to get her bearings back.

"All right, you look," said the first voice.

"You gotta open it up, silly," said the deeper voice.

The chamber moved sideways again, tossing her against the wall.

"Get your fingers outta there!" said the first voice.

"I just wanna see!" said the deeper voice.

"Wait," said the first voice. There was a pause.

Annie dared not move.

"What?" asked the deeper voice.

"I think it's dead," said the first voice.

"How do you know?" asked the deeper voice.

"It's not moving," said the first voice.

The roof of the chamber came clean off and Annie wasted no time. Changing into light form, she sped off into the sky.

"What was that?" asked the second voice.

"I dunno!" said the first voice. "Let's see what I've got."

Disoriented, Annie found herself careening through the air.

"You got nothin'!" said the second, deeper voice.

"Really?" asked the first voice.

Annie righted herself and picked out the boulder where she had been sitting, amongst all the other boulders that were swimming in her vision, but she couldn't see the Valenblade. She flew down, looking for the missing blade in the jumble of rocks nearby, paying no attention to the giants.

"Wait!" whispered the deeper voice. "There's another one!"

"No! That's the same one!" insisted the first voice. "That's mine!"

Annie cast about, looking for a glimmer of metal. It had to be here somewhere.

"Get it!" hissed the second voice.

Annie looked up, poised to switch to light form and escape. A giantess was approaching, eyes wide, hands ready to grasp her again. Embedded like a thin sliver in the heel of one of those massive hands was the Valenblade. The Faerie switched to light form and shot toward the descending hand. She grasped the Valenblade by the handle and yanked it free.

"Oh-Oh-Oh! Ow! Ow! It stings!" howled the giantess. "Nasty thing!"

"I'll get it!" bellowed the giant, swatting at the escaping Faerie, but Annie was long gone, just a flicker of light headed deep into the mountains of the Oryxx.

* * *

Jehzik perched on a familiar rock and eyed the spiky towers which he had hoped never to see again. He hadn't decided if he should venture a look. The place seemed deserted. There was no movement in the watchtowers or in any of the windows or doors that were visible from this spot. For years he had used this perch to observe the fortress in secret, watching the comings and goings of Black Warriors and the Golrakken, even the occasional visit by the Interrogator. The thought of it made his stomach churn. He waited there for a long time, just thinking.

If the furball (what had she called it again? A "gruffen?") was held prisoner in there, he was going to be hard to get back out, especially if he was hurt. Chances were good that he was hurt. Jehzik found a small pebble and instinctively snatched it up for his craw. Then he spat it out. He wanted no more of this place.

Periodically, he scanned the sky, looking for the Faerie. It would be a pity if she blundered into this place only to be captured. How would he get both of them out? At least the rain had finally tapered off.

Sometime later, there was still no sign of movement in the fortress and no sign of Annie. Flying low, Jehzik slipped out from his observation post and looked for some indication that a gruffen had passed by. The only thing he found was a series of impressions in a gravel slope cutting across a switchback. The slope was too steep for a horse.

Rather than returning to his perch, Jehzik patrolled a wider area. The upper peaks of the Oryxx were hidden in clouds, and if the Faerie missed by one pass, she might bypass the fortress entirely without realizing it. He followed the rising air current up the ridge and sailed over the top of it, scudding along at crest level so as to keep an eye on both sides of the ridge. When he came to the first peak in his way, he slipped to the outside of it. He would work around the backside of the great peaks surrounding Uzzim-Khail, slipping back inside for another lap around the rim.

He completed his first loop and was about to slip inside when he caught the telltale flicker of light off to his left. Immediately, he began a series of tight circles out of sight of the fortress on the Faerie's side of the ridge. When the flicker of light stopped on the rocks just shy of the saddle, he flew over and landed.

Annie materialized and looked around. "I can't believe I found you!" said the bedraggled Faerie.

"Likewise," croaked Jehzik. "I'm amazed you escaped."

"Twice," said Annie. "Once from the Golrakken and once from two giants."

Jehzik looked at her sideways. "That far north?" he said. "That's way out of the way."

"I know," said Annie.

"How did you find this place?"

Annie held up the Valenblade. "I saw Black Warriors, too, a huge army of them. Brian wasn't with them." She shuddered.

"You saw...*him*, didn't you," said Jehzik, his feathers standing on end.

Annie nodded.

"So the Dark Master is on the move," said Jehzik. "Something must have changed drastically. He has not left this place in all the years I've been here." He hopped up on a boulder and peeked over at the darkened fortress. "Then it is empty," he said. "Maybe."

"What if Brian's trapped in there?" said Annie.

Jehzik's heart sank. "I had the same thought."

"I have to know," said Annie. "If it were me in there, he would come after me."

"Yes, and probably get himself caught just as easily," croaked Jehzik. "I don't mean to be cruel, but the chances of going in and freeing a furba—I mean a gruffen—are very slim, especially if you also want to get out intact. I can't imagine what kinds of traps have been left behind."

Annie rested her head in her left hand as her right hand kept hold of the Valenblade.

With a flurry of wings, Jehzik hopped back to where she sat. "Can you use that far sight to see into the fortress?" He thought about it for a minute. "On the other hand, that would be just the sort of thing he'd notice."

"I can try," said Annie.

"Just quickly," said Jehzik. "Back out, or whatever it is you do, if anything moves."

Skin prickling with goose flesh, Annie brought the ring in contact with the metal guard and looked over the ridge. First, she took a peek inside one of the upper windows. It was entirely dark. Another peek into an open doorway at the end of a long catwalk was no better. She tried several other windows. They were all so dark they might as well have been opaque.

"I can't see anything," she said, quickly moving her ring away from the metal.

"You don't seem to have set off any alarms," said Jehzik.

A great roaring sound wafted across from the fortress. Then it stopped. Annie froze, ready to move at any moment. There it began again, like the sound of an angry bear, only deeper and more massive.

"What's that?" hissed Annie, crouching.

Jehzik shook his head. "Nothing to worry about," he said as another roar echoed off the mountainsides. "It's Blorg snoring."

"Who's...Blorg?" asked Annie.

"The gate troll," said Jehzik. "That could be good news."

"Why?" hissed Annie, eyes wide as yet another roar rang out from the fortress.

"Listen," he said. He waited for one roar, then another. "Six," said Jehzik. "If he does a seventh, I'd say the place is abandoned."

A deep, resonating roar blasted out across the rocky faces of the Oryxx.

"I think we're in the clear," said Jehzik. "They never let him snore like that more than a few times without causing him some serious pain." The crow nodded toward the fortress as still another great snore issued forth. "I want to have a talk with him."

"Why?" asked Annie.

"He may know if the gruffen was ever here," said Jehzik.

"Why would he tell us?" asked Annie.

"It pays to be good at stealing food now and again," squawked the crow. "I've shared more than a few morsels with the gate troll of Uzzim-Khail." He hopped closer to the ridge. "You can stay here, or you can come with me," he said. "Either way, keep an eye out for me, would you?"

"I'll come with you," said Annie. "I want to hear what he has to say."

"All right," said Jehzik; "but stay out of sight of the guard tower, probably on the wall someplace. Blorg doesn't handle surprises well."

"But how will I hear him?" asked Annie.

"Don't worry," said Jehzik. "You will."

They took to the air and quickly landed on the outer wall. The place made Annie's hair stand on end. She crouched behind the battlements, trying not to breathe, partly from fear, partly because the stench was awful.

The rhythmic roaring stopped with a great, guttural howl. Annie shrank down even further.

A huge voice bellowed out from the base of the guard tower: "OH NO! WHAT ARE YOU DOING HERE?!"

There was an almost inaudible croak.

"EVERYBODY OUT!" bellowed the voice.

Another nearly inaudible croak was followed by another bellowed response: "WHY DIDN'T YOU GO OUT WITH EVERYONE ELSE? I ALREADY SHUT THE GATE AGAIN! WHY DIDN'T YOU GO OUT WITH THAT LAST ONE?"

A pause.

"THE BROWN, FURBALL ONE!"

Another pause.

"I DON'T KNOW!"

A longer pause.

"HE MADE ME OPEN THE GATE! EVERYBODY GONE!"

A nearly inaudible croak.

"LONG TIME AGO!"

Another pause.

"BROWN! FURRY! GONE! WHY ARE YOU STILL HERE?"

A longer nearly inaudible croak.

"DO YOU NEED ME TO OPEN THE GATE?"

Short pause.

"OH! THAT'S RIGHT!"

A bit longer pause.

"GOT ANY OF THOSE MEATY BITS?"

Short pause.

"TOO BAD! I LIKED THE MEATY BITS!"

Longer pause.

"SHOULD I OPEN THE GATE?"

Slightly audible croak.

"OH! THAT'S RIGHT! OFF WITH YOU, THEN! GO ON!"

Annie followed as Jehzik flew off over the battlements. Together, they raced over the pass and across the forbidding landscape for several minutes until Jehzik finally brought them down under a sheltering outcrop.

"Rrraack!" said the crow, shaking out his feathers. "I owe that stinky fellow some meaty bits."

"So he saw Brian?" asked Annie.

"Yes!" said Jehzik; "as I'm sure you heard. Amazing! The furball walked out of there on his own two feet, all by himself, it seems."

"Gruffen," Annie corrected him.

"Maybe so," said Jehzik; "but even Blorg called him a furball."

"An easy mistake to make," said Annie. "I'm guessing that Brian would head straight west. He wouldn't stick to the road."

Jehzik let out a sigh. "At least we didn't have to go into the fortress to look for him," he said. "I wasn't looking forward to that."

"Me neither," said Annie, shivering. "Now we just have to find him out here."

"Yes," said Jehzik; "and there's a lot of 'here' out here. One can easily get lost in the Oryxx. Once you're out, you have to cross the great valley, and then you still have to get through the Mirrak-Haas."

"I know; you said so," said Annie. "Let's get going. We know he left after the Black Warriors, so we should search between here and the army."

"True," said Jehzik. "Where did you see the army?"

"In a wide valley," said Annie; "near a river."

"That cuts our search area in half, but it's still a lot," said Jehzik.

"Let's go," said Annie. "And stay north. Brian will take the shortest route, but he likes being uphill."

A light drizzle began to fall as the crow and the Faerie soared off northward.

* * *

Brian crested yet another high pass and looked out over the barren landscape. He was high enough and close enough now to see that he was approaching the wide valley he had seen from the air a few days ago. He could just make out the river coursing through the middle of it. For a moment, he wondered how he would cross such a wide river. Then he shook his head. He'd have to figure that out once he got there.

He had just come through a low point in the broad shoulder of the peak. A wide spur swept off to the north and curved back westward. A row of blunted spikes marked the upper edge of the spur, but it flattened out a bit down slope before dropping off precipitously into the ravine below. The flatter section would allow him easy passage to the end of the spur which connected to the far ridge. Dropping to all fours again, he loped off down the rocky slope toward the flatter section of the spur.

The gruffen had been ignoring his stomach for a couple of days now. It had been a long time since he'd felt this hungry. So far, he had not seen hide nor hair of any game. The scrub that clung to the rocks was bitter and tough. Up this high, even moss was scarce. Perhaps he would find something edible closer to the river.

* * *

Jehzik watched as Annie drifted down and landed by a rocky overhang out of the wind and rain. Taking a last look around, he flew in and landed beside her.

"You all right?" he croaked, cocking his head sideways to fix her with a bright eye. "That weakness getting to you again?"

"Just tired," said Annie. She found a spot where she could sit and lean back against the stone wall. "And hungry," she said.

The crow bobbed his head up and down. "I could use a little grub, myself," he said. "I know a place not too far from here where I might find some." He thought for a moment. "No, not something you could stomach, I don't suppose." He thought again. "There's another place where I sometimes find food. It might take me awhile but I could try there."

Annie looked at the big crow and smiled. "You're very nice," she said. "You must be as hungry as I am."

"Probably so," said Jehzik; "which means I'm probably just as selfish as I am nice."

"Do you want some help?" asked Annie.

"No."

Annie looked out at the rain. "Maybe we should just keep looking for Brian while we look for food."

"We could," said Jehzik; "but you're not as used to this place as I am. I've lasted out here for ages. I'll go find food and bring some back. In the meantime, you stay put."

"It's going to be dark soon," said Annie.

"Easier for the thief, harder for the cook," said Jehzik. He looked around. "You picked a good spot: I can find this place even in the dark, and you can't easily be seen. I'd better get going or we might miss dinner." He hopped over to the side of the shelter and looked over his shoulder at the Faerie. "I'll caw three times when I'm back," he said.

"Thanks," said Annie. "You're sure you don't need any help?"

"You wouldn't be a help," said Jehzik. "No offense."

He shot down a long gully that he would later follow back to find the Faerie again. Once he got to the end, he turned to his right and soared past one rocky spur after another. He followed the line of the mountains for a long time, his wings beating hard to counter a slight headwind. Climbing up to a saddle between two massive peaks, he crossed over and began a long descent down the other side. Wet snowfields gave way to talus. Eventually, the drainage collected enough little streams to create a creek which cut its way down to a valley at the feet of the mountains.

Daylight had almost faded by the time Jehzik finally reached the lake at the base of the mountains. As it was everywhere else in the Oryxx, there were no trees, only scrub. The crow remained high in the sky, sailing around the perimeter of the lake, until his sharp eyes found that glimmer of fire. The smell of smoke reached him a moment later.

Oh, good, thought Jehzik: fish for dinner.

The fire was in a rocky windbreak, a notch in the stony cliff by the gravelly beach. Jehzik flew down to the cliff top to have a look. Peering over the edge, he could see the cooking fire. Suspended over top of it, half a dozen good sized fish were roasting nicely. They had been skewered onto a stick that was jammed into a crack in the stone.

The huge, green-skinned cook was sitting nearby, watching the roasting process with great interest. The fish were nearly done and the ogre kept reaching over and then pulling his hand back as if to wait just a little longer. Finally, the ogre pinched off a bit of one fish and quickly licked his fingers. A great growl of satisfaction rumbled in his chest.

Jehzik hopped nervously, watching intently for an opportunity. As the giant green fellow began to reach for the stick, the crow launched himself off the cliff. Once the ogre had removed the stick from the fire, Jehzik dove right at his bald head, pecking at it, and then pulling up.

The ogre looked up, but Jehzik was behind him. The crow wheeled back around and pecked the ogre on the back of the neck. The ogre spun around, to look, still holding the fish skewer with one hand. Jehzik wheeled again and pecked him on the top of his head, pulling immediately back up out of reach. The ogre slapped hard but succeeded only in clapping himself resoundingly on the scalp. Next, Jehzik dove down and pecked the giant ogre right in the middle of the forehead, pulling away just before the massive green hand whacked against the green skull again. Peck after peck, the crow pestered the ogre. The big fellow bashed himself on the forehead, the cheek, the ear, the scalp—everywhere the crow pecked him. Getting hit so much was affecting his coordination. He became clumsier and clumsier.

The hand that wasn't swatting was waving the skewered fish distractedly. A few roasted morsels had already fallen off. Jehzik pecked the back of the giant ogre's head, turned sharply and pecked him again on the nose. One more time, the big hand came flying up and slammed into the green face.

The ogre staggered backward on the uneven ground, unable to focus properly. The skewer dropped from his hand. Jehzik pounced on it and broke free a good-sized chunk of meat. Letting that lie, he pecked at the stuff still on the skewer, eating as fast as he could.

"Hey!" bellowed the staggering ogre, coming back to his senses. "That's MY fish!"

Jehzik choked down one last bite, seized the freed chunk of fish and flapped away furiously as the ogre picked up a rock from the beach and heaved it after him. The crow instinctively turned out over the water. The rock sailed harmlessly past. Ignoring the curses and insults that followed, Jehzik sped off with his prize, back up the long drainage. He flew quickly up and over the pass, down the other side, on and on across the steeply undulating landscape of the Oryxx. Despite his earlier confidence, the crow had some difficulty retracing his path. Several of the long spurs coming down from the higher peaks looked the same, especially in the darkening gloom.

By the the time found the gully that led to Annie, he'd been flying for over an hour. Relieved, he headed for the outcrop that marked Annie's sheltering rock. He almost forgot to crow three times. There was no response. Concerned, he landed a short distance away and set the cold fish down on a flat rock.

"Annie?" he called.

No answer.

"Annie? Are you there?" he called again.

Something stirred in the rock shelter.

"Annie, it's Jehzik," said the crow. Again he crowed three times.

"Jehzik?" said Annie's sleepy voice.

"I'm back," said Jehzik; "and I've got dinner."

"Fish!" said Annie as the crow brought it over.

"Courtesy of the lake ogre," he said, laying beside her in the dark.

Annie felt around for it, brushed bits of dirt off it and bit into it hungrily. "'S good!" she said.

"He's the best cook in the Oryxx," said Jehzik.

"I wish we didn't have to steal it," said Annie; "but I'm so hungry, I'm just glad to have something to eat."

"That's the way it works in the Oryxx," said Jehzik.

"Wait, did you get any?" asked Annie.

"I already ate," said the crow.

"When?" asked Annie.

"I got mine fresh and hot," said Jehzik. "Don't you worry about me. That cold bit's yours. Sorry I couldn't carry more."

"Mmmm," said Annie. "No, it's good. Thanks!" She sat back against the rock wall and licked her fingers. "Ogre's actually cook."

"They do," said Jehzik.

"Gruffens can, too. Brian does when he wants to," said Annie. "I hope we find him soon."

"Me, too," said Jehzik. "Maybe then we can all get out of here. For now, though, I think I'll get some sleep."

"Good idea," said Annie. "Thanks again for the fish."

"You're welcome," said Jehzik. Hiding his head under his wing, he fell asleep.

* * *

The next morning the wind had picked up but it wasn't raining. Annie and Jehzik were flying as soon as it was light. They resumed their systematic search of the area, flying a measured pattern some distance apart, working their way eastward. It was slow going, but they kept at it.

"Maybe we should go find the army and work our way back," said Jehzik when they stopped to rest. "That way, if he's going westward, we'll be sure to see him. The way we're doing it, he could be just ahead of us and we'd never find him."

"Let me see if I can find him from here," said Annie. "You keep an eye out, though. Last time I did this, I got caught."

"Go ahead," said Jehzik, flitting up to a boulder where he had a better view.

Annie touched the ring to the Valenblade and scanned the landscape, letting her eye rove up one ridge and down another. She didn't want to look too far westward. The idea of seeing that dark face again gave her the chills. Still, she forced herself to look further and further out. Where could he be? She hoped he hadn't fallen somewhere they couldn't find him. If he was trying to hide, he was certainly doing it well.

"Wait!" she said, suddenly. "There!"

"Where?" said Jehzik.

Annie let her sight come back to her immediate surroundings. "Follow me!" she said. "Come on! Let's go!"

*　*　*

It was, indeed, a big river. Brian stood by the banks and asked himself if he thought he could swim it. The answer was no. He'd come to the narrowest spot he could see from the foothills behind him but there was clearly no good way to cross it at this point. He looked upstream and downstream. The river looked about the same up and down the entire valley, at least from this vantage point.

He had been traveling through this wasteland for a day and a night but he had seen few trails and no roads. He looked upstream and downstream again. Nothing moved but the river. He didn't like being out in the open like this. He turned southeast and headed back to the edge of the foothills where the route was free and clear. He picked up the speed, loping smoothly across the desolation.

He kept this up for a couple of hours, covering quite a distance, still not coming across any sort of road. The river down in the valley looked the same as always. Sometimes it was a little closer, sometimes further away, but it seemed no easier to cross.

The ground began to undulate a bit more sharply. The river narrowed as the slope of the valley steepened. Brian continued forward, slowing only a little as the talus in the foothills became coarser and looser. Eventually, he came down closer to the river. By that time, the watercourse was cutting a steeper gulch into the valley.

"Brian!"

The gruffen shook his head and kept going.

"Brian!"

He slowed slightly and looked around, sure this time that he had heard that familiar voice calling his name.

"Brian! Brian!"

Flashes of blue and black dropped out of the sky and landed on the rocks just ahead of him. Brian came to a halt, stood up, and stared, mouth open.

Annie didn't wait for him to recover. Setting the Valenblade on the ground, she leapt on him and threw her arms around his neck. "Oh!" she cried, tears streaming down her face. "You're all right! We found you!"

Brian wrapped his arms around her and picked her up. "What are you doing here?" he asked.

"We've been looking for you for two days!" she said, her face buried in his wet beard.

"Who's we?" asked Brian.

Annie leaned back to look at him. "Oh!" she said. "That's Jehzik. He's a crow."

Brian looked over at the black bird bobbing its head. "I can see that," said Brian.

"Good to meet you finally," said Jehzik.

"It talks!" said Brian.

"Yes, he does," said Annie. "He's been helping me look for you all this time. He even brought me food yesterday."

"Good," said Brian. He looked over at the crow. "I forgot: what's your name?"

"Jehzik," croaked the crow.

"Put me down," said Annie. "I brought the Valenblade!"

"How? I lost it in the river."

"I caught it," said Annie, going over to get the blade. She picked it up and handed it back to Brian.

He took it and looked it over. "Something's different," he said.

"Like what?" asked Annie.

"It's got a butterfly on it," said Brian.

Annie took a closer look. Sure enough, in a shade slightly lighter than the rest of the handle, she could see a faint image of a butterfly.

"Something happened when my ring touched it the first time," she said. "Now I can see really far whenever my ring touches the metal. It's like flying, only I can do it just by looking harder in any direction I want to see."

"Just like in the Crimson Tower," said Brian.

"That's what I thought," said Annie.

"Maybe that's what the ring was for," said Brian.

"The Blade is definitely different," said Jehzik. "Something bad seems to have left it."

Brian turned it over in his hand again. "It doesn't feel different." He knelt down and drove it into a rock, slicing into it easily. "Still cuts everything," he said, pulling it back out. He slid it into the sheath that had become so familiar he'd forgotten he had it on. Then he looked around. "You should go. I still have to get out of here."

"We're not leaving you here alone. Where were you going?" asked Annie.

"Looking for a crossing," said Brian, pointing at the river.

"There's only one good one," said Jehzik, jerking his head to point downstream. "The road leads right to it."

"Should have stayed on the road, then," said Brian, shrugging his great shoulders. "How far?"

"Just over that rise," said Annie. "We could see it from the air."

"Then what's the best way there?" asked Brian.

Jehzik cocked his head. "For you? It depends. The main road is really the fastest way. I just don't know how you would get past the Black Warriors once you catch up with them. Anything else is a long trip north or south, and you still have to come back to the southern fords to cross the Volgan River."

"What about the bridge?" asked Brian.

Annie and Jehzik looked at each other.

"The bridge is gone," said Annie. "But don't worry, Grisbane and the other Small Giants are all right."

Brian took a deep breath and glanced around again. "Let's go then," he said. "The road is fast. I'll go there."

Brian dropped down to all fours and took off with renewed energy. Annie flew along beside him just over his left shoulder while Jehzik went on a bit ahead.

In about an hour, they had come to the road. Jehzik flew off to scout the way. When he came back, he flared and landed on a boulder.

"The bridge isn't guarded," he said. "Judging from all the hoof prints, the army has already passed through. I haven't seen them yet."

"Can I cross?" asked Brian.

"Yes," said Jehzik. "Go quickly. From here to the Great Gates, it's nothing but wide open flatland. Anything and anybody can see you out there."

"What's out there?" asked Annie.

Jehzik shrugged. "Could be anything: ogres, goblins, trolls, Black Warriors, Golrakken. Who knows? Havvac might even come back. I hate to paint it black, but it's just not a good place to be on the ground."

"Let's go then," said Brian.

With Jehzik in the lead, they headed down the road. Brian was glad to be moving west again.

CHAPTER 54

Into the Mirrak-Haas

The Dark Master approached the towering structure on foot. Even in their ruined state, the Great Gates of Ulvanoth soared above them. Morvassus allowed the Twin to guide him under the central arch. He could feel the power of the fountain just beyond. Energy flowed from it in a constant upward stream, similar to the pool at the foot of his throne in Uzzim-Khail. He followed the sensation directly to the edge of the fountain.

Placing both hands on the edge of the low wall surrounding the lowest pool of the fountain, he leaned over slowly to place himself directly in the flow of energy.

The force hit him full in the face. Startled, he pulled back. Something was wrong.

"What is it, m'lord?" asked the Black Warrior captain standing behind him.

Morvassus did not answer. He removed the Twin from his eye socket and slowly extended his arm. He could feel the rush of energy increase as the hand holding the marble of pure black drew closer to the stream. With a slow, deliberate motion, he pressed into that flow. The Twin burned in his hand. The deeper into the flow he pushed his hand, the more painful was the burning sensation. When his whole hand was engulfed in the flow, the fire began to spread up his arm to his shoulder, across to his neck. Quickly, he jerked his hand back out again.

All the way from Uzzim-Khail, his strength had slowly drained, but he knew that once they reached the Great Gates, it would be renewed. Now he felt it draining even faster.

Once more he gripped the Twin in his fist. This time he drove it deep into the roaring stream of power. He was forcibly ejected and sent spinning to the ground. Standing up slowly, the Dark Master fitted the Twin back into his eye. Once again he could see shadowy shapes around him.

"Tainted," he said.

"M'lord?" asked the Black Warrior captain.

"The pool is tainted," said Morvassus, quietly. "Bring me a soldier."

"You!" barked the captain, pointing at a Black Warrior. "Dismount and present yourself to the Dark Master."

The Black Warrior did as ordered.

Morvassus could see the dark form in front of him. "Remove your helmet and kneel," he said.

The Warrior removed his helmet and went down on one knee.

The Dark Master also knelt, facing the soldier. "Now bow," he said.

"Yes, m'lord," said the Black Warrior. He lowered his head to his knee.

Morvassus reached out and gently placed a hand on either side of the warrior's face, his fingers slipping around the soldier's ears. Then he leaned forward and placed his forehead on the back of the Black Warrior's bowed head.

For a brief second, the Black Warrior stiffened. Then his whole body began to tremble. The Dark Master's hands caressed the sides of the soldier's face as he hummed softly, tunelessly, his voice slipping up one moment, and down the next. As he caressed, he began to explore the edges of the Black Warrior's ears with a fingertip. He continued the strange humming. The soldier shuddered as with each caress, the Dark Master's fingertips slipped just inside the ears, first gently, then firmly, then insistently. Now the Dark Master held the soldier's skull completely still as he drove his fingers progressively deeper and deeper until they were buried inside the black head. The soldier convulsed violently, his body jerking while his head remained glued to his knee. His skin began to emit thin wisps of dark black smoke. His arms went limp and his hands twitched uncontrollably. The humming continued.

The horses stamped and gnawed at their bits nervously, eyes wide. Their riders held them firmly in check. No one dared speak.

Still holding the soldier's head in his hands, his fingers deep inside it, Morvassus began to rock back and forth, back and forth, back and forth, his forehead keeping contact with the back of the warrior's skull. With every rocking motion, the Black Warrior's bodily convulsions became more random and violent. His head remained locked between the Dark Master's hands. All at once, the Black Warrior's back gave out and the body collapsed. The warrior became a limp form in Morvassus' hands, elastic, pliable, bending almost without structure or resistance as the Dark Master rocked back and forth. The soldier's body was becoming transparent now, as if the skin was but a dark vapor surrounding nothing but air. Slowly, the body dissipated into nothing, leaving only a smoking black head in Morvassus' hands. The Dark Master pressed his hands closer and closer together, reducing the head to a swirling ball of black vapor. Soon, that, too, dissipated and vanished.

Morvassus brought his palms together and touched the tips of his thumbs to his brow. Then he rose to his feet again. He looked around at the amorphous shapes of his warriors. "Bring me my mount!" he called. "We must ride quickly."

* * *

"Annie!" yelled Brian, still loping along at full gruffen speed.

The Faerie was flying high over his right shoulder, her eyes scanning the area for signs of the enemy.

She dropped down low beside him. Jehzik circled above, riding the wind.

"What is it?" asked Annie.

"You said you can see far," he said, coming to a stop and pulling the Valenblade from its sheath.

"You want me to take a look?" she asked.

"You scared?" asked Brian, noticing the look on her face.

"Yes," she said. "I don't want to see *him* again."

"I'll try then," said Brian. He held the Valenblade and stared hard into the distance. Nothing happened.

"Did it work?" asked Annie.

"No," said the gruffen.

"I have to touch the metal part with the ring," said Annie. "That's when it works for me."

"Maybe if you do that while I hold it," suggested Brian.

"We could try," she said. "Let me stand in front so we can both see."

She leaned back against his chest while he held the Valenblade in front of them. She brought her hand up and touched the ring to the metal guard. A shock raced through them both, causing Brian to roar and Annie to cry out unexpectedly. Jehzik circled back quickly, alarmed.

Blue lightning shot from the Valenblade, tracing random, forking patterns along Brian's and Annie's arms, and flickering across their bodies. It lasted for only a moment, but when it was over, both of them were gasping for breath.

"That's like what happened to me the first time!" said Annie, still holding onto the Valenblade with Brian.

"Ugh!" said Brian. "That hurt...wait...hey! I can see far."

Annie looked out across the wide plain. "So can I," she said. "What if I let go?"

"Try it," said Brian, still staring off into the far distance, trying to get used to the extended sight without actually sitting solidly on the Crimson Throne. "Did you let go yet?"

"Yes," said Annie. "You can still see?"

Brian nodded. He could look anywhere he wanted to and see as far as he liked.

"What if I step away?" asked Annie. She ducked out under his arm and stood up again.

Brian stared hard to the west. "I see them," he said.

"Black Warriors?" asked Jehzik, landing close by.

"Many," said Brian. "The ones that left the fortress."

"Careful," said Annie, reaching out and touching his arm. "Oh!"

"What?" asked Brian.

"I can see, too!" she said. "All I have to do is touch you."

Brian brought his sight back in close and looked at her. She was staring off into the distance. "Can you still see?" he asked.

"Yes," said Annie turning her eyes in another direction. Way off in the north, a massive dragon lifted off. "There's a dragon flying."

"Which dragon?" asked Jehzik.

"The big brown one that caught Brian," said Annie. She took her hand from Brian's arm. "Now I see normally."

Brian put the Valenblade back in its sheath and stared hard. He saw nothing different. "Me, too," he said.

"We'd better keep moving," said Jehzik. "Where were the Black Warriors?"

"Big gates and a fountain," said Brian. "Middle of nowhere."

"The Great Gates of Ulvanoth," said Jehzik. "Were the warriors at the gates?"

"Not yet," said Brian; "but they will be soon."

"At this speed, they'll reach the foothills of the Mirrak-Haas by nightfall," said Jehzik.

"How about us?" asked Brian.

"That depends on how fast you can run," replied the crow; "and how clear the road is ahead. Did you look?"

Brian shook his head. He brought the Valenblade back out and held it so that he was touching the metal guard. Staring hard, he looked down the road, farther and farther, faster and faster until, once again, he found the Black Warrior army. He quickly pulled back.

"Nothing ahead," said Brian. "Nothing between us and them."

Jehzik took a deep breath and hacked. Shaking his head, he looked back at his companions. "Well, I guess we just go as fast as we can then," he said.

The gruffen raced along the road as the Faerie and the crow climbed up to keep watch. Even in such dangerous territory, Brian was running with ease. League after league slipped under his leathery hands and feet. He ran without stopping, almost without tiring, it seemed.

The dull landscape never changed. The flat, barren plain extended out in all directions, bounded on the east by the now-misty mountains of the Oryxx and bounded on the west by the Mirrak-Haas, which seemed to loom larger but never draw closer. To the north and south, there was only flat, rocky, plains as far as the eye could see.

Late in the afternoon, Jehzik called Annie and they both flew down to talk to Brian on the ground.

The gruffen slowed his pace a little. "I can keep going," he said.

"I haven't seen the Great Gates yet," said Jehzik; "but if we could pass them and get into the foothills, I'd feel a lot better, especially if there's a dragon about."

"I say we keep going, then," said Annie.

Brian picked up the pace again, charging forward with even more urgency.

Not long after that, Jehzik shot ahead and then came back. Once again, they descended to talk to Brian.

"Don't stop," said Jehzik. "We're not close to them yet, but there are goblins on the road."

"Where are they going?" asked Annie.

"I don't know. Same direction we are," said Jehzik.

"How many?" asked Brian.

"Fifteen or twenty," said Jehzik.

"A lot," said Brian.

"Not that many," said Jehzik. "It's just a loose band, I think. I don't see any more in the area. Morvassus sent most of them to the southern fords."

Brian loped along. "How soon till we meet them?"

"Not long now," said Jehzik.

"Stop," said Annie. "I want to take a look."

Brian came to a halt and stood up, taking the Valenblade out from its sheath. Annie landed next to him and laid her hand on his arm. They both looked down the road.

"I see them," said Annie.

"Me, too," said Brian.

"They're not moving very fast," said Annie.

"Like I said," returned Jehzik; "they seem to be on their own."

"They're in the way," said Brian. "Can we go around? I don't need the road."

"It's going to be nighttime soon," said Jehzik. "You probably don't want to keep going in the dark with this lot anywhere nearby."

"Should we just stop?" asked Annie. "As long as they're going away from us, we can just let them keep going."

"We'll just catch up with them tomorrow," said Jehzik.

"Maybe they go somewhere else," said Brian.

"True," said Jehzik. He thought for a moment. Looking up at the darkening sky, he asked, "Can you run at night?"

"Yes," said Brian.

"Good," said Jehzik. "Since you don't need the road, we two will stay low and you can follow me to the north a bit. We'll pass them by in the dark and they'll never know it. We'll stay off the road if we stop for the night."

"Go!" said Brian.

Jehzik launched into the air, followed quickly by Annie and then Brian. The crow angled his path off the road and they raced full speed in a straight line until they were some distance from the main road. They continued on as long as they could still see. No one said a word. When darkness fell, Jehzik turned them to the left until he thought they were traveling parallel to the road.

Brian continued onward, feeling his way across the rocky plain, considerably slower than he had been moving before. Annie stayed close beside him. Jehzik flew just ahead.

"Wait," croaked Jehzik. "Stop."

They slowed to a stop.

"What?" said Annie.

"Something's up there," said Jehzik.

"Where," said Brian, breathlessly.

"Up ahead," said Jehzik.

Brian sniffed the air. "Dark magic," he said.

"Yes," said Jehzik. "A lot of it."

"Where are we?" whispered Annie.

"I thought we were north of the road," said Jehzik. "Now I'm not so sure."

"Why?" asked Brian.

"I think we're near the Great Gates," said Jehzik.

Brian brought out the Valenblade and touched the metal. Staring hard, he had something like the "moonlit" view he had from the Crimson Throne, only this was clearer. "I can see in the dark," he said.

"I'll try," said Annie, reaching out and touching his arm. "I can see, too."

"Those are the gates," said Brian. "The road is right over there."

"The goblins are still on the road, coming this way," said Annie.

Jehzik fidgeted nervously, but kept his voice down. "What's going on at the Gates? Rraaack! Something feels very bad."

"Nobody there," said Brian. "But I can smell it."

Annie looked around. "There's a fountain on the other side. Does it always glow like that?"

Jehzik stared into the darkness. "I don't see a glow," he said. "Ugh, this is making me sick." He hopped a few steps away and began to gag and retch.

"Come on," said Annie. "We can't stay here."

"Over there," said Brian, pointing to a rise in the ground that announced the beginning of the foothills. "Won't be seen."

"You lead," said Annie. "I'll get Jehzik." She gently lifted the crow off the stony ground. The poor bird continued to heave. He could hardly breathe.

"Give him to me," said Brian. Cradling Jehzik in the arm that held the Valenblade, he rambled along on two feet and one hand in a lumping gait that was still fairly fast. Annie flew just over his shoulder. Periodically, she would touch his shoulder so she could have a look. Ever so slowly, it seemed, they covered the long distance to the foothills.

"A cave," said Brian, finally. "Good."

They brought Jehzik inside, out of sight. When they found a good place to lay him down, Annie settled in next to him and Brian went back to the entrance to keep watch.

"Where are we?" asked the crow.

"Brian found us a cave in the foothills," said Annie. "Are you all right?"

"I think so, but I can't see a thing," said Jehzik.

"Neither can I," said Annie. "It's just dark in here."

"Oh," said Jehzik. "Rraack! That was awful."

Annie stroked his feathers in the dark. "You were pretty sick."

"Thanks for the help," said Jehzik.

"You're welcome," said Annie. "Brian did all the work."

* * *

The lead goblin sniffed the air. "What is that?" he asked.

The rest of them sniffed, hands on their weapons.

"Smells like Black Warrior," said one.

"Burnt Black Warrior," said another one.

"Roasty, toasty, blackened Warrior," said another.

Someone sniggered.

"Shut it," said the goblin leader. "That's not what I'm talking about. Use your nose. What is that?"

They sniffed again.

"I smell sweet," said one with a squeaky voice.

"You stink like all the rest of us," said another.

More sniggers.

"Stuff it, the lot of you!" growled the leader. "Something's different at the gates. I don't like it."

"No, no! I *do* smell sweet," insisted Squeaky Voice. "Kind of like Faerie sweet."

"Don't flatter yourself," said another.

"I'm not talking about myself, idiot!" said Squeaky Voice.

"Who you calling idiot?"

The leader sniffed. "He's right, idiot," he said. "And there's a musty smell, too, but I'm talking about that sharp smell."

"Oh go on with your smells," said another. "Are we stopping?"

"Not here," said a different one. "That burnt Black Warrior smell gives me the creeps."

"No," said the leader. "I don't like it. We'll keep moving."

"Good," said Idiot. "Just keep Faerie Sweet Bum downwind of me."

"Shut it," said Squeaky Voice.

* * *

Brian watched as the goblins continued on up the road into the mountains. Once he was sure they were gone, he let his gaze drift back to where he was. Then he started a long, slow search across the open plains.

For a long time, the gruffen sat at the cave entrance, Valenblade in hand, looking for anything that moved. For a long time, nothing did. Finally, he found a more comfortable spot a bit further inside the cave where he could still see out and sat down again.

Then, for the first time in what seemed like a long, long time, Brian fell asleep.

* * *

"Keep looking," said the big troll. "It's going to be too light soon."

"I'm looking, I'm looking," said the small troll. "You're the one who wanted to come down here."

"I thought I smelled something," said the big troll.

"And you had to come find it," said the small troll. "What did you think it was?"

"I don't know. Something sweet," said the big troll. "It was right around here, I know it."

"You'd better be right," said the small troll; "and it had better be quick or we'll be using these clubs for shovels."

"Wait, this is it," said the big troll. "Smell that?"

The small troll nodded, a big grin stretching across his face. "I like it!"

"See what I mean?" said the big troll. "Sweet, eh?"

The small troll nodded. "But there's a musty something, too."

"It's down there," said the big troll.

The small troll looked around. "We've got to get underground," he said.

The big troll crept down the hill a bit further and pointed. "In there," he said.

The small troll caught up to him and saw the opening. "Our lucky day," he said.

They came down to the cave and peered inside. The big troll pointed at the ball of fur by the wall and then pointed at himself. The small troll nodded. Taking a last look around, the big troll crept inside the cave.

* * *

Brian looked up groggily. Had he fallen asleep? Something smelled bad. He jumped to his feet, Valenblade in hand. Next thing he knew, he was crashing into the stone wall. Somehow, he hung onto the Valenblade. Before he could get his breath, he was picked up and thrown deeper into the cave. He rolled over twice and staggered upright.

"Trolls!" he yelled, backing up deeper into the cave.

The monster swung its heavy club. Brian parried with the Valenblade, slicing neatly through the tip of the club but slowing it not a bit. The club slammed into the wall and came swinging back the other direction, showering dust and broken rocks all over. Brian scrambled out of the way. Everything hurt.

"Run!" he yelled. He staggered further into the cave, searching frantically for his friends. Since he was still holding the Valenblade, he could actually see in the pitch black cave. Up ahead, Annie and Jehzik were blindly groping their way along.

"Run!" he yelled again, racing toward them as fast as his aching body could go. He scooped up the startled crow with one arm, grabbed Annie around the waist with the other, and took off down the passageway at a dead run on two legs, still holding the Valenblade.

The great trolls crawled in after him.

Brian thumped onward, following the only route available, a rising path that, for the moment, continued straight ahead. He stole a glance over his shoulder. The trolls weren't gaining on him, but they were moving surprisingly fast for something so big in such a restricted space. The gruffen scanned the walls for cracks, crooks or crannies—anywhere he might be able to hide or through which he might pass without being pursued.

The cave narrowed slightly and the passage grew more crooked. Though it slowed Brian just a bit, there was still enough room for the trolls behind him. Finally, off to the right, he found a thin opening where he might just fit. He would have to put down his cargo first, though.

"Quick! Inside!" he said, dropping Jehzik and Annie at the opening.

The crow and the Faerie worked their way inside but Brian was too big. Taking the Valenblade, he carved out chunks of rock. The trolls were coming closer every second.

"Go deeper!" Brian yelled, still hacking away at the rock. He tried again, but he still didn't fit. Carving great slices of stone, he finally widened the opening enough. He shuffled in sideways and got blocked again, but he was out of the main passageway, at least mostly out of it.

The troll club smashed against the opening Brian had just carved, pelting him with broken stones and enlarging the gap even more. Brian focused on cutting his way deeper. Another smash of the troll club bashed an even bigger hole. Brian wriggled in further as the big troll's face peered into the gap.

"They're in there!" said the big troll, reaching in.

Brian felt the great fingers touch his back and he instinctively cut backward with the Valenblade. A deafening howl went up at the other end of the arm. Brian continued to hack his way deeper into the passage.

"Look out!" he yelled. No one answered him.

The troll hammering started again, showering the gruffen with more dust and rocks.

Once Brian squeezed through a little further, he burst into a larger chamber. Annie and Jehzik were nowhere in sight. Still holding the Valenblade, he looked around the room until he found an exit. Annie and Jehzik were climbing up a steep, bouldery section. Brian followed as the hammering and howling continued behind him.

"They won't get in soon," said Brian.

"I wouldn't count on that," croaked Jehzik. "Trolls are champion tunnelers."

"Brian, where does this go?" asked Annie. "Can you see ahead?"

Brian stared up the passageway with his extended sight. For a long time, there seemed to be nothing but boulders, like where they were now.

"Stairs!" said Brian.

"What?" said Jehzik.

"Lots and lots of stairs," said Brian, still following his extended sight.

A thundering crash behind them sent them all climbing again, chased by a choking cloud of dust.

Brian grabbed Jehzik and climbed up beside Annie.

"Get on my back!" he bellowed.

As soon as she touched him, she could see again. "Go!" she yelled, coughing from the dust.

Brian scrambled up from boulder to boulder, the Faerie clinging to his back and the crow tucked into the crook of his arm. More clouds of dust billowed up from below. Brian kept climbing. The way steepened considerably.

"Let me perch on your shoulder," said Jehzik. "I won't be—aawkk! Ow!— I won't be in the way so much."

"All right," said Brian. He lifted the crow up and helped him crawl to a decent perch.

It did help. Brian hung onto the knife but he was able to use his arm more and made better progress. The pounding below was getting further and further away, but the choking dust kept coming. After a particularly difficult, steep section, the way leveled out a bit more and Brian was able to weave his way between the relatively close cave walls. The floor of the cave was wetter here. He splashed through a few puddles. The clouds of dust didn't seem to drift all the way up here.

"Nice to be able to breathe again," said Jehzik on Brian's shoulder. "I hear water. If you find a puddle deep enough, I'd love to get some of this grit out of my feathers.

Not long after that, they came to a wider section. Off to one side, a trickle of water leaked out of the wall and filled a small pool.

"Here's your bath," said Brian.

He helped Jehzik off his shoulder and placed him beside the pool. Annie slid off his back and joined Jehzik by the water.

The crow took a few tentative hops into the pool. "Oh, this is luxury!" he said. "Stand clear!"

"Go ahead," said Annie.

"Ahh," sighed the crow. Then he ducked his head under repeatedly, shaking his feathers out and spraying water everywhere.

Annie covered her face and waited for her turn.

"Well," said the crow, shaking himself one more time and hopping back to the edge of the water. "No time for the whole ritual, I suppose, but that was the most welcome bath I can remember in the last hundred years or so."

Annie laughed and felt her way over to another side of the pool where she could shake the dust off and wash her face, arms and legs. Brian splashed water on his face, but he dared not shake himself for fear of showering them all with dust again.

"Not big enough for you, eh?" said Jehzik sympathetically.

"Doesn't matter," said Brian. "Later, maybe."

* * *

Brian and Annie stared up the stone staircase allowing their extended sight to fly up flight after flight, seemingly interminably.

"Where do they go?" asked Jehzik, sitting on Brian's shoulder.

"Don't know," said Brian, still staring.

"There," said Annie.

"What?" asked Brian.

"Keep looking," said the Faerie. "See that straight sliver of light?"

"Oh," said Brian. "There."

"What is it?" asked Jehzik.

"I'm not sure," said Annie. "It appears to be some sort of door."

"So this leads to a structure somewhere," said Jehzik. "That's good news and bad news, I suppose."

"Why?" asked Brian.

"Good news because it means that this stairway leads to the surface, most likely," said Jehzik. "Bad news because I can't imagine any structure in the Mirrak-Haas that I would want to be in."

"Is there nothing good out here?" asked Annie.

"Nothing good that I know of, besides us three," said Jehzik. "There are neutral elements, I suppose, but they're so used to the bad stuff that they react with violence to any encounter at all."

"Did you see another way?" asked Brian.

"Another way out?" asked Annie. "No."

"Let's go then," said Brian.

He took Annie's hand and they began to climb the steps together. Now that the troll danger was behind them, they went at a slower, steady pace. The Snowdaughter kept her wings folded behind her; there wasn't room to fly in the narrow stairway. Tired thought she was, she dared not stop.

The steps followed the natural veins of weaker rock, turning this way and that as the folded strata dictated. As they progressed further and further up, the rocks they tread changed from cold and black to gray with shiny flecks speckled throughout. The flights of steps grew longer and straighter. This went on for hours on end. Once in awhile, Brian and Annie would stop to rest, but then there was nothing more to do but keep climbing.

* * *

The Dark Master called a halt in a flatter space where several horses could stand abreast. The mounted army of Black Warriors strung out in a line down the mountain trail. Slowly, he dismounted and walked a short distance ahead of the army.

"Captain," he said. "Bring me a soldier."

"You!" ordered the captain, singling out one of the riders a bit further down the line. "Off your horse! Present yourself to the Dark Master."

The Black Warrior hesitated.

"Now!" barked the captain.

Still, the Black Warrior did not move.

"That is a direct order, soldier," growled the captain.

The Black Warrior did not comply.

The captain rode up beside him. "You are not deaf, soldier," he said in a low voice. "You are commanded to present yourself to the Dark Master. Now dismount and obey."

The Black Warrior's hand went to his weapon but he never reached it. A spear pierced his neck from behind. The soldier crumpled in the saddle and slid to the ground, taking the spear with him, its sharp point jutting out between his breastplate and his helmet. The body turned to smoke and disappeared.

"Well done," said the captain. "Retreive your weapon, soldier. We may need it again." He pointed to another warrior. "You! Present yourself to the Dark Master."

Slowly, deliberately, the next soldier dismounted and walked over to stand before Morvassus.

547

"Remove your helmet and kneel," said the Dark Master.

Very slowly, the soldier complied, dropping to one knee and placing his helmet on the ground.

"Now bow."

The soldier slowly bowed until his forehead rested on his knee.

The Dark Master knelt before him and reached for the soldier's head.

In a flash, the soldier pulled a dagger from his boot and drove it up under Morvassus' exposed chin, but as the blade drew closer to the dark flesh, the soldier's movements became slower and slower. The dagger never found its mark.

Morvassus gently placed his hands on both sides of the warrior's head, even as the blade drew ever closer to him. Just as slowly and deliberately, the Dark Master rested his forehead on the back of the warrior's skull. The tips of his middle fingers pressed into the ears of the bowing soldier. The Black Warrior's body jerked once. His hand dropped the dagger. As the Dark Master's fingers burrowed into his ears, the Black Warrior began to spasm violently. Once again, the Dark Master rocked back and forth. The Black Warrior's body grew limp and pliable, then translucent, and then finally dissipated into smoke.

The Dark Master rose and climbed back onto his mount. He turned to face the Black Warrior army.

"Remember," he said. "I made you, I sustain you, and I can unmake you just as quickly. Those who follow me may sacrifice from time to time, but ultimate victory lies with me. The faithful will be rewarded. Those who betray me will be punished as I see fit. I assure you, it will not be as pleasant as what you have seen here." He paused. "If I perish, you all perish. Some of you seem to have forgotten that."

He motioned to his captain. "Forward," he said. "We waste time."

The army fell in line. For the next several hours, they continued up the narrow, winding path that threaded through the Mirrak-Haas. Around mid-afternoon, the partially rebuilt towers of Akka-Illin became visible. The long line of dark riders climbed the switchbacks to the fortress.

"Do you trust the Golrakken, m'lord?" asked the Black Warrior captain.

Morvassus took a deep breath and laboriously let it out. "An interesting question," he said. "Especially from a Black Warrior captain with ambition."

"Your assessment of my motivation is clear, m'lord," said the captain. "Akka-Illin is well situated. The force that controls it commands a wide area. If you deem it wise, I would know your answer."

Morvassus smiled. "That's why you are a captain, soldier." He leaned back in the saddle, stretching his back. "I trust Dragonhelm no more than I trusted the Interrogator," he said, finally.

"Understood," said the captain.

"And no more than I trust you, Captain," added Morvassus, looking straight ahead. Taking another laborious breath, he slumped forward on his mount.

"Shall we pause again, m'lord?" asked the captain.

Morvassus shook his head. "We are within sight of the fortress," he said. "The power in that place will give me far more than the life of another warrior."

Within the hour, they were calling for the portcullis to be raised. The Black Warriors guarding the fortress opened the gates and stood back to allow the Dark Master to enter the broad central courtyard. A company of warriors entered with him. The rest of the dark army remained outside, ready to move when the order came.

The Dark Master dismounted slowly, carefully. Even maintaining the magical illusion that concealed the full extent of his weakened condition from his soldiers cost him a great deal of energy. Still, he dared not diminish the tremendous stream of magic he kept directed at the Midnight Stone in the Shioroth. He could feel the pull, the desire of the Twin in his hand to unite with the one in Ender's hands. Morvassus was counting on that desire. The power he had been accumulating for hundreds of years was now being spent on this quest for a final confrontation. He must continue to exert pressure on the Midnight Stone in the Shioroth, disrupting any attempt by the Stonekeeper to use the Midnight Stone to his own ends.

All at once, he stopped, mid-stride. Something had changed in the Shioroth. This was the mistake he had been waiting for! In response, the Twin nearly leapt from his empty eye socket. He seized it in his hand and held it tightly. Concentrating his strength, he amplified the message that his dark Stone was sending across the Mirrak-Haas, across the Abandoned Land, over the Volgan River and the eastern fields to the great monolith of the Faeries.

It was a single-minded, compelling call: "COME!"

The force of the transmission dropped Morvassus to his knees. At a shout from the captain, twenty Black Warriors formed a tight circle around the Dark Master, weapons facing outward. For a moment, Morvassus knelt there, hardly able to breathe.

"Take me to the pool," he said, trying to stand.

The captain ordered two guards to enter the circle and help the Dark Master to his feet. "Show us to the Interrogation Room!" he ordered.

The two guards half led, half carried the Dark Master to a door in the corner of the wide central courtyard. He seemed not to notice them, his face vacant, as if focused elsewhere. His feet moved mechanically as the guards helped him follow the dark stairwell that led down into the bowels of the fortress. At the landing at the bottom, they turned left, heading for a single door at the end of a long hall, the Black Warrior captain following close behind.

The outgoing message continued to reverberate.

"COME!"

* * *

Breathing hard, the gruffen braced his back against the trapdoor and pushed again. The door refused to budge.

"I can't see," said Jehzik, a few steps down the staircase. "Are you sure it's a door?"

"It sure looks like a door," said Annie, her hand on Brian's calf so she could still see as he held the Valenblade. "It's even got a handle."

"Is there a lock or something?" asked the crow.

"We've looked it all over and I don't see anything like a lock," the Faerie answered.

"Doesn't move,"said Brian, leaning against the wall to rest.

"Must be magic," said Jehzik. "I have a bad feeling about this place."

"Me, too," said Brian. "But nowhere else to go." When he had caught his breath again, he said: "Get back. I'm going to dig out."

Annie reached down and picked up the crow. "We'll stay behind Brian," she said to him.

The trapdoor seemed very thick and was reinforced with heavy iron. The gruffen carved out a rough chunk of wood and iron. With a great clattering and clanging, the pieces bounced down, down, down the stairs, finally coming to rest somewhere far below. He waited, listening. There was no sound on the other side of the trapdoor.

"Faster now," he said.

Hacking and chipping, he carved away at the heavy door. Bits, pieces and big blocks of it clattered down the stairs. When he had made a hole big enough for light to enter, he stopped and sniffed the air. The smell made his fur bristle. His skin itched.

"Dark magic," he grunted.

"I don't hear anything," whispered Annie. "Let me take a look."

She used her extended sight to look out beyond the trapdoor. The light they could see through the hole was clearly not sunlight or torchlight; it was more diffuse, like moonlight. Annie let her gaze rove around the large, stone-walled chamber. The room was unoccupied. The source of the light was a circular pool in front of a dark throne. Light from the pool seemed to rise in a flowing column but it did not illuminate the ceiling high above. A single door appeared to be the only exit. Fortunately, it was directly across from where they were standing. They would not have to pass the throne or the pool to get to it.

"No one's up there," said Annie; "and the door to the outside is close by."

"Good," said Brian. "We need to go."

"Wait," said Annie. "Can you see past it? I can't."

Brian stared. "Past that door? No. That's strange."

"Wait," said Jehzik, when the hole was big enough for him to fit through. "Put me out there first."

Annie handed the crow off to Brian who held him up to the hole. Jehzik flitted up through the hole and perched on the edge of it.

"Oh no," he croaked. "No, no, no! This is the Interrogation Room! We can't stay here! Go, Brian! Cut! Cut! Cut!"

Brian cut great crescents of wood and iron. As soon as he could, he shoved Annie through the hole and then kept carving.

Annie found her way to the door, pressed her ear against it and listened.

"Someone's coming!" she hissed.

Brian carved out one last great chunk of the trapdoor and hauled himself out of the stairwell.

CHAPTER 55

The Wall

When the supply of eligible prisoners dwindled to nothing and the flashing lights finally stopped, the Surgoths numbered nearly two hundred. The watchers on the Southgate battlements could not be sure what had happened to the weak or elderly prisoners who remained, but the cooking fires had begun shortly after the transformations ended. There seemed to be plenty of roasting meat. The brooding sky matched the dark mood of the defenders on the wall.

For the last few hours, the Birdman had been roving among his goblin troops, speaking to the leaders of each platoon, congregating Surgoths here and there. Now he approached the eastern edge of his vast army. With a wave of his hand, he dispersed the thin, purple-tinged shield wall that had remained in place since the day before. As it vanished, so did the green wall that had matched it from the other side.

"He's ready to move," said Holren, clutching his staff.

Falnor nodded. "Archers ready!" he called.

Tania quickly climbed to a perch in the tree wall on the eastern side of the battlements. All archers of the Green Stone had arrows on the string, ready to pull. Arrayed on the street behind them, one hundred Faerie archers were poised to launch skyward.

The Birdman's hands and arms were moving quickly, repeating the same pattern over and over. Holren stared at him, trying to discern the pattern.

"A fire spell!" said Mari, grabbing her husband's arm.

"He intends to burn the wall," said Holren. "Come!"

The two of them raced down the stairs and headed eastward around the cobblestone road that rimmed the city just inside the tree wall. Moments later, a great flash silhouetted the tree wall and lit the sky above them. The shock of the blast was felt in everyone's chest. Holren shot ahead, quickly leaving Mari behind. Another flash followed, then another, and another, and another! Holren rounded the bend to see a section of the tree wall about thirty paces wide burst into flame. Tongues of fire licked in between the mighty trunks and branches. Within seconds, the entire section was engulfed in flames. The searing heat drove the wizard back down the cobblestone road.

When Mari caught up with him, Holren was casting a water spell. She did the same. A huge, white spray of water showered onto the roaring fire. Steam billowed into the sky, mixing with the thick, black smoke. Again and again, the two cast the water spell. It slowed the spreading but the fire continued to burn. Soon, Holren and Mari were turned back by the intense heat. Following the roads, they skirted the area, working their way through the deserted neighborhoods to find a place where they could directly face the breach in the wall. Overhead, armed Faeries were already flying there.

A crackling flash lit up the low clouds. One of the mighty trees had exploded. Shortly afterward, two more trees blasted to bits, showering burning debris in all directions, scattering the Faeries flying overhead. Holren and Mari came around a corner to find a wall of flames. The trees at the initial point of attack had now burned to the ground, creating a gap wide enough to allow six horses to pass abreast. Holren started to build a protective shield wall only to be driven back by another exploding tree. Still another explosion drove them even further back. Holren, Mari and the Lammethan gathered together a safe distance away, preparing now for an attack through the widening gap.

The smoke and heat made breathing difficult. The gap continued to widen as trees on either side succumbed to the fire. Through the veil of smoke, hundreds of goblins could be seen surging toward the gap.

Holren sent a ball of green fire through the breech. Somehow it was swallowed up, disappearing before it reached the enemy. Quickly, Mari did the same but that spell had no effect either. The goblin army advanced unhindered. Within moments, the enemy had reached the breech.

"Stop the flames!" hollered Holren. "You go that way!" He turned and ran off in the opposite direction.

Mari raced back through the deserted streets the same way she had come. Running seemed so slow. With a flick of her wrist, she became a hummingbird, streaking off above the cobblestone road. When she reached a safe place, she reverted back to her own form. Already she could feel the strain of casting the spells. The denseness of the Dark Magic on all sides seemed to make every effort more difficult. Concentrating on the water spell, she blasted a stream of spray at the leading edge of the flames. The trees that were already engulfed continued to burn, but, again, the advance of the fire was slowed. She focused on the flames at the base of the tree wall, sending up great clouds of steam.

Out of the cloud rushed a goblin, coughing and spluttering. Mari redirected the next water spell and struck the creature full in the chest. The goblin was thrown backwards into another one bursting from the cloud of steam just behind it. The sorceress changed the pattern of her hands and sent a ball of fire racing toward the two goblins as they regained their feet. The closest one took it in the shoulder, spun around and landed hard, splattering black blood on the cobblestones. The goblin in the back drew a dagger and flung it at Mari, narrowly missing her as she ducked. Before she could recover, the goblin was dashing straight toward her, sword drawn. She flicked her wrist again and turned back into a hummingbird, flying swiftly out of the way. She landed on a rooftop, changed back into her own form and continued to put out the fire as best she could, ignoring the goblins that staggered out of the churning steam and into the deserted streets. She was beginning to tire. A goblin arrow whizzing past her head forced her to retreat. The hummingbird flew off in search of Holren.

* * *

At Thadris' signal, the Faeries assigned to the Eastgate rose into the air and surged over the top of the tree wall, sweeping southward to flank the attacking goblins. A volley of arrows shot from Golrakken longblows flew up to meet them, catching a few mid-flight and dropping them out of the sky. The rest of the Lammethan rained arrows down on the attacking goblins rushing toward the breech in the wall. Dozens of the enemy fell, only to be trampled by their fellows in the mad rush to the gap. The Faeries climbed up out of reach as the goblins at the perimeter stopped and returned fire. Still, a few goblin arrows hit their marks, sending the winged creatures plummeting earthward.

More goblins surged through the gap in the tree wall as Faerie archers from the Southgate sailed over the wall and closed in from the opposite side. Now nearly a third of the goblin army stationed on the east side was moving across the fields toward the gap. The Faerie archers rained arrows down on them but their quivers would not last long and many of the sharp tips embedded themselves in goblin shields that were held overhead.

* * *

"Now!" cried Eulian raising her sword high.

The huge latch was lifted and the doors of the Westgate were hauled open. The Elven princess and Arvon Dustrider rode out with a hundred and fifty Elven warriors on horseback. Turning immediately southward, they rounded the city and drove hard into the western flank of the goblin army, leaving a bloody goblin swath in their wake.

Arvon swung his sword down and sliced into goblin flesh between the helmet and shield. The creature fell lifeless as the Dustrider pulled his weapon free to parry an attacking blow from the other side. Two more goblins fell to his sword. As Arvon leaned from his mount to yank his blade from the chest plate of yet another goblin, the horse reared, almost throwing him from the saddle. When the front hooves came down again, Arvon felt something strong grab the reins. The horse's head was jerked violently to the side and Arvon found himself looking directly into the dark visage of a Surgoth. The monster grinned.

Still off balance, Arvon brought his sword around toward the grinning face. The Surgoth deflected it easily with his forearm and dragged the horse's head to the ground, buckling its knees. Arvon pitched forward out of the saddle and rolled away from his falling mount. The Surgoth let go of the reins and reached for Arvon. The Dustrider's mighty two-handed swing and beat back the reaching hand but the Surgoth continued to advance. Arvon backed away, ducking under and batting away the Surgoth's second reach. The Dustrider's sword was long enough to get in under the Surgoth's long arms, but the creature was fast and Arvon knew that a cut to the body was useless. He turned to run only to have to fight off the goblins that had come racing up behind him.

He hacked his way through the first wave of them and ran forward, leaving the dead and dying between himself and the Surgoth. The monster simply stomped over them and reached for him again. This time, the dark creature got both hands on the back of Arvon's leather jerkin. Arvon swung his sword in a wide arc over his own head, sweeping the area behind him. The sharp tip of his blade found the one place it could cause damage. Instinctively, he arched backward to drive the tip home. The powerful hands still clung to his jerkin. The monster stumbled forward, dragging Arvon to the ground.

Arvon twisted away, yanked his blade free and staggered to his feet to face the next oncoming wave of goblins. He had nowhere to run. Stroke after stroke, parry after parry, he fought the goblins, somehow holding them all at bay.

Then, a long, dark arm reached around him and pinned Arvon's sword arm to his side.

* * *

Eulian sounded the retreat. The goblins closing in behind them would soon cut them off from the Shioroth. The standard bearer on her left side turned northeastward as planned, heading for the tree wall where Falnor's forces were ready to open the Southgate. She brought her sword down on a goblin, felling it in one blow, but when she looked up again, she realized Arvon was no longer beside her. The Elven forces were riding hard toward the Southgate.

"Keep going!" she yelled, waving them on as she wheeled her horse around to look for him.

"What is it?" called a young Elf pulling up as he drew near her.

"Arvon!" she said, still looking for him. "I can't find him!"

The young Elf turned the other way. "There!" he shouted. "Follow me!"

Eulian spurred her horse forward to where she had just seen a flashing blade driven into the eye of a Surgoth. She could see Arvon's red beard just before he went down. Another Surgoth was already coming up from behind to join the attack as a wave of goblins closed in.

The young Elf charged ahead, knocking goblins aside as he rode toward the red-bearded figure who had once again gotten to his feet to fend off the goblin challenge. Eulian held the reins in one hand along with her sword, drew her dagger and focused on the Surgoth, urging her steed to go faster. The young Elf crashing through the goblins in front of Arvon with Eulian's horse not far behind, galloping in parallel. The Elven princess came up behind the Surgoth, just as the dark monster wrapped its arm around the Dustrider. Before it could reach up to snap Arvon's neck, Eulian leaned over and jammed her dagger into its eye socket. Leaving it there, she pulled hard on the reins with both hands.

The Dustrider broke free of the falling Surgoth and spun around. Eulian wheeled about and Arvon pulled himself up behind her with his free hand.

"Go!" he hollered, hacking at the closest goblins.

Eulian galloped ahead. The young Elf raced up beside her, keeping his mount between the princess and the surging wave of goblins that was quickly cutting off their escape route. The Southgate was closing. A flurry of arrows from the battlements slowed the oncoming goblins.

"Get in!" yelled Eulian.

The young Elf obeyed, spurring his horse forward and shooting through the closing gates at a full gallop. Eulian and Arvon barely slipped in behind him, clattering to a stop a short way down the road. The three of them paused a moment, dazed and breathing hard.

"I owe you again," said Arvon when he could speak.

Eulian reached back and leaned on his thigh. "No," she said. "We both owe him." She bowed toward the young Elf who was still catching his breath.

Wide-eyed, the young fellow simply nodded. Black blood dripped from his sword onto the cobblestones.

* * *

Even before the last of the Elves had ridden through the Westgate, goblins came spilling out of the western woods from two separate places. They were met by a shower of arrows from Dwarven archers on the battlements but they did not stop. A dozen Surgoths emerged from the woods, carrying a great tree trunk between them, their heads bowed low, eyes down. The Dwarven arrows bounced off harmlessly as the Surgoths charged straight for the gates. Despite their heavy load, the monsters quickly outstripped the advancing goblins.

The gates were slow to close. It was clear to Roggin that they would not be latched in time to seal out the attackers.

"Ready!" He ordered, racing for the stairs. "Leave the gates!"

Fifty Dwarves positioned themselves on the street a short distance from the slightly open gates, archers in back, arrows ready. Yorgun Steelsmith stood in front with the rest of the company. For a moment, all was quiet.

Then the great tree came bursting in. The unlatched gates offered little resistance. Surprised by the minimal impact, the Surgoths staggered forward. The first two were felled immediately by Dwarven arrows. The second two plowed into their fallen predecessors. The momentum of the massive trunk dragged the rest of them forward a few paces before everything ground to a halt.

Goblins poured in through the open gates, streaming around the tree.

"Fire!" ordered Roggin.

The Dwarves on the battlements sent a storm of arrows down on the backs of the intruders, clogging the entrance with dead goblins. Even so, more goblins clambered in over the top of their fallen comrades. Dwarves waiting in the wings closed in on them from both sides, cutting off any retreat. The archers on top of the gate returned to the outer battlements and continued to fire on the remaining attackers outside. Below, steel clashed against steel as the swords and battle axes of the Dwarves met the blades and bludgeons of the goblins.

Abandoned their battering ram where it lay, the Surgoths waded into the Dwarves, cracking skulls, tearing limbs and tossing aside any who attacked. One of the dark monsters went down with a dagger in the eye. Then another fell.

Owler reached for another dagger but he had used them all. Ducking in, he retrieve one from the fallen Surgoth. When he stood up again, he had to leap aside to avoid the slashing swords of advancing goblins. A few quick paces took him out of range, but the battle was closing in from all sides. Swinging his sword, he beheaded the first goblin to get within reach and parried the blow from a war hammer with the backstroke. Another sweep of the blade cleared an escape route. He leapt through it and immediately rejoined the battle next to a knot of Dwarves whose axes were building a grizzly pile.

The Surgoths continued their rampage through the ranks of the Dwarves. Three of them fell lifeless to the ground, a testament to Dwarven bravery at close range. The remaining five wreaked havoc.

Roggin's axe chopped the knees out from under a great goblin. He smashed the creature's skull with the butt of the axe head and jumped up on top of the body to take on the next enemy. This goblin wielded a long, two-handed sword and swung it with considerable strength. Roggin deflected the first swing with the flat of his axe and ducked under the second stroke. Before the goblin brought the long blade back around, its belly had already been torn open by Roggin's axe.

The wiry Dwarf shouldered past the falling goblin and swung hard at the next thing in his path. His sharp axe did not even dent the dark skinned shin but it got the full attention of the shin's owner. Roggin scrambled between the Surgoth's legs and took a few steps toward open space when a swift kick in the back sent him flying. He landed face down with the breath knocked out of him. His axe skittered across the cobblestones. Unable yet to gasp for air, he struggled to his knees and crawled after it. A great hand shot out and grabbed him by the ankle.

"Oh, no you don't!" bellowed Yorgun Steelsmith, bringing his double-bladed axe down on the Surgoth's wrist. It didn't do any damage, but it freed the younger Dwarf from the monster's grip. The Surgoth roared and swung its other fist, cuffing the Chief of the Dwarves hard on the side of the head and knocking him off his feet. Yorgun's helmet went rolling down the street.

Roggin scrambled after his lost axe, gasping for air. When he turned around, Yorgun was back on his feet with his back to Roggin, standing between him and the monster. The Surgoth brought his fist down toward the Dwarf's white-haired head. Yorgun side-stepped but the blow glanced off his hip. When the Chief of the Dwarves tried to stand firm, his leg gave way and he fell.

The Surgoth reached down to grab the old Dwarf. Still dazed, Roggin flung his axe at the monster's face. His aim was too low; the spinning axe missed the Surgoth's vulnerable eyes and flew straight into the open mouth. The Surgoth choked, spat out the axe, and coughed as Roggin grabbed Yorgun with both hands under one arm and pulled him away.

"Take my axe!" said Yorgun.

Roggin ignored him, still hauling him across the cobblestones.

"Take it!" said Yorgun again.

The Surgoth shook its head, coughed again and looked around.

"Take it! That's an order!" said Yorgun, shoving his axe handle into Roggin's chest.

Finally, Roggin looked down.

The Chief's white beard was wet with blood. "Take it," said Yorgun. "Do something good with it!"

Roggin seized the axe. The Surgoth shot out a hand and grabbed the Chief of the Dwarves by one leg, yanking him off the ground, snapping him like a damp rag and flinging him aside, but Yorgun's axe was already on its way. Before the Surgoth even let go, one of the double-blades was buried in its brain.

A tall fellow with close-cropped, blonde hair leapt over the Surgoth as it fell, forcefully yanked the axe from the dead monster's face and tossed it back to Roggin. With a grim nod, Owler turned to face his next foe, dispatched him with a few well-placed strokes and set off to find another.

* * *

"It's the Birdman, sire," said the Faerie lookout. "He is with the Black Warriors." He pointed to the northeast.

Rohidan nodded. "I assume we are next then," he said.

Smoke from the burning tree wall between the Eastgate and the Southgate swirled slowly around the stone monolith of the Shioroth, obscuring the towers on the lofty summit. Mid-afternoon cloaked itself in shadows darker than dusk.

Another flash lit the sky, this time between the Eastgate and the Northgate. Those at the Northgate could now see what had alarmed those at the South and Westgates already. Flash after flash exploded with the sound of thunder. The tree wall burst into flames, turning the stormy sky to orange.

"Archers ready!" called the Faerie commander.

Two hundred Lammethan archers set an arrow on the string and awaited the order to fire.

Rohidan watched as the tree wall around his beloved city succumbed to the flames. Some of the great trunks disintegrated completely, blasting to bits and scattering fiery debris across the abandoned streets. Rooftops and backyard gardens were burning. The fire seared a dark, empty hole in the wall and lit tree after tree in both directions, roaring with wild fury. In a few minutes, the initial blast zone was just a blackened gap. One hundred and fifty Lammethan soldiers had been sent to the area and now provided the only ground defense at that point. The sounds of battle echoed off the walls of the Shioroth, barely audible over the roaring flames.

The Golrakken and the Black Warriors congregated in the northeastern portion of the fields, combining their strength, ordering their positions. They did not attack.

"The Birdman contines westward," said the lookout.

"Indeed," said Rohidan.

"Why doesn't Ender do something?" asked the lookout. "No disrespect, Lord Rohidan, but if I had the power of this Midnight Stone, I'd have wiped out the enemy, doused the fire and restored the wall by now."

Rohidan looked over at his kinsman. "I can imagine what I might do," he said; "but neither you nor I have that power, nor do we have the responsibility of managing it. Why he shows such restraint is beyond my understanding."

The thick, orange-tinted cloud of smoke billowed up into the sky.

The Elder Faerie shook his head. "I hope the Stonekeeper chooses well," he said; "for all our sakes."

* * *

Goblins streamed in through the southwest gap in the blazing tree wall, some of them burning themselves in the mad rush to get in. Lammethan archers in the air and Pelnaran archers on the battlements had felled many, but there were goblins to spare, and arrows were running low. Most of the fighting was now hand-to-hand.

From her perch on the tree wall, Tania set her sights on the Surgoths. Their tall, dark bodies were easy to pick out on the ground. Few of them bothered to protect their eyes now. Most simply waded into the fray and attacked without restraint or mercy. The valiant Men of the Green Stone did their best to steer clear of the monsters but those who were caught rarely escaped. Whenever she had a clear shot, Tania let an arrow fly. Doing so felt like the most natural thing in the world. Her skill proved itself over and over. She had lost count of the number of arrows she had used. Somehow, whenever she reached for one, her quiver always had a few remaining.

A thunk in the tree trunk by her head broke her concentration on the battlefield below. She looked down for the shooter. A goblin on the rooftop nocked another arrow but Tania had already fired back. Even as the goblin pulled the bowstring, it took a green arrow to the throat. The creature pitched backward and tumbled off the roof. It was dead when it hit the ground.

Smoke from the growing blaze obscured Tania's view below. She could feel the heat building as the flames leapt from treetop to treetop. Quickly, she climbed down from her perch and took her place amongst Falnor's archers on the battlements. They were hard pressed to keep the swarming goblins from taking the gates. One by one, the archers ran out of arrows, drew their swords and ran to join the others blocking the road that ran along the inside of the wall. Tania remained above, firing into the mass of goblins that now clogged the side road. One after another fell, but the fighting was fierce and the goblins had far greater numbers.

The dark-skinned woman spied a Surgoth approaching from a side street, followed by a band of goblins that were much larger than the normal rabble. She nocked an arrow and trained it on the leader, waiting for the right moment. For a short time, she lost sight of it behind the buildings. Keeping one eye on its expected exit point, she fired a few quick shots into the goblin mass on the perimeter road. The Surgoth emerged, as expected, only it was traveling much more quickly now. It smashed through the defenses of the Green Stone, not bothering to enjoin them in combat, intent on reaching the Southgate from the inside. Tania could not get a good bead on its eyes.

She saw the captain of the Green Guard step into the monster's path and fling a war hammer directly at its face. The hammer snapped the Surgoth's head back and glanced off. Another soldier off to one side swung his sword at the monster's legs. The well-aimed blow made no cut, but it effectively slowed the monster. The captain quickly closed in on the Surgoth. Thrusting his sword into the monster's face, he caught it under the jaw. The monster stopped in its tracks, grunted and swiped at the sword, knocking it out of the way. With the other hand, it seized its attacker. The captain slashed with his weapon and twisted away from the grip but the Surgoth did not let go.

The archer on the battlements had no time time to think. Heart pounding, she let fly.

* * *

A high pitched sizzle sounded over Captain Falnor's head. He ducked reflexively. The risky shot found its mark. The stricken Surgoth released its grip on Falnor and crumpled to the ground. No sooner was the captain free than he plowed into the pack of heavy goblins behind the fallen monster. Black blood streamed from his Pelnaran blade as he sliced his way through the advancing enemy. His troops acted as one, mowing down all who approached.

The Green Guard would protect the Southgate. Every soldier on the ground would do so or die trying.

* * *

Lia smacked the flat of her sword against the oncoming goblin blade, knocking it into the rusty axe that had also been swung at her. The axe hooked the goblin sword and locked the weapons together just long enough for Lia to drive her heel into one goblin's thigh. That goblin went down with a cry as Lia swung her blade in a measured arc, catching the axe-wielding goblin in the upper arm, slicing into the sinews but not into the bone. She slipped her blade out and swung it down to parry a weak stroke from the goblin at her feet. The strength of her blow knocked the sword from its hand. She stabbed it quickly in the throat and backed away to stay out of range of the dagger that the axe wielder stabbed her direction with its off hand. Two strokes from her sword deflected the dagger and cut through flesh and bone, leaving the goblin's hand dangling by a tendon. The goblin screamed and charged, head first. Lia stepped aside, shoved hard on the goblin's back, sending it face down into the street. Then she turned to take on a behemoth of a goblin that rushed her immediately afterward. She ducked inside its raised blade, reached up with her free hand and wrapped it around the goblin's arms. Spinning and pulling down, she rolled the goblin over and broke its hold on its huge sword. The weapon clattered to the ground and the massive goblin tumbled to the cobblestones. Continuing her movement, Lia brought her own blade around on the follow-through, cutting deeply into the goblin's neck.

A blow from her blind side sent her staggering. When she got her balance, she took a few steps toward a clear space and turned around. Grabbing her sword with both hands, she squinted through the searing pain. With a howl, the Surgoth charged, shoving goblins out of its way. Lia reached for a dagger and aimed for the eyes. The Surgoth deflected the throw easily, but Lia knew it would have been wide anyway. Swinging her sword with both hands, she spun around and hacked a path through a knot of goblins that had closed in behind her.

Every few steps, Lia had to fight her way past another foe, leaving a trail of black blood. Still the Surgoth advanced, stepping over the fallen, pushing others aside, fixated on its prey.

Lia turned up a deserted street. All at once, nothing was in her way. Her ears were ringing, her vision was blurry and she had a metallic taste in her mouth. She wiped her face with the back of her armored wrist. The leather shielding slid across skin slick with her own blood. She stumbled down the pavement, a shock of pain searing through her head with every footfall. She could no longer hear the noise of battle. Still she continued forward.

A heavy blow struck her between the shoulder blades. Her head snapped back and she felt her breath empty through her open mouth. For a moment, she caught a glimpse of the orange tinted cloud of smoke that surround the Shioroth. Then she landed hard on the ground and lost hold of her weapon. Instinctively, she rolled sideways, unable breathe, struggling to get out of the way. A kick to her rib cage sent her rolling across the cobblestones.

Her arms reached out to stop herself. Blindly, she got to her knees only to be seized by the shoulders, lifted up and thrown back down again. She landed on a dead goblin, sliding off to the side on the greasy black blood. Her hand closed instinctively on a wooden handle. The Surgoth came over top of the fallen goblin and leaned over, grinning widely, reaching for her again. Lia flung the goblin axe at the sound of the monster's breath. She could barely see. It was almost a lucky shot. The Surgoth turned its head at the last second and the axe head smashed into the outside edge of its right eye. It was a glancing blow, just a delay.

Lia reached around for another weapon and found a heavy goblin sword. She hauled it up off the ground as she struggled to her feet. Everything was spinning around her. The shadowy form of the Surgoth swung a long arm at her and she batted it away with the heavy goblin sword. The monster closed in a step and swung again. Lia shoved the jagged end of the blade at its face. The Surgoth grabbed the weapon and yanked it out of her slick hands, tossing it aside and shoving her backwards to the ground. She hit hard. For a second, she almost blacked out.

Two strong hands seized her by the throat, abruptly cutting off her next breath. She felt the weight of the heavy haunches sitting on her knees. Hammering at the Surgoth's forearms had no effect. She felt around on the ground for something—a rock, a stick, anything. She couldn't breathe. Her hand grabbed a fistful of dirt and she flung it at the shadowy shape. The hazy world spun haphazardly in all directions. Then everything went dark and silent.

* * *

Aaron swung his two handed longsword, parrying a goblin stroke with the flat and slicing into the goblin's neck with the sharp edge. He kicked the falling goblin back into two more. They were disabled long enough for him to deal with a taller one who had a war hammer. Redirecting the first hammer blow, he threw the big goblin off balance. His next stroke took off the goblin's head and sent it rolling down the street. He kicked another goblin in the groin, knocking it senseless to the ground with the pommel of his sword as it doubled over.

Quickly, he parried a strike aimed at his knees, shoving the sharp steel aside and lifting it slightly. A rapid twist of his blade broke the goblin's grip and tossed the enemy weapon a few feet away. With short, swift strokes, he cut the goblin once, twice, three times, and then stabbed it just above the breastplate. Yanking his blade free, he turned to address the next brute.

The flow of goblins seemed unending but he would rather these than the big, dark-skinned monsters. He had faced two Surgoths already and didn't relish the idea of running into another. They could be beaten back, but unless he could get inside the long reach of their arms, killing them was difficult. The first one had parried heavy sword cuts with its forearms, completely unharmed. It went down only after he had pitched a goblin spear into its face. The second Surgoth refused to give him a good shot at its eyes. Only after he had fought it back repeatedly had one of Tania's small green arrows killed the thing.

He stepped to his right, reached with his free hand and grabbed a thrusting sword arm, pulling the goblin forward and tossing it to the street. Another goblin came at him from the other side, a buckler in one hand and a sword in the other, crazily swinging both. Aaron brought his two-handed sword down on the buckler, splitting it in half and cutting into the goblin's arm. The insane creature struck out with the sword in its other hand as if nothing had happened. Aaron parried the blow on the flat and brought the back of his forearm across the goblin's face as it continued forward. Drunkenly, the goblin swung the remaining half of the buckler, catching Aaron on the upper arm. Aaron countered with a heavy backstroke, cutting through the goblin's leather armor and slicing deep into its collarbone.

Looking up, he suddenly ducked below the fist of a Surgoth. He swung hard, connecting solidly with the monster's knees. Unbalanced, the Surgoth pitched forward toward him. Aaron took the glancing body hit down low, upending the monster and dumping it into the pavement and then took a few running steps to put some distance between himself and the Surgoth. Goblins attacked from the left. He beheaded the first, skewered the second through the entrails and slammed it into a third as he pulled his sword free. The skull of the last goblin was split in half.

Aaron jumped over the fallen goblins and turned to face the Surgoth again. He batted its hands away with his blade, looking for an opening, but found no advantage. Aaron backed up again and again, unable to get in close enough for the kill. Finally, he saw his chance. The Surgoth overreached. Aaron drove the tip of his long sword straight up, catching the inside of the overhanging brow. The Surgoth's knees buckled and the creature crumpled to the ground, the sharp steel tip of Aaron's weapon stuck in its skull. Aaron stepped on the monster's face and yanked his sword free.

Out of the corner of his eye, he saw another Surgoth on its knees, throttling someone on the ground. The monster's prey was still fighting. Aaron took off running, bashing aside any who approached, his eyes on the struggling fighter. The Surgoth's great hands were choking off the windpipe, but the fighter on the ground flung a handful of earth at the attacker. The Surgoth shoved away from its intended victim and reached for its own face, wiping at its eyes and then shaking its head violently in all directions.

Aaron plowed into the blinded Surgoth, shoulder first, knocking the creature off balance. Before it could recover, Aaron thrust hard with his sword, aiming at the face. He struck the Surgoth in the temple. Stabbing again, he struck it in the ear. The monster turned away from him instinctively, swinging a wild fist as it spun away. Aaron ducked away and kicked the Surgoth in the hip, making the monster spin faster. As the ugly face came back around, Aaron jammed his sword into its eye.

Glancing around for enemies, he saw three goblins, all dead, all of them shot through by Faerie arrows. A male Faerie archer landed a few feet away, watching the empty street.

Aaron dropped to his knees by the fallen fighter, but what he saw confirmed what he already knew. Red blood covered half of Lia's face. Gingerly, he lifted her head and listened for her breath, but felt no warmth on his ear or cheek.

"Let me take her," said the archer, quickly stowing his weapon. "I can get her there faster."

Aaron looked at him wordlessly and nodded. The Faerie took Lia from his arms and flew off toward the Shioroth's central garden.

Picking up his long sword once more, Aaron stalked back toward the next advancing band of goblins. There were plenty more where these came from. The wall was still burning. He had work to do.

* * *

Smoldering ashes were all that remained of the northeast portion of the ancient tree wall but the flames on either side of the still-widening gap leaped high into the stormy sky. Dark smoke billowed upward like an angry beast.

A series of explosions from the northwest announced the third attack on the wall. A moment later, smoke began to rise there as well.

The Black Warriors and Golrakken who had been patiently assembling for the last quarter hour now charged toward the wide gap in the northeast. The thundering of hooves mixed with the roar of the fire.

The Lammethan responded immediately. Over a hundred of the Firstborn turned to light form and flew high over the heads of the advancing army, just out of arrow range. The flickering lights flew clear past the charging horses, wheeled around and attacked from behind. Black Warrior archers from the squadrons still assembled before the Northgate attacked the Firstborn from the flank, but the high-flying Lammethan were out of reach. Faerie arrows rained down on the rear ranks of the charging Black Warriors and Golrakken, felling many.

The Black Warriors merely turned to smoke and dissipated as they fell, but the Golrakken dropped lifeless to the ground, their spirits screaming and crying in the ears of the Firstborn. A few of the Faeries succumbed to the Golrakken magic and responded. Instantly, the Golrakken spirits entered the Faerie bodies, forcing them to the ground below. The beautiful winged bodies began to change. Their skin turned gray and stretched taut over their skeletons. Their wings shriveled up and fell off. Their eyes retreated deep into their skulls, leaving hollow sockets with only a dull glow. Their lips peeled back into a perpetual grin, and they stood to their feet to join the rest of the gray army facing the Westgate.

The sight of their kin turning into their enemies struck fear and horror in the hearts of the Firstborn. The counterattack faltered and the captain called a retreat. Once again, the Firstborn sailed high over the charging Black Warriors and Golrakken, but by then, the enemy was already within the city walls.

✴ ✴ ✴

Ender stood in one of the guard towers of the Eastgate, the same place in which he had been standing for the last several hours. Though he held the Midnight Stone in his hand, he had assiduously avoided fighting back. All of his efforts had been directed against a power that he knew no one else could feel. A darkness no one else could see had rolled across the fields from the east. Its influence had hastened the demise of the tree wall, emboldened the enemy, and deepened the defilement of the earth beneath the Shioroth. Ender had resisted it continuously, but it would not be vanquished.

His own thoughts had turned dark. He no longer wondered why the enemy advanced. The need to conquer and subjugate, to rule utterly, seemed obvious, unquestionable, even reasonable. Still, he strove to keep this great power contained. The struggle existed as much within his own mind as it did out there in the physical world. For much of the time, Ender had focused inward, his eyes open but not seeing. The relentless pressure had taken a toll.

Now he looked out the window of the guard tower and saw how much the world had changed. Fire and smoke rose high into the air to the north and south as the blaze consumed tree after ancient tree. Faeries fell from the sky, tricked by the Golrakken voices. Mounted Black Warriors and Gray Warriors poured into the city through the northeastern gap in the wall. Further South, the Men of the Green Stone fought bravely but the inflow of goblins could not be stanched. From time to time, there was a blast of colored fire as Mari or Holren cast a spell. The bellowing Surgoths roared throughout the city. Everywhere Ender looked, he saw the dead and dying. He felt the power of the Birdman's magic strike the tree wall even before the explosions began.

Enough!

In the space of a thought, Ender broke off the struggle with the darkness from the east and vanished into smoke, sailing through the guard tower window and into the air where he could get a better view. He could see the energy of the enemy sweeping in from all sides. With a sweep of his invisible hand, he turned the fields around the Shioroth to mud, miring the charging horses that had not yet entered the city and slowing the Surgoths and goblins that, up till now, had surged ahead unhindered. With another sweep of the hand, he extinguished the fire on the walls. Even so, thousands of the enemy were already within the city walls. He must stop them. One more time, he raised his hand, this time to strike.

Only then did he realize his mistake. No longer was he grounded, thinking clearly and deliberately.

"COME!"

The call of the Twin reached out and wrenched him away from the Shioroth, hurtling him across the eastern fields, past the ranks of the Golrakken and over the Volgan River.

A whisper began inside his mind. "We shall be one. We shall be one. We shall be one."

The phrase repeated itself over and over until it occupied almost every corner of his consciousness. Some part of him recognized what was happening and struggled to countermand it, but the insistence of the call was consuming.

Deep within him, he now knew the struggle of centuries, the lust for power, the deeply held belief in destiny and in justice on one's own terms, revenge and finally conquest. It was only right. The triumph of might and superior intelligence over mere philosophy was clearly not only appropriate, but inevitable.

Sailing over the Abandoned Land, Ehrmahann Jahrmahann could feel the conviction that the part he had played in this game up till now was only to weed out Morvassus' weaknesses, to force him to find different sources of strength, to consolidate control and to bring all possible allies under his sway. He had stepped in to carry the Midnight Stone at exactly the right time. He was the transition. His strength was well-honed, but logic demanded that he unite with one who already knew how to wield the Stone properly. Indeed, this merging was already in progress. He could feel it as he drew closer to the rising peaks of the Mirrak-Haas. Not much longer now and he would present the Midnight Stone to its rightful owner, joining with him as he was predestined to do.

Somewhere deep within his mind, a solitary voice screamed desperately that all of this was a lie.

CHAPTER 56

One

The Golrakken and the Black Warriors surged into the city, trampling Faeries and Elves as they came. The defenders of the Shioroth fought valiantly, but were beaten back without mercy.

Grisbane and his kin stood on both sides of a gap in the wall, smashing the legs out from under any horse that turned to take the perimeter road, crushing the riders with blows from their heavy staves. Though they grew more bloodied and battered, the Small Giants allowed no one access to the road. The smoke from the Black Warriors rose along with the shrieks of the fallen Golrakken. The Small Giants merely unhorsed another rider and grimly smashed him into the ground. None of them said a word.

* * *

Karkaan Dragonhelm led the troops into what had once been the home of his people. Even after centuries, the streets were familiar. He sent several patrols down smaller roads to flank the defenders as he brought the main company around to the south to attack the Eastgate from the inside. With the help of the Black warriors, the Golrakken had arrived with overwhelming force. The conquest of the Shioroth should be short, thought Dragonhelm.

* * *

The stream of cavalry pouring through the gap stopped abruptly. Muck and mire had appeared under the pounding hooves of the armies of Morvoth, trapping over a thousand enemy riders before they could reach the city. The astonished Elves and Faeries inside closed ranks in front of the huge gap in the tree wall, blocking the entrance and shutting off any escape for those already inside.

* * *

Brian rolled clear of the trapdoor and scrambled across the room to join Jehzik and Annie. They flattened themselves against the wall by the door to the outside.

Someone on the other side of that door shuffled nervously through a set of jingling pieces of metal.

One of them was fitted to the door only to be removed. The jingling resumed.

"Get on with it, soldier!" said a rough voice that clearly belonged to a Black Warrior.

"Yes sir," said another Black Warrior voice.

"That one," said a third.

Someone else was breathing laboriously.

"Hurry!" said the first Black Warrior.

Another metal bit was inserted into the door. A mechanism clicked once, twice, three times.

Brian raised the Valenblade and held his breath, heart pounding.

The latch lifted and the door opened. The torch in the hallway cast long shadows on the floor of the Interrogation Room. Brian couldn't tell if there were three people or four.

"Go in!" barked the first Black Warrior.

Brian brought the Valenblade down on the first shape to appear in front of him. The Black Warrior guard let out a cry and fell to the stone floor, dark liquid and smoke issuing from a great slice that ran from his shoulder halfway down his arm. As Brian turned toward the next enemy, the hard heel of a boot sent him reeling back into Annie.

"Keep going!" barked the Black Warrior captain.

Annie picked herself up off the floor and turned herself to light form. The Black Warrior captain stepped back into a defensive position, startled by the flickering light. Annie dove on the fallen guard and pulled the sword from his scabbard. While she was down, the captain swung at her fiercely. The Faerie rolled onto her back and parried the stroke without thinking, surprised at the power in both his stroke and her own block. The captain attacked again. Annie rolled away once more, using her speed to keep clear of his slashing blade. She got to her feet and faced the captain head-on. The Black Warrior attacked in earnest, his powerful strokes clashing against her sword. She held her ground, parrying every stroke, matching his strength with hers. She darted sideways, out of his reach and then ducked behind him and leapt high into the air. He whirled about, sword swinging in the direction he had last seen her. The sharp metal blade sliced through emptiness.

Annie's borrowed sword came crashing down on the Black Warrior's helmet, knocking him to the ground. Annie flew straight down, sword point first. The steel punctured the leather and drove clear to the dark heart. With a burst of smoke, the Black Warrior captain was dead.

* * *

Brian got up on his feet. The other Black Warrior with the dark figure was very close.

Time slowed to a crawl. With his enhanced vision, Brian could see a shadowy figure pull away from the arm of the guard. The shadow looked directly at the gruffen. Brian recognized it now. This was the same dark entity that had departed the fortress. How had they had come to meet him once again all the way here? He was actually within reach, if Brian could only move. His body felt like it was fighting through wet clay.

The shadow raised a fist and aimed it at the gruffen. Brian swung the Valenblade but his arm could not move fast enough. Something that might be described as blindness, or perhaps a complete extinguishing of light, was growing outward from the fist, coming directly at Brian. The gruffen could almost feel the power as it approached. Time slowed even further. Every motion took forever. He brought the Valenblade down, down, down, down. Onward came the darkness, closing in on Brian's chest. He did not waver. Down came the Valenblade.

The magical blade bit into the shadow's wrist, cutting cleanly through skin, muscle, tendon and bone, severing the hand completely. The blindness that had been seeping from the fist vanished as the fingers slackened. A tiny marble of infinite black bounced free as the disembodied hand hit the floor.

Time returned to normal with a brilliant flash and a shockwave that knocked everyone to the ground.

* * *

The archers' arrows were spent. Thadris arrayed his troops to counter an inside attack on the Eastgate. The thunder of hoof beats approached from around the bend ahead.

"Steady!" he shouted.

Hearts quailed at the sight of the Golrakken army and the Black Warriors charging around the corner. A few moments more and the Elves and Faeries knew they would be overrun. Everyone stood firm.

Then something shifted. Everyone felt it. The effects were immediate.

In an instant, the entire army of Black Warriors simply vanished. The defenders suddenly found their blades slashing through wisps of dark smoke which quickly dissipated. Though the northwestern gap in the tree wall grew wider, there were no troops to ride through it.

In the same instant the Black Warriors disappeared, the enchanted horses on which the Golrakken rode also vanished in smoke. The Golrakken riders dropped to the pavement. Limbs were broken, backs were snapped, and helmets cracked against the stones. The defenders of the Shioroth fell upon their enemies and drove them back, ignoring their taunts and cries.

The gray warriors fought fiercely. Karkaan called the remainder of his army to himself. They stood together, bristling with weaponry, calling out to the defenders who surrounded them, bating, insulting, cursing and threatening. It seemed to be a standoff.

Then, out of the sky flew Rohidan, the Eldest of the Faeries. He landed between Karkaan Dragonhelm and the Eastgate.

"A parley!" sneered Karkaan. "What a useless gesture! One word from you, Rohidan, and your soul is mine. You know you cannot win this fight. We will conquer you whether we ride or march; it matters not to us. More than a thousand Golrakken are still pouring through your precious wall, or did you not notice?"

Rohidan drew his sword and approached Karkaan slowly. "You are wrong, Karkaan," said the Elder Faerie.

Everyone gasped. Those nearby drew back in alarm and stared, horrified.

"Ha!" crowed Dragonhelm. "The old winged one succumbs at last. Your transformation will be the sweetest yet, old fool! Prepare to kneel!"

Rohidan took a step forward. "Not so, my old friend," he said.

He was unchanged! His skin had not turned gray, nor had his wings shriveled up and fallen.

"Do not call me 'old friend,'" spat Karkaan.

"As you wish," said Rohidan; "though you were that, once."

"That time is long past, old fool," rasped the Golrak.

"Three things you appear not to know, Karkaan," continued the Elder Faerie. "First, the Dark Master's enchantment has left you. I could not stand here and speak to you otherwise. The voices of the Golrakken have no effect. Second, your reinforcements are not pouring in through the gap. They are mired in a band of mud that now surrounds the city."

"You lie!" growled Karkaan.

"If you could see for yourself, you would know I do not lie," said Rohidan. "Third, you and your kin are no longer immortal, vulnerable only to the Valenblade. Common steel can kill you now."

"Another lie," sneered Karkaan.

"Test me and see," said Rohidan. "I, myself, am proof of the truth."

"I will sever your head and run the rest of you through," said Karkaan.

"I think not," said Rohidan, quietly. "Your time ends today."

"So you have come to fight, my 'old friend?'" asked Karkaan.

"Yes," said Rohidan. "Today we finally lay you to rest."

Karkaan Dragonhelm stood back and said to his fellows: "If they wish to fight, then a fight they shall have, but no more wasting time with this fool."

"Thadris!" called Rohidan, keeping his eyes on Dragonhelm.

"Yes, Lord Rohidan!" said the Elven prince.

"Are our people ready?"

"They are, sir," came the reply.

Rohidan nodded. "Goodbye, Karkaan," he said. "I would that it had ended differently."

The Golrakken leader did not respond.

"We attack on your command, Thadris," said Rohidan quietly.

Thadris looked around at the Faeries and Elves surrounding the Golrakken. "Now!" he cried.

The defenders rushed the Golrakken from all sides. Steel clashed against steel. Blood flowed on both sides. Rohidan, himself, struck down a Golrak who had come between him and Karkaan.

"Proof, Dragonhelm!" shouted the Elder Faerie as he withdrew his sword from the gray skull. "Look!"

Beneath Rohidan's feet, the body was already decomposing. Rohidan rolled the decaying corpse over with his boot. The body armor was rapidly corroding, and dust leaked out between the seams. Another shove with the boot, and even the armor crumbled away, leaving nothing but a pile of bits and dust at Rohidan's feet. All around them, the same thing was happening.

"The Golrakken can be killed!" sounded the cry. "The Golrakken die!" With a roar, the forces of the Shioroth pressed forward.

The soldiers of the gray army saw their wounded dying and disintegrating at their feet. For the first time in many centuries, their cold hearts quailed. Every weapon held against them had suddenly turned lethal. The ranks of the Golrakken collapsed inward.

Karkaan's leering expression did not change. "I will not rest," he rasped; "not today, Rohidan das Lammethan, not until I have carved the last breath from your throat and driven my sword through your heart." He strode forward to meet the Elder Faerie.

His swiftly cutting Golrakken blade met with an equally swift parry from the Elder Faerie. Their swords flashed in a deadly dance, stroke after stroke, parry after parry, each one pushing for an advantage. The ferocity of the fight was matched only by its discipline. For a long time, neither could gain the upper hand. Karkaan drew first blood, a cut into Rohidan's shoulder, not much more than a tear in the fabric that quickly stained red, but enough to encourage the Golrak to swing with even greater force and speed.

That was when Rohidan found his opening. The sharp edge of his Faerie blade cut deeply into the exposed gray neck.

Karkaan's sword fell from his hands. Rohidan cut from the opposite side, slicing deeply into the gray flesh again. The dragon helm pitched forward as Karkaan fell lifeless to the ground. The Elder Faerie turned on the next Golrak and began anew, stepping over his fallen foe as the gray body turned to dust beneath him.

"Karkaan is dead! Karkaan is dead!" The shout rang off the walls of the Shioroth as Thadris' forces pursued the fleeing Golrakken.

Even as they fled, the Golrakken were cut down. Soon, the defenders were striking at brittle, dusty flesh and rusty armor. Not much later, they had no one left to pursue.

The sounds of battle continued in the south. "Follow me!" cried Thadris. "To the Southgate!"

Rohidan stepped back through the rush of Faeries and Elves. Kneeling down, he plucked a dark red stone from the ground, rubbed a little dust off of it with his thumb, and carefully placed it in a pocket in his robes.

* * *

The faint voice in the far corner of Ender's mind grew suddenly clear. "STOP!"

The Stonekeeper dropped like a rock from his lofty arc. The force that had hauled him clear across the Abandoned Land and over the summits of the Mirrak-Haas had suddenly released him. He had returned to physical form only to fall from the sky.

"STOP!" the voice cried again.

Ender's speed slowed but the jagged rocks were still rising to meet him at an alarming rate.

"STOP!" shouted the voice. Finally, Ender recognized it as his own.

The Midnight Stone responded, bringing him to a complete stop with his feet planted firmly on a slab of rock. Ender drove all other thoughts from his mind and focused on staying exactly where he was. He couldn't tell if his vision was clouded, or if he was merely in the fog. Slowing his frantic thoughts, he stared down at his feet. Stay grounded, he thought. Stay grounded.

Something had changed. His connection with the mind behind the Twin had been cut and he was starting to think clearly again. Holding the Midnight Stone, he could feel the call, but the force that pulled him through the sky no longer existed.

"ONE!" begged the Midnight Stone.

Ender called to the Twin, but the Midnight Stone in his hand only screamed in agony. The Twin could not respond.

"ONE!" cried the Midnight Stone.

Ender's vision cleared and he found himself staring down at the battlements of Akka-Illin. The fortress was deserted. Dark smoke was drifting away on the wind, dissipating as it went.

"ONE!" cried the Midnight Stone.

The Stonekeeper calmed himself again and listened to his own thoughts as he watched for any movement in the fortress. Nowhere could he sense the Black Warriors or their enchanted mounts. He listened again, searching the corners of his mind for stray intentions.

Stepping off the cliff, he vanished once again. This time, he flew exactly as he intended, over the high walls of the fortress, down into the empty courtyard, across to the open door in the corner, down the dark stairwell to the torchlit hallway and in through the open door at the very end.

* * *

Once the fires had gone out, Holren had focused on blasting the Black Warriors streaming in through the gap in the northeast section of the tree wall.

Their sudden disappearance had left him without a target. Racing through the streets, he came to the Northgate.

"Where is the Birdman?" he called up to the lookouts in the Northgate towers.

"He's gone into the forest where the Dwarves came out yesterday," one of them called back.

Holren quickened his pace and soon reached the gap in the northwest portion of the tree wall. He did not slow as he cast his spell. Anyone looking at him now would see only a shift in the light, or perhaps a shadow. When he got to the mud, a dry path opened up in front of him. Once he had run the length of it, the dry path turned to mud once again. He curved around to follow the line of trees that marked the boundary of the woods. Though he saw a smattering of goblins and a few Surgoths hiding inside, he did not yet see the Birdman.

He could feel the magic, though, a dark force radiating out from somewhere in the woods, moving southward. Slowing his pace, he quietly entered the forest. He continued to close in on the source of the Dark Magic, careful not to disturb the goblins hiding behind trees here and there. He always felt as if the Birdman was just ahead, up around the next corner, the next boulder or the next tree, just out of sight. Holren's path took him deeper into the woods, around a rocky spur and down into a small ravine. By now, he had a good look at the tracks he was following. They were very much like large human feet but the claws left deep impressions in the soft earth. Holren tried to remember what the Birdman's feet looked like.

He had just scrambled up out of the ravine when he was struck hard in the chest by an invisible force. He tumbled backward halfway down the steep slope before he recovered. A small, shadowy figure above him threw another invisible bolt before turning and disappearing back into the woods. Holren fended off this attack and quickly climbed up out of the ravine. His attacker was nowhere to be seen, but Holren could still feel him, and the trail of broken branches and trampled moss was obvious. He raced through the woods now. Up ahead, he got another glimpse of his shadowy enemy. Holren's old apprentice, Taron Kaiss, clung to the back of a Surgoth that was carrying him very quickly through the forest.

The wizard wove a fire spell. Just as he released it, the small, dark figure on the Surgoth's back sent out a broad wall of magic which smashed the fireball into a million sparks. The heat was intense enough to set the underbrush on fire, but it did no harm to the fleeing pair.

Holren broke through the broad wall, dousing the fire as he went. Quickly, he conjured another fire spell. It was met with the same defense. The Surgoth charged southward unimpaired.

The wizard quickened his pace and began to close the gap. He sent three fireballs in quick succession. The first two were deflected. The last one struck the Surgoth in the back of the legs. The small figure on the back of the Surgoth let go of his mount and tumbled to the ground as the stricken monster stumbled and crashed into the undergrowth, half of its right leg burned away.

Holren drew his sword as he charged forward. A few more steps and he would drive the point of it home.

The force that struck him full in the chest stopped his forward motion and dropped him to his knees, unable to breathe.

Quickly, he put up a shield of green tinged light. No sooner had he done so than a bolt of lightning came shooting up from the hooded figure on the ground, blasting against his shield and pushing him even further down.

The figure of the Birdman rose from the ground. Gone was the small, misshapen apprentice. The towering creature waved its hands, casting spell after spell without stopping.

Holren was hard pressed to maintain his shield. A counterattack was impossible. He still hadn't gotten up off the ground or gotten his breath back, and he could feel his strength being used up little by little. The Birdman advanced a step or two, relentlessly pounding the kneeling wizard with first one kind of spell and then another: water, fire, lightning, wind, rocks, back to fire. The attacks increased in intensity as the Birdman focused all his attention on the spells.

Still maintaining his green-tinged shield, Holren reached down and found the simplest weapon. The rock struck the Birdman full in the face, knocking its head back and breaking its concentration.

Holren jumped to his feet and immediately went on the attack, casting spells of confusion, paralysis and weakness. The Birdman staggered back but soon recovered. Flashes of lightning were met with flaming bolts. A torrent of water was blasted into a massive spray. The forest lit up and resounded with the sounds of their battle. Fire crackled and thunder roared but neither of them gave ground.

In the midst of the fight, the Birdman began to shriek, a long, sustained, ear-splitting howl that cut through all other noise. Holren kept his focus on his attacks and defenses. The howl continued, loud enough to drown out the sizzling lightning and pounding water.

Their battle had blasted a clearing around them. For twenty paces on all sides, there were no trees. The bare ground beneath their feet was scorched and hot one moment and frozen solid the next. Still the fight continued. They stood only a few paces apart, hammering at each other with spell after spell.

Into the clearing came the Surgoths. Fifty of the dark skinned monsters rushed in from all sides and formed an ever-tightening ring around the two fighters. Holren cast a series of fire spells to drive them back. The Birdman countered with ice and water. The Surgoths closed in, undaunted.

Holren immediately broke off the attack, dropped to one knee and built a shield bubble around himself. The Birdman slammed at the shield with fire, lightning, heat and cold. Holren held firm, but he could not move. All his power was focused on the shield.

The Birdman quickly changed tactics. He formed a wall of force that fully enveloped Holren's shield bubble. Then he leaned on this new shield and exerted all his power. Purple light shot out all around the shield. Holren renewed his defenses. Still more purple light emanated from the Birdman's clawed hands, racing around and around the glowing egg that surrounded the wizard. The lights changed from purple to blue, to red, to white, and then back to purple. A few moments later, Holren was encased in a cage of lightning that forked incessantly around his shield.

The Birdman changed back into his old form.

"Well," said Taron Kaiss. "I may not be able to see your face, but I know fear when I feel it. You did not expect such a match, I suppose. You always considered your powers superior. Little do you know, old master, so very little do you know."

Crouching inside the shield, Holren said nothing. His mind searched for any weakness in the cage around him, any means by which the spell could be taken apart from the inside. So far, he had found none.

"It's a puzzle, isn't it?" said his former apprentice. "This is beyond your skill, wizard. The spell perpetuates itself, growing stronger each time the pattern repeats. It even feeds on your resistance. When your strength fails, the cage will collapse on you and nothing you can do then will save you from it."

The blind apprentice turned to one of his Surgoths. "You, bear me away from here. I need to rest. Those who remain, watch the prisoner. If he does get out, tear him apart."

The Surgoth closest to him knelt down to allow him to climb up and the others gathered around the lightning cage to wait.

Holren felt increasing pressure from the cage. It had already grown incrementally more powerful.

* * *

The high shrieking sound from over the wall sent a shiver down Roggin's spine, but the effect it had on the Surgoth he faced was a blessed relief. The hairless, dark skinned monster turned swiftly away, smashing through the swarming goblins as it ran. All the Surgoths appeared to be on the run, heading toward the gap in the wall. The wiry dwarf turned Yorgun's double-bladed axe on the goblins immediately nearby.

* * *

Arvon Dustrider swung his longsword in short, deadly strokes, cutting into the mass of goblins that swarmed around the gap in the wall. The inflow had suddenly stopped, but the sheer numbers of the enemy already at hand were as much as he could handle. He bashed away a goblin war hammer and brought the sharp of his blade across the wielder's neck, sending the goblin to the ground. The goblins behind that one stepped over their fallen comrade and kept coming.

"Surgoths!" yelled Tania from the rooftop.

The Dustrider cleared a space in front of him with his sword and took a quick look around. The dark, hairless monsters were racing toward him. Another flash of the great longsword kept the goblins back long enough for him to jump up onto a fence and swing himself onto the roof of another house. The goblins followed, clambering up onto the fence. Arvon cut them down one by one as they reached the roof. Hammers and axes flew up toward him. He ran down the roof line and escaped down a back alley to come around and fight from another angle.

* * *

Mari watched the Surgoths converging on the southwest corner. Flying as a hummingbird once more, she lifted up over the rooftops and followed. The high shriek coming from the western woods seemed to have called the monsters away. The tall creatures ignored the battle as they left the city. More than a thousand goblins were trapped in the thick mud that surrounded the tree wall.

That must be Ender's doing, thought Mari.

The Surgoths simply stomped on the mired goblins, trampling them deeper into the mud as they ran for drier ground. Eventually, the Surgoths themselves became mired in the muck. They waded through it slowly, climbing over the fallen goblins whenever they could. Even so, dozens of them reached solid footing and raced toward the western woods.

From this position, Mari could now see the flashes of light that flared in the western forest. The Surgoths were heading straight for it. Her blood turned cold. She flew across the tree wall and over the muddy fields, sailing over the woods toward the blazing lights. Smoke was rising from the scorched battleground ahead. Explosions and flashes of lightning were followed by clouds of steam and billowing smoke, forcing Mari to turn away. She flew a short distance and landed on a high branch. The hummingbird form took too much energy. She transformed herself into a falcon and lifted off again, soaring up on the rising air currents to see if she could get a better view from higher up.

Skirting the smoke and steam, she rose higher and higher until she was able to get a look straight down. Her sharp falcon eyes could see fine details on the ground below, even from this height. The Surgoths were rushing toward the Birdman and the wizard. In a moment, they would be upon him. Instinctively, she dove down. When her husband created a shield around himself, staving off all attacks, Mari pulled up again. There was no way to reach him behind that shield. She circled higher once more, formulating a plan, keeping her eye on the action below.

To her horror, she saw the Birdman build his cage of lightning around Holren. Now she had another obstacle to overcome. Catching the rising air, she circled higher still. Her energy reserves were low. She had been fighting goblins and Surgoths all night. To ensure the success of her intended spell, she would have to abandon her falcon form. Her plan was risky, but if she climbed high enough, she might have enough time to free her husband and escape, herself. If she failed, neither might survive.

The Birdman was stepping back from the lightning cage which imprisoned her husband. She had to move now. Positioning herself directly over the circle of Surgoths, she started her dive and flicked a wingtip, releasing her transmutation spell. Back in human form, she continued to free fall, headfirst, toward the ground.

Carefully, she formed the words, piecing together the elements one at a time as the ground came up to meet her faster and faster. Each portion of the spell was woven to release the exact amount of power in the precise direction needed to break the lightning cage that wrapped around her husband's shield.

At the last second, she sent the energy out, flicked her wrist and transformed back into a falcon, pulling up sharply to avoid crashing into Holren's shield. She barely cleared the heads of the Surgoths as she sailed off to the side and up over the treetops.

The spell she had built during free fall contacted the cage and sent the lightning flying in all directions, away from the protective shield. The ring of Surgoths took the full force of it. Lightning blasted great holes into their dark flesh, igniting the monsters' insides. They roared in pain. A moment later, the fire had consumed them from the inside out, and they were nothing but glowing cinders.

* * *

Holren stood to his feet, his protective shell destroyed by whatever had just happened. A falcon was flying over the treetops, apparently circling back. Taron Kaiss had been thrown to the ground. He lay stunned beside the smoldering ashes of his Surgoth.

The exhausted wizard drew his sword and rushed toward his former apprentice. With a mighty swing, he brought the blade down on the dark hood. Steel met skull and cracked it.

Taron Kaiss rolled away, his hands still working spasmodically. Talons formed on his fingertips. His body began to stretch and lengthen. A beak began to protrude from the dark hood. The creature continued to crawl away but Holren struck again, hard, just above the hip. The creature turned face up. Its hands continued to spasm. The bird-like face began to emerge as the cloak and hood disappeared. Holren brought the sword down again, this time at the joint where the neck and skull met. The creature jerked but kept working its clawed talons. Holren raised his weapon and stabbed straight down, driving his sword point directly into the Birdman's chest.

The talons stopped their spasmodic movements and reached for the hands that gripped the sword. Holren yanked the blade free and staggered back, gasping for air. The Birdman traced a pattern weakly in the air, as if drawing a figure or words on the wizard's chest.

"No!" said Mari, from a few paces away. Summoning the last of her own strength, she sent a ball of fire directly into the wound opened by Holren's sword. "That's enough!" she said.

Light began to burn inside the wounded Birdman.

"Mari?" The Birdman's voice sounded more like a frightened young man. "Mari?"

Light began to show through cracks in the Birdman's skin. Brighter and brighter it became, splitting through the flesh, like a hungry fire licking at a dry log.

"Mari!" wailed the Birdman.

The fire grew. The taloned hands fell to the ground. The hideous head rolled to the side, its great beak open and loose. Then the light consumed the body utterly and burned it to ash.

Holren stumbled to Mari's side as she stood bent and trembling.

"The woods are full of goblins," he said. "We'd best get out of sight."

She nodded and followed him deeper into the woods.

* * *

The black crow shook its feathers and looked hastily about, stunned. The Faerie was getting up off the floor on one side of the room. The gruffen had been thrown across to the other side and was just now getting to his feet. The dark figure of Morvassus was kneeling near the pool, his wounded arm cradled in his lap, feeling around with his remaining hand for something on the stone floor. Jehzik spied what Morvassus was looking for just before the Dark Master did.

Frantically, the crow dove for the small black marble, knocking it away. Morvassus lunged, but Jehzik was quicker. He pounced on the Twin and snatched it up with his beak.

Instantly, Jehzik's vision changed. Everything in the room became frighteningly alive. His whole sense of direction was askew. He tried to take off but he simply crashed to the floor again. Desperately, he scrabbled about, not knowing where to go or how to get away.

"Give it to me," said a dark voice very close.

Jehzik felt the hand on his tailfeathers. Pain seared through his entire body.

"Give it to me," insisted the voice.

Jehzik's head jerked this way and that, but he did not release the black marble in his beak. All he knew was that he wanted the hand to let go, for the voice to go somewhere far, far away and leave him alone. A surge of power shot through his entire body, from his beak to the tips of his wings, into every claw, and all the way down to his tailfeathers.

"Go away!" he croaked.

As he did so, the Twin slipped from his beak, but the hold on his tailfeathers had been released. The black marble rolled away.

* * *

Brian stood up and tried to get his bearings. Somehow he had ended up across the room near the throne by the pool. Closer to the door, Annie was on her feet. The Black Warriors were all gone. Over on this side of the pool, Jehzik and the shadow figure were chasing after something on the floor. He started over toward them. Jehzik seized something, but now he seemed unable to fly. Brian saw the figure's arm reach out and grasp the crow by the tailfeathers. Racing forward, the gruffen dove at the shadowy figure, driving the Valenblade deeply into its back.

One moment the shadow was beneath him, and the next moment, Brian was face down on the floor, the Valenblade buried to the hilt in stone. Something splashed into the pool.

✳ ✳ ✳

Still panting, Annie looked around for more enemies. She had no weapon, but she would fight with her bare hands if it came to that. The dark shadow figure had disappeared. In fact, the entire room was empty except for the three of them.

"Brian! Jehzik!" she called. "You all right?"

"Where did he go?" asked Brian.

"I don't know," croaked Jehzik. "I'm just glad he's gone."

A shadow darkened the doorway and Brian leapt back to his feet, blade at the ready.

"It's all right," said Ender, coming into the room.

"Healer!" cried Jehzik. "Oh, is it good to see you!"

Ender knelt down and reached toward a crack in the stone floor.

A sharp pain stabbed through his palm. He waited, but nothing further seemed to happen. That was all. When he opened his hand again, it held a single deep black stone. No more voices cried for reunification. The urge to destroy was gone.

He looked around the room. Annie and Brian still stood where they were when he entered.

"Where is Morvassus?" asked Ender.

"Vanished!" croaked Jehzik, hopping a bit closer; "just as you arrived!"

"I heard a splash," said Brian.

"So did I," said Annie.

Ender went over to the pool. The light inside was fading, but he could still see the column of energy emanating from it. He held the Midnight Stone over the pool and looked into it. The water began to swirl slowly. Even as he watched, the light dimmed and went out. The swirling motion ceased. The pool merely reflected the torchlight from the doorway.

That was when many things began to shift back into place, back to where they had once belonged many hundreds, even thousands of years ago.

* * *

At the Southgate, the archers' arrows were spent. Only Tania's quiver remained full. She continued to shoot from rooftops and dark alleys, constantly changing her position. Falnor and the remaining Men of the Green Stone fought toe to toe with the enemy. They were supported by the Lammethan, who attacked from above. The Faeries did their best to keep the enemy from spreading deeper into the city.

The ring of mud around the tree wall had slowed the goblin army's advance to a crawl, but the remaining troops were forming a living bridge across it toward the large gap in the southwest. At any moment, the onslaught of fresh goblins would begin again. The Surgoths which had been stuck in the mire, now emerged to fight again. The shrieking sound that had called them away had stopped. In fact, the intense flashes of light in the western woods had also stopped.

"They're coming!" cried a lookout on the battlements.

"So are the Elves!" shouted Thadris as his troops surged into the southwestern streets. The defenders of the Southgate roared as the news spread. The Faeries which had been defending the Eastgate dove down on the enemy and chased many of them from the alleys and side streets.

Already, though, Surgoths were stepping onto the living bridge, their dark skin covered with dripping and drying muck. A few of the weaker sections of the bridge failed, but the Surgoths merely climbed back up and continued forward. Work to repair the damage started immediately, even as new troops piled onto the living bridge.

The enemy was partway across the mud when a cry went up from the goblins still waiting behind: "Dragon!"

Confusion reigned. "Which one? What color? Whose is it?" Nobody knew.

Repair on the bridge came to a halt and everyone looked skyward. Out of the east, diving directly at the goblins in the mud, came a winged lizard. No one could identify the creature by its shape from such an angle.

Before they could determine if it was friend or foe, it opened its mouth and spewed fire on the mass of goblins in the mud. The heat was intense enough to incinerate the Surgoths who had almost reached the city. It also hardened the mud wherever it touched, sealing in the hundreds of goblins who remained mired in the muck. Goblin arrows flew into the air. Those that found their target simply glanced off the hard scales. The dragon wheeled about, diving back down for another pass, torching the enemy even as the massive retreat began.

Now that he had forced them to abandon the attack, Gasslic began herding the enemy together, cutting off their escape with fire. The stench of burnt goblin rose into the air as he seared through their ranks time and again, scattering them one minute and rounding them up the next. When he was finished, neither Surgoth nor goblin was left standing within view of the city walls. Half buried corpses filled the dried mud south of the city.

Winging his way over the wall, Gasslic looked for somewhere else he could aid in the fight, but he could not separate friend from enemy. Within the city, a blast of fire could cause more damage than good. He sailed over to where the Lammethan from the Northgate had come to the aid of the Elves and Dwarves who guarded the Westgate.

He caught sight of a Surgoth fighting two valiant Dwarves. Diving down, he seized the monster's hairless head in his mouth, lifted into the air with the creature, coughed once and spit out the flaming remains beyond the wall.

When he circled around again, he saw Aaron's bald head. The warrior was waving him down. Gasslic landed on a roof.

"Have you seen Holren or Mari?" bellowed Aaron.

"No," said Gasslic.

"Go look!" yelled Aaron. "Lots of flashing in the woods!" Not waiting for an answer, he stepped into the path of a pack of goblins trying to escape down a side street and bloodied his sword yet again.

The dragon thundered away over the wall. He spied an obvious hole in the forest canopy. He circled the area first, looking for signs of life. There were none. A smaller circle in the middle of the clearing was as dark as coal. The whole place still prickled with residual magic but nothing moved. The dragon circled lower, searching the edges of the circle. Still, he saw no movement.

Rising up again, he circled wider, scanning the woods. Through the canopy, he could see scattered goblins running randomly through the woods. They seemed to have no direction. As he followed the air currents along a row of low hills, he spied two figures on the backside of a rocky outcrop, huddled in each other's arms. He recognized them immediately. He curved back around and glided to a landing on the huge boulders.

"You have been busssssy, I sssssee," he said.

"Yes," said Holren. "Taron Kaiss is dead."

The dragon nodded his great, scaly head. "A sssssssad but necesssssary ending," he said. "You two sssssseem to have ssssssssurvived the encounter."

"Just barely," said Holren.

Out of the corner of his eye, the dragon saw movement, first in one area, then another. "Thissssss placccccce isssss not sssssafe," he said. "We sshhhhhould not tarry. I will get you out."

"Can you take both of us?" asked Mari.

"A ssssshort dissssssstancccce, yesssss," said Gasslic. "You ride. I'll grab your hussssssband."

Holren helped Mari up onto Gasslic's back. "Are you sure you can carry both of us?" he said.

"Make yourssssssssself into a ball," said Gasslic. "It will be easssssier for me—quickly!"

Holren did as he was told. Gasslic beat his powerful wings and lifted up from the boulders, seizing the wizard in his claws as he did so. The dragon's wings snapped and thundered like great sails in a fickle wind. He turned downhill and skimmed the forest, bashing the tips of his wings into the treetops as he tried to climb. Slowly, slowly, he was able to get high enough to clear the rest of the woods without dragging Holren or his own tail through the trees.

When he was clear of the forest, he settled down and left Holren on a wide stretch of open field, fully exposed, but out of range of any weapon. The only goblins nearby were burnt corpses.

"What happened here?" asked Mari.

"I'll exsssssssplain later," said the dragon.

"Take her to the central garden," called Holren. "Neither of us will be fit for battle for awhile."

Gasslic took off immediately. When he came back, he bent down so the wizard could mount.

Holren stood on shaky legs, looked up at the high perch on the dragon's shoulders and fondly patted the scaly neck. "I'm sorry, my friend," he said. "I haven't the strength to climb up."

"Then into a ball with you," said Gasslic.

The wizard obliged. Gasslic lifted him off the field and sailed over the tree wall, over the houses of the Green Stone where the battle still raged, over the inner wall and into the central garden.

* * *

Ender lifted out of Akka-Illin, bringing Brian, Annie and Jehzik with him. No longer did he feel the pull of another Stone, the influence of another force, the desires of another mind. The Midnight Stone was completely at peace in his hand.

They sped quickly over the Mirrak-Haas. Had their mission not been so urgent, the experience would have been utterly exhilarating. Ender simply held the Stone and they all flew effortlessly, high over the rocky crags. Here and there, the late afternoon sunlight began to peek through the clouds. The storm overhead was finally beginning to break up.

They crossed the Abandoned Land in a few breaths, or so it seemed to Brian. The last time he had flown at this height, he couldn't enjoy the view. Now, with nothing visibly holding him up, he still could not quite relax. He clutched the Valenblade, looking for enemies even as they flew over. So far, he had seen only a few bands of goblins.

Annie gasped as they passed over the Volgan River. Though she knew what to expect, it was still startling to see that the beautiful bridge was no more. Down below, whitewater churned over the rubble and around the last remnants of the great stone supports.

Ender and his charges sailed over the fields toward the Shioroth. Brian looked ahead to see what was happening.

"The wall burned!" he shouted.

"Yes," said Ender. "I see goblins and Surgoths, but the Black Warriors have vanished, just like they did in Akka-Illin, and I see no evidence of the Golrakken or the Birdman."

By the time he had finished saying this, he was landing on the street just inside the Eastgate. He set down his companions. Annie found a Faerie sword on the ground, turned to light form and set off behind Brian who was already racing on all fours after a band of goblins that was running through the streets.

Ender rose up high into the clearing sky, disappearing from their sight as if shot from a bow. From his height, with the vision provided by the Midnight Stone, he could make out every living creature below. He could see Gasslic landing in the central garden and depositing a very weak Holren on the grass. He could see Calicia offering Mari a place to lie down. He could see Rummel Stoneboots looking up at him with an expression of both concern and relief. He could see Tania felling yet another goblin with her small, green arrows. He saw Captain Falnor, bloodied and weary but undaunted, fighting alongside Thadris who was in no better shape but just as determined. He could see Arvon Dustrider fighting back to back with Eulian as if the two were one warrior. He saw Aaron with his sword and Roggin with Yorgun's double-bladed axe. Owler wielded his sharp sword and a stolen goblin dagger. Rohidan fought alongside three Small

Giants, driving the enemy from the side roads. Faeries, Elves, Dwarves and Men fought together and individually throughout the southern half of the city.

Hundreds of goblins still remained along with a handful of persistent Surgoths, fighting with the ferocity of cornered animals. Another two hundred goblins gathered into knots and small bands in the western wood. Off to the southwest, some residual fire continued to burn itself out, the last evidence of what appeared to have been a tremendous battle.

All of this Ender perceived in an instant. He looked deeper.

Saturating the earth around the Shioroth was the ring of defilement that had killed the tree wall and kept Rummel Stoneboots trapped in the central garden. Though the Birdman who had invoked it was dead, the strange power emanating from the ground continued to empower the goblins and Surgoths. With the sight provided by the Midnight Stone, Ender could now see the complex system of spells that knit all this together. The life of the Shioroth itself was sustaining the elements of its own destruction. All he had to do was break the connection.

For a moment, he studied Brian who was racing along the street, routing goblins from their hiding places, slicing his way through steel and muscle with Annie assisting from the air. He watched Jehzik searching for and calling out other enemy hiding places. He turned to find Gasslic who had found and killed another Surgoth. Satisfied that these would be unharmed by his actions, he looked for the ever-moving point where the connection between the defilement and the creatures created and sustained by it could be broken.

There it was. "Release," he said.

Down below, the earth shuddered. Ender watched the deep brown stain of the defilement recede instantly. The ring around the Shioroth grew thinner and thinner, fading rapidly away until it was completely gone.

As it did so, goblins and Surgoths disappeared into thin air. Even the creatures in the western woods vanished in the blink of an eye. Within a few seconds, the battle weary defenders had no one else to fight. A great shout rose up from the city as the sun broke through the clouds for the first time in days, bathing the Shioroth in golden light.

CHAPTER 57

Endings

E nder looked about again. There was not an enemy in sight. Quickly, he dropped down from his great height, landing in the central garden. He went straight to the room where the most grievously wounded defenders had been laid. The life of some had already left them. He set about working on the weakest first. Holding the Midnight Stone over their injuries, he focused on knitting the bones and sinews back together, stopping the bleeding and restoring their strength. Healing each one took time. Not bothering to keep a physical form, he moved quickly from one to the other, ensuring that no more were lost.

As he became more adept at this, he was able to expand his reach, working on several at once, all in different locations. The Elves and Faeries assisting with the wounded would sometimes notice injuries healing even as they cleaned them. Their own efforts seemed to be enhanced. Calicia could feel her husband's spirit throughout the infirmary. Deep gratitude filled her as she went from room to room, giving comfort and healing to both the wounded and their caregivers.

Rummel Stoneboots and the Lammethan brought more of the wounded from the streets below until the halls were overflowing.

Still, the grief over those who had perished was an ever-present specter. Hundreds of Faeries had been lost. Over three hundred Elves had died and nearly four hundred Dwarves had given their all in defense of the Shioroth. Of the Small Giants, only Grisbane, Thisvane and Gullen remained. Defgar and Rifgar had battled to the end, finally falling at the hands of Surgoths. The Men of the Green Stone had been reduced to a handful. Falnor, himself, had received numerous wounds and had simply refused to go to the central garden until all of his men had been accounted for. Shortly thereafter, Rummel had found both him with Thadris, and had convinced both of them they were losing too much blood to be out there much longer. They reluctantly agreed to be carried to the infirmary.

The Lammethan who were not needed at the infirmary poured out into the city to care for those who had fought so hard in their defense. Doors were opened and the tired and hungry were invited in and given food and shelter. Brian used his great nose to sniff out fallen defenders hidden under debris. He lifted overturned carts and toppled fences, and dug people out of damaged buildings, using the Valenblade whenever the pieces were too big to move. As soon as he had found someone, Annie flew off to find Rummel or a couple of Lammethan who could transport the wounded to the infirmary. If no one was available, Brian carried the wounded himself until someone else came along to help.

* * *

A bloodied warrior descended the stairs into the Shioroth's central garden. He no longer wore his leather jerkin or carried his heavy axe or his two-handed sword, but he still carried two daggers in his well-oiled belt. A nasty scrape in his bald scalp had been roughly cleaned and left open to dry. A bloody cloth was wrapped around his sword arm where a goblin axe had cut through his leather armor. His face and hands were riddled with cuts and scratches, some of them deep enough to still be seeping.

He strode directly across the grass to the infirmary.

Calicia's heart fell as she saw Aaron coming through the open doors. "This way," she said.

They entered a long hallway lined with very still bodies laid neatly side by side. The race of each body varied: Faeries lay beside Elves who lay beside Dwarves and Men. Their injuries were sometimes gruesome and obvious, sometimes not, but the reason for their stillness was the same. Some had been covered with a blanket. The faces of others were hidden by a garment or just a cloth.

Aaron recognized a pair of boots and nodded to Calicia who stopped and allowed him to pass.

"Was she alive when she got here?" he asked, looking at the large stain of blood where the cloak covered her head.

"No," said Calicia. "Not even the Jalice had any effect. I tried."

"Thank you," he said.

"I'm very sorry," said Calicia.

Aaron stared down at Lia's supine form. "Thank you," he said, not looking up. "I'll just stay here a moment. You have others to tend to."

Calicia nodded and left quietly.

Slowly, Aaron knelt down at Lia's feet and placed his big hands on her booted ankles. He held them firmly and squeezed, bowing his head. He looked up again and ran his hands up to her knees, massaging them gently, unable to breathe. Closing his eyes once more, Aaron leaned all the way over, his whole body shaking. Then he took a deep, ragged breath and buried his face between her knees. He clutched her legs tightly, gasping for air and silently soaking her torn breeches with tears and blood.

* * *

The sky had grown dark when Brian and Annie finally sat down for a long-awaited meal with Arvon and Eulian in the barracks of the Blue Stone at the Westgate. After everyone else was finished, Brian was still eating. Annie volunteered to deliver a message to the Northgate. She was heartened to see lights in the windows of the city once more.

On her return, she flew the long way around on the east side of the Shioroth's central garden wall to see the full moon. As she flew over a moonlit terrace, she noticed a figure sitting on the ground by the stone wall. No one else was around. Dropping down, she came in close, recognizing the Elder Faerie.

"Are you hurt?" she asked.

Rohidan shook his head. "Not in the way you mean, young one," he said.

Annie landed and sat down beside him, feet crossed, leaning back against the wall, just as he was. Neither said anything for a long time.

"Everything changes, Annathía," he said.

"I know," she said, quietly.

The Elder Faerie looked at her. Then he smiled. "Yes," he said. "I suppose you do." He reached over and took her young hand in his wrinkled one. "I'm glad you're here."

Annie smiled back at him, studying his craggy face.

"The end of so many things has come," said Rohidan. "The Lammethan are a dying race. My gracious wife is gone. And, today, I killed my closest friend and most bitter enemy." He looked out over the burned tree wall. "I wondered why I should remain here. What point was there in my survival?"

Annie squeezed his hand and said nothing.

"But with you beside me now, I cannot help but think that this full moon brings something new," Rohidan continued. "I wonder what that is."

"I don't know," said Annie. She nestled in beside him and laid her head on his shoulder. "I hope you'll stay and find out with me."

He caught a breath, reached over and patted her cheek. "Bless you, young one," he said.

"One more thing," said Annie. "Can I ask a favor?"

"Of course."

"Can I call you 'grandfather?'"

Rohidan squeezed her hand. "I should like that very much," he said.

* * *

There was a knock on the door.

"A patrol from Pellían, Commander," said the messenger

"I will be there in a moment," said Falnor. He rose from his bed, pulled on his breeches, tucked in his shirt and pulled on his boots, amazed again at how quickly Ender had restored him to health. Strapping on his sword belt, he strode to the courtyard of the Southgate where fifty men had just arrived. From the state of their horses, they had ridden hard to get here. They stood at attention as he approached.

"Welcome," said Falnor. "Please be at ease."

"Lieutenant Belwin, sir," said the patrol leader, bowing in salute.

"What news, Belwin?" asked Falnor. "We have been told that the city was attacked by a Birdman with goblins and Surgoths, and that he wiped out Captain Achor's regiment and took many prisoners. Tell me what is going on back home. How does the king fare? No need for formalities. You're speaking to a friend."

"King Raealann is dead, sir," said the Lieutenant. "Word is that he was poisoned. We suspect Captain Achor, but no one can prove it."

"Go on," said Falnor.

"As you said, sir," Belwin continued; "Achor's men were wiped out, save for a few who tried to warn us. Clearly, Gerran succeeded in bringing this news to you."

"He did," said Falnor.

"By the time Achor's survivors reached us, we were already under attack," said the Lieutenant. "Half of my regiment was killed, including Commander Elford. Captain Distel took charge brilliantly and we were able to regroup. We kept the enemy to the eastern portion of the city, but they took many prisoners, anyone they could lay hands on. Our attempts to rescue them were brutally beaten back. Judging from our heavy losses, their attack on the city was hardly full strength. We strengthened our defenses. Every citizen who could be armed was prepared to fight. After it became obvious there would be no second attack, we sent scouts. None of them saw any sign of the enemy until they came here." He paused and looked around. "This patrol was sent to rescue prisoners but we seem to have arrived too late. We've seen no sign of them or the enemy."

"It's a long and painful story, Belwin," said Falnor. "Have the men come in and rest. Dorsen will care for the horses."

* * *

Ender left the infirmary and finally placed the Midnight Stone back in his pocket, feeling a mixture of exhaustion and exhilaration. He had been working among the wounded for hours, but the Midnight Stone seemed to be much easier to manage. He stood for a moment, watching the full moon which had passed its zenith an hour earlier and begun its descent toward the Western Mountains.

A great shadow came up over the far ridge. From the gait, Ender knew Rummel Stoneboots had returned. Within a few steps, the Lord of the Mountains arrived at the Shioroth. bent down and let someone slip from his shoulder to the ground at the central garden.

"Lady July!" said Ender. "Your timing could not be better. I have done what I can. Now they need what you can do."

July bowed slightly and entered the infirmary.

"I have noticed something new," said Rummel.

"What is that?" asked Ender.

"The remainder of the tree wall is beginning to fail," said Rummel. "The soil is good, but the trees themselves have been irreparably damaged."

"You seem not to be upset by this," said Ender reached into his pocket and touched the Midnight Stone.

"Look carefully and you will see why," said Rummel.

Ender looked. Indeed, the trees were rotting slowly, but there was a spark of life beneath each one, as if a new ring of life had formed just outside the dying tree wall. "How is this possible?" he asked.

Rummel grinned. "This is the marvel," he said. "All that is needed to rebuild the wall is a living sacrifice from any one tree. The trees remember what they are supposed to be. Every portion of the tree has everything required for a new tree."

"Where did you find a living sacrifice?" asked Ender.

"One of the great trunks was too thick to be defiled so soon," said Rummel. "When I approached it after you removed the defilement, I could see that its heart was still alive. With that sacrifice, I was able to plant a new ring around the city."

"I can see it," said Ender.

"As the old trees rot, they enrich the soil for the new growth," said Rummel. "Even in death, they grant life."

Ender looked at the tiny specks of green glowing with life all around the city. Already they were twice the size they had been when he first saw them.

"If you gave them a boost, I'm sure no one would mind," said Rummel.

The Stonekeeper smiled and imagined the new wall springing up from the ground. As he did so, the old trees disappeared quickly into the soil. The bright green glowed even stronger. In a moment, tiny sprigs broke out into the moonlight. A few minutes later, they were saplings casting shadows on the perimeter road. Not long after that, they were as tall as the battlements and still climbing.

"It takes no power to do this," said Ender. "I feel no drain at all."

Rummel nodded. "It's the trees," he said. "Somehow they always give more than they receive."

Ender let go of the Stone and watched, amazed, as the new tree wall began to bond to the Westgate, the shiny leaves rustling in the wind.

* * *

In the coming weeks, many other repairs were made to areas in the Shioroth that had suffered during the battle. Healing the hearts of so many who had lost friends and loved ones took much longer. Each night, as she walked the wall around the central garden of the Shioroth, the Lady July blessed the sleep of all those within the city.

Captain Falnor and Tania returned to Pellían with Lieutenant Belwin's patrol. Ender, Calicia, Holren and Mari spent some time there as well, their powerful magic helping to restore the heavily damaged east side of the city. Aaron kept himself occupied with training both the new recruits and the advanced forces. Captain Distel was placed in charge of the new Green Guard at the Shioroth.

Owler traveled westward with Thadris, Eulian and Arvon Dustrider, along with the Elves who had survived. A contingent remained behind at the Westgate of the Shioroth, as always.

Bostler and the other Elves were fetched in groups by Rummel Stoneboots and returned to Val-Ellia. The strange pool in the wine cellar seemed to have disappeared and no obvious remnants of magic remained. Thadris insisted the portly Chief Chef had gained weight while waiting in the Western Mountains.

"There was nothing to DO!" said Bostler. "I think we ate well, though, despite the limited ingredients. It's all my staff's fault. If they would leave SOMETHING for me to manage, I wouldn't have time to enjoy any of this marvelous repast myself. Now, if you'll excuse me, I have the most marvelous dessert for tonight, but it will be simply *ruined* if I don't go now!"

Roggin Steelsmith led the remaining Dwarves back into the Western Mountains after a day in Val-Ellia. Owler promised to visit soon.

Gasslic and Jehzik set about exploring. Never had there been a happier pair than those two. Grisbane, Thisvane and Gullen returned to their home by the Volgan River where everything already suited them. "I'll get the urge to travel again, I'm sure," said Grisbane. "For now, I'd like to rest the old bones a bit. Then I might take a jaunt into the Abandoned Land. It's been a long, long time since I've seen the sun set on the Mirrak-Haas."

* * *

With a splash, Brian pulled out a fish. He had been waiting for a nice big one.

"Fish!" he said.

"Nuts!" said Annie, coming over with her pockets and hands full of them. "Now we have lunch."

Brian started the fire and sat back to roast the fish.

"We should make a house out here," he said.

"In a cave?" asked Annie, looking around for a good rock with which to crack the nutshells.

"Maybe," said Brian. "What do you think?"

Annie looked around. Sunlight filtered down through the canopy overhead. There was a nice stream nearby. Not far away, there was a fading thicket of blackberries that would be just as wonderful next year as they had been this year.

"Maybe so," said Annie. "We should talk to Owler. He knows how to make good houses in places like this."

"Yes," said Brian. "This is good."

"What is?" said Annie, cracking a nut open. "Good, I mean."

"This," said Brian, thumping his big, furry chest.

"You feel good?" asked Annie.

He nodded.

"So do I," she said, handing him a nut. "It's good to be home."

EPILOGUE

It had started as a low rumble, deep in the bedrock under Uzzim-Khail. As the days went by, bits and pieces high atop the lofty towers broke off and fell, down, down, down, exploding into powder as they struck the pavement below. The rumble continued, building louder one day only to become louder yet the next day. One by one, the high catwalks connecting the towers shattered into pieces and fell. The bridges began to crack, then to crumble. They gave way and pounded into rubble that lay strewn across the battlements and courtyards below. Black dust rose into the sky and drifted away.

The rumbling grew louder still. Even greater cracks appeared in the towers. Whole sections of their stone walls broke off and crashed to the ground.

Finally, late one afternoon, the towers themselves began to fall. One by one, they came apart. The second tallest tower split down the middle. One side crashed into the great central tower and broke apart, scraping away all evidence of the old bridges as it slid into the central courtyard. The other side of it smashed against another tower further out. Like a massive tree, the outer tower tilted sideways, cracked, and pitched off the cliff. The next highest tower burst in the middle, and collapsed directly downward, filling the courtyard with heavy debris. Then the smallest tower of Uzzim-Khail bent forward, cracked and crashed headfirst into the courtyard.

The rumbling increased. A huge crack appeared in the great central tower, running diagonally from the base at the back around to the front where one of the highest bridges had once stood. Still vertical, the massive tower began to slide backwards off of its ancient foundation. It hit the outer wall, crumpled, shattered, and continued on down the cliff, breaking into countless fragments that rolled out onto the valley floor.

The rumbling continued, echoing off the rocky peaks of the Oryxx.

Finally, the entire outer defenses of the fortress started to give way. Slabs of ancient stonework tumbled down from the mighty cliffs on which they had stood for millennia. The massive gates groaned and twisted, breaking apart and crashing outward to slide down the steep road. The rumbling grew even louder.

About this time, the snoring in the guard house stopped.

The gate troll of Uzzim-Khail awoke with a start. The rumbling noise was deafening. He covered his ears and tried to stand up. The ground was shaking so violently that he could not get to his feet without using his hands, but every time he used a hand to steady himself, the noise hurt too much, so he covered his ears again, losing his balance and landing with a thump.

The guard tower was breaking into pieces all around him. Huge chunks of masonry fell from the ceiling. The great wheels that opened and shut the gates were creaking and moaning. The mechanism behind them ground away like the teeth of some metal behemoth.

"OPEN THE GATES?" he bellowed through the noise. "CLOSE THE GATES?

No one responded.

He tried to climb the wheels, but they were skewed to the side and would not turn. More stonework broke off of the ceiling and walls, pelting him on his hard, hard head.

"NO!" yelled the troll. "NO!"

He crawled around, trying in vain to keep the walls from shaking. Jagged cracks had appeared, and the walls themselves seemed to be swaying, flexing, breathing in and out as the rumbling continued.

"NO CRACKS! NO CRACKS!" wailed the troll. "NO SUN! NO SUN NO SUN NO SUN NO SUN!"

He implored the walls to hold but they could not. The great wall of Uzzim-Khail was crashing down, taking most of the guard tower with it. Groaning and twisting, the mechanism that worked the gates broke into to pieces. Gears and wheels rolled away into the valley.

"NOOOOOO!" wailed the gate troll. "NOOOOO, NOOOOO!"

The rumbling grew even louder, rattling the high perch of bedrock on which the mighty fortress had been built. Rubble was shaken off in all directions, pouring down on the new slope of dark talus that had formed below the cliffs.

The gate troll continued to wail, his fists pressed into his eyes, tears streaming down his filthy cheeks.

"NOOOOO! I DON'T WANT TO BE STOOOOOOONNNNE!"

On and on he wailed as the walls of his prison came apart and crashed down off of the cliffs.

Then, finally, everything stopped. The troll rocked side to side, crying and sniffling as the wind coming down from the summits of the Oryxx blew the dust down the valley.

After a few minutes, the gate troll rubbed his eyes, and peeked between his fingers. Puzzled, he got to his feet and looked around. The dust was still settling, but the results were obvious. The only thing still standing on the foundations of the ancient fortress of Uzzim-Khail was himself.

He squinted at the sky. The storm was clearing. Dumbfounded, he just stood up and stared. The sun was sinking toward the horizon, but a shaft of it shot straight through a notch between two mountains, landing full on the gate troll.

He covered his eyes with his forearm. The warmth on his body actually felt kind of nice. He stood that way for several minutes as the light shifted off of him and left him in shadow once more. Looking around again, he realized he was still alive. Why, he had no idea. A big grin stretched across his face. Walking jerkily, with legs and feet unaccustomed to covering any distance, he took several steps toward the steep, rubble-strewn road. Then he thought better of it. Getting down on all fours, he crawled backwards down the soft slopes left by the new landslides. It took a long time, but his tough hide garnered hardly a scratch from the rocks and dust.

He reached the bottom, stood up again and turned his clumsy steps toward the only road he knew, up and out of the valley. Small quakes continued. Every time the ground shook, he sat down and waited until it went away. Then, seeing that he was still all right, he bumbled his way forward once more.

When he was a third of the way up to the pass, the rumbling started again in earnest. He dropped to the ground, crouching on hands and knees. The mountains shook all around him. The rocks underneath him shifted a little. Far across the way, a section of the mountainside slid off, scraping a path to the valley floor. Down in the valley, Uzzim-Khail's massive rock outcropping broke apart and collapsed in a heap, spreading clouds of dust in every direction. Then, just as it had started, the rumbling stopped.

The former gate troll of Uzzim-Khail waited as the dust storm blew over. Then he stood up again, shook off the silt, rubbed the grit out of his eyes and ambled awkwardly up the path.

Yes, he decided. Today was a very good day for a walk.

ACKNOWLEDGEMENTS

I am grateful for so many people who have accompanied me on various parts of this journey. Thanks to Louanne Cole for all of her support in the early years. Thanks to fellow author Craig English, whose insightful, incisive and practical editing wisdom—and unflagging enthusiasm—helped me work through that first major review. I couldn't have asked for a kinder, firmer hand than his wielding that red pen. Thanks to Danielle Comby Havens for graciously taking the time to edit portions of a later draft. Thanks to Fran Teaster who warned me she would not be nice about it, read the manuscript, and then badgered me for years to get this story published. (It's here, Fran!)

Thanks to my family: to my late mother, Lucille, whose love for words surely engendered my own; to my father, Richard, whose generous gift allowed me to move from paper to PC; to my sister Kathryn, who listened to me talk about this forever and was still excited to see it all come together; to daughters Lauren and Sarina who were there almost from the beginning, and whose creative talents inspire me to make the most of my own; to my wife, Ping, who passed around loose-leaf pages with sons Ryan and Alan as they all read an early draft and gave me the thumbs-up (and, yes: you were so right about Annie!).

A special thank you to Ping for making crucial comments at key points, always believing that this book could and should be a reality. Thank you for gently, persistently, insistently fanning that spark inside me that loves to tell a tale.

Finally, thanks to you, dear reader, for making this story part of your world.

Mark Ivan Cole
Taipei, Taiwan - September 28, 2017

ABOUT THE AUTHOR

Mark Ivan Cole is an avid musician, a published poet, and an award winning artist whose paintings have been shown on both sides of the Pacific. He grew up in the Ecuadorian Andes, and he and his wife, Ping, have hiked many miles in North America's mountains and canyons, as well as in various places in China, Southeast Asia, Europe and South Africa. Cole's affinity for rugged landscapes is often reflected in his creative work. He and his wife currently live in Taiwan. The Valenblade is his first novel.

https://thevalenblade.wordpress.com
https://markivancole.wordpress.com

Facebook: Mark Ivan Cole

Made in the USA
Middletown, DE
12 April 2021

37423934R00357